*"I just wanted to tell a good story,
because that's what life is all about, I think."*
LUCIA ST. CLAIR ROBSON

Born in Baltimore, Maryland, and raised in the Florida Everglades area, Lucia St. Clair Robson has been a Peace Corps volunteer in Venezuela and a teacher in a Brooklyn ghetto. She lived in Japan for a year and later earned her master's degree before starting work as a public librarian in Annapolis, Maryland, where she lives today in a rustic 1920s summer community.

Lucia Robson's library experience of presenting programs to audiences ranging in age from 2 to 90 trained her in the craft of storytelling. She brings to the task of researching a historical novel a reference librarian's dogged persistence and an insider's awareness of how to find obscure sources of information.

While tracing Tiana Rogers' story, she camped in the Ozark region of Arkansas and Oklahoma to become familiar with the flora and fauna. When she wrote of chiggers in *Walk In My Soul*, she did so with first-hand knowledge.

Ride the Wind, Lucia Robson's first novel, became a national bestseller within weeks of publication. She is currently at work on her third novel and now devotes herself full time to her writing.

WALK
IN
MY
SOUL

Lucia St. Clair Robson

Ballantine Books · New York

Grateful acknowledgment is made for permission to use translations of Cherokee incantations from the following:
Walk in Your Soul: Love Incantations of the Oklahoma Cherokees by Jack Frederick Kilpatrick and Anna Grits Kilpatrick. Copyright © 1965 by Southern Methodist University Press.
Run Toward the Nightland: Magic of the Oklahoma Cherokees by Jack Frederick Kilpatrick and Anna Grits Kilpatrick. Copyright © 1967 by Southern Methodist University Press.

Library of Congress Catalog Card Number: 84-91666
ISBN: 0-345-30789-5

Manufactured in the United States of America
Cover design by James R. Harris
Cover painting by Tom Hall
Text design by Amy Lamb

FIRST EDITION: June 1985

10 9 8 7 6 5 4 3 2 1

I dedicate this book to the wisest of teachers, my mother and father. If their souls are not in balance it is because the scale is weighted so heavily with love.

And to Ulisi, Gram, who has journeyed to the Nightland.

I want to thank Owen Lock for telling me I could do this, and Pamela Strickler for telling me how.

Thanks are also in order to the wizards of Maryland's Anne Arundel County Public Library Interlibrary Loan Department. They can make rare and obscure items appear from thin air. This book would not have been possible without them.

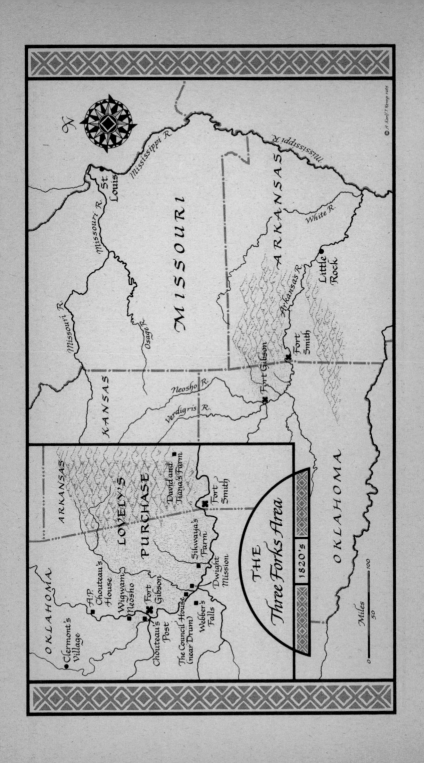

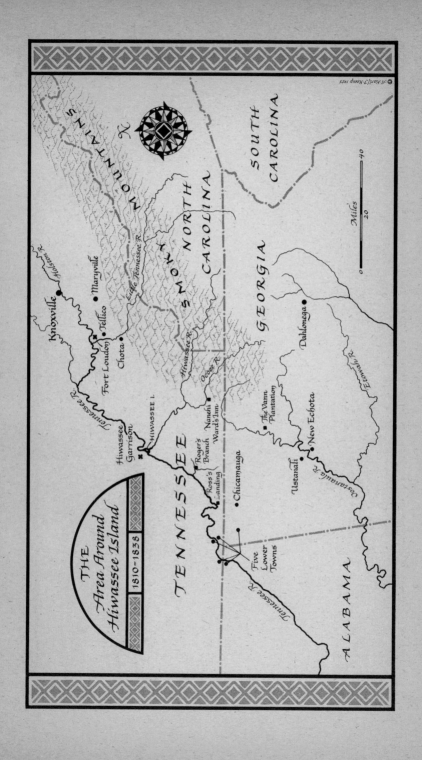

THE
Area Around
Hiwassee Island
1810–1858

© H. Karl / J. Kamp 1995

Miles
0   20   40

SMOKY MOUNTAINS

SOUTH CAROLINA

NORTH CAROLINA

GEORGIA

TENNESSEE

ALABAMA

Holston R.

Little Tennessee R.

Tennessee R.

Hiwassee R.

Ocoee R.

Oostanaula R.

Etowah R.

Knoxville

Maryville

Tellico

Fort Loudon

Chota

HIWASSEE I.

Hiwassee Garrison

Nunelii
Ward's Inn

Roger's Branch

Ross's Landing

Chicamauga

Dahlonega

The Vann Plantation

New Echota

Ustanali

Five Lower Towns

Cherokee Syllabary

ᏣᎳᎩ ᎠᏕᎶᏆᏍᏗ

After 1828

D a		R e	T i	Ꮩ o	O u	i v
Ꮔ ga	Ꭴ ka	Ꮄ ge	Y gi	Ꭺ go	J gu	E gv
Ꮀ ha		Ꮅ he	Ꭿ hi	Ꮠ ho	Ꮁ hu	Ꮑ hv
W la		Ꮶ le	Ꮕ li	Ꮆ lo	M lu	Ꮭ lv
Ꮙ ma		Ꮙ me	H mi	Ꮺ mo	Y mu	
Ꮎ na		Ꮄ ne	ᖏ ni	Z no	Ꮕ nu	Ꮓ nv
Ꮕ hna	Ꮐ nah					
Ꮖ kwa		Ꮽ kwe	Ꮝ kwi	Ꮴ kwo	Ꮝ kwu	Ꮑ kwv
Ꮜ sa	Ꭶ s	Ꮞ se	Ꮟ si	Ꮠ so	Ꮡ su	Ꮢ sv
Ꮤ da		Ꮥ de	Ꮧ di	V do	S du	Ꮯ dv
W ta		Ꮦ te	Ꮨ ti			
Ꮬ dla	Ꮭ tla	Ꮮ tle	C tli	Ꮯ tlo	Ꮰ tlu	P tlv
Ꮐ tsa	Ꮶ tse	Ꮪ tsi	K tso	Ꮫ tsu	Ꮳ tsv	
Ꮹ wa		Ꮺ we	Ꮻ wi	Ꮼ wo	Ꮽ wu	Ꮾ wv
Ꮿ ya		Ᏸ ye	Ᏹ yi	Ᏺ yo	Ᏻ yu	Ᏼ yv

EAST

The Sunland

1809

Is one of the fairest portions of the globe to remain in a state of nature, the haunt of a few wretched savages?

—WILLIAM HENRY HARRISON,
Governor of Indiana Territory
1810

Cherokee government produces a society of peace and love, which . . . better maintains human happiness than the most complicated system of modern politics enforced by coercive means.

—WILLIAM BARTRAM, *Naturalist*
1791

Chapter 1

Nine-year-old Tiana Rogers stamped her foot and glared up at her father. To spite him, she shouted in Cherokee, knowing he had never mastered its complexity. But it was difficult for Tiana to stare and shout. Her mother had taught her the Indian way of averting her eyes and keeping her voice low. Besides, a child almost never defied her parents. Rudeness was bad enough. Rudeness to a parent was almost unthinkable. Tiana's younger sister, Susannah, and her older half-sister, Nannie, silently urged her on.

"This one won't go to school!" Tiana shouted, using the formal third person. "She won't!"

"Oh yes you will!" Jack Rogers roared in English. He had lived almost thirty years with the Cherokee and he knew how hard it was for her to argue with him. He admired her spunk, but he also pressed his advantage. He held her dark, blue-gray eyes with his own pale blue ones, and worked himself into a good imitation of fury. "I'll not be having ignorant little heathens for daughters. You're Rogers. You come from fine Scots stock. You will be educated," he reached full volume, "or by the holy God, I'll beat refinement into you!"

"Tiana is *Ani Yun'wiya*, one of the Real People," the child yelled, leaning backwards to look up at him. She switched to the English she had learned from him. "I'll not be shut up in a stinking school with a purse-mouthed, bowel-locked, religious prig." Tiana's voice rose shrilly. She could feel her control slipping and tears stinging her eyes. She gave one last volley in her defense. "I won't!" She whirled and sprinted through the open door. Nannie and Susannah followed her across the wide porch and leaped the three stairs down into the yard. Their short smocks flew up to flash bare bottoms. They ran across the trampled barnyard and disappeared into the bushes.

Jack Rogers watched them from the doorway. The six-foot, two-inch lintel barely cleared his head. He smiled a little. Damn, but it was good to let loose and rip now and then. Indian courtesy was wearing on a man not raised to it. Arguing with a Cherokee was like trying to fell a reed with an ax.

The little scamp, he thought. She pretended not to understand English when it served her purpose. But she had heard her father rant about the missionaries often enough. She could repeat his words, even to his slight brogue. She was a quick one.

As Jack went back into the house, he felt the chill in the air. His two wives were pointedly ignoring him.

"Ah, Jennie, lass, I wouldn't really beat them."

"I know." Jack's second wife, Jennie, concentrated on her spinning wheel. Elizabeth, his first wife and Jennie's mother by a former husband, gathered up her carders and baskets of wool and left the room.

"Then what is it?"

"So it's heathens we are, are we?" Jennie spoke quietly, as always. She didn't take her eyes from her work.

"I didn't say that."

" 'Ignorant little heathens,' you said."

Hell-fire. He had forgotten he said that. What memories women had. They could fling a man's hasty words back at him years later. Maybe his neighbor, old Campbell, was right. He didn't teach his wives or children English and he never bothered to learn Cherokee himself. They were a singularly happy family. But shouting at Tiana had invigorated Jack and he felt conciliatory.

"They were inconsiderate words, lass, without meaning." But Jennie wasn't to be conciliated.

"The Cherokee path is good enough for me, and for you too, husband, when white ways don't suit you." A strand of cream-colored wool ran through Jennie's delicate, calloused fingers. She leaned into her work, poised on the ball of her bare left foot. She spun the wheel gently with a peg in her right hand and drew out the yarn with her left. It twisted and quivered like a living thing in her fingers. She walked forward to let the yarn wind onto the spindle. Then she backed up and started over. That day she would walk twenty miles, a step or two at a time. The humming of the spinning wheel was constant, like a low, distant wind sighing through grass.

"The Indian path isn't good enough for your daughters, is it?" she continued. "Do you want them to be like the black robes and their gloomy women? Do you want them to think laughing is . . ." She searched for a word. "*Uyo'i*, bad, like they do?"

"The Council told the missionaries they want education for their children, not religious claptrappery. I know. I wrote the letter for them. Gave me great satisfaction." Jack paced from the plank floor onto the rag rug and back again. His heavy, brass-toed work shoes rang loud, then muffled. The sun had been up nearly an hour and he had work to do. But he knew he had best settle this issue now. The Cherokee were polite. They didn't like to contradict anyone. But they were also tenacious. They worried a question until it was answered to their satisfaction.

"At least Blackburn and his staff are dependable." Jack said. "You know how many schoolmasters we've had here. They're either drinkers or gamblers or whoremongers or loafers or worse. They're often but little better educated than their pupils." Rogers barely stopped himself from saying that only a worthless man would be in this howling wilderness teaching a brood of half-breed brats for a dollar a week and board. Jack Rogers loved his family, but he had few illusions. "I want the girls to marry well. They need some polish put to them."

"You want them to marry white men, you mean."

"Dunna be telling me what I mean, woman."

Jennie knew she had pushed him as far as she could. She tried another approach. Her English was adequate, but halting.

"Give them each a present. Give them ribbons for their hair. And something they can use in school. Penknives from the factory. The ones with the buttonhooks on them."

"They won't wear anything that buttons. They'll rarely even wear clothes," he said in exasperation.

"They'll wear clothes to school. Make school an adventure. A dare. Use honey instead of vinegar to attract flies."

"You attend to it, then. I can't fettle around here all morning. I'm riding to the garrison to see how Charles is doing at the factory. The yearly report is late again," Jack grumbled. "And I'll be getting the usual reprimand." Jack was never satisfied with the way his oldest son ran the factory, the government trading post, for him. "I'll bring home the knives." Jack snatched his low-crowned straw hat from the peg by the door. From habit, he rolled the sides of the wide brim to make them turn up. But the old hat's brim had long ago assumed the shape he wanted. He jammed it onto this head and left.

With a small sigh of relief, Jennie watched him go. He would never accept the fact that he wasn't in charge of his own family. He was the father of five children by Jennie and six by Elizabeth. But no matter how much he might bluster, he wasn't really in charge of them.

Clan membership was passed through the mothers to their children. And family responsibility fell to members of the mother's clan, usually her older brother. After all, a woman could easily marry another husband, and often did. But she had only one oldest brother. Jack said that clan nonsense was over, past. But it wasn't. Not yet. Charles, Jack and Elizabeth's oldest son, would escort the girls to school and enroll them. It was his duty, not their father's.

Nannie Rogers walked along a high ridge. The other two followed single-file, padding barefoot over the narrow animal trail. Nannie was ten, a year older than Tiana. Seven-year-old Susannah skipped to keep up with the other two. Below them, their father's fields cut into the dense forests of the lush Tennessee River valley. The children could see smoke spiraling up from the huge stone chimneys hidden by the trees.

The Real People called their country the Land of a Thousand Smokes. Pale smoky haze lay thick in the valley. It wreathed the tops of the hills like islands in a tranquil sea. To the east rose the mountains. Their sides were covered with a spring carpet of purple, pink, and lavender rhododendrons. The blue peaks themselves were shrouded in mist. The mountains were the home of countless spirits. Spirits inhabited each large rock and high pass, each bald and cave and ravine. They lurked in each stream and sang with the wind in the treetops.

The trail swerved to avoid a thicket of twisted laurel ablaze with orange flowers. Then it narrowed and threatened to lose itself in the maze of rocks and tangles of grape vines and blueberry bushes. The air grew cooler as they entered a stand of yellow poplars two hundred feet high. Sunlight knifed in straight shafts through their canopy.

There were black oaks whose furrowed trunks measured thirty feet around. There were chestnut trees rising from the litter of their own sweet nuts, and beeches and gums a hundred and fifty feet high. But their size didn't awe Tiana. The trees were her friends. She had special ones she talked to and gave nicknames. They stood guard over her.

The noise of water bubbling over rocks grew louder. Ferns called *yan utse'stu*, the Bear Lies On It, crowded the path. The stream was one of thousands that began in the mountains and threaded their way through steep ravines or cascaded from towering cliffs. The fallen log that led to the other side of the stream was wide enough for the three of them to walk abreast. A misty spray kept the log's carpet of moss a brilliant green. It felt cool and spongy under Tiana's feet. Small ferns sprouted where the wood was soft with decay.

Tiana pushed through the dense bushes around their favorite glade. It was bordered on two sides by a limestone cliff covered with ferns and moss and glistening with rivulets of water. At the foot of the wall was a deep pond that reflected the pale spring leaves of the trees above it. Water, backed up from the stream, flowed over a limestone ledge into the pool. Birds and insects were trying to out-sing each other.

The floor of the glade was covered with tiny flowers. The Real People had given them names like "Greensnake" and "Partridge Moccasin," "It Wears A Hat" and "Little Star," "Deer Eye," "Fire-Maker" and "Talker." Dainty, translucent white Indian Pipes pushed through the black loam. Tiana hunkered and fingered one of the drooping, waxy flowers. She half-expected Tsawa'si, one of the handsome Little People, to peer out at her from the cluster of slender stems.

Someone must have quarreled here. Quarreling angered The Provider, the Great One who lived in Heaven somewhere above the sun and moon. He changed those who quarreled into Indian Pipes to remind others to keep the peace. The smoke that hung over the mountains was another way The Provider reminded them of peace pipes.

"'What are we going to do?" asked Nannie.

"I don't know." Tiana stared gloomily into the green-tinted water.

Susannah lay next to her with her chin on her crossed arms. They kept a wary eye out for the huge red-and-white-striped leech who lived in pools like this. He was a vague, shifting shape in the water until he sent up a wave that washed the careless into his domain. "They beat children in those places," Tiana said. "They tie them up and beat them."

"How do you know?" asked Nannie.

"James told me." They believed everything their older brother told them. To be beaten was unthinkable. Their father had once whipped their oldest brother, Charles, long ago, before the girls were born. But the silent grief and outrage of Jack's wives had stopped him from ever doing it again. He threatened from time to time. But the threats were no more real than the wicked bogle man he had frightened them with when they were younger.

The older Rogers children, Charles, Aky, Mary, John, James, Joseph, William, and Annie, had learned to read, write, and cipher from teachers hired by their father. Jack had no love for the missionaries. They hadn't named him "Hell-Fire Jack" for nothing. He had resisted sending his youngest ones to the new Presbyterian school at the abandoned Tellico blockhouse, but he had finally decided to do it.

"We'll have to run away," Tiana said finally.

"Where?" asked Nannie.

"Here."

"Here?"

"Yes. We'll live the way the Real People used to." Tiana's sisters looked dubious. "We'll hunt and fish and make cloaks of feathers and furs. We'll be *Ghigau*, Beloved Women and warriors, like Nanehi Ward."

"We can live in a cave," said Nannie.

"And we'll never have to milk or fetch wood or haul water," added Susannah.

They whiled away the morning weaving flower wreaths for their hair, swimming, and searching for early berries and ramps. They took turns pretending to be Nanehi Ward saving poor Mrs. Bean from being burned at the stake. They dreamed of becoming *Ghigau*, Beloved Women like her. She had killed a man in battle. She was privileged to speak in the highest councils with the men. And she could save the lives of captives if she chose. Although there were no battles or captives anymore. There had been peace between the Real People and the white men for fifteen years.

The day began to darken early. Heavy black clouds scudded overhead. A chill wind found their hiding place by the pool. The leaves above them began to flutter, as though stirred by an unseen hand. The birds fell silent. Far away, the girls heard the rumble of thunder. Anisga'ya Tsunsdi, the sons of the Great Thunder, must be talking to each other. Or the other Thunder Men, who lived in the high cliffs and under waterfalls, were traveling from peak to peak along their invisible bridges.

"I'm hungry," Susannah said. A few hard berries and some raw ramp bulbs were not very satisfying. Tiana began to regret her idea of running away. The thought of spending the night in a cold, dark cave was not as appealing as it had been that morning.

"I saw an opening at the top of the hill, not far from here," said Nannie. "I never noticed it before. A rock must have rolled away from the entrance."

Tiana shivered as the wind blew colder and the thunder growled louder. She wished she knew the right prayers to appease the Thunder Men. Usually the Real People were friends with Thunder, but it didn't hurt to cajole him a little.

The girls crouched to peer into the blackness of the cave. A dazzling flash of lightning, a crash of thunder, and large, icy drops of rain drove them inside. They hovered at the entrance, adjusting their eyes to the darkness.

"I want to go home." Susannah began to sniffle. "There might be Little People living in here."

"They'll be kind to us," said Nannie. "They help lost children."

"They won't be kind if we disturb them. They don't like to be disturbed. They'll bewitch us."

"Quiet." Tiana didn't want to hear about bewitching. Nannie screamed and grabbed her.

"*Tla'meha*, a bat," Nannie said sheepishly. Tiana felt more bats brush by, like flying cobwebs.

"At least it's dry," she said.

"This isn't fun anymore. Can't we go home?" Susannah had subsided to a whimper now. She clung to the frayed hem of Tiana's smock. The air in the cave was musty, undisturbed for years. Vague shapes of tumbled boulders loomed in the dimness. Some looked like animals. Or worse, bogle men.

Susannah was crying softly, hopelessly. She had been on these escapades with her sisters before. She knew they would stay here all night rather than admit defeat. And she was too afraid to go out into the thunderstorm alone. Outside, the rain was falling heavily. The world seemed alien and afire with fitful lightning. Susannah jumped at each crash of thunder.

"It's all right, little sister," said Tiana. "I'll make sure there are no animals or Little People in here." She advanced farther into the room, holding a stick in front of her. She tapped it against a dim shape by the wall. The stick made a muffled thud, and dust rose. Tiana sneezed. The hair at the nape of her neck began to stir with dread.

"What is it?" hissed Nannie.

"Let's go," wailed Susannah. She was sobbing now.

"I don't know." Tiana's heart was pounding as she tapped the object gently again. A bolt of lightning, then another and another flashed nearby, illuminating the cave. For an instant the girls saw what was at the end of the stick.

Propped against the limestone wall was a large cane basket, broken open and frayed at the rim. Sitting in it was a mummified human body. The brown, leathery skin was stretched over the empty skull in a hideous grin. A tiny brown bat hung from one eye socket. A skeletal hand rested on the edge of the basket as though the corpse were about to pull itself from its coffin.

Then the cave was black again. Tiana was too terrified to move. She was disoriented in the sudden darkness, and afraid she would bump into the corpse. Or perhaps the thunder and lightning had jolted it back to life. Maybe it was reaching for her even now. She could feel its bony grip on her shoulder, its cold fingers caressing her cheek. She wanted to run but her feet had turned to stone, and her knees weren't strong enough to lift them. She felt hot urine stinging her legs.

Susannah broke the spell with a shriek. Screaming, they jostled each other as they crowded through the opening. Lightning lit the way as they scrambled down the hillside, heedless of the rocks and brambles.

The day's light was fading fast as they raced for home. Icy rain turned to hail. Tiana tried to shield her face with her arm as chunks hit her head and shoulders. Her feet were numb with cold and bloody from the rocks. Susannah slipped in the mud and Tiana stopped to haul her to her feet. They were all sobbing now.

The yard of their house was a shallow, swiftly flowing river when they splashed up to the front steps and onto the porch. They stopped at the big wooden door and wiped their feet on the mat of woven corn shucks. They stood panting and shivering while they gathered courage to go in. Tiana was relieved to see the latchstring out.

She took a deep breath and tugged at the string. It pulled the bar up inside so she could swing the door open. She winced as it creaked on its wooden hinges. Silently, the three girls filed into the warm room, lit by a huge fire and rush lights in wire holders. Tiana could hear the rhythmic "frump, frump" of Elizabeth's loom in the next room, where large balls of wool and cotton yarn, dyed yellow and rust, brown and black and indigo, hung from the rafters.

Jennie was mending by the fire's light. Jack sat in his throne, the only comfortable chair in the house. He was studying the chessboard on an upended log in front of him. On the other side of the board Jack's tenant farmer, Elizur Schrimshear, sat on a three-legged stool. He was a taciturn man, but dependable. His lanky legs sprawled on either side of the log table. A goose quill toothpick stuck from the side of his mouth.

Tiana was glad her brothers Joseph and William were still visiting their uncle Drum in Hiwassee Town. They teased her and her sisters whenever they could get away with it. Fifteen-year-old Annie was weaving a basket of dried river canes, but her mind was on boys as usual. She had blossomed late and was making up for lost time. Tiana's half-brothers, James and John, were watching the chess game. Fancy, the black woman who lived with them, was asleep in her small room under the eaves of the attic.

The girls lined up on the cold plank floor. Muddy puddles formed at their feet and they dared not stand on the rag rug.

Jack glanced up from his game. "It's rapscallions I'm raising. You've taken to rooting with the hogs, have you?"

Tiana struggled to catch her breath and stop shivering. Why was she always left to do the talking?

"We were caught in the rain, *Skayegusta*, Well-Dressed One," she said. She hoped to placate him with the honorific title.

"You don't say so, lass," said Jack mildly. "You look like you've been consorting with the Great Leech in the river mud."

Tiana closed her eyes briefly in relief. He had a terrible temper, but he didn't carry a grudge. Actually, Jack had taken one look at the three of them and had decided they'd been punished enough.

"*Atu'n*, young woman, get them some food," said Jennie to Annie.

She followed Annie into the summer kitchen attached to the main house. Tiana heard her pulling the big wooden tub across the floor. She returned with a kettle of water to heat for bathing

Life looked brighter to Tiana when she was clean and dry and fed. She huddled in a wool blanket, softened by wear, and stared into the fire. Never had Grandmother Fire seemed so cheerful and comforting. Tiana fingered the small leather bag around her neck. It contained a piece of Grandmother Fire's charcoal to protect her. Tiana's favorite cat lay in her lap. Tiana leaned over to listen to her purr. Jennie claimed cats were counting, "*Taladu, nuhgi, taladu, nuhgi,* sixteen, four, sixteen, four," when they purred.

From the corner of her eye, Tiana gauged her father's mood. After losing the chess game, Schrimshear had gone to his tiny room attached to the barn.

It was good he had lost. Winning always put Jack in a good humor.

Jack Rogers looked harmless enough now, with his feet propped on the stool and his long, soapstone Cherokee pipe between his teeth. Tobacco smoke floated around the red calico turban he wore to cover the bald spot on the back of his head. He had on moccasins and lumpy wool socks. Annie had knitted them many years earlier with more good intentions than skill. His favorite old striped hunting shirt had faded the same gray as his slops, the baggy breeches of homespun.

Jennie Rogers wore a simple dress in the high-waisted French fashion. At thirty-five, Jennie was still slender, but she had full breasts that swelled over her low neckline. Her thick, coarse black hair hung to the backs of her knees when she stood. Her elfin face was lovely and unlined. It was easy to see why Jack had beem unable to resist her when she was a girl of fourteen.

"Mother," said Susannah. "We saw a ghost."

"It wasn't a ghost, it was a dead person," said Tiana.

"Where?" Jack understood Cherokee much better than he spoke it.

"In a cave in the hills. It was dried up and sitting in a basket," said Tiana.

"There was a bat in its eye." Susannah shivered.

"It was ghastly," added Nannie, using one of her father's favorite words. The Rogers children spoke a strange mix of English and Cherokee.

"It must have been one of the Old Ones," said Jennie. "They used to bury their dead that way."

"But it still had brown, wrinkly skin on it," said Nannie.

"The nitrous soil in some of those caves preserves flesh as neat as Fancy's cucumber pickles," said Jack.

Tiana sucked in her cheeks. She widened her big eyes and rolled her eyeballs back in their sockets. Moaning far back in her throat, she slowly extended one hand, tensed into a claw, out of the blanket and toward Susannah. The shadows thrown by the fire's light made her face ghastly indeed.

"Stop, sister." Susannah's lower lip trembled.

Annie yawned, took a rush light, and bid them good night. John followed. In the other room, the sound of the shuttle stopped. Elizabeth had gone to bed.

"Your father has something for you, daughters." Jennie glanced at Jack. He grunted and scowled as he searched through the deep pockets sewn into his pantaloons. This smacked of bribery, and it wasn't his style. But he passed a knife to each of them.

"Those are for sharpening quills," he said brusquely. "And you know what quills are for."

"Yes, *udoda*, father." They were too happy to be home to argue about school.

Tiana wondered if school would be like the council house where the old men sat around the sacred fire and shared their knowledge with the boys. She had often stared at the dusty books over the tall desk where Jack stood to write his reports and figure the accounts of the government factory. There were eight volumes of Rollin's *Ancient History*, Brook's *Gazeteer*, and Morse's *Geography*. Books were so mysterious to Tiana. They held dead people's words trapped on leaves. Magic like that surely must be reserved for the wisest, for the Curers Of Them.

Finally, James collected the sleeping Susannah from the rug, wrapped her blanket around her and carried her upstairs. Nannie followed. Tiana stood with her blanket clutched around her and looked at her father. He gave a reluctant smile and she climbed into his lap.

They sat for a while in silence while she fingered the small bag hanging from a thong around his neck. Jack said the bag held a piece of Little Deer's antler. If so, it was a precious amulet. Little Deer was chief of all the deer tribe. A bit of his antler would bring deerskins to the man who owned it. Jack called it superstitition. But he always wore it.

"I'm sorry I shouted at you, Father," Tiana said.

"It's all right, lass." He stroked her hair a bit roughly. His hands were big and calloused and unused to subtle motions. All eleven of his children were acceptable-looking and smart enough. Thank God there wasn't a simple one in the lot. But this one was special.

When the children gathered, Tiana was the one people noticed first. Her long, black hair was thick and silky and often tangled. Her huge, dark blue eyes flashed from behind the curtain it formed. She was tall and slender, with fine features, like her brother James. She seemed to run everywhere she went, sprinting through life on lanky, coltish legs.

"I understand why you don't want to go to school, daughter," he said. "I never liked it much myself. But it's only the summer term, three months. And you're fortunate to go at all. The Council had to insist that girls as well as boys be taught. It's time for you to get a proper education. A very wise man, of the Greek tribe, once said, "He who knows nothing, loves nothing.' " For an instant Jack wondered what his daughter would do with her education. Would she be the belle of eastern society? A half-breed squaw? Hardly. *Take things one at a time*, he thought. *Let tomorrow look after itself.*

Tiana looked sleepily at the familiar room. Some of Jack's best tobacco leaves hung from the low, massive rafters. They would cure there near the fire. Tiana could smell the same aroma of tobacco and smoke in her father's rough shirt. Slices of apples and pumpkin and long, twisted shucky beans were strung on thread and hung from the ceiling too, along with bunches of dried herbs and ears of seed corn, their husks turned back and braided together.

Baskets of fruit and corn and white and purple and speckled beans lined the walls. Shelves held pickled corn, beets, green walnuts and tomatoes, cucumbers and dandelion buds. There were crocks of preserves and marmalades and apple butter, the overflow from the root cellar and the kitchen. Near the hearth stood two jugs of Jack's homemade corn liquor. Jack had put several splinters of scorched hickory wood in each jug. In three weeks the liquor would be as red as bonded whiskey. Jack said it tasted like wild flowers and made a man fart fire.

On one wall hung a bag of dark wool plaid, with Jack's *piob mor*, the great highland warpipes given him by John Stuart, his brother-in-law. Stuart had received them from old Ludavic Grant, the family patriarch, and the grandfather of Elizabeth and her sisters.

The Rogers' wigwam was the grandest in the area. The hewn log walls were squared and matched. Inside, the chinks were covered with split boards. The stone fireplaces were big enough for Tiana to stretch out in. As she watched the flames Tiana began to drift off to sleep. She heard the rattle of the copper curfew cover as her mother laid it over the raked coals. She heard the quiet whoosh as Jennie blew out each rush light that hadn't guttered already.

Jennie climbed the stairs, holding a bright torch of lighter pine. Jack followed with Tiana in his arms. He turned sideways so her long legs wouldn't hit the rough walls. He laid her gently on the soft feather bed, next to Nannie and Susannah. Tiana burrowed under the covers and smiled at her mother and father.

"That Greek was wrong," she murmured.

"Why?" asked Jack.

"I don't know anything, and I love you and mother. And Grandmother Elizabeth, and Fancy and my sisters and . . ." Her voice dropped, giving in to fatigue. Jennie and Jack tiptoed from the room.

Chapter 2

Tiana screamed when she felt cold hands grab her, jerking her awake. She heard Nannie yelling.

Susannah was bouncing on the bed and flailing at William and Joseph with her pillow. Feathers escaped from the ticking's seam and floated around them. William nibbled up and down Tiana's shoulder and arm. Between bites he made horrible cackling noises. Joseph was trying to bite Nannie and shouting that the Water Cannibals would eat her. He grabbed Susannah's ankle and pulled her down into the melee with them. Susannah shrieked. She was terrified of the Water Cannibals who stole children's souls.

"*Halehwi'sda, ungida'*, stop, elder brother!" Tiana struggled to break free as all five children thrashed in a tangle of arms and legs and covers. The hempen rope lacing that supported the mattress on the massive wooden bedframe creaked under them. Downstairs they could hear their father bellowing a favorite song.

> *And where they get one hell, may they also get ten.*
> *May the devil double rubble trouble damn them, said*
> *the sailor, Amen!*

The children stopped their horseplay briefly to chorus in on the "Amen!"

"*Agwetsi*, children," called Jennie's soft voice from the doorway. "*Nu'la*, come." She repeated the word, raising the pitch to change the meaning. "*Nu'la*, hurry. Grandmother Sun will rise without us."

The children fell silent and separated themselves from each other and the bedclothes. The girls giggled and whispered as they straightened the covers and followed Jennie downstairs.

The eight Rogers children who still lived at home and the black woman, Fancy, filed out the back door with their mothers. They scattered into the bushes to urinate. No one bothered to use the necessary. The older children had never gotten into the habit, and the younger ones were sure a latrine demon lurked in the murky hole.

The black of night had turned to pale gray, and the world seemed shrouded, mysterious. It was the special time of promise, the birth of a new day. Tiana had seen almost every dawn in the nine years since she was born. But each one still awed her.

The family crossed the cluttered back yard, ignoring the hens and ducks and honking geese that flocked around, demanding to be fed. Tiana ran her hand along the rough, weathered side of the old wagon, standing like a patient horse under the overhang of the barn. Then she hurried to catch up with Grandmother Elizabeth and to take her right hand. Susannah held Elizabeth's left one.

Tiana walked solemnly along the narrow trail to the stream, but she wanted to dance and sing. It was April, *Anoyi*, the Strawberry Moon. The air was perfumed with flowers and new leaves and moist earth. It was time to visit Hiwassee Town for the corn planting festival.

Tiana skipped once with the joy of being alive on such a beautiful day, and felt a slight squeeze of Elizabeth's strong fingers. Greeting the sun today, the time of the new moon, was serious. The entire family had to be purified against any possible tainting from the women's monthly cycles.

As Jennie led them upstream Tiana heard the faint sound of *ama'tikwalelunyi*, the rolling water place. They greeted Grandmother Sun every morning at the waterfall where Long Man, the river, spoke in a voice like Thunder's.

The children faced east and lined up, according to age, so their bare toes touched the water. While Tiana tried not to let her teeth chatter in the early morning chill, Elizabeth stood behind each in turn and recited a prayer to the river.

Gha! Listen! Now you have come to hear, O Long Man
O helper of people, you let nothing slip from your grasp.
Let the white staff of long life be in my hand.
Let my soul stand erect in the seventh heaven.

When Elizabeth had prayed over Susannah, the youngest, they all pulled off their nightshirts, and waded into the water. Tiana held her arms across her bony chest, knelt down, and sucked in her breath as the icy water closed over her naked body. She scrubbed herself vigorously with the gritty river sand, as much to keep warm as to get clean. When they had all washed they stood, shivering and looking east again, as Elizabeth finished the morning prayer. She asked the Provider, the Creator of the sun, the moon, and fire, to purify them, and to bless the family with health and long life. Tiana smiled as the golden crescent of the sun appeared over the hills.

"Good morning, Grandmother Sun," she murmured. "Smile on me today and help me be *u'da'nuh't*, a person of soul and truth and feeling, a kind person." A red-tailed hawk sailed across the sun's face, and soared on the morning breeze.

"Good morning, Hawk," Tiana said in a low voice. The hawk screamed its hoarse, piercing call, dipped its wings, and disappeared into the trees. Tiana felt goosebumps that weren't caused by the cold. Her heart thumped faster. She was sure the hawk had called her name. It was possible. Her mother and grandmother said every living thing had a spirit. And sometimes those spirits spoke to human beings.

"*Tawodi,*" Tiana murmured. "Hawk." She like the sound of it. Maybe the hawk was giving her its name. She'd often wondered what her secret name would be, and how she'd receive it. This must be it. Hawk. It was a good name.

As Tiana joined her brothers and sisters she smiled to herself. Not one of them noticed she had changed, that something important had happened to her. She hugged the secret inside her. Jack Rogers sauntered down the trail toward them, as he did every morning.

"Good morning, children." He nodded to them.

"Good morning, father," they answered. He stopped in front of Tiana.

"Why are you grinning like a baked 'possum, lass?"

"It's a beautiful day." She hesitated. "And a hawk spoke to me."

"Do you say so, now? And what would a hawk discuss? Mouse

bowels perhaps?" He boxed her affectionately on each side of the head.

She watched him stride to the stream, and strip off his nightshirt. His hairy white legs and buttocks were as familiar to her as the trees and boulders around the stream. And they were as much a part of this ceremony as Grandmother Elizabeth's prayers, although no one would say so. Jack dashed into the water as though charging an enemy's breastworks. He splashed and cursed the cold and sang as he washed. While he bathed, Jennie and Elizabeth led the children back toward the house and the morning's chores.

The ancient wagon creaked as it rocked along the narrow, rutted trail. They were going to visit their uncle, Drum, the headman of Ayuwasi, Hiwassee Town. The road had been worn down until Tiana could almost reach out and touch the sides of it at a level with the wagon bed.

Jack called the wagon Old Thunder, because its name in the Real People's language was *tikwale'lu*. It meant the rolling, crashing sound that thunder and wagon wheels and waterfalls made. They passed a stream of people, on foot and on horseback, all bound for Hiwassee Town and the corn planting festival. They called greetings as Old Thunder passed.

William and Joseph sat on the back edge and shot at birds and squirrels with their blowguns. James and John had ridden ahead. Jennie and Grandmother Elizabeth sat with the girls on corn shuck pallets laid on the floor of the wagon bed. They leaned against the stiff folds of the Osnaburg tent, and Tiana's cat slept in one of its valleys. They were surrounded by digging tools and baskets of clothes and food, bedding, utensils, and presents for their family and friends in Hiwassee Town.

Grandmother Elizabeth sucked tranquilly on her small white clay pipe. She had been gaining weight steadily in the past few years, and Susannah liked to sit on her soft lap and trace with her fingers the maze of deep lines around her grandmother's eyes and mouth.

Elizabeth's hair was streaked with gray and her beauty was blurred by the years. One had to search to find the delicate features she had passed on to Jennie and Tiana. But her eyes were still large and dark and somewhat wistful. And she was wise with the knowledge of the Real People. She talked around her pipe now as she told them stories. Tiana and her sisters leaned forward to hear her quiet voice over the noise of the wagon.

"Do not look at the new moon for the first time through trees, or you will be ill in the month to come," she said. "When you see the new moon, say 'Greetings, Grandfather. When you shine again we will be seeing each other.' That means you will live to see Grandfather Moon again."

"How do you know that?" asked Tiana.

"The great cannibal, Stonecoat, said so. He was a terrible giant who killed people and ate their livers." The girls knew that, but they liked to hear the story, because they could act in it. "Not even the greatest of our warriors could capture him. But a wise curer told the Council they must find seven maidens whose monthly flux came at the time of the full moon. He told them to lie down along Stonecoat's path and uncover their legs." Annie, Nannie, Tiana, and Susannah stretched their legs out in front of them and pulled their skirts up. " 'Well, well,' Stonecoat said. 'Beautiful women.' " And Elizabeth pinched their legs while they squealed and wriggled to get away.

"But as Stonecoat passed each maiden he became weaker and weaker and began vomiting blood. Finally, he fell down and was captured by the people. They tied him to a stake and burned him there. As he burned, his spirit rose and sang out all the stories and knowledge and customs of our people. Some of the songs were for hunting, and some for war. Some were for curing and some for love. Even after he died, the Real People could hear his spirit singing in the sky."

They passed the hours of the journey with songs and stories until they reached the Hiwassee River. Jack and Punk Plugged In, the ferryman, loaded the wagon aboard the rickety platform built between two large dugout canoes. They had to line the horses and wagon up carefully, or the boat would tilt precariously. On the other side, Jack paid Punk Plugged In with a twist of his tobacco. Punk Plugged In was a young man, but he seemed old. Tiana could not remember hearing him say more than a few words, and she had never seen him smile.

As Old Thunder lurched up the muddy slope of the riverbank and onto Hiwassee Island, Tiana stood up to look over the wagon's side. They passed the first house, far from the center of the village. It was the oldest of the few still built in the ancient style.

Upright poles supported walls of wicker latticework. The walls had once been covered with a plaster of red mud mixed with grass and deer hair. The wicker work showed underneath where great slabs of plaster had fallen away. The ground around the shack was littered with the debris. The remnants of the roof were thatched with broom sage and furry with moss.

The owner's name was Raincrow, but the children called her Spearfinger because she reminded them of the mythical old woman who haunted their dreams. Spearfinger lived in the side of the cabin's single room that still had a roof over it. The other side was open to the elements and overgrown with weeds.

Spearfinger was squatting, as usual, on an upturned barrel next to her door. She clenched a clay pipe upside down in her teeth. The children fell silent and avoided her eyes as they passed. The Spearfinger of their legends was a terrible ogress whose skin was like rock. She had a forefinger sharpened to a wicked point to stab children and eat their livers.

The children were never sure which was worse, to have her shout spells at them or to see her smile. When she smiled she flashed two complete sets of teeth. She had the evil look of a gar fish peering from a tangle of gray hair, like dead river grass. Many said she was *u'ne'go'tso'duh*, evil, with a blackness of soul.

She was surely mad. No one had ever seen her sit on the ground or on a chair. She was always perching on something. No one walked under a low-hanging tree without looking up first to make sure she wasn't lurking there. She claimed to be on friendly terms with the shades of every soul who had lived in her house. She talked to them loudly. Tiana imagined the ghosts following her like a flock of squabbling crows.

After Spearfinger's house the farms formed a neat, irregular patchwork of red clay fields bordered by grass strips. Most of the seventy or eighty cabins that made up Hiwassee Town stood alone in the middle of their fields. Dark green hedges lined the pathways connecting the cabins. The paths from the cabins to the fields were always carefully swept so *Selu*, the corn spirit, wouldn't stray.

Each cabin had a half-buried, conical sweat house across from the front door, and mounds of mussel shells and ridges of ashes in back. Some had beehives in black gum stumps. The bees made a steady hum and flowers bent and waved under their weight.

Most of the cabins, no matter how small or shabby, were shaded by apple and peach and plum trees. A few had storerooms or root cellars or separate kitchens. Most had open pavilions for summer living and corn cribs on tall, spindly legs. Hollow gourds hung on high crosspieces attached to poles. Martins flitted in and out of them. Tiana breathed in the heady aroma of smoke and horse pastures, blossoms and middens.

Above the trees at the center of the village rose the town house. It was built on top of a large mound, left there by the Old Ones. The low cone of the town house roof was covered with a layer of dirt where flowers and grasses had taken hold. From a distance it looked like a small mountain. The wagon skirted the *gatayusti* ball-field where a few boys rolled a stone and threw javelins at it.

Jack drove through the center of the village and stopped the wagon in front of the palatial cabin of Sally Ground Squirrel, Drum's wife. With two large rooms, separated by an open hall or dog trot, it was the biggest house in Hiwassee Town. It had a kitchen in back and a porch along the front. The doors and windows were open to let the breeze blow through. It had a privy house, storage sheds, two sweat lodges, and two cabins where Sally Ground Squirrel's six slaves lived.

Off to one side of the cabin was the tiny room where Drum sold a few trade items. Tiana loved Drum's store. It had things her father's did not. Drum stocked eel skins for tying back one's hair, silver bracelets and nose wheels and earbobs, rings and large round or crescent-shaped gorgets, necklaces of silver or engraved and polished shell.

There were plumes and strings of shiny white and deep purple wampum beads, painstakingly cut from quahog shells. There were small baskets of sinew and nettle fibers for the women who thought the trade thread snarled and broke too easily. Other baskets held lumps of soapstone for pipes or strings of trade beads in brilliant colors. On rainy afternoons, Tiana and her sisters liked to sort the beads by colors and sizes. They also liked to measure things on the scale Drum used to weight the brass pots and kettles sold at so much per pound.

Drum was sitting on the porch when the Rogers arrived. He rose a bit ponderously.

"*A'siyu*, I am good," he said in greeting, as Tiana and Nannie and Susannah threw themselves at him. "What is this?" He looked astonished as he pulled a chunk of crystallized sugar from Tiana's ear. He pulled another from Nannie's hair and, with a flourish, a third from Susannah's nose. They giggled as they took them. They hadn't figured out how Drum did that trick, but they were happy to think it magic.

Ahu'lude'gi, He Throws The Drum Away, had more white blood in him than Cherokee. If he had not been wearing the traditional fringed hunting coat, leggings, and turban, he would not have looked Indian at all. He was forty-five, with gray streaks in the curly auburn whiskers that almost reached his round chin. His wide, brown eyes were mild and good-humored and slightly bulging. He was beginning to sport a belly that hung over the bright, woven belt he wore wrapped twice around his middle. The belt's tasseled ends reached his knees and swung when he walked.

Jack settled down to talk with Drum. Jennie and Elizabeth went to the open kitchen to help Sally Ground Squirrel with the evening's feast. The girls ran off to play. There were many members of their mother's clan, The Long Hairs, in Hiwassee Town and the girls went in search of the cousins they called "sisters" and "brothers."

Tiana slipped away from the horde of children who raced through the village. She followed a path to a huge old cedar. The path led to its base and stopped, because Tiana wasn't the only one who considered the cedar special. It was a holy tree, fragrant and straight-grained and red, like the skin of the Real People. From time to time people came here to collect twigs to burn. The aromatic smoke of the cedar frightened away *anisgina*, ghosts.

Tiana stood with an arm outstretched, her fingers barely touching the fibrous bark. She threw her head back to look up the tall, straight trunk and into the branches.

"*A'siyu, Ajina,*" she said. "Greetings, Cedar. The hawk spoke to me today. I think it was giving me its name. Do you think it was?" A small wind stirred the needles near the top of the tree, as though in answer. Tiana put her arms around the trunk and pressed her cheek against the rough bark. "*Wadan*, *Ajina*, thank you, Cedar."

"Does The Cedar speak to you, child?"

Tiana whirled at the sound of the voice.

"I think so, Beloved Woman. But maybe not," she stammered. "I'm only a child. I know nothing." Tiana had never spoken alone to Ghigau, the Beloved Woman Nanehi Ward. She lived in Chota, a town to the north, but she visited Hiwassee often. Beloved Woman had adopted many orphans. They swarmed around her and called her *Ulisi*, She Carries Me On Her Back, the Real People's word for grandmother. But Tiana could never be so familiar with her. She couldn't even think of anything to say to her.

"The spirits speak to whomever they choose," Ghigau said. "If they speak to you, they have their reasons. They see something special in you." Ghigau stared hard at Tiana. "Will you not help plant the corn?" Nanehi Ward smiled, and Tiana felt better. From the distance she heard Drum's voice, calling from the town-house roof. He was telling everyone where to meet for the planting.

"*Hayu*! Yes!" Tiana said.

"Then come with me." The Beloved Woman held out her thin hand and Tiana took it.

"Ghigau." Tiana slowed her steps to Nanehi's regal pace. "Does your name mean Path, or Spirit People?"

"It means Path, little one. I wouldn't anger the immortals by taking their name."

"And is Nannie, my sister, named after you?"

"Maybe. I'm honored if she is." Nanehi knew there were hundreds of girls called Nannie in the Cherokee nation and that most of them were named in her honor.

It wasn't difficult to talk to Ghigau. The Beloved Woman wasn't so different from Tiana's own *ulisi*, Grandmother Elizabeth. Tiana knew Nanehi Ward could answer a lot of the questions that bothered her. She took advantage of the time alone with her.

"And is the cedar really red because people cut off a wicked magician's head and hung it in the top of one and the blood dripped down the trunk?"

"That's what the old women told me when I was a girl."

"Why does Drum sit and chant in that hut in the middle of the fields at corn-planting time?"

"He is calling to Selu, Mother Corn. If you listen carefully, you might hear the rustling sound of Selu bringing the corn."

"I'll listen for her, Beloved Woman." Tiana was excited. Older people rarely discussed planting and hunting rituals with young children. They were very sacred.

"Beloved Woman." This was a sensitive subject, but Jack Rogers always said she would not learn anything unless she asked. "When you were a young woman you fought with the warriors, didn't you?"

"Yes."

"And my mothers say you once killed a man in battle."

"Yes, I did."

"Was fighting in battle with the men exciting?"

Nanehi Ward paused. No one had ever asked her that question. She considered it a moment.

"Yes, it was."

"But later you counseled peace, didn't you? And you warned the Americans about an attack from us."

"Yes."

"The young men talk of how wonderful it would be to go to war again. Would it? Is war better, or peace?"

Ghigau picked up a twig. She was tall, so she squatted to be closer to Tiana. She adjusted the stick on one finger until it hung there, perfectly balanced.

"Now you do it," she said.

Tiana did.

"How does it feel?"

"Light. Almost alive, the way it teeters there."

"Life is like this," Ghigau said. "It must be always in balance. Kindness and *duyukduh*, justice, must balance evil. Wisdom is balanced by age, life by death. If your life is in balance, your soul will be as light as that twig. Your soul will fly."

They entered the village, and Tiana watched wistfully as the children jostled for Ghigau's attention. But she was soon laughing and joking with her cousins as they all ambled toward the fields in a long procession. The women's bright kerchiefs and belts and the men's calico shirts made it look more like a party than work. The men would do the heavy labor of clearing the fields. The women would plant together until they finished the portion Drum had assigned for that day.

Tiana left her moccasins at the edge of the field, near one of the ax blades set on a short pole. The blades faced the four winds. They were there to break up thunderstorms that might damage the crops. As Tiana walked out into the harrowed field, she felt as though her feet were taking root in the warm, red soil. She imagined herself growing straight and tall and fruitful, like the corn. She felt connected to the earth and everything that grew in it and lived off it. The hawk had spoken to her, and so had the cedar and the Beloved Woman.

She worked in rhythm with the others as she built up small hills with her mattock and watched Jennie drop seven corn kernels into each hill. Four was a sacred number, but seven was even holier and more magical. Tiana whispered a short charm of her own to each handful of corn as she covered them with earth. She wished them warm rains and gentle winds and she promised to visit them as they grew.

Chapter 3

Twenty-year-old Fancy grumbled loudly as she banged the pots around. She was tall, ebony black, and deceptively fragile-looking. Her full, loose dress was dyed a butternut brown. It was patched and faded and didn't quite reach her thin ankles. The sleeves were rolled up above her elbows. Her feet were bare and her hands were calloused.

She moved around the cluttered kitchen with the grace of a leopard. She had the long head and the fine features of her Ashanti ancestors. She preferred to speak Cherokee but she mixed it with English. She spoke both with an African accent she had recently picked up from frequent visits to the Vann plantation.

"I don't understand why you girls want to learn white ways," she muttered. "Except for Captain Jack, there ain't a white person worth hanging. White folks don't give black folks nor red folks nothing but abuse. And you'all is cluttering up my kitchen with your frippery. How'm I to cook for the Pharoah's army that lives in this house?"

Tiana looked up from the litter on the kitchen table.

"Father's making us go to school. And we have to make ink somewhere."

"Well." Fancy dried her hands in the folds of her skirt. "There's nothing more I can do here. You children are thick as mice in the corn cratch. I'll be in the garden." She took her straw hat from a peg and her hoe from among the tools leaning against the kitchen wall. As she walked out into the bright May sunshine, cats ran from all directions. Purring, with tails up, they milled around her legs.

The cats were supposed to eat mice in the barn and the cratch, the slotted wooden bin where the corn was stored. But Fancy slipped them scraps from time to time, and they were always on the mooch. Fancy planted cat mint at the edge of the garden. She said it was to keep insects away. But she and the children loved to watch the cats cavort among the grayish plants.

"*Wesa, wesa*, pussy, pussy," she called in her husky voice as she scattered stale cornbread. The chickens eyed the bread from afar. When the cats left they would find the crumbs.

Behind Fancy's tranquil face she was worried. Her life had been safe and comfortable for the past fifteen years. She had lived with the Rogers ever since Hell-Fire Jack had found her hiding beside her dead mother by the river. He had buried the mother in an unmarked grave and had brought the frightened child home, riding behind him on his horse. "I brought you a fancy present," he had told Elizabeth as he handed the child to her. And she had been called Fancy ever since.

Fancy couldn't tell them where she and her mother had come from or how they happened to be by the river. From the scars on the mother's back and the emaciated condition of her and the child, Jack assumed they were runaway slaves from far to the south. It took weeks for Fancy's body to fill out and for her belly, swollen by malnutrition, to return to normal. The Rogers hid her until they were sure no one would come looking for her. Then they raised her with their children.

As she hoed a corner of the large garden, the sun shining through the straw hat made a checkered pattern of light on her dark face. Thoughts turned over in her head. More and more whites were sneaking into Cherokee country. They came to trade or preach or squat on the Nation's land. To many of them any free black person was valuable property to steal and sell farther south.

This school was one more excuse for whites to be where they did not belong. No good would come of it. At best, those people would train the girls to be servants. That's all they considered black and red children suited for. Fancy shook her close-cropped head as she hacked viciously at the clods of rust-colored dirt.

In the house, James showed the girls how to make copybooks

while Jennie boiled ink. An iron kettle of water and crushed walnut shells simmered slowly while Jennie added vinegar and salt to set the color. Later she would pour in a bit of brandy to keep the ink from becoming moldy.

The oak table top was littered with gray shavings from the lead plummets the girls would use to draw lines. Blotting sand and lamp black for the ink had spilled. Tiana had a black smudge on her nose from the soot. There was fine gravel from the soapstone James was reaming out to make another inkwell. There were quill shavings and tiny shreds of paper from the trimmed edges of the copybooks. There were feathers and ferules and ink holders, wood shavings and walnut shells from the girls' snacks. Tiana was happily arranging her supplies in the square tea tin Jennie had given her when she heard hoofbeats outside.

"Mother Jennie, brother, come quick!" shouted Fancy. "They've killed James Vann."

"I feared this," said Jennie as they ran outside.

James Vann had killed a member of her clan in a duel two years before. The Real People didn't distinguish between types of murder, and James Vann was half Cherokee. Self defense, premeditation, accident, negligence, it was all the same in their law. The ghost of the dead man could not go to the Nightland until his death was avenged. The clan was honor-bound to avenge their dead member.

Fancy held the bridle of a big roan gelding. Sitting loose and easy in the saddle was a young black man. In his right hand he trailed a line back to a second horse. There was a body lying across it. The slave touched his hand to the brim of his tattered corn-shuck hat and bowed slightly. Three small diamond-shaped scars decorated each cheek, but otherwise his face was smooth and brown. His large eyes were remote under dark lashes. His nostrils were flat and flaring.

"You remember Coffee, Mother Jennie," said Fancy. "From the Vann place."

"Yes. What happened, my friend?"

"Marse James and I was hunting that thief what's been stealing livestock. The master was drinking at Buffington's tavern near Womankiller ford. Someone shot him through the chinks in the wall. I's on my way to take master's body home now. I thought you'all might want to know about it."

"Thank you," said Jennie. She turned to Fancy. "Dark daughter, get Coffee something to eat. Be quick. He had best be on his way before the day gets much hotter. Brother, find your father. He's in the lower field with Elizur." James ran off with Nannie and Susannah trailing behind. "I'll saddle a horse and go with you," said Jennie. "Daugher, tell *Ulisi* I've gone to the Vanns' with Coffee."

"Don't go, mother," said Tiana. "They might kill you."

"No, child. It's settled now. I must comfort Peggy Vann and take presents to cover the bones of the dead."

Coffee followed Fancy to the kitchen. Tiana shadowed them. She had never seen a back as broad as Coffee's. He had a short waist and long legs extending from heavily muscled haunches. He loomed over Fancy, yet he was just as graceful, in his own way.

Fancy's hand shook as she put leftover corn cakes on a plate. She threw a rasher of bacon into a skillet and set it on a long-legged trivet over the coals. While the bacon crackled and sputtered, she slipped Indian bread and dried apples and jerked beef into a leather wallet. When she spoke, there was fear in her voice.

"Did you do it, Coffee?" She pronounced it Kofi, his Ashanti name. He had been cargo on a slave ship eleven years earlier.

"No." He glanced at Tiana, who tried to look as though she weren't listening.

"Child, you're supposed to give Mother Elizabeth a message."

"Yes, sister." Tiana left reluctantly.

"I didn't kill him," continued Coffee. "But you know I wanted to. When Master was drunk he was as mean a man as God ever wattled a gut in."

"Why didn't you run when you had the chance?" asked Fancy.

"If I ran they'd think I killed him. Besides, I ain't ready yet. The new Cherokee police make it harder to escape. They'd have caught me, unprepared as I was." He leaned down and spoke softly in Fancy's ear. "And I wouldn't have left without you."

"Who do you think it was?" asked Fancy as she heaped Coffee's plate with bacon and cornbread and greens. He ate standing up, leaning against the oak table.

"I don't know and I don't care. The bastard's dead and there are few to mourn him. I expect his son, young Joe, will take over."

"Will he sell you?"

"Not likely." Coffee chuckled. "I do the work of three of his lazy niggers." Coffee cupped a huge hand on either side of Fancy's slender chin. His palms covered most of her thin face and curved around her large, brown eyes. His thumbs felt the pulse beating in her long neck. "I know how to bow and scrape, make myself necessary to Joe Vann. Then, when he doesn't expect it. . . whoosh. I'll steal path and go. And you'll come with me."

"When?" Fancy leaned against him and he wrapped his arms around her. She was tall enough for him to lay a cheek against the top of her head.

"Soon."

"When will I see you again?"

"Saturday night. The usual place."

"But the patols are looking for runaways here, on the Nation. The Georgians are behind it." Fancy hit her fists lightly against Coffee's chest. "Damn the whites! The Cherokee copy the worst in them—police, patrols, greed."

"Hush, Fance, hush. Will you be there Saturday?"

"Of course."

"I'd best go then."

"Are you ready?" Jennie called from outside. Coffee slung the wallet of food over his shoulder. He kissed Fancy quickly on the mouth, his fingers entwined in the tight curls on the back of her head. Then he went outside.

Tiana stood in the wreckage of her bedclothes. Even the hard, lumpy cornshuck mattress was on the floor. As she heaved one end of it back onto the sagging rope lattice on the bed frame, she fought back tears. Most of the thirty girls in the long dormitory were in the same predicament. The room looked like a tornado had blown through.

Mrs. Seeth MacDuff, stiff and straight in whalebone stays and wooden busks, patrolled the aisle between the two rows of cots. This was her first teaching job. She was nervous, as afraid of her charges as they were of her. The fear made her harsh. She tapped the bed posts and pointed out errors in bedmaking with a flexible willow rod. She hadn't hit anyone with it, but Tiana could imagine her doing it. Now and then she ripped the covers off a bed and the child started over. There was no talking.

One of the youngest children was sobbing in a corner, her nose pressed against the wall. She had wet her bed, been humiliated and sent to a corner. Susannah was standing in another corner. It hurt Tiana to see her there, so small and alone. Now and then Susannah would wipe her nose on her sleeve and peek sideways at her sisters.

Tiana wished she could change places with her. It was her fault

Susannah was there. Tiana had encouraged her to crawl into bed with her the night before, and they had been caught. Susannah had pulled their old trick of stuffing her small pillow and extra clothes under the blanket so it would look like she was still there.

"Wicked, sinful child," Mrs. MacDuff shouted when she discovered them. "Wicked!"

"Wicked" and "sinful" were new ideas for Tiana. She knew about being bad, of course. But wicked and sinful seemed to mean bad with something added. Something sinister and lingering. When Mrs. MacDuff said the words they carried a whiff of brimstone and a whimper of agony. Tiana already knew enough about Mrs. MacDuff's religion to think she didn't want to learn any more. It sounded ghastly, as her father would say.

As Tiana carefully folded the coarse sheeting to make the neat corner Mrs. MacDuff required, she glanced up at the ceiling. There was a dark spot on it that filled her with dread. A man had been killed in the attic of this school. The stain couldn't possibly be his blood, but it haunted her nonetheless. She could almost hear the angry voices of Doublehead and Ridge and the others. Old Doublehead had signed away some of the Real People's land in exchange for secret payments to himself. The national tribal council had condemned him to death for it, and he had fled here to hide.

Tiana could picture the old headman, his jaw and hip shattered, fighting his executioners. She imagined Ridge sinking his tomahawk into Doublehead's skull and the blood spurting. It had all happened up there, over her head. The Rogers children spoke of it secretly because their father had been involved somehow, at the beginning. What if Doublehead's vengeful ghost still lurked in the school's attic?

Even though the dormitory was crowded with beds and children, it had seemed bare and lonely that first night. Seeth MacDuff had sat up, knitting by the light of a tin lantern that threw shadows on her lean, stern face. She had a nose much too long for her. Even though she was young, there were fine lines radiating from her mouth as though it were gathered with thread into puckers. Her eyes were the blue of indigo dye water after the third or fourth dipping. She was encased to her sharp chin in a voluminous black dress with a high collar. Her pale brown hair was pulled so tightly into a bun, Tiana wondered if it gave her a headache.

When Seeth had finally gone to sleep behind a screen, Tiana had whispered for Susannah to join her. She had never slept by herself. Why should she and Susannah be miserable alone when they could comfort each other?

Now it was the morning Tiana had thought would never come as she lay awake aching with homesickness. Obviously they wouldn't all troop down to the river to bathe and greet Grandmother Sun. Grandmother Sun was already over the horizon. Tiana propped the shutter open with a stick that lay under the small window near her bed. She leaned her arms on the sill and looked out. It was a beautiful May day. Over the noise of the girls making beds and struggling with the buttons on their new clothes, Tiana could hear the birds. A pair of swallows swooped around their nest site in the eaves just above the window.

The last of the girls had used the chamber pots. The beds were finally made, and everyone dressed. Each student had found a small pile of clothes and a pair of shoes waiting for her on the long shelf that ran the length of both sides of the room. They had swapped until each had something that would fit. But Tiana's shoes were already beginning to pinch. A few older girls came in with basins of water and everyone crowded around to wash.

"Faces and hands only, children," said Seeth MacDuff. "Be quick." Tiana hurried, trying to hide her distaste at the water, which was gray by the time her turn came. She was eager to be away from this drab, chilly place and outside in the sun. She would take her shoes off as soon as she was out of Mrs. MacDuff's sight, and find a stream to bathe in properly.

"Stand at the foot of your bed, each of you."

Tiana ignored her. She waited for one of the older students to translate. She had learned that pretending not to understand English could be useful.

"Now kneel down. We are going to thank the Almighty God for this opportunity to improve your savage and wretched state."

After ten minutes of kneeling on the cold floor, Tiana was in despair. She was hungry and her knees and back hurt. This was obviously going to happen every day. Tiana began plotting excuses to go home.

Prayers were followed by scriptures. Scriptures were followed by singing and more prayers. Then they all stood, painfully, for the lecture on their duties at school. They would grow their own food, cook it, preserve it, serve it, and clean up the kitchen and dining hall. They'd tend the school's animals, and help with the milking and butchering. They'd make, mend, wash, and iron their clothes and the schools' linens. They would carry water and wood and clean the dormitory and school room, the barn and the outbuildings, after they'd made the brooms to do it.

There was more—embroidery, candle- and soap-making, carding, spinning, etiquette and deportment. But Tiana stopped listening. She rolled her eyes at Nannie and made a face. When would they have a chance to read or write?

Tiana spoke aloud in Cherokee. Her words rang out in the silence that followed Mrs. MacDuff's speech. They startled even Tiana, but her mouth was set in the line Jack Rogers used when he was angry.

"This one came here to learn to read and write, not feed the hogs."

Every head swiveled in her direction. The children could not believe one of their own was starting an argument. But the Real People were stubborn in defense of *duyukduh*, truth, or justice. Tiana felt justice was being threatened.

"What did she say?" Seeth MacDuff asked her interpreter. The girl translated. Seeth drew herself up inside her stays. "Child, you will do as you are told. If you learn nothing else here you will learn discipline and Christian humility."

"This one's father will not tolerate her coming home without learning to read." Tiana used the formal third person in an effort to state her case in an adult manner. "Her father paid money to send her here for an education."

"Too much education is unseemly in a girl. It encourages vanity. You will aspire above your station and bring down the wrath of God."

"Better that than the wrath of my father," Tiana blurted in English.

"Blasphemy!" Seeth paled and sucked in her breath. "What is your name, you poor, ignorant child?"

"Tiana Rogers." Tiana answered obediently, but she was appalled that someone would show such a lack of respect as to ask her name.

"I should have guessed. What can one expect of a child whose father is a depraved blasphemer openly living in sin?"

"Don't call my father names!"

"Diana . . ."

Tiana let this error pass. If this woman was so ignorant of proper behavior she would call someone by name, it was better she not use the correct one. And if she did know the unspoken rules about names, she might be using Tiana's to bewitch her. Tiana was glad she now had a secret name, a spirit name. It made her feel protected.

"Diana, you will kneel here while we eat breakfast. You will ask the Lord's forgiveness for what you have said. If you do not obey, I will send you home to your father. He shall not receive his money back. That is the agreement. I doubt he will be pleased to see the report I will send home. And I understand your headmen discuss discipline problems in council."

Tiana glared at her. Mrs. MacDuff was no fool. She was right. Jack Rogers wouldn't be pleased about losing the tuition money. And the thought of having her name mentioned in the council of headmen terrified her.

As Tiana kneeled, she clenched her teeth. She would stay. She would get her education.

Chapter 4

The mission school where Tiana was struggling for her education stood between her uncle Drum's town of Hiwassee and the nearest white settlement of Maryville, to the north. Maryville, Tennessee, had been settled on the site of the old Cherokee town of Ellijay, after the Real People had ceded that part of their nation to the Americans. It was a strange location for a town. The terrain was precipitous and laced with ravines. The countryside around it was beautiful, with mountains looming over it. Less could be said of Maryville.

Ragged stumps protruded from the trampled earth of the town. Few trees had been left standing in the scramble for building and heating material. It was August, 1809. It had been raining for three days. The unpaved streets between the crude cabins and taverns and the blacksmith shop were a morass of mud. The only signs of life were the horses standing dejectedly outside the taverns, a few dogs sheltering under wagons, and a hog the size of a small calf wallowing blissfully at the end of Maryville's main street. The street ran along the highest ridge in town, and cabins clung like barnacles to the sides of the hills and ravines around it. Water cascaded down the ravines and flowed into Pistol Creek as it paralleled Main Street.

In the center of town, the half-finished Blount County courthouse was surrounded by construction rubble. It looked as though it were melting back into the red mire around it. The tiny jailhouse and stocks were empty. The troublemakers must have been too damp or too melancholy to cause problems. The hard drinkers, a large proportion of the town's population, had gone to ground in the three taverns.

The favorite, Cunningham's, was next to Houston's new store. It had the only billiard table in town. The clack of the wooden balls could be heard there night and day. When the rain slacked or the wind shifted, sixteen-year-old Sam Houston could hear men swearing and shouting over their dice games and grimy cards, or singing exuberantly off-key.

Sam didn't particularly like the crowd that frequented Cunningham's, but he wished he were there anyway. He wished he were anywhere but where he was.

"Sounds like all hell's pounding bark next door," he said in his slow Virginia drawl. "Must have rained out the fair at Calamity Corners. And saved female purity, no doubt."

"What?" Sam's older brother, James, looked up from the account book. "Sam, you're not paying attention. I'll explain this once more." James chewed on the end of his pencil. It was an extravagant act. The old Faber was the only one in town. "You deduct the tare and the trett." James scribbled on a scrap of stained brown paper. His figures were cramped and tiny to save space. "Then you divide the suttle by the amount given. The quotient will be the cloff. Subtract that from the suttle and the remainder will be the neat weight."

"Neat," said Sam wearily. "What's the tare?" He idly watched the steady trickle of water that leaked through the wooden shingles and dropped loudly into a tin bucket underneath. Flies buzzed listlessly around the smoked hams hanging from the ceiling.

"I told you what the tare is," said James.

"I forgot."

"The tare is the allowance to the buyer for the weight of the container the goods come in."

"And what's the trett again?"

"I told you that too."

"Bad memory."

"You can memorize poetry. What's the matter with you?"

"Poetry's important. It's easy to remember. It rhymes. If this rhymed, I'd remember it."

"You can't eat poetry. This store can earn us a living."

"If you call this living," muttered Sam.

"Would you rather be clearing the south field?"

"Naw. Can't dance and it's too wet to plow. I might as well be here. What's the trett?" he said with resignation. He leaned his elbow on the counter and rested his chin in his hands.

"This is the last time." James was pushed to the edge of his patience. He spoke slowly, enunciating carefully. "The trett is the allowance of four pounds in every hundred and four pounds for waste—dust, chaff, insects."

"Four pounds of insects? Quite a crop. Maybe we should sell them separately," said Sam. "And do you divide the cloff into the suttle or the flummery?"

"Dammit! This is not flummery. This is serious business." James broke the pencil in a fury. He looked at the pieces in horror, then flung them through the open door of the potbellied stove and into the fire. He grabbed his hat from atop a buxom dress form and stalked out. He paused in the doorway to jam the hat on his head and turn on Sam. He pointed a finger at his younger brother and shook it.

"Stay here until closing time. Dust everything. Add the week's accounts. Empty the ashes. Beat the blankets so the moths don't eat them. And keep out of trouble." He turned and ducked his head to clear the wide, sloping eaves. He cursed as he sank calf-deep in mud that flowed over the top of his boot. The suction almost pulled the boot off when he yanked it out. Rain water from the eaves poured down his back when he tilted his head. "And fill in this hole," he shouted. "A mule could drown in it."

Then Sam was alone and restless. He was at that impossible age when he considered himself a man, but no one else did. He craved adventure like a bear craves honey. He daydreamed that a lathered horse would gallop down Main Street, its rider shouting that the Indians were coming. He pictured the painted warriors drifting through the forest around the town. Only Sam and his friends could save Maryville from destruction. Sam grabbed a hoe from the ones leaning against the wall. He leaped the tall counter and crouched behind it. He peered over the top of it, scouting the enemy.

"Bang, bang." He fired the hoe at the dress form, half-hidden by a stack of crates. "Zach, I got one!" Then he realized how foolish his voice sounded in the cluttered store. Sixteen and playing childish games. Still, Indians had attacked Maryville well within the memory of the older settlers. It was the most exciting thing Sam could imagine, but he put the hoe back a little sheepishly.

He tried to pace. He was six feet tall, and still growing, and there was little room to spare in the store. The low ceiling was lowered even further by the things hanging from it.

Dangling from the beams were boots and kettles, skillets and animal traps and hanks of strong-smelling twine. There were ox yokes, bridles and hackamores, waffle and wafer irons, long-handled spatulas, chocolate and coffee bean roasters. There were cheese drainers, washboards, candle molds, and snuffers.

Hoes and shovels, scythes, pit saws, splint brooms, axes, gun worms, and grain cradles leaned against the wall. The floor was covered with barrels and kegs and crates of powder, lead, nails, salt pork, pickles, tobacco, soap, dried apples and peaches, flour, lump sugar, and ardent spirits. The shelves were piled with boxes of handkerchiefs, combs, knives, flints, hard soap, hose, snuff, tea, sealing wax, scissors, and sewing notions.

The only color in the store was the corner with the cards of ribbons and bolts of cloth—strouds and calicos, canvas and linen and Irish Osnaburg. Sam held a length of sky-blue dimity, the color of his eyes, against his chest. He wrapped it around him, togalike, and squinted at his reflection in the small mirror next to the ladies' bonnets.

" 'But that imperious, that unconquered soul,' " he thundered, his voice powerful for one so young, " 'no laws can limit, no respect control.' " He folded his arms across his broad chest. "You handsome dog," he said to his reflection. "You're far too fair a lad to be dogging a plow or dusting a counter." He put the cloth back and ran his fingers through his thick, chestnut hair.

He idly sifted white corn meal through his fingers and wondered how many pounds of insects were in the barrel. There were several pounds of rat shit, he'd wager. "Two quarts make a pottle," he muttered, walking a few paces, turning and retracing his steps. "Two bushels make one strike. Two strikes make a coom. Two cooms make a quarter. Four quarters make a chaldron. Five quarters make a wey. Two weys make a last." Measuring and counting. Sam tried to picture himself, fifty years hence, still standing at this counter, his life measured in ells of cloth and cooms of corn. And he would never understand the currency exchange. There was English standard and the new federal decimal system, the dismal system, Sam called it. There were state currencies, Continentals, Johannes, Pistoles, Moidores, Dubloons, not to mention bartering. *Well*, he sighed. *It's better than plowing. An evening with a priest of the Inquisition is better than plowing.*

Sam stretched over the counter and pulled the bottom wooden box from a stack of them. He felt around inside it, under the corset. He took out his copy of Pope's translation of the *Iliad*. The new French fashions made corsets less in demand these days, and James never opened these boxes unless he had to. Sam had found a safe hiding place for Pope.

The boy emptied the bucket under the leak. He pulled a chair closer to the stove and threw a small chunk of hickory into the fire. The rain had brought a chill with it. He propped his feet on the ash box, which was overflowing, and grabbed a withered, shriveled apple-john from a basket. The fruit looked terrible, but it kept two years and tasted good. A small mouse swung wildly from one of the bags of seed hanging from the ceiling. Sam saluted him, wished him well, and opened his book.

He wasn't expecting any business on a rainy afternoon, so he jumped when a movement caught his eye. He swung his feet to the floor with a thud of his heavy boots. There was a boy, about fifteen years old, standing six feet from him.

"Hullo," Sam stood, feeling nervous and awkward. He was too startled to be frightened. Indians rarely came to Maryville.

James Rogers managed to look solemn and noncommittal at the same time. His slender brown body was naked except for a sodden linsey-woolsey loincloth. His long black hair was braided. He was wet. Two mud-coated objects dangled loosely in his hand. It took Sam a few seconds to realize they were moccasins. James raised his right hand in a mockery of an Indian greeting.

"How," he said.

"How," said Sam, raising his own hand. He saw the hand still held the *Iliad* and dropped the book on the chair. "I didn't hear you come in."

"I took sneaking lessons in school." James was the best English speaker of the Rogers children. He spoke it better than most people in Maryville. "I was quite good at it. Advanced to the first form in stealth. Besides, I've read Rousseau. I know how to act."

"I'll be damned." Sam finally noticed James's dark blue eyes.

"That's not for me to say." James grinned. "Actually, I damned you roundly when I stepped into the lake at your door." He held up the moccasins. "Have you considered raising trout there?"

"Whales. I ordered a pair from Noah when he sailed by earlier. Put your foot gear in front of the fire."

Sam cleared off another chair and dragged it near the stove. James set his moccasins neatly in the sand box under the stove's ornate, paw-shaped feet. He looked with distaste at the cigar butts and tobacco that had turned the sand dark brown, but he made no comment. Sam tossed him a white linen towel, which turned reddish brown with mud as James dried himself on it.

"What tribe are you from?" Sam asked, leaning his back against the counter and crossing his arms.

"Scots," said James.

"No, really."

"Really. I'm part Cherokee. A woods colt that's been domesticated, you might say."

"Oh." There was an embarrassed silence. A breed. Well, to hell with what the town might think. Sam held out his hand. "Sam Houston," he said. "Sam, to friends."

"James." The boy took the hand firmly. "James Rogers."

"Are you cold?" Sam thought he saw James shiver.

"No." James smiled. "An Indian would have to be frozen solid before he'd admit he was cold."

"Well, I was just going to make myself a hot flip. Man can't drink alone." He stuck the flattened end of an iron flip dog into the fire to heat while he poured beer into a heavy, two-quart glass. With a pair of sugar scissors, he cut chunks of brown sugar from a loaf and added them to the beer. "Now for the best part," he said.

"Kill Devil," said James.

"Correct." Sam drained two gills of rum from a cask. With an elaborate sweep of his arm, he pulled a silver nutmeg holder from his pocket and shook the hard kernel into the palm of his hand. He grated it on the perforated lid of the holder and shook the powder into the glass. Then he stirred it with a stubby flip stick. James plunged the glowing end of the flip dog into the glass. The liquor foamed and steamed, saturating the air with the smell of hops and nutmeg.

The boys slouched contentedly in their chairs. They warmed their bellies and the palms of their hands with the hot glass they passed back and forth between them. They sniffed the fragrant steam that rose in their faces and savored the flip's burnt, bitter taste. Outside, the rain drummed hypnotically. Mice played tag among the boots hanging over their heads. A cricket chirped in the corner. Sam enjoyed the moment as he enjoyed the drink. There was no one in Maryville to whom he felt closer than he did to this stranger right then. Sam had many friends in town, but none with this air of exotic mystery about them.

"What brings you to Maryville?" he finally asked.

"Trade. My father runs the government factory at Hiwassee garrison. But he doesn't have nearly as many wonderful things as you have here. This is truly *uskwiniye'da*."

"*Uskwiniye'da*?" Sam asked.

"It means 'every kind.' Our word for store."

"*Uskwiniye'da*." Sam rolled the word around on his tongue. He liked it.

"Father just has hatchets, knives, beads, blankets, mirrors, trinkets. Things that appeal to the childlike primitive mind." James flashed another of his dazzling grins. Sam realized the smile showed more than humor. Being both white and Indian must have been difficult. A smile was something to hide behind.

"We stopped to see our sisters," James went on. "They're in school at the old Tellico blockhouse. My brother John is with me. He's seeing to the horses over at Russell's inn. We had planned to spend the night there, but Russell seemed none too pleased to see us." A sudden shout and pistol shots from Cunningham's made James flinch.

"It's all right," said Sam. "They're only shooting at each other." But Sam knew James had reason to flinch. Most of the houses in Maryville had heavy shutters to repel arrows and musket balls. Peace had only been made with the Cherokee a year after Sam was born. A treaty didn't wipe out fifty years of warfare and rancor. Hatred was rooted more deeply in the settlers than the huge stumps in their fields.

"What do those men do for a living?" asked James.

"Name something illegal," said Sam wryly. There was another comfortable silence.

"We brought civilized clothes with us," said James finally. "But the weather's been so hell-fired ghastly, we didn't want to ruin them."

It wouldn't matter, thought Sam. *Loincloth or cravat, there's no denying this lad's an Indian.*

There was a clatter and a creaking outside. John Rogers drove Old Thunder under the eaves, built wide to shelter the unloading of freight. The wagon sounded as though each board and metal fitting were operating independently.

"God-damn it! Hell-fire!"

"John found the hole." James rose reluctantly and went to the door.

"How do you curse in Cherokee?" asked Sam, following him. It might prove a useful bit of knowledge.

"We don't."

"Not ever?"

"No. We never found it necessary until we met white men."

"Hell-fired hole!" John was still swearing as he stalked through the open door and dropped a basket of peaches on the floor. "Help unload," he said abruptly in Cherokee, ignoring Sam. He stamped out, his work boots vibrating the floor boards. James looked apologetically at Sam.

"Someone must have insulted him at Russell's."

Sam shrugged. *I wouldn't be surprised.*

The wagon canted sharply to the left, the rear wheel deep in the hole. John was hauling back the heavy, sodden cover with ferocious tugs. The smell of the canvas—coarse, wet cotton and mildew—almost choked Sam.

"*Hadawesoluhsda, unginili.* Rest, elder brother." James laid a hand on John's arm. "They don't matter."

"Not to you." John heaved a keg of whiskey onto one broad shoulder. "But if I had a choice, I'd draw and quarter them, after I'd burned them alive and scalped them." John was stockier than James and shorter, with the powerful muscles of his father. His brown eyes were smaller and more closely set in his square, brown face. His dark brown hair was braided and hung down his back. His baggy homespun trousers clung wetly to his sturdy legs. He wore no shirt.

They finished unloading in silence. They piled everything in the middle of the floor, the only space available. John stood defiantly in front of the heap, as though defending it.

"Father say come here." His accent was heavier than James's although he was a year older. "He say Houston only honest man in town. All others have miller's thumb, cheat on weights."

"Glad to hear we have a good reputation," said Sam. Much as he disliked his brothers, Sam had to admit they were honest. Their mother made sure of it. "What have you to trade?"

"Beeswax, honey, peaches, baskets." John held up one of the beautifully woven cradles coveted by the settler women. "Whiskey from father's distillery. Tobacco, Orinoco, stemmed. Good. Strong. Preserved food, ginseng, indigo, deerskins, several bucks worth here." A deer hide, or buck skin, had been the medium of exchange with the Indians for years. A buck had come to mean a dollar.

The boys spent the rest of the afternoon sorting and weighing and haggling. Sam disliked store-keeping, but he had a natural bent for it. When James and John had picked out what they needed, they loaded the wagon. It took all three of them to lift the last item, a barrel of dry plaster. Then they settled down in front of the fire again with a fresh glass of flip.

John bit off a chunk of tobacco from a black twist of it. He chewed slowly as he stared into the fire. From time to time he shot a brown stream into the sand box under the stove. He had picked up the habit from his father.

"Fellow from here, one of the old Wataugans, Moss Greeley, went into Knoxville the other day," Sam said conversationally. "Slow as pond water, Moss is. He stayed at the new hotel there. And a sumptuous place it is too. Lavish appointments, all gilt and glitter." Sam slouched, stretched his long legs, and hooked his thumbs under the braces that held up his baggy homespuns. The other two boys slid down further in their chairs, the better to enjoy the story.

"Well, ol' Moss set his besmirched carcass in a red velvet chaise in the lobby and proceeded to chaw his quid of long green. Now and then he'd project a sluice of amber onto the pristine floor." John punctuated the story with a sluice of his own as he concentrated on Sam's extravagant vocabulary. Sam continued.

"An employee of that eminent establishment brought over a gleaming, refulgent cuspidor and placed it in front of our local worthy. Ol' Moss squirmed on the chair so he was pointing in a different direction and let fly again. The lackey put the cuspidor in front of him. And again Moss politely swerved to avoid it. This happened several times, until Moss's neck began to ache from twisting it every which way. He fastened a baleful eye on the earnest young man with the cuspidor. 'Now see here, son,' he said. 'If'n you don't take that damned thing away from here, I'll spit right in the middle of it, dire-reckly.' "

James and John chuckled and there was another serene silence.

"What were you reading when I came in?" asked James.

"Pope. The *Iliad*. Have you read it?" Sam leaned forward eagerly.

"No. It's as Hippocrates said. 'Art is long and life is short.' I want to read it someday though."

"We could read it together. Stay here awhile."

"Can't," said John. "Must go back to Hiwassee Town. Russell say, 'You turds be gone by sunset.'" John drew his finger across his throat and scowled.

"Russell would say something like that." Sam didn't mention that Russell had lost family in the war against the Cherokee.

Sunset wasn't far off. Sam considered inviting them home. His mother would be as courteous to them as she was to everyone. But Sam doubted his brothers would be. Sam liked James Rogers and even dour John too much to see them humiliated in his own house. But the thought of them climbing into their rickety wagon and driving out of his life was intolerable.

"I wish you could stay," he said wistfully. "It's dull as damp powder here." There was another shot from next door and the sound of breaking glass.

"Doesn't sound dull to me," said James.

"Take my word for it. It is."

"Come to Hiwassee," said James. "Stay with us."

"I couldn't."

"Why not?" asked John.

"Your people wouldn't want me. A white boy."

"Sure they would," said James. "You could live with my uncle Drum. He relishes company."

"He doesn't even know me."

"That makes no difference to Drum. Living at our house isn't that different from your own, I'll wager. But you'll like Drum and Hiwassee Town. It's more like the old days there."

"I have a family here."

"So? A man has to go off on his own to find his purpose. Our people understand that. Yours will too."

"Anyway, this place stinks." John dismissed Maryville with a wrinkle of his nose. Sam smiled at him.

"It was better before people got civilized and built backhouses. Now the shit piles up. The tannery's odiferous. When the wind's right, the smell will coat your teeth."

"Sam." James sat eagerly on the edge of his chair. "Come back with us. We'll have a wonderful time, I promise you."

"Can we go hunting?"

"Every day if you like."

"Would it be safe? I mean, the Cherokee have no reason to trust whites."

"Mother trusted father," said John laconically.

"Of course it's safe," said James. "You'll be my special friend. Like Uncle John Stuart." Sam looked puzzled. "Back in 1760 Chief Aganstata liked Captain Stuart, my mother's sister's husband. He saved him from being massacred with the rest of the soldiers at Fort Loudon. A special friend is always safe. Drum made my father a special friend thirty years ago."

Why not? There was a long silence while Sam sipped his flip and considered the idea. He poked it and pried it. With three slaves and four other sons, his mother didn't really need him. Sam suspected she insisted he work at the store to get him from underfoot. And she was used to his running off for days at a time to go coon hunting. Maybe this time he'd stay a little longer. A week or two. She wouldn't worry.

This was what Sam's brother John called "opportunity," although probably not the kind he had in mind. Who knew when one was likely to pass his way again.

"How far is this Hiwassee Town?" he asked.

"About sixty miles."

"I'll do her." Sam jumped to his feet. "Let me throw a few things into a poke." He scurried around the store, filling a feed sack with items he thought he might need. "What does Mr. Drum like?" He asked.

"He likes brandy," said John.

"French, if you have it," said James. "But he'll drink Barbados."

"His name is Ahu'lude'gi, He Throws The Drum Away. But we call him Drum. When white people are around he calls himself John Jolly," added John.

"Why is that?"

"Oh, funny custom, I guess. One doesn't tell possible enemies one's name. Gives them power over you." James changed the subject. "He'd like calico for a new coat. The brightest you have. Red, preferably."

Sam began filling another sack. "Now I need some mitchin."

"What?" asked John.

"Mitchin. Tucker. Tuck-a-nuck. Viaticum. You know. Food for the road. And beverage too, of course." He rolled a keg across the floor. "It's only swipes," he said apologetically. "Small beer. You'd need an ocean of it for a first-class toot." Sam brushed the flies off a ham hanging from the ceiling and unhooked it. "Now I'll filch some duds and I'll be ready."

"Filch some duds?" James and John both looked confused.

"Hook some togs. You know. Steal some clothes. I thought you spoke English."

"So did I," said James.

"You steal, we blamed," said John.

"I'm not stealing," said Sam. "I'm taking a few things on credit. They owe me for two weeks hard work here. I'll leave an I.O.U. for the balance."

"Will you leave a message telling your father where you are?"

"Hell no. I don't want my brothers coming after me. Anyway, my father's dead."

"Listen." John came to attention.

The rain had stopped. Somewhere a wagon started up with protesting squeals and the loud sucking plop of wheels through mud.

"It's getting late," said James nervously. He and his brother were young and alone in hostile territory. Night was coming on.

"Let's git while the gittin's good," said Sam.

The ride down Main Street was interminable. Sam told himself it was because he didn't want his brothers to catch him before he escaped. But sitting there, high on the shaky seat of the clattering wagon, he felt like a very large, moving target.

The street was empty except for the patient horses at the hitching rails, their coats steaming as they dried. And there were the dogs and the wallowing pig and a few bedraggled chickens wading in the puddles and pecking at drowned bugs and earthworms. One of the dogs detached himself from his nest in a burlap bag under a porch and pursued the wagon. He snapped at the rear wheel, more from a sense of duty than the joy of the chase.

Sam's skin crawled as though the stares from behind the cracks in the doors and shutters were palpable. Not everyone in Maryville hated Indians. The tolerant merely looked down on them. There just weren't very many tolerant folks.

The wagon inched past Russell's inn and stable, then past the shack where Love built beaver hats and saddles. The boys approached Porter Academy, standing alone in a meadow off Main Street. Sam hooked his thumb nail behind his upper front teeth and flipped it, making a loud, disdainful click in the school's direction.

"What's the matter?" asked James.

"Learning would be a great pleasure if it weren't for schools." Sam had spent one term at the academy. He had left in a huff because, he said, they couldn't teach him the classics in the original Greek and Latin. However, the rumor in town was that he didn't like the academy's rules. No drinking, gambling, swearing, or fighting. No horse races or balls or other "frolicking assemblies." Sam figured that was like throwing away the sweet kernel of life and eating the chaff.

The boys almost made it out of town without trouble. They only had to pass the Wayside Inn. The Wayward, Sam called it. The lanky sow wallowing out front was as good an advertisement for the tavern as any. Sam's mother forbid him to enter the place. That was probably because of Smitty. Smitty was a lady of pleasure. Her tiny room was attached discreetly to the rear of the Wayside, with a view of the tavern's necessary. A man could relieve himself in more than one way behind the Wayside.

No-'count Maryville, Sam thought. *Small potatoes and few to the hill.* Sam held his breath as they drew parallel to the sagging front porch of the tavern. It sounded crowded inside. The boys jumped when the door slammed open, breaking one of its wooden hinges and dangling askew. A small, filthy man, arms and legs spread, flew backwards through the opening. His momentum carried him, flailing for balance, off the edge of the porch and into the street. He landed on his back with a splash. It was obviously the most contact he'd had with water in a long time. The sow surged to her feet with a grunt and a twitch of her kinked tail. As she walked off with an air of injured dignity, the swarm of flies around her divided, some preferring to stay with the newcomer.

The Wayside's doorway filled with men, hoping for a fight. But the man in the puddle just lay there. He stared serenely at the gray sky and swore steadily at his assailant, a cadaverous fellow who looked down at him from the porch.

"God-damn your god-damned old soul to hell-fire and damnation, god-damn it," said the man in the puddle. "And god-damn your father's god-damned soul to hell-fire, and your god-damned grandfather's god-damned hell-fired soul, and your hell-fired ancestors, all the god-damned way back to the damnable, hell-fired son of a god-damned bitch that spawned your god-damned hell-fired, damnable line." His voice trailed off with the effort. "Damnation!" he muttered. He struggled to rise, but the mud sucked him back to its bosom. He probably preferred the mud to his bed at the inn. It was softer and had no bedbugs. The water drowned the man's fleas, and he didn't have to share the puddle with fellow travelers. He fell asleep, snoring in little hiccups.

The man on the porch swayed, steadying himself with one hand on a shifty post. His watery blue eyes, rimmed with red, focused on the wagon. He pointed a finger at Sam and his new friends.

"Injuns!" he shouted. "Little Sammy Houston's takin' up with Injuns."

"Can you prod these nags along any faster?" Sam asked John from the corner of his mouth. Sam was too big to fear most of the men in town, but he did fear Dirty Dutch. Even sober, Dutch had the look of a man who cared little for his own life, much less anyone else's.

"What if they shoot at us?" asked James.

"They won't," said Sam. "They have to check their pieces at the door. Anyway, they couldn't hit a barn if the door was swinging. Po' whites and piney woods tackies, we call their kind."

"Trunk," muttered John.

"They are indeed drunk," said Sam. "How about more speed?"

John flicked the whip casually. He didn't want to tuck tail and run from this scum, but he didn't want to face them either. A dozen men moved off the porch in a pack and followed the wagon on foot. They had not the collective wits among them to mount their horses. Dirty Dutch loudly described the tobacco pouches that could be made from an Indian's scrotum.

"Either of you boys armed?" Sam asked.

"We aren't crazy," said James.

"White men see Indian with gun, shoot first," added John.

"We have a blowgun," said James.

"Just thought I'd ask." Sam resigned himself to his fate.

"String them along, brother." James glanced over his shoulder. "Wear them down, draw them away from their horses."

"Can't go too fast," said John. "Horses plenty tired."

"You have an idea, James?" asked Sam.

"Maybe." James stood and faced backwards, bracing his knees on the jolting seat. He put one arm up and pumped it, wriggling his balled fist obscenely at the end of it. "That's what I'm going to do to your mothers and sisters, you barnyard bungholers," he shouted.

"Are you demented?" Sam put his arms over his head and ducked. With a howl, the mob broke into a run. Rocks hit the back of the wagon.

"How far away are they?" asked John. He was concentrating on the holes in the road.

"About a stone's throw," Sam mumbled to his knees.

"You've got their range, brother. Keep that distance." James was cool now and smiling wickedly. Sam didn't know James had a temper. Few people knew it. He hid it behind his smile. Sam glanced at John and saw he was grinning maniacally and driving with considerable skill.

"I thought you said you weren't crazy," wailed Sam, clutching the side of the rocking wagon.

"When I give the word, slow down, brother," said James.

"Slow down!" Sam looked wildly at the ravening pack behind them. "Oh, Lord, whatever I did wrong in this world of care, I'm sorry for it."

"Now!" said James. John began reining in the horses slyly, so they seemed to be tiring on their own. James climbed over the back of the seat, and moved carefully toward the rear of the bucking wagon bed.

The men were tiring, but they thought they were gaining. That spurred them on. The look in Dutch's eyes wasn't even remotely human anymore, and he wasn't wasting breath shouting. There were flecks of spittle at the corners of his mouth. James could see the green scum on his teeth when he snarled.

"If he catches you, James," Sam shouted over the din, "he won't stop skinning at your balls. You'll be the biggest god-damned tobacco pouch ever made."

James dodged the few rocks the men had the energy to throw. He pried the lid off the big barrel by the tail gate.

"Father skin you if they don't," John called over his shoulder.

"I'll take my chances with father." James freed the barrel from the ropes holding it. He stuck his tongue out at Dutch, to encourage him. Sam's knuckles were white on the edge of the wagon seat, as much from fear as from holding on. But he realized what James had in mind, and he smiled too.

"It'll work," he shouted. "The wind's right."

Dutch was almost within reach of the tailgate. With a triumphant gleam in his eye, he grabbed for it. The others were close behind. James braced the barrel of plaster against the wagon gate and lifted it from the bottom. Using the tailgate as a fulcrum, he tipped the barrel so its contents poured down on Dutch and the others. The powdered lime rock and horse hair blew into their faces and eyes. A helpful wind blinded them with it, setting them to sneezing and coughing. It coated them with white dust before the plaster settled into the mud. The men's feet churned it into a thick, hardening mass.

James heaved the empty barrel over the edge of the wagon and it rolled in the men's path. He laughed as most of them fell in a tangle, with Dutch on the bottom. They thrashed in the white mud until they were all thoroughly coated.

"Let's go home," said James, still laughing. He held onto the tailgate board with one hand and waved at Dutch.

"Tsi'stu wuliga' natutun' une' gutsatsu' gese'i," said John.

Sam looked at James, who was settling in between him and his brother.

" 'The rabbit was the leader of them all in mischief,' " James translated. "We have many stories about the rabbit outwitting bigger, more ferocious enemies."

"Do you suppose I'll hear some of them?" Sam asked.

"Of course."

"Whoo-o-o-ee!" yelled Sam. He skimmed his tattered old hat back toward their fallen foes. "Whoo-o-o-o-ee!" he shouted again. He was filled to bursting with laughter, relief, and joy.

As he watched his hat settle at Dirty Dutch's feet, Sam wondered what kind of reception he'd receive when he returned from his holiday with the Cherokee. Maybe he'd stay three weeks, to give this prank a chance to die down. But he didn't worry much. That was too far in the future. All he could think about was what adventures he would have with the Indians. Folding his arms across his broad chest, he settled back on the hard seat.

"How do the Cherokee say 'Howdy-do'?" he asked.

Chapter 5

"Tiana Rogers, drop that snake!" Seeth MacDuff shrieked across the dusty schoolyard. She broke through the crowd of girls waiting their turn at scotch-hopper and headed for Tiana at an undignified run. Tiana looked up from the slender green snake she held stretched between her hands.

"Don't worry, Mits MacTuff," she called. "I won't harm him." Assuming she had mollified her, Tiana continued nibbling up and down the snake's back. She was careful not to break its dry, satiny skin with her teeth. Mrs. MacDuff ran faster.

"Hurry, Tiana," whispered Nannie, "or I won't have my turn."

"I get him next," hissed Susannah.

The snake didn't seem to care who had him. He laid his emerald-green head and chartreuse belly along Tiana's wrist, enjoying her warmth. He seemed reassured by her promise not to hurt him.

"Drop it this instant, Tiana. Kill it." Seeth waved her hands frantically. She looked like a startled stork trying to become airborne. The hems of her rusty black skirts had erased the scotch-hop lines drawn in the dirt and raised clouds of dust in her wake. She stopped a safe distance away, her face warped with revulsion and fear.

"Kill the nasty thing, Tiana."

"I can't do that," Tiana said.

"You'd best drop it," said Nannie wistfully. "I'll have to find another. And this one was such a lovely, big snake."

"Good-bye, *Salikwa'yi*, Brother Greensnake." Tiana watched the snake slither away. Seeth MacDuff approached cautiously.

"Where is it?" She peered into the bushes.

"Gone," said Tiana.

"Whatever possessed you to do such a nasty thing?" Seeth didn't wait for an answer. "Go wash your mouth with soap. Savagery! Eating a live snake." Seeth shooed the air behind Tiana, trying to hurry her along without touching her.

"I wasn't eating him," Tiana said over her shoulder. "Biting snakes gives children strong teeth. I explained it to him." As the girls parted to let them pass, they giggled. Tiana was in trouble again. It happened almost every day.

"Pagan superstition. God gives you strong teeth if you deserve them," Seeth said.

"Maybe God chooses to look like a snake sometimes," Tiana said. "If I were God and could do anything, I'd try different bodies. What fun that would be."

Seeth looked as though, when lightning struck, she didn't want to be in Tiana's vicinity.

"God doesn't have fun. And it's blasphemy to even think you might be God." She raised her eyes to heaven, imploring aid from a higher source.

The trouble with Mits MacTuff, thought Tiana as she trudged toward the soap and the water, *is that she has no imagination. Of course God has fun. Why else bother to be God? Did Mrs. MacDuff really think God existed only to punish people?* If so, Tiana felt sorry for both God and Mrs. MacDuff.

"If I were God I'd be a hawk and fly high in the clouds, looking down on the lovely world I'd made." She was caught up in the whole glorious idea of omnipotence. "Ouch!" She rubbed the crown of her head where Seeth had rapped her with a thimble.

"Thimell pie, thimell pie, Tiana's eating thimell pie," taunted one of the girls.

"*Utsu'tsi*, titmouse," Tiana hissed scornfully. Everyone knew the titmouse was a tale-bearer and a liar and much disliked among the Real People.

"Tiana spoke an Indian word, Mits MacTuff." Like most of the Real People, the child had difficulty distinguishing between d's and t's in English.

"I didn't hear her, Mistress Lucy, and the Lord loves not a snitch."

Snitch? Surely Mrs. MacDuff didn't have a sense of humor. But at least she was fair. She hadn't taken the word of a tattler, and Tiana wouldn't receive the hated metal token. The token was passed to any student who slipped into her native tongue. The one who had it at the end of the day received three blows across her palm with her hornbook. A mouthful of soap for biting the snake would be bad enough. Tiana hoped whoever had made the soap had put extra sassafras in it to make it taste better.

Tiana was always in trouble, but she was not always guilty. Nannie had put the molasses in Mrs. MacDuff's inkwell and the frogs in her bed. It was Nannie who locked her in the privy house, wedging a stout stick between the wooden door handle and the ground. It must have been the glint in Tiana's eye and her laugh that made Seeth accuse her first. Tiana never denied it. She wasn't a snitch. And she didn't want Nannie or Susannah punished. But Tiana could not bring herself to play tricks on Mrs. MacDuff, even though the woman punished her for the strangest reasons. Like when she stripped to her drawers one hot August day to run out in a rain storm. Or when she took her shoes off to splash in puddles, or when she was late to meals.

Tiana felt sorry for Seeth MacDuff. She somehow understood that she herself would return to her life with the Real People, but her teacher was trapped forever in the prison of her own rigid beliefs. She saw Seeth as more of an exile, far from home and loved ones, than she herself was. Seeth had recently married William MacDuff, the winter term teacher, but they treated each other as cordial strangers. Tiana couldn't imagine Master MacDuff patting his wife on the bottom the way Jack Rogers did Jennie.

As for Seeth MacDuff, she couldn't understand why every theological discussion with this simple, pagan child left her so confused. Why was she unable to stay angry with her? And why, in spite of all the trouble she caused, was Seeth going to miss her when she left?

Seeth's first teaching experience was a difficult one. She had started with thirty children who spoke little, if any, English, and came from a different culture. She had yet to learn that the worst troublemaker was often the brightest. She did not realize that a good teacher was as often changed by her students as they were by her.

The school's dining hall overflowed with people. Mothers and fathers, brothers and sisters, aunts, uncles, cousins, and grandparents had come to see the girls perform. The Real People wore their best clothes, though some were faded and patched neatly. They sat patiently on the hard wooden benches. They lined the walls, stood in the doorways, and looked in the windows. Younger children played Peep, Squirrel, Peep or You Can't Catch Me among the wagons and tents in the school yard. It was time for the "Breaking Up," the exhibition at term's end.

Reverend Gideon Blackburn and William MacDuff were there for the occasion. Seeth wore her most elaborate black dress. She looked like she was drowning in the lace and ruffles of her high collar. She wrung her lace-edged handkerchief as she gave orders to the girls.

Several of the fathers had built a simple stage at one end of the hall and the girls had decorated it with greens and candles they had made. It looked elegant. Tiana sat with the rest of the class on the benches arranged in a semicircle on stage. Her palms were sweaty and her stomach twitched. Her whole family was sitting in the audience. Jack Rogers had walked down the aisle with a challenge in his eyes and both wives following him He knew it was far easier for the missionaries to overlook polygamy in Indians than in a white man.

Seeth turned to inspect her children one last time. Their black hair was shiny and braided, their dresses starched and ironed until they stood out like cardboard. Their shoes were lined up precisely, and their hands were folded in their laps. Seeth was overwhelmed with tenderness for them. They would never know how much they meant to her. It pained her to think that many of them disliked her and, worse, thought she disliked them. Seeth's tears blurred their serious, frightened faces. They had all worked so hard for this day. Seeth prayed they did well.

She needn't have worried. She didn't realize the miracle she and her children had accomplished. In three months the girls were reading, writing, and speaking rudimentary English. They knew simple sums and could recite testament verses from memory. They knew the arts of the needle and had embroidered some stunning samplers. Each had labored over an elaborate exhibition piece of her penmanship. They had worked from sun-up to sundown, six days a week to do it, but they had nothing to be ashamed of. If Seeth hadn't been so preoccupied with the state of their souls, she would have been amazed at the keenness of their minds.

After singing several hymns from Rippon's *Selections*, the girls began their recitations. The speeches and poetry and Bible verses seemed to go on for hours as Tiana waited for her turn. Finally it came.

" 'There is a just God who presides over the destinies of nations.' " Her voice sounded small and faltering until she gathered herself to deliver her speech as she had been taught. It was a favorite speech for occasions like these, but hearing it from a Cherokee child's lips moved Seeth deeply.

She had tried to convince Tiana to recite something religious, as most of the other girls were doing. But Tiana had insisted on this one. She had called on that much-used word, *duyu'ghoduh*, right, justice. It was her right to recite whatever she wished, within the bounds of propriety. Then Seeth realized the room was hushed as Tiana's young voice rang out. She took special pains to pronounce her d's.

Is life so dear, or peace so sweet, as to be purchased at the price of chains and slavery? Forbid it, Almighty God! I know not what course others may take, but as for me, . . .

Tiana paused, her timing perfect.

. . . give me liberty or give me death.

She stood a moment, poised with her arm raised in the dramatic gesture Seeth had taught her. When those interpreting for families and friends finished whispering, there was absolute silence. The Real People appreciated drama and oratory.

"Tell them about it, child." Fancy's husky voice broke the hush.

Tiana curtsied at the applause and nodded to Nannie, who handed her a scroll tied with a red ribbon. Tiana curtsied again in front of Mrs. MacDuff and gave her the scroll. As she untied the ribbon, Seeth had a fleeting fear that this was another of Tiana's pranks. Then she began to cry in earnest, mopping her eyes and nose with her tattered handkerchief. Written in Tiana's childish hand, with artistic flourishes around the margins, was a schoolgirl's well-worn verse.

Many, many a voice will greet me
In a low and gentle tone,

But its music will not cheer me
Like the cadence of thine own.

It was signed simply "The Hawk."

"The ribbon will look pretty in your hair, Mits MacTuff," Tiana said. "Red means the east where the sun rises. It means life and bravery and success. You were brave to leave your home and come to a far land to teach us. We're grateful to you."

"Thank you, child." From her chair, Seeth hugged Tiana, enveloping her in the smell of lavender and starch.

"I'm sorry for the sorrow I cost you," whispered Tiana. "Do you forgive me?"

"Yes, child." Seeth wiped her eyes as she watched Tiana walk down the aisle to where her family awaited her. Seeth had no way of knowing Tiana had given her most precious gift. She had shared her secret name, The Hawk. It was a measure of her appreciation for the education she had received.

Seeth MacDuff would always remember her first class. She would especially remember Tiana, The Hawk, the child who wanted to soar with the birds and look down on God's creation.

The morning after the breaking up, the mission school was deserted. Bushes in the yard and the woods beyond were broken where wagons had driven over them and children had cut them for toy bows and arrows. The area was littered with bits of hides, horns, and bones, cracked for their sweet marrow and dragged here and there by the dogs. There were circles of charred wood and ashes where the families had built cooking fires. Smoldering in the embers were Tiana's rigid, leather school shoes with the loose peg that had hurt her for two months.

It was late August. The moon was growing fatter each night. When it was full the Real People would celebrate their most important religious ceremony, the annual Green Corn Dance.

Reverend Blackburn had worked with the Cherokee long enough to know the futility of inviting them to a church service. Even as he invited them after the breaking up and even as they grunted noncommittally, Blackburn knew they would not come. In the past five years they had brought four hundred of their children for him to educate. But even though the adults rarely converted, he had to keep trying. It was unbearable that they would risk their immortal

souls in that ungodly saturnalia. Whiskey had given the Green Corn
Dance all the loathsome characteristics of a Roman orgy, as far as
Blackburn was concerned.

Seeth MacDuff came out just after dawn to greet an empty yard.
She had tied Tiana's red ribbon in her hair which flowed in a pony
tail down her back. She carried her own small Bible as a present for
Tiana and her sisters. She looked around her, bewildered, wondering
if she had dreamed the whole school term. Her husband took the
liberty of putting an arm around her waist to comfort her.

"You'll have to learn to let them go, Seeth."

She nodded without speaking. They walked to breakfast in the
echoing dining hall.

It was just as well Seeth couldn't hear Tiana and her sisters telling
about their time at school. Tiana stood in the rocking wagon bed,
her legs spread to steady herself, and acted out Seeth MacDuff locked
in the privy house. Fancy laughed so hard she almost fell off the
back of the wagon where she sat with her long legs swinging. Conversation passed back and forth among the family like the clay pipe
and the jug of homemade whiskey.

It was good to hear the rich language of the Real People again,
with all its subtleties and colors. It was soothing to Tiana's ears after
the harsh sounds of English. There were so many thoughts English
couldn't express. Cherokee was a musical tongue anyway. And the
dialect spoken by the mountain bands, the Overhills, was the most
lyrical of all. They substituted l for r, giving a trill to their words.

The trees and bushes closed in around and above them, forming
a winding corridor of yellow light and green shadow. Red-gold dust
from the wagon wheels danced in the shafts of sunlight. Tiana began
singing verses of a revival tune Seeth had taught them, and the
family joined in on the chorus. Jack sang bass and Fancy tenor.
Everyone else ranged in between. They sang lustily, feeling the
swing and drive of the simple melody.

Shout O——— glo———ry, for I shall mount above the skies,
When I hear the trumpet sound in the morning.

Tiana stood with her knees braced against her father's back and
searched for her cousins and friends. Tonight she and Nannie and
Susannah would hunt lightning bugs with them and play hide and

seek in the dark. When they came in sight of the cornfields, stretching over the surrounding hills and all the way to the center of town, Tiana pounded on her father's shoulders.

"*Halehwiśda*! Stop! I want to say hello to the corn."

Jack shook his head, but he pulled on the reins. Tiana climbed over the wagon's side and onto the running board. She jumped off before Old Thunder had stopped moving and ran toward the first field. It had already been harvested and was empty of people.

Toward the center of the village, the fields were dotted with harvesters picking the last of the new corn. Men, women, and children moved at a leisurely pace among the plants, dropping the tender ears into big baskets. They waved at the Rogers as Old Thunder passed.

"*A'siyu*, Selu, greetings, Mother Corn." Tiana walked among the clumps of straight stalks that reached over her head. A breeze rippled the slender, fluted leaves. Tiana knew it was Selu sighing for her lost fruitfulness. In the old days, corn grew overnight, and was ready to harvest in the morning. But people had disobeyed Mother Corn's instructions. They hadn't watched all night while the corn grew. Now their descendants had to watch it and tend it for weeks.

But Mother Corn couldn't complain about how the Real People cared for the corn now. The plants stood three or four to a mound. Bean plants grew up their stalks, and gourds, squash, and pumpkins rambled between the corn hills. There were few weeds.

Tiana walked among the plants that closed over her head. She ran her hands lightly across their leaves and talked to them. High above her, a raven screamed as it folded one wing close to its body and fell in a plummeting dive. Tiana knew the raven was playing, but his call sent a tic of fear through her. Raven Mockers cried like that when they came to steal an ill person's soul.

Tiana caught a glimpse of teeth and Spearfinger's wrinkled face half obscured by the greenery. She gave a small scream and felt her heart pound in her chest. She turned and ran, dodging among the corn until she arrived, breathless, at Sally Ground Squirrel's house. She slowed to a walk, struggling to catch her breath. Drum said Spearfinger wouldn't hurt anyone, but that was hard to believe.

Tiana couldn't be frightened long. It was too wonderful to be home. As she neared the cabin, she stripped off her smock. It was hot, and in Hiwassee Town, few children wore clothes until they were Tiana's age or older.

As usual, Drum was in his seat of honor, a rocking chair in the last stages of palsy, and held together with linn-bark rope. There was the usual group of men with him, including James and John. But a stranger was there too. Tiana was only wearing her loose cotton drawers and carrying her smock balled up in her fist, so Sam could be excused for not knowing whether she was a boy or girl. What could not be forgiven was his considering her of little consequence.

"*A'siyu*," he said absently when Drum introduced her. She flushed angrily when he glanced over her head and began talking to the adults. This pale stranger was getting the attention she had intended to have for herself. She looked him up and down as he joked with James and John and Drum, just as though he were of their clan. *He can't even speak our language*, she thought scornfully.

His thick, wavy chestnut hair was clubbed into a queue at the nape of his neck. His blue eyes were good-humored, but Tiana would have said he looked vain. He was much larger than average, well proportioned and solidly built. He stood above most people in any normal gathering. He wore buckskin leggings on his long, sturdy legs and a loose, blue calico coat with a large frill around the V-shaped neck. Like Drum's, the coat was belted at the waist. A silk scarf was knotted at his throat. He carried himself a bit awkwardly, but with the confidence of someone used to being liked by everyone. Already the young women were in a dither over him. Tiana watched them watching him.

Don't you consider yourself the handsome one, Tiana thought. *Flirting with all the girls*. He was arrogant. He was much too smug. "Pride goeth before a fall," Seeth MacDuff was fond of saying.

No one noticed the glint in Tiana's eyes as she and her sisters ran off with their cousins.

Sam sat grinning at the people around him, at Drum and Sally Ground Squirrel and their enormous family. *Pleasant surprises*, he thought. *That's what makes life a fair truck*. He was pleased with the trade life had made. Two years of drudgery and boredom in Maryville, the harrassment of his brothers, in exchange for this. *Fair truck, indeed*.

The main room of Sally Ground Squirrel's cabin was crowded. The dirt floor was covered with woven mats for guests to sit on. There were so many guests it was difficult to walk among them without stepping on a hand or foot. The overflow sat outside. Yet, in spite of the crowding, in the two weeks Sam had been there, he had never heard an argument or a harsh word.

Sam had spent the previous night sleeping on the floor with a dozen or so other people who had come for the Green Corn ceremony. The dug-out sleeping hut and the open pavilion had been full. Sam had slept with his head under a table so no one would step on it on the way outside to relieve himself.

He suspected someone young and female had tried to crawl under his blanket with him the night before. If so, it would certainly be one of life's more delightful surprises. Maybe it had been a case of mistaken identity. If it wasn't, Sam still didn't know what the rules were. He had pretended to be asleep until she left. Where Sam came from a man could get into serious trouble abusing hospitality that way.

Besides, there were too many people sleeping around him. Sam was not shy, but he had his limits. He wouldn't admit it, but he was inexperienced in love. It wouldn't do to be caught off-balance his first time out of the starting gate.

"Uh, *unginili*." He nudged James Rogers.

"*Unginutsi*," said James.

"What?"

"*Unginili* means older brother. Unless a girl is speaking. Then older brother is *ungida*. I'm younger than you. Younger brother is *unginutsi*, unless you're a girl."

"Right." Sam despaired of ever getting the complicated family connections straight. "I think someone, a female someone, tried to crawl under my blanket last night. I ignored her. I was afraid of making your uncle angry. Did I do the right thing?"

James laughed. "That depends."

"On what."

"On what clan she belongs to. You aren't a member of a clan yet, so I'm not sure the rules apply."

"What rules?"

"We marry our grandmothers."

"You marry your grandmothers?"

"Yes. The Real People call members of their mother's father's clan and their father's father's clan grandmother or grandfather. They can tease and flirt with people from those clans. And they pick mates from them. Of course, in my family our mothers'

fathers and our father's father were white, so we're a little confused."

"Well, I'm glad to hear it," said Sam, "because I'm mighty confused."

"But," James had an afterthought, "we call our mother's mother
grandmother too, but we would never marry her. She's of our own
clan . . . and much too old, besides. We have to treat members of
our own clan with respect, except our brothers, uh, and the cousins
we call brothers, although, come to think of it . . ."

"Never mind," said Sam. "You can tell me about it later." Sam
looked around. There were six or seven young women staring at
him even then, with as open an invitation in their eyes as Sam had
ever seen. If he could just figure out the system, there might be a
whole lot more to this life than he had expected.

A huge pot of stew bubbled and plopped on the hearth against
the side wall. Most of the smoke rose through the mudcat chimney,
a precarious affair of sticks chinked with a mortar of clay and cattail
fuzz. From time to time, fallen mortar exposed wood, which ignited,
adding excitement to the occasion. The fireplace didn't draw well,
and smoke escaped in puffs around the top edge of it. It filled the
room with a thin haze. Late afternoon sunlight poured through the
open door, which faced east. Now and then someone passing the
door would set the illuminated smoke to swirling in sinuous patterns.

The door was open for light and ventilation and as an invitation
to share the roof and the meal. Sam had given up trying to guess
who was a relative, who was a friend, and who was a total stranger.
Drum and Sally Ground Squirrel treated them all the same. There
was always food bubbling on the hearth, and guests were fed as
soon as they arrived.

There was little furniture in Sally Ground Squirrel's cabin, but
tan cane mats woven with black geometric designs covered the walls.
Their main purpose was to stop drafts, but they were beautiful too.
A few dogs lay in the doorway with their muzzles on their paws.
They mournfully watched the bowls being passed out and eyed the
platters of meat being brought in from the roasting sides of beef
outside. There was no corn served, though. That would have to
wait until after the ceremony of the first fruits.

"Do you know why the head of *suli*, the buzzard, is bald, my
friend?" Drum asked Sam. James chuckled as he translated.

"No."

"The buzzard's head wasn't always bald, you know." Everyone

crowded closer to hear. This was a favorite story. "This is what the old men told me when I was a boy. Once the buzzard had a beautiful topknot. He was too proud of it to eat carrion with the rest of the animals. 'You may have it all,' he said to them. 'It isn't good enough for me.' " Drum lifted his chin in a haughty pose and looked down on the people around him. "So the animals and birds decided to punish him for his pride.

"They convinced the buffalo to play dead. When the buzzard passed overhead, the crow and the magpie pretended to eat the buffalo. 'Come taste this, Brother Suli,' they called. 'The meat is fat and sweet.' 'Oh no, you can't trick me,' he said. But he circled, as buzzards do, closer and closer to see what they were doing. The buffalo never moved. Finally the buzzard landed and bit the buffalo's eyelid. The buffalo didn't stir. Then the buzzard bit his nose, and still the buffalo didn't stir.

"Finally, the buzzard went to the buffalo's rump and ate a piece of fat there. Believing the buffalo was truly dead, he entered his anus. It was very dark in there." Drum pretended to peer ahead into darkness. "He went deep inside and bit off a delicious piece of fat. Then another. But the buffalo squeezed his anus tightly shut and stood up. 'Oh, please, Brother Buffalo, let me go,' the buzzard cried. 'No,' said the buffalo. 'Not until you've learned a lesson.' The buzzard cried and pleaded, but the buffalo held onto him.

"When the buffalo finally let the poor buzzard go, all the feathers had been stripped off his head and his scalp had been rubbed raw. It's red to this day. The buzzard was so ashamed he began to eat dead meat, no matter how decayed.

"Now, my young friend, tell us once more how you and my nephews escaped from Maryville."

Sam was glad to oblige. He wasn't sure if it was his story-telling or James's translation that brought the laughter and applause, but he was pleased with himself anyway.

"When is the ball play I've been hearing about?" he asked, when the story was finished.

"The day after tomorrow," said Drum. "We call it *Anetsa*, Little Brother To War. Tomorrow we fast. Will you join the game?"

"Does a chicken have lips?"

"Maybe you'd best watch, brother," said James.

"Naw. I'll play. Wouldn't miss it. I'll go easy on the boys, seeing as how I'm bigger than most."

"It gets rough."

"Rough! Not likely. I've played foot-ball with Mad Mountain McCabe. Three hundred pounds of unalloyed meanness. The genuine article. Anyway, I've been practicing all week. The rules are just like back home. There aren't any."

One of the younger Rogers girls handed Sam his bowl of stew. He pulled his wooden spoon from his belt in anticipation. He was starving, but he waited patiently for Drum to throw a bit of liver into the fire as an offering to it before anyone ate.

"I can take care of myself." Sam didn't notice Tiana staring at him after she served him. He did notice something swimming in the grease on top of the stew. He poked it with his spoon and it paddled frantically away and tried to climb the smooth, inwardly sloping side of the maple-burl bowl. When Sam cleared away the lumps of pumpkin and potato and the chunks of venison, he saw a small, red newt with a limp collard leaf draped over its slippery back.

Sam tried to act nonchalant. He looked around to see if anyone else was biting into a live salamander. He had heard about the infamous Black Drink of the Green Corn ceremony. Drum had told him there were many rituals involved. And Sam had heard that the Real People ate bullfrogs from time to time. Maybe this was a test. Maybe Drum was seeing if, like *suli*, the buzzard, Sam was too proud to eat anything that was put before him. Sam wanted desperately to fit in here. Dare he ask about the beast? If it had gotten into his stew by mistake would he embarrass Drum or Sally Ground Squirrel by calling attention to it? He leaned over to James.

"Is it part of the ceremony to eat your meat on the hoof?"

"What?" James stared into the bowl. As Sam tried to flick the leaf off the salamander's back for a better view, James looked for Tiana. He saw her weak with silent laughter and hanging onto a window frame. She winked at him.

"Why yes, brother," James whispered solemnly. "But I can understand your reluctance. They taste too much like mud for me. Why don't you just slip it down the front of your shirt until you can rid yourself of it."

Sam looked gratefully at James. He surreptitiously fished the salamander out by the tail and stuffed it into his shirt. He squirmed a bit as it wriggled, wet and greasy against his bare skin. But it was better than eating it.

"Excuse me," said James. "I have to answer nature's beck." He left quickly and joined Tiana behind the cabin. Laughing helplessly, they both lay across the rain barrel.

Chapter 6

Tiana sat in the darkness near the edge of the high, flat mound in the center of Hiwassee Town. No one was sure who built this mound, or the smaller ones on the island. Some said the builders were the Old Ones, the Real People's ancestors. Some said the Yuchi, the Faraway People, had built them. It was the highest point on the island and Tiana liked to sit there.

Below her, light from the new hearth fires glowed through the open cabin doors. Now and then sparks flew from the chimneys in a shower that fell upward. Where fires had been built out of doors, she could see the forms of people around them. Torches moved, disembodied, like *atsil'dihye'gi*, the ghostly fire carriers.

Last night, the village had been dark. Everyone had put out their fires after they had burned the old mats and stools, baskets and gourds. All day people had filed up the log steps set into the side of the mound. They walked quietly through the council house with new containers for embers from *atsi'la galunkw'ti'yu*, the sacred fire.

Tiana loved the Green Corn ceremony. It was a time to start life fresh, to erase past mistakes and to be forgiven for wrongdoings. The whole village vibrated with excitement. Women cleaned until a haze of dust hung over the cabins. Old utensils and containers were replaced with new ones.

The communal storehouses were full of donations from the harvest. Baskets and sacks and mounds of food lay piled around the entrances. There were beans and squashes, peanuts and corn, especially corn. There was six-weeks corn, the roasting kind. There was parti-colored hominy corn, with hard red, white, blue, and yellow kernels. And there were the large white ears of flour corn. Any family in need was welcome to take from the communal stores. No one went hungry among the Real People unless they all did.

Jennie and Grandmother Elizabeth had given each of their daughters something new for the celebration. Tiana and Susannah and Nannie had gotten their first white dresses to wear at the dances after the ball play tomorrow. It would be Tiana's first time performing with the women and older girls, and she was nervous. Tonight she would practice with the other beginners.

Even now she could hear the drums and chanting of the men dancing in front of the council house, not far away. They had been dancing since that morning. Many of them now moved in an exhausted trance. Even though they fired their weapons every half hour as part of the ceremony, Tiana flinched when the guns went off again. The noise was deafening and left her ears ringing.

"Sister!" Tiana heard Nannie calling her.

"I'm here," she called back.

"Come quickly. Ghigau is going to tell us a story." Nannie and Tiana worked their way through the crowd watching the dancers and slipped inside the small door of the council house. The other girls sat on the benches at the rear of the large, dim room. They were in the section reserved for members of the Wolf clan, because Nanehi Ward was a Wolf.

Tiana looked around her. She never sat in this part of the council house. Everything looked different from here. Then, with her feet up on the bench in front of her, her elbows on her knees and her chin cupped in the palms of her hands, she leaned forward to hear Nanehi Ward. Tiana wanted to stroke the Beloved Woman's long white hair to see if it was as silky as it looked.

Ghigau had waited until Tiana and Nannie and a few other strays were settled. Story-tellers believed everyone should hear a story from beginning to end. If someone came in late, Nanehi would start over again.

"Did you all just notice the full moon tonight?" Ghigau asked, in the recent past tense.

"Yes," the girls answered.

"When I was a girl, this is what the old women told me they heard when they were girls. The sun and moon are sister and brother. Long ago, they shared the sky together. The sun was very beautiful. One night, when her brother, the moon, was in its dark time, the sun was visited by a man. Because there was no light, she couldn't see his face, but he spoke sweetly to her. He told her she was standing in his soul, and he touched her heart. They became lovers.

"Each month, at the dark of the moon he visited her, and though she shared her bed with him, she never saw him. Nor would he tell her who he was. Finally, she was so curious she had to know. When he came to see her she exclaimed, 'Your face is cold,' and she rubbed his cheeks with her hands. She had dipped her hands in ashes and smeared them on his face so she would recognize her lover when she saw him in the light.

"The next night her brother, the moon, rose with his face covered with gray spots. 'You're the one,' she cried in horror. Her brother was so ashamed he kept as far away as he could. To this day, when he comes near his sister, the sun, he makes himself as thin as possible so he can hardly be seen. For everyone knows brothers and sisters of the same clan must not mate."

"Thank you for the story, Beloved Woman," Tiana murmured with the other girls.

"*Agwetsi*, children," called Sally Ground Squirrel.

"It's time for you to practice the dance," said Ghigau. The girls slid off the benches and lined up in front of Sally Ground Squirrel.

Sam stood bleary-eyed between James and John and tried not to sway. He knew if he did he would fall on his face. The priest had been chanting for an hour and the end seemed nowhere in sight. Sam wondered how the other twenty-four ball players could stand so rigid and still, with their ball sticks crossed at their bare chests.

Sam's stomach growled loudly. Fasting for twenty-four hours was bad enough. Not sleeping for twenty-four hours didn't help either. And his eyes burned from sitting in the smoke of the council fire all night, watching the dancers and listening to the monotonous chanting.

All that would have accounted for his exhaustion and hunger and the pain behind his left eye. But he also had taken the Black Drink. It was viler than James had described it. It was worse than the noxious decoctions his mother had poured down his throat when he was a child. He had barely made it outside before he was vomiting bile and the little food left in his stomach. The thought of it made his stomach churn even now.

He had retched helplessly, heaving until he thought his vitals would join his meal on the ground. It was small consolation that all around him, others were doing the same. And the stench didn't help his queasiness. If the Black Drink was designed to clean out the body and prepare it for renewal, as Drum said, it was admirably suited for the job.

All night they had gone to water, the most sacred of rites. At the river they'd listened to old Dik'keh, The Just, as he chanted his incantations. They had dipped their ball sticks in the water and splashed themselves. Then they'd returned to the dance. Every now and then John, who had been chosen Talala, Woodpecker, would leave the festivities and run out into the darkness. Sam could hear his peculiar cry, three yelps and a long quaver.

"What's he doing?" Sam asked James.

"He's telling the other team they're already beaten. The call terrifies them and makes them lose heart."

"And what's the other team doing?"

"Their *Talala* is yelling the same thing at us, of course."

"It doesn't make sense."

"When did religion ever make sense?" asked James.

At sunrise, after choking on billows of smoke from green pine branches, the players started toward the ball field, several miles away. Their path followed the river, and as they walked, The Just led each of them to the water to purify them individually. While he chanted, the others sat and waited.

Sam and James leaned against each other's backs because they weren't allowed to lean on anything else. Some of the young men adjusted the feather ornaments in their hair or talked about the game. Others twisted extra strings of linn bark and repaired their sticks. James had showed Sam how to make his, bending the end of a hickory sapling and tying it in a pear-shaped loop. The loop was filled in with a woven basketwork of leather thongs or the stringy inner bark of the basswood tree.

"Make the weaving tight," James had said. "The other team will bring a small ball, hoping it will pass through our baskets."

Now, while they waited for the curer, The Just, James untied the two stuffed bats on his sticks and passed them to Sam.

"You'll need these more than I will," he said.

"I thought you didn't believe in superstition."

"I believe in nothing," James said. "And I believe in everything. Anyway, they'll be an inspiration to you. Bats are fast, the best at dodging. They won the first ball play between the birds and the animals. The animals wouldn't have Tla'meha', the Bat, on their team because he was so small. But the birds made him wings from an old leather drum head." James was silent for a moment.

"My people believe there's a spirit, a force, in everything, animate and inanimate," he said finally. "I can't say they're wrong. There are many things in nature I can't explain. Stay with us, friend. Live in these hills and mountains. Listen to them. Listen to the trees and rocks. Listen especially to the water and the wind and the animals. You'll understand what I mean."

John returned from his trip to the river with The Just and sat next to James and Sam.

"How many men play on a team?" Sam asked.

"Ten, a hundred," grunted John. "Doesn't matter."

"What's allowed?"

"Everything but murder."

"You'll have one particular opponent," said James. "If he's knocked out of the game you'll have to leave too, so the sides stay even."

"What if I'm knocked out?"

"Don't worry." James smiled. "We'll drag you off the field before you're trampled. Anyway, they only try to hurt the skilled players. You'll be safe."

"Thanks."

"He gonna soak?" asked John.

"Good idea."

"What do you mean?" asked Sam.

"When we stop next, go downstream and sit in the water up to your neck until we call you," said James.

"Why?"

"So your skin will be soft for the scratching."

"What scratching?"

"Ritual," said John.

"Will you boys soak?"

"No."

"Then neither will I," said Sam.

"Suit yourself." James shrugged.

"I don't suppose we could grab us a bite to eat, could we?"

John looked horrified.

"I didn't think so," said Sam wearily.

The Just drew a square in the dirt to represent the playing field. He took a sharpened stick from a bundle of them and pointed it at John. He drove the stick into the ground, marking John's position for the game. He did the same for each player so they would all know where to stand. Then he delivered a long harangue. Sam couldn't understand the words, but they inspired the others. Men shook their ball sticks and punctuated the talk with shouts.

"Take off your breechclout," said James.

"Why?"

"Scratching." John untied his belt and let the loincloth drop. James looked at Sam hard. "Now we see what you're made of under that white skin."

The Just held a short comb firmly in his hand. The teeth were sharpened splinters from a turkey leg bone set into the shaft of a turkey quill.

"Good God!" Sam muttered under his breath.

The Just grabbed James's arm and stabbed the splinters into it at the shoulder. He dragged the comb down the arm to the elbow, making seven white lines that quickly turned red as blood rushed to the surface. He repeated the operation three more times on that arm, then did the same to James's other arm. Sam could hear the ugly rasping of the splinters tearing into the boy's flesh, but James only smiled. Sam's knees wavered and his head began to spin. He shook it to clear it.

When The Just finished, blood ran from almost three hundred gashes on James's arms, legs, chest, and back. With a shell, James scraped off the blood as it dried so more would ooze out.

"You can still quit," he said. "And go back to Maryville." It was tempting, but Sam grinned weakly at him. In for a dime, in for a dollar.

"Naw. Can't dance and it's too wet to plow. I'll stay."

James gave him the old Roman thumbs-up sign. Hunger, nausea, and exhaustion forgotten, Sam clenched his teeth and waited for his turn.

When all the young men were scratched and painted grotesquely with their own blood, The Just gave each a piece of root that had sacred tobacco smoke blown across it and charms said over it. Sam chewed the root and followed James's example, spitting the juice into his palms and rubbing it on himself.

Then they went to the river one more time. The water was icy when it hit the warm blood. Sam shivered and gulped to keep from grunting with the cold. He wanted to cry, not from pain but from the realization that as much as he liked James and John, he was an outsider in their lives. He was an outsider in a million ways so subtle he couldn't even imagine what they were.

He felt shut out of a society where colors and compass points had life and personalities. Where Thunder was a friend and animals gave hunters permission to kill them. The Real People seemed so content with their place in the grand scheme of things.

All Sam had known was change, restlessness, the search for some-place to call home, always somewhere else. His stubborn Scotch-Irish people could not accept the world as they found it. They had to change it or destroy it. They attacked the magnificent old trees as though they were enemies. Sometimes they shot game just for the pleasure of it, something a Cherokee would not understand. Sam dressed slowly, sunk in his gloomy thoughts. He jumped when he felt a hand at his waist.

"What are you doing?"

"Loosening the belt on your loincloth," said James.

"If you do that it might fall off."

"Exactly. If someone grabs you it'll come off before you're thrown down and stomped on."

"But I'm not wearing anything else."

"So what?"

Sam shrugged. It seemed foolish to point out the obvious, that he would be naked in front of several hundred women and girls. He nervously fingered the ornament fastened in his thick braid. The eagle feather would give him keen sight. The deer tail would make him fleet. The snake's rattle would frighten his opponents. The amulet seemed firmly fixed, but its weight bothered him. He won-dered which he would lose first, the ornament or his loincloth.

Sam also wondered if there might be something to The Just's medicine. His fatigue was gone. The scratching made him intensely aware of his body, heightening the sensations on his skin. Every hair seemed to feel the gentle breeze brushing it. He felt strong and fast and invincible. His hard muscles gleamed under the layer of grease smeared on to make him slippery. With his bare feet he felt every pebble and twig in the path. He had never felt so alive.

His exhilaration rose with the noise around him. The shouting was supposed to bear the players to victory, like trees carried on the flood by Long Man, the river. And Sam did feel carried along by the cheering. He had come through the ordeal with the best of them. He had been tested and he'd passed.

Friends crowded around the players, encouraging them. Scarves and shawls fluttered around them. They were thrown across the outstretched ball sticks by the women and girls. Sam was surprised to see three of four laid across his own. Annie Rogers blocked his path. She draped a red handkerchief over the others and stared up at him.

"*Ule'stuyasti aginay'li* ," she said sweetly. She stood on tiptoe and kissed him on the lips. Sam blushed a deep red. James and John laughed.

"What did she say?" he asked, as she slipped away in the crowd.

"She said 'My very good, brave friend,' " James answered.

"Sam standing in her soul," said John. "She looking at him with white eyes, love eyes."

"Maybe Beloved Man, Drum, should name our friend Heart-stealer," said James. Sam felt the heat in his face and neck, but he was pleased. *Sam is standing in her soul*.

The team from a village across the river marched onto the field and a frantic commotion erupted. Hundreds of people held up things they wanted to bet and called for stakes to match them. Sam watched two old women, wizened and bent, screaming nose to nose at each other. One waved a twilled trade blanket and the other a pair of lace-and-linen drawers.

Sam also noticed a small cluster of white men standing away from the crowd, in the shelter of the trees. They were whiskey sellers, no doubt. Sam clenched his teeth in anger. Drum must have known they were there. But there was little he could do. They weren't stupid enough to have the illegal whiskey with them. They'd have hidden it in a cave somewhere. They would make contact here with customers and arrange to meet them somewhere for the sale.

By the end of the afternoon, many of the Hiwassee men would be drunk. The Real People sometimes referred to disease as The Intruder. That's what these men reminded Sam of. They were intruders who brought their own disease, alcoholism, with them. And they or others like them were everywhere. There was hardly a celebration without whiskey peddlers skulking around the edges of the dancing. Sam looked away from them and tried to put them out of his mind.

The clamor faded a bit and the gamblers retired to the sidelines. A man from each town stood watch over the heap of goods that had been staked. The players formed two lines, each team facing the other. There was a shuffling as the men rearranged themselves. Then each laid his ball sticks in front of him, pointing them at the player across from him, the one who would be his counterpart.

Sam went over the simple rules in his head. The ball couldn't be picked up with the hands, although once it was off the ground, it could be carried that way. The team that carried the ball twelve times between their goal posts won. There were no fouls, other than *Uwa'yi Guti*, With The Hands, picking the ball up. Sam tensed into a slight crouch as he waited for The Just to finish his last speech.

"*Ha! Taldu-gwu*'! Now for the twelve!" The Just threw the tiny, leather-covered ball into the air. Within seconds the game was a collieshangle, as Jack Rogers called it. It was a noisy, raucous, brawling affair. Sticks clashed as men swung on the ball and on their opponents. The screaming from the sidelines almost drowned the shouting of the players.

Sam lost sight of the ball early in the game. He was caught in a tangle of greasy, sweaty arms and legs. He jumped into the thickest of the fray, punching and yelling and gouging with the rest of them. From the corner of his eye he saw John leap triumphantly from the pile and sprint for the goal. He held his two sticks clasped together to keep the ball in the basket. Sam raced after him to protect his rear. Everyone dropped their sticks and chased them.

One of the team members was gaining on them. There was murder in his eyes. He was about to lunge for John when Sam clenched his hands together, extended his arms, locked his elbows, and swung with all his might, catching the man in the stomach. He doubled over, gasping for breath, and his friends dragged him off the field. His counterpart on the Hiwassee team left too.

Then the pack was on them and Sam and John went down under the weight of it. Sam lay still, collecting his breath and mentally checking for broken bones. The players took their sticks from the men whose job it was to pick them up when they were dropped in the excitement. There was a shout from the Hiwassee crowd. John, who lay face to face with Sam, grinned.

"James make goal."

"James!"

"You betcha. I no have ball."

Groaning, Sam pulled himself to his feet and limped to the center of the field. As captain of the scoring team, James threw in the ball for the next inning.

For five more hours the game raged up and down the field. Sometimes the players swarmed in a single pack. Sometimes they broke into smaller mobs. Men leaped over other players or dove between their legs. They tripped each other, they got into free-for-all fist fights. They howled and shouted and yelped like foxes.

Occasionally two men would roll on the ground, locked in their own private struggle. Then the drivers ran from the sidelines and beat them about the shoulders with switches until they broke their hold. The maimed were dragged off the field and dumped without ceremony. Punctuating everything were cries of "*Uwa'yi Guti*," With The Hands, With The Hands.

The score was ten to eleven, in favor of Hiwassee. The crowd was close to hysteria. Someone threw the ball in a high arc that flew over the spectators' heads. Shouting, the teams charged through the crowd, scattering people in all directions. Players tripped over squalling babies and dogs in their frantic scramble.

Once the tiny ball was lost and had to be replaced. While another was brought, the teams took a break to drink a sour juice of green grapes and wild crabapples. As the afternoon wore on, Sam realized the other team was concentrating its efforts on James. He was agile as an otter and fast as a deer, and he was under attack.

Sam began dogging his friend. If they were going to hurt James, they would have to get by Sam first. He might not be fast, but he was big. He wasn't ready when James suddenly turned to him and passed him the ball. "Go!" he shouted.

Confused, Sam looked at the lumpy, frayed object in his small basket. It was almost the only time he had seen it all day. It hardly seemed worth the fuss. Then he saw the other players bearing down on him.

"Hell-fire!" he shouted, and began to run. He was almost to the goal when he felt a tug at his loincloth. He jerked sideways and twisted violently, leaving his belt and the cloth dangling from his opponent's hand. He clamped the net of the second ball stick over the first to keep the ball inside. He held the two sticks over his head as he raced, naked and shouting, between the goal posts. He had made the winning point.

The mob ran screaming onto the field. Over their noise he could hear Annie Rogers's high, melodious voice.

"*Utana wa'toli. Asgayeguhsda uge'sani.*"

"What's she saying?" he asked.

"Big cock," said James.

"Handsome arse," said John.

"Congratulations." James handed Sam a blanket to wrap around his middle.

The white peace flag hung limply outside the council house. There were no windows in the building and only a small hole in the peak of the conical roof for smoke to exit. But most of the smoke hung around and combined with the body heat of those inside to make the atmosphere very close.

Tiana craned to see around the rustling, fidgeting line of women and older girls ahead of her and into the small door of the council house. The women fingered the long, colored ribbons that twined with their hair and fell loose down their backs. Or they admired each other's dresses and jewelry. They were waiting for their cue from the driver, the man in charge of the dance that night.

Overhead, thunder rumbled and lightning flashed. Behind them the men's line waited too. Tiana heard the driver, the leader of the dances, give his gourd rattle the rapid tremolo that signaled the start of a new performance. Sally Ground Squirrel paced down the line giving final instructions. The women and girls were arranged by height, with the youngest, smallest, at the end. That was where Tiana and her sisters stood.

Sally Ground Squirrel wore her best clothes, but the waist of her long, gathered skirt rode up over her round belly and met her ample breasts, hanging soft and loose in her full blouse. Her broad face was framed by a red bandana. She had a pointed chin and a hawk's nose that looked out of place on her plump body and face. But she was the civil headman's first wife and as the head of the Women's Council, she was often consulted on village affairs.

Now, as leader of this dance, she wore rattles made of the shells of box turtles. The shells had been dried so the plastron and carapace held pebbles. Then they were tied to a piece of leather strapped around the calves of Sally Ground Squirrel's stubby legs. The clustered turtle shells made her legs look even thicker and somewhat deformed.

"Do you remember the signals of the rattle?" she asked Tiana, Nannie, and Susannah.

"Yes, Beloved Mother," they answered.

"Remember to keep close to the dancer in front of you, and don't be nervous," she said. "You'll do well."

The driver beckoned, and Sally Ground Squirrel took her place at the head of the line. She began keeping the beat with quick, small shuffles of her feet, and the dancers moved forward. Tiana caught a glimpse of hundreds of faces in the dimness of the town house. Then she concentrated on her feet and the sound of the drum, the singers' chanting and the driver's rattle.

She bent her knees slightly and leaned forward, like the others. She moved with small, quick steps onto the dance floor in the center of the town house. Somewhere, her father and mothers and brothers were watching. Her line intertwined with the men's as they all circled in a narrowing spiral toward the big, central fire.

Along with the others, she went through the graceful motions of preparing the corn meal and pouring it into the men's hands. She was a little surprised to notice her older brother Charles, dancing across from Ghigau's daughter, Rachel. Not only that, Tiana was sure she saw Charles tickle Rachel's palm as they pantomimed the pouring of the corn meal. Tiana knew her staid brother was in love again. But Nannehi Ward's daughter?

When they had all gotten as close to the fire as they could, they formed a double circle facing it. The dance leader shook his gourd rattle in short, hard strokes again and Sally Ground Squirrel shouted, "*A'stayi'distiyi*, faster, harder." The drum picked up tempo and the dancers stomped heavily in place.

Tiana was exhilarated. She pressed her elbows to her sides so she could stamp as hard as possible. Her legs and arms and head felt as light as the foam on Long Man. Finally, the men gave a whoop that was answered by the audience, and the drum beat slowed again. Tiana danced out with the other women, and stood, trembling and sweating outside.

Now she could relax and enjoy the evening. Drum had already sacrificed part of the first fruits to Ancient Red, the sacred fire, so she and her sisters could eat as much as they wanted. She knew there would be baskets piled high with fresh steaming corn, roasted in the husk. They would eat corn all night, and still not tire of it.

Sam watched the women dance gracefully out. James and John had told him this was where boys could flirt, and pick mates. So Sam was paying careful attention. He sat with the other ball players on a bench of honor near the council fire.

He had a full belly for the first time in two days and a weariness and ache that stopped only at his bone marrow. His burning eyelids, one of which was purple and swollen, drooped and fell closed. His head jerked as he snapped back awake. There would be dancing all this night too. He wondered if he'd be able to hold out.

To stay awake, he studied the seven-sided council house. The roof was supported by a circle of seven columns made from the huge trunks of trees. The fire in the center of the room threw flickering shadows on them. The three or four hundred people of Hiwassee Town sat on tiers of benches around the walls. Members of each of the seven clans sat together.

The women wore scarves on their heads and bright calico dresses, full and flowing. The men wore turbans of flowered calicos and silks, depending on their means. They wore long, belted hunting shirts with tassels and fringe. The children wore little or nothing. Jack Rogers sat on a front bench with the respected elders of Hiwassee.

Nancy Ward stood in the center of the room. As she spoke, she turned slowly to face each of the clan sections. There was almost absolute silence as she talked. *No one's even farting.* Sam was impressed. Beans were a big part of the Real People's diet and breaking wind backwards was always good for a laugh. After about thirty minutes, Ghigau came to the end of her speech. James translated for Sam.

"My children," she said. "The Real People will only be strong as a nation while each of you is strong as an individual. There are forces in the world that would divide us, lead us down an evil, dissipated path. We of the Seven Clans stand in the Sunland. We are the friends of Thunder. We leave our footprints on the White Path. My children, I am proud of you."

Sam watched Nancy as she sat back down between her nephew, Drum, who was the Peace or Civil Headman, and De'gata'ga, Standing Together, the War Headman. Like Drum and Standing Together, she wore a headdress of slender white egret feathers that bobbed and danced when she moved, which wasn't often. She sat so still, she might have been a statue. She looked twenty years younger than the seventy-two she was. She was still strikingly beautiful.

Her people called her Beloved Woman, or Pretty Woman or War Woman. She was, or had been, all of those. Sam tried to imagine her taking up her fallen husband's spear and killing a man. It was easier to think of her saving Mrs. Bean from being burned alive at the stake. He had heard the story from her great grandson, Jesse Bean, often enough. In gratitude, Mrs. Bean had taught her to spin and weave. And Nancy Ward had taught her people.

"Sam Houston." James nudged Sam to stand and face Drum, who was talking to him, or about him. Sam wasn't sure which.

"*Gha*! Hear me!" Drum was impressive in his graceful headdress and cape made of the downy feathers from a turkey's breast. "Today Sam Houston has proven himself worthy of being one of the Real People. Listen, all of you! I this day and forever, call Sam Houston my son." Drum blew tobacco in the wind's four directions and over Sam's chest. He began to chant. His speech had the sacred number of seven lines to add to its power.

> *He is a Wolf and one of my clan, the Wolves.*
> *He will live in a White House.*
> *His pathways through the country of the Seven Clans will be white.*
> *The Yellow Mockingbird will laugh with him.*
> *No one will climb over him.*
> *The Sons of Thunder will walk behind him.*
> *The White Lightning will show him the way.*

"And I give him a new name. *Gha*! Hear me! From this day on, his name will be Kalanu, The Raven. Hear me, Great Wizard, I am just telling you. His name is Kalanu. His clan is Wolf."

"You will live in a house of peace and prosperity," James murmured to Sam. "Your path in the world will be peaceful, your future happy. The Yellow Mockingbird is a powerful spirit. He will bring you wealth and love. No one will defeat you. You will be protected by the Sons of Thunder and helped by Lightning. The Raven of Hiwassee was a famous war chief and the title given to a new headman. You are now Drum's son." Then James stood and moved to stand in front of the fire. He beckoned to Sam to stand next to him. He spoke loudly, while John took over the task of translating.

"I call Kalanu, The Raven, my brother. I will love him and protect him and stay with him for life." He took off his shirt and handed it to Sam. Sam hesitated, unsure of what to do. Then he gave James his shirt in return. James's frock strained as Sam pulled it over his head.

"I will draw thorns from your feet." Sam recited the familiar traveler's greeting in Cherokee. "And we will walk the White Path of life together." He exchanged moccasins with James. "I will love you like a brother of my own blood."

"I will wipe tears from your eyes and put your aching heart to rest when you are sad," James said. He gripped Raven by the shoulders, then hugged him.

Sam's heart was so full of love for Drum and James he could hardly talk. It was just as well. The Real People spoke in the backs of their throats, while Sam's language used the tongue. He had great difficulty pronouncing Cherokee. But he tried, keeping it simple.

"*Wadan, sgidoda*. Thank you, Father." He turned to James. "I love you, brother," he said in English.

Chapter 7

Tiana, Nannie, and Susannah lay on their bellies and peered over the edge of a large boulder. They were watching the scene below with interest and amusement. Unaware of their presence, The Raven, Sam, worked happily on, his bare buttocks pumping enthusiastically. His rear end had goose flesh from the chill, early spring air. Annie Rogers's legs were locked around his back, keeping time with his rhythm. They lay entwined on a thick bed of moss by the river.

"Stay here," whispered Tiana. Carrying a small leather sack, she wriggled through the bushes toward the clothes Raven and Annie had left in a heap. Her sisters waited in suspense until she reappeared. They pressed their hands tightly over their mouths to keep from snorting out loud, and they rested their cheeks on the cold, damp rock. They watched the pair below finish in a wondrous fit of moaning, writhing passion.

Ten or fifteen minutes of rolling and tickling and giggling followed before Annie reached for her dress. Raven tied on his loincloth. He had that self-satisfied look Tiana detested. Absentmindedly, he pulled on his left moccasin, then his right one. He froze with the moccasin half on. His face went from complacency to astonishment to disgust, and finally settled on anger. Tiana squeaked before she could smother her mouth again.

Raven glared up, searching for them, but they had ducked behind the boulder. With a sigh, he took off the moccasin and reached into it. He pulled out a huge, slimy mass of salamander eggs. Some of the gelatinous mess oozed through his fingers. The rest was squashed between his toes. He shook his fist toward the laughter floating over the top of the boulder.

"*Unegihldi*! Ugly!" he shouted at the children's retreating backs. It was as close to swearing as the Real People came. "*Ahyeli'ski*, mocker," he muttered. "I'll get you." Then he regretted his anger. They were only children, girls at that, and beneath his notice. He should not give them the satisfaction of seeing him riled. But they had tormented him all winter. A man had only so much patience. His dignity was under constant attack and he had no privacy at all. If this kept up, he would be too nervous to perform.

On one of her visits to Hiwassee Town that winter, Tiana had sneaked into the dug-out sleeping lodge while Raven and Annie were trysting there, happy to have the place to themselves. Tiana had piled green branches on the fire. She filled the small room with smoke, screamed "Fire!" and laughed while the pair ran out coughing and naked into the snow.

Raven remembered the girls' laughter as a bale of hay showered down on him and Annie in the Rogers' barn loft. Sneezing and gasping, they had struggled from under the hay. Once Tiana had simply taken their clothes, forcing them to wait until dark to sneak back into the village behind cut branches.

Tiana even knew his personal habits. She knew when he was likely to disappear with Pope's *Iliad* into Drum's pride and joy, the privy house. Raven usually had a long session in there each morning. One day Tiana greased the seat. Actually, she didn't have to know when Raven was most likely to use the backhouse. He was the only one in the family who did. The others thought it was dirty and smelly. So it stood, a monument to progress, meant only to be admired.

When the girls were visiting, Raven never went to bed without checking carefully under the robes and blankets. He had found everything from snakes to frogs to thistles. He also checked his clothes and food. For the most part he quietly disposed of the items and kept his mouth shut. He knew that galled Tiana more than raging at her. Besides, they were hard to catch. Their favorite retreat was the vast maze of canebrakes stretching for miles along the river.

Now he shook his head as Annie rocked with glee. She took all this with amazing good humor. But then, he didn't know she planned to get even later. Raven cleaned his moccasins as best he could and wiped his hand on the moss.

As bad as the children were, it was hard to stay angry at them. He watched them scamper through the huge ferns that carpeted the forest floor. Their delighted laughter rang in the cool air. They were dwarfed by the towering columns of the tree trunks. With their bare brown bodies painted in dappled patterns of sunlight filtered through a green filigree of leaves, they looked like *Nunnehi*, the Little People, benevolent spirits who peopled their world. Raven wasn't sure these particular spirits were benevolent, though.

Carrying his moccasin in one hand, he took Annie's hand with his other and limped to the rushing river to wash his foot. He glowered at Annie as she giggled from time to time. No respect. A man couldn't get respect from women here.

Still, it was a good life. Raven's two-week vacation had stretched to eight months. And he had no desire to return to Maryville. If there was a lovelier spot than the Hiwassee River, Raven hadn't found it. The cold, black water rushed over rocks and sang its own endless song. A green wall of trees hung over it, making peninsulas where the bank had eroded from around their roots. Small, green islands floated serenely in the calmer waters along the shore. Raven and Annie walked along a series of sandy, crescent beaches, climbing over occasional fallen trees.

" 'When the North wind his boisterous rage has spent . . .' " Raven recited from Pope, adding more lines to the hundreds he already knew. He orated with passion, flinging his arms wide and shouting over the noise of the water. Annie's eyes began to glaze in boredom. She was inventing an excuse to leave when she saw the canoe rounding the bend.

"*Ni!* Look!" she said, pointing.

"Hell-fire!"

"What is?" Annie's English was the worst in the Rogers family. Raven couldn't honestly say he loved her for her mind. But then, she didn't love him for his, either.

"They're my real brothers, James and John. They've found me." He waded out to catch the prow of the dugout. The boat was heavy, a typical Cherokee canoe, hollowed from a solid log.

"What took you so long?" he asked. Together they heaved the two-hundred-pound canoe onto the bank.

"Beloved friend," he said to Annie, "meet James and John, my older brothers. This is Annie Rogers, uh, a friend of mine."

"*A'siyu,*" said Annie, dropping a slight curtsy and averting her eyes politely. Then she ran ahead, her long, black hair bouncing on her shapely rear end.

"Well," said John as he followed Raven up the path. "I can see why you didn't come home, Sam. She looks an easy tit. Do the Indians share their squaws?"

Raven rounded on his brother. His voice was ominous.

"She's the niece of the head chief and daughter of a fine family. And she speaks English. Many of them do. So watch your mouth. And when you talk to the Real People, don't look into their eyes. It's not polite."

"The Real People?" John said.

"That's what they call themselves."

"A bit of arrogance, that."

"White people wrote the book on arrogance."

"What about our stuff?" shouted James from the canoe.

"Leave it," said Raven. "We can come back for it."

"Someone might steal it."

"Not likely. You're not in Maryville, you know." The day was ruined for him. He walked in silence toward Hiwassee Town.

Sally Ground Squirrel's cabin was the finest in the village. But suddenly it looked small and shabby to Raven. The first crop of spring flies was buzzing around the midden of mussel shells and bones. A pair of pigs rooted through the fresh garbage there. The yard was full of boxes and barrels, a new shipment of goods for Drum's trading post. There were bundles of cane poles and oak splints for baskets and a litter of basket-making scraps under the big maple. More flies buzzed around the green hides tacked to the cabin walls to dry.

The clutter around the cabin had always seemed so natural. Everyone worked outside in good weather and a bit of disorder was inevitable. Now Raven saw it through his brothers' eyes. He hoped they wouldn't ask him why there was a buzzard feather over the cabin door. He didn't want to admit it was to scare away witches.

As he dipped the gourd ladle into the *kanahe'na,* the sour hominy gruel in an earthen jar on a bench by the door, he noted the look of distaste that passed between James and John. Raven took an extra swig.

"Want some?" He offered them the ladle.

"No. Thanks anyway," John said hastily.

"I'm not thirsty. Or hungry." James wasn't sure which need the gruel was supposed to take care of. It was obvious the ladle served everyone, and that the gruel was rancid. The flies seemed to like it though.

"*A'siyu igali'i*, hello, friends." Drum bustled, beaming, from behind the house where he had been hoeing the kitchen garden. He carried his crude wooden mattock. His pantaloons were rolled above his knobby knees. He was wearing his oldest calico hunting shirt. He had a faded kerchief tied around his forehead to keep the sweat from his eyes. His curly, auburn hair stood out in disorder above it. His feet were bare and red with loamy clay.

"Howdy," said John. "What'd he say?" he murmured to Raven.

"He said, 'Greetings, friends.' That's the headman, Ahu'lude'gi, Drum. He speaks English. He just prefers not to."

"Don't worry, Sam," said James. "We'll be civil to your friends."

"Hello, Chief," said John Houston jovially. "You must be the famous John Jolly. It's a pleasure to shake your hand, sir."

Damn! Raven thought. He had forgotten to mention it was an extreme lack of respect to call someone by name. And John spoke too loudly, as though volume would make English more easily understood. *Let them try to patronize Drum. Better men have tried and failed.* Raven had become used to the Real People's soft-spoken talk. His brothers' voices seemed harsh and booming.

Drum moved his old rocker under the vast branches of the ancient maple that shaded the cabin. James and John Rogers arrived and sat on logs. The Houston boys were given stools. Before he sat down, Raven stared up into the leaves overhead.

"What's the matter?" asked John Houston.

"*Yunwi Tsundi*," said Drum, chuckling.

"Little People. Spirits," Raven translated.

"Don't tell me you've gotten superstitious."

"Just cautious." But apparently Tiana and her sisters had other fish to fry, as Mrs. Houston would say. Now that his brothers were here, Raven thought of his mother. It was as though they had brought his whole past, invisible, with them.

As Sally Ground Squirrel served them chilled madeira from the springhouse, Sam realized she was not at all like the elegant Mrs. Houston. Her daughers brought corn cakes and buttermilk and the first berries of the season in thick yellow cream. They spread the bowls and baskets of food on mats.

The Girth, Drum's only son, lumbered up to join them. Drum always said The Girth could smell food a mile away and with the wind behind him. If The Girth was a disappointment to Drum, he never said so. The Girth went happily through life with a friendly smile on his broad, innocent face. He wasn't a simpleton, like Watty Ridge, he just wasn't very bright.

When they finished eating, there was an awkward silence. Raven glared at his friends. James and John Rogers were playing dumb. The Girth didn't have to play dumb. Drum was being bland and unilingual.

"Do you speak Cherokee, Sam?" asked John Houston. "You've been here long enough to learn."

"You must be joshing," said Raven. "Cherokee is the most infernally difficult form of communication ever devised by man. There are dozens of ways to say 'father.' Greek and Latin are as easy as bean farts compared to Cherokee."

James and John Rogers smiled.

"Aha!" shouted John Houston, "You do speak English." They all laughed. The morning passed pleasantly enough. After noon, Raven walked with his brothers back to their canoe.

"Sam," said James. "We know how you are. You get these wild hairs up your arse from time to time. But it's time to come home."

"This is home. I'm part of Drum's family."

"You're such a romantic, Sammy," said John.

"Don't call me Sammy. I'm not a child. I'm Kalanu, The Raven."

"We need you at the store. You have responsibilities."

"I would far rather measure deer tracks than ribbon," said Raven a bit pompously.

"What shall we tell Mother?"

"Tell her I love her."

"How can she believe that?" asked John. "She misses you, you know. Did you really think you could run off for months and not hurt your mother?"

Raven hung his head.

"Tell her I'll come home soon. After the spring planting here. I owe them that much help at least."

"When you come," James took in Raven's hunting shirt and leggings, "wear decent clothes. You walk into Maryville in that get-up and they'll hang you like as not."

"Actually, Sam, it's a good thing you stayed away," said John. "Dirty Dutch was waiting for you. But he lost his temper a month ago. Gouged a man's eyes out. Left town ahead of justice."

"Justice? Things are changing in Maryville," said Raven.

"They are. The place is growing. There's opportunity there. You shouldn't be wasting your talents here with savages." John held up his hand before Raven could answer. "Yes, I know. They're nice folks. But think of your future, man."

"Think of Mother," added James.

"I am. I'll be home after the planting here. Be careful," he shouted as the canoe labored off under their inept handling.

As much as Raven hated farm work, he didn't mind it in Hiwassee. The Real People made it something of a party. On mornings when the communal fields were to be worked, Drum climbed to the roof of the council house and shouted out where and when people were to gather. Raven fell in with the rest of the villagers as they strolled out to work.

When Raven finally decided to return to civilization, as he had promised, the spring planting somehow spilled over into the summer hunts and the harvest and the Green Corn ceremony, which Raven didn't want to miss. He had outgrown the few clothes he had brought with him a year earlier. He wore leather leggings, moccasins, and an elaborate hunting shirt Sally Ground Squirrel had made him. A red calico turban was wrapped around his head, and a feather hung from the braid that now reached the middle of his shoulder blades.

Drum seemed willing to go on providing for his adopted son forever, but Raven knew he couldn't accept such generosity indefinitely. And John Houston was right about one thing. There were few opportunities to make a living here. Subsistence farming might be all right for a time, but it wasn't much of a career. Besides, if he didn't like Maryville, he could always come back.

Raven ignored Tiana as he walked toward the path that ran by Sally Ground Squirrel's cabin. The path led to the Great War Trail that would take him back to Maryville. He carried a satchel of clothes, food, and presents from the friends who followed him. James and John were going with him to the rim of the white settlement. They would cover the miles in an easy lope, until James heard Raven's breathing begin to labor. Then he would slow the pace.

They each carried a pouch of parched corn, a flint, a knife, and a cane blow gun and darts. For them a hike of sixty miles was little more than an outing.

Raven whistled as he sauntered by the wagon where Tiana and Nannie and Susannah lounged, sucking on long stalks of sugar cane. Then without warning, he dropped his satchel and made a grab for Tiana. She squealed and dodged and darted across the yard with Raven in hot pursuit. The other girls scattered like chickens when one of their number was destined for the stew pot. Tiana might have gotten away from Raven if James and John hadn't headed her off. Raven slung her, kicking and screaming, over his wide shoulder.

"Put me down!" She hammered on his back with her small fists. Her shaggy hair hung in her eyes. Her long, thin legs waved in the air. Her narrow rump formed an inverted V over his shoulder.

"Aha, my proud beauty," said Raven. "Now you'll pay through the nose, as my people say. The Great Leech is going to eat your nose. And it'll be just as well. You won't be able to smell his fetid breath as he drags you off to a slimy, watery grave."

As he talked, Raven paraded through the village with James and John and a throng of curious cousins trailing after.

"I've found where the Great Leech lives," Raven said over Tiana's screams. "When he pulls you under, toads and salamanders and little fish will feast on your flesh." He pinched her bony haunch. "Not that there's much to eat," he added.

"Ouch! Stop."

"Feel the little beasts crawling over you." He held her with one arm and tickled her with his free hand. "You'll turn into mud and fish shit."

"Put me down!"

"I'll put you down. Deep down."

He led the parade through the forest to a deep, black pool. To tell the truth, it gave even Raven a feeling of dread. The place had a haunted, evil air about it. The Real People avoided it because the pool's opaque waters probably hid demons too ghastly to contemplate, much less tempt with a dangling arm or leg. Besides, the water was unusually cold. There were far pleasanter places to swim.

The pond was shaded by a huge, twisted oak that had been blasted by lightning. The charred part of the wood was considered very powerful. Only the most capable of shamans dared possess it. The tree was so gnarled and mutilated and covered with hairy moss and ferns, it seemed like a crippled beast standing silent sentinel. Yet it still put out leaves.

Raven climbed onto a large boulder at the pool's edge. He posed dramatically on its flat top, his eyes lifted piously to heaven. He waited for his audience to assemble for the full effect. Clouds hid the sun. A thin mist rose from the water's black surface, like steam from a witch's caldron. Even though it was absolutely still, the water seemed to seethe just below the surface. Tiana redoubled her efforts to escape. Fear crept into her voice. Some of the other children began to look alarmed.

"*Gha! Asa'we'hi*! Hear me, Oh, Great Wizard!" Raven shouted.

"No!" Tiana shrieked. She was terrified. Wizards had boundless powers. They weren't to be trifled with. Even if this foolish white boy didn't know what he was doing, he could unleash forces over which he had no control. Several children began to cry, sure they were seeing Tiana for the last time. But Raven was enjoying himself.

"*Vini, vidi, vici. E pluribus unum*," he recited slowly and solemnly. When he finally threw Tiana in a high arc, she seemed hysterical with fear. She hit with a loud, satisfying splash. Raven folded his arms and waited for her to surface and swim to shore. James had even brought a blanket to wrap around her.

When she came to the top, she seemed too frightened to help herself. She screamed once, then went under and stayed there. Raven searched the black water that spread outward from the center of the pool in phosphorescent ripples. Not even bubbles appeared. Children began to wail and the adults muttered. The seconds seemed to turn into minutes.

Raven could stand it no more. Leather leggings, turban, and all, he dove into the pond. He shuddered as the icy water closed over him. He found Tiana rising to the surface and hauled her to shore. He laid her in the grass and hovered over her. His turban had collapsed into a dripping wreath around his neck. James draped the blanket over her. There was a bluish tinge to her golden-brown skin. Her black hair, plastered to her head and shoulders, made her look even thinner and more wan.

Raven panicked. Had he taken the joke too far? He shook her gently by the shoulders and rubbed her small, cold hand. He searched for a pulse in her thin wrist which dangled limply. She shivered, then shivered again. Raven was relieved to see it, but then he feared she'd go into convulsions.

"Oh, Lord." He looked helplessly at James and John. He lowered his face closer. "I'm sorry, little sister," he whispered. "Please don't die." Tiana's eyes flew open. She spit a solid stream of water directly into his eye. He dropped her wrist to protect his face. Her aim was precise as well as powerful.

"*Unegihldi!* Ugly!" she shouted. She wriggled out from under him, leaped to her feet, and ran off crying. Everyone laughed with relief. Raven wiped his face and wrung out the dripping length of cloth he used as a turban. His leggings were probably ruined. His shirt was cold against his back and chest.

"I forgot to tell you," said James. "Sister can hold her breath to the count of a hundred. She's the champion."

"You forgot to tell me," Raven grumbled. "Whose side are you on, anyway?"

Laughing, they all walked back to Hiwassee to pick up Raven's satchel of belongings. *I'd better check it carefully for varmints*, he thought.

Chapter 8

Jack Rogers sat in front of the fire, staring, hypnotized, into the flames. His old chair was tilted back and his feet were propped up against the stone hearth. An October wind moaned around the corners of the house. Like the rest of his family, Jack was listening to Fancy tell a story.

Jack knew Fancy had been visiting the Vann plantation. He wrote the passes for her and worried until she returned. If he didn't give her a pass, she would sneak away. And it was easier for her, a freedwoman, to go to her lover. But it was still dangerous. There were men who stole blacks and sold them farther south.

Fancy brought these stories back with her from the slave quarters at Vanns'. She swore this one came from Africa, but Jack had heard it from old Cherokee story-tellers. The Indians merely substituted a rabbit for a spider as the main character.

Where did they start, these stories? Jack felt a fleeting kinship with all people everywhere who stare into a fire at night and tell stories. Perhaps God was nothing more than a cosmic story-teller, weaving a tale of his own. Jack puffed futilely on his pipe and reached with his long, slender tongs for an ember to relight it. He gave his attention back to Fancy. When she told stories her dark eyes grew even bigger and more compelling.

"So, Anansi, The Spider, say to the gum man, 'If'n you doan let go my hands and foot, I'll kick you wif my lef' one.' But the gum man, he doan say nuffin. So Anansi rares back and lets fly. An' doan you know, chillun, his foot sticks tight in that gum man. 'Let go my foot!' screams Anansi. An' he butt the gum man wif' his head. Anansi be so stuck in that gum man he can't move no way a'tall."

Grandmother Elizabeth puffed on her pipe as she listened and carded yarn. Fancy called her Anansi, The Spider, always spinning and weaving. Jennie was making a double weave basket to carry water. The hundreds of supple cane strips waved over her head as she worked. James was pretending to read, but he was probably listening. The other children sat on the floor at Fancy's feet.

Jack studied Fancy's handsome profile as she talked. Her face was lit with the images she called from the air and gave life in everyone's minds. *How does it end, God, this story of Yours? Not well, I fear.*

Jack had welcomed white settlers at first. They brought amenities and the company of his own kind. But now Jack wasn't sure what his own kind was. He had forgotten what white people were like. Or maybe he thought they'd changed in the years of his exile among the Indians. But they hadn't. They were still voracious for land, and unscrupulous in obtaining it.

And there were the old animosities between the fiercely patriotic Scotch-Irish from Ulster and the Highlanders who had sworn allegiance to the Crown. The Highlanders had pledged that allegiance under duress, to obtain pardons after the disastrous War of the Pretender. They hated the British too, but their word was iron. They had fought against the rebels in the late war. Jack had fought with them as a scout.

Now the Ulstermen's offspring were pushing down from places like Maryville. They were brave and sturdy stock, but they were also stubborn and contentious and single-minded in getting what they wanted. What they wanted was land. They had no love for Jack and the other Tories. And they certainly had no love for the Indians.

Worse were the religious groups trickling into the Indian nation. They argued with each other over the possession of souls the way the Scotch-Irish argued over land. Jack knew the missionaries despised him for his two Indian wives and his brood of children by them. But even though for years Elizabeth had been more a sister to him than a wife, he refused to renounce her as his mate. She would have a place of honor in the family for as long as she lived.

And to hell with the preachers. The Real People called the Methodists The Loud Talkers. *A good name for them*, he thought bitterly.

"Captain Jack."

"Yes, Fancy girl."

"I want to go to the camp meeting over to the Vanns'. I'll leave here Friday morning. Maybe I'll go to water with The Loud Talkers and be baptized."

"I didn't know you'd gotten religion, Fancy."

"Why sho." She fell into the dialect of the quarters.

"Maybe I'll get the jerks, and come crawling to the mourners' bench." She rolled her eyes in mock piety. "Sides, it's always a good show." She jumped up and flung her head back and her arms heavenward. "Come to Jee-e-e-zus!" she shouted. "And be *saved*!"

"You wouldn't want to go to the Vanns' on account of that handsome stud there, would you?"

"Captain Jack!" Fancy's eyes widened in innocence.

"May we go, father?" Tiana, Nannie, and Susannah ringed his chair.

"No."

"Why not?"

"Because those preachers will put foolish notions in your heads."

"They're too sensible for that," said Jennie softly, not looking up from her basket.

"All right," grumbled Jack. Cherokee women. They never knew their place. Just because Jennie was right she thought she could contradict him in front of everybody. And the mad thing of it was, he loved her for it. Poor, mad Ferguson, the poet, said it well. "Ask her in kindness, if she seeks, in hidling ways to wear the breeks." Jack was never certain who wore the breeks, the breeches, in his house. He wasn't even certain it was his house. He stubbornly referred to it as his, but he knew that among the Real People, the Nation owned the land and the women owned the houses.

"Someone will have to go with them." Jack capitulated as usual.

"I'll go," said James.

"Take the new rifle."

"I will."

Fancy and the children arrived at the Vann plantation late Friday night. They rode up the sweeping, circular carriage drive of Vann's huge brick mansion. It was the grandest house for a hundred miles around. James Rogers dismounted there to pay his respects and deliver gifts from his mothers. A servant took the horses, and the girls followed Fancy to the slave quarters.

Pine knots blazed all through the quarters. Tiana heard the sound of drumming and singing.

"Why aren't they asleep?" she asked Fancy.

"Because of the camp meeting tomorrow and the funeral."

"What funeral?" asked Susannah.

"A man died. They're burying him tonight. Didn't you feel it?"

"Feel what?" Tiana felt a tantalizing prickle of fear.

"The warm air as we came up the drive. That was *asgina*, his spirit passing. He was fanning the air with his wings."

"Fancy!" Coffee ran toward them, dodging the people who crowded the narrow path between the two rows of cabins. While he and Fancy embraced, the girls looked around them.

Vann had over fifty slaves at that plantation and more at his other two farms. The number was multiplied now by visitors who had come with their masters and mistresses for the revival meeting. Tiana felt a hand plucking at the hem of her smock. A woman squatted on the ground and rocked back and forth.

"Can't you hear him?" she asked. When she looked up at Tiana her face was wet with tears.

"Hear who?"

"My boy. Can't you hear him crying? They're whipping him. He's calling me. Can't you hear him?"

"Come, little one." Coffee guided her away.

"What's the matter with her?" Tiana asked.

"Her only child was cried off yesterday. She's a bit touched by it."

"Cried off?"

"Sold," said Fancy.

"How could Joseph Vann sell her son?"

"Come, sister, watch the dancing." Fancy pushed her between the shoulder blades.

The sound of the drumming grew louder. It was nothing like the simple, monotonous beat of the Real People. This drumming had patterns so complex Tiana couldn't begin to follow them. The dancing was like nothing she had ever seen either.

In the flickering light of torches, people writhed and twisted. The dancers clapped and stamped and chanted responses to the singer

who led them. Tiana began to sway too. She and Nannie and Susannah were too fascinated to notice Fancy and Coffee slip away.

They returned an hour later, as the rough pine box was brought
out. Coffee took his place at one corner, and he and three other men
hoisted it to their shoulders. Joseph Vann, James Rogers, and Bryson, the overseer, joined the procession that fell in line behind the
widow.

It was a happy, shouting parade that wound along the path through
the tall trees. Only the dead man's wife and children seemed to care
he was gone. That bothered Tiana.

"Didn't anyone like the dead man?" she asked.

"Of course, child. Everyone liked him."

"Then why aren't they crying?"

"We're singing him home."

"Where's home? Heaven?"

"I don't know, *tsikilili*, my sweet-singing chickadee, but it's better
than here. I guarantee you that."

It was midnight. The full moon was bright overhead. Tiana shivered. Midnight was a powerful time, when malevolent spirits were
at their strongest. She saw a strange, twisted form ahead, like a
person in agony, or a demon with spindly arms uplifted from the
swirling mist.

"What's that?" she asked.

"That's a grave marker black folks make back in Africa," said
Fancy. More of them rose from the misty gloom. Each one was
different, but they were all eerie. The singing had slowed to a dirge
to match the mood of the place.

Tiana and her sisters crowded together in the middle of the path.
The usual wooden grave markers were canted at crazy angles, sinking
unevenly in the swampy ground. It was a dismal spot. It was the
only land permitted for the slaves' cemetery because it wasn't suitable
for planting. A pale blue light flitted through the trees in the distance.
White people called it foxfire, but Tiana knew it was *atsil'dihye'gi*,
fire carrier, a ghost. For reassurance, she caught a fold of Fancy's
skirt.

The widow laid a quilt over the coffin. They heard the box splash
as it was lowered into the swampy hole. Then Coffee and the other
pallbearers began shoveling dirt over it. Tiana heard the first muffled
thuds as clods hit the wooden lid.

Bryson, Vann's overseer, sidled up next to Fancy. His stomach
hung over the waist of his baggy pantaloons. He had a florid, puffy

face and small, close-set eyes threaded with red lines. He smelled of onions and sweat, whiskey and decay.

"Evening, Fancy," he said in a low voice. "I'm Bryson, the foreman here."

Startled, Fancy flinched and moved away a little. She considered which personality to adopt. Humble was no good. Humble was what he expected. It was what he wanted. And she wasn't very good at humble anyway.

"I know who you are." She turned her head away and pretended to be absorbed in the burial.

"I like your look, girl. I have a proposition you'll find to your advantage."

"I'm spoken for, Mr. Bryson."

"Who?"

Fancy didn't answer. She dared not name Coffee. Bryson could make his life a torture.

"Some nigger mule is tupping you, I'll wager. He's ramming that big black cock into you, eh?" The thought excited Bryson.

"Mr. Bryson, there are children here."

"Just Injuns. They don't understand the Christian tongue." But he lowered his voice. "Don't cross me, girl. I've taken a fancy to you." He laughed at his own poor joke and people turned to look. Fancy knew she had to get rid of him before Coffee saw him.

"Come to the Rogers' next week," she murmured. She was stalling. Maybe he would find someone more willing. Maybe he'd decide she wasn't worth the thirty-five-mile ride. And Captain Jack would help her discourage him.

"I'll do that." He walked away.

"What did he say?" asked Nannie.

"He's only a singing bird," she told them in Cherokee. She tousled Nannie's and Tiana's hair. "You girls will sleep at the big house tonight. James says Joseph Vann has laid the inside walls in oils. Red and green and blue, like the clay and the sky and the corn plants outside those big, glass windows."

"We want to stay here," said Tiana. "One of the children said there'd be music all night. A fiddler's come from another plantation. And he can fair make a fiddle talk, they say."

"It's late. You go with James. I'll see you tomorrow."

She watched them walk up the hill toward the mansion, jumping when Coffee laid his arm across her shoulders.

"What's the matter?" he asked.

"Nothing. Let's go." She pulled him toward the meadow where they often met.

"You in a hurry, woman?"

"Ain't I always?"

"That's why I love you."

Later that night they lay wrapped in the blanket Coffee had brought. Fancy's head was cradled in the hollow where his arm met his shoulder. With her long fingers, she traced the bulging muscles of his chest.

"I have a surprise for you, Coffee. I've been saving my egg money and the money from the indigo I sold. I have a lot."

"Fancy . . ." There was pain in Coffee's voice.

"No, listen, my love. I'll talk Captain Jack into making up the difference and we'll buy you. You could live with us. Do carpentry, help around the farm. Maybe we could have a farm of our own."

"How much money do you have?" If Fancy hadn't been so excited she would have noticed the weariness in his voice.

"More than seventy dollars." Coffee was silent. "How much do you think we'll need?" she asked. "You have some money from your carpentering, don't you?"

"About a hundred dollars. Maybe a little more."

"There. We can do it. Almost two hundred dollars." It was an enormous sum to Fancy.

"Fancy." Coffee rolled over and held her tightly in his arms. She felt his hot tears on her neck.

"We can do it, love," she said over and over, rubbing the nape of his neck to soothe him. "We can do it. How much you reckon we'll need?"

"Vann said he wouldn't sell me for less than twelve hundred dollars." Coffee's voice was muffled against her shoulder.

"Twelve hundred dollars!" There was awe mixed with the despair in her voice. "There's not that much money in the whole world!"

"You're right, my sweet, fancy lady. There's not that much money in the world for the likes of us. But for the Vanns, it's not so much."

"Twelve hundred dollars." She was too stunned to cry. She lay dry-eyed, all night, looking up at the stars.

For days people had been arriving at the plantation. They had set up a city on the rolling meadows behind the house. There were tents of canvas, sheeting, sacks, and oiled cloth. Other folks camped under their wagons and ate off the tailgates. Black women wandered through the crowd and sold ginger cakes and whiskey. Still the roads were crowded. By Saturday morning there were several thousand camped at the Vanns'.

Tiana and her sisters found more playmates, black, white, and red, than they had ever had. And they had always had plenty. The children ran in packs from one end of the sprawling encampment to the other. They swung from the trees and splashed in the river. Fancy watched them and shook her head.

"Law," she said to the slave women around her. "Where do they get the go?" She'd been quick to volunteer to cook for those who hadn't brought enough provisions. Joseph Vann donated the food. His house and field slaves baked corn bread and boiled huge kettles of beans and fatback and greens. There were crisp chitlins for the children. Tiana was fascinated with the way they melted in her mouth, leaving just a salty, ham taste.

Bryson had been busy supervising the slaughter of the hogs now roasting in deep pits nearby. Fancy began to relax. Probably he had been drinking the night before and had spoken on a whim.

As night fell, lines of people with torches marched to the meeting place.

"What should we do?" asked Tiana.

"Just watch," said Fancy. "There are black folks here, so it'll be a good time. Maybe they'll do some fuguing tunes."

"What are those?"

"Oh, the music chases itself up and down and round and round, like you children been doing all day."

Tiana eagerly led Fancy by the hand through the crowd to the front of the congregation. They had to crane their necks a bit backwards to see the stage. *Whatever's going on, that child has to be in the middle of it*, Fancy thought.

Chills went through Tiana as the music gathered force and the harmonies and dissonances of thousands of voices soared. As she watched people overcome with rapture, tears streamed down her own face. Mrs. MacDuff had never told her the white man's religion was like this. On stage, a Methodist circuit rider raised his arms and his face to the cloudy night sky. The crowd hushed.

"I take my text from Second Thessalonians, chapter one, verse eight," he shouted. " 'In the flaming fire take vengeance on them that know not God and that obey not the Gospel of our Lord, Jesus

Christ.' " He glared out at the silent congregation. Tiana wanted to cough, but didn't dare. "Brothers and sisters, can you feel the heat of flames flickering at your feet? Can you hear the screams of souls in torment? Will you raise your voice in agony among them? Will flaming black vultures peck your eyes throughout eternity, my brethren? Will you sink into the lake of fiery brimstone for your lying?"

"No, Lord!" someone shouted.

"For your drinking?"

"Mercy, Jesus!"

"For your whoremongering?"

Tiana shook her head. Why did Christians have to be terrified into being good? It made no sense to her. Their god was no better than the bogle man. The white woman next to her began to moan. Her eyes rolled back in their sockets and she swayed. Her long, heavy hair fell from under her cap. Combs flew as she began to jerk violently, sending her hair whipping around her head. Tiana tugged at Fancy's sleeve.

"Is she sick?" she asked. "Should we help her?"

"No. She's just getting the call. Leave her be. If it's a good meeting the ground'll be littered with folks before too long."

The woman stood suddenly with a shrill cry. She babbled in a strange tongue, then her body went rigid. She crumpled and lay still.

"Brother Dave," called the preacher on stage. "I've struck fire. A brand's been plucked from the burning. Help the sister in the front row."

Susannah started to cry and Fancy took her in her lap. She hid her face between Fancy's breasts, but the other girls watched openmouthed. The people around them began to froth or speak gibberish or fall to the ground and writhe. Others danced at their places to some inner music.

"Sisters," said Fancy, "I'm taking the little one to the big house. I'll be back soon." Fancy carried the sleeping child up the dark path toward the rear portico of the house. She was on her way back when a hand grasped her arm, and whirled her around. Tonight, whiskey was stronger than onions on Bryson's breath.

"You've bewitched me, woman." There was a wild look in his eyes. He had not slept the night before and he had been in a fever all day. He had watched her moving, tall and haughty, through the crowd. He had fantasized that her long, slender legs were wrapped around him and that her full lips were kissing him. "I want you now," he said drunkenly.

"You're hurting my arm, Mr. Bryson." Fancy looked desperately around. If she raised a cry, Coffee would find them and attack Bryson. He would die for it. "Please let go. I'll do whatever you want. Just let go."

"Oh no, my black beauty. I'm not so stupid." He tightened his grip and began marching her toward the bushes. She became docile and slumped in submission. When she felt his grip relax, she made a break. She jerked and twisted her arm, hitting him with her free fist. She almost escaped, but he was quicker than he seemed. He swung his heavy whip handle and hit her on the back of the head with it. He caught her as she fell against him.

She woke up stripped and gagged and lying on her back. Her hands were tied together, then tethered to something solid behind her. One ankle was tied to a post set firmly in the dirt floor. She looked around. She was in an abandoned shanty, somewhere on Vann's property. There was a foul-smelling straw pallet under her and a stubby candle burning on a wobbly table nearby.

Bryson sat tilted back in an old chair. His bullwhip lay across his lap. It looked as though he had used this place for this purpose before. Fancy groaned as pain shot through her head. Bryson rose and stood over her. He trailed the tip of the rawhide whip down her chest and belly. He flicked her lightly on the thigh with it.

"Black bitch." He said it quietly, but it was the ugliest sound Fancy had ever heard. "Think you're too good for a white man, do you?" He flicked the whip again and she felt the sting on her breast. She closed her eyes. *Oh, Provider,* she prayed. *Help me.*

"I can hurt you bad, woman. I can hurt you inside so no one will see it under that sooty skin." He straddled her thrashing body. He held the whip handle, ten inches long and three inches in diameter, with the lash trailing behind him. "But I ain't gonna hurt you. You won't feel no hurt. You're gonna feel good. I'm gonna love you up like you never been loved. You ain't gonna forget old Bryson."

Fancy closed her eyes and screamed into the gag. She filled her head with silent screaming. But she still felt the weight of him as he lay across her. She still smelled him. She felt the rough end of the whip handle pushing against her. She tried to comfort herself with the thought that this wasn't a human being. It was an animal.

But the brutal, searing pain tore at her as he pushed the handle into her, and ripped the soft, tender flesh.

"Fancy!"

"Fancy, where are you?" Somewhere far away, she heard James and Coffee. She felt the weight lift from her. She heard Bryson's boots thudding out the door. She lay, waiting and choking on her tears.

"Oh, my sweet Fancy." Coffee knelt over her. James held the pine knot torch while he took the gag from her mouth. He covered her with his big shirt and felt under it for broken ribs and bones. James cut the ropes holding her hands and foot. Coffee held her close as she sobbed. When she had calmed a little, he asked her.

"Who did it?"

"Take me home."

"Tell me, woman. I'm a man. They can only push me so far." He shook her in his rage. Then he realized what he was doing and hugged her to him. "I'm sorry, Fancy. I'm sorry, girl. But I have to know."

"He'll kill you."

"He'll have to hurry, before I kill him."

"They'll come after you with dogs and guns."

"Tell me."

"No. Take me home. Please, my love. Brother." She turned to James. "Take me home."

"Let us go, friend." James put a hand on Coffee's shoulder. "We have to get away from here. We can find out who did it later. My father will hunt the man down and see he's punished."

"Punished!" Coffee looked up at him with hatred in his eyes. "This is white work. They ain't gonna punish no white man for raping a black woman. Don't talk to me about punishing." He sobbed in rage and frustration and anguish.

"This is the Cherokee Nation," said James. "There's justice here."

"There's slavery here. Is that justice?"

"Let's go." James helped Fancy to her feet, and Coffee picked her up easily in his arms.

Chapter 9

Fancy stolidly gathered the apples that had been aging in the sun. She and Tiana, Nannie and Susannah had peeled, cored, and quartered the apples, then bruised them with rolling pins. They had left them spread on a bed of straw while thirty gallons of cider boiled down to fifteen. Now the girls crawled over the straw, brushing bits of it off the apples and putting the fruit into the baskets they dragged behind them.

Even though it was October, Fancy perspired from the heat of the fire. She wiped her face with her apron as she stirred the cider to see how it was thickening. Jack followed her around.

"Fancy, lass, you must tell me."

"Leave me be, Captain Jack."

"I have to know. I'll get him. I just can't let the man go. He must be punished. He's harmed one of my own."

"Nothing you can do."

"Dammit, woman, tell me!" Jack was losing patience. He'd been trying for days to find out what had happaned to Fancy. But she refused to tell him anything. Thousands of people had been at Vanns'. Any of the men could have done it.

Jack blew out his breath in exasperation as Fancy began dumping the baskets of apples into the huge kettle of boiled-down cider. Tiana and Nannie stood by to stir it. It took both of them to wield the long paddle. The terrible, undefined thing that had happened to Fancy preoccupied them far more than the apple butter they were making. They watched the struggle between Fancy and their father.

"You must tell me, if not for your own sake, then for the girls. The man can't be allowed to run loose like a mad dog."

"Sisters." Fancy turned to Nannie and Susannah and Tiana. "Run into the house and fetch the molasses and quinces and sassafras."

"But we won't need them for a long time," said Tiana.

"Go get them now." When the girls were out of hearing, she said, "It was me only he wanted." Her voice broke. "I'm afraid. I'm afraid he'll find me here, but I can't tell you, Captain, I can't." She swayed, and Jack caught her. She sobbed against his chest. "Please don't ask me."

Jack put his arms around her and patted her. He rocked her in his arms, as though soothing a child to sleep.

"I'm sorry, lass. I'm sorry. This business has made me a little daft. If you can't tell me, you can't. But whoever he is, he won't hurt you again. I'll find out, I promise you. I'll leave his carcass for the wild animals to feed on."

Jack stopped hounding her, but Fancy began having bad dreams. Every night she would wake, screaming, and the family would gather around to comfort her. After a while Nannie and Annie, Susannah and the boys would plod wearily back to bed, but Tiana stayed. Each night she listened while Jennie and Elizabeth sat at the edge of Fancy's straw pallet and questioned her.

"Was the dream about a house burning or people singing?" Jennie asked gently. Fancy shivered and shook her head.

"Did a wolf or fox bark in the dream, or did you hear an owl?" asked Elizabeth.

"No," said Fancy. "Someone was chasing me. I couldn't see his face. But I kept stumbling, and people stood in my way, and he was coming closer."

Jennie and Grandmother Elizabeth shook their heads. Someone had obviously put a spell on Fancy. They knew which dreams meant death, and which meant sickness or insanity. But these dreams of Fancy's were beyond their understanding. Fancy didn't protest when they insisted she go with them to Hiwassee Town for the annual Great Medicine Time.

She thought perhaps Drum or The Just could cure her of the dreams. Even if they didn't, Hiwassee Town was farther away from the Vann plantation and Bryson. Each night, after Jennie and Elizabeth and Tiana went back to bed, Fancy cried silently for Coffee. But she dared not try to see him. A trip to Hiwassee Town would at least occupy her mind.

Long ago plants had promised to help the Real People cure disease. In autumn, when the leaves fell into Long Man, the river became a vast medicine kettle. Its eddies and rapids resembled the boiling of the curers' decoctions. In October the Seven Clans bathed in Long Man to prevent sickness.

In the dim light of pre-dawn, Tiana held Fancy's hand as they waded into the river with the rest of their family. The Rogers children and grandchildren numbered close to twenty now, and they all gathered here for the Great Medicine ceremony. They joined the hundreds of people ranged along the bank of the river. Mothers carried infants, the well supported the sick. Most wore only loincloths as they stood in the roiling water. There was a light breeze, and leaves rained from the huge trees lining the river.

The water always seemed different at this time of year. As Tiana walked farther out into the stream, it swirled around her body like a powerful beast. Streams and rivers were roads to the underground homes of spirits. Sometimes the spirits lured people down there to live with them. In the water's movement, Tiana thought she could feel invisible hands tugging at her.

Always, at the beginning of this ceremony, she felt like she was entering a magician's spell, or a witch's caldron. The air shimmered with magic and mystery. She tried not to wince when the gold and red leaves brushed against her on their whirling journey downstream.

Then she calmed herself. There was nothing to fear. The people around her loved her. The plants were her protectors. Long Man was her friend. Everything was alive and she was at the center of that life. She felt the life force in every stone under her bare feet, and in every leaf that caressed her as it passed. While The Just chanted his songs to The Provider, Tiana smiled and lifted her arms to greet Grandmother Sun who was just stepping over the treetops. *Good morning, Grandmother,* she thought. And she knew the sun heard her.

As they all walked quietly out of the water, the mystery seemed to dry up and disappear with the drops on her skin. As she and

Fancy found their clothes, left in a heap on the shore, Tiana tried to cheer her.

"We'll dance all night, sister," she said. "We'll dance to keep awake while the medicine simmers in the pots. And The Important Thing won't climb over us for another year." Like everyone else, Tiana often referred to illness as The Important Thing. One never called disease by name. That would attract its attention.

Fancy smiled at her with sad, brown eyes. "I know, sister," she said. "And the boys will tease the girls. The men and women will tell embarrassing stories about each other."

"Dark daughter," Jennie called to Fancy. "Stay here beside Long Man. The Beloved Father will try to help you." Jennie held out an old, tattered shirt for Fancy to put on. When Drum finished his ritual Fancy would throw it into the river to move her bad dreams downstream with it. Tiana returned with Fancy, but Jennie gently pried her fingers loose and propelled her toward the village.

"I want to watch," Tiana said.

"You cannot, daughter." Jennie's voice was kind, but firm. "This magic is too dangerous for the inexperienced." Tiana wondered how she would ever become experienced if she were chased away from the rituals. She followed the path until it curved and carried her from her mother's sight. Then she doubled back through the bushes. On her stomach, she wormed through the dense cane stalks until she could see Jennie and Elizabeth, Fancy and Drum.

Drum was holding his hands out in front of him, his thumbs and forefingers pinched together. Tiana strained to see what he was doing and she wondered why he was doing it.

"*Gha*! Listen!" Drum said. "This is Fancy. Her clan is the Long Hair," chanted Drum. Tiana realized then how fortunate it was Jennie and Grandmother Elizabeth had adopted Fancy into their clan. Otherwise she would have no protection against harm from people or spirits. Tiana concentrated on the archaic images of Drum's charm.

Gha! *Evil things were being given her.*
Where is the assigner of this evil?
Gha! *Listen, O Brown Beaver, your Saliva walks Above.*
Evil had been given her, but now her soul is released.

Fancy shouted the name of a village far downstream, the destination for her bad dreams. Then she sank under the water, rose and sank again six more times. Finally she tore the shirt off and stood naked. She flung the shirt into the river and watched it float away. Even after Drum and the women left, Fancy stood staring downstream.

Tiana began to wriggle silently backwards. She was at home here, in the cool dimness among the slender cane stalks that grew six or eight inches apart. The long, narrow leaves sprouted horizontally a few feet from the ground and formed a thick green ceiling over her head. The plants grew fourteen feet high. With their knives, Tiana and her sisters liked to hollow out small rooms and corridors in the canebrakes and play there.

Now there was a rustling sound coming toward her. She looked for the cow that was probably making the noise. Cows liked to forage on the tender young leaves and shoots. Jack was always cursing the cane for hiding stray cows and blessing it for sustaining them through the winter.

She bawled softly, like a calf. "*Wahga*," she called. "Sister Cow." Then, like one of Fancy's persistent nightmares, she caught a glimpse of Spearfinger's wrinkled face leering at her from among the stalks.

Tiana dared not scream. There was no knowing what kind of trouble she'd get into for spying on sacred rituals. Drum might call her name out in council, or scratch her arm with his bone comb to let everyone know she had been bad. So she watched in horror as Spearfinger duckwalked at a crouch through the cane toward her. The two stared at each other and for a few moments there was no sound but the rattle of the cane tops.

"Thunder feeds on your soul." Spearfinger's voice was dry and brittle, like the voice of the cane. Tiana stared at her in wide-eyed terror. Was the old woman a shape-taker? A demon masquerading as a human being? Was she putting a spell on her? Tiana's heart pounded as she stood rooted to the ground.

Spearfinger smiled and exposed her double rows of teeth. Maybe she smiled to reassure Tiana, but she only released her from the spell of her fear. Tiana turned and crashed blindly through the dense cane stalks. Above her the thickly woven leaves thrashed and trembled with her flight.

Her friends, the cane, had changed into something sinister. They clutched at her as she pushed blindly through them. Their leaves had turned into tongues that sang, *"Su-sa-sai, su-sa-sai."* It was the song Spearfinger crooned to lull little girls before she stabbed them with her sharpened finger, and ate their livers. The cane's song seemed to pursue her all the way to the village.

Tiana was out of breath when she rounded the corner of Sally Ground Squirrel's cabin and found the women setting up their day's work. In good weather, Sally Ground Squirrel and her friends usually gathered under the old maple. Some of the women had spread their clay and greenware out on mats. They were shaping pots or using carved paddles to pat designs on the unfired vessels. Others pounded corn in the upright logs hollowed out at the top to form mortars. The rhythmic thud of their weighted pestles was soothing to Tiana. Some women mended clothing, or with heavy wire combs, picked seeds from cotton. Jennie had brought out the basket Tiana was working on as well as her own. She had been teaching Tiana to double weave so the basket would hold water. She didn't think it strange Tiana was panting and sweating. The child was always running.

When Tiana had caught her breath, and before the morning's gossip started in earnest, she asked a question.

"Is . . ." she paused. She wasn't sure how to phrase this. Accusing someone of witchcraft was serious. People accused of it were often killed. "Is there a witch in this village?"

"One can never know for sure," said Sally Ground Squirrel. "Why do you ask?"

"This one is just curious," Tiana said.

"Has Mother Raincrow frightened you again, daughter?" Jennie asked.

"A little."

"If she is *uyai gawe' ski gewa*, a Speaker Of Evil, a conjuror, she harms no one in Hiwassee," said Sally Ground Squirrel. "There are some who go to her for charms."

"Then I should not fear her?"

"You should be cautious, granddaughter," said Elizabeth. "She is powerful. One should always treat persons of power with respect."

"I will, grandmother." Then, while the women shared the latest news and scandal, Tiana concentrated on her own small, slender fingers and the hundreds of cane splints. Even though she was creating them she was always amazed at the intricate geometric patterns growing under her hands.

James and John Houston had been right. Maryville had changed in a year. The flat land had been built on. Now cabins jutted precariously out over the sides of the steep ravines. Hunched against the chill autumn wind, Sam walked stealthily through the bushes in the deep gorge of Pistol Creek, behind Main Street. He felt furtive, creeping through the back side of town, but he didn't want to be seen.

Maryville's garbage had prospered too. Sam idly kicked a tin that had once held smoked oysters. *Pretty soon this ditch'll be full enough to build on*, he thought. *Well, more than one town has a firm foundation on garbage*. Hiwassee certainly had. The children were always finding treasures scattered among the debris and ancient mussel shells of the mounds there.

Sam didn't have to look at the blank back walls of the buildings lining the street above him. He could tell where he was by the contents of the avalanche of trash spilling into the gully. There were old mill stones and grind stones, broken wheels and rotten, bleached canvas.

He knew he was passing Russell's inn by the blue china shards and fish bones. Russell still had that black cook who fixed river trout fit for the gods. Scraps of beaver felt littered the ground behind Love's hat factory. Then Sam began to find broken glass, green and brown, mostly, and hundreds of stubby, white clay pipe bowls.

This was it. The owner of the Wayside still rented long-stemmed clay pipes by the evening. When a man finished smoking, the end of the pipe was soft with spittle. So he broke it off before he turned it in. The pipe was ready for the next customer. Sam climbed out of the ravine, toward the back of the Wayside. He couldn't have gone much farther anyway. The privy was built out over the gully. Sam could smell the result.

Sam peered over the top of the ravine. There was no one in sight, except a few chickens settling in a row on the eaves over Smitty's door. They looked at home there. It hadn't occurred to Sam that the Wayside's chickens might belong to Smitty. He walked along the plank path toward her penthouse. She had planted flowers and a rose bush in front of the small lean-to attached to the Wayside's back wall.

The one tiny window was closed, but crude flowers had been drawn on the shutter with charcoal. The red clay mud in the cracks between the logs had been whitewashed. But the clay had shriveled as it dried and the wash was chipping off. Sam stood a moment, summoning the courage to knock.

"Who is it?"

"A customer," he stammered. He could do better than that. "Sam Houston."

"Come on in."

Sam pushed the door open and ducked to enter. He bumped his head on the low rafters and moved farther in where the roof sloped upward to meet the tavern's back wall. There was little room to spare between his head and the ceiling.

Smitty was lounging on her bed, knitting by the flickering flame of a rush light. Her hair was hidden by a mob cap of gathered muslin. There was a flowered cloth on the small table next to the bed, and a matching cushion on the room's one chair. A faded Turkey carpet decorated the dirt floor by the bed. Old newspapers covered the walls. They were probably for insulation. Sam doubted Smitty could read. There were advertising posters over the news-papers, an attempt to decorate the place.

There was no hearth. One of Ben Franklin's stoves crouched in a corner and gave a cheerful glow. On it, a steaming teakettle whis-tled softly to itself. Perfume bottles, toilet articles, and a few old portraits in chipped gilt frames stood on a shelf. Smitty laid down her knitting and patted a spot beside her on the bed.

"Sit down, boy. I won't bite. Not unless you pay extra."

Sam sat gingerly on the far end of the bed. The corn-shuck mat-tress rustled loudly.

"You're a handsome, strapping lad. Good to see you back."

"You know who I am?"

"Everyone knows everything in a town this size."

Sam winced.

"Besides, I watched you leave a year ago at the head of that parade. People have been talking of your plaster stunt ever since. Dutch woulda killed you if he'd caught you." Smitty laughed and slapped her broad thigh. Sam studied his hat, trying not to stare down the front of her pelisse. The blue satin robe was loosely fastened. He could see the soft white breasts. *Like Ma's dumplings*, he thought. The satin robe was worn thin, but it was lined with a lighter blue silk. Smitty had known better times. She coyly brushed a loose lock of hair under her cap.

"It's good to be back," said Sam. Then he fell silent.

"I don't suppose you're here for knitting lessons." Smitty loosened her robe more. The light from the burning rush outlined the whiskers over her upper lip and shone on the powder caked in the creases of her face. Her tiny painted mouth was almost lost in the sagging jowls that blended into her neck. She hadn't a chin to speak of. There were puffy pouches under her pale blue eyes. Without the underpinnings of stays and corsets, her torso was lumpy and dimpled.

"It's my night off, actually," she said.

"Oh, I'm sorry, ma'm. I didn't know you weren't, uh, open for business." Sam hoped the relief in his voice wasn't obvious. Sam had nothing against older women. He just wasn't used to anyone waging such all-out warfare on the ravages of time. "I'll go and leave you in peace." He rose hastily.

"Sit. Sit. I can use the company. In my establishment, talk is cheap." Smitty had been in the business a long time. She knew Sam had changed his mind. And she was lonely. Not many people dropped by to talk. "I hear you've been living with the wild Indians. What was it like?"

Sam told her. She fixed them each a cup of tea, pouring hot water over the powder she shaved from a large black tea brick. While they sipped their tea from the saucers, Smitty sat with her feet up and her pelisse open, but unnoticed. Sam was still talking half an hour later when there was a loud knock at the door. Smitty sighed. "I told Bartlett not to send anyone back here." Sam realized he was sorry to leave.

"Mrs. Smith, this is Reverend Moore." Sam and Smitty rolled their eyes at each other.

"The Reverend Mark Moore?" Sam whispered. "The head of Porter Academy?" Smitty nodded.

"I have a customer now, Reverend," Smitty called. "Come back in a half hour."

"Mrs. Smith, the Reverend is not here for that," said a woman's voice. "We want to talk to you. Let us in, please."

"Ohmygod!" Sam's face went pale, then red. He rushed wildly around the tiny room, like a squirrel in a mouse trap. "That's my mother!" he hissed. "How did she know I was here?"

Smitty laughed. She fell back on the bed laughing. Her laughter would have been contagious if Sam hadn't been in such a panic.

"This isn't funny, Smitty. Where can I hide?" The pounding on the door had started again. Sam looked under the bed, but it was too high off the ground. He'd be in plain sight. He opened a trunk and found it full of lacy underthings.

"Hide?" Smitty could hardly talk. "I'd as easily hide a panther in a pisspot as hide you in here."

"What'll I do?" Sam was almost in tears. His mother was the only person in Maryville who awed him.

"Take it easy, dearie. It's me they want to talk to. Just stand behind the door."

Sam flattened himself against the wall and stopped breathing while Smitty adjusted her robe and cap. She stepped outside and closed the door behind her. Sam could hear the low murmur of voices through the log wall. When Smitty came back in, she slumped onto the bed. She leaned her elbow on the brass rail and rested her chin, what there was of it, on her palm. She stared across the room at the closed door.

"What is it, Smitty?"

"Concerned citizens. A committee of them. You know a place is civilized when people start forming committees."

"What do they want?"

"A view of the back of me, leaving town."

"You don't hurt anyone."

"I'm a bad influence." She went to the small wardrobe that held two or three dresses, in a style ten years gone. She pulled a bag from under their flounces.

"Where will you go?" asked Sam.

"Knoxville maybe. Or farther west. Some place bigger or smaller than Maryville. Maryville's at that awkward stage of growing up. Just big enough to have pretensions. But I was getting to like it. It's gonna be a real nice place someday. I was thinking of retiring here," she said wistfully. "Maybe taking in needlework, knitting. Maybe make hats. I'm good with my hands, you know."

"Why don't you do it?"

"No. They know me here. Your ma's a decent woman, Sam. No offense, but there are few creatures more ferocious than a decent woman."

"I'd best go, Smitty," Sam said awkwardly. "It's been real nice meeting you."

"Good night, Sam," she said absentmindedly. When he left, she was dusting her portraits with a bundle of chicken feathers and packing them carefully among her underwear in the trunk.

The Mounted Gunmen gathered for their weekly muster in front of the new Maryville courthouse. They were a motley mob, young mostly, and armed with everything from the latest 1808 model musket to hoes. Sam had joined and played the drum for their drilling. His drumming had a distinctly Indian beat.

Affairs went well enough until the official muster was over. Then the captain, John Cusack, and two helpers rolled out the whiskey barrel as usual. They set it up under the only tree left, an oak they called their Liberty Tree. The twenty-five volunteers fell into a jostling line and set to work on the contents of the barrel.

As the afternoon wore on, they became louder and more affectionate. Arm in arm, they sang lustily, swaying to the beat of Sam's drum and ending each chorus with a bump that sent the last man in line flying. Cusack jumped onto a wagon bed and delivered a speech, damning Britain to hell and the four quarters. The British navy had been impounding American sailors and they were stirring up trouble among the Indians to the north again. In fact, the British were usually blamed for anything that went wrong. Sam jumped up next to Cusack. He pounded on the wagon side with his drum sticks to get everyone's attention. Then he began reciting from the *Iliad*.

> Oh, tyrant, arm'd with insolence and pride,
> Inglorious slave to interest, ever joined with fraud.

"Huzza!" the men shouted. "Down with Britain!"

> But let the signal be this moment given,
> To mix in fight is all I ask of heaven.

"Huzza!" they roared again.

"Cusack, what's that infernal noise?" A man appeared on the courthouse steps. "Keep your men in check. The court can't hear the cases."

"The field of combat fits the young and bold," Sam yelled drunkenly at him. "The solemn council best becomes the old."

"Huzza!" agreed the militiamen.

From his perch on the wagon, Sam spied Smitty. She was in front of Russell's livery. She wore a huge calash, a traveling bonnet that looked like the folding top of a carriage. Clogs kept her skirt from the mud of the street. Her trunks were piled behind her and were surrounded by round hat boxes, bags, and cages of chickens. A forlorn, leafless rose bush, its roots wrapped in burlap, stood sentinel over her possessions.

" 'Ah, like fair Laodice in form and face, the loveliest nymph of Priam's royal race.' " Sam pointed in Smitty's direction. "They're evicting a grand lady, boys. What say we give her a royal send-off, to show our appreciation for her contribution to the cultural life of Maryville."

"Huzza!" The men about-faced and quick-marched to Russell's. Sam beat a tattoo with all the strength in his brawny arms. They didn't notice the judge, the sheriff, and the county officials storming out of the courthouse. They were followed by the plaintiffs, the defendants, and the court hangers-on. The militiamen surrounded the coach and handed the boxes up to the driver, who stowed them on top of it. Under her powder, Smitty turned bright pink, but she was pleased.

"Mind the rose bush," she called. "Have a care with it."

"Farewell, Mrs. Smith," shouted Sam over the noise of his drum. "You take our hearts with you!"

"Yes, sir," hiccupped Cusack. "Right there in the cage with the chickens."

Smitty hugged each of the men. When she came to Sam, she stood on tiptoe, pulled his face down, and kissed him while the men cheered. She boarded the stage and waved out the window at them. They waved back until she was out of sight. They turned to finish their party, but found the sheriff blocking the path. He stood about five feet five inches, vertically and horizontally. He was angry.

"Cusack, Houston, what do you think this is?"

"A farewell party?" Sam asked innocently, trying to go around him to reach the whiskey. The sheriff moved sideways, blocking him.

"You boys have had enough. Go home."

"There's whiskey left."

"No more for you," called the judge, peering around the sheriff's bulk.

"Pish tosh," said Sam. He beat a tatoo on the sheriff's bald head and, with his drum, shoved him out of the way. The judge was almost trampled in the rush for the whiskey barrel.

Ordered, that John B. Cusack be fined Ten Dollars and Samuel Houston Five Dollars for disorderly riotously wantonly with an Assembly of Militia Annoying the Court with the noise of a Drum and with force preventing the Sheriff and Officer of the Court in the discharge of his duty against the peace and dignity of the State.

Sam looked over his mother's shoulder as she read the order. "They could use a grammician over at the courthouse," he said. "This is no laughing matter, Samuel," said Elizabeth Houston. "Have you no respect for your own mother?" shouted John.

"Please." Sam held his throbbing head in his hands. "Lower your voice. Silence is the language of wisdom, Drum says."

"I won't lower my voice because you drank too much and behaved vilely yesterday and are sick today because of it. You're a disgrace." John continued to shout. His face was much too close to Sam's for comfort.

"That's enough, John." Elizabeth Paxton Houston's soft, slow voice was much more effective than John's shouting anyway. She was only a few inches shorter than Sam. Her thick, chestnut hair was streaked with gray. She wore it Grecian style, pulled back and falling in ringlets on her neck. She had gained weight over the years, but she was still handsome. And Smitty was wrong about her. She was more than a decent woman. She was a good woman. And a strong one. She had an iron will neatly encased in perfume and velvet.

She was the daughter of a rich planter, one of Tidewater Virginia's aristocracy. Her people had been encouraged by England to emigrate to northern Ireland. The Crown hoped the influx of Protestants would crush the Catholic Irish resistance. But the Scots had prospered there, so much so that the English drove them out again with high rents. In doing that, they spread the discontent to America. The Scotch-Irish settlers were fiercely independent and determined to have their own land. They would pay no more rent.

Elizabeth came from a line of survivors who flourished wherever they settled. So her family had not been pleased when she announced her intention to marry Samuel Houston, Sam's father. In their eyes he was an uncouth highlander, one of those who pushed on into the coves of the mountains and hacked out crude farms there.

But it was clear that eighteen-year-old Elizabeth had made up her mind to marry him. He was a dashing young captain in Morgan's Rifles and he did have an estate, left him by his father. So the Paxtons acquiesced.

Nine children and hard times followed. Samuel Houston, senior, was rarely home. He became a major in the Virginia militia, a brigade inspector. For twenty-three years he made his rounds of the forts in the state. But it was peacetime. There was little advancement. He had a family and slaves to support and a farm that was sliding into bankruptcy. He dreamed of moving west. There were fortunes to be made there, if not with Aaron Burr's ephemeral schemes, then in the wars he was likely to stir up. But President Jefferson squelched Burr's machinations. Peace rolled inexorably on.

When Major Samuel Houston died, far from home, in 1806, he left Elizabeth a "waggon with chain and gears compleat for five horses." He left her a bankrupt farm and debts and paperwork for a land grant in east Tennessee. Methodically, Elizabeth Houston made a list of assets.

There were three adult slaves and two black children, an iron-gray mare, a riding chair and harness, a sword, a card table, and three tea boards. Wine. Bed linen. A woman's saddle, bridle, and martingale. An umbrella. The relics of a better life. What was left after paying the debts she packed into the new wagon and the family's old one. She loaded the children and the slaves and set out for Tennessee, over the mountains and three weeks away.

In the four years since then, she and her sons and bondsmen had built a sturdy, two-story log house. It stood on a slope overlooking the wooded valley of Baker's Creek, ten miles from Maryville. They had cleared much of the four hundred and nineteen acres patented to them. But they had done the past year's work without the help of young Sam. Now Elizabeth Houston was calling him to task.

"You were drunk in the public streets. You assaulted an officer of the peace and a member of the bench."

Sam hung his head under the lash of his mother's calm voice.

"You made the Houston name a laughingstock and a disgrace. Worst of all, you were seen by the decent people in town embracing a woman of low degree. How could you do this to me, Samuel? How can I show my face in Maryville after this?"

"I'm sorry, Mother."

"Sorry!" John Houston exploded. "Is that all?"

Elizabeth Houston raised a hand to quiet him. She shook her head sadly. "I've tried to teach you right from wrong. I've raised you to be honest and upright and God-fearing. Where did I fail?" Through all the trials that had beset her, Sam had never seen his mother cry. Her tears made him feel baser than all John's lectures.

"You did nothing wrong. I couldn't have had a better, nobler mother." He hugged her stiffly. He smelled the rose-petal perfume she always wore in her hair. Elizabeth Houston was not a woman to flaunt affection. It was the first time Sam could remember hugging her. "I'll reform. I'll work hard and make you proud of me."

Sam tried to keep his promise. He went diligently to the store every day for a month. He held his temper, although barely, when James or John scolded him. But he refused to pay the five-dollar fine. And he was tiring of John's heckling him about it.

"John, it's payday."

"You'll get no pay."

"Why not?"

"It's going to pay the fine you owe, plus interest."

"I said I wasn't paying it."

"You don't have to. I will. The Houston honor will be upheld, even if you don't care about it."

"I do care about it. That's why I refuse to pay. I won't be charged and fined like a common criminal."

"Then don't behave commonly."

"I'm warning you, John, if you don't pay me I'll take the money from you."

"You and the drunken Mounted Gunmen, I suppose."

Sam leaped the counter and jumped his brother. He was younger, but far bigger. The two of them rolled on the floor, bringing goods crashing down around them. They were still fighting when they burst through the door and out into the street.

"Fight! Fight!" People ran to watch them pommel each other. Sam was pushing John's face into the dust of the street when he called, "Pax." Sam let him up, and the crowd dissolved.

"Give me my money," said Sam.

"Go to hell." John brushed himself off and wiped the dirt from his mouth and face. He spit out some sand, mounted his horse, and rode away.

Sam went back inside. He took items valuing a month's pay and threw them into a sack. He thought a moment. Then he gathered more things, as much as he could carry. He left an IOU for them. Where ·he was going he wouldn't need money, but presents were always welcome. He would need them to get back into Annie's good graces. She had been distraught, then angry with him for leaving. But Sam wasn't worried. *You'll soon have her back, you winsome cavalier.*

He banked the fire in the stove and added the price of a wool coat to the IOU. With a piece of charcoal he hastily scrawled "Gone traveling" on the outside of the door. He turned his key in the heavy padlock and slid the key under a warped board in the door. Then he headed south at a fast walk.

He followed the well-marked Wachesa Trail, the trade road from North Carolina through the Cherokee Nation to the Hiwassee and beyond. Once he passed Sam Henry's mill and the cabins around it, he walked for a day through steep hills and dark forests.

Then he began seeing paths branching off and disappearing among the hills. He knew there were Cherokee farms and cabins at the ends of them. He began to pass the tiny settlements of the Real People, each with its town house and ball field and dance ground.

He crossed the Hiwassee on the old ferry guided by Punk Plugged In and climbed onto the bank of Hiwassee Island. Once there he felt like Kalanu, The Raven again. As he hiked down the tree-shaded path he broke into song.

> *Best of all! She has no tongue,*
> *Submissive, she obeys me;*
> *She's fully, fully better old than young,*
> *And still to smiling sways me;*
> *Her skin is smooth, complexion black,*
> *And has a most delicious smack;*
> *Then kiss and never spare it,*
> *'Tis . . . a bottle of good claret.*

He danced a little jig and gave himself a whirl under his favorite old chestnut tree spaning the trail.

" 'Tis . . . a bottle of good claret."

"Yeee-e-e-e-i-i-i-eeaa!" The scream sent prickles chasing down Raven's spine. His blood turned to ice water. He screamed in answer and looked up. He saw teeth. Lots of them. Then he was rolling on the ground with the creature wailing and cackling on top of him, apparently intent on eating his ear. He flailed blindly at it, but it was strong, and seemed to have more than the usual complement of arms and legs. He doubled up and tried to protect his head with his arms.

"Leave off, mother," a voice called. Raven was relieved.

"Father, pull her off of me!"

"Mother, mother, that's no way to treat a friend."

Raven scrambled to his feet when he felt the weight lifted from his back. He waited, panting, while Drum murmured to Raincrow, old Spearfinger, in his calm voice. She stood, hunched over and frail looking, her head to one side like a bird. Her hair stuck out in tangled spikes from under the filthy green kerchief askew on her head.

"He's my son, Mother. Be kind to him." Drum rummaged through the scattered contents of Raven's satchel. He found a corncob pipe and offered it to her. She jammed it upside down between her two sets of teeth. With a final shriek, she disappeared into the underbrush.

"Welcome home, my son." Drum embraced Raven.

"Thank you, father. She's some reception committee."

"She's harmless enough."

Raven rubbed his ear where she'd fastened her teeth into it.

"Why does she always put her pipe in her mouth upside down?" he asked.

"She says demons can't enter her through the pipe when it's upside down. It confuses them," Drum said.

"Isn't that like locking the hen house after the fox is inside?"

Drum laughed. Raven didn't bother to ask Drum how he knew he was coming. Drum always seemed to know everything. When Raven asked him how he knew, he would only wink mysteriously and say "*Tsikilili*, a singing bird told me."

It was good to be with Drum again. Raven felt at peace walking silently next to him. He had a lot to tell Drum and to ask him, but it could wait. "White people talk too much and too loudly," Drum had once told him. "They never take time to listen. When Drum leaves a group of white people, his ears ring for a long time after. Silence is the voice of the Provider. In silence he gives us his most important messages. In silence we can hear the voices that must be felt with the heart rather than heard with the ears."

Finally, when they were near enough to Sally Ground Squirrel's cabin to hear the thud of her corn mortar, Raven asked the question that had been on his mind.

"Are James and John here?"

"They're at their father's."

"I'll visit them."

"They'll look on you with white eyes," Drum said.

Chapter 10

Tiana was exhausted. She took several seconds to awaken. Two nights ago, her family had been up until dawn, celebrating the announcement of Annie's marriage to John Fawley and Charles' taking Rachel Ward as his second wife. Nanehi Ward had been there. The *ghigau* was now related to Tiana.

The Rogers' neighbors and friends and relatives, their slaves and white tenant farmers had gathered for a party. Two hundred people had feasted on the steers roasting in the yard. The tables had sagged with food and there had been fiddling afterward.

Raven had been stunned by the news of Annie's marriage. Tiana enjoyed the look on his face. He seemed more distraught that it had taken her less than a month to replace him than by the loss of her. *His pride is certainly large enough. He won't miss this little chunk of it.* Besides, there were many young women interested in Raven. He hadn't lacked dance partners.

The last guests had finally left the afternoon before. The Rogers family had gone to bed with the setting sun. But Fancy had had another of her nightmares. Her cries had echoed through the quiet house and Tiana offered to stay with her. It took courage. Fancy's dreams meant a sorcerer was at work.

Now Tiana lay next to Fancy on the narrow pallet in the tiny attic room, the cock loft. While Fancy thrashed and moaned in her sleep, Tiana stared at the low, sloping ceiling and listened to the night sounds—a restless cow in the barn, a whippoorwill whose call meant someone had died, or soon would. A bear or raccoon splashed in the creek behind the house.

It seemed as though Tiana had just fallen asleep when something waked her again. It would be daybreak soon. Jennie would call her children to go to water and greet the day. The first rooster had crowed. He was always early. The guinea fowls had started po-tracking in the wood lot. Soon the ducks and geese and hens would join in and the cows would low to be milked. Tiana was used to those sounds. They wouldn't have waked her.

There was a small rap on the shuttered window. Another fol-lowed, like pebbles thrown against the boards. With her heart pound-ing, Tiana padded barefoot across the cold floor to open the shutter.

The bright moon was almost down. It gave a silvery light to the zigzag fence, the garden plowed under, and the trees along the creek. There had been an early frost that made the young birches look as though they'd been shriveled by intense heat. Their leaves were still green but the edges of them had curled up, giving them a frizzy look. Tiana knew the leaves would fall green and crumble to fine powder under her moccasins.

Coffee stood in the moonlight and beckoned to her with both hands together over his head. Tiana heard the faint clink of chains. She lowered herself on her stomach over the sill, her bare feet search-ing for purchase on the cedar shakes of the cat slide outside her own second-story window. She dropped, landing lightly with her knees bent. She walked down the slope of the cat slide, the roof of the summer kitchen, and squatted at the edge. Under her toes, she could feel the soft moss growing on the rotted edges of the shingles. She shivered with the cold. Coffee held out his arms and she jumped, grabbing him around the neck.

"What happened, Coffee?" she whispered when he had set her awkwardly on the ground. His wrists were manacled and his shirt was shredded and covered with blood.

"No time to 'splain, Tiana. Got to talk to your daddy, and Fancy. But we can't wake anyone else, or I'm a dead man."

It was impossible to keep Coffee's arrival a secret from the family. Jack, James, John, Raven, Fancy, Tiana, and Nannie gathered with Coffee in the barn. Joseph and William were gone, as usual. Jennie and Elizabeth stayed at the house to fend off any patrols that might come. Susannah was sleeping peacefully. While Fancy bathed Coffee's lacerated back and smeared it with an ointment of boiled basswood root, he told them his story.

"Bryson found out about me and Fancy, I guess. I didn't know why he was meaner 'n usual. Then yesterday he put these on me." He rattled the manacles and the length of chain attached. "Said he couldn't trust me. He chained me to a tree and sent the other niggers off. Started to whip me. Said I'd been lying to master about him. But that wasn't it. He said he was going to kill me, whip me till there was nothing left. Then he tole me what he did to Fancy. Taunted me with it.

"I went crazy, Captain Jack. I tore that tree limb off and broke it on him. Then I beat him with the chain. I never gave him no chance to defend himself. No more'n he gave me."

"Is he dead?" asked Jack.

"I reckon. If he's alive, he's wishin' he wasn't. He didn't have no face left." Tiana winced. "I hauled him to the gully behind the quarters and threw him in. Don't think anyone saw me. Don't know if they've found him yet or not."

"This'll be the first place they look when they miss you."

"I know. But I didn't know where else to go. And I had to see Fancy."

"James, John, Sam, bring those boards from the loft. Fancy, help me clear this trash out of the wagon. Girls, run to the kitchen and pack food for a trip. Be absolutely quiet. If anyone comes to the house, they must think we're still asleep. We have to get Coffee to Hiwassee garrison."

"The garrison?" asked Sam. "Isn't that walking into the lion's mouth?"

"David Gentry, the smith there, can take these irons off. He does all my smithing. I don't keep the necessary tools here, and I might hurt Coffee if I try to do it. The garrison is farther north, away from Vann's place and in the middle of the Nation. The Georgians will not be as likely to make trouble there. Vann'll want to recover Coffee, but you can be sure those white crackers from Georgia will be out for his blood. They'll try him by Lynch's law."

Tiana listened, as they all did, for the baying of hounds.

"I did the best I could to cover my trail," said Coffee. "I waded the river."

"In any case, we have to hurry," said Jack.

When Tiana and Nannie returned from the house, the men were laying a false bottom on the wagon bed. Coffee held Fancy tightly and wiped her tears on the tail of the shirt Jack had given him. John was a big man, but Coffee's shoulders threatened to burst the seams.

"I'll come back for you, Fancy girl. We can live with the maroons until we can get to the north." He climbed into the wagon and stretched out under the boards. The last plank had a knothole in it so he could breathe. Jack began lowering it.

"This is going to be hell-fired uncomfortable, Coffee," he said apologetically. Coffee put his hands up to stop the plank.

"Captain Jack—" His voice choked. "I know I can't thank you for what you're doing, but I have to try."

"Later, man, later." Jack had seen what white mobs did to slaves accused of murder or rape. He would not have that on his conscience. The plank dropped in place. The boys loaded whatever they could find on top of the second floor.

"This'll have to look like a trading trip," said Jack. "If anyone stops you, say you're taking goods to the factory to sell."

Tiana and Nannie threw their traveling bags into the wagon. Tiana was climbing over the side when her father picked her up under the armpits, swung her around, and dropped her to the ground.

"Oh no, lass. You're staying here."

"But we want to go," Tiana said.

"No." He turned to give more orders.

"Come Nannie." Tiana retrieved their bags from the wagon.

"But—"

"Come!" Tiana dragged her sister off. They raced for the apple orchard and the shortcut to the road.

"I'll trap that pair of skunks that's been living under the house," Jack said. "I'll kill one on the trail Coffee took here and one in the barn. I'll scatter their scent all over the area. That should confuse the dogs. James, John, you drive to the garrison. If anyone stops you, tell them you're going to the factory. You may make it without being stopped. But they'll come here sure. I have to be here to talk to them."

"Sir," said Sam. "I'll go with James and John."

"No sense you getting mixed up in this. Best you go home to your family. Things will get ugly here."

"But, sir, they'd suspect me less, a white man and a slaveholder and all. And you know James can't lie and John's English lacks polish. I'm a good actor, if I do say so myself."

"He's right," said James.

"It's against my better judgment."

"I was going back to Hiwassee Town anyway," said Sam. "The garrison isn't far out of the way."

"All right. That frees John to take Fancy to Drum's by the back route. Drum will know where to hide her. I don't want any mobs getting to her." John ran to saddle two horses. "Now move, all of you!" said Jack.

As he watched the horses and wagon scatter, Jack realized his hands were shaking. *Well, Jack,* he thought, turning to find the traps for the skunks, *it won't be the first time you've been in a scrape. It's too bad Coffee got to Bryson first. I'd have enjoyed killing him myself.*

He remembered the day, over thirty years ago, when he had saved the Jennings boy from torture at the hands of the hostile Cherokee. He had been young and idealistic then. He couldn't understand how his new friends, the Real People, could be so cruel. *You had a lot to learn about cruelty, lad,* he said to himself.

James drove at a fast clip. He wanted to put as much distance as possible between them and the patrols. Yet he drove carefully. He knew it must be excruciating for Coffee, with his torn back pressed against the hard floor boards.

"Can we trust this Gentry fellow?" asked Sam.

"Sure. He's my sister Mary's husband."

"It figures. You're related to everyone in the Nation, aren't you?"

"Just about." James grinned at him.

"Any idea what Coffee will do when he gets the irons off?"

"One thing at a time, Raven." Then they saw the girls in the road ahead. Both were panting and sweating in the cold air.

"Whoa." James stopped a few inches from Tiana, hoping to force her out of the way. But she stood her ground. She reached up to grab the horses' corn-shuck collars.

"Go home!" James yelled. "We're in a hurry. You heard Father."

"We're coming with you." Tiana walked between the big horses so James couldn't drive them forward without running her down. She climbed onto the wagon tongue and from there to the seat. She stepped over the seat, steadying herself with a hand on each boy's head. Nannie attacked from the side. She hung onto the brake lever as she stepped onto the axle and then over into the wagon bed. The girls settled themselves there, plumping up some bags of beans to lean against.

"You can't go," said James. "It's too dangerous." Raven had a feeling James would lose this argument.

"You need us," said Tiana.

"We do not. Of what use are two girls?"

"A patrol won't be as suspicious if there are children along. You can say I'm sick and you're taking me to the garrison to see the doctor. That'll give us an excuse to hurry. Move along, James. Time's wasting." She waved imperiously.

James put his head in his hands.

"Help me get them out, brother."

"I hate to admit it, but she's right."

"Father will be furious."

"So? That's nothing unusual," pointed out Raven.

Tiana rapped softly on the floor boards.

"Don't worry, friend," she said. "We'll take care of you." As they drove off, she opened her satchel and pulled out a smaller sack. Dipping into it, she smeared ashes onto her face and neck, arms and legs, giving her skin a gray, unhealthy appearance. Then she rummaged through the small leather case she always wore around her neck.

"Is that your *etui*, *Ulisi*, Grandmother?" asked Raven. He and Tiana had an uneasy truce. He'd begun calling her the affectionate name given any female member of one's grandfather's clan. Intermarriage with whites had confused the clan system, but the name was still popular.

"What's an etwee?" Tiana asked.

"A little traveling case a lady wears pinned to her bodice."

"That's sister's *juju*," said Nannie. "Fancy says Tiana has the 'hand.' She keeps her magic in there."

"Looks like charcoal to me," said James.

"Smear this under my eyes, sister," said Tiana, ignoring the boys. "Blend it in so I'll look sickly."

"Did you realize your sister's ten years old and going on forty?" Raven asked James.

"That's all right." James clucked to the horses. "When she's forty she'll probably act ten."

Tiana began eating the apples she had picked in the orchard. She was on her fourth when they heard hoofs pounding behind them.

"Halt!"

"Oh, Lord," breathed Raven. "The *posse comitatus*."

"You girls keep quiet," said James. "It looks like a patrol." He let the ten men catch up. They were a surly lot, but there was a feeling of excitement about them. They reminded Tiana of hounds, hot on the scent and eager for blood. They were heavily armed with pistols, muskets, and long knives. Most chilling of all were the coils of ropes with nooses at the ends.

The leader was a burly man with a five-day growth of black beard and a buck tooth. His Springfield musket was held carelessly across his lap, the muzzle pointed at James and Raven.

"Good morning," said James. "You men huntin'?"

"You could say so. We're huntin' a runaway nigger. Killed a white man in cold blood."

"Can't say as we've seen an outlyer. You haven't seen one, have you, Sam?" Raven shook his head.

"How long he been missing?" Sam asked.

"Since yesterday."

"I hope you catch him and give him what he deserves. Killed a man, you say?" Raven turned to James. "Maybe we'd best hurry along if there's a rogue nigger loose."

"We'll check your wagon first." The man moved closer.

"You can see we're not carrying anything but goods for Hiwassee and my sisters," said James. "One of them's real sickly. She's got to see the doctor right away."

"Soon as we deliver the child I'd like to come back and help you hunt," added Raven. He felt the gun under his feet, but he knew it wouldn't be of much use. Sweat beaded on his forehead. No one noticed Tiana uncork a small vial and gulp its contents. The man leaned over the wagon's side and stretched his hand down to pull away some of the boxes stacked on the false floor.

With a loud gagging and retching, Tiana threw up all over his hand, his arm, and the floor of the wagon. She moaned piteously and rolled her eyes until only the whites showed. She heaved again, spewing bile and partially digested food, mostly apples. The man backed his horse hastily away and wiped his hands on his pantaloons.

"What's she got?" he asked. Tiana moaned again.

"The cholera." Nannie started to cry. "We didn't want anyone to know."

"Holy shit for a shoeshine!" one of the men wheeled his mount in a tight circle and galloped back down the road. The rest followed him. Only their leader watched the wagon until it was out of sight around a curve.

"You little buzzard, you," said Raven, when it was safe. "That was some act."

"It wasn't an act." Tiana retched again. "I feel ghastly. Boneset tea really works. That and the apples."

"Do it downwind, grandmother," said Raven cheerfully. He passed his big bandana to her. "First stream we come to, you can wash. Whew! You stink!"

"Sister, you were a soldier too," James said to Nannie.

"Brother!" shouted Tiana after a while. "Stop!"

"What's the matter?"

"Boneset tea works at both ends." She leaped out and disappeared into the bushes. Raven and Nannie had to help her into the wagon when she came back. She shivered convulsively.

"Think what they would have done to Coffee if they'd caught him." Tiana shivered again. Raven put a finger to his lips. There was no sense talking about it, especially in Coffee's hearing. *Imagine what they would have done to us*, Raven thought.

"I've been thinking."

"What is it, little sister." There was respect in James's voice.

"We shouldn't take Coffee to the garrison."

"Where do you suggest?"

"Tahlequah, the school at the blockhouse."

"What school?" asked Raven.

"The mission school, at the old Tellico blockhouse," said James. "We could hide Coffee there and bring David to him. There'd be less chance of discovery."

"Would they countenance that?"

"Mits MacTuff will help us. I know she will," said Tiana.

"She might. The missionaries hate slavery. And the school's been used as a sanctuary before, a few years ago."

"Won't people suspect it then?" asked Raven.

"No," said James. "White people don't notice if it's just Indians killing Indians."

Seeth MacDuff had packed her trunks and was ready to leave. Reverend Blackburn's poor health had finally forced him to close the school. It was empty now. There would be no winter term. Seeth stood in the silent classroom as darkness fell. She ran her hand over one of the benches, polished to a high sheen by the bodies of students. The bench was scarred with initials. Mrs. MacDuff didn't notice the tiny letters, T.R., as her fingers passed over them. Tiana had been unable to resist trying out her new penknife a year and a half earlier.

"Mits MacTuff!" Seeth whirled at the sound of the timid voice in the doorway.

"Tiana! Nannie!" She beamed at them. "What brings you here?"

"Trouble, Mits MacTuff. We need help."

"Oh, dear God in Heaven!" Seeth saw James and Raven helping Coffee from the wagon. His legs were cramped from being stretched for hours in the same position. His shirt and the rags stuffed under him as a cushion were stuck to the blood from his back. He was exhausted from two days without sleep.

"Get him inside quickly. Nannie, lead the horses to the barn. Tiana, show the boys the way to the attic stairs. I'll get some candles and medicine. We can take a pallet upstairs."

"It's a dangerous undertaking we ask of you," said James.

"I know that."

Tiana grinned at James and Raven. "I knew she'd help."

They made Coffee as comfortable as they could in the cold attic. He fell into a deep sleep while they told Mrs. MacDuff his story. Raven noticed the broad brown stain on the attic floor.

"Is that what I think it is?" he asked.

"Yes," said James.

"No one's going to die here now," said Seeth. "You boys can bring David Gentry in the morning. I'll stay with Coffee. Mr. MacDuff's away and we won't mention this to him. Slavery! What an abomination. 'And will ye even sell your brethren?' "

"You girls stay here with Mrs. MacDuff," said James.

"We can't," said Tiana. "If anyone checks our story and finds I didn't see the doctor, they'll suspect. I'll have to eat the rest of the apples," she said wearily.

"And when the doctor finds nothing seriously wrong with you?" asked Raven.

"We'll praise the Lord that I don't have the cholera after all."

"Grandmother," Raven grinned at her, "you are a caution."

As James made ready to drive away the next morning, Seeth handed a bag of food over the wagon's edge to Nannie.

"Thank you for helping us, Mits MacTuff," Tiana said.

"The Bible says, 'Remember them that are in bonds, as bound with them; and them which suffer adversity, as being yourself also in the body.' Hebrews, chapter thirteen, verse three. It's all in the Bible, Tiana, Nannie. Everything you need in life. Have you been reading it?"

"No." Tiana was shamefaced. "But we will. We promise."

Once at the garrison it was easy to find the blacksmith's shop. The sound of the hammer on the anvil rang over the usual uproar. A group of small boys stood around the large double doors. They collected there each day to watch David shape solid iron. There was also a pack of dogs trying to get in. It was always warm in the smithy.

David Gentry's shop was cluttered. The outside walls were hidden under the junk leaning against them. There were old iron rods and parts of machinery and axles. There was a rusted stove, half a carriage, and items whose identities were obscured by time and David's cannibalization of pieces of them. Behind the shop was a stack of horseshoes that reached the eaves.

The inside was almost as littered as the outside. A long wooden rack held stock metal, bar iron sixteen feet long and in various shapes. The workbench was covered with carpenter's tools, wagon parts, shavings, and bits of metal and wood. The floor was paved with parings from the hoofs of horses and oxen.

David stood at the forge, which glowed bright red in the center of the shop. Except for his leather apron, he was bare from the waist up. He wasn't very tall, but his shoulders were massive and his arms thick and corded. He handled the heavy bar of iron easily with his tongs as he heated it and pounded it thin. He was beginning to bend it slowly into a hoop when James, Raven, Tiana, and Nannie entered the shop.

"Hello, brother," said James.

"*A'siyu*, brother. What brings you here?"

"We must talk to you."

"Then talk."

"We need to talk in private."

"I'll be with you in half an hour or so. Soon's I finish putting this tire on a wheel."

"Brother," said Tiana, "it's important. We need you right away."

"I can't leave now, little one."

"You must." She tugged at his apron in her anxiety.

"Child, when you're working with iron, patience isn't a virtue, it's a necessity." A shock of blond hair had escaped from the bandana twisted and tied around his forehead. He blew it out of his eyes. "If you want to speed things up, take over the bellows from Tyler there. He's wearing thin."

"I'm not," the towheaded boy said.

"I need you to go tell Adoniram I won't be needing him for an hour or more." He turned to James while the rod reheated in the fire. "Adoniram's my striker, a Cherokee who's learning the trade. You can take his place. Hold the rod while I hammer it." He glanced at Raven.

"This is a friend of ours," said James. "Sam Houston."

"Pleased to make your acquaintance. Sam, close the doors, will you." Raven shooed away the small mob of admirers. The lucky dogs who managed to stay locked inside the warm shop kept their heads low, trying not to be noticed. Raven and James stood close to David as he worked. They talked in the intervals between hammer blows.

"Where is he?" asked David.

"Where's who?"

"The slave you're hiding."

"What slave?" Raven tried to look nonchalant. But his stomach jumped and he glanced furtively around.

"Word's out there's a killer on the loose. 'Bludgeoning white men and raping the fair flower of Southern womanhood.' The whole garrison's up in arms. There's the usual talk of a slave rebellion." David went on hammering calmly.

"It's not like that," said James.

"It rarely is. And when you four came bursting in, I figured you were mixed up in it somehow. That one," he pointed at Tiana and grinned his crooked smile, "is always in the pot when something's stewing." He gave the iron a ringing blow. "What do you want of me?"

Tiana flinched as David's hammer and chisel rang in the still attic. She feared it could be heard for miles. If there were search parties nearby, they would know what the sound meant. The manacles fell off Coffee's wrists. Seeth gently rubbed salve on the raw skin where they had been. Now came the difficult part. Coffee broke the silence.

"I thank you. You folks have done enough. I can strike out on my own now. There are caves where I can hide until I find an outlyer camp."

"Friend, those camps are made up of people who are only runaways," said James. "They haven't killed a man. The whites will hound you until you're caught."

"You boys bring my big trunk into the school house below," said Seeth. "Hurry. Mr. MacDuff is due back anytime. We'll take Coffee to Connecticut with us. David, you'd best get back to the garrison before you're missed. Coffee, you stay here until I call you." Seeth, stiff and straight and proper as always, led the procession downstairs. She began pulling clothes from her huge trunk of leather wrapped on a wooden frame. She fed the clothes, a piece at a time, into the stove.

"What are you doing, Mits MacTuff?" asked Nannie.

"If I leave these someone might wonder why." Her hands trembled. This would take too long. "Bring the rest and come with me." She gathered up an armful of the voluminous dresses and ran to the privy house. She began stuffing her clothes down the hole of the three-seater.

"You're throwing away all your things," said Tiana.

" 'Ye can't serve God and mammon.' Bring buckets of barn soil. We'll dump it in here, on top of the clothes."

"Aren't you going to tell Mr. MacTuff what you're doing?" asked Tiana as she emptied the manure into the privy holes.

"Not until I have to. Brother MacDuff is a poor liar. So am I. But they might not bother to ask me. I'm only a woman, after all. What would I know?" Tiana thought she saw Mrs. MacDuff wink.

Seeth promised Coffee he could send for Fancy as soon as they reached safety. The boys drilled small holes in the trunk and situated Coffee in it as comfortably as possible.

"The first day will be the worst," Seeth told him. "Once we're a day's journey north we can think of another plan. Later, we can pass you off as a servant."

William MacDuff arrived soon after the trunk was closed. He looked worried.

"Armed parties are scouring the countryside. They're in an ugly mood. They'll probably shoot someone by mistake before this is over."

"Everything's ready here, Mister MacDuff. The children helped me load the wagon. They returned to say good-bye," said Seeth.

"Let's leave before a patrol comes. I don't want to talk to such savages." She hugged Tiana and Nannie.

"Aren't you afraid?" Tiana whispered in her ear while her husband checked the load.

" 'Whoso harkeneth unto me shall dwell safely, and shall be quiet from fear of evil.' " Seeth smiled and definitely winked as she climbed primly aboard the wagon.

"Please write us," said Tiana.

"I will." She waved until she was out of sight.

"A brave woman," said James.

"I hope they make it." Raven looked down at Tiana. "Grandmother, why is she called Seeth?"

"It's from the Preacher Book. 'The Lord seeth not as man seeth, and my child shall be called Seeth.' " Tiana clutched the Bible Seeth had given her. "What does 'mammon' mean?"

It was a weary, shaken group that pulled into the yard of the Rogers wigwam. Only four days had passed since Tiana, Nannie, Raven, and James had left for the garrison with Coffee. But it seemed to Tiana they had been away for years. They had been stopped three times on the trail home. The men in the patrols had ransacked the wagon each time. It was fortunate James and Raven had thought to dismantle the false floor and scrub up the fresh bloodstains left by Coffee's wounds. As they pulled the horses to a stop, they heard a wailing from behind the barn. Dogs howled in sympathy.

"What in blazes is that caterwauling?" asked Raven.

"Bagpipes. My aunt's husband, John Stuart, taught Father to play them. It must have gone badly here."

"Why do you say that?"

"He usually plays them when he's angry or agitated about something. They calm him down."

"Calm him down," said Raven. "It's a wonder."

Tiana and Nannie were out of the wagon before it stopped rolling. They raced through the front door, to find Jennie and Susannah sweeping up broken pottery. Grandmother Elizabeth was sorting through her scattered yarns and putting her spinning wheel together. Susannah burst into tears when she saw them.

Jack Rogers ran to join them.

"What happened here, Father?" asked James.

"They came looking for Fancy and Coffee." Jack turned and hung up the pipes so no one would see the tears in his eyes. When he turned back again, he grabbed Tiana by her thin shoulders and shook her hard.

"Don't ever do that again!" he shouted. "Don't ever disobey me like that!"

"Your father's been worried about you," said Jennie softly.

Worried didn't describe it. Jack had cursed himself constantly for sending the boys on such a dangerous trip and for letting Tiana and Nannie slip away from him. If he hadn't been so distracted, he would have known Tiana was up to something. She hadn't given him the usual argument. He could expect her to risk her life for Fancy or someone Fancy loved. Fancy had been adopted into Tiana's clan. *It's no wonder we mule-headed Scots get on so well with these stubborn Cherokee. We understand this tribal clan system very well,* he thought.

"They made a mess," said Tiana, stooping to pick up a piece of pottery Jennie's broom had missed. She put her arms around her father's waist. His anger gone, he hugged her to him.

"Aye, lass. That they did. Tell me of your trip. Is Coffee safe?"

Chapter 11

Raven hefted the heavy *gatayusti* ball and squinted down the field. The two teams lining the ball's path were tense. Each player held his seven-foot pole ready to throw. The ball was a quartzite disk, six inches across and two inches thick. It was convex on one side and concave on the other. It was highly polished and almost perfectly round.

This was Raven's first time throwing the ball. He wanted to do it right. He studied the terrain while the players fidgeted. Finally, he drew his arm back and rolled the stone in a wide arc across the field. Whooping, the boys chased it, throwing their poles at it and at each other's. There was a loud clatter when the poles collided. No one hit the ball, and when it stopped everyone, including the spectators, shouted and argued about which pole had landed closest. Raven paced around the poles and studied the marks carved on them to measure their distance from the stone.

"The Girth!" he called. Drum's son waved his arms and grinned. Everyone collected his pole and lined up for another round. The game would go on for hours, sometimes days, until a player had earned one hundred points, two at a time. By the middle of the afternoon, Raven's shoulder and arm ached. He was glad James suggested they quit for dinner.

They walked in a tired, ragged line up the path. Thickets of winter grapes brushed against their leggings. Raven shifted his pole to relieve his arm. He shivered as the cold wind dried the sweat on his body.

Raven heard the distant rumble of an approaching flock of wood pigeons. The light around them dimmed as the birds flew overhead, a vast, gray cloud blocking the sun. There were millions of them. Raven and the boys hastened under a tree to avoid any mementoes they might leave. In all likelihood this bunch would be an hour or two in passing. Raven decided to ask James and John to go on a pigeon hunt with him soon. The roost couldn't be too far from here.

It was November, 1810. The brilliant reds of the sumac and maple and golds and ambers of the sassafras and sweetgum were fading to shades of dingy brown. Many leaves had fallen, exposing bare tangles of black limbs against a gray sky. The leaves on the branches rattled in the wind like the bleached, delicate bones of birds. Others drifted silently through the haze of smoke that flowed in layers among the trees. The women were burning the debris on the forest floor. When the flames died, they gathered the nuts that lay exposed underneath.

The corn had been shucked and the cratches were full. The communal storehouse overflowed with the brightly colored ears of hominy corn. Raven glanced over his shoulder. Somewhere in the high hills and mountains to the east was a cave where Fancy hid. Drum refused to tell anyone where she was.

"She's hidden like the winter wren that vanishes in the laurel thickets," he would say whenever Raven asked him. In the old days Fancy would have been safe in Echota, the village where Nanehi Ward grew up. It was a peace town. Anyone could ask for sanctuary there. But whites had no respect for that tradition. Patrols were still searching the villages for Coffee and Fancy.

Raven balanced his long pole under his arm and held the smooth disk in front of him. He turned it over, admiring the work in it.

"Who made this?" he asked. James shrugged.

"*Gatayusti* balls have always been around." The balls were considered town property. Whenever a new village was built, its site was· located near a good area for a *gatayusti* field. Before the town house or communal granary or cabins were started, an acre was cleared and leveled for the game. During breaks from raising the women's cabins, the men would play. Or maybe they built the cabins during lulls in the *gatayusti* game.

After dinner, Raven, James, and John walked with the men of

Hiwassee toward the town house mound. Tiana and her sisters and cousins followed with the women and children. Many people carried unlit torches and horn or pottery containers with embers. The council would end after dark and the torches would be lit with the embers. No fire could be taken from the sacred council house hearth. Even the pipes must be emptied before the men left with them.

Drum and his friend, fiery old De'gata'ga, Standing Together, led the way. De'gata'ga's name meant, roughly, two people standing so closely together in thought as to be one. Standing Together was as lean as Drum was round. He was as volatile as Drum was calm. He was as good a choice for war leader as Drum was for civil leader. He was a full-blood who clung obstinately to the old ways. He wore his hair in a style that hadn't been popular for fifteen years. His head was shaved except for a small patch of hair on the back of it. A few feathers and strings of shell wampum beads dangled from the topknot. The shaved scalp emphasized the magnificent nose that slanted out from his high, sloping forehead and dominated his ferocious face. Standing Together always looked like he was ready to take the raid trail at any moment.

Drum looked like a contented country squire with his ruddy cheeks and round belly hanging a bit over his belt. He wore homespun pantaloons and a starched white linen shirt with a wide lace collar. The soles of his shoes were nailed on with wooden pegs. The shoes were clumsy, but he wore them whenever he dealt with white authority.

Tonight was one of those occasions. Return Jonathan Meigs, the United States agent to the Cherokee Nation, walked between Drum and Standing Together. The Real People called him White Path. Meigs was seventy, a frail, white-haired man, dwarfed between Standing Together's height and Drum's breadth.

He wore gray knee breeches and an ill-fitting, rusty black coat, frayed at the collar. One of his black silk stockings had a run in it. His chin was hidden in his stiff, high collar and cravat. The other men slowed their pace, but still he had to hurry to keep up.

Sik'waya, Opossum Place, a nephew of Drum's, limped along beside Kah-nung-da-tsa-geh, Walks The Mountain Tops. Walks The Mountain Tops was called Ridge by the whites. He was a full blood, who had become a successful planter with huge orchards, hundreds of acres, a fine house, and fifteen slaves. He dressed like a white man. His eighteen-year-old son, Watty, was nowhere in sight. That was just as well. Watty was harmless but hulking and simple. He could disrupt a council very effectively with foolish questions.

The last member of the group around Drum was a young man only a few years older than Raven and his friends. John Ross was the son of a Scottish trader and a Cherokee mother who was three-quarters white. He was short and stocky with a square face and serious blue eyes. He was well educated in English and spoke the Real People's tongue somewhat haltingly.

The day's light would be gone in half an hour. Already bats were darting around Tiana. Tiny winter wrens were singing their call and response. One would begin a high-pitched trilling, then another would take it up when that one ended, and another after him. From the smoky woods nearby came the haunting song of a cedar flute in a minor key. Tiana paused to catch her breath at the top of the mound, and to look out over the peaceful village.

Inside the town house there was the usual rustling and coughing and muffled talk and laughter as the Real People found their places on the benches. Everyone in the village came to general councils. Before the talk was over, many children would be asleep on their mothers' laps.

If the town house had been smaller, it would have been cluttered. Behind the last row of seats, tools for working the communal corn-fields leaned against one wall. Nested baskets for collecting the harvest stood next to them. There were piles of sticks with their bark stripped off so they would smoke less when burned.

There were boxes and baskets for the *gatayusti* balls and for the pipes and tobacco smoked in council. Some baskets held ceremonial capes and headdresses and the leaves for the sacred Black Drink. Others had extra rattles for the dances. One held baskets and dice for the basket game, and carved animals and cornhusk dolls to amuse the children. There were stacks of bearskin robes and blankets for those who didn't bring enough to winter meetings.

Near the fire, piled at the base of the seven central columns, were round hand drums and water drums. The water drums were logs hollowed from the soft buckeye wood. They stood upright and were filled to varying levels with water, giving each a different tone. The drumheads were woodchuck skins stained red with pokeberry juice and held in place with hickory hoops. Cane flutes, strings of pebble-filled tortoise shells, and hawk bells hung on the columns next to grotesque masks. There were bundles of feathers and gourd rattles covered with a hard, shiny paint of crushed shells.

Tiana took an apple from a basket of them and found her usual place in the section reserved for the Long Hairs. Tiana yearned for the day when she'd be old enough to sit farther forward, where she could see. Beloved Women sat with the headmen and elders. But there were no Beloved Women anymore, except for Nanehi Ward.

"Sister," Nannie whispered to her. "I have to piss."

"Now?" Tiana was exasperated. Nannie picked the worst times. She couldn't urinate near the town house. They would have to clamber back down the stairs.

"It's urgent. And at least it's not dark yet."

"It will be by the time we get back." But Tiana slipped outside with Nannie.

The girls were still gone when several armed white men burst into the large room. A murmur rose as people craned to see them. Raven recognized the leader. He was the same man who had stopped him and James when they were smuggling Coffee to the garrison.

"Those crackers won't leave off until they have Coffee roasting slowly over a fire," Raven said to James. James nodded. The men wore bandanas tied loosely around their necks. If they had known Meigs would be here they probably would have pulled the kerchiefs up to cover their faces.

"We're looking for that rogue nigger," shouted the leader. "We hear his woman might be hiding here."

"We're hiding no negro woman here," said Drum through James. As always, he spoke the absolute truth.

"We're gonna search anyway." The man nodded around the dim room.

"The white flag of peace hangs over the door," said Drum. "You may look, but not with weapons on you."

"We ain't asking permission and we don't go nowhere without our guns."

Scowling, and with his arms crossed over his chest, Standing Together stepped in front of them.

"Tell him to move," the bucktoothed man told James. "Or I'll have to hurt him."

"You'll do no such thing, Ben Abbott." Return Meigs moved up next to Standing Together.

"You gonna stop us, old man? Your gummint ain't worth a pot of piss here." But his voice lacked conviction. He had been recognized by someone in authority. *Very good, White Path*, thought Drum. *If you can name a man, you can control him.*

"Georgians," muttered James to Raven. Of all the settlers, the ones from Georgia hated Indians the most.

The two groups were tense. Only Drum seemed at ease. But then, nothing seemed to bother Drum. Meigs had shaken the white men's resolve, but pride wouldn't let them back down. Raven was wondering, almost with Drum's detachment, what would happen, when help came from an unexpected source. Everyone jumped at the sound of a child screaming outside and horses whinnying and stampeding.

"Daughter!" Jennie cried. She knew Tiana's voice, even distorted in a shriek. She and Grandmother Elizabeth hurried along the benches, as people moved out of their way. Confusion broke out. The screaming stopped, but over the noise they could hear the shouting of the white man left in charge of the patrol's horses. Abbott and his mob rushed outside and the Real People crowded after them. Raven and James got to the door in time to see the last of the horses disappear into the forest around the village.

"We'll be back," Abbott called over his shoulder as he and his men ran down the steps or slid down the mound's steep sides.

From the top of the mound, Raven watched them scatter through the village in the pale evening light. It would take them a while to find their horses in the dark. A figure materialized from the smoky gloom of a grove of trees and old Spearfinger stood in Abbott's path. She held her finger in front of her beaked nose and shook it at him and the men with him. The fingernail curved out in a sharp, filthy claw an inch and a half long.

"I'll eat your livers," she screeched again and again in Cherokee. The dogs in the village howled at the sound of her voice. She spit on Abbott. Her saliva was powerful. It held her life force and transferred it to whatever it touched. It would make her curse even more effective. Abbott was about to knock her down when Watty Ridge, all six foot six and two hundred and eighty pounds of him, lumbered out of the bushes and loomed at her shoulder. He smiled his foolish grin at the white men.

Abbott and the others detoured around them. Spearfinger screamed one last incantation and snatched some fringes from Abbott's buckskin shirt as he jogged by. With a sly smile, she tucked them in the folds of her shrunken bosom. She would use them later to put a curse on him. Then, for good measure, she threw a few stones. Watty waved cheerfully at the men's retreating backs.

It took a while for the people to file back inside and quiet down. Tiana and Nannie were a little out of breath, and Jennie and Elizabeth sat them between them. They put their arms around them to make sure they didn't go anywhere. Tiana snuggled against Grandmother Elizabeth. Her heart was still pounding, but there was a small smile on her face. To hide it, she looked innocently up at the precise, cross-hatched pattern of the ceiling's smoke-blackened laths and bark shingles. The familiar pattern was cut into wedges by the heavy beams radiating out from the center post, an oak log five feet across and twelve feet high.

"Girls." Drum's head was wreathed in smoke. "Are you all right?" Tiana jumped when she realized he was speaking to her and Nannie.

"Yes, Beloved Father," she answered.

"What happened?"

"Their horses became frightened," said Tiana.

"Tell them the rest of it," said Nannie. Tiana only shrugged. "That one threw rocks at them." Nannie dropped into the formal third person she was used to hearing in council. "Sister told this one to make a noise to distract the white man. Then she screamed and waved her arms to frighten the horses. She stabbed them in the rumps with her penknife too."

"She gave that trash leg-bail at a mighty rate," Raven whispered to James. "Grandmother is something else." James chuckled.

There was a stir as the door creaked on its wooden hinges. Everyone turned to watch two men enter. Walosi, Springfrog, and his lieutenant, Goksga, He's Smoking It or Smoker, were large. They each stood about five feet eleven inches tall and weighed over two hundred and thirty pounds. They were dressed in heavy boots, trousers of homespun, loose, billowing shirts, and leather jackets. Their broad brown, Indian faces, and long black braids looked odd under dented felt hats.

"One hears there was trouble here," said Springfrog, twisting his hat in his hands.

"There was," said Drum. "Where were you?"

"Gambling, as usual," grumbled Standing Together. "Playing Black Eye, White Eye, no doubt. Pay them fifty dollars a year and they're never around when you need them." Standing Together had opposed the Light Horse when it was formed two years before. He said the Real People had gotten along without police for hundreds of years. It was the whites who needed police, he said.

"The trouble has passed." Ridge shifted to make a lot of room for them at the fire.

"The girls frightened them away." No one missed the slight taunt in Drum's words even though there was none in his voice. Springfrog belonged to the clan of Drum's father's father. Drum could tease him if he wished. "After the council, you can help the white men find their horses. We don't want them here any longer than necessary," Drum added.

Actually no one questioned George Washington Springfrog's zeal, or that of his assistant, Lieutenant Smoker. The year before, in exasperation, Smoker had put his own brother's eye out with a knife because he refused to stop stealing horses. Springfrog and Smoker and the four privates had been elected because they were the largest men in the village. Captain Springfrog received fifty dollars a year, his lieutenant forty, and each private thirty. The money came from the annual annuities paid the tribe for lands they'd ceded to the United States.

"I'll speak to Captain Armistead at Hiwassee garrison," said Meigs. "Abbott's been causing trouble for a long time. The soldiers evicted him from Cherokee land two years ago."

"If we can't use the Light Horse to protect ourselves from white men, what good are they?" asked Standing Together. "It's the whites who cause trouble. If one of us steals horses it's to get back what's been stolen from him. If one of us causes trouble it's because he's drunk on the whiskey the whites sell."

Springfrog and Smoker were silent. They knew their jobs were futile where the whites were concerned, and ridiculously simple when it came to policing their own people. The Real People weren't adept at lying. Lawbreakers usually admitted their guilt and often turned themselves in for punishment. They knew if they lied about their guilt their ghosts would not be able to enter the Nightland when they died. They would be condemned to roam the earth in limbo. It was threat enough. A headman had only to ask the accused "Do you lie?" to get the truth. But the families of the Light Horse had come to depend on their princely salaries, so the men doggedly tried to fulfill their obligations.

"We're like the animals," said Standing Together. And everyone knew this council would start with a story. "This is what the old men told me when I was a boy."

Raven glanced down at the pipe James passed him. The wooden stem was carved in the form of a naked woman reclining voluptuously. Raven always felt sheepish handling it. At least it wasn't as bad as the one Drum had. The bowl was a man kneeling, facing the smoker. The base of the stem was the figure's huge phallus.

"Many years ago," Standing Together continued, "the animals were much bigger and stronger than they are today. They had chiefs and councils and town houses, just as we do. They could speak our language. The animals invented the sacred ball play. And they were so powerful, they and the insects brought disease to us to revenge our hunting them. But as time passed, one by one, they went up to *Galun'lati*, the world above. The beasts who live here now are but poor, weak imitations of those great ones. Like the animals, each succeeding generation of the Real People seems weaker."

"Everything has been different since the Delaware took the box with the sacred relics in it twenty years ago," said Drum. "When they stole the holy box, they stole the power."

"Possessions," said the slender, quiet man next to Ridge. He sat with his left leg out stiffly in front of him. A disease in the knee joint had crippled Sik'waya. No longer able to hunt or farm as well as before, he earned his living as a silversmith. Sik'waya had made Standing Together's large, cresent-shaped silver necklace.

"Too many of the Real People think only of possessions. When a person has too many possessions that one becomes the possessed. That one must care for them and protect them. There's no time for the spirit, for the mountains and the seasons, for dawn and twilight when the spirit world is closest to our own." He stopped abruptly and went back to staring into the fire. It was a long speech for Sik'waya.

"Beloved Fathers, I would speak." Sally Ground Squirrel rose from her place just behind the respected old men of the village. Tiana craned forward to see better.

"The women's council discussed what Standing Together has said about the Real People losing the power they once had. They have asked me to tell you what is in their hearts."

"Tell us," said Drum.

"The women are your mothers. They tend the hearth fires and care for Ancient Red, the Provider's gift." Sally Ground Squirrel moved down to stand in front of the benches of men. Most of them knew what she was going to say, and they looked uncomfortable. "They have always spoken in council with you, their sons. They are brave too, and have their share of wisdom. These young daughters proved that tonight when they chased away the white men. Yet women are not as welcome to speak to you here as they once were.

"That's why the Real People aren't as strong as in the old days. The white men have made you ashamed to listen to your mothers' and sisters' advice. They tell you women aren't as good as men. They say it so often you are beginning to believe it." Sally Ground Squirrel paused. "And what is far worse," she went on, "the women are beginning to believe it too." She sat down in a murmur of women's voices.

"You touch our hearts with your words," said Drum. "Our mothers and sisters and daughters will always be welcome to speak here." The old men grunted agreement. Many of the young men didn't. "White Path has come to smoke with us," Drum went on. "He has brought Tsan-usdi with him. Tsan-usdi had been to the Nightland and will tell us what he saw there."

Return Jonathan Meigs' knees cracked loudly when he rose. As he spoke, people translated in each clan section.

"My brothers and sisters, Tsan-usdi, John Ross, has just brought a letter from your brother, Ata'lunti'ski, out on the Arkansas." He adjusted his spectacles and squinted at the pale ink on the smudged paper.

> My Friend and Brother, White Path,
>
> Tell my friend, Rogers, that I have commenced digging a salt well. I have sworn off drinking whiskey until I find salt. I have got solid rock and would be glad if he would send me some augurs and powder for boring.
>
> I am your *kanalee*, friend.
> Tahlonteeskee

"At least he's found someone on the Arkansaw who can write," commented Jack Rogers. "I'll be glad to send him augurs."

"Perhaps you'd like to take the augurs to him," said Meigs. He was here to ask the Real People to move west to join the small number who had already emigrated there. Jack knew why Merigs was here and ignored the remark. He didn't feel like making the agent's job any easier.

"I saw a tomahawk claim the other day," he said.

"What's that?" Tiana asked Jennie.

"Someone has marked a claim by blazing the bark of a tree, a witness tree, on Cherokee land."

"How can white men claim Indian land?"

"Hush, daughter. I can't hear."

"I'll see to it," said Return Meigs. "I know the evil some white men do. They squat on the land, clear it, build shanties before they're caught. They profess ignorance of the fact that they're trespassing. They tease the government to purchase the land since it's already settled. If they are moved, they complain of hardship, while they are the sole cause of all they suffer. The soldiers ran three such families off last year."

"And the government tries to persuade us to cede more of our country," said Ridge.

"There's plenty of land to the west," said Meigs. "Young Ross here has just visited Ata'lunti'ski and seen it. The government is offering it to you." Meigs knew if he could influence Drum and Standing Together they in turn would try to sway their clans to join Drum's brother, Ata'lunti'ski, on the Arkansas. Unanimity was necessary for council decisions to be carried out. It was devilishly difficult to get unanimity on this question.

"It's good land, though rocky to till," Ross said. "The best that can be said about it is there are few white people."

"The Seven Clans will not move west," said Standing Together loudly, and with great finality.

Here it comes, thought Meigs. *President Madison has no idea what things are like here.*

"The west is *wudeliguhi*, the darkening land. The land of death. It is *tsusgina'i*, the ghost country where spirits go. We will not go there. Not now. Not ever. Not until we are dead. There will be no more talk of it."

Meigs wisely dropped the subject, although he knew it was only postponed. He knew the Real People believed the spirits of their dead lived in settlements in the Nightland. They hunted and grew corn, just as mortals did here. But there was a horror of the place. Meigs couldn't blame the Real People for that. He himself didn't like to imagine the shades of the dead carrying on a grotesque parody of normal life.

"In any case," said Jack, "it's time to ride the marches."

"Hear! Hear!" said his sons. They enjoyed the old Scottish custom of tracing the boundaries of common land and looking for encroachers. It made them feel not quite as helpless before the steady, obstinate invasion of settlers.

As John Ross stood to make his report, Tiana curled up on a thick bearskin and pulled a blanket over herself. She was lulled to sleep by the crackling fire, the talk, and the faint moaning of the wind around the town house. She woke up when Raven shook her by the shoulder. James and John each picked up one of her sleeping sisters and followed the men from the town house. Drum banked the fire.

"It's time for bed, Grandmother," said Raven. He picked her up easily and was among the last to walk out into the cold night.

Chapter 12

For Raven, the best part about leaving Hiwassee Town was coming back. He was returning from one of his occasional trips to Maryville for clothes in a larger size for himself and presents for his friends and lover. Drum had given him a simple incantation to make the journey shorter. Raven wasn't sure what it meant, but he always said it as he was setting out and it seemed to work.

> *Provider, Provider,*
> *I have just picked him up.*
> *The Big Moon is coming up the road.*
> *A'hulu! A'hulu! A'hulu! A'hulu!*

Perhaps he had merely adopted the Real People's attitude of enjoying the going as much as the arriving.

Raven's spirits started to flutter when he stepped onto the rickety ferry at the Hiwassee. He chattered to taciturn Punk Plugged In as he poled the boat across. The round birthmark on Punk Plugged In's cheek grew a deeper red when anyone talked to him. As usual, he avoided Raven's eyes and mumbled his thanks when Raven paid him for the trip.

With his pack on his back, Raven marched along the tree-lined road until he came to the huge old oak. It was bare of leaves now, in the early days of February, 1811. Roosting like a moody owl on a low-hanging branch was Spearfinger.

"Good day, mother." Raven bowed, sweeping the ground with his battered felt hat. "I trust your health is well." He reached over his shoulder and pulled out the gaudy red scarf he'd packed on top of his rucksack. He knotted it and tossed it up to her. She caught it neatly and smiled hideously. He detoured in a wide arc. Still waving cheerfully, he backed away from the tree.

He sang as he passed the bare fields freckled with foraging crows, and he collected a crowd of laughing children around him. He bowed to everyone he passed. In his broken Cherokee he complimented all the women as they wove mats and baskets, or patted clay pots into shape or pounded corn, or swept their yards and the paths around their cabins. He inquired into each family's health. Coming home to Hiwassee was better than a gill of rum. His spirits took flight when he saw Drum.

The Real People shook hands with those who weren't friends. They called acquaintances "those one only holds by the ends of the fingers." So Drum never just shook Raven's hand. He grabbed his arm in both hands, then embraced him.

"My son, I thank The Provider for protecting you along the road. I greet you with delight in my heart. Come, let me wash the dust from your feet." Drum was overjoyed to see his adopted son. Whenever Raven traveled to the settlements, Drum feared he wouldn't come back.

Sally Ground Squirrel waited for Raven at the door of her cabin. She laughed when he hugged her and tried to lift her off the ground. He made a great show of straining under her weight.

"How are you, my brother?" asked James, holding Raven's forearm in both his hands.

"Shittin' in high cotton." Raven grinned. "Have you been keeping my sweethearts warm for me?"

"You can warm them yourself at the dance tonight."

The Real People didn't need much excuse for a feast or a dance. Raven's arrival was more than enough cause. But there was another. The village council had asked Standing Together to kill a golden eagle, the Pretty-Feathered Eagle. They needed the feathers for headdresses and for the wands used in the eagle dance. But eagles were sacred. Only the most respected could wear their feathers. And very few knew the ritual necessary to appease the spirit of a slain eagle.

Standing Together spent eight days in the mountains, fasting and singing the proper songs. When he returned, he said a snowbird had died. That confused other vengeful eagles. The feathers now hung in a deerskin in a small, round hut built near the town house. A dish of corn and venison was set in front of the feathers so they could eat.

The eagle dance was only done in the late fall or winter, after the crops were harvested and the snakes were asleep. If an eagle killer practiced his craft in the summer, frost would kill the corn. And the songs of the eagle dance would anger the snakes. Tonight, the people would give Standing Together presents and the older men of the village would perform the eagle dance. It was a dance for young men, but the young men had no battle deeds to boast about while they performed it.

Raven sat in the crowded council house and fortified himself with some of Jack Rogers' best extract of corn. The liquor was homemade, but there was no need to be ashamed of it. It was clear and smooth. It slid down Raven's throat and set fire to his chest and stomach. Outside there was a barrel of more common spirits, the kind Jack called Tiger Spit. Raven knew the party would become rowdy before dawn, and he intended to enjoy it.

The drummers kept up a steady beat and the singers chanted. A long line of young women entered the council house. They were dressed in white gowns decorated with beads and ribbons. Bracelets jangled on their arms. Their black hair hung down their backs. They answered the musicians in low, sweet tones. Then they formed a semicircle, the two lines back to back, and moved slowly around, facing the spectators. Raven smiled when he saw Tiana's serious face near the end of the line. He was always a little surprised she could move so gracefully on her thin stalks of legs.

The young men and boys trotted in with a loud whoop. They wore shirts and loincloths and leggings, bracelets and round shell necklaces, and high, waving plumes in their turbans. They faced the women and moved in time with them. The bells and turtle-shell rattles on the women's legs kept rhythm with the drums. The first two dancers rose on their toes, then the next pair, and the next. They made a gentle rise and fall in the line as it moved slowly around the room. The first couple whirled and changed places, whooping as they did it. Their movement was repeated by each pair in turn.

Raven's legs were pleasantly wobbly and his head seemed to spin on its axis. He felt like he couldn't move if he had to. It was a combination of the hypnotic fire, the powerful whiskey and the drumming, the sensuous dancing and the dim light. Dawn wasn't far away when James tugged at Raven's sleeve. Raven followed him outside where the cold air revived him a little. Eight or nine young men were dressing for the next dance.

"Get dressed, Raven. You can do this one with us." James began sorting through the pile of costumes.

"Oh no, brother. Not I. I'll make a colossal ass of myself." Raven had difficulty speaking, and his eyes couldn't agree on what to look at.

"Of course you'll make an ass of yourself. That's the point."

"No." Raven belched, then hiccupped. "Someone might recognize me."

"Here." James handed Raven a pile of rags. "The mask will cover your face and the robe will cover your body."

"I can do the other dances. But I'm not drunk enough for this one."

"If you become any drunker you'll pass out. Or start reciting Pope to the multitude as usual. Hurry. It's almost time."

"Not this mask," wailed Raven.

"It's the only one left," said James. "We saved it for you."

"I'll trade with someone."

"No time. Hurry."

Raven swayed as James and The Girth tied the robe of multicolored ribbons and rags and strips of leather around his neck.

"This is ridiculous." His voice was muffled by the wooden mask they fastened over his head. Most of the other masks were carved to look like old men. One was made of the papery globe of a hornet's nest. Its opening formed the mouth and it looked like a hideous, diseased face. Raven's mask was different. There were two slits to see through and one where the mouth should be. But instead of a nose, there was an obscenely shaped gourd, with rabbit fur glued to its base to resemble pubic hair.

"What's my name?" Raven resigned himself to his fate.

"Sweet Cock."

"Wonderful. Who are you?"

"Makes The Pudenda Swell." Raven had to laugh. If his brothers could see him now.

"Do you know what to do?" asked James.

"Yes. I've seen this dance plenty of times." Raven took the gnarled staff James handed him. Using it as a cane, he fell in line behind the last dancer as The Girth led the way. Now that he was committed to the Booger Dance, he began to enjoy it. He relaxed and let the whiskey carry him where it would. He hunched over and shuffled, cackling and wheezing, along with the rest.

The ten of them burst into the council house. They yelled and cavorted, causing consternation among the people in their path. Those farther away stood on benches to see them. Pregnant women hid their faces so their unborn children wouldn't be as ugly as the masks. The Girth had filled a long-necked gourd with water and tied it between his legs. The rags of his costume fell away from it and he brandished it, waving it so a stream of water arced out. Children shrieked with laughter and scrambled to get out of the way. Everyone knew it was only water, but that wasn't what it looked like.

Raven sang the bawdy song with the others, mumbling words he didn't know. The Booger dancers whooped and shrieked and spun, sending their motley clothes flying in tatters around them. They ended the dance in progress and soon had the entire council house in an uproar. Hobbling and leering, they chased the women, frightened the children, and threatened the men. Raven had a wonderful time. He sidled up to Galidoha, Climbs Around, his latest sweetheart. Giggling, she tried to hide behind her mother's broad back. He poked his long nose obscenely at her. He cackled while she put her hands in front of her round face to defend herself.

"Go away, beloved friend."

"How did you know it was me?"

"Your feet."

Raven tried to see his feet through the slits in his mask.

"No one in the village has feet that big."

Raven pulled his mask up, leaned down, and quickly kissed Climbs Around on her full mouth. Then he rejoined the dancers. They all gathered in the center of the council house and quieted a little. Drum conferred with The Girth, whose mask was painted white and topped with skunk fur for hair.

"We have visitors from a far-off place," announced Drum. "They're from the white settlements." Everyone laughed. "What do you want?" Drum asked The Girth.

"Women!" The dancers shouted, and rushed to catch some. The women screamed and laughed and ran.

"You can't have our women," said Drum. "What else do you want?" The Girth whispered to Drum, who relayed his answer. "*Di'lsti*," he shouted, and everyone laughed. The Girth was mocking white people who confused *di'lsti*, fight, with *dilsti'*, dance. "We are at peace," said Drum. "We don't fight. Tell us your names."

"My name is Melodious Farts." The Girth broke wind loudly three times to prove it. He began to shuffle in a clumsy parody of the graceful eagle dance. But instead of telling of his prowess in war, he boasted about his conquests in bed.

"What'll I do?" Raven whispered while The Girth performed.

"Tell a bawdy Cherokee story," said James. "There are lots."

"I don't know any well enough to tell. I'm still learning your infernal language."

"Tell a simple one. One from your own people. If you need help, I'll translate," said James. "And don't worry about giving yourself away. Everyone knows who you are."

"I know," said Raven. "My feet." James laughed.

When Raven's turn came, he staggered to the center of the dance floor. He launched into a shuffling, stomping imitation of the eagle dance. Then he ran around the hall, poking his nose at the women. The more everyone laughed, the more ridiculous he acted, until the crowd was clapping and stamping with delight. Then he raised his hands for silence.

"I once knew a hairy white man, with lots of whiskers, who went into Maryville one Saturday night to sell his goods. Of course he stopped at the tavern to have a few drinks and wash away dull care." Raven turned slowly so everyone could hear. His strong voice carried to the back rows of benches in the darkness against the walls.

"This man's friends persuaded him to have his hair cut short and to have his whiskers shaved off. When the barber finished, he looked as though Tala'tu, The Cricket, had been at work." Raven waited for the laughter to fade. The cricket was called The Barber because he ate the nap from furs.

"That night, the farmer went home very late, weaving down the trail like this. He tiptoed into the house and undressed quietly. He slipped into bed without saying a word so he wouldn't wake his wife. But she woke up anyway. She ran her hands over his smooth face and said, 'Young man, if you're a'going to do anything, you'd better be quick about it, because Old Whiskers'll be here any minute.'"

Raven bowed low to the applause. Then he lost his balance and fell sprawling in the dust.

The next thing he knew, he was waking up naked on his corn-shuck mattress in Drum's *asi*, the hothouse dug into the hillside. The small fire had burned low, but it was still very hot inside. In the distance Raven could hear Drum's voice calling from the roof of the council house.

Drum announced the day's news every afternoon, and Raven listened to find out what had happened while he slept. He usually missed most of the report and Drum repeated it for him in broken English at the evening meal. But this afternoon, Raven could understand almost everything.

He sat straight up in bed, bumping his head on the low ceiling near the wall. For two years he had struggled with the Real People's language. He spoke it and heard it every day, but he despaired of ever learning it well. Each verb had hundreds of forms, depending on the characteristics of its subject and object. His understanding now was an unexpected gift. Drum was telling the people of Hiwassee Town that the black woman had gone north on a boat. Fancy was safe.

Raven lay back down, his head throbbing. He smiled gratefully at Sally Ground Squirrel when she pushed aside the hide door with her shoulder. She crawled in, balancing a bowl of stew and a gourd of cold water. The ceiling was too low to stand up, so she knelt on the mats and furs covering the dirt floor. Raven took a long drink. His mouth felt like he'd been eating plaster, and his stomach churned. He groaned, and Sally laughed.

"I'll never drink again, Beloved Mother," he said. "At least not until the next time." Sally laughed again as she added a few peeled sticks to the fire and left.

Pulling his blankets after him, Raven moved gingerly to the bed shared by the younger children. Theirs was the one nearest the door. Drafts entered around the edges of the hide door. But the dugout was so hot Raven lay on his blankets, using them to cushion him from the lumpy mattress.

He propped the door open so he could see out. The cold winter wind was invigorating on his face. Snow began to drift silently through the trees. Raven lay on his stomach with his chin on the backs of his hands and watched it fall. He wondered if he would ever be able to float comfortably with the seasons, as Drum did. The seasons reminded Raven of his own mortality. They reminded him of how fast the years flew.

Raven knew he couldn't stay on this small island forever, no matter how pleasant it was. The question of what would happen in years to come bothered him every now and then. But it was difficult to worry and watch the snow too. So he watched the snow and listened to the silence.

He was feeling much better as darkness fell. Drum would say night was throwing her sable cape over the world. Raven saw a torch flame wavering toward him through the night. It illuminated the snowflakes, and they in turn gave the fire a cold, spectral quality.

Drum pushed the torch in front of him through the opening. He laid the blazing pine knot on a large, flat rock by the circle of stones that made the hearth. The torch burned cheerfully, lighting the small, domed room. Drum went out and returned with an armload of peeled sticks. The fire would have to burn all night.

Drum wore his ceremonial gorget, a large, round shell disk with the figure of Uktena, the Great Snake, etched on it. River pearls set in it to represent stars flashed in the firelight. Drum had promised to teach him and James and John tonight. Drum and Raven shared a pipe until James and John entered. Without a word, the pipe was passed to them, and they all stared into the fire. Drum threw a bit of raw liver, as a sacrifice, into the flames.

"We call the fire Ancient Red or Grandmother, but we must never be familiar with her," Drum said. "If you spit into the fire, your teeth will fall out. If you urinate into her, worms will attack your bladder. When you hunt, you must always sacrifice some of your kill to her. The night before you go on a hunt, drop a piece of deer liver into her. The direction the fragments pop out of the flames will show you where to hunt. If you wave your moccasins and leggings over her smoke, she will protect you from snakes."

James watched Raven tend the fire and relight the pipe. Drum had obviously been teaching him the ritual. For an instant, James was envious. In less than two years this white boy had become as much a member of the Real People as James was. James tried so hard to adopt the white man's ways, his knowledge, and Raven was trying just as hard to be an Indian.

Drum really did love Raven as a son. It was easy to do. He was big and handsome, quick and eager to learn. Drum would share with him knowledge reserved for those destined to become headmen or curers. Would Raven stay long enough to use the knowledge he was given so generously? James doubted it. Raven had a way of making any place seem too small to contain him long. *We must each choose our own path*, Drum often said. Raven would come to a fork soon. He would have to choose a trail and forever wonder about the one not taken.

"We can learn much from nature," Drum was saying, almost as though he were talking to himself. "Everything in nature has its own purpose, no matter how hidden it may be from us. We learn patience from the spider. We learn to leap like the panther."

"Beloved Father," said Raven. "Will you give us war charms?"

"There is little use for war charms now. The red flag of war never hangs in front of the council houses. No longer do the warriors stream from the villages like skeins of geese after the war leaders. Peace is a good thing. I do not like the sound of mothers weeping for their dead sons. But there is no glory in peace."

Drum paused again, thinking. "War is the greatest test a man must face. There may come a day when you will be so tested. I cannot leave you without protection.

"It's possible to put your soul, your life force, in the treetops so *ga'ni*, arrows and bullets, can't reach you. Once a man dared his enemies to shoot him. They did, but they couldn't kill him. Then one of them shot into the trees and the man died. Here is *i'gawe'sdi*, a charm to hide you from ambush and to protect you from arrows and bullets.

> *Red Lightning!* Gha! *You will be holding my soul in Your Clenched Hand.*
> Gha! *As high as the Red Treetops my soul will be alive and moving.*
> Gha! *It will be shining here below.*
> Gha! *My body will become the size of a hair, the size of my shadow!*

"After saying that you must spit on your hands and rub the saliva on your face and chest. This symbolizes going to water, and it protects you with the power in your saliva. When you rehearse a charm, repeat it only three times. To say it a fourth will release its magic. You may improvise new charms, but you must never change the old ones."

The hours went by, but Raven hardly noticed. He was entranced by Drum's quiet voice, telling of battles long past, and bloody deeds. As dawn approached, Drum told Raven to build up the fire. Sweat began to run from them as the temperature rose even higher in the dug-out. The sun was almost ready to pounce over the hills when

Drum lifted the hide door and looked out. Light was turning the sky from black to gray, and sending blue shadows across the deep snow. It was time to go to water.

The four of them crawled out of the dug-out. Their sweaty bodies steamed in the cold air. The world was white, with its edges softened and rounded. It was hung with curtains of mist. Frost made lacy patterns in the trees. They whooped to scare away water cannibals and other evil spirits.

The boys stripped at the river, ignoring the goose flesh and the cold. Drum scratched them with his bone comb. Then they waded into the icy river while Drum recited prayers over them. Raven stared, fascinated, at a golden leaf encased in thin ice. At dawn he always felt as though he owned the world, as though it were created new and fresh each day, especially for him. It was indeed a time of magic.

Jack Rogers pulled his old wagon under a spreading oak. Little of the hazy rain penetrated the canopy of its leaves. On the mountain-sides all around, the brilliant spring colors seemed to glow in the dove-gray mist. This was sparsely settled country, out at the edges of the Real People's land. Jack looked up at the mountains, veiled in clouds.

"They pleasure the eye and soothe the soul," he said.

"They do," said Charles. In the back of the wagon, James and John covered their rifles with a tarpaulin cloth and opened the basket of food Jennie had packed for them. They offered some of the Indian bread and fried bacon to Jack and Charles. Jack peered suspiciously between the slices of crumbly bread.

"My cooker is taking on airs with these sandwich things." Jack always felt uncomfortable referring to as his sons' half-sister as his wife. He avoided it by using the Cherokee terms for wife. "She must think she's nobility. Barbarous custom," he mumbled around his food.

"Someone else has been eating here." James pointed to peanut shells littering the ground.

"White people." John nodded to a dead box turtle. There was a bullet hole in its shell. "They kill things and leave them to putrify."

Jack sighed. He thought they would find whites on Indian land. That was why he rode the marches every year. He used to take a certain grim pleasure in it. He felt like the sword of justice when he ordered trespassers off, or sent the garrison soldiers after the more recalcitrant ones. But every year there were more squatters. And they were becoming surlier. More and more of their faces looked familiar. He was sure many left, only to return again. Or perhaps they all looked alike to begin with.

The Real People had no stomach for this sort of thing. After a hundred and fifty years of contact with whites, they still believed their own honor was a universal virtue. They had difficulty understanding that whites would settle on land that didn't belong to them.

Jack rewrapped his meal and pulled the large collar of his wool hunting coat up around his neck. It and the wide brim of his hat would shed some of the rain. But he was chilled to his bones. He cursed the necessity for this. Charles settled down in his blanket and pulled the edge of it over his head. Jack flicked the reins and snapped the whip at the reluctant horses. It would be best to finish this before nightfall. Some of these people were capable of killing witnesses so they could go on unhindered a while longer.

"Can you find them, James? John?"

"Yes," said James. "They seem to shed trash as they go, like a snake sheds its skin. And their tomahawk claim must be somewhere nearby."

James was right. They found the witness tree with a hatchet slash in it. Before long they were atop a high ridge overlooking the new homestead. The tiny cabin huddled against the far wall of the mountain cove like a cornered animal. The timbered slope swept up a mile or more, almost from the cabin's back wall. A bit of land was cleared around the cabin, but it was only a nibble from the dense forest. A column of smoke rose from the trees near the house. The squatter must have been clearing a field by burning it. In his other field, corn stubble stood among the tall, girdled trees and huge boulders.

For a few seconds Jack almost pitied the man. It was a hellish task to start fresh in this country. It was enough to wear any man to the bone, fighting that avalanche of a wilderness. Was it hope or desperation that drove men to take on so much with so little? As they drew closer, Jack saw that the fence around the tiny pasture was sagging, but new. The gray-green lichen hadn't begun to grow on it yet.

The cabin itself was made from the straight yellow poplar trees that grew in abundance. But the logs were undressed and unseasoned. In wet weather, and there was plenty of that here, they would rot under the bark. As they dried they were already shrinking and leaving large chinks between them. Leaves and mud and sticks and rags had been stuffed in the widening cracks. It always amazed Jack that these places could look weatherbeaten before they were even finished.

Three dirty children dug in the mud with broken roof shingles. They reminded Jack of the white urchins who used to come into his store at the garrison. They had no money nor goods to barter, so they stood and looked with big, hungry eyes at the splendor around them.

These children were surrounded by bits of iron, a bottomless kettle, bones, pieces of hide, a barrel with half the staves missing and the hoop at a rakish angle. There were split shingles, discarded sedge brooms, a length of rusted chain, and an abandoned wagon bed that would never roll again. The wheels had been taken off to make a log drag. But now the wheels too were broken. There were piles of sodden sawdust and ashes, corn husks and cobs, and stacks of firewood, most of it green. One of the children ran to the door, which was too badly warped to close tightly.

Jack's pity vanished. Damn the man! Winter would laugh at that hovel. The squatter would watch his woman and children sicken or freeze.

"How be you, strangers?" The squatter cradled his old musket as he ducked to clear the low door frame. A woman with a yoke across her thin shoulders trudged up the slope from the creek. She looked like many of the women on the frontier. Her gaunt face may have been lovely once, in a pinched and grudging way. But now the cheekbones were too prominent and the nose and chin too sharp. There were folds in her eyelids, giving her eyes a drooping, haggard look. Everything about her, from her face to the dress she wore, seemed gray. She beckoned the children with her head and sidled into the cabin. That wasn't normal. Women out here were starved for company and news. She must know they weren't supposed to be there.

The man was thin too. There was a gap where his two front teeth should have been. His long, pale hair was slicked back on his bony head. His features were too small for his face. Jack would have said he had a fever and ague complexion. A sullen boy came around the corner of the cabin and leveled a gun at them.

"We ain't got much to share with you," the man said. Then he looked more closely at James and John and Charles. "You can come in, mister, if you're hungry." He nodded at Jack. "But your niggers'll have to stay out here."

Jack stretched his arm out behind Charles's back and motioned for John to stay calm.

"We didn't come to visit. You're trespassing on Indian land. You must leave immediately."

"This ain't Injun land. Ain't no Injuns for fifty mile, 'ceptin' those." He nodded at James and John. "I'm claiming this land fair and square."

"You aren't claiming anything fair and square and you know it."

"Listen, mister." The man's voice rose to a whine that grated on Jack's nerves. "I got a family to support."

"And you're doing a piss-poor job of it."

"I've made improvements. You can't throw me off."

"This boil on the arse of creation"—Jack pointed to the cabin with his whip—"is not an improvement."

"What's your authority to come on my land and threaten me?" The squatter tried to look belligerent. He wasn't very good at it, but Jack knew the man had him. Jack had no real authority, except the tacit approval of the National Council. That meant little to white people.

"I have the authority given me by Captain Armistead of Hiwassee garrison," Jack lied. He waved an unredeemed bank note he happened to have. At least it would be good for something. Chances of receiving any money for it were slight. And like as not, the man had never seen one.

"You and your authority and your niggers can jist clear off my land." The man raised his gun and pointed it at them. The boy did likewise.

"We'll be back," said Jack.

"Come armed," said the man.

Chapter 13

The crowd that gathered at Hiwassee garrison to greet the monthly boat from Knoxville was even bigger than usual. People filled the dock and overflowed along the banks. The surrounding woods were dotted with the tents and shelters of the Real People. The women and children had come with their men who were heading south for a big council at Ustanali. Not many could afford the price of passage on the keelboat. They were there to buy provisions for the trip and to hear what news the boat brought.

The boat was a day and a half late arriving. The river was low, making rocks and shoals, rapids and snags even more difficult to avoid. Tiana, Nannie, and Susannah were impatient. It was August of 1811. The heat was intense, and the extra wait was an added burden.

Stripped to their fancy new drawers, they roamed the crowded garrison. They had watched David Gentry at work until they could bear the forge's heat no more. They wandered out of the stockade to the gristmill where it was cool and damp. They watched the corn rush out the hole in the middle of the millstones and pour into the battered wooden bin below. They were chased back out into the heat when the miller caught Tiana burying herself in the bin of cool corn meal.

The girls explored every cranny under the building. They climbed on the massive beams that held the mill's floor twelve feet off the surface of the pond. Then they played in the wooden flume that diverted the cold creek water over the huge mill wheel. When they were chased from there they contented themselves with frolicking under one of the cascading leaks in the flume.

From the distance they heard the loud clanging of a bell. "The boat's here," Nannie cried and the three of them left on the run. The officers' ladies drew their skirts away in distaste as the girls pelted by. They were dripping wet and covered with red mud. Their bare feet left damp prints behind them on the planks. Tiana rushed up to her father, who stood at the end of the pier with Return Meigs and Captain Armistead. She grabbed Jack's hand and leaned out to see past the thick pilings.

"Ach, lass! Look at ye!" said Jack. Startled, Tiana stared down at herself. She ran her fingers through her wet, tangled hair and hitched up her linen drawers. The hated pantalettes had slipped until they were about to fall off. The ties at the knees had come undone and the lace frills at the hems clung limply to her thin calves. It would have been impossible to say what color the pantalettes had originally been. Tiana retied the cord at her waist and the ones at her knees.

"Go change your clothes," said Jack.

"But the boat's coming."

"Go," he thundered. Tiana and her sisters flew back down the dock, against the stream of traffic. They tore across the deserted drill field and burst into the small cabin their older half sister and aunt, Mary, shared with David Gentry. They rushed out again, still pulling their dresses over their heads.

At times Tiana had to crawl between the men's legs, but she got to the end of the wharf just as the keelboat was docking. The usual river traffic of skiffs, dug-out canoes, barges, and crude hide boats schooled around it. Tiana dodged to avoid the men standing by to tie up *Suck Runner*.

"Old Suck" was a keelboat, fifty feet long and fifteen feet wide. With its upcurved bow it was slender, graceful, and elegant of line. But the elegance was hidden by the old clothes and filthy, torn bedding hanging from every line or draped on the roof of the low deckhouse. It had rained hard the day before and soaked everything. The rest of the deck was covered with lashed-down boxes and kegs and tarpaulin-covered sacks of grain. There were canvas tents for the crew and passengers to sleep in.

Suck Runner's sides were scarred. Her name was painted in white on her algae-stained bow, but most of the paint had scraped off on rocks and snags. A faded scrap of cloth hung from the twenty-five-foot mast, but it was impossible to tell what country the flag represented. Only a dozen men were needed to guide the boat downstream. But *Suck Runner* seemed aswarm with humanity, all of it unkempt. In the August heat, most of the crew wore full beards, sweat-stained flannel shirts, and baggy butternut pantaloons tucked into heavy boots.

They waved their broad-brimmed black hats and shouted invitations to the women. There were few tavern keepers in the crowd. They were all battening down the hatches for the coming storm of business and for the fights that would inevitably follow. Putting up with the boatmen was the surcharge on the cargo they carried.

Suck Runner took its name from The Suck, the narrow, roiling channel where the entire Tennessee River forced its way through the Cumberland Mountains. Shooting The Suck was thrill enough to last the average person a lifetime. But these men did it on a regular basis. Old Suck was the same boat that had taken Fancy upriver on the first part of her journey to Connecticut, Canada, and Coffee. She had gone with a party of black-frocked Moravian missionaries, or Ravens as the Real People called them.

Old Suck's captain leaned hard on the eight-foot sweep and the keelboat veered toward shore. It hit the pilings with a shuddering thud Tiana could feel through the soles of her bare feet. There was a long, high-pitched squeal of wood rubbing against wood. The *bosseman* stood on the upswept bow, swearing in French and shouting garbled instructions to the good-natured helpers on the dock. People scattered as the huge knots on the ends of the thick, tarred lines flew through the air.

In the middle of the happy turmoil, tears stung Tiana's eyes. She remembered Fancy standing there, her life's belongings in a shabby canvas bag. Her egg and indigo money, plus what Jack could give her, was sewn into the hem of her new dress. A man's woolen great coat hung about her thin shoulders. A crisp red bandana, worn Cherokee style, covered her cropped hair. The skin on her bare legs had been dry and gray and flaking in the cold air.

It had been the most dismal day Tiana could remember. Fancy had knelt to enfold her and Nannie and Susannah as they sobbed against her chest. The girls had taken over Fancy's flock of chickens as they promised they would. They used the earnings to pay postage on letters to her. They received a letter in return, a simple message in Fancy's hand.

"I am in good health," her letter had read. "Everyone here is kind. Coffee and I will be marry soon. I miss you. I cry for you every day. I love you. Your loving *udo*, sister, Fancy."

Now Tiana hid behind a hogshead and watched the unloading. Men trundled sacks and barrels toward the shore. While they worked, Tiana stared up the river. She tried to imagine the keelboat carrying Fancy through the steep, green, mist-hung valley of the Tennessee River to the Ohio. From there she tried to follow Fancy all the way to Connecticut. She concentrated hard, trying to picture a town with carriages and tall buildings of brick, like the Vann house.

She considered the marvelous idea that all of it was within her reach. If Fancy had gone to Connecticut, she could too if she wanted. It was a remarkable concept, the thought that there was a world different from the one she knew. Long Man, the river, could carry her far away. She shook her head at the wonder of it and ran to find her father.

Jack Rogers was relaxing in his favorite tavern when Tiana found him. He was enjoying a quiet game of backgammon before the boatmen finished their work and shattered the tranquility. Their custom wasn't encouraged here, but that never stopped them.

Conger's inn was the nicest within a fifty-mile radius. The huge fireplace was bare and scrubbed. The floor was freshly sanded and the six tables were scoured with sand until they gleamed. A tall writing desk stood against one wall. The high bar was enclosed at both ends by barred gates that reached the ceiling. Mr. Conger had closed and locked them to discourage customers from helping themselves to the tavern's stock. But enthusiastic patrons had been known to dive over the high counter itself.

Jack looked up from his game as Tiana ran in. She was out of breath, as usual. It seemed to Jack he rarely saw her any other way.

"Father," she said, "I want to go to Ustanali with you."

"No." Jack tried to concentrate on his game.

"Why not?"

"Because this will be an important council for the headmen of all the Overhill and Valley towns and the chiefs of the other tribes. Tecumseh himself may be there. They will be discussing war. Passions may run high. It will not be a place for children."

"I'll stay out of the way. I only want to ride on the boat."

"No."

"John Ridge is going with his father. And he's younger than I am."

"No." Jack never took his eyes off his backgammon pieces. Tiana sometimes had the feeling she was no more than a buzzing mosquito to him.

"Please."

"Tiana."

Tiana knew the tone. Her mothers never said their children's names aloud. To do so would be offensive. And Jack had fallen into the habit too. When he did call one of his children by name, it meant he was angry.

"For the love of Lucifer!" A beam of light blinded Tiana. "Come out of there. The boatman's grim face was much too close for comfort. She could smell the garlic and tobacco on his breath, and her stomach was already queasy. He crouched as he held up the lid of the crate where she had been hiding for a day.

"I can't get out." She sniffed. "My legs won't move."

"Jacques, you were right," the man called. "There is a large rat in the hold."

A second face appeared. With his swarthy skin, wild, curly black hair, and eyepatch, Jacques looked like a pirate. But Tiana wasn't sorry to be discovered. She had been in the box since before Old Suck left the garrison. She had left it only to relieve herself in the bilge water behind the stack of goods. It didn't make the water smell any better. And she had a horror of the heavy boxes and barrels breaking loose and pinning her while she squatted. She couldn't stand in the crowded hold because the ceiling was only four and a half feet high. The box was too small to stretch her legs.

She had eaten all her meager provisions the first day. She'd spent the night and this morning sick from the boat's rocking and the strong smell of tobacco, raw cotton, tar, lumber, and the stagnant water in the stifling hold. She'd had more than enough time to reflect on her folly as she lay in the narrow box, listening to the rats scamper around her and the heavy boots thud overhead.

The cargo creaked and groaned ominously whenever the boat hit a stretch of bad water. But she'd been afraid to call out. She knew her father would be furious if he found her. Now the decision was out of her hands.

"Hell-fire!" Tiana heard Jack's voice booming from the deck above. "A girl-child, you say. I think I know who she is."

Tiana started to sob as the two men hauled her, not ungently, from the box. A ring of dirty, bearded faces fringed the opening to the hold. As she poked her head through the hatch, Jack Rogers caught her roughly by the wrists. His strong grip hurt as he swung her out of the hold in a wide arc. She landed hard on her feet and swayed, blinking up at her father in the bright sunlight. Tears streamed down her cheeks and her lips trembled, but she held her ground. Jack glared at her in a fury.

"One of your litter, is she, Rogers?" asked the captain mildly. "Audacious spratkin."

"Ay." Jack shook his head grimly. "She's one of mine. I'll pay you for her passage and take it from her hide."

But James Rogers winked at her from behind his father's back, and the men laughed. Jacques lifted her onto his broad shoulders and paraded her around the boat.

It took her the rest of the journey to win her way back into her father's good graces, but she was fast friends with the crew in short order. She followed Jacques around like a puppy. After they gathered fuel at each wooding place, she gave an Indian yell with the crew as their keel wheeled into the current. And she sang out with them.

> Hard upon the beech oar!
> She moves too slow.
>
> All the way to Shawneetown,
> Long while ago.

Tiana passed the remaining few days fishing off the stern as they drifted lazily with the current. When the mosquitoes and gnats were bad she smeared herself with mud as the men did. She helped the cook prepare meals and clean up afterward. She mended clothing and aired bedding. She scrubbed places that had never seen a brush before. She wove Jacques a bright, tasseled belt to replace the filthy cord holding his pantaloons in place.

In the evenings the crew taught her knots and whittling, stories and songs, and bits of French. Propped against the sacks on the roof of the deckhouse they waved mosquitoes away and watched the magnificent night sky. They speculated about the strange new star that progressed slowly across the heavens with a bright tail streaming after it.

"*Atsil'tlunts'tsi*, Fire Panther," said Tiana, pointing it out to Jacques.

"It's a comet, daughter, not a panther," said her father. But where it came from and what it meant, none could say.

As they traveled south, the Real People's towns along the river changed slightly. There were fewer orchards and fields and herds of cattle. These were the Cherokee of the Five Lower Towns. They were called the Chicamaugas, after Tsikamagi, River of Death. They had broken with the Overhill and Valley towns in 1777 and had fled here, farther from white intrusion. They had held out against the Americans after the rest of the tribe surrendered in 1794. The conservative element was strong here.

As Old Suck entered the part of the Nation that bordered Georgia, Tiana began to feel anxious. She remembered hairy men with cruel eyes and nooses dangling from their saddle horns. Idealists said Georgia had been colonized by England's poor, the debtors. Jack Rogers said it had been settled by rabble.

By the time Old Suck reached Rossville near the sacred Lookout Mountain, Tiana could play a simple melody on Jacques's fiddle. She could bluff her way through a three-card game called *poque* and she knew some English and French phrases of which Seeth MacDuff would not have approved.

"*Ah, ma petite puce*, my little flea." Jacques lifted Tiana up and hugged her good-bye at John Ross's wharf. "Are you sure you do not want to shoot The Suck with us? It will be a ride you will not soon forget."

"*Non, mon frere*." She kissed him on his bristly cheek, under the eyepatch. Then she dodged out of the path of the men pulling the planks back aboard and preparing to push away from the dock.

"Back out," shouted Jacques to the men. "Throw your poles wide and brace off, you sons of dogs." He waved to Tiana as the boat moved sluggishly into the middle of the stream. "I shall miss you, little flea of my heart," he shouted. Tiana waved until the boat was out of sight, then she turned to explore the bustle at the Ross estate.

Twenty-five years earlier, John Ross's trader father, Daniel, had built a solid, two-story log house for his bride, Molly MacDonald, who was one-fourth Cherokee. Over the fireplace in the main room was a plaque that read FLORET QUI LABORAR. The motto had been granted to the Earl of Ross in 1681. Over the years the Rosses had flourished in the new world. Now young John Ross and his brother, Lewis, had gone into partnership with John Meigs, White Path's grandson. Their store at Rossville was always busy, as were the Rosses' mill and tavern and ferry. But they had never been this busy.

People from all over the Cherokee Nation were converging on the sacred refuge town of Ustanali for the council. Rossville was a convenient way station for many of them. Drum and Standing Together and fifty people from Hiwassee Town had arrived in a fleet of canoes two days before. They had camped overnight, then had left to thread the maze of streams that would eventually take them to Ustanali.

Jack Rogers hired four horses for himself and his three sons. Tiana rode behind her father. For ten miles she listened to him grumble about the highwayman who charged a king's ransom for the miserable jades he called horses. Then he muttered about the heat and the dust and the road jammed with families on foot and slow-moving wagons and reckless riders.

"I should have stayed home," he said for what seemed the hundredth time. "Leave my fields and trade to rush off, hand over head, to hear some red Demosthenes preach death and destruction. Lunacy. Hell-fired lunacy." While he ranted, Tiana caught the eye of a girl about her own age. In a matter of minutes they were old friends, and Tiana rode the rest of the way with her on her horse.

Tecumseh was more than a humanitarian, a genius, an orator, and a soldier. He was a showman. He waited until the meadows and forests around Ustanali were filled with thousands of Cherokee tents and shelters. Then he made a triumphal entry with his retinue of twenty mounted Shawnee warriors. He staged a great ceremony, with magnificent costumes and dancing. And he waited until nightfall to speak. Darkness covered the distraction of people arriving. Darkness focused attention on Tecumseh as he stood on a raised dais in the light of a huge bonfire. Tiana worked her way to the front of the crowd and stood open-mouthed as he spoke.

In Shawnee, Tecumseh meant Panther Passing Over. He was named for the meteor that flamed through the black sky the night he was born. There were many who said the comet, the Fire Panther, overhead now was a sign of his power. Tiana believed them. Not since the camp meeting at the Vann plantation had she seen so many people affected so deeply by a speech.

Ideas seemed to pour from Tecumseh's lips in a passionate avalanche. His words were simple. It was said his mother was one of the Real People, and he spoke without a translator. His strong voice carried easily in the silence that was broken only by the crackling of the huge fire and the occasional neighs of horses and the distant bark of a fox or dog.

Tecumseh lowered his voice now and then, forcing his audience to lean forward and to strain to catch his words. He drew them closer that way, pulling them into the web of his personal vision. Unlike the camp meeting, the thousands of people filling the clearing and standing among the shadowy trees were solemn and quiet. There was no hysteria here.

"Brothers!" Tecumseh shouted. "We all belong to one family. We are all children of the Great Spirit. Now trouble brings us together to smoke the pipe around the same council fire.

"Brothers! We are friends. We must help each other. The blood of our brothers and fathers has run like water to satisfy the greed of the white men."

Tecumseh's eyes, emphasized by lines of red paint radiating out onto his cheeks, seemed to glow with a fire brighter than the one behind him. He was dressed in moccasins and loincloth. His bare body glistened with sweat and trembled with emotion. Tiana didn't have to be told what the egret feathers in his hair meant. The white feather was for peace between the Indian nations, and the red one was for enmity with the white man.

Tiana inched forward between the Shawnee warriors standing like statues in front of the dais. She had to throw her head back to look up at Tecumseh. At forty-two, he was still a handsome man. His face was long and patrician. His teeth were white and even. His carriage was erect and graceful. He was made even more attractive by the inner fire of his dream of a united Indian coalition. It was the same dream that had taken him on a crusade from Canada to the Gulf of Mexico.

"Brothers! When the white men first set foot on our ground, they were hungry. They had nowhere to spread their blankets or kindle their fires. Our fathers felt sorry for them and shared whatever they had. Brothers! The white men are like snakes. When they are chilled, they are feeble and harmless. But give them warmth, and they sting their benefactors to death. At first they asked only for land for their lodges. Now nothing will satisfy them but all our hunting grounds from the rising to the setting sun.

"Brothers! The Great Spirit gave us strength and courage to defend our land. If we do not use it we are doomed. Where are the Pequot today? Where are the Narragansett, the Pokanoket, and the other once-powerful tribes? They have vanished before the white man's greed like snow before the summer sun. Will we let ourselves be destroyed too, without making an effort worthy of our race?"

"Never!" Caught in Tecumseh's fervor, Tiana's voice rang out in the silence that followed his speech. She turned scarlet and tried to hide. But Tecumseh only smiled down at her.

"Shall we give up our homes?" he continued. "Shall we surrender our land? Shall we abandon the graves of our dead? Shall we forsake our pride and our courage? I hope you will cry out with this brave child, 'Never!' We can only enjoy peace if we are prepared to defend ourselves when wronged." Tecumseh held up a piece of cedar, long and tapering, like a flattened obelisk. One face of it was carved with symbols.

"*Ani Yunwiya*, Real People, join in this holy struggle to prevent your own extinction. If you do, Pathkiller, your principle headman, will receive one of these sacred slabs. It has two meanings. We tell the white man it is a heaven stick. It stands for family and earth, water, lightning, trees, and wind.

"But the message to our red brothers is different. When a great sign from heaven is given, we will leave the hunt and the fields. We will travel like lightning to meet at Detroit. We will drive the white man away."

Tecumseh held up a bundle of cedar sticks. He took one out and beckoned to Tiana. She looked around in confusion. Tecumseh crouched at the edge of the platform and held out a hand to her. There was no mistaking his meaning. One of the Shawnee warriors lifted her to stand next to Tecumseh.

She was close enough to see the weariness in his mild, hazel eyes. He had traveled thousands of miles, trying to unite people who had been at war with each other since before any of them could remember. He rarely slept in comfort. He rarely slept at all. Now he rested one slender hand lightly on Tiana's shoulder.

"This twig is weak," he said. He passed it to Tiana and murmured, "Break it." She looked at it as though seeing her hand through someone else's eyes. She was aware of the thousands of people watching her. "Break it, child," said Tecumseh again. She snapped it in two and gave him the pieces. He held them up. "Even a child can break a single twig. But a strong man cannot break a bundle of them." He demonstrated, straining until the muscles of his arms bulged. Tiana climbed down, her moment of glory over almost as fast as a meteor could shoot across the sky. Tecumseh went on. "United, strong in the old ways, the white man can never break us. Divided, alone like this twig, we will be destroyed, tribe by tribe." He took sticks from the bundle until there were only four left. Then he retied them with a thong.

"Each town leader who joins us will receive a bundle of four cedar sticks. He will break one at each full moon. When one stick is left, there will be a sign in the night heavens. Then each leader will cut the last stick into thirty pieces. He will burn each piece at dawn. He will burn the last piece at midnight. Then I will stamp the ground with my foot and shake down the houses. In the middle of the night, the earth will tremble and roar. Great trees will fall when there is no wind. Rivers will run backward and lakes will form. When the sign appears, you must pick up your guns and gather at the river near the fort called Detroit.

"You of the Real People must decide. Join the Seminole, the Creek, the Shawnee, and all who will fight with us. Throw away the whiskey and tools and trinkets of the white man. Kill the sluggish cattle whose meat is unfit for warriors. Kill the useless cats that swarm around your wigwams. Join us in a great and proud nation."

When he paused, Ridge shouted from the crowd.

"Such talk will lead to war with the United States. It will mean ruin for the Seven Clans." Those around Ridge turned on him. They might have killed him if his friends hadn't surrounded him and hustled him away. Tecumseh went on as though nothing had happened.

"Become with us a sacred fire spreading over the land, consuming the race of dark souls. Accursed be the race that has seized our country and made women of our warriors. Our fathers from their graves reproach us as cowards. I hear them now in the wailing wind. Their tears drop from the weeping skies.

"The white men corrupt our women. They trample the ashes of our dead. We must drive them back down the trail of blood. We must drive them back to the Great Water whose accursed waves brought them to our land." Tecumseh's voice rose to a hoarse shout. "Burn their houses! Slay their stock! Slay their wives and children that the very breed may perish! War now! War always! War on the living! War on the dead!"

Tecumseh finished and stood still. Sweat glistened on his face and body. A murmur grew as people shifted and discussed his words. Drums began a steady beat that intensified as more joined in. Tecumseh wouldn't stay for the dancing or feasting or the debate that would rage for days among the headmen of the Real People. He had many more miles to travel, and little time.

The brash young United States and Britain had been drifting aimlessly toward another war, as Britain searched United States ships, impressed her seamen, and interfered with trade. The United States certainly wasn't prepared for war. Neither side wanted it. But neither side was making any effort to stop it. If Tecumseh was going to form his Indian army into an independent force he would have to hurry.

Tiana stood absolutely still in the midst of the turmoil. Tecumseh's words echoed in her head and tears filled her eyes. She felt alone and forlorn and frightened. "Slay their wives and children that the very breed may perish." He was talking about her white father. He was talking about her family. He was talking about her.

Chapter 14

Jack crossed his arms on his chest and glared at Elizabeth. She was squatting next to a big trunk by her narrow bed and searching through its contents. Hanging from the rafters above her were huge hanks of her yarn, dyed in tones of yellow and brown. Her big loom stood in the corner. As always, she avoided Jack's eyes as she went on packing a few clothes into saddlebags.

"It's too dangerous, Old Woman." Jack used the affectionate Cherokee term for wife. He had tried forbidding Elizabeth to go and he'd failed. Now he was resorting to wheedling. After thirty years he still hadn't found the way to change a Cherokee woman's mind. And after thirty years he still couldn't get used to being thwarted.

"I've hunted *a'taliguli*, The Mountain Climber, for fifty years, My Supporter."

"But whites are hunting ginseng now. And some of them are vicious. People far away, across the big water, will pay handsomely for the roots of your precious Mountain Climber. Whenever someone will pay a lot of money for something, there are white men who'll do anything to get it."

"Granddaughter and I will be careful." She turned away from Jack as though the matter were settled. Jack blew out his breath and stomped from the room.

Without speaking, Tiana followed her grandmother through the main room of the house and out into the yard. Elizabeth tied their bags onto rings sewn to a broad leather strap around the mare's flanks. Tiana hugged Susannah and Jennie and her father. Then Jack lifted her onto the horse in front of Elizabeth. They both would ride bareback, although Elizabeth put her moccasined feet into stirrups attached to a surcingle. Jack laid a hand briefly on his first wife's arm as she gathered in the reins.

"Old Woman," he said in a low voice, "there's evil in the mountains that comes not from your Great Snake and Stone Man and Little People. Have a care."

"I shall, husband."

The two rode to Hiwassee and spent the first night there. Then they rode all the next day without saying much. Tiana was relieved to be away from people and their talk of Tecumseh and war. A Creek had killed a woman of the Real People and renewed old hatreds. The headmen had decided not to ally with Tecumseh and the Creeks. Life seemed to go on as usual but for the constant speculation about Tecumseh's signs and his holy war. Still, Tiana felt burdened with worry. She felt much older since the council at Ustanali.

The hills became steeper and the trees taller as they neared the mountains. It was *Dulisidi*, Nut Month, September. The brilliant orange of the maples spread like flames amidst the green of the trees. Finally, when Tiana had to throw her head back to see the tops of the tall peaks rising in front of her, she asked what was on her mind.

"Ulisi, why have you brought me with you?"

"It's time for you to go to school." Elizabeth gave her small smile when she said the English word "school."

"School?"

"*Tsacona-ge.*" Elizabeth pointed toward the ragged layers of peaks, like solid blue haze. "The Place Of The Blue Smoke. That's our school. In the old days the wise men went to the mountains and camped for seven days and nights. They shared what they'd learned in the previous year, and they told stories of the bravery of their hunters and warriors.

"On the night of the seventh day the wise men were quiet. All night they listened to the Little People who live in the mountains. The Little People sang and danced and told stories from ages past. They had listened to the old men too, and added those new stories to the old ones. Thus the knowledge of our people was passed from generation to generation." Elizabeth paused. "Ayasta, Spoiler Campbell, is suffering from palsy. It's time for me to gather the roots of the Mountain Climber here to use in healing her. I wanted you to come with me, to the mountains, to the center of our country's soul."

"Why did you bring me and not my sisters?"

"What clan do we belong to?"

"*Ani Gihlahi*, The Long Hairs." Tiana was used to her grandmother following a question with another question. She knew if she were patient her questions would be answered.

"What's the other name for our clan?"

"Sometimes we're called the Pretty Woman clan."

"Pretty Women or Beloved Women haven't always come from our clan, but they have more often than from the others."

"There aren't any Pretty Women anymore, except for Ghigau."

"When we need a Beloved Woman one will appear."

"What has that to do with me?" Tiana turned to look at her grandmother and Elizabeth smiled at her. She loved this child, with her huge eyes like the dark star sapphires found here, and her wild mane of black hair.

"Perhaps nothing. But even though the old men no longer come to the mountains to share wisdom with the Little People, knowledge must be passed on. When the hearth fires are relighted at the Green Corn ceremony, not every clay vessel can hold embers from the sacred flames. We choose only the best, those bowls that fired well, without cracks, and with the deepest, richest colors. So we look for the children to carry our special knowledge. You're such a one."

Tiana thought about that as they rode up into the cool stands of red oak, and cedar, birch, redbud, locust, and magnolia. Above her the sky seemed to pulse with the intensity of its blue color. The air became cooler, and Elizabeth passed Tiana an old wool coat her brothers had outgrown. When she put it on, the hems of the sleeves dangled almost to her fingertips.

The sun had slid below the peaks and shadows were stretching like fingers up the slopes when Elizabeth decided to make camp in a fragrant stand of red cedar. She stopped by a grayback, a huge gray sandstone boulder that seemed to be pushing up out of the forest mold around it. Frost had heaved it loose from its place far up the mountainside ages before. Gravity had pulled it, inch by inch, down the slope until it rested here, far from its original home. Tiana used it to dismount. As her foot sank into the cushion of moss and wintergreen on the boulder, mice exploded from a hidden nest.

Startled, Tiana tumbled off the boulder when the mice bounced in all directions, like popping corn, and disappeared into the mat of plants. As Tiana picked herself up she smelled the faint skunk odor of the Rugel's ragwort that grew like a ruffled collar around the boulder. She brushed the leaves and forest mold from her coat, then held the horse while Elizabeth climbed laboriously down. Elizabeth wouldn't be riding horses much longer. They were both stiff and sore from the long hours on horseback.

Elizabeth picked a few of the bright red berries from the wintergreen. She crushed them so Tiana could smell their aroma.

"I'll take some of these leaves to make a tea for Susannah," Elizabeth said. "It'll help her sore tooth."

Together, they built a small fire. While Elizabeth mixed corn bread dough, Tiana waded in the nearby creek. She cornered and caught a huge bullfrog and begged his pardon before she twisted his head off. She skinned him in the flowing water so his meat wouldn't become bitter. She caught another and did the same.

While she warmed her numbed feet by the fire, Elizabeth parboiled the frogs in a small kettle, then set them on green stakes to roast.

"Tomorrow I'll make a blowgun and hunt bigger game," Tiana said. Elizabeth only grunted. Under her breath she was singing a charm to make the food cook faster. She had patted the corn meal into flat cakes and pressed them onto large pieces of chestnut bark. She stood the bark in front of the fire so the cakes could cook.

Tiana and her grandmother sat in the shelter of their small cedar lean-to and watched the flames dance and chuckle to themselves. Now and then stray drops from a misty rain hit the fire, making it hiss. It was easy to see the fire as a living being, a magical spirit, sent by the gods. It warmed them and entertained them and comforted them in the vastness of the mountain forest. It carved a warm room of light from the cold blackness around them.

Tiana was grateful to Grandmother Fire for that. The trees here were even larger than the ones back home. The steep gorges and ravines were dark and mysterious. She could easily imagine Uktena, The Great Snake, lurking in a barren mountain pass with the lonely wind mourning around him. Without wanting to, she strained her ears to hear the drums of the Little People. The high, bare balds were their dance grounds.

Tiana pricked chestnuts with her knife and put them in the hot ashes of the fire. When they'd roasted, she and Elizabeth breathed in their steamy fragrance as they peeled them. While they ate, Elizabeth began Tiana's education. As was usual among the Real People, she started with a story Tiana already knew.

"This is what the old women told me when I was a girl," Elizabeth began. "Long ago, when the world was new and every living thing spoke the same language, birds and beasts and plants and humanity lived happily together. Then humans began to multiply. They invented weapons and fish hooks. They began killing the other beings. Finally, the animals became angry and held a council.

"The small animals, the fishes and turtles and lizards, all spoke about how cruel humans were. The insects complained that people stepped on them and swatted or crushed them. The big animals complained too. Only the ground squirrel spoke out for people. He made the other animals so angry they tore stripes on his back with their claws. You can see the stripes there still.

"After discussing and shouting for days, the animals decided to invent disease to kill human beings. The deer decided to send rheumatism to every hunter who failed to ask his victims's pardon. The others thought up all the horrible illnesses people now suffer. The grubworm was so happy about it he fell over, laughing, and has wriggled on his back ever since.

"But the plants took pity on people. They promised to help cure the diseases. When a curer doesn't know what to use, the spirit of the plant will tell her. She can go into a field or forest and look carefully. The right plant will nod to her."

"Then why must we study plants, if they'll speak to us when we need them?" asked Tiana.

"Because, child, plants will only nod to you when the situation is very grave. We must learn about the world ourselves. We can't sit on a mountain top and wait for Thunder or the Great Wizard or the Yellow Mockingbird to bring knowledge. We must watch and listen and apply what we've learned. Almost anything can teach us, if we can hear its voice."

"Father once told me of a wise man named Bacon who said 'Knowledge is power.' " Tiana looked out at the vegetation massed around them. In the fire's light the beads of rain gleamed on the leaves like millions of eyes. There were as many kinds of plants as grains of sand in Long Man's bed.

"Bacon was right."

"But how can I ever learn all there is to know?"

"No one can learn everything. But you know a great deal already. How do you prevent poison ivy from giving you a rash?"

"I call it my friend. And if I get a rash anyway, I rub it with the flesh of a crayfish."

"Can you think of anything else?"

Tiana stared into the fire as though she expected it to give her answers.

"If a mother chews *aniwani'ski*, bugle weed, and rubs it on the lips of her children, they'll become great speakers." A thought occurred to Tiana. "Did you or mother do that for us?"

"Yes, we did," said Elizabeth. "What else do you know?"

"If one puts a cocklebur into water from a waterfall, then drinks it, she'll have a good memory. If a woman washes her hair with the pounded roots of *distai'yi*, catgut, her hair will be strong. And I know bonset tea cleans one out."

"If you think hard, you'll remember many, many things. Here are some you may not know."

Elizabeth talked until Tiana's eyes began to droop. Then they both crawled into their blankets and slept snuggled together amid the spicy cedar boughs of their bed. Tiana woke to the songs of the birds. She looked out at the banners of ground fog drifting around the huge tree trunks.

After going to water and eating a breakfast of cold corn bread, she and her grandmother rode higher into the mountains. Their mare's hooves clattered on the rocks of the narrow, twisting path. Banks of sodden moss hung over the trail. The tree trunks gleamed wetly. Pools of black water lay among their knobby, sinuous roots. A blanket of ferns covered the forest floor. Across precipitous gorges, silver ribbons of water plummeted from clouds of mist. Tiana began to breathe deeply, drawing in the redolence of fir and spruce and pine. She wanted to fill her body with the odor until she smelled like the fir.

Seventy-five feet over her head, the tops of the trees creaked in the wind as though conversing with each other up there. When Tiana stopped to relieve herself, she stared into a drop of water poised on a leaf. In it she saw the veins underneath magnified by the lens of the drop. She stared into it, entranced by the mystery of it. She had a vague, exhilarating feeling that she could see and understand the whole world in this tiny drop of water. She felt surrounded by magic. And she felt magical herself.

Elizabeth continued to guide the mare upward. Often they had to dismount and lead the animal around huge logs that had fallen across the trail. When the going was smoother, Tiana rode languidly, her long legs dangling and finished fastening a feathering of thistle-down to darts of black locust wood.

She slid the darts in and out of her new blowgun, the way James had taught her. She was making the dart fit tight enough to build up the necessary air pressure. James had taught her to use a blowgun too. She was a fair shot. When she was done, she had a dozen small darts in the pouch slung at her hip.

About midafternoon, Elizabeth turned onto a slope that faced east. "You must be quiet now, and listen only," she said. She tied the mare to a tree and searched through the tumbled boulders and scrub. Tiana followed close behind.

Elizabeth found the plants hidden among clefts in the rock. She spread out an ell of white cloth that her patient, Spoiler Campbell, had given her. She circled the plants four times counterclockwise, each time chanting an incantation, she faced east while she dug up the roots. Tiana craned to see them. They looked so much like a tiny man she could almost believe, as many did, that they shrieked when they were pulled from the ground.

Elizabeth laid the roots on the cloth and wrapped them. She chanted to them again before she packed them away in the saddlebag. Then she carefully scattered the ginseng's red berries so they would propagate. When they were making camp again for the night, Tiana dared ask a question about them.

"Grandmother, are those all the roots you're going to take?"

"Yes."

"But you came so far. Why don't you take many roots, so you'll have them. There are enough."

"I don't need many. Curers only take what they need for the near future. We prefer to collect herbs fresh, when their life force is strong."

While Elizabeth finished the lean-to, Tiana took her blowgun and went to the creek to hunt small game for dinner. As she was coming back with a rabbit slung in one hand and her blowgun in the other, she heard the voice of *tsikilili*, the chickadee. She stopped to listen carefully, trying to interpret what he was saying. Chickadees often warned of events to come or carried news. Instead of news, she heard a man's voice.

Tiana dropped to her hands and knees, put down the rabbit, and crept toward her camp. Her grandmother wasn't alone. Tiana's heart pounded and her mouth felt dry when she saw the white man. He brandished his rifle like a club and shouted at Elizabeth, but she faced him calmly. She pretended not to understand him.

A *sanger*, Tiana thought. A ginseng hunter. Ginseng hunters were a solitary lot. A surly pack of dogs, Jack Rogers said. Jack said they didn't care whose land they hunted on. He said most of them didn't care if they stripped an area of the valuable plants. And they didn't care if they killed someone while they did it.

Tiana put a hand over her heart, trying to still its thumping. The man had grabbed Elizabeth's arm and was shaking it. He raised the gun higher, and brought it down. Elizabeth dodged, and the rifle stock hit her a glancing blow across the shoulder and head. Tiana's first impulse was to charge at the man. But she didn't. With trembling hands, she loaded a dart into the blowgun.

She raised it, took a deep breath, and blew. There was a muted, hollow "thuk" as the dart exploded from the barrel of the cane. It hit the man in the neck and buried itself almost to the hilt. Before he could do more than raise a hand to the wound and look surprised, Tiana had another dart and fired. This one punched through his cheek and into his mouth. The feathering seemed to sprout from his face.

He wasn't hard to hit. He was much bigger than the rabbits and birds and squirrels Tiana usually shot at. With a strange detachment, Tiana wondered if she could hit his eye with the next one.

Tiana tossed a stone so it rustled the bushes off to one side. Cursing and bleeding, the man looked wildly around at the tangled masses of dog hobble laced among the trunks and branches of dripping rhododendron and laurel. He had no idea how many Indians were lurking there, or what gruesome tortures they had in mind. He didn't seem inclined to find out. Tiana heard a crashing of underbrush as he mounted his horse and galloped away.

Tiana ran to help her grandmother get up. She brushed back the hair to see the ugly welt forming under Elizabeth's ear.

"You can help me make a poultice for it," said Elizabeth.

"Grandmother, we have to get away from here. He might come back."

"Why did he leave?" Pereplexed, Elizabeth looked around her.

"I shot him," said Tiana. "How shall I make a poultice?" She wanted to change the subject. She had shot a white man. She wasn't sure what consequences might follow.

"You shot him? With your blowgun?"

"Yes. We must fly from here, grandmother."

Elizabeth laughed.

"When you are an old *ulisi*, I pray you have a granddaughter as full of surprises as you yourself are. She'll make life interesting, even after you think you've seen everything."

"Grandmother, he might come back."

"I know a back trail, an animal path that's well hidden. We'll take that," said Elizabeth. She was still chuckling as Tiana pulled her to her feet. She grunted and swayed and put a hand to her head, but with Tiana's help she managed to mount the mare.

The night seemed endless. Tiana jumped at every cracking twig. A skunk bumbling through the underbrush terrified her. They traveled slowly, illuminating their way with resinous splinters of lighter pine. By morning they were well down the mountain.

"Will we go home now?" asked Tiana.

"Not yet. I want to show you one more place."

"Where?" Tiana only wanted to reach the safety of her family. But it wouldn't have occurred to her to argue with her grandmother.

"Everything in its time."

They spent the night at Tellico blockhouse. Then, instead of heading south, toward Hiwassee, Elizabeth turned the mare north and east. As they rode, she passed the time telling Tiana stories or pointing out plants and giving their uses. If she felt pain from the bruises on her shoulder and head, she said nothing about it. Finally, she stopped at the crest of a hill overlooking the Little Tennessee River.

Around them were grass-grown trenches and the vine-covered remains of crumbling log walls and palisades. Elizabeth walked the mare around the ruin of the five-sided fort. Then she and Tiana dismounted and stood looking at the tranquil ruins. A rusty cannon ball lay half-buried at Tiana's feet.

"Do you know where you are, granddaughter?"

"Fort Loudon."

"Why do you think I brought you here?"

"Because it was a great victory for the Real People? They laid seige to the fort and forced the white soldiers to surrender. They avenged themselves of the treachery of the English."

"More than that. There were women here too. Do you remember what they did?"

"They defied the war leaders. When the English soldiers had only rats to eat, they took food to their white husbands inside the fort."

"The war leaders threatened to kill them. Do you know what they said?"

"They said to go ahead and kill them. Their clans would avenge them. They were brave, grandmother."

"Yes, they were. Men make war. They glory in it. Eagle feathers in their hair count more to them than their lives or the lives of their brothers. But the men have always listened to our counsel for peace. Sometimes they do not follow our advice, but they listen. When a woman feels strongly enough about something, she may defy the warriors and the war leaders."

"Like Nanehi Ward did when she warned the settlers of an attack?"

"Yes."

"Did she really save Mrs. Bean?" Tiana had always assumed Mrs. Bean was named for the plant.

"Yes, she did. I was there. I was young. It wouldn't have occurred to me to stop it. The men were too many and too strong and too drunk with blood and victory. I'll never forget the time." Elizabeth's eyes seemed to focus far away, or long ago. "The Beloved Woman was angry. She strode out into the center of the dance ground and held up her ceremonial swan's wing to stop the drums and the dancing.

" 'No woman shall be burned at the stake while I am Beloved Woman,' she said. She was magnificent. The warriors stared sullenly at her, but they made no move when she untied that poor captive. We women have always had the final word about captives. I suppose that's because we adopt them into our clans. Those were proud days, granddaughter."

After leaving Fort Loudon Elizabeth approached Sik'waya's wife's farm with caution. Because Sik'waya spent his days mumbling to himself and marking on pieces of bark many people believed he was *dida'hnese'sgi*, a Putter-In And Drawer-Out Of Them, a sorcerer.

"It looks uncared-for," said Tiana. "Maybe he's been sick." Weeds grew high in the harvested fields. His wife's few cows were gaunt.

The yard around the cabin's door was littered. Elizabeth was worried.

Many years before, just after Sik'waya's leg became so crippled he could no longer hunt well, he had turned to keeping a tavern. He wasn't successful at it because he grew too fond of his wares. But he'd finally sworn off whiskey. He'd taught himself blacksmithing and silver work. Now, Elizabeth feared he may have gone back to drinking. But even as a drunkard he had been a kind, gentle man.

Sik'waya hobbled from the doorway of a tiny shack off to one side of his wife's cabin. His thin, aesthetic face lit with a smile. He was appraoching forty seasons and his hair was sprinkled with gray. He was wearing spectacles balanced on the tip of his narrow nose. He had on a tattered shirt, and patched leggings and moccasins. He waved his pipe at them.

"Beloved kin, my heart sings at the sight of you. Let me wash the dust of the trail from your feet and make you as comfortable as humble circumstances will allow."

Sik'waya was understating the case. His circumstances had gone far beyond humble. The windowless cabin was dim. Most of the light came through the hundreds of chinks in the cabin wall, or the hole where the roof had rotted. The hearth was a shallow depression in the center of the small room. Smoke was supposed to exit through a hole in the roof peak, but most of it collected at the blackened ceiling.

Sik'waya offered Tiana and Elizabeth the cabin's only two stools. He hammered the leg back into one by pounding it on the dirt floor. His wife, U'ti'yu, dropped a small kettle of thin gruel in front of them. She did it with such ill grace that some sloshed over into the dirt. She left without a word of greeting. Sik'waya smiled apologetically as he brought them horn spoons to dip out the hominy gruel.

"My cooker is blue," he nodded after his wife. "Someone must have spoiled her saliva, made her unhappy." While he asked politely about his guests' trip, his five-year-old daughter, E'yagu, Pumpkin Setting There, slipped in and sat cross-legged on an old hide. She and Tiana shared a spoon. While she ate, Tiana made the mistake of asking Sik'waya what he had been doing. He broke into a smile.

"I'm devising a way of drawing our language. I'm making a symbol for each word." With a stick, Sik'waya began sketching crude pictures in the dirt of the floor. He drew and recited the words for a half hour or more.

"But there are so many words," he said sadly. "I listen to people when they speak. I rush home and make new characters for the new words I hear. I already have hundreds. It's becoming harder and harder to remember them all. My cabin," he gestured vaguely toward the nearby shed, "is full of words marked on pieces of bark. And those are just the names of things. The action words are very difficult to draw."

"Brother," said Elizabeth gently, "we all know the Real People are not supposed to have writing. They lost that right long ago, when they neglected the books the Provider gave them. The white man took them and left us the bow and arrow. Now the white men have writing. It is theirs."

"I don't believe that, sister. I'll find a way. Why is the white man so powerful? Because he has writing. He loses nothing. He can capture words on talking leaves. He can tame the wild animal that is knowledge. He can pass it to his sons and daughters without losing any of it."

Sik'waya's father had been white, an emissary from George Washington, some said, or an itinerant German pedlar. Others claimed he was one of the soldiers beseiged at Fort Loudon fifty years before, although Sik'waya didn't seem that old. Whomever he was, Sik'waya had never known him. He neither spoke nor understood English. He had been raised by his mother, who never remarried. All she would say about Sik'waya's father was that his name had been Gist.

"But I've been rude," Sik'waya said. "It's late and you must be tired."

"Father," said E'yagu timidly. "I smell smoke."

The four of them ran outside to find Sik'waya's work room in flames. The dry wood burned quickly. Elizabeth and Tiana and E'yagu had to hold Sik'waya to keep him from running inside.

"My work," he said, over and over. "More than a year of work. I had hundreds of words drawn and organized." Then they noticed U'ti'yu standing off to one side, watching the fire. She was smiling.

"Brother," said Elizabeth, "granddaugher and I will go. We have a long way to travel." Sik'waya hardly seemed to hear her.

"May your path be white," he said. "And may the Red Mountain Lion go before you."

Chapter 15

"Father, am I red or white?" Tiana threw a dried leaf into the fire and watched it turn a glowing, pulsing red. The veins were outlined in light before the leaf shriveled in the flames. She didn't see Jack Rogers glance over her head at Jennie and then to Drum.

"Why do you ask, lass?"

"Curiosity."

"Come here." Jack opened the blanket draped around his shoulders. She left her place between James and Raven and climbed into her father's lap. He wrapped his arms around her and enfolded her in the blanket. Across from her, Joseph and William passed the pipe between them. They had only recently been allowed to smoke on special occasions and they tended to put on airs about it. Nannie and Susannah were asleep on their bed of pine boughs under the lean-to. They had piles of furs and blankets over them and a pan of hot stones at their feet. But they still lay curled together like squirrels in a nest.

It was mid November, 1811. The Rogers family was camped on a ridge overlooking a deep valley in the Mountains of the Blue Smoke. There was snow in the high passes. It was a strange time for a trip here. And even stranger, Jack had made no argument when his daughters asked to come along.

"I want you all there," he had said. "I want you to see there's nothing to Tecumseh's hocus-pocus."

There had been a general exodus to the mountains as the date of Tecumseh's first sign, a Fire Panther, approached. With the others, the Rogers had threaded their way up the steep paths until they were among the fragrant evergreens. Campfires flickered among the trees on the slopes below them and on the ridge across from them. The Rogers had set up their camp with Drum and Sally Ground Squirrel and their children.

Finally Jack spoke.

"So you're curious to know what color you are." He took Tiana's arm from under the blanket, pulled back her sleeve, and pretended to study her skin by the fire's light. "You're the color of the sacred cedar." He sniffed the arm. "Fragrant as smoke, and soft and velvety as a flicker's breast."

"She asked a serious question, husband," said Jennie softly.

"So she did." Jack sighed. As the hour approached midnight, they all glanced from time to time at the star-strewn sky. "You're neither red nor white, lass. You're yourself. Let ignorant folk try to put people into categories. Let them ignore the fact that each person is unique. We know better. You're like no one else. You're the best of both races. Though what good you got from me, I can't say. All the good came from your mother, to be sure."

"Oh." Tiana was silent again.

"Have Tecumseh's words upset you, daughter?" asked Jennie. She had noticed how unnaturally quiet her daughter had been since the council at Ustanali.

"Yes. He said the whites were an accursed race. Father's white. And I'm mostly white."

"Tecumseh himself knows every individual of a race can't be condemned for the bad actions of some," said Jennie. "It's said he loves a white woman, and he asked her to marry him. But he wouldn't give up his people for her. Surely he wouldn't kill her."

"But he's telling the Real People to kill all the whites, even the women and children. Or drive them out. If they drive us out, where will we go?" Tiana had been brooding about the question for three months.

"Your father is one of the Real People," said Drum. "He's a Special Friend. No one will harm him or his family. And you are as much a part of the Seven Clans as anyone." *Perhaps more than most*, Drum thought to himself.

"Will I have to kill my cat?"

"No," said Jennie. "No one will be killed."

"But what if Tecumseh turns all the tribes against us?"

"You might as well try to gather the clouds or ally the wolf and the panther as unite the tribes," said James.

" 'Who hath gathered the wind in his fist? Who hath bound the water in a garment? Who hath established all the ends of the earth? What is his name?' " said Drum, staring at the sky.

"Is that from the preacher's book, Beloved Father?" asked Tiana.

"Yes. I asked Raven to read parts of it to me. I especially like the proverbs. They're as beautiful as the ancient incantations of our people. It's a fine book. And so old. I wonder that white people are still so evil after having that book so long."

The wind carried a faint shout from across the valley.

"Hell-fire!" said Jack under his breath.

"I hope not," said Raven. But his flesh crawled anyway.

Tiana's stomach jumped. All the terrible things she feared were now possible. Without thinking, she spit. Spitting when a shooting star passed over meant she would keep her teeth when she grew old.

Despite what her father said about Tecumseh's hocus-pocus, a brilliant, greenish trail of fire was streaking across the sky from the southwest. It arced gracefully over the valley and disappeared into the northeast, the land of the Shawnee and Tecumseh.

"What did Tecumseh say the final sign would be?" spoke Raven into the silence that followed the meteor's spectacular display.

"He said he would stamp on the ground and shake down the houses." Drum pulled one red cedar stick from his coat. With his knife, he began scoring it off into thirty sections. He had voted not to join Tecumseh, but like many headmen, he was keeping track of the time anyway.

"This was a coincidence," said Jack.

"And when did he say his sign would happen?" asked Raven.

"A month from now," said Drum.

On December 16, the night Tecumseh's final sign was to come, the Rogers wrapped themselves in blankets and sat out on the porch. If Tecumseh did carry out his threat and make the ground shake, they wanted to be near home. Besides, it was winter now. The mountains were shrouded in snow. To Tiana they seemed like old men in ermine mantles, hunched against the cold.

Tiana and Nannie shared a blanket with Jennie. James and John sat on the porch floor with their backs against the house's wall. William and Joseph sat on the steps. Mother Elizabeth dozed in her favorite chair with the bent hickory rockers. Her mouth was open and she snored lightly. Susannah lay in her ample lap. Even Elizur Schrimshear, the tenant farmer, was there. They all shivered as they waited around a cheerful pile of coals in a barrel of sand. Tiana envied her father, warm and serene and snoring in his big bed by the fire in the main room.

The sky was clear. The stars glittered like ice shards in the cold light of the moon. They were so bright, they gave the yard and trees a silvery glow.

"Midnight," said Jennie. As long as there were stars shining Jennie always knew what time it was. Tiana tensed. She had been dreading this day and hour ever since she had seen the meteor a month before.

"Wal," said Elizur at last. "I reckon the earth ain't gonna tremble tonight." He stepped off the porch, his lanky legs carrying him past the middle two steps. "I'll fix that loose step for you in the morning, Miss Jennie. Good night."

"Good night." Jennie herded her daughters inside. The boys followed.

As Tiana lay awake in her bed, Nannie and Susannah breathing softly beside her, she stared at the ceiling. She knew she should be relieved the world hadn't ended tonight. She fell asleep wondering why she was vaguely disappointed. She woke up an hour and a half later and lay with her eyes closed. Even in her half-asleep state, she was sure she was moving.

"William, Joseph," she muttered. "Stop shaking the bed." She tried to roll over, but the heavy wooden frame bucked and sent her flying onto the floor.

"What's happening?" asked Nannie. Susannah began to cry as she hung on to the bed post. Tiana tried to stand, then fell again. She heard a loud rumbling and pottery breaking downstairs.

"Mother! Father!" Tiana screamed. She couldn't walk on the dancing floor boards so she crawled toward the door. The rumbling grew louder.

"Girls, get out of here!" Jack Rogers clung to the lintel. "Hurry!" He picked Susannah up. The other two held onto the tail of his long nightshirt as they staggered down the narrow stairwell. Tiana braced herself with her hands against the rough, swaying walls and tried not to scream. The logs trembled until she was sure they would collapse and crush her and her father and sisters.

They reached the main room and ran through it, dodging tumbled furniture, broken vessels, and scattered tools and food. The strings of pumpkin and apples danced at the ceiling. The floor was awash in applesauce, jellies, and preserved food spilled from smashed jars. Apples rolled crazily around the room. Tiana could hear the roof shingles clattering overhead. Jennie and Mother Elizabeth waited for them in the doorway. Their arms were piled with blankets and quilts.

"Get outside!" shouted Jack. "Move!" He roared when they hesitated. If it was this bad in here, what was it like outside?

In bare feet and wearing long flannel nightgowns, they huddled in the yard as the porch roof collapsed. Cattle bellowed and fell in the corral, where they lay kicking helplessly. From the barn came the crash of the loft falling and horses screaming. Elizur ran from the barn, hauling Jack's prized racehorse after him. In a panic the horse reared and balked. Elizur dodged a massive beam that fell from the overhanging and pinned the horse. Elizur sobbed as he tugged futilely at the three-foot-thick timber.

Trees swayed and crashed, their roots making tearing sounds as they ripped from the ground. Tiana heard explosions like cannon fire all around her. Boulders rolled down the hillsides, smashing trees and crushing everything in their paths.

But more terrifying than the loud noises was a much quieter one. A crack opened in the earth twenty-five yards away from Tiana and her family, who clung to each other. Tiana heard a distant murmur from it, like David Gentry's forge when the bellows blew on it. A flash of light came from the opening. Perhaps Seeth MacDuff had been right after all. Perhaps this was the day of judgment.

Tiana was afraid to look at the crack. Maybe she'd see damned souls fleeing from the Burning Place. Maybe Auld Horny, the devil himself, would pull himself out of the opening. Tiana could smell sulphur. Under her feet, the ground felt warm. It buckled and seethed. Stones rattled. The old wagon, its driver's seat eerily empty, rolled off across the yard. The roaring and crashing and rumbling went on until Tiana thought it would deafen her.

"What's happening?" wailed Nannie, over and over. Susannah sobbed hysterically as Elizabeth tried to comfort her. Joseph and

William stared, wild-eyed, around them. They clung to Jennie as she crouched with an arm around each of them. James and John ran from the house with their parents' big feather mattress between them. They threw it over their mothers and sisters and brothers. Then they crawled under it with them.

"Where's my cat?" It was too much for Tiana to accept. She focused on something smaller. "Where's my cat?" she repeated, staring from under the mattress. "Wesa, wesa, wesa," she called softly.

"James!" Jack shouted to be heard over the din. "Did you put out the fire?"

"I forgot. I'll go."

"No. I'll do it."

"Father, come back!" screamed Tiana. But Jack staggered inside, climbing over the rubble of the fallen porch roof. The house creaked and groaned as though in pain. With a quilt, Jack smothered the fire. Then he ran outside. The house shuddered, but stood.

The tremors returned all through the long, cold night. They only subsided as the aura of dawn stained the eastern sky, outlining the blue mountain peaks in a deep rose color. The tranquil sunrise seemed to soothe the angry earth. But the hazy morning light showed the extent of the destruction. There would be a lot to do.

Tremors continued to shudder through the ground at irregular intervals. For a week, while the Rogers cleaned up the debris and buried dead animals, they slept in makeshift tents in the yard. They dared not spend much time indoors, even though snow fell and they were always cold.

Refugees passed through for days. On foot or on horseback they trailed silently into the yard. They carried heavy packs and bundles or drove carts piled high with possessions. Most of them were headed for the garrison. Some were fleeing to the mountains where Tecumseh had said they'd be safe. Tecumseh had promised war. It was now obvious Tecumseh kept his promises. There was protection at the garrison, and maybe food and tools to replace what people had lost. The government seemed to have an endless supply of such things.

Four days after the first quakes, a party of Seminole from the south rode into the yard. They were heavily armed and painted for war. Tiana and Nannie and Susannah hid in the wagon and watched through knotholes as their father signed with the warriors. Then the party rode north to join Tecumseh at Fort Detroit.

A group of Chicamauga Cherokee arrived too. They intended to ignore the National Council's decision and ally with Tecumseh. Using James as interpreter, Jack smoked with them around an open fire in the littered yard. After three hours, he convinced them to turn back.

Tiana watched the council from the window. When the sullen Chicamaugas finally mounted and returned the way they'd come, Tiana wanted to cry with relief. She thought of how Jack talked about the Rebellion of 1776. In her mind she heard his voice, heavy with homemade whiskey and the intoxication of memory.

"Those were the days," he would say, gesturing broadly with his pipe. "Those were the days when war slipped its bonds and came rampaging down the valleys." Tiana was never sure if he were speaking of war with approval or not. But the image of a colossal, slavering, ravenous War demon trampling down her peaceful valley kept her awake nights.

Raven dug frantically until his shovel struck something soft. He dropped to his knees and scraped with his hands. Tears streamed unheeded down his cheeks as he cleared the dirt from around a tiny arm.

"I've found someone!" he called, choking on his own sobs. It was hard to make himself heard over the keening of the women as they searched for loved ones or mourned the dead. The child's father ran to help Raven. Together, they cleared the last of the dirt from around the dead girl. Raven gently scooped dirt from her open mouth. He was still crying as he watched her father carry her to where the other bodies were neatly laid out. Old Spearfinger darted among the wounded. She smoothed on her salves and chanted curing incantations.

Many people in Hiwassee Town had been saved because they had been outside watching for Tecumseh's sign. They had gathered around small fires on the bare dance ground outside the town house and talked in hushed voices. Most of those who slept were in the dug-out hot houses, which held up better than the cabins. Even so, some suffocated when the dug-outs' dirt walls and roofs fell in on top of them. And many of the casualties were children who had gone to bed early.

It was an hour before dawn. The village was lit by the fires that broke out when chimneys tottered and collapsed in showers of sticks and stones and dried mortar. Chickens and birds, roused from their roosts, rose squawking into the air. The animals in the pastures cried in terror. There was a continous grinding sound as the timbers of the cabins wrenched apart. All over the village, cabins shook, then fell inward and the screams started.

From the town house mound, Raven had watched it all happen. In a matter of seconds the peaceful village turned into a nightmare. Never in anyone's memory had such a thing happened. But Tecumseh had predicted it.

Now, as he remembered Tecumseh's words, Raven felt the hair stir on the back of his neck. "I will stamp on the ground with my foot and shake down the houses." Heartsick and weary, Raven went back to work clearing away debris and uncovering those still trapped. As he heaved away heavy timbers, Raven wondered if the destruction had been as bad around Maryville. He prayed it hadn't.

"Will you go to your other family, my son?" Drum worked with Raven, helping him dislodge a wedged beam. Drum always seemed to know what his son was thinking.

"I must," said Raven. Perhaps his mother was dead or hurt. Perhaps all she had struggled to build had been destroyed. He pictured her with her long skirts pinned up and her petticoat hems stained with the red mud as she planted and harvested along with her children and slaves.

He saw her standing on the scaffolding as the walls of her house rose under her keen eye. He saw her with her sleeve rolled up, reaching far inside a cow's birthing canal to help a calf. He saw her strong, handsome face, with gray hair blowing in wisps around it as she stood on a hill and discussed with her sons which fields to plow. He saw her sitting, her head buried in her arms, amidst the ruins of her hard life.

He wanted to go to her. But he heard the moans and cries of those around him. He loved these people as much as he loved his own family. He couldn't leave them now, not when his strength might save another person.

Raven couldn't know the extent of Tecumseh's sign. From Canada to the Gulf of Mexico, the country had been devastated. And the devastation was only beginning. The quakes would go on intermittently for ten more years.

The ground in west Tennessee had split. Dark, sulphurous hot water spewed out, along with geysers of white sand. The Mississippi River rose fourteen feet in a few hours. It turned back on itself and flowed upstream, hissing and roaring. Massive bluffs toppled or slid into the river. Hundreds of boats were lost in the maelstrom of its waters. Near the border of Kentucky and Tennessee, a vast depression formed and filled with water. Thousands of acres were destroyed or made barren and ugly.

Perhaps Tecumseh's omen had been too powerful. It was one thing to leave the hunt and fields to go off to war. It was quite another to walk away from a home in ruins and a family hurt. Even so, many warriors from Tecumseh's allied tribes journeyed to meet him. Even skeptics became convinced. They just didn't see the need to travel to the Detroit River to make war. They commenced hostilities wherever they were. All over the frontier, white settlers once more armed themselves and went about their daily tasks with apprehension in their eyes.

Raven intended to leave Hiwassee Town as soon as the dead were found and the wounded cared for. He knew Drum would understand. The communal granary had been destroyed and much of the village's food supply had been lost. The women salvaged what they could, but the meal was mixed with sand and mortar. The people of Hiwassee had always shared everything they had with Raven. They had taken him in as one of them. He couldn't walk away from them when they needed help. He thought about taking a wagon to Maryville for supplies, but he already owed a hundred dollars there for things he'd bought in the past. He doubted anyone would give him credit, especially not to help Indians.

Besides, he knew that if he went to Maryville he wouldn't return. His loyalty was like a lodestone. The attraction was strongest to that which was closest. So he stayed in Hiwassee Town and hunted with the men. He helped rebuild the cabins so families could have shelter from the winter. But he always watched the trail from the north. "Evil rides post, while good news stops at every tavern," the saying went. His family knew where he was. Raven consoled himself with the thought that if something had happened to his mother, his brothers would have sent for him.

Five weeks after the first tremor, another one hit. It wasn't as bad as the first. People escaped from their trembling cabins, but Raven realized it was time to go. He could neglect his mother no longer. Drum walked him to the ferry.

"*Sgidoda*, Father, I regret leaving you and my family here," he said as they waited for Punk Plugged In to pole across from the far shore. "I'll work in Maryville, repay my debts, and bring you things to replace what was destroyed."

"Don't burden your heart with replacing anything. When one has little, the loss of it doesn't matter. Pity the rich who are too heavy to rise, have too much property. You yourself are the best gift you can bring me. My heart will cry like the lonely hawk in the empty sky until I see you again."

"My soul shall be empty without you," said Raven.

"Give your mother my greetings. She must be a Beloved Woman to have borne so fine a son."

Raven hugged Drum. As he settled himself on the keg that served as a seat on the ferry, Drum inquired about Punk Plugged In's family. Punk Plugged In stared at the ground as he answered and the round birthmark on his cheek reddened like the glowing tinder for which he'd been named.

As the boat pulled away, Raven heard Drum begin to chant in his rumbling, conjurer's voice. He was protecting his son on his journey.

The water of the Hiwassee River was much higher than usual. Some of the cabins in the village had been flooded. *When Tecumseh sends a sign, he doesn't give half measure*, Raven thought. *I wonder if he parted the Detroit River for his army to cross?*

Raven walked through countryside that looked as though nature had been waging war. The umber sun shone dully through a thick haze of smoke and dust that seemed to cut off heat as well as light. He had to detour around fallen trees whose trunks were thicker than he was tall. Rivers and springs had disappeared or changed course. Fish lay rotting in dry beds where streams had been. The small villages of the Real People were often in shambles or abandoned. Raven's anxiety increased when it became obvious Maryville couldn't have escaped damage.

The settlers' shanties and the jagged stumps in their half-cleared fields reached farther south than before. Raven resented them. They meant he would have to start his mental readjustment earlier. Reluctantly, he began the change from the red to the white way of thinking, from The Raven to Sam Houston. It was always like waking from a pleasant dream and finding his house had fallen into disrepair while he slept.

He walked into town as the sun was setting, washing the buildings in an unnatural reddish glow. *Rather like hell*, Sam thought. Then he smelled Toole's tannery. Toole had added more hide houses, open sheds that did little to contain the odor. *More like hell's privy.*

The streets were littered with trash as usual. There were piles of construction materials for new buildings, and ruins of those that weren't rebuilt after the earthquake. There were forty families in Maryville now. Some of them weren't careful where they threw their household garbage. Not all of it ended up in the ravine of Pistol Creek. But there was a big new church and more stores. Russell had added to his inn. Two stage lines stopped there now. One of them went from the Carolinas to Nashville, and the other from Georgia to Knoxville.

"Wal, looky here," someone called out. "A buzzard's come home to roost." Sam turned to look into the pale eyes of Dirty Dutch. He was back in town. *I'd've thought someone would've given him an extra buttonhole long ago.* Sam stared silently at him, as though viewing an insect through a lens. He was too tired and unhappy to argue with him. Dutch started to say something, thought better of it, spit in Sam's direction, and turned away.

Sam was too weary to gloat. He didn't realize how much he had grown and how strong he had become in his two and a half years with the Real People. His broad shoulders were straining the latest hunting shirt Sally Ground Squirrel had made him. He wore his leggings and moccasins, his loincloth and blue-and-white three-point trade blanket with careless grace. But in the streets of Maryville, such clothes carried an air of savagery.

Nor was Sam aware of a look in his blue eyes and a set to his muscular body that hadn't been there when he'd left town the first time. Dutch couldn't have described the changes either, but his instincts recognized them and avoided tangling with him.

Sam only knew he was hungry and thirsty and tired. The small amount of fallen snow did little to cover the town's disarray. Most of it was mud-spattered or churned into an icy mire under a steely sky. The bleakness matched Sam's mood. He pulled his blanket tighter around him. He knew it was irrational, but as a white man, he felt the cold more.

His moccasins padded softly on the boards of Russell's porch. He pushed open the door and entered the noisy, smoky room. The noise stopped.

"Howdy, stranger," said Russell from behind the bar. "What for you today?"

"I ain't no stranger, Rus, and you know it. Give me a drink of black jack. No. Make it two."

"Sorry, Sam. Didn't recognize you in that get-up." Sam leaned his back against the high bar. He propped his elbows behind him, on the top of it, something few were tall enough to do. He surveyed the roomful of men. Most of them resumed their conversations and arguments around the tables. *More dandies in the crowd*, Sam thought. *More buckled shoes and kneebreeches. Maryville's importing a higher class of riff-raff.*

"Sam Houston, you old savage. Bring your tail over here, dust it off, and sit it down," shouted John Cusack. His boots slid off the table and hit the floor with a thud as he stood up.

Sam grabbed a dried salted fish from the bunch that hung over the blackjack barrel. With two glasses clenched in one big hand, and chewing on the fish, he wended his way among the tables. He avoided the dark puddles of tobacco juice where he could. Wading through tobacco juice in moccasins wasn't the same as doing it in boots. His friends were sitting in a corner, near the fire.

"How are you, John?" Raven asked.

"Fine as frog hair," said Cusack.

"Same old swipers, I see." Sam grinned.

"Sit." Cusack pulled over another chair.

"Thanks, but I'd rather stand." Sam shook hands with Zachariah Woods and Jesse Bean and embraced Cusack, slapping him on the back. Cusack was thirty and the silver in his brown hair and beard made him seem older. Zach Woods was sixteen and Jess, although as big as a man, was barely fourteen. They regarded Cusack as a man of infinite age and wisdom.

"Been killing chickens?" asked Zach. "You got feathers in your hair."

Sam pulled the falcon feather from his long, thick queue and twirled it absentmindedly in his fingers. The headmen had awarded it to him for being the strongest man on the village ball play team.

"Just part of a mosquito I swatted. They grow them big down on the Hiwassee."

"If you're a sample, I'll believe that," said Cusack. "If you were a steer I'd say you were ready for market."

"Soon he'll be so tall he can get his hair cut in heaven and his shoes shined in hell," said Zachariah. Jesse lifted the hem of Sam's hunting shirt.

"What are you doing, Jess?" Sam jerked away and swatted him.

"Just wanted to see what you injuns wear under those shirts."

"The suit God tailored for me. And if you want to keep the hair He gave you, you'll watch your hands."

"Brash as a young colt, Jess is," said Cusack. "We caught him smuggling a red ear into the corn shucking a few months ago. He intended to produce it so he could kiss a gal. Our boy's growing up." Jess blushed. His round, smooth face turned even redder than usual. He took a long pull at his drink.

"Look at him swipe it off though," said Sam.

"Be careful, Jess," said Zachariah. "Last time you drank too much you tried to help a rain barrel across the street."

"It was dark," muttered Jess.

"To chivalry." Cusack held up his tankard.

"To revelry," added Zachariah.

"To ribaldry," said Sam.

"It's good to see you back, you miserable walkabout," said Cusack.

"It's good to be back." Sam was relieved to find he meant it.

"It's been dull as preaching without you," said Zach.

"What persuaded you to leave the Indians? Did Tecumseh's twitching shake you from the nest?"

"I'm worried about my mother and sisters. Was there much damage here?" Sam asked.

"It's hard to tell," said Jesse. "We're never sure from day to day if the buildings are going up or coming down."

"The place is growing." Sam stirred the fire with a poker and threw another log on.

"It's growing to admiration," said Zach.

"Your family's all right, Sam," said Cusack. "That's one helluva house your mother built. It stood through it all. I reckon she'll be glad to see you."

"Speaking of the late excitement," said Zach. "I had a hell-fired ride the other day."

"Zach's about to load up lies and scatter them broadshot," said Cusack.

"This is the truth, boys."

"Zach," said Sam. "You wouldn't know truth if you fucked it."

"Was it an elephant you rode, Zach?"

"Naw. I was up in the mountains huntin' bear. And the ground commenced to rumble and bump like a dog with fleas. So I grabbed ahold of a maple. Me and that maple rode four acres of land two hundred yards down the side of that mountain."

"To veracity." Sam extended his glass in another toast.

"To mendacity."

"To audacity."

"Say," said Jesse, weaving a little. "Did I ever tell you boys about the time my grandmother was tied to the stake with faggots piled around her feet. And a thousand screaming savages ready to broil her?"

"No more'n a thousand times," said Sam. "I met the woman who saved her. It pains me to admit it, boys. But that tale Jess has been spinning for years is actually true."

The noise in the room increased as talk turned to argument. Men began to shout and gesture wildly.

"Actually, Sam," said Cusack calmly. "We've had more important matters to discuss than earthquakes and such." He nodded around them. "Fun's a-foot. There's talk of war."

"With Britain? There's been talk of that for years," said Sam.

"Wal," said Zach. "Dame Rumor's jaw must be plumb wore to a nubbin these days."

"There's a quantity of war news from young Henry Clay and his Hawks," said Cusack. "But Papist that I am, I'll wait for the sacrament of confirmation."

"I reckon I'll be going out to the farm now," said Sam. "It's a long walk, another ten miles." He drained his second glass of blackjack, then gestured with it at the ragtag assembly in the tap room. "Don't let these sons of Mars start the war without me."

"Will you enlist?" asked Cusack.

"Not for a while. I have to pay off bills in town."

"How do you plan to do that?" asked Jesse.

"I'll think of something."

"You're not considering work, are you?" asked Zach. "You've been a shining example, an inspiration in the endeavor of loafing."

"The Mounted Gunmen still muster every Saturday," said Cusack. "We'll save you a place in line."

"Are you sure you can't stay awhile?" Zach looked around with satisfaction. "Passions are rising. There'll be a bully row before the evening's aged much. And you can tell us about life with the red-skinned gentry."

"Later," said Sam.

Outside, the Nashville stage had arrived, and the taproom filled with more people. Smoke lay thick in a layer just above everyone's head. A line of cloaks and jaunty, low-crowned beaver hats with upturned brims hung from pegs near the door.

A traveler approached Sam and his friends. He was dressed in a waist-length velvet frock coat with tails that reached the backs of his thighs. His skin-tight yellow nankeen trousers disappeared into slate-gray boots that came almost to his knees. The boots were unusual in that they fit him well, had delicate pointed toes, and they were clean. His ruffled white linen shirt had a high, stiff collar with a red silk cravat tied in a floppy bow. The ends of the bow were tucked into the man's coat.

As he walked, he ran his fingers through his hair to disarrange it properly. It stood out all over his head in what was called the hedgehog style. He must have had Republican tendencies, because he was wearing his hair in a French fashion. And he wore the long trousers of the Republicans, the liberal party. Zach whistled.

"Togged out in first-rate style, ain't he, boys."

"Hairdo looks like he's been hiking backwards through a hurricane," muttered Jesse.

"Don't reckon he shovels much soft fodder in that outfit," observed Sam.

The man put a manicured hand on the back of the chair Sam had never used. His long, lace cuffs fell over his fingertips.

"Pardon me, gentlemen, my party begs the use of this chair."

"Our friend here will be returning in a few days," said Zach, nodding toward Sam. "We're saving it for him."

"Give him the chair, you latrine lizard." Mad Mountain McCabe graced them with a look that seemed to have mass and weight all its own. He wasn't being chivalrous, just belligerent. The stranger smiled nervously at him. He wasn't sure he wanted McCabe for an ally.

"Is this wise, Zach?" muttered Sam.

"Of course," said Zach, rolling up his sleeves. "I'm a horse. My father can lick any man in Tennessee, and I can whip my father. I'm a screamer and a son of a screamer." Zach turned to McCabe. "Forgive me, McCabe," he said sweetly. "I didn't know this here frogeater was your girlfriend."

Sam backed gingerly toward the door as McCabe began the slow process of surging to his feet. His rising was an undertaking that occurred in stages, as though coordinating his entire body at once was too difficult a task for his brain.

As Sam crossed the porch, he heard the first table go over in a shattering of glass.

Chapter 16

Sam ignored the laughter as he tacked his notices up around town. Even his friends had started calling him Professor Houston. And they weren't being respectful.

"Do you really think your degree from the Indian University qualifies you to teach?" asked Zachariah.

"You're only nineteen, Sam, not much oldern'n your pupils will be," Cusack gently reminded him.

Sam walked down the splintery plank sidewalk. Without comment, he nailed another handbill on the courthouse bulletin board. It hung there along with lists of jurors, advertisements for lost cattle, slaves, and hunting hounds, legal notices, and the tavern lottery numbers. Sam had been getting the same reaction ever since he announced his intention to start a school.

"Eight dollars a term!" Cusack whistled as he read the handbill.

"That's two dollars more'n they charge at the Academy." Jesse craned to see over John's shoulder. He couldn't read, but he wouldn't admit it.

"I'm only asking for one third of it in cash," said Sam. "The rest can be paid in corn and calico."

"You gonna hold classes in Russell's tavern? You do a lot of lecturing there," said Zachariah.

"I'll use the old Kennedy schoolhouse. Maybe board with the Kennedys."

"I wish you well, Sam. But if the venture should . . . uh, not arrive at your expectations, you can do carpentry with me," said Cusack.

In the hour after dawn, Sam stood in the doorway of his small schoolhouse and looked out over his kingdom. It was mid May, 1812. Spring planting was over. Children would have no serious duties until harvest time. It was the first day of Sam's school term.

The one-room cabin stood on a hill covered with flowers. It was shaded by oaks and maples, hickories, pecans, and sourwoods. The trees and hills were the new, brilliant green of spring under an indigo sky. To the east, ranks of gray-blue mountains faded and became gauzier with distance. Hundreds of birds clamored overhead. The cold spring nearby muttered its way over moss-covered rocks. A raccoon ambled by, realized he wasn't alone, and hustled off through the bushes.

As idyllic as his corner of the world was, Sam had no illusions about his students. Most of them wouldn't be here because they wanted to be. Sam couldn't blame them on a day like this. He was almost grateful only nine boys had registered. Sam rarely had doubts. But he had some now, as from the regal height of the cabin's third step he watched his pupils assemble.

They shouted and jostled. They hit each other with knots tied in the ends of their handkerchiefs. They insulted and cuffed each other, and peeked into each other's lunch baskets. They snatched caps off the smaller boys' heads and skimmed them into the branches overhead. Some of them were so clean they looked like they had been scrubbed with a stiff brush. Others looked like they had already put in a windy day behind a plow.

Sam rapped loudly on the doorframe with his lead knuckles. He pointed his switch at the loudest, dirtiest boy.

"What's your name?" he asked.

"What's it to you?" the boy said sullenly. One tooth was broken and his greasy hair almost covered his sallow face.

"Well, Mr. Whatsittoyou," said Sam, "wash up at the spring before you come in. That goes for you and you and you." He pointed his switch at three others.

"I shall not," said the first boy.

"Then you shall not enter," said Sam. The three smaller boys filed off to the spring. The biggest one didn't move. *It seems I'll have only eight pupils*, Sam thought. With his switch, he motioned the others inside. Except for the two youngest, they chose to sit on benches at the back of the room.

The three freshly washed boys joined them. They had left more dirt on then they had cleaned off, but Sam wasn't going to quibble. He had made his point. While he sharpened his quill and the two six-year-olds passed out the pens Sam had made, the others kept up a steady murmur and fidgeting. *Like a coopful of chickens with mites.* The door slammed open. Sam nodded pleasantly to the scowling boy in the doorway.

"Thank you, Mr. Whatsittoyou. You look much better." *God will forgive me that small lie,* Sam thought.

"Smith," the boy muttered as he stalked by Sam's tall desk.

"I beg your pardon?" Sam asked politely.

"Name's Smith."

"Sir." Sam, still pleasant, tapped his switch lightly and casually on the edge of his desk.

"Sir." The answer was almost inaudible.

"I beg your pardon?"

"Sir!"

"Good. Welcome, Mr. Smith." *This will be a long day,* he thought. He flashed the class his most engaging smile. "This first day of school reminds me of the farmer who sent his hound to college." As he told the story, he walked among the benches looking at the books the boys had brought with them. Most of them clutched tattered bluebacks or primers that had been in their families for years. One had a copy of Shakespeare. Sam began asking each in turn to read for him, if he was able. The beginners, the third form, would be the largest group.

He assigned the bigger boys their places at the high tables running along three sides of the building. The tables were formed by the long wooden shutters that were hinged at the bottom, lowered downward and propped in the horizontal position. When school was over, they were closed to cover the windows. The windows were slits made by leaving out part of a log in each wall. Daylight was the only illumination.

Sam was careful to place each boy with more than an arm and a ferule's length between them. Any less space and they'd be hitting each other. The boys would write standing up.

The spacing didn't last. The second day, there were two more students. The day after that, three more. Word had gotten out that

Professor Houston was as amusing as he was instructive. The class grew, until Sam had to order more benches from John Cusack. By June the room was crowded with thirty-five students, and Sam was turning away the overflow. The boys used the writing desks in shifts, and they worked elbow to elbow.

The last student to apply before the class was filled was Jesse Bean. He arrived late and stood a bit defiantly in the doorway, twiddling his sweat-stained hat in his hands. His new shoes were tied together and thrown over his shoulder to keep them from getting dusty on the five-mile walk to school. He had wet his long, blond hair at the spring and plastered it to his head.

"Morning, Jess," said Sam. "Bill, Jonas, make room there for Mr. Bean. You're in time for lunch. But classes start at seven of a morning."

"Yes, Sa . . . ." Jess faltered. "Sir."

Lunch was Sam's favorite time of day. He ate with his students under the trees. He often swapped food with them, bartering what Sarah Kennedy had put up for him. While the boys ran and played ball, he would cut a sourwood stick and trim it in spirals. Then he'd thrust half of it into the stove if the morning was cool. The flames turned that half blue, leaving the other half white.

One day, about the middle of June, he tarried after sending the boys inside to begin their parsing. One of the two six-year-olds had been stung by a horsefly. The child tried not to cry while Sam hunkered down to inspect the welt.

"Barnaby," he said conspiratorially. "I'm going to give you an ancient Indian remedy." Barnaby sniffed and looked impressed. Sam chanted a charm Tiana had taught him for spider bites. It was common with the children of the Real People.

"*Ghananisgi saghonige, ghananisgi une'guh. Gha! Nigada.* Blue Spider, White Spider. Now! Both of you!" He repeated it four times. Then he spit on the welt and rubbed the saliva into the wound. "Feel better?" he asked. The child smiled and nodded. Sam rose and followed him slowly to the schoolhouse. He was congratulating himself on how well he was handling everything when he heard the crash of falling benches.

"Fight! Fight!"

He cleared the top step in one bound. His kingdom was in chaos. Smith and Jesse were rolling on the floor. Other fights had broken out among their supporters. Sam didn't try to separate them. He waded into the fray. He grabbed boys by the backs of their collars and the waists of their trousers and threw them into a pile on top of Smith and Bean.

Ignoring the muffled cries of those on the bottom, he continued until there were twenty boys in a squirming heap. Then he began to flail at them impartially with his rod and rap heads with his lead knuckles. He got grim satisfaction from the solid crack of metal on skulls, and from the howls of pain. When his arm tired, he let the pile sort itself out. Its parts limped back to their benches and sat gingerly.

"There'll be no fighting here!" Sam roared, working himself into a good imitation of fury. But inside, he blamed himself. It was Friday. He should have known better than to leave the boys alone on Friday. He had soon learned that no serious work could be done then. So he'd begun recitation time. Each student had to commit something to memory and recite it. This Friday, nine-year-old Alexander Kennedy volunteered to begin. He shuffled nervously to the front of the class. Sam prepared to enjoy himself. Alex usually recited an original composition.

"Sheila McGuire's Courtship," he said. "By Alexander Kennedy."

Sheila McGuire, come set you down by me and I'll tell you your doom.
Your eyes are like dogwoods when they are in bloom.
Your long turnip nose shall ne'er be forgotten.
Your teeth, by Jobe, are every one rotten. . . .

"War!" The door slammed open and Zachariah Woods stood panting in the opening. "War! Billy Phillips just rode through town, headed for Nashville. It's war. Come on, Jess, Sam. Cusack's calling up the volunteers."

Within seconds the classroom was empty. Sam heard the boys yelling, their voices becoming fainter as they pelted down the path toward Maryville. Zachariah turned to follow them.

"Zach, are you sure?" Sam called.

"Hell yes, Sam." Zachariah's brown eyes were almost crazy with excitement. "Phillips left Washington less than a week ago to carry the news. He's been riding hell-bent for leather ever since—almost a hundred miles a day. Following in his dust was a recruiter. Governor Blount is calling for volunteers. Each man gets a horn of powder, a dozen flints, and lead for a hundred bullets."

"One hundred bullets," said Sam wryly. "They obviously expect a war of short duration. And do they provide horses or uniforms?"

"Naw. But they want you to bring a rifle and not a smoothbore. And dark blue or butternut homespuns for uniform." Zachariah could linger no longer. "Hurry, Sam," he shouted over his shoulder.

Sam didn't follow him right away. He closed the shutters and swept out the school, jobs the boys usually did. War had finally come, but he had agreed to teach thirty-five students until mid November. And Sam Houston kept his word.

Tiana sniffed as she turned the handle of Mother Elizabeth's weasel, a spidery contraption that wound yarn into skeins. At regular intervals the wooden gears clicked to mark off the twentieth turn. Susannah silently counted the clicks. Six clicks and a skein was wound. As Tiana and Nannie sang, Tiana tried to turn the handle so the click of the weasel matched the key word in the song their father had taught them.

> *All around the mulberry bush,*
> *The monkey chased the weasel.*
> *The monkey thought 'twas all in fun.*
> *Pop! Goes the weasel.*

"You're turning it too slowly," said Nannie. "Let me do it." Tiana gave up the handle. Her arm was tired anyway. But she went on singing, partly to cover the sound of voices in the other room, and partly to keep from crying.

> *A penny for a spool of thread,*
> *A penny for a needle.*
> *That's the way the money goes.*
> *Pop! Goes the weasel.*

At breakfast, James and John had announced their intention to enlist as scouts in the United States Army. Now Jack and Jennie were trying to dissuade them. Joseph and William watched with interest. They wanted to go to war too, but dared not mention it to their father. Jack's face was livid as he paced back and forth in front of the fire. Tiana could hear him over the sound of her own singing.

"Why should you risk your lives for the bloody Americans? They despise you, don't you know that? And they make little secret of it." Tiana's singing faltered and died. She didn't want to hear, but she couldn't stop herself from listening.

"We're not joining the local volunteers, the Tennesseans or the Georgians. We're joining the army. They don't hate us."

"Ah, lad." Jack shook his head. "They're all of a piece, the Americans. God's chosen. They hate everyone not of their color or politics or religion. And what about the farm? Who'll do the planting?"

"It's November. The corn and tobacco are harvested. You won't need us until spring," said James. "We want to uphold the honor of the Real People. Show the Americans we too are brave."

"We want to share in the glory," said John.

"Glory," said Jack. "Now there's an airy commodity. How do you think your mothers will feel when you're brought home like sacks of wheat, all the glory leaking from the holes in ye."

"We'll be scouts, not soldiers. And we'll be careful." This was very difficult for the boys. Children of the Real People didn't defy their parents. But war didn't happen along every day, not like in the old times. They might never have another chance to win honors and eagle feathers and to boast in the eagle dance.

Jennie spoke up from her darning.

"If you're killed, brothers, Mother Elizabeth and I will grieve the rest of our lives," she said. "But you may have to kill others. Have you thought on that?"

"We'll do what our duty requires."

"The Real People stopped killing." There was irony in Jennie's voice. "The white men convinced us it's uncivilized to wage war."

"This is different," James mumbled. "We have to defend our homeland."

"British recognize the Real People's right to their land. The Americans don't," said Jennie.

"The Council decided to ally with the Americans. And all our clan brothers are going."

Even as Jack argued, he knew it was futile. He had seen that look in young men's faces before. He had seen it in a mirror thirty-five years ago. Patriotism. Loyalty. It was all a jig to the tune of circumstance. There were Americans who still hated Jack for being a Tory in the late war. Now his own sons would side with the Americans their father had fought.

Tiana and Nannie and Susannah stood in the doorway and heard their father capitulate.

"If you're going, you may as well be equipped," he muttered. "Hell-fired government thinks an army can win wars on air and empty promises and outmoded weapons. Damned muskets'll hit just about anything, as long as you aren't aiming at it." He took two rifles down from their pegs over the mantle. "You'll have to go afoot. We have no horses to spare."

"Please don't go!" Tiana threw her arms around James.

"Don't fret, sister." He smoothed her soft hair. James and Tiana had an special affinity for each other. Maybe it was because, with their long black hair and dark blue eyes, they resembled each other.

Jennie went upstairs to gather the boys' clothing for the trip. Mother Elizabeth went into the kitchen to pack food. Jack sat brooding in front of the fire.

"A pox on war," he grumbled, loudly enough for all to hear. "Spend all that time and money to raise sons, only to have ha'pence worth of lead snuff them out." *And will your strong, young bodies fall and decay? Will you become flowers of the forest?* he thought. Jack hadn't used the most telling argument to keep his sons at home. It would have had no more effect than the others. And it would have upset the family. When the Real People decided to join with the Americans, they declared war also on the Creeks, their neighbors.

The Rogers family might well need its sons to defend itself from more than the Creeks and the British. There were Americans who refused to consider any Indian an ally. War excused acts that weren't as likely to happen in peace.

Silently, Jack planned. They would need stouter shutters for the windows, and an opening from the house to the root cellar. They should stock a cave or two in the hills, for sanctuary, in case they couldn't get to the garrison. They would have to sell less crops and hoard more. They would need more fire buckets. And powder and lead and weapons, if there was any for sale. Jennie and Elizabeth should practice shooting, though they could each drop a squirrel at fifty yards. "Hell-fire," he muttered around his pipe. "I thought we were done with this lunacy."

"Daughters." Jennie's arms were piled high with clothes. "Check these for mending, and darn the socks. Sons." She nodded to Joseph and William. "Get the lead stock from the barn, and fetch a ham from the smokehouse. Bring one of last year's." James had already laid the family's guns in a neat row and was mixing vinegar and salt for cleaning them. John was preparing bullet molds.

With tears in her eyes, Tiana sorted through the patched panta-

loons and shirts, the linen small clothes and jackets, all of which
had seen service on more than one Rogers boy. Tiana was sad not
only because she would miss James and John. She wanted to go
with them. The song she had been singing echoed in her head.

> *I've no time to sit and sigh.*
> *No time to wait til by and by.*
> *Kiss me quick, I'm off, good-bye.*
> *Pop! Goes the weasel.*

It was October 14, 1812. Maryville was in an uproar. Sam had been
obliged to cancel classes, even though there were only a few weeks
left in the term. Now he stood watching the volunteers of Captain
Cusack's company assemble.

News from the north had been bad all summer. The war was not
going well for the Americans. A doddering General Hull had lost
Detroit in August and hundreds of weeping, raging American soldiers surrendered their guns. Tecumseh, forced by circumstance to
ally with the British, watched them. In Maryville, someone whitewashed the letters "Roast in hell, Hull" on the side of Russell's
livery. It was up to the Southerners to save the nation's honor.

There were faded banners of red, white, and blue bunting left
over from past Fourth of July celebrations. Everyone for miles around,
including the dogs and pigs, lined the main street. People waved
small flags with seventeen stars scattered randomly in the blue field,
and greeted each member of Cusack's company with loud huzzas.
Even the brilliant reds and golds of the trees seemed to celebrate
with bursts of color.

A small corps of homegrown pipers and drummers shared a makeshift reviewing stand with Maryville's officialdom. As clerk of the
court, Sam's brother John sat up there. *A big frog in a small pond*,
Sam thought, with a pinch of malice. The pipers were approximating
"Yankee Doodle" to the ragged cadence of the drums. The Reverend
Mark Moore peered over the edge of the stand, as though gauging
the distance to the ground in case of collapse. The circuit judge's
lips moved silently as he practiced his speech. Children eddied in
and out under the platform like the autumn leaves that blew about.

Since September Sam's class had dwindled as the older boys
mooched off to drill with the volunteers, or to just hang around to

hear the latest war news. Many of them, like Jesse Bean, lied about their age to enlist for this sixty-day period.

Sam knew his students were disappointed in him for not joining Cusack's company. They idolized Professor Houston and wanted him to be a hero. For that matter, he wanted to be a hero. He wanted it desperately. There were times when he physically had to resist the urge to throw down his sourwood rod and slam out of the classroom. He wanted to buy Andrew Kennedy's rifle, mount a horse, and ride off to war.

Sam's bill in town was paid and he had money left over. But he still owed a debt to the boys who frowned over their splotchy copy work or whooped when they spelled a word right at the weekly bee. This term would probably be the only schooling most of them would get. And the term wasn't over. Sam wasn't going to cheat them.

"Halloo, Houston!" Zachariah Woods rode toward him, against the flow of men gathering at the reviewing stand. Zach wore the dubious uniform of brown knee-length frock, trousers, and moccasins. The knap of his brown felt slouch hat was worn bare. His straight, dark hair fell to his shoulders. "Where's your horse?"

"In the stable."

"Well, mount up, man. Time's a-hastin'. The Brits and the Spaniards are about to take New Orleans. And we're going to conquer all of Florida. It'll be a thundering good time. There'll be loot and then some."

"Will there be?" Sam said dryly as the boy swayed on his father's plow horse. Zachariah apparently hadn't stopped celebrating the night before. He had been champing at the bit all summer for this. He had even appeared for three out of every four of the Mounted Gunmen's drills. He was ready to beat the British all to smash, as he put it.

"I'm going to sit this one out," Sam said. "But you enjoy the dance."

"But Sam—"

"I'm not going, dammit!" Even drunk, Zach could hear the misery in his friend's voice.

"Come on, Zach! We'll miss the speeches and the whiskey." Jesse waved at them.

"Good-bye, Sam. I wish you was going. It won't be near as much fun without you." Zach leaned down and put out his hand. Sam grasped it firmly.

"Dodge the lead, you landloper. And leave a few of the ladies in New Orleans unconquered. I plan to get there myself before this is over."

"You'd best hustle then. We're going to finish this off in jig time. Sixty days at most." Zach grinned. His handsome face was boyish and innocent. Sam realized he loved him. He loved Jesse, too, and even crusty Cusack. They'd had some rousing coon hunts together in the past year. He would miss them. He was glad they'd only be gone two months.

"Where's your coat?" Sam asked. He knew Zach's family was poor, but the boy needed a coat.

"Ain't got one."

"Take this." Sam stripped off his own sheepskin one and handed it up to him. "Winter's coming."

"Oh, hell, Sam. Thanks. But I won't need it. Mammy was a polar bear and Pappy was an Eskeemo. I got ice water in my veins. Besides, we're headed for the sunny south. We'll be back before first snowfall."

"Take it as a memento and give it back when you return."

"As a memento, then." Zach tucked it under the leather straps holding his rolled blanket. He touched his fingers to the brim of his hat, wheeled his horse, and trotted down the street.

Sam hardly heard the speeches. He felt caught in the cage of his responsibilities. How could he let his friends ride off without him? What if the war did end before their enlistment was up? Over the noise of the shouting and music, Sam heard Drum's soft voice. *Wisdom is knowing what to ask and whom to ask. You can learn grace from the panther, power from the bear, patience from the spider. And of those three virtues, patience is the most important.*

And the most difficult, Beloved Father.

" 'Shall we who have clamored for war, now skulk in a corner?' " The judge was quoting that Nashville lawyer, Jackson, the one Governor Blount put in charge of the West Tennessee forces. He hadn't much experience as a general, but he was a fighter, they said. Wolfish about the head and shoulders. His friends said he was unpolished. His enemies, and he had plenty, said he was uncouth. But Sam had to admit he earned good marks on rhetoric.

" 'Are we the titled slaves of George the Third? The military conscripts of Napoleon? Or the frozen peasants of the Russian Czar? No!' " The overweight circuit judge was working himself into a lather with Jackson's words. " 'We are the freeborn sons of the only republick now existing in the world. The period of youth is the season for martial exploits. How pleasing the prospect to promenade into a distant country.' "

The speeches ended three hours later. Cusack's company of thirty-five men rode slowly out of town with guns firing and a shouting throng behind them. Those who wore slouch hats had stuck ever-green sprigs in their hatbands. Others wore their usual coon- or fox- or mink-skin caps with the tails dangling. The tassels and fringe on their hunting smocks swung jauntily.

Each man carried a small-bore rifle and wore a tomahawk and scalping knife in his waistband. The brass and silver inlay on their rifles flashed in the sunlight. The tow cloth of their shirts and breeches had been steeped in a tan vat until it was the color of dry leaves. It was much more practical for wilderness warfare than the scarlet and white and blue uniforms of the regular army.

They were men with bark on. Even if it was only two months, they would be telling stories about this adventure for years. Sam wondered if he would ever have stories to tell. Would he ever get a chance to prove himself worthy of the name Drum had given him, The Raven?

"Damnation," he muttered. "Damnation and hell-fire."

Chapter 17

A month passed. Sam ended the term with the traditional breaking-up ceremony. His scrubbed and starched boys recited to a full house. Even Alexander Kennedy, who had recited only comic verse all term, waved the flag.

> *See our western brothers bleed.*
> *British gold has done the deed.*
> *Child and mother, son and sire,*
> *Beneath the tomahawk expire.*

December brought terrible cold. The old timers swore they couldn't remember a worse winter. The chill seemed to match the winter in Sam's heart. Rumors said no foe had appeared at Natchez and the promised battle at New Orleans hadn't taken place. But although the Mounted Gunmen's two-month enlistment was up, there was no word of them. It was as though the vast, dense forests to the south and west had swallowed them without a trace.

Tavern talk that winter was of Napoleon's invasion of Russia. Napoleon had been keeping the British busy in Europe, diverting forces they would have used against the Americans. If Napoleon were defeated, the Americans would feel the pressure of an enemy with only one front to defend. The Russian winter was proving a formidable foe. It might accomplish what the combined forces of Europe could not.

Sam spent a lot of time in the taverns. At home he had to listen to his mother talk about the virtue of honest labor. The only alternatives Sam could see in Maryville were farming and shopkeeping, and neither appealed to him. To hold his mother at bay and to delay decisions for a while, he applied for the winter term at the Porter Academy.

The threat of working for a living was an effective goad to learning. Sam endured three months of discipline and rules. But it was clear he wasn't cut out to be a serious student either. When he wasn't in school or asleep, he was in Russell's tavern.

He was there now, sitting alone in a corner and feeling sorry for himself. He was lonely, more than half drunk, and brooding about life. Without his friends to distract him, the Indian crept back into Sam. Looking out over the usual crowd in Russell's he felt like a predator—a wolf or a catamount or a silent hunter of the Real People, stalking his prey. He didn't belong here.

He had a sudden stab of longing for the musical talk of the Real People, for Hiwassee Town and the hunts with James and John. He thought about going back to see Drum. It was tempting. But James and John had marched off to war. And Sam couldn't bear to slink back to Drum without earning honor in battle. He would return to Hiwassee in triumph, and worthy of his name, The Raven, or he wouldn't return at all.

Sam propped his big boots onto a chair in front of him and tilted his own seat back against the wall. He half closed his eyes, which made the smoke-filled room even more dreamlike.

He was so deep in his revery he thought the drum was only part of it. Finally he shook his head and realized the tavern was emptying and there were several drums playing outside. His boots crashed to the floor and his chair overturned as he bolted out of it. He joined the crowd converging on the square in front of the courthouse.

It was what Zach Woods would have called a bully show. An army recruiter was there with a company of men, and a real, live brass band. Every man was dressed in a blue coatee with red collar and cuffs, white pantaloons, and brown gaiters. Their low shoes were polished with lamp black. They wore natty, black beaver hats in civilian style, with white pompoms on the side. The brass buckles on the white belts crossed over their chests flashed in the late March sunlight. They were carrying smoothbore muskets instead of newer rifles, but to Sam the soldiers looked magnificent.

He craned to see over the crowd as the men of the color guard snapped through a precision drill with their flags. Sam stood on one foot and then the other while the sergeant rambled on about the glory and adventure of war. Finally he put a handful of silver dollars on the dirty head of a drum and called for recruits. While the two trumpets, a fife, and a tuba assaulted everyone's sensibilities, Sam elbowed his way forward. He was the first to collect a dollar.

"Ho, Houston," someone shouted. "Gonna be a private? Gonna kiss some officer's arse?"

Sam whirled and glared into the crowd of roughs from Russell's.

"And what have you craven souls to say about the ranks?" he roared, hands on hips. "Go to hell with your stuff! I would sooner honor the ranks than disgrace an appointment."

"Private Houston, polish my boots." Someone else took courage and jeered from the anonymity of the center of the pack.

Sam advanced on them, and they all drew back just a little.

"I'll polish my boots with your backside." He surveyed them with contempt. "You shall hear of me." Then he added in a quieter voice, "You shall hear of me."

When Sam walked up to his mother's house that evening, he paused on the gallery to admire the view. The house stood on a shelf that sloped toward the east where the mountains rose like old friends. He would finally be leaving this. Sam went inside and found his mother in the walnut-paneled main room.

Elizabeth Houston stood, straight and stern, in front of the glass-doored cupboard that held her cherished family china. When she struck that pose, she always reminded Sam of royalty holding audience.

"Samuel," she said.

"Yes, ma'am."

"Doctor Anderson visited while you were in Maryville. He says you do not apply yourself to lessons."

"I—"

She held up a strong, calloused hand with a plain gold band on the ring finger. "He says you lead the other boys in mischief during recitation and then charm your way out of retribution. He says he often determines to whip you. But you serve up such a pretty dish of excuses, he cannot."

"I plead guilty as charged." Sam didn't mention that Doctor Anderson probably lacked nerve to whip a lad who towered head and shoulders over him. "We mean no harm by the pranks we play. And Doctor Anderson's teaching of geometry is uninspiring."

"Don't criticize your elders. He says you've been dueling."

"It was only a prank. We pretended to fall out with each other, Will Bates and I. Our seconds loaded one pistol with poke berries and the other with corn mush. Someone snitched to Doctor Anderson. We waited until he and Reverend Moore stampeded from the school to prevent bloodshed. Then we blasted away at each other. The crimson juice on Will's shirt and the mush on mine made us seem mortally wounded. We fell, writhing and moaning on the ground." Sam staggered. " 'I am killed! I am killed!' " He grasped his belly with his hands, contorted his face in agony and sank down the wall until he sprawled, head lolling, on the floor.

Elizabeth laughed in spite of herself. No one could stay angry with Sam. It was like trying to hold a grudge against a big, friendly, if troublesome, puppy.

"Mother." Sam picked himself up. "I wish you could have seen their faces." Elizabeth realized with a pang how closely Sam resembled his namesake, his father. "When they found out they'd been deceived, they gave us 'Hail, Columbia,' I can tell you."

"What will I do with you, Samuel? Will you never grow up? You have just turned twenty years of age. You cannot travel the hard road of life in a sulky of smiles. Is there no occupation that appeals to you?"

"Yes, there is."

"For the love of the Almighty, what is it?"

"I enlisted today. I've come to beg your leave to join the army. I want to be a soldier."

"A soldier." Elizabeth bit her lower lip, a habit she had when perplexed. He was like his father in more than looks. His brothers were content to be shopkeepers and farmers and the courthouse clerk, but not this one. "A soldier," she said again.

"Yes. A recruiter, a sergeant, came through town today with a squad of men. Every one of them had white pantaloons and a waistcoat. And boots, black and shiny. They had flags, fluttering smartly in the breeze. They were splendid!"

Elizabeth had to smile. Back in Virginia she had been raised in the richest family in the valley. She had ridden in a carriage whose driver and footmen wore white pantaloons and waistcoats and shiny black shoes.

But for all Sam's reading and mother wit, for the past six years his world had been confined to an Indian village and Maryville and environs. His friends were the illiterates of the forests and taverns. Of course the sergeant looked splendid. Perhaps the army would be good for him. It might educate him in a hard, but effective, school.

"And you enlisted?" she asked.

"I took the silver dollar from the drumhead, yes." Sam pulled the coin from his pocket and flipped it in the air. He rubbed its surface with his thumb, partly to hide his nervousness.

"As what rank?"

"Private." Sam saw the disappointment in his mother's eyes. He had known it would be there.

But Elizabeth knew better than to forbid Sam's going. It had never worked in the past. And maybe this would be best. She did what mothers and fathers all over the frontier were doing. She reached for the gun that hung over the fireplace.

"It was your father's when he served with Morgan's Rifles." Sam knew that, of course. Elizabeth rarely spoke of the past. But during the rare times Samuel Houston, senior, had been home, he had gathered his children around him and reminisced. "Morgan's Brigade was the most famous and most honored in the Continental Army," Elizabeth continued. "If you ever disgrace your father's memory, my door is closed to you. I would rather all my sons fill an honorable grave than one of them flee to save his life."

"I won't disgrace you."

"I know you won't. When do you leave?"

"In a month. I'm to report to Knoxville the first of May."

Elizabeth Houston rotated the gold band on her finger and tugged at it until she was able to work it over her knuckles. When she gave it to him Sam read the single word etched inside: "Honor."

"Thank you," he said.

It took Sam thirty days to rise to the rank of sergeant. He was drilling a platoon when the remnants of the Maryville Mounted Gunmen straggled into the Knoxville encampment. They were part of a sorry column of old wagons and weary men on foot. It was early June, 1813. The Maryville men had traveled a thousand miles and back. They had been gone more than seven months. Sam recognized Zachariah Woods and John Cusack walking beside one of the wagons. Sam dismissed his men and ran to meet them.

"Zach! John! I thought I'd never see your raggedy arses again. Where are your horses?"

"Et 'em," said Zachariah.

Sam gripped each one in turn by the arm, then hugged him. He stepped back and noticed their bare feet.

"I thought you had five toes on each foot when you left, John," he said. "Where are the other two?"

"They froze and fell off." John wiggled the three remaining toes on his filthy, calloused foot.

"Great God, man! What happened to you? Where's Jesse?"

"Sad about Jess," said Zach. "He left his blankets to piss one night. Froze solid. We found him next morning."

"That's terrible!" Sam was horrified.

"Naw. It weren't so bad. We hung a lantern on him. Used him for a light post."

"He's lying as usual, Sam." Jesse's wan voice came from the wagon. Sam climbed onto the running board and peered over the high side. The stench of bile and feces was almost overpowering. Most of the men were suffering from fevers and the flux. Sam tried to ignore the smell and the buzzing of flies. Jess lay crowded in with the others, some of whom moaned and tossed. Others lay unnaturally still. Jess was pale and thin. His beard covered his face in a fine fuzz.

"Just seeing you improves my health." Jess smiled. "A dram might do me wonders." He crawled toward the tailgate, mumbling apologies to the men he jostled on the way. Sam helped him from the wagon and supported him, his arm around the boy's waist and Jess's arm around his shoulders.

"I have some fuel in my tent that'll stiffen your bones and starch your collar."

The four of them walked across the busy parade ground to the line of neat, white canvas tents. They sat on the two cots while Sam poured each of them a shot of rum. Then he sat on the box that served as a table.

"We heard Congress put a lid on Madison's plans to take Florida," he said. "The rumor was you all were vacationing at Natchez."

"Freezing our butts," said Zachariah. "I thank you for the coat, by the way. It saved my life. 'Course, it got stole somewhere toward the arse-end of February. I'm sorry, Sam. Red-hot stoves were safe from some of our thieving comrades in arms, but that's about all."

"Don't trouble yourself over it."

"Old Hickory was—"

"Old Hickory?" asked Sam.

"Andy Jackson," said John. "He's a tough one, he is. Earned the name on the march from Natchez. He walked the entire way. He commandeered food, supplies, wagons. Helped the sick, worked right alongside his men, clearing trails, building bridges. Ate what we did. When we did. Which wasn't often."

"Anyways," continued Zachariah. "Old Hickory was ready to place the eagle on the ramparts of Mobile, Pensacola, Saint Augustine, anywhere the government wanted to hang its hat. We were ready, Sam. We were willing. We were able."

"We were screwed." Jesse, too weak to sit, stretched out on his back on the empty cot.

"You have such a simple way of clarifying issues, Jess," said Cusack. "We were indeed screwed."

"How so?"

"Most of us, thinking there was glory . . ."

"And loot," added Zach.

"And loot, to be had in Florida, enlisted for another two months. But at the end of that time, about mid February, the Secretary of War sent orders to disband. Turn in all supplies and funds to that puffed-up pile of pigeon puke, General Wilkinson, and go home."

"And us a thousand miles from aforesaid home, in the middle of the worst winter anyone could remember," said Jesse.

"Well, Old Hickory was fit to be basted and barbecued," said Cusack. "He swore Wilkinson didn't have as much brains as the head on his beer."

"We always gathered around when Old Hickory commenced to rip. Unless he was ripping at us," said Zach. "He warms the air, he does. We made it through winter by the heat of his oaths."

"Wilkinson thought he had us militia where he wanted us," continued Cusack.

"By the balls," added Jess.

"He sent his recruiters to our camp to sign us up for the regular army. And truth to tell, we didn't have much choice. Weren't any of us thrilled with the prospect of a thousand-mile hike on an empty stomach through three-foot snowdrifts." Cusack stared gloomily into his tin mug. He drained it and held it out for a refill. "But Jackson put an end to Wilkinson's plans. He caught the first recruiter and held him off the ground by his shirt front." Cusack grabbed Zach to demonstrate. "Choked the man purple. Told him if he tried to seduce a single Tennessee volunteer into the regular army, he'd be drummed from the lines and a few other acts which discretion bids me not discuss."

"So Jackson put up his personal note to cover wagons and supplies and marched home at the head of his troops, in direct defiance of the Secretary of War's orders. There's a man for you." Zach held up his mug in toast.

"It weren't much fun," said Jesse before dropping off to sleep.

At thirteen, Tiana still had the smooth, golden-brown skin and huge innocent eyes of a child, but she was losing her coltish look. Her long legs were less knobby and no longer covered with scratches and scrapes. The angles of her body were softening. Her face was filling out, becoming the perfect frame for her strong, arched nose. She took more care with her waist-length hair these days. It was always clean and brushed and shiny.

She wore a cape of supple doeskin to keep out the October chill. War or no war, it was the time of the Great Medicine ceremony, when the Real People bathed in Long Man. Tiana had come to Hiwassee with her family, but she couldn't take part in the ritual. She had just begun her monthly flux. She felt lonely and shunned. This was the first Great Medicine ceremony she had ever missed.

It was just after dawn and she had come here to talk to the sacred cedar about it. She could feel the blood, warm and sticky on her thighs. The raw cotton Jennie had given her to bind between her legs with rags was soaked and smelly. Tiana was miserable. When she had told her mother about the blood, Jennie had taken her off by herself and given her a flint razor to shave the hair from the soft mound where her thighs met. She also gave her a small mirror and a pair of brass tweezers, to pluck hair from her face.

"You're a woman now," Jennie had said. "When your flux comes, you mustn't bathe in Long Man. You'll defile him and ruin the fishing besides. You mustn't cook or handle food or you'll make the men sick and weak. You can't allow the menstrual blood to fall on anything someone else might touch."

Tiana knew all that. She couldn't help but notice there were times when her mothers and sisters didn't do their usual chores. When she was young she thought them lucky to have the time to themselves. Now the price seemed too much to pay. If this was being a woman, she wanted none of it.

She was supposed to separate herself from the family too, but Jack said that was nonsense. "What do you mean, woman?" he would yell at Jennie whenever the subject came up. "Are my wives and daughters to sleep in an overturned barrel like the hounds?" But the shame was still there, no matter how much he denied it.

So Tiana was simply avoiding everyone. She came here to be alone. All day, the others would be feasting and dancing at the town house, and she felt too miserable to join them. She had the irrational fear they would know she was bleeding. The fact that all women went through this was of little comfort. Inside, her bowels cramped. Outside, she felt dirty. She sat at the base of the cedar with her cheek against the rough bark.

"*Gha*! Now! Brown Spider, You have just scattered my soul all about." The quavery voice startled Tiana, and she looked up, alarmed.

She tracked the sound to a dense thicket of laurel that shivered with the passage of something through it. Tiana clung to the tree and stared at the trembling leaves as the thing drew closer.

"Black Spider, You have just scattered my soul all about," said the shrill voice again. "Blue Spider, You have just scattered my soul all about. Red Spider, You have just scattered my soul all about." At the words "Red Spider," Spearfinger emerged from the bushes about ten feet from Tiana. Tiana gave a small cry and shrank back, but she didn't run away. Spearfinger had been reciting a simple charm to dispell enmity. It was so common even Tiana knew it. It wasn't the sort of charm a witch would say.

The old woman advanced slowly, holding out her right hand so Tiana could see that her right forefinger was normal. Tiana stared at it. The mythical Spearfinger had a long right arm, weighted at the end with her grotesque, sharpened finger.

"We are of one mind," Spearfinger said. "Everywhere you look, let there be a blue haze."

Tiana stared into Spearfinger's grimy face. She had never been this close to her. The deltas of deep wrinkles around her eyes and mouth were outlined by the dirt caked in them. Grandmother Elizabeth had told Tiana witches never looked anyone in the eyes, so she tested Spearfinger. The old woman seemed to know what she was doing. The two stared at each other for a minute or more.

"Do you want something of me, grandmother?" Tiana kept her voice calm, although her mouth felt dry. What if Grandmother Elizabeth were wrong?

"You will be attired in the Red Sunrise."

"What do you mean?" Tiana asked.

"The White Red Smoke has been aimed at your soul."

"Please, grandmother. I am young. I do not know the *idi gawe'sdi*, the ancient incantations."

But Spearfinger wasn't going to explain. That would lure her into the dull, still waters of sanity. She cocked her head and grinned. Tiana shuddered at the spectacle.

"Follow Grandmother four times above the treetops," said Spearfinger. "Sing her to her rest four times. She will dress you in her glowing robes."

"Where must I go to follow her, grandmother?" Tiana assumed Spearfinger meant the fast boys went on to become better hunters. For four days, they had to follow the sun with their eyes.

"The Place of the Blue Smoke."

"And what must I sing to her?"

"A Hawk song." Then Spearfinger cackled, spun around four times and hopped erratically off into the bushes like a mother bird luring a snake away from her nest.

Tiana thought about Spearfinger's words. She had never heard of a girl going on a fast. Her father wouldn't hesitate to let James or John or William or Joseph go. But he would forbid her. Of that she was sure. Four days alone in the mountains. She thought of the ginseng hunters and the bears and the Little People. She remembered the spirits that swarmed among the boulders and in the high passes, and the Thunder Men who strode along their invisible bridges from peak to peak.

Besides, a war was being fought. The young men of Hiwassee Town were in a ferment. The war songs and dances had been revived. The countryside was unsettled. There was no reason to go off alone. Spearfinger was crazy. She didn't know what she was talking about. But the longer Tiana sat, the stronger the feeling grew. She had to go.

When she went back to Sally Ground Squirrel's, the village was deserted. Tiana heard the drums and singing at the town house. She rolled a blanket and tied it so she could sling it across her back and checked her knife in its sheath on her belt. She put a flint in her pouch along with a whetstone. She took no food. If she needed any, she could easily find it. Elizabeth had taught her what plants were edible, and how to trap fish. And she could always make a blowgun.

With charcoal, she left a short note on a cane mat. She told her family not to worry. She would be back in five or six days. She set out for the mountains at an easy lope. She was used to traveling on foot from home on Rogers Branch to Hiwassee Town. Her long legs would carry her effortlessly for miles.

She climbed until she found a spot on the first ridge that seemed right, a small bald, covered with grass the color of unbleached muslin. It was surrounded on three sides by oaks and maples, all gold and red. On the fourth side the bald sloped downhill, giving her a view of a river slicing through the hardwoods of the cove floor. It narrowed as it threaded among the hills, and was finally lost to sight.

Tiana made sure there was water nearby for bathing at dawn. The stream flowed down a series of rock ledges. The huge rocks in and around it were covered with dark green moss. Tiana explored her meadow like an animal staking out territory. It seemed safe enough, except for the huge oak down the slope, near the stream. It had been struck by lightning that split its trunk a few feet above the ground, but left it alive.

Tiana circled it warily. Lightning-struck wood was full of Thunder's power. To touch it could cause her hand to crack open, like the wood. She set her blanket down in the meadow and sat in the middle of it. It was late afternoon and her stomach was growling loudly. She chewed on a piece of grass and from the corner of her eye watched as wispy gray clouds formed striations across Grandmother Sun's orange surface. Tiana knew Spearfinger didn't mean she should look directly at the Sun. Grandmother Sun didn't like that. It made her children squint and look ugly. She punished those who did it by giving them fevers.

When the last sliver of Grandmother Sun's face disappeared below the hills, Tiana felt very much alone. She regretted her rash decision to come up there. "You act without thinking, lass," her father always said. Tiana wished Jack were there, or Jennie or *Ulisi*. The air grew cold, and Tiana drew her blanket around her shoulders.

She began to hear night noises, rustlings and chitterings in the thick brush surrounding the bald. An owl called and Tiana shivered and fought off tears. What if the owl were a witch? She tried to make herself as small as possible in the blanket, pulling it over her head and drawing her feet up so only her face showed.

After what seemed like hours, a rabbit screamed somewhere nearby. Tiana stood and stared into the darkness around her. A wolf howled, then another. A crashing sound seemed to be coming up the slope. Tiana stumbled along the narrow trail to the oak tree that stood like a black, gnarled void against a sky made lighter by Grandfather Moon. Tiana laid a tentative hand against the rough bark. She was ready to jerk it away at the slightest indication the oak would harm her.

"May I sleep in your arms, friend?" she asked. There was no answer. But the oak made no effort to hurt her either. The wolves howled again, this time closer.

Grandmother Elizabeth said if one's intentions were good she had no need to fear. Tiana couldn't really say what her intentions were in coming here, but she certainly had nothing evil in mind. So, taking a deep breath, she threw her blanket up into the hollow created by the lightning and climbed after it. The cavity was dry and full of leaves. She wrapped the blanket around her and nestled down in them.

The next morning, she sat on her blanket and watched the sun progress across the sky. The first day all she could think of was food. The second day, she felt sick, but at least the bald seemed like home. By the second day the animals had gotten used to her. A pair of mice chased across her lap. A bird landed briefly on her head.

The third day, she thought she would die if she didn't eat. And still she saw no purpose in coming here. *Patience*, she heard her grandmother say. *Learn patience from the spider. Everything has its time and its reason.* The fourth day, her head was light, and she moved slowly so she wouldn't become dizzy. But she felt elated. She heard and saw with sharper clarity than she ever had.

On the fourth day she saw hawks. They began flying over alone or in pairs or groups. There were merlins and red-tails, Sharp-shins and peregrin falcons. Finally, as Tiana stared in amazement, a vast flock of broad-winged hawks flew over. There were thousands of them. Their whistling cries filled the air. Tears streamed down Tiana's face and she felt she could soar up to meet them.

"Good-bye, brothers," she called to them. "Safe journey, sisters." She looked up at the sun, shielding her eyes from its glare. "Thank you, Grandmother."

Tiana's legs and arms seemed detached as she started down the ridge toward Hiwassee. Bright points of light danced in front of her eyes. Her ears rang with the song of the hawks. She was singing a hawk song of her own as she entered Hiwassee Town. And when her father started scolding her, she smiled beatifically at him and fainted.

Chapter 18

General Andrew Jackson sat as rigid as a ramrod on his gaunt horse. Jackson was thin anyway, but dysentery and starvation rations had made him cadaverous. He winced as pain shot through his bowels. When the spasms were too intense he would dangle his arms over a horizontal pole and hang there until they eased, although the pain never stopped entirely. But he ignored it now. His men must see no weakness in him.

The crest of bristly gray hair on his high forehead made him seem even taller than his six foot one inch. In the icy December wind the left sleeve of his threadbare coat was ripped open along the seam to allow for the sling on his arm. In Nashville the summer before, his volcanic temper had involved him in a street brawl with his own officers. He was paying for it in pain from a shoulder wound that still hadn't healed.

His high-pitched voice was hoarse from swearing at a company of mutinous soldiers. He had tried to reason with the men when they decided to leave. He had appealed to their patriotism and honor. Now there was nothing left but threats.

"Retreat? Stuff your god-damned, lily-livered retreat!" His gravelly voice was venomous, his haggard face was livid. The veins in his skinny neck stood out purple in the cold. The muzzle of his gun lay across his horse's neck because Old Hickory's wounded shoulder was too weak to support it. There was no doubt in anyone's mind he was ready to use it. But his eyes were what held the entire brigade of defiant men at bay. His eyes glittered. They were sunken into his hollow cheeks and they seemed to glow from the dark caves under his brow, like a dangerous animal at bay.

"No one in my command retreats unless it's in a god-damned coffin. Any of you dastardly fart-suckers wants to volunteer for a hell-fired coffin ride, by the Eternal, just drag your rat-arsed carcass forward. I'll mince your shivering slats."

The uneasy silence was broken only by the clinking of hardware, the shuffling and snorting of horses, and an occasional low muttering from the ranks. Colonel John Coffee and his mounted troups rode quietly up behind Jackson. They wore dingy woolen hunting shirts and copperas pantaloons. They were an unkempt lot. Those without regulation jockey caps wore hats of animal skins like the foot soldiers. But unlike the foot soldiers, they had a fierce loyalty for Coffee and, by extension, for Jackson. They leveled their pieces at the mutineers.

One by one, the hungry, angry, shivering men turned back toward the bleak palisades of Fort Strother. Jackson gave an inaudible sigh of relief.

"Say, Sam," said Davy Crockett as he slogged through the calf-deep mud, "you reckon James or John could teach me Cherokee on this campaign?"

Sam laughed.

"You haven't fooled me with your act, Davy. You're far wiser than you pretend to be. But I doubt you're wise enough to learn Cherokee in less than a lifetime. See this?" He held up his brass canteen. "The Cherokee word for it means the-handled-container-that-shines-soldiers-they-to-carry-them-solid-they."

"You don't say." Crockett studied his canteen as though he had never seen it before. He was silent a while as they trudged along. Jackson's army had hiked over the Raccoon Mountains in a cold March rain. They were headed for William Weatherford's stronghold, To-ho-pe-ka, the Great Horseshoe. Weatherford had built a wall across the narrow neck of a hundred-acre peninsula, bounded by a huge curve of the Tallapoosa River. Jackson's scouts said Weatherford and the remnant of his beleaguered Creek army were waiting there now.

The trek over the mountains had been grueling. What made it bearable for Sam was Davy Crockett and James and John Rogers hiking beside him. The Rogers boys had joined the Thirty-Ninth Infantry as scouts. They could find a trail where most white men would have sworn there was none. Sam enjoyed the distinction of having close friends among the Cherokee. The men of east Tennessee might claim to despise Indians, but they considered it the greatest of compliments to be compared with them.

Before James and John left Hiwassee Town the village council made them wolf scouts. It was a great honor. The dancing and ceremonies had gone on for days. James claimed he and John had to beat the young women away with sticks.

Over their uniforms they wore short mantles of wolf pelts, with the forepaws fastened around their necks. Sam envied the barbaric look of the thick pelts with paws and tails dangling. He knew the prestige that went with them.

When they neared the Creek barricade, James and John moved off with the Cherokee Unit. As Sam and Davy marched the last few miles, Crockett told one of his famous stories.

" 'I'm the ragman,' he screamed at me. 'The very devil himself. And I'm for any man that insults me. Log-leg or leather breeches, green shirt or blanket-coat, land-trotter or river-roller. I'm the man for the massacree!' 'Well,' says I, 'I don't value you.' I looks him up and down, kinda slanticular. 'I'm the yellow flower of the forest,' I says. 'A regular pissabed, I am. A dandelion. I got the truest rifle, the fastest racking horse, the prettiest sister, and the ugliest dog in *Ten*nessee.' " His story was interrupted by a loud wail. "Lordy!" He spun around. "Who's got a catamount by the tail?"

"James Rogers," said Sam. "He's playing his father's bagpipes. That's what the Scots call a *brosnachadh*, a summons to war. James says the great war pipes were considered a weapon because they inspired men to fight."

"I can understand that," said Crockett.

The music grew louder as James approached. The drummers fell in line behind him because James wouldn't tolerate their marching in front of him. Affecting a heavy brogue, he would quote his uncle, John Stuart, on the subject. "Aye, and will a fellow who beats a sheepskin with two sticks go ahead of me? And me a musician?" The drum's slack heads made a throbbing, hollow beat that counterpointed the steady drone and wail of the pipes. The hair along

Sam's neck prickled with the sound of it. The music was savage. It was primitive. It was ghostly. It was the perfect voice for war.

As James played the pipes, his face had a wild, faraway look on it. He had painted jagged red lines on his cheeks. James might deny it, but he believed the paint made him invisible. Drum had mixed a certain type of butterfly with the hematite, to make the wearer agile. The paint was incongruous with the ill-fitting uniform of short, blue roundabout jacket and loose trousers that didn't reach James's ankles. He had tucked them inside his high, laced moccasins. Like Sam, James wore a belt with loops for his bayonet, knife, and canteen. He carried spare flints in the cartridge box slung across his chest.

Twenty-five hundred men, their faces closed and grim, marched in slow step to James's music. Sam thought his friend and brother had never looked so handsome. His throat tightened and his nostrils stung. He blinked back tears as he watched James leading the men to battle, and, for some of them, to their death.

Sam didn't think about his own death. His soul was in the treetops where death couldn't find it. At dawn he had gone to water with James and John and some of their clansmen. He could feel the scratches from The Just's bone comb tingling under his itchy wool trousers and jacket.

Sam's heart pulsed with the pipes and the drums. He could feel the blood coursing through his veins. His feet moved of their own accord in step with the thousands around him. The ground trembled under their heavy tread.

Through the trees and brush Sam caught a glimpse of the Creek barricade. It was impressive. The wall swept in a concave curve along the three hundred and fifty yards of the peninsula's neck. It was made of green logs laid horizontally five to eight feet high. Double rows of portholes were situated to catch attackers in a lethal crossfire. Weatherford had planned well.

James's song ended. The pipes' keening subsided to a moaning, then stilled. He handed them to a trusted drummer and ran to join the Cherokee. Three hundred of them were guarding the bluff across the river from the village at the rear of the stronghold. They were to shoot any Creek warriors who tried to escape.

The men formed into ranks. In the relative quiet, Sam could hear the Creeks shouting insults. Sam checked his men's weapons. Most of the soldiers had used guns since they were children. But it was easy to load out of sequence in the confusion of battle.

"Tie up your overcoats and blankets," Sam said. "If you've priming in the pan, empty it. Pick your touch holes and prime anew." Most of the soldiers in Sam's platoon were little more than boys.

"Aren't you afraid, sir?" one asked him.

"My heart's fluttering like a duck in a puddle." Sam winked.

"Looks like we're to be in front," another said.

"Yep. You'll like it here. There's less dust." He grinned and gave them the old thumbs-up sign. "If you're smart lads, you'll have a bit of blanket about you or an old hide to wet. You can wrap your piece in it, to cool it down when the fighting heats up." That was a bit of advice Davy Crockett had passed along to him. "Spare the women and children," Sam added.

"Kill the nits and you will have no lice," someone muttered. Sam glared at him.

"Jackson doesn't make war on women."

There was a shuffle and rattle of sabers and bayonets as soldiers found their places. Their ranks filled the woods as far as the eye could see. The shuffle became a vast, nervous fidget. Men coughed, stamped, scratched, and inspected their weapons again. They wiped their faces, hitched up their pants, and adjusted their braces or their cartridge boxes. Some rattled their bayonets to make sure they were firmly seated. Others pulled their hats down or pushed them up out of their line of vision. Somewhere, a man sneezed. The minutes dragged by while Jackson conferred with his officers.

Sam used the time to compose himself. For all his brave talk, this was his first battle. He half closed his eyes and summoned Drum's calm voice. *There is a way to put your soul in the treetops where arrows and bullets can't find you.* Sam repeated the charm to himself four times.

Surreptitiously, he spit on his hands and rubbed the saliva on his face. He slipped the hand into his jacket to rub his chest too. He knew, in his head, it was foolish. But in his heart, he wasn't sure.

Finally, there was a flurry of activity around the field pieces. Men cheered the first puffs of smoke and the dull explosions. They leaned forward, eager to rush through a breach in the wall. But despite the cannons' steady roar and the gouts of acrid black smoke, no breach appeared. The grapeshot rattled harmlessly on the logs, or sank into them and the Red Sticks jeered. The bombardment went on for two more hours and the barricade stood solidly intact.

"Look!" A man pointed over the heads of the Creeks. Smoke rose above the trees behind them. The Cherokee had attacked the Red

Sticks' unprotected rear, capturing the village there and setting fire to it. When the cannons stopped, the soldiers could hear the distant sound of gunfire and the Creeks milled in confusion. Breach or no breach, it was time to charge.

On a hill, Jackson stood with his sword raised and drums beat a rapid tatoo. The sword dropped. With a long, yodelling yell, the soldiers raced forward, firing and loading as they ran. Sam screamed a war cry of the Real People as his long legs pulled him well ahead of the pack. He smelled the burning powder and saw the blue smoke settle thickly. He felt the arrows and balls whirring around him, but they were harmless as flies. He was as small as a fox and swift as a deer.

He glanced above the treetops and saw a raven soaring there. He knew his soul was with it. He looked back down quickly. It wouldn't do to give away his soul's hiding place. White men would never think to look there, but the Creeks might.

He saw Major Montgomery climb the barricade at one of its lower points. He saw him raise his sword and shout, his words lost in the din. He faltered and toppled backwards off the wall, and lay without moving. Sam looked over his shoulder and saw the soldiers wavering.

He unsheathed his sword and ran until he could feel his legs pull in their sockets. Yelling at his men to follow, he headed for the spot the major had climbed. He covered the last ten yards in a few strides, and saw Montgomery would never rise. The side of his head was gone.

With one tremendous leap, Sam scaled the barricade. He swayed on top, then regained his balance. He stared down at the painted faces beneath him, and at the bristle of lance heads and arrows, knives, tomahawks, and guns. Suddenly, it didn't matter if anyone was behind him or not. He could kill them all.

"You Wizards," he screamed to the spirits. "I am as much a Wizard as You!" Then he jumped down into the swarm of Indians. They seemed to close in over his head while he hacked methodically with his sword. He saw the blood spurt from those he hit, but it didn't seem connected with anything human. He felt a strange calm, as though he were merely doing a piece of necessary work.

Sam didn't see the men of the Thirty-Ninth climb the wall. When they arrived, he was at the center of a ring of warriors and flailing about him like a madman. He was only barely aware of flashes of blue coats at the periphery of his vision. An arrow shaft projected from his inner thigh, but he didn't feel it.

After half an hour of fierce fighting, the outnumbered Red Sticks were slowly driven from the barricade. They took shelter in the trees of the high ground, and the battle became a series of hand-to-hand skirmishes through the thick underbrush. Sam tried to run after the fleeing Creeks and fell. He tugged at the arrow in his leg, but he couldn't remove it.

"Sir," he called to a lieutenant. "Take this out." The lieutenant pulled at it gingerly.

"Harder." Sam gritted his teeth.

"I can't, man. It's barbed. Go find the surgeon."

Sam grabbed the lieutenant's sleeve and waved his sword at him. "Pull harder, damn you!" he bellowed.

The lieutenant braced his boot against Sam's leg while Sam leaned against the breastwork. With both hands and perhaps a bit of malice, he yanked at the arrow, ripping the flesh as he pulled it out. Blood gushed from the ragged gash.

The excruciating pain brought Sam to his senses. As though waking from sleep, he heard the gunfire and shouting and saw the smoke around him. He felt the weariness in his arms and shoulders from hacking with his heavy sword. He knew he couldn't fight until he bound the hole up. Cursing, he limped off to find the surgeon. He was lying on the ground, recovering from the job the harrassed doctor had done, when Jackson rode by.

"Are you the man who took the redoubt?"

"I am, sir."

"Injured, I see. Have they taken care of you?"

"Yes, sir."

"Good. You won the day. Rest here. You've earned it. What's your name?"

"Houston, sir. Ensign Sam Houston, from Maryville."

Jackson dismounted and took Sam's hand in a firm clasp.

"Thank you, Sam. I won't forget you. You have my word." Sam had never seen eyes that burned with such fanaticism and unswerving will as Jackson's did.

"It's an honor to serve under your command, sir."

Jackson remounted and rode slowly among the dead and wounded. Sam saw him stop to weep over Major Montgomery's body. He waited until Jackson was out of sight, then he struggled to rise. The surgeon motioned him to lie back down, but Sam ignored him. He had told the roughs of Maryville they would hear of him. They wouldn't hear of him if he spent the war on his back. Nor would he earn eagle feathers and the right to keep his name, The Raven. He grimaced with pain as he fixed his bayonet and staggered toward the fighting.

For the next five hours he moved quietly, stalking human prey through the chaos around him. While the other soldiers thrashed and shouted, Sam ghosted through the thick underbrush. In his mind he was a black panther prowling at night, dark and deadly. He felt like he could see everything, even behind him, and no one could see him. At a glimpse of red paint or sweat glistening on brown skin, he crept up silently, raised his bayonet, and plunged it in with all his considerable strength.

Toward the end of the afternoon, the fighting slowed as the ground became thickly sown with bodies. Groups of soldiers ranged through the peninsula. They were surrounding and bayoneting or bludgeoning lone Indians. Not a single Red Stick surrendered, not even when a bayonet was at his breast. Those who tried to escape by the river found their fleet of canoes gone. James and John and other Cherokee had stolen them to ferry their men across and attack the redoubt's village. Red Sticks who tried to swim to safety were shot by the Cherokee and cavalry on the bluffs.

Sam lost count of how many men he killed. He only remembered the last one. Sam and the Creek saw each other at the same time. Under the paint Sam could tell he was only a boy, perhaps fourteen or fifteen. He seemed so young, so small, so fragile and so frightened, Sam hesitated. The boy didn't. With his bloody tomahawk raised, he charged.

Sam dodged and felt the air rush by his ear as the blade grazed it. He whirled and lunged with his bayonet. The Creek slashed with his tomahawk again. It hit the bayonet with a loud ring and snapped it. The blow spun the hatchet from the boy's hand, but his knife appeared so fast that Sam never even saw him pull it from its sheath.

He crouched, and he and Sam circled each other. The boy's eyes were wild, his lips were curled back in a snarl, and his teeth were bared. It was plain he'd never give up. Sam dropped his empty rifle and held his sword raised in both hands.

"Your pathway is Black," he chanted in the Real People's tongue. "Your soul is walking toward the Nightland. Your Black entrails will be scattered on the path to the Nightland. Your soul will wake there." Then he spit. The sputum hit the boy on the cheek. The Creek flinched. He knew the power of saliva.

Sam took advantage of the moment. He swung his sword with

both hands and cleaved the young warrior from the crown of his head to his chest. Brains splattered all over Sam and blood continued to pump after the body had fallen. As Sam stared at the mutilated corpse, he was wracked with sobs. Still crying, he bent over and vomited. He leaned against a tree until he had regained his composure. Then he went in search of his men.

The sky seemed afire along the horizon, but the blaze was only the sun going down. There were few warriors left to flush and dispatch. Smoke from the guns and the burning village rolled over the peninsula. Sam had to walk around the heaps of bodies. He felt permeated with the smell of blood and entrails. Already buzzards were circling overhead.

Sam found Jackson and most of his men discussing what to do with the last group of resisters. They had holed up in a fortified embankment at the bottom of a deep ravine. They must have known their cause was lost. But they seemed determined to take with them as many enemies as they could. They fired on Jackson's peace emissary and sent him back bleeding.

"By the Eternal!" Jackson raged. "Who will lead an assault on that vipers' nest?" He looked surprised when Sam stepped forward.

Sam had picked up another bayonet from a dead soldier. Now he fixed it and waved to his men to follow. He charged down the ravine to within five yards of the wall and leveled his rifle. He saw the sparks from the Creeks' weapons as they opened fire. A ball shattered his right shoulder, and another buried itself in his right arm.

He dropped his gun and his men faltered, then ran for safety. Alone and under fire, Sam clambered back up the ravine. He reached the top before his outraged body finally had enough. His legs buckled, and he fainted. Two men carried him to the makeshift hospital of blankets laid out under trees.

Darkness was shrouding the carnage when soldiers lit piles of brush and threw them over the edge of the ravine. The fire caught in the dry grass and bushes, and the slope turned the refuge into an inferno.

The Creeks held out as long as they could. Then they climbed over the top of the ravine and ran toward their enemies. Their hair and clothing blazed in the wind created by their running. They turned into living torches that lit up the undersides of the trees' leafy canopy. Jackson's men shot them as they appeared. Given the circumstances, it was the kindest thing they could have done.

Chapter 19

Perhaps a few Red Sticks escaped during the night. But there couldn't have been many. Two hundred and fifty women and children were penned in a hastily-built corral. They wailed or sobbed or stared stonily at nothing. Most of them sat, unmoving on their blankets, throughout the cold night.

When morning came, Jackson walked all over the desolate stronghold. He inspected every body carefully, shoving apart piles of corpses with his boot. His own scouts were right. William Weatherford, Red Eagle, wasn't among the slain. Five hundred and fifty-seven warriors were dead, not counting the hundreds killed in the river. There was no way of knowing how many had drowned. The bodies would be washing up on shore for a long time to come. Jackson ordered his own dead soldiers sunk in the river to prevent their being mutilated by Creeks later.

To keep an accurate tally, the men had sliced off the nose of each Red Stick so the body wouldn't be counted twice. Some of the dead warriors were missing their scalps or strips of skin. Souvenir hunters had cut the strips to tan and braid into bridle reins. The skin had been flayed from one man's back and a soldier was boasting he would cover the family Bible with Creek leather. Others took big pieces from thighs to make high moccasins. Jackson didn't like the practice, but he didn't try to find the culprits. The men had little enough incentive in this war. Jackson himself had taken a child's quiver and bow for his adopted son, Andy.

Old Hickory was disappointed that he had missed Weatherford. He was the leader of this rebellion and the one Jackson wanted. But if Weatherford had been at the Horseshoe, neither the village nor the canoes would have been left unguarded. He was far too crafty for that. The soldiers told stories about Red Eagle. They talked about the day he and his fine gray thoroughbred had been trapped atop a high bluff. He urged his horse over the cliff's edge and into the churning water far below. The American soldiers had lined the bluff to watch him and his magnificent horse struggle against the current and finally swim out of sight. The Tennessee and Kentucky sharpshooters could have killed him, but they didn't try. They were too impressed with his courage and audacity and style. No, it would be unthinkable to find Weatherford dead, mere carrion. Jackson didn't waste time wondering what would drive a man to turn his back on his white blood and education and side with a hopeless cause.

James and John also walked across the corpse-strewn peninsula looking for their friend and brother. Then they searched among the American wounded. They found Sam, pale and shivering, under a pile of blankets. The surgeons hadn't expected him to live till morning and had left him to die while they attended others. He had spent the night alone on the cold ground, but even in the cold he was perspiring heavily. He struggled to rise to greet his friends. James hunkered and pushed him gently down. His skin felt cold.

"Glad to see you, fellows," said Sam, panting. "I reckon we ought to celebrate." He tried to grin. "You bring the whiskey, I'll bring the thirst."

"Lie still," said James. "The surgeon says you lost oceans of blood and you're in shock."

"Pshaw! What does he know. I'll be fine. Just need a little drink to recover from the hangover the doctors gave me last night."

Jesse Bean and Davy Crockett found them. They'd recovered their knapsacks from the supply wagon and were ready to march.

"We've come to say good-bye," said Davy. "Our bunch is moving out. Looks like you'll be able to ride back in style, you lucky dog."

Sam grinned weakly.

"Sam says he has a hangover," said James.

"Yeah," said Sam. "Those sawbones gave me a canteen of whiskey so I couldn't fight back while they tortured me. 'Waste not, want not,' my mother always says. I drank it all."

"Did it kill the pain?" asked John.

"Not that I could tell. They excavated in my arm for nigh unto an hour. Never did unearth the bullet."

James pulled Crockett aside while Sam was telling John and Jesse about taking the redoubt.

"The doctors say he won't live. He lost too much blood."

"I'm real sorry to hear that," said Crockett. "Wish I could give him some of mine."

"John and I have permission to go with him to Fort Williams with the rest of the wounded. Will you tell his family of his deeds? We'll try to send word of his condition."

"I will. Do you need help?"

"No. We skinned a dead horse and made a litter of the hide." James stared at the ground. "He's been a good friend," he said softly. "Like a brother." Crockett laid a hand lightly on James's shoulder as they walked to where Sam lay. Davy squatted so he could grasp Sam's hand.

"We're going on one of Old Hickory's promenades," he said. "We'll all have a drink in Maryville."

"Good-bye, Davy. Good-bye, Jess. It's been a frolic."

"Good-bye, Sam."

Crockett grasped James and John each in turn by the arm. Then he hugged them both.

"It's been an honor to serve with you," he said. He unslung his knapsack and untied the rolled blanket from the top. He gave it to James, along with a silver dollar. "Ain't much," he said. "But it might buy you some provisions along the way. I'd give you more if I had it." James nodded. Everyone knew Davy would give away his shirt if someone needed it.

"He looks bad," said Jesse when he and Davy were out of hearing.

"Jess," said Crockett, "you were talking to a dead man."

A week later, James and John lowered the stretcher onto the ground outside Fort Williams. They and Sam and the rest of the Thirty-Ninth had built the small station as a supply post six months earlier. It was almost deserted now, with a minimum force. The other wounded had arrived earlier, riding the sixty miles in the over-crowded wagons or on horse litters. A few offered to help James and John with their burden, but they stubbornly refused aid. They knew the wagon or horse litter would jolt him, causing him more pain than he already suffered.

It was dark when they reached the fort's closed gate and the wound on Sam's leg was green and puffy. He moaned and called out, "Stab him! Stab him!" In his mind he was sinking his bayonet into flesh, over and over. Sometimes he would run it all the way through the body and sometimes he would strike bone. It was a nightmare even his pain couldn't drive away.

John pounded on the gate.

"Who are you? What's the countersign?" the watch called from the parapet twenty feet above them.

"I don't know, damn it. We just came from the battle at the Horseshoe," said John.

"Let us in," shouted James. "Our friend is hurt." He held up a pine torch so the soldiers could see his face. James wore moccasins and homespuns. His hair was braided. He was obviously an Indian.

"Take him over there." The man gestured vaguely behind them. "There's a cabin about half a mile from here."

"Open the hell-fired gate." John was losing patience.

"Can't. Orders. Wouldn't even if I could. Might be a trick. You boys stay over at the cabin. Clear out, come sun-up. Even if you're not hostiles, we can't take refugees here. Not enough grub for our own."

"We're not refugees. We're Cherokee scouts. Members of the Thirty-Ninth. I can tell you who all the officers are."

"Hell-fire!" roared John. "We built this pigsty! This man's an ensign. He's bad hurt."

There was no answer save for faint laughter from behind the wall. In a rage, John hammered on the logs with his rifle butt. He and James heard the ring of a metal ramrod on steel. The light from their torch gleamed on the barrels of three muskets poking through the small loopholes at the top of the parapet.

"If you ain't gone by the count of ten, I'll put you all out of your misery. Breeds," they heard him mutter. "Probably some of Weatherford's sons of bitches." Thunder rumbled and a cold mist began to drift down.

"Bastards!" shouted John. They heard the click of a musket lock.

"Come, brother." James took the pine torch from his pack and lit it with the guttering one he held. The pine burned with a steady flame that hissed when a larger raindrop hit it. James laid the stem of the torch along the pole of the litter frame so he could hold them both with one hand. James willed his aching arms to carry his friend half a mile farther.

They laid Sam in the most sheltered part of the abandoned cabin. Then they made a bed of leaves that had blown in through the empty doorframe. Exhausted and shivering, they huddled together all night and slept late the next morning.

James was awakened by a boot rapping sharply against the sole of his moccasin. He and John looked up at a ring of grim-faced soldiers. John glowered at them, but James smiled in his charming, ingenuous way.

"Morning," he said, gently pushing aside a musket barrel so he could stand. He squatted next to Sam and checked his heart, as he often did each day. He had a horror of Sam's slipping away from him. He pulled the blanket from around Sam's neck. Sam was still wearing the bloody blue coatee and white stock of the Thirty-Ninth. James wiped his friend's perspiring face tenderly with his sleeve and looked up at the circle of men.

"His name's Sam Houston. He's from Maryville. Is there a doctor at the station?"

The lieutenant pulled the blanket farther off Sam's body, and the stench of his thigh wound hit him. One of the men gagged, and the lieutenant hastily dropped the blanket back in place.

"Sorry about last night." He stared down at Sam. "Can't take chances, you know."

"Is there a doctor?"

"Naw. No doctors anywheres around here. Why wasn't this man with the rest of the wounded? They all left this morning for Fort Jackson."

"The wagons and horses jolted him too much," said James. "We fell behind. He shouldn't be moved any farther anyway. We'll stay with him."

"We have to go back," John reminded him. "Leave only good for two weeks. Have to go now."

"At least eat something first," said the lieutenant. "Private, take them to the mess area. See they're well fed. Give them some supplies. We'll take care of your friend, give him a decent burial."

"Brother." James leaned close to Sam's face. "Brother." Sam opened his eyes.

"Are we home?" he murmured.

"No. We're leaving you with people who'll care for you. We have to return to the Thirty-Ninth." He wasn't sure if Sam heard him or not.

"Did you see me leap?" Sam whispered.

"What?"

"Did you see me leap the wall? I learned that from the panther."

"Brother of my heart . . ." What does one say to a brother one will never see again in this life?

"I hear you," Sam said. "Give my love to Drum and Sally Ground Squirrel and your family. Buss little Tiana, Grandmother. She's a stitch, she is. Take care of them till I get back."

"We will."

"One more thing."

"What?"

Sam grunted in pain as two soldiers lifted his stretcher. James and John walked beside him.

"Kiss old Spearfinger hello for me."

James and John couldn't help laughing.

"Good-bye," said Sam. "And thanks, brothers."

"Good-bye, my brother," said James.

Chapter 20

Tiana lifted her mask so she could peep through a crack in the window shutter. She had woven the mask of corn husks and decorated it with fur eyebrows, moustache, and hair. The white sheeting she wore draped over her head dragged the ground. She motioned over her shoulder for Nannie and Susannah to stop giggling.

Twelve-year-old Susannah was wearing a mask she had carved of soft buckeye wood. On the porch in the dark, Susannah's white shroud and the vacant eyes and gaping mouth hole of her mask sent a shiver of fear through Tiana. She hugged herself in anticipation of the fright they would give the children inside.

"Let me see," whispered Nannie. Nannie had painted her own face with charcoal and ratted her long, black hair until it stood out in tangles around her plump face. She pulled her sheeting around her as she took a turn at the crack.

The main room of the house was filled with warmth and light and dancing shadows. Rush lights and pitch pine torches flickered on the mantel and shelves around the room. A huge fire crackled in the fireplace. The men talked and smoked in front of it while the women and older girls worked in the fragrant kitchen.

A dozen or more children played near the table boards set on trestles for the meal. They were building cabins and a redoubt of dried cornobs and attacking the Red Stick village at the Horseshoe.

Their cannons and musket fire and the cries of the wounded and dying carried over the talk in the kitchen and around the hearth.

The entire Rogers clan and their friends and neighbors had gathered to help Jack celebrate his fifty-seventh birthday. It was also October 31, 1815, the Scottish *Samhain*, the night the dead walked. When the girls were young, Jack had frightened them on *Samhain*. He would lurk outside in the dark, screaming like a banshee. Or he would paint his face and leer in the windows. His sons had done the haunting for a few years. Now the girls were taking over.

It was a perfect night for *anisgina*, ghosts. The full moon was shrouded in a thin veil of clouds. Its bluish aura was ringed in orange. Far away, two wolves howled a mournful dialogue. A light wind rattled the dry leaves, gave them life, and sent them skittering across the bare yard. The same wind seemed to pluck at Tiana's sheet like cold fingers. An owl hooted nearby, and Susannah crowded closer to her older sisters. The Real People knew witches disguised themselves as owls.

Mary Rogers Gentry opened the door a crack and peeped out, squinting to see them in the darkness.

"Are you ready?" she whispered.

"Yes," said Tiana. She felt a little sorry for Mary, her mother's sister. Mary had been beautiful all her life. Now, at twenty-seven, she seemed to dread losing that beauty. She dressed extravagantly for the simple life of a blacksmith's wife at Hiwassee garrison. And she quickly grew impatient with conversations that weren't about her. She was like a lovely flower with an unpleasant smell. But she was being a good sport tonight.

She signaled inside to Aky and Annie, who began to snuff the rush lights. Jennie draped a dark cloth over a frame in front of the hearth. The children looked up, startled, as the warm, friendly room suddenly turned dark and eerie. The girls outside heard the children squealing and corn cobs rattling across the floor.

"Who's out there?" Jack put a nervous quaver in his voice. "Did you hear something, children?" he asked in his abominable Cherokee. "Could it be Spearfinger? Could it be Water Cannibals or witches? Is the Important Thing coming to get you?" That was the worst. Children often heard about the Important Thing, a euphemism for disease, but they weren't sure what it was. There was silence while the children listened, and tried to imagine what the Important Thing looked like.

Tiana moaned loudly as the door creaked on its wooden hinges.

Nannie cackled and leered. Susannah shrieked and raised her arms, fingers tensed into claws under the sheeting. Children screamed and fell over each other as they scuttled for safety. There was pandemonium as the girls chased them around the room, behind furniture, under the table boards, and between adult legs. Towers of nested baskets toppled and apples and beans rolled out on the floor.

Tiana went after three-year-old Patience Gentry, who climbed into her father's lap, pulled David's full white shirt out of his pantaloons and put it over her head. While she burrowed up under it, Tiana tickled her. David laughed. He had wondered where Tiana was that evening. Now, it wasn't hard to guess who the three goblins were, nor which was Tiana. She was taller than her two sisters. David put his arms around Patience, shirt and all, and hugged her to him. But he winked at Tiana.

While the children calmed down and Jennie relit the rushes and sticks of pitch pine, the girls dodged through the press of women watching from the kitchen door. Laughing, Tiana and Susannah stripped off their masks and shrouds. Nannie washed her face and began the difficult task of combing her hair.

Tiana could see there was more than enough help in the kitchen, so she joined the men gathered around the fire. As Grandmother Elizabeth shoveled another loaf of bread from the oven built into the stone hearth, she smiled at Tiana. Although Tiana had said nothing about shooting the sanger or going on a four-day fast, Elizabeth told all her friends. Soon everyone in Hiwassee knew about it. The women included Tiana more in their discussions. The men tolerated her presence.

William and Joseph were envious. They glared at her, but she ignored them. She knew the women rarely mingled with the men, but it was her right to be here. David moved over to make room for her on the bench.

"Thank you, husband," she said lightly. Among the Real People a man often married his wife's widowed sister. A woman referred to the man her sister married as "husband." Tiana thought nothing of it and David shouldn't have either. But he gave her a strange, glancing look before he returned his attention to the discussion.

The men were talking about the battle at New Orleans. Jackson's victory over the British there ten months before had ended Jemmy Madison's war. The men were always talking about New Orleans or the Battle of the Horseshoe. John Rogers insisted on being called

Captain John now. Tiana had heard all his stories and everyone else's too. For the first time in her life, she dared interrupt.

"What happened to Tecumseh?" she asked.

"He was killed when he forced the British horse's arse, Proctor, to stand and fight," said James. "All Proctor was good at was retreating. I hear souvenir hunters stripped Tecumseh of everything, including his hair and skin."

Tiana felt a rush of sadness. Handsome, eloquent Tecumseh, Panther Passing Over, mutilated by white savages. Even if he had been her enemy, she wished him a nobler death than that.

"I heard differently," said David. "A trapper came through the garrison a few months ago. Said he was there. Said a fellow named Kenton sneaked Tecumseh's body away and gave it a decent burial. Those men skinned some other poor sod."

"I'm glad," said Jack. "He was a hell-fired troublemaker, but he deserved better than to become razor strops and boot laces for that rabble."

"And has no one heard from The Raven?" Tiana asked.

"I fear he's dead, sister," said James gently. "I hardly recognized him when he came through the garrison in that charnel wagon a year ago. Only someone as strong as The Raven could have lasted as long as he did. He didn't know me or Drum. He was dying then." James drew a long puff on his pipe and stared sadly at it. "He would have written us or come back if he'd lived."

Elizabeth rang the dinner bell, and everyone converged on the table boards. While women carried out the last baskets and dishes of food, Jennie lowered the heavy candlebeam, carefully playing out the rope that held it up. David had forged it from an iron hoop with candle holders attached. With his usual artistry, he had added a delicate, wrought-iron filigree of vines and leaves. It wasn't used often. Candles were time-consuming to make and costly to buy. They were burned sparingly.

Jennie lit the precious candles and raised the beam again. It swayed slightly, throwing a festive, golden light on the table boards under it. Tiana sat as far from it as possible, though. It sometimes dropped hot wax. The children rushed to the far end of the table, where they would stand to eat. Seats were reserved for the adults. Tiana had been sitting with the adults for a year or more.

Everyone looked expectantly at Jack, at the head of the table. He carved a piece of beef from the platter in front of him and threw it into the fire as an offering to Ancient Red. Privately, Jack called the custom mumbo-jumboism, but he knew no one would eat until he'd done it.

It wasn't a large party by the Rogers' standards. There were no more than forty or fifty people. Only one pig and one steer had roasted on spits all day, instead of the three or four beeves barbequed at Christmas. At Christmas two hundred people celebrated here for days.

But food was plentiful nonetheless. Pitchers of small beer and dandelion wine and flasks of Jack's best whiskey stood on the table boards, along with ewers of buttermilk and cider. There were baskets of steaming pumpkin slices and hunks of fresh bread, basins of mashed squash with honey, snap beans and collard greens with fatback and vinegar. There were berries in cream and sweet potato pudding and corn and apples cooked a dozen different ways each. A huge earthen pot held steaming baked beans and ham.

There were mounds of pale butter, and platters of chicken and hickory-cured bacon. There were venison steaks and bass fried in cornmeal. A roast suckling pig sprawled on a huge platter. The largest basin held the hotch pot, a stew of vegetables and mutton. Tiana wondered how she was going to fit everything onto the big wooden trencher she shared with Nannie.

Jack stood and held up his tankard.

"May sweet peace perch on our army's standards," he said. "To General Jackson and the gallant men who fought at the Horseshoe and New Orleans."

"Hear, hear!" everyone shouted, raising their glasses.

"And to us all, *Slainte Mhath*, good health."

"*Slainte Mhath*." They pronounced the old Scottish toast "Slantchy Va." Then, David stood. Jack's whiskey had made him unusually extroverted.

"To this repast," he said. "And to the women who have stirred around in the kitchen like a six-horse team in a mudhole." He sat down abruptly amid the laughter.

"To the lasses," said Jack.

"To the lasses," the men echoed, toasting their favorite. Tiana looked up to see old Campbell's youngest son holding his glass out to her. She smiled uncertainly at him. He had been trying to capture her attention all day, mostly by throwing hickory nuts at her. He was sixteen, but he seemed so young. His hands and feet were too big, as though the rest of him hadn't caught up with them yet.

Tiana wore a new red dress of store-bought checked gingham. It flowed from her shoulders to the tops of her best moccasins. It was caught under her small breasts with one of her own belts, woven in diamond patterns of red and blue and yellow. The dress was gathered at the neck and cut low, like her mother's. The long, full sleeves were caught at the wrists, leaving a ruffle that lay in soft folds on the tops of her hands.

This was the first time she had worn one like it, and she wasn't entirely comfortable in it. Her hair fell in black ripples to her waist as she concentrated on her food. When she glanced up the table to avoid Daniel Campbell, her dark blue eyes met David's light brown ones. He gave her a hint of his crooked smile and raised his glass to her. "Save me a dance." He mouthed the words. She smiled and toasted him back. He was really quite winsome, David was. And a graceful dancer. Then she was too busy eating to notice him staring at her. For a while, the only noise was the clatter of spoons on wooden trenchers.

Jack Rogers finished eating first, belched loudly and slumped in his chair at the head of the table. He was tired. He'd spent the morning with James and John chasing cattle through the dense cane-brakes along the river. Then there had been the throwing of the tabor before dinner to prove he was as vigorous as ever. *Every man desires to live long*, he thought. *But no man would be old.*

Jack propped his elbow on the arm of his old chair, rested his chin on his palm, and surveyed the boards with satisfaction. They were loaded with the fruits of his fields. He studied the faces lining the table. Old Campbell with his wild, white thatch and beard and David Gentry with his unruly blond hair seemed out of place. The overall impression was of dark hair and eyes and brown faces, even though most of them had white blood in their veins.

For a moment, Jack realized he was a stranger in a strange land and that those he loved were alien from all his people had ever known. What would his parents, long buried in the rocky soil of Scotland, think of his wives and children? Then the moment passed and the faces were again more familiar than the family he'd left so long ago. He couldn't imagine being prouder of his children if they'd been freckle-faced towheads, educated in the finest British schools.

Jack stood, mildly embarrassed by his bare white knees that poked out between the cuffs of his argyle trews and the hem of the red-and-blue wool plaid kilt. One end of the plaid was tossed over the shoulder of his white linen shirt. A purse of badger hide, decorated with silver and tassels, hung at the front of the kilt. He carried a dirk in a sheath at his waist. This was his old uniform, the one he wore as a scout for the 71st Highland Regiment in the late war of rebellion.

The tartan smelled musty. It was riddled with moth holes. He had to belt it with fewer pleats to fit around his middle. The draft he felt on his crotch discomfited him. Looking down at his pale knees, he realized they were knobbier than he remembered them. He would go on wearing the uniform on special occasions. It was his way of honoring his father-in-law, old Ludavic Grant, the patriarch of this mob, and John Stuart, Jack's fiery-haired brother-in-law. The Real People had loved Stuart. They had called him Bushyhead. Jack had loved him too. As a young scout he'd idolized Stuart and had wept for days when he died. Even now a child with flame-colored hair would appear among Stuart's offspring, the Bushyheads, and bring a pang of memory.

Jack tapped his spoon on his tankard and cleared his throat.

"May I have your attention," he thundered. "Tonight the Rogers wigwam is a *ceilidh* house, a place where we can all share stories and music and dancing, even as we've shared this meal."

"And can we duck for apples?" asked Patience Gentry from the end of the table.

"Aye, lass. That we can."

Tiana and Nannie, Susannah and one of the Campbell girls piled the dirty dishes into big baskets they carried between them. Soon the table boards and the trestles were gone and the benches were pulled back to line the walls.

Using the handtalk the Campbell family had developed over the years, Campbell's youngest daughter asked her father to play. It was well they had another form of communication. Old Campbell was deaf now. David had offered to make him an ear trumpet, but Campbell declined. He said the news was all bad anyway, and he'd just as soon not hear it. His deafness didn't affect his music, which had never been particularly good anyway. But he was the only fiddler around and he was in great demand.

While old Campbell fussed with his battered fiddle and James brought out the drums and rattles, Tiana sneaked up behind David and tickled him.

"Husband," she said. "Wrestle me. I can beat you now."

David ducked his head and grinned at the floor.

"Not tonight, niece," he said in his low voice.

"Do you fear my pro . . . my protigious strength?"

"Do it, brother," said James. "She wants humbling."

"Another time," said David. But Tiana grabbed his hand and kneeled down, forcing him to his knees on the opposite side of the bench. David thanked Providence for the Cherokee custom of avoiding another's eyes. Tiana might be young, but if she ever looked into his eyes she could surely read his heart there.

He stared instead at their hands, locked together with arms touching and elbows braced on the bench. He could manage to dance with her once or twice a night. It was difficut, but he could do it. When he was away from her, in his shop, he thought often of dancing with her. Then, when he had the chance, he was too nervous to do anything but concentrate on his feet, terrified he'd stumble and embarrass himself.

But this was different. The sensation of her fingers and the smooth warmth of her forearm seemed to lengthen and slide down his body, into his groin. He could imagine, all too easily, her entire body bare and straining against his, the way her arm did. They had been playing at arm wrestling ever since she'd been a small child. But lately, it had become torture for David.

"Husband, you're not trying." Tiana grimaced as she tried to force his hand down onto the bench. Her irrepressible hair fell across her face and trailed across his hand and arm until David thought he would die of longing. He didn't hear the good-natured betting going on around them. He stared only at the hair where it curtained her face and hid her eyes. When he could stand her touch no longer, he let her push his hand down.

"You allowed me to win," she said.

David shrugged. "I did. But I'll tell you truly, you're becoming very strong." David's hand and arm still tingled with the feel of her skin as he went to join the men around the fire.

Tiana sat with Nannie and Susannah on a thick bearskin. She knew there would be stories later and apples baking in the ashes, mulled cider simmering and nuts in baskets. When he got drunk enough Jack would sing his endless ballads, probably "The Minstrel Boy." And he had promised they would duck for apples in the big washtub. After Campbell's rigadoons and raspies, his reels and jigs, they would do the dances of the Real People until dawn. Campbell would cavort and buss all the women and try to balance a glass of beer on his head. Tiana supposed she would have to dance at least once with Daniel Campbell. She didn't want to hurt his feelings.

"A new song is popular at the garrison," David said, during a lull in the chatter. His voice was young, but with a slight huskiness to it, as though rusty with lack of use. Patience was curled in his lap. His other daughters, Isabel and Elizabeth, sat leaning against his knees.

"The garrison's copy of the *Register* arrived from Baltimore with the words and music. The tune is an old drinking song, 'Anacreon in Heaven.' Anacreon was a Greek who wrote his best poems, so they say, while intoxicated." David raised his glass to that idea. "At any rate, they're singing it in all the taverns."

"What is it about?" asked Tiana.

"Oh, the flag. The war. It's patriotic, I suppose. It's called the 'Bombardment of Fort McHenry.' "

"How does it go?"

David gave his shy, crooked grin.

"I'm not much at music, and it has a hellacious range."

"Sing it for us," they all begged.

Tiana had often seen David sing to himself at the forge, but the noise of the hammer and the bellows made it impossible to hear him. Now, as he began, she was surprised at what a soothing, resonant voice he had.

"Oh, say can you see, by the dawn's early light . . ."

Chapter 21

The sun was still well below the horizon, and the sky just turning from charcoal to the color of ashes. Tiana had been lying awake on the bed of juniper boughs a long time, long enough to hear Nannie sneak in. She pretended to be asleep while Nannie pulled her coat and moccasins off and crept under the covers. Nannie must have found a young man whose sap was rising. Probably the Price boy. Tiana envied her.

It was late February, sugaring time. Ostensibly the Seven Clans came here to the mountains to collect the sweet syrup of the maple every winter. But the young people waited for it all year for another reason. When the campfires melted the night around them into glowing pools of light, teenagers snaked their blankets and fur robes from the lean-tos and sneaked away to trysts.

Everyone knew about it, but as long as the lovers were discreet, no one said anything. Nine months from now there would be a few children born whose fathers were invisible, as the Real People delicately put it. Tiana had heard the crunch of furtive moccasins passing her shelter throughout the night. She could distinguish them from the normal tread of people going off to relieve themselves.

Now she waited until Nannie was breathing deeply before she slipped out from under the blankets. Moving slowly and silently so Nannie and Susannah wouldn't wake up, she adjusted her long wool dress. She pulled on her high, fur-lined moccasins and laced them. She wrapped one of Drum's thick white trade blankets around her shoulders and stepped out into a white world.

In the pale gray light, she looked like part of the landscape as she drifted among the shelters and piles of gear mounded with snow and the winking embers of the banked fires. A ghostly mist shrouded the trees around her.

In the next clearing, light glowed from the flames under the huge boiling kettles. She heard the faint sound of voices and the crackling of the wood as it burned. Women stayed with the kettles all night. They used spruce branches to brush froth off the top of the bubbling syrup. Each watch gossiped and joked the hours away until the next came to relieve it.

Tiana walked to her favorite place far from camp and sat on a snow-covered boulder jutting out over a half-frozen stream. She watched the water slide like silver silk over black rocks. It made its way down a series of ledges and through the frozen latticework formed by its own cascades.

She thought of what Grandmother Elizabeth often told her. "In silence we hear the voices of the spirits most clearly." And in winter the mountains were the quietest. Up here Tiana felt as though she could see the entire world and hear it speak to her, in silence and in the music of the water.

The north slope below her was covered with rhododendron thickets sculptured in morning hoarfrost. Each bush wore a delicate coat of white lace. A white-tailed deer stopped to nibble the first tender shoots of an alder. A wren whistled his song somewhere in the tangle of bare, black limbs overhead.

Along the creek the small white flowers of the pepper-and-salt pushed through the snow. In another week or two the aroma of the spice bush would perfume the forest. In a month, Tiana could walk through columns of warm air, as though entering a room from the outside. Pale green growth would soften and blur the harsh outlines of the trees and slopes.

Tiana came here to greet Grandmother Sun. But she had another purpose too. She was going to try a magic ritual for the first time in her life. This wasn't the familiar morning chant to the sun. It wasn't one of the common charms children knew to cure insect bites or make food cook faster. This was special. It was magic Spearfinger had given her. And any magic belonging to Spearfinger made Tiana nervous.

Before Tiana had left to come sugaring, she had found Spearfinger in a semilucid state. Or rather, Spearfinger had found her. She must have regarded Tiana highly to venture into sanity to communicate with her. With a cock of her head and a crook of her dirty, gnarled finger, the old woman beckoned to Tiana as she was digging wood fern roots for one of Grandmother Elizabeth's remedies. Tiana assisted her grandmother often with simple cures. And more and more often, women were coming to Tiana herself for help.

The sight of Spearfinger's double set of teeth and her amulets of shriveled mole and wren dangling from a thong always set Tiana's old fears to chittering in her head. But she calmed them. Spearfinger had been leaving her small presents over the years. Or at least Tiana assumed it had been her. Spearfinger had a habit of exchanging one thing for another, like a crow.

Tiana had lost a steel sewing needle that way, and a small mirror. But she had found in their stead a smooth, purple-veined pebble, probably for divining, and the polished sphere of matted hair and saline clays from a cow's stomach. It too was undoubtedly powerful. Tiana carried them in the small bag she wore around her neck in hopes someday Spearfinger would explain them to her. It looked like this might be that day.

Spearfinger had perched on a high root of a yellow birch that had taken hold in a fallen tree years before. The log had rotted away from under the seedling as it grew. Now the birch was standing on stiltlike roots that formed a cage around the phantom log, totally gone now.

Grinning down at Tiana, Spearfinger had pulled a thin book from the bosom of her dress. There was no telling where she had gotten it. Spearfinger had adjusted her glassless spectacles on her pointed nose, opened the book and moved her lips, turning the pages now and then, as though reading them. She had even pushed her glasses to the end of her nose and peered over them, just as Seeth MacDuff used to do. Then she glanced slyly at Tiana.

"Very powerful magic." The old woman spoke around the upside-down clay pipe in her mouth and tapped the open book. Its soft leather covers draped over the outspread palms of her skeletal hands.

"Yes, Mother Raincrow." Tiana's curiosity overcame her old fear. A new book was worth some risk. She climbed onto one of the lower roots of the birch so she could peer over Spearfinger's shoulder.

"The child of the Long Hair can hear the voice of these leaves," Spearfinger said.

"Yes, Mother. This one can hear some of what they say." Tiana took the book and leafed through it while the old woman waited patiently. "It's about phrenology." She sounded the word out. "It talks of the white man's . . ." She searched for a word. "Magic. A white curer can feel the bumps on a person's head and look into that person's soul or tell her future." Tiana had never had anything like a conversation with Spearfinger. She spoke slowly and cautiously, uncertain of what Spearfinger's response might be. And she was poised for flight.

Much of Tiana's education had come from sitting on the steps of the garrison's taverns and listening to the talk that drifted through the open doors. Or, if she was lucky, David Gentry hooked her a back issue of the *Niles Register* before it was worn too thin to be legible. At any rate, Gall's and Spurzheim's new theory of phrenology had been a popular subject lately.

With reckless abandon Spearfinger plunged one hand into the uncharted wilderness of her own matted hair. She ran a finger over the drawing of a hairless human head, sectioned off and labeled. She was intrigued, but not awed.

"White men know with their heads," she said, obviously pleased to find proof for what she had always believed. "The Seven Clans know with their hearts. You can sing the songs of the talking leaves to me."

"Yes, Mother."

Spearfinger cackled. She jumped down from the root and did a small shuffling dance step. She caught her spectacles neatly when they fell off her nose.

"Raincrow will make you strong."

"There's no need to pay me, Mother. It makes my heart glad to sing you these songs."

"This one will cover you with Red Attire. She will clothe you in knowledge." She beckoned Tiana closer and looked suspiciously around her. Then she whispered a charm for re-beautifying a person.

"Mother, this one can't use this. She's not *didahnuhwisgi*, a Curer Of Them."

With her bony knuckles, Spearfinger thumped Tiana on the chest. "The plants call you sister. The trees speak well of you," she said. "The hawk sends her greetings."

Tiana forgot herself and stared at Spearfinger for an instant. How did she know about the hawk?

"Sing this song four times at dawn at the river when you want to attract a man. Do not repeat it four times before then, or you will start it working before you desire it to." Tiana started to speak, then closed her mouth. She had no trouble attracting men. She needed a charm to repel them now and then. But she did need a charm to call the one she could love. She was beginning to wonder if he existed. "Your Pathways have just come to a turn," the old woman went on. "When you return from the Blue Haze, we will walk and sing together."

Spearfinger cocked her head and stared fixedly over Tiana's shoulder. When she started chattering brightly, Tiana looked cautiously around. There was no one there, of course. Tiana stood, rigid, waiting for Spearfinger's spirits to fly past her. She could almost feel the air stir. She was relieved when Spearfinger hopped and swerved down the trail, her spirits in tow. She left a certain stillness behind her, as though she had gathered up all the restless, gibbering demons in the area and had taken them with her.

But she had left Tiana a charm to re-beautify, to make herself radiant and irresistible. Maybe it would help. Maybe she wasn't beautiful enough to attract the happiness that eluded her. So she had brought the charm with her to the stream that morning.

With a sigh, Tiana stood and threw down her blanket. She piled her hair on top of her head and pinned it there with bone combs. She lay her pouch on top of the blanket and took off her moccasins and leggings. She pulled her long dress over her head. The powdery snow crunched and compacted under her bare feet.

Naked, she stood with her arms lifted toward the first rays of Grandmother Sun. Her skin seemed to have absorbed some of the gold from the sun's light. Her black hair glittered with sparks from it. Her long legs were slender extensions of the curves of her small, firm breasts, tiny waist, and rounded haunches.

"Good morning, Grandmother," she said. "Bless me today." Then she recited the usual incantation four times.

> *Where the Seven Clans are, so am I.*
> *There will be no evil in front of me.*
> *I stand in the very middle of the sunrays.*
> *I stand facing the Sunland.*

She broke through the thin ice at the edge of the water. Her feet slipped on the smooth stones as she moved out to a deep hole in the streambed. She drew her breath in sharply as the frigid water closed over her body. A thousand needles seemed to be pricking her. She closed her eyes and concentrated on the sensations on her skin. stayed there until she began growing numb. Then she waded out.

Sunlight turned the beads of water on her body into sparkling jewels. Now that Grandmother Sun was awake, the snow carpeting the mountains' folds shone in subtle, shifting shades of white and gray, blue and purple, with gold highlights. They were pale against the heaps of slate-colored clouds that faded to dove, then a silvery pearl. The clouds became brilliant white where Grandmother's rays poured through a gold-rimmed opening. To Tiana it seemed like a doorway into another world. Looking up at it, she could easily believe Seeth MacDuff's stories of heaven.

She faced east, with her arms extended and recited the charm to re-beautify herself.

> Gha! *Listen. You Red Hawk who live above.*
> *I am as beautiful as the Hummingbird.*
> *As the Red Cardinal is beautiful, I am beautiful.*
> *As the Blue Cardinal is beautiful, I am beautiful.*

She brought her arms toward her body as though gathering in something. She faced north and repeated the ritual, then did it again for the west and south. She did not use the tobacco Spearfinger had left in her moccasin one morning. She had showed it to Grandmother Elizabeth, who went pale under her brown skin.

"It's dangerous, granddaughter," she had said. "Give it back to Mother Raincrow. It must be *tso lagayuh' li*, Ancient Tobacco. Only experienced curers can handle it. If you use it in a spell, the person you direct it against may fall ill and consult a Curer. If he finds that Ancient Tobacco caused the illness, he may return the evil to you."

The loud, slurred call of a cardinal sounded above Tiana. *Are you red or blue?* she thought. *Joyful or lonely?*

She hunkered down and tried to see her reflection in the clear ice at the edge of the stream. She crossed her arms on her knees and stared at her blurred image. *I'm growing old. Almost sixteen. And I don't have a lover yet.* Nannie was considering marriage to the Price boy. All Tiana's cousins were spending time with someone special.

Yet there was no one Tiana wanted to touch in the way the women described when they talked about love.

The sun's weak warmth on her back couldn't keep Tiana from trembling with the cold, but she stayed there, staring at her rippled image. *Why am I here, Grandmother?* she asked. *Will I always be alone, watching others travel life in pairs? Will I always walk the lonely Blue Pathway? Will there be no footsteps echoing behind me?* She waited a few moments longer, but there was no answer. Shivering, she dressed and started back to the camp.

Sugaring had always been a special time, when the daily routine was left behind. She and her sisters used to wait for it impatiently. In late January they would begin checking the ends of the maple twigs for sap. They prayed for clear weather in the mountains during the early part of the winter and then a heavy snow. That meant the ground would freeze more deeply than usual and the sugar would taste better. They kept their belongings packed so they could leave with as little delay as possible.

The Rogers and their friends went together. It was a large sugar bush, a thousand or more taps, and they all shared the work. In a long line, their horses and mules hauled the clumsy sledges with curved sourwood runners up the steep icy trails. When they reached the campsite, the younger children ran laughing in all directions. The older ones helped the adults set up camp.

While the men began cutting wood, the women pulled back the layers of weathered mats in the storage sheds. They uncovered piles of nested bark and wooden dishes for catching the sap and buckets for hauling it. The buckets were stained a rich yellow inside or aged to a deep mahogany color. Any cracked vessels were mended with balsam gum, and new ones were made. They also pulled mats off the log troughs and inspected them for cracks.

Tiana loved the rhythmic toc-toc of axes as the adults cut firewood and repaired the lean-tos. They burned the centers out of new butternut logs while the children gathered kindling. But mostly, the children played. They stole rides on the huge log drags and created small blizzards with snowballs. Like the boys, Tiana and her sisters had contests to see who could sit longest in the cold streams. Or they threw greased, eight-foot poles called snowsnakes down the snowy slopes to see whose would glide the farthest.

As children, Tiana and her sisters and cousins had tunneled into drifts and hollowed out rooms. When the sap began to fill the wooden dishes under the taps, she sneaked fingerfuls of it.

Now, as she topped the high ridge above the camp, she saw that everyone was awake and busy. Steam rose from cooking fires, and she could smell meat roasting. She picked up an old steer hide left by the children the day before. It was stiff and slick from being used as a sled. Tiana shook the snow from it. Then she lay on her stomach, gave a push with her hands and toes, and rode down the steep hill on it.

She gathered speed until she was careening wildly off the bumps in the slope. She managed to steer it around the outlying shelters, and plowed into the snowbank near the boiling-down kettles. She tumbled off the sled and climbed laughing out of the drift. She brushed her earlier unhappiness off with the snow and grinned at the women around the kettles.

"*A'siyu*, sisters." She turned to Grandmother Elizabeth and, coming to attention, snapped one of Jack's salutes. "Private Rogers reporting for duty, General," she said. She draped her blanket over a limb and rolled up her sleeves. She pulled her thick, black hair back and tied it under a red bandana like the other women wore.

"Stand next to me, daughter." Jennie smiled and held out a flat basket of dumplings. Tiana took one, dipped it into the syrup, and gnawed on it while she warmed herself at the fire. The long, thin dumplings had been shaped from corn meal and water, and boiled. Then Jennie had let them cool, split them in half, and toasted them lightly over a fire. She had left them outside the shelter overnight to freeze. Now they were a tasty snack.

"One wonders where her granddaughter has been," Elizabeth said to Sally Ground Squirrel, and the other women there. "She was gone very early this morning, or perhaps she found somewhere warm to spend the night."

"*Ulisi*," said Tiana. "I was at the river, alone."

"A pity," said Elizabeth. "When one is old, one needs small children to carry on one's back."

"You have more grandchildren than pea blossoms on a vine."

"One can never have too many grandchildren."

One of the grandchildren, Aky's son, Aaron, tugged at Tiana's skirt. He was flanked by Pleasant and Levi, two of Charles's children, Elizabeth and Isabel Gentry, and one of the many Bushyheads. They were already caked with snow from their play until even their eyebrows were dusted with it. Tiana knew what they wanted. She dipped a wooden ladle into the simmering syrup and dribbled a stream of it onto the clean snow of the bank. When it hardened into candy, she broke it into pieces and gave it to the children.

"Is it good?" she asked Tadpole Bushyhead. The child nodded, her wild hair bristling like burning straw around her head. Then they ran off to play.

Tiana took the maple-wood paddle from her grandmother and began stirring the syrup. Elizabeth sat heavily, with a weary sigh, on a stool and went on gossiping with the others.

"One hears there's a witch in Coosewatee Town," Tojuhwa, Redbird, said. "He put a spell on Spoiler Campbell." Redbird had recently married Drum's son, The Girth. Everyone agreed they were a well-matched pair. She was spherical. Her small head and feet contrasted strangely with her ballooning bust, waist, and hips. Keeping a house was at times more than her simple intellect could grasp. The women were used to helping her out.

"There's talk in council of making it against the law to kill witches," said Sally Ground Squirrel.

"Law," said Jennie. "So much talk of laws. I don't understand why we need so many laws."

"Perhaps it's time we spoke to the Beloved Men," said Sally Ground Squirrel. "They're becoming enchanted with the white man's laws. Soon we won't be able to defecate without a decision from the council."

"We're not welcome there anymore." Charles's second wife, Rachel, didn't sound unhappy about it. She was just reminding them of a fact they may have forgotten. Tiana always listened carefully when Rachel spoke. She was Ghigau's daughter, after all. But Rachel never had much of importance to say, which disappointed Tiana. She was curious to know what a young Beloved Woman would be like.

"Sisters, we must not surrender our right to speak in council." Jennie rapped the rim of the kettle with her paddle for emphasis.

"The Council of Women decides things for us," said Annie Rogers. "They represent all the clans. And Sally Ground Squirrel speaks for them. We don't have to concern ourselves."

"Councils are boring," said Mary. "The old men drone for hours."

"Here come the boys." Nannie ended the conversation. She wiped the sweat from her forehead and straightened her scarf.

"You're blushing, sister," said Tiana.

"I'm not. It's the heat of the fire."

But Tiana knew better. After the boys emptied their heavy sap buckets into the kettles, they usually stayed to stuff snow down the backs of their beloveds' dresses. The teasing would become more sensual as night drew nearer. Tiana also knew Daniel Campbell would shadow her all day, trying to get her alone. He had already tackled her once and stolen a kiss while they floundered together in the soft snow. She hadn't enjoyed the kiss. He had planted it wetly off center, somewhere between her mouth and nose.

To avoid him, she stayed at the kettles most of the day. But the sight of her bare arms and chest glistening with perspiration and her face flushed in the fragrant steam of the kettles drove more than one boy to distraction. If Tiana was still alone on the Blue Pathway, it was of her own choosing.

Chapter 22

Maryville
November 30, 1816

Lt. Sam Houston
Nashville

Sam,
Perhaps I ventured too far after hearing from you respecting the affair between yourself and M———. Things stand in a remarkably unpleasant situation with respect to you & the queen of "gildhall." She has thrown W M sky high and is ready to leave mother home friends and every thing dear to her, and forsake them and go with you to the earth's remotest bounds. I know & you know that J. Beene is your friend & if I were to advise you it would be to speedily marry M——— by moonshine or any other way most handy.

Yours Sentimentally,
Jesse Beene

"Damnation!" Sam slammed the letter on the desk and pushed his chair away from it. He winced as pain shot through his shoulder. From New Orleans to New York, an army of army doctors had worked over that old wound. After two and a half years neither that one nor the one on his thigh had healed.

Sam padded back and forth in his stockings. He wore two pair to insulate his feet from the draft coming through the cracks in the cold, wooden floor. "Send Jesse fishing and he catches a frog. He has no more sense than a flustered duck," Sam muttered to himself. "I ask him to explain to the girl that I can't possibly marry her. That I'm not good enough for her. That I have a hay wagon full of debts and no prospects, and this is what happens."

He sat on the corner of his desk and surveyed his tiny, bare room, a lieutenant's quarters. His furlough home in September had been short, only long enough to fall in love and get in trouble. Sam knew it was unreasonable to blame Jesse for his predicament when his own wayward charm was responsible. But he blamed Jess anyway.

He considered the alternatives. Marriage was discarded immediately. He couldn't tell Mary the truth, that with time and distance his ardor had cooled. Should he write her and plead poverty? No. There was no predicting to whom she'd show the letter. The thought of his confession circulating through Maryville like smoke around tavern tables was unbearable.

He leaned his knuckles on the desk top, scarred with the carved names and initials of other lieutenants. Squinting in the dimming light from the window, he reread Jesse's blotchy letter. Jesse's hands were too used to handling a plow. He always pressed too hard on the quill and sent ink flowing in puddles around his letters, or in sprays across the page. *Hell-fire*, Sam thought, *he misspelled his own name*. "To the earth's remotest bounds," he read again. "To the earth's remotest bounds."

With a desperate glint in his eyes, Sam found a clean sheet of foolscap and a sharpened quill in his desk drawer. When he blew on his fingers to warm them, his breath made a frosty cloud in the air. He rose and put another log on the small fire, and brought a brand back to light a candle.

He stirred the ink in its stone pot and dipped the quill. For a time, the only noise was the scratching of the pen across the heavy paper and the distant sounds of drilling and drums below his window.

December 20, 1816

Major Genl Jackson
Cmdr, So Div
Nashville

Sir,

   In my continued service to my country I am pleased
to volunteer for any special duty requiring my presence
in the Wilds of our Frontier. I have given ample proofs
of my Valor and Fidelity in the cause of Liberty. I ask
only to continue to serve you in whatever capacity you
might desire.

Your Hble Servt
Sam Houston
Lt 1st Regt Infantry

David Gentry looked up as Tiana came through the door of his shop.
As usual, his heart speeded up and his throat grew dry when he
saw her. He could feel the blush spreading across his face. He bent
closer to the glowing forge so the color might be mistaken for the
heat from it.

"Good day, niece."

"*A'siyu*, husband." She stamped snow from her tall, fringed moccasins and shook the powdery flakes from her black hair. She hung
her ankle-length cape on a peg by the door. Even in December she
had no need of it in David's shop. The sleeves of his muslin shirt
were rolled up over the bulging muscles of his upper arms. A twisted
bandana held his thick blond hair out of his eyes.

"Father sends you some of his best whiskey. He says it's an un-
commonly good run." She pulled a corked bottle from the basket
she carried. "Christmas cheer."

"Thank you. I have need of it." His last words were lost in the
ringing of his hammer on the ax head he was making. "Would you
blow for me? My striker is spending the holidays with his parents."

"I didn't know Adoniram was a Christian."

"Only at holiday time," said David. "And there's not much work at
this time of year. He might as well go. He sees little of his family as it is."

"I can strike as well as blow," she said. "I'm strong enough." She
pulled with both hands on the cord tied to the shaft that closed the
bellows and blew air into the forge. The bellows were so big an
entire ox hide was used to cover the lungs.

"I don't doubt you're strong enough," he said. "But striking takes more than brute strength. It wants skill. You must know where to hit the hot iron to shape it to your desires." He held the ax with his tongs and heated the blade's edge until the pale straw color deepened to orange, then brown. When purple spots appeared in the brown, he plunged the steel into water. Steam rose with a loud hiss.

"I can learn to strike," Tiana said. "But I want to be a carpenter or a joiner. Will you teach me? You know how to do everything."

"A carpenter? You have strange notions, niece."

"Don't lecture me, husband, about the place of women. Mrs. Meigs has already wearied me with it."

He looked at her in mild surprise. There was a new tone in her voice. He had known for a long time she wasn't a child in body. Now he realized she had grown up in spirit too.

"If you want to learn to build, I'll help you. But it's hard work. You can't lift beams alone."

"Neither can you. There are ways to do it. Blocks and tackles, and apprentices. Or I could make furniture."

"How old are you, that you're so concerned about a career?"

"Almost seventeen. It's late to start, I know. But I'd work hard and make up the time I wasted."

"Have you thought of marrying?" He feared her answer, but he had to ask. She must have had proposals already.

"No." She followed him to the work bench and waited while he chose a handle from the pile he had carved of springy ash.

"No? That's all? Not ever?"

"Not until much later. There's no one who interests me now. Not many men are as educated as you or father. I want a man I can talk to."

"Nor any beaus?"

"None I care to encourage. Men want a servant, not a wife. And their pride is such a fragile thing. I fear I'm too clumsy in the handling of it."

She leaned her elbows on the table so she could watch him fit the handle into the eye of the ax head and drive the wedge into the slot to hold it in place. David took a deep breath and willed his pounding heart to be still. As she bent over, the low neck of her dress showed the curve of her firm breasts. A leather bag hung in the cleft there. David fought the desire to kiss the spot where it lay. He was sure his love for her would throttle him. It had been growing inside until it seemed he would burst with it. And he was much too shy to tell her so.

"I'm through here." His husky voice was under control, but with an effort. He felt the panic rising in his chest. He had to get away from her. "Thank your father for the whiskey. I'll take it on home. Where are you staying? Where's your family?"

"They're at Hiwassee Town. I came to see you and Mary and the girls. And to wish you all a happy Christmas. I made the trip on Sterling."

"Your father let you ride his racehorse?"

"Not quite. Father was in council with Drum and Standing Together and mother was off somewhere, visiting. I left a note saying Sterling and I would be here."

David chuckled. He banked the charcoal fire in the forge and put out all the lanterns but one. Outside, it was dark.

"You never change." He put on his big coat made from a bear hide with the fur inside. Tiana tied her wool cape about her shoulders and adjusted the hood over her hair. As he held up the lantern, he saw that the deep blue of the cape matched her large eyes under their heavy fringe of black lashes. She was almost as tall as he was. Five feet eight inches at least.

Together they walked across the fort's deserted drill field as the snow fell more heavily. In places, sparkling flakes danced around their ankles. David pushed open the door of his cabin and held it for Tiana to pass. He set the lantern on the bare table in the middle of the room.

"It's cold in here," Tiana said. "There's no fire. Where's sister?"

David busied himself at the hearth, laying a fire and lighting it.

"Gone," he said finally.

"Gone?"

"She left a few days ago. Split the blanket. She took most everything. It was hers anyway. I've been sleeping at the shop. I'll bed there tonight. You can sleep here." He pulled coverings from a trunk, fussing nervously with the bed. "She left some blankets and a comforter. You must be hungry. There's a little food. Some ham out back, and bread Mrs. Meigs brought. It's a little stale. The fire will warm the place soon."

"Friend." Tiana grabbed him gently by the arm and stopped him in mid-career as he searched distractedly through the clutter on the one shelf that held his belongings. With Mary gone, Tiana realized how little he had of his own. "Pour us each a glass of Father's whiskey. I'll see to things. They want a woman's hand." She opened her basket. "I brought Mary a present, a linen board cloth." She shook the creases out of it and laid it over the table. David placed the bottle and the two small, chipped glasses on it. Then she pulled out a pottery jar of apple butter and a loaf of fresh bread wrapped in oiled paper and a cloth. She laid it with a flourish next to the whiskey.

As she reached for her cape, David watched her with sad, honey-colored eyes.

"I'll be back," Tiana said. "Find a knife to cut the bread and spread the apple butter."

She returned with her arms full of fragrant cedar and pine boughs. She laid some on the table and put others along the mantle and on the empty shelves. Soon the room was pungent with their smell. She found a few stubby candles and put them in save-alls, wire frames with pins to hold candle stubs. They burned cheerfully among the greens between her and David. She crossed her arms on the table and took occasional sips of the whiskey. David focused on his glass.

"What happened?" she asked.

"She left. A fast-talking high roller rode through a fortnight ago. A gambler, I think. Dressed well. A regular spark. Glib tongue. He said gold had been found in Georgia and he intended to get some." David didn't mention the gold had been found, supposedly, on Cherokee land. If that were true, a Cherokee wife would be convenient. "Mary said she was bored here. She went with him to Georgia, I suppose. She said she'd let you all know when she found a place to live."

"And the girls?"

"She took them. They're hers too, by your Cherokee law." There was a bitter edge to his voice. Tiana reached across the table and took his hard, calloused hand. He refilled his glass with his free hand.

"I'm sorry. You love them so much."

"I do. More's the pity."

"You must come back to our house with me. We'll all have Christmas together. Drum loves to celebrate it. He says aside from the Preacher Book it's the only good idea Christians have." Lights danced in Tiana's eyes. "We'll eat so much food we'll waddle around for days." She puffed her cheeks and crossed her eyes.

David laughed and Tiana realized, with a start, how much she loved his lopsided grin and his shy eyes under his wild, blond hair. She squeezed his hand. He was more than winsome. He was actually very beautiful. Why had she never noticed before? There was an awkward silence.

"You'll need more wood." He went out in his shirt sleeves.

Tiana pulled the big down comfort from the bed and laid it in front of the hearth. She filled the kettle and hung it over the flames. She had brought some precious coffee in her basket too, as a present for David. They could put their whiskey in it for warmth. Already there was a glow in her chest. Her head and legs felt light. She realized she was a little frightened and there was a slight churning in her bowels. *Why should I fear David?* she wondered.

David piled the wood in a neat stack next to the hearth. He laid a few more logs on the fire so it blazed up.

"Sleep well. I'll see you in the morning." But he couldn't move toward the door. He couldn't take his eyes off her.

"Stay here a while longer." Tiana patted the comforter, and he sat stiffly next to her. He stared fixedly into the fire. "There's coffee brewing," said Tiana. "And whiskey still in the jar." Tiana pulled the comforter around them both. "You're cold. Finish this glass and I'll pour a dram in your coffee."

"Tiana . . ."

"You're lonely, aren't you, beloved friend?"

He nodded.

"So am I. My soul is blue with loneliness." She held his cold cheeks in her warm hands and turned his head so she could stare into his eyes. Perhaps there *was* something good about looking into someone's eyes, she thought. They spoke so many things his tongue might never say. David buried his face in her hair and wrapped his arms around her. She felt him trembling as she held him close. "Everything will be all right," she said. "Raincrow knows a charm to compel a runaway mate to return. I'm sure she'd teach it to me. She's taught me so much this past season."

"I haven't loved Mary for five years or more. I stayed with her because of the children." He was astonished and disoriented by this fantasy suddenly become reality. "I love you. I think I've always loved you, even when you were a harum-scarum child."

They lay nestled in the comforter and listened to the fire snapping. Tiana rested her head in the hollow of David's shoulder. She was amazed at how happy she was, and at peace.

"There is a charm, a song, to attract a loved one," she said. "Mother Raincrow sang it for me." She laughed. "Mother Raincrow is quite a romantic, you know."

"The old woman with the spare set of teeth?"

"Yes. Her life must have been very sad. To bring love to others, yet never have it herself."

"Sing me the song, though it could hardly attract me more."

As she sang it in the Real People's language, David closed his eyes and listened to her voice. He didn't understand the words, but he understood the feelings well enough.

"What does the charm say?" he asked when she finished.

"The words mean, 'Look at me very beautifully. Let us talk very beautifully. There is no loneliness. So let us talk.' " She opened the collar of his shirt and blew on his chest. He shuddered and held her more tightly. "For the charm to work, one must blow on the breast of the desired one," she said, her lips brushing his skin.

David untied the cord that gathered the neck of Tiana's dress and loosened it slowly. He pulled the neckline open, his hand caressing her breasts, and he pushed the cloth away from them. He bowed his tousled head and blew gently on each one. As Tiana stroked the back of his neck and ran her hand up into his hair, she felt the stirring and warmth in her groin intensify. She moaned far back in her throat.

"Look at me very beautifully," David whispered as he kissed one dark brown nipple. "Let us talk very beautifully." He kissed the other. "There is no loneliness. So let us talk."

David slid his hand under her skirt and moved it up her leg with agonizing slowness, as though he feared to shatter the moment. Tiana's whole being was under his hand, feeling it caress her. His fingers reached the top of her thigh and spread to cover the smooth triangle between her legs. He held the soft ridges cupped in his hand for several breaths until Tiana's groin began to ache, physically, with longing for more.

Then his fingers began to probe, to explore her. When David found the tiny center of her pleasure, he circled it lightly with his finger and Tiana cried out softly. Unable to control the sensation surging through her, she gripped his shoulders and squeezed them hard. She felt his finger slide inside her, then another. She felt suspended there, and weightless on his hand, like the stick she'd held balanced so long ago. It *was* possible for a soul to fly.

With her eyes closed, she began undressing him. He leaned over and kissed her tenderly on the mouth. When he spoke, he did so with his lips still against hers.

"I have loved you always," he said. "And I will always love you."

The open pavilion was littered with the remains of the feast. Dishes and bowls and baskets were scattered on the mats that covered the ground. Tiana's younger friends and relatives were arranging their clothes and giggling among themselves as they prepared to escort her to the nearby council house. The older women, supervised by Sally Ground Squirrel, were already cleaning up the mess. On the other side of the town house, in another bower, the men were feasting with David. More than a few of them must have been drinking. The women could hear their loud laughter.

Jennie put a hand on Tiana's arm and motioned to the others to wait for them at the door of the town house.

"Daughter," Jennie said, when they had gone. "I want to give you some counsel you may find strange."

"What is it, mother?" Tiana wanted to tell Jennie how much she loved her and admired her. She wanted to let her know how much she would miss her. Now that she was leaving Jennie's house, she realized how little she knew about her. Instead, she was the dutiful daughter, carefully avoiding her mother's eyes.

"It's my duty to tell you of your obligations as a wife," Jennie said in her low voice. "I should tell you to work hard to make a home for your husband. And to raise many children. But I don't need to tell you those things. You have always worked hard. You'll be a good mother and a loving wife.

"There is one more thing I must tell you." Jennie paused. Her gentle, beautiful face was suddenly remote with some unspoken sorrow. "Do not lose yourself, your soul, in your family. Do not think only of them and forget your duty to your people. And do not think me unfeeling to give such counsel. I love my husband as my life. I love my children as much. If I had to start over, I would want everything to be as it has been.

"But you are different, beloved daughter. There is a light in your soul that can make other people's paths easier. People see that light in your face. They hear it in your voice. The old ways are changing. The new ways are not always good ones. The path the Seven Clans must follow is dark and twisting. We will need your light. To walk ahead of the others on a dark and dangerous trail will not be easy. In spite of your husband, in spite of your children, there will be times when you will be terribly alone. The special ones are always surrounded by people, and always alone. Do you understand me?"

"Yes, mother. I think so."

Jennie threw her arms around Tiana and held her close.

"Mother," she said. "I'll miss you. I wish I could have known you better."

"Your daughters will know me. I'll be *ulisi*, She Carries Me On Her Back. And someday you will have grandchildren to carry on your back."

Together, Tiana and Jennie walked toward the crowd waiting at the door of the council house. Even though Tiana was three inches taller than Jennie, it was easy to see they were mother and daughter.

Tiana walked ahead of David into the dim council house. She wore an ankle-length white dress of supple doeskin. Long blue and red and yellow ribbons flowed with her hair across her shoulders and almost to her knees. Tiana turned and smiled quickly at David. The lights dancing in her eyes and the curve of her mouth made his legs feel weak. He was glad he didn't have to speak much in this ceremony. He didn't trust his voice.

He and Tiana waited on opposite sides of the dance floor while the men and women of Hiwassee took seats facing each other across the room. Drum stood in the center with his eagle wand raised. He nodded to Tiana and David, and they advanced until they were standing face to face.

Tiana thought David had never looked so handsome. He was dressed in the leggings and moccasins of the Real People. He wore a white ruffled shirt with red beaded bands around his upper arms. A crescent gorget of silver lay on his broad chest. His blond hair strayed from under the blue turban. Mrs. Meigs, White Path's wife, stood next to him. She had agreed to act as his mother.

David carried a leg of venison, which he held out to Tiana. She took it and passed it to Jennie, who in turn handed her a basket of corn meal to give to him. Then Mrs. Meigs and Jennie handed them each a blanket. They passed them to Drum, who held them up for everyone to see. He folded them together and gave them back to David. Like the blankets, Tiana and David were now united.

David knew the ceremony was over, but he had asked James if there was anything appropriate he could say. He had rehearsed it in Cherokee, not caring if he repeated the charm four times. It was an incantation to cause a wife to be happy in her new home.

"I just consumed your heart," he said. "I just consumed your soul. I just consumed your flesh. I just consumed your saliva."

Together, without touching or saying anything more, David and Tiana left the council house. They walked down the stairs alone and in silence, mounted horses, and rode toward David's cabin at Hiwassee garrison.

Chapter 23

Raven and James and John Rogers sauntered single-file along the narrow track made by the light tread of forest animals over the years. It was late May, 1817. The morning's rain had stopped, leaving the tumbled green slopes and ravines of the mountains sparkling. A gentle wind had swept the sky clear of clouds. A spider web strung with irridescent drops of water hung like a necklace between two twigs.

Birds and insects filled the world with a cheerful cacophony. Silver curtains of water covered rock outcroppings where tiny springs seeped to the surface through fluted, bluish-gray lichen. The Real People called the lichen *utsale'ta*, pot scrapings, because they looked like the thick film that formed in the bottom of hominy pans.

The silver of the springs and the raindrops was repeated in the fluttering leaves of the cottonwoods on the next slope. Silver flashed from the wings of butterflies clustered on the trunk of a birch tree. Huge gray boulders, covered with a fine pelt of dark green moss, stood in the midst of ferns.

Raven was in high spirits. When he had walked into Hiwassee Town several days before, James and John had almost knocked him down in their joy to see him. Even dour John had grinned from ear to ear. It had been three years since Raven, unconscious or raving, had passed through Hiwassee garrison in an army freight wagon.

Everyone except Drum had assumed he would die. But Drum refused to mourn him.

Now Raven was back and very much alive. He let everyone think he was only on furlough, which was true in a way. But when his furlough ended, he had an important job to do. If James and John wondered why he wore his tight uniform trousers and blue tunic, they said nothing. The three of them were bound for Hiwassee garrison, but they were taking the long way around. This was like the old days, when they had gone hunting in the mountains for a week or more at a time.

They were in high spirits for another reason. They had breakfasted on venison roasted on sourwood sticks to flavor it. Then they'd smoked a pipeful of dried hemp leaves. The hemp lightened their steps and their heads. Raven felt as though he were walking through a timeless corridor of green leaves and bird song. He thought he could hear each bird and insect in the babel around him.

Raven held his army musket by the long muzzle, with the stock over his shoulder. He swaggered just a little, imitating the Tennessee and Kentucky mountain men. James carried his old rifle balanced loosely in his hand and swinging in time to his easy stride. They both also carried bows strapped across their backs, and arrows stuck through their hair.

John had a dozen darts in the pouch slung at his side. The darts' thistledown feathering showed at the opening of the pouch like a nest full of fledglings. John had rifled the blowgun barrel with spiral grooves, making it very accurate. As he walked, he whittled an arrow shaft from a piece of switch cane that grew in the uplands.

John was in charge of bringing down small game. Raven and James were keeping desultory watch for larger prey. More from habit than anything else, James softly sang an old Natchez hunting song over and over. "*Tsi-hla-hi-he-tsi-no-ma.*" Neither James nor John, nor even Drum knew what it meant. A group of Natchez had lived with the Real People for a hundred years, and their magic was believed to be powerful.

Once away from the garrison, Raven took off his red sash and stuffed it in his pack. He opened the top buttons on his coat and turned down the high, stiff collar. He swiveled his head from side to side, glad to be free of the hindrance. He tied his black boots across the top of his pack along with his leather "tombstone," his tall, cylindrical hat.

Now he was remembering how to walk in moccasins. He placed his heels carefully and rolled his soles forward, so there would be no abrupt snaps or crunches from twigs underfoot. He walked lightly, as though he weighed no more than the cottonwood seeds that blew by on their silky white hairs. His euphoria kept him from feeling fear when he saw a rattlesnake coiled and whirring in the path.

"Brother *Utsa'nati*, He Has A Bell, is here," he said.

"So I see," said James. None of them tried to kill the snake. He Has A Bell was Thunder's necklace and valuable to him. Besides, the Real People knew that if a man killed one, another would come seeking vengeance. John held up a piece of campion root, Rattlesnake's Master. Hunters carried it for protection.

"Let's not see each other again this summer, O Chief of the Snake tribe," said John politely. The three of them waited until the snake uncoiled and slithered away through the dense bushes.

"Someone's been here," said James. "And they didn't want to be seen."

"How do you know?" Raven looked around for signs. John pointed ahead of them, to the acres of tangled laurel covering the slope of the ridge they were traveling. Raven squinted, trying to see what James and John saw.

"There?" He pointed to where the leaves of the laurel had been disturbed. Their lighter undersides showed in a line where bodies had passed. From the size of the swath, there must have been a lot of bodies. Instinctively, the three lowered their voices.

"Traders?" asked Raven.

"Not hell-fired likely," said John. "The tobacco road is on the ridge west of here."

"Sangers?" asked Raven hopefully, although he knew ginseng hunters usually traveled alone. Whoever had passed this way did so in large numbers. Raven and James loaded their weapons.

James squatted to run his finger through drops drying on a rock and held the blood up for them to see.

"Damn!" breathed Raven softly.

"Slavers," said James.

"Mebbe," said John. They both looked at Raven. He was, after all, in the uniform of the United States government. If the trail was left by slavers, they were almost certainly doing something illegal. Raven considered a moment.

"Let's go get them," he said. They began a slow trot that would cover ground quickly, with a minimum of effort. The only noise from them was the muffled thud of their moccasins and the rhythmic sound of their breathing in unison. The trail they followed grew fresher. While James and John sorted out the various footprints, Raven rubbed his aching shoulder and leg.

"Two pair of boots, one with a loose peg in the sole. Two pair of moccasins, one of them Cherokee," announced James. "Ten or twelve shoeless."

"White men," said John.

"Not necessarily," said James. "But white or Indians, there are four we must face. The rest are negroes. Chained in a coffle, no doubt. One has cut his foot. The blood is smeared in the print. Another is bleeding from the chafing of the manacles, or he's been whipped. He's leaving blood in drops."

"If two of them are hurt, they can't be traveling very fast," said Raven. He fell wearily in line behind his two friends. The peacetime army hadn't prepared him for this kind of exertion.

Finally, they heard the faint rattle of chains and the brutal crack of a whip from a bend far ahead by the winding trail, yet just across the open space between them and the next curve. Ears straining, the three trailed their quarry silently.

The rhythmic clanking ahead broke into a jangle. Then there was silence. The slavers must have been allowing their merchandise a brief respite. Raven heard the crack of a whip, then another, and another. By the fifth lash, the screaming started and Raven began to run. He burst into the small clearing with his rifle leveled.

"Halt!" he shouted at the man with the whip. Behind him, James pointed his gun at two slavers who stood close together. John aimed his blowgun at the fourth man, an Indian who froze. White men tended to consider the blowgun a toy; Indians knew better. John could easily lodge a dart in his prey's eye. It was obvious from the look on John's face that he'd do it without hesitation.

But the man with the whip wasn't impressed, either by the weapons or Raven's uniform. It was clear he intended to stop only when the man crouched at his feet was dead.

"Go to hell." He brought the whip down across his victim's back again. The men chained on either side shrank away to avoid being hit. All of the ten blacks were barefoot. Most wore only tattered canvas trousers cut off at the knees. One, a woman, had on a shift of coarse sacking. For a brief moment Raven thought she was Fancy, and his blood chilled. He was wrong, but she could have been Fancy.

Slavers didn't care whom they sold, as long as their merchandise had negro blood in them. They looted the north for freedmen and Florida for blacks who lived in Spanish territory. They kidnapped men, women, and children. They fattened sick slaves, greased them to give them a healthy shine, and plied them with whiskey to make them sprightly. In doing so, they often spread plagues of various kinds. They trafficked in criminal slaves, falsifying warrants of good character. With glib promises to keep families together, they bought them from kindly owners, then sold the mothers, fathers, and children separately.

"I said stop," Raven called again but the slaver ignored him. His tobacco-stained mouth was twisted in rage. His close-set eyes were unfocused. His arm rose and fell steadily. The man he was whipping moaned, his pleas for mercy coming out in an ugly, bubbling garble. The others were silent.

Raven had a moment of panic. He would have to shoot the scoundrel. Raven wasn't accustomed to murder, even of a man like this. In war the enemy was usually faceless. In duels the opponent could shoot in his own defense.

While Raven hesitated, James swiveled. His rifle cracked, and the whip flew in the air. The man sank to the ground, clutching his shattered hand. Raven covered the other two while James reloaded.

"Thank you, brother," he said.

"Think nothing of it," James said. "He was close. An easy shot." The other three dropped their guns and spread their arms out in front of them, palms up.

"You'll regret this," said the injured man. "I have friends in high places."

"I never counted hell a high place." Raven turned his collar up so he'd look more official. "Where are the bills of sale for these unfortunate creatures?"

"Go to blazes."

"I'm a lieutenant in the United States Army."

"I don't care if you're God's grandmother."

"I have authority to arrest you for illegally trafficking in human flesh. It would give me great pleasure to do so."

With his good hand the man pulled a dirty sheaf of papers from inside his shirt and tossed them on the ground in front of him. Cradling his rifle in one arm, with his finger on the trigger and the muzzle aimed at the man, Raven picked them up. He shuffled through them.

"There are six bills of sale here. And they look none too authentic."

"I lost the others." The man held out his hand so the blood from it would drip onto the ground. "I have to bind this," he said.

"You may do so after we discover who is illegally chained and set them free. You can save time by telling me. Otherwise, we shall have to guess from the descriptions on the papers." Raven sighed and gave a look of insincere regret. "These appear to be old papers. Perhaps they don't belong to these folks at all. You might bleed to death before we sort it all out. Pity." He turned to the nearest black. "Where are you from, fellow?"

"Florida."

"I thought as much." Raven turned to the smuggler. "Perhaps your grasp of geography and the boundaries and perogatives of nations is weak. Florida belongs to Spain. Negroes there are free, or the property of the Seminoles who do not sell them. Now tell us which four are not included in these bills of sale."

"The woman," said the slaver. "That saucy scoundrel there." He pointed to the beaten man, who was mercifully unconscious. "The second to the last in line, and that one."

"Now I must trouble you for your keys." Cursing, the man tossed a large ring of iron keys at him. Raven unlocked the four free blacks, who clung to him, thanking him in Spanish, Seminole, and English. The woman threw herself at Raven's knees and sobbed. Raven motioned for the slavers and their Cherokee guide to take the blacks' place in the coffle. He transferred the heavy packs from the blacks' backs to theirs. The manacles closed around their wrists and ankles with a loud, satisfying clank.

While John and one of the freedmen made a stretcher of blankets for the unconscious one, Raven distributed food from the packs to the blacks still in chains. Then they turned the coffle around and headed for Hiwassee garrison. If the bills of sale were bogus, they could be checked there and the unfortunates set free.

Raven swung his worn, patched canvas knapsack to his left shoulder to give his right one a rest. He had packed it carelessly that morning, and something gouged him when he wore it on his back. He could have repacked, but he was too close to Hiwassee to stop. Soon he would see the gnarled old oak where Spearfinger usually perched like an affable buzzard. Where the trees were widely spaced, fragrant flowers carpeted the forest floor. A purple mass of rhododendron flowed down a nearby slope and into the trees. The large, well-worn roots in the deep trench of the trail were like old friends. Raven had stubbed his toes on more than one of them in his midnight sorties as a youth.

Raven had delivered the slavers to Captain Armistead at Hiwassee garrison and had seen justice done. James and John had gone home to help their father on the farm. Now Raven was going to visit Drum. He was feeling pleased with himself and sang as he marched along.

> *Yankee Doodle, keep it up.*
> *Yankee Doodle, dandy.*
> *We'll soak our hides in homemade rum*
> *If we can't get French brandy.*

He wore a faded calico hunting shirt loose over his tight army trousers. He knew Sally Ground Squirrel would make him clothes more appropriate for his mission.

He stopped and listened. The breeze carried the faint sound of women's laughter from their favorite bathing spot at the river. He laid his knapsack by the path and crept stealthily up to the rock ledge from which he and James and John used to spy on the girls. He felt like a boy again, bent on devilment.

As he lay on the warm rock looking down, the scene below was even better than he remembered it. And he remembered it as being wonderful. The Hiwassee and Tennessee rivers met below this southern part of the island. A lagoon had formed, with a sandy, crescent beach. A spit of land almost closed it off from the rivers themselves. Tall bushes and trees lined part of the beach. The other half was bordered by a rolling meadow of grasses and wildflowers. Strawberries grew there in profusion. Raven smelled jessamine and wisteria and allspice.

Brightly colored dresses lay in heaps on the beach, while five or six young women splashed in the water. Two others sat naked on shore and rinsed their hair in water from leather buckets. *Spunk water, no doubt*, Raven thought. He knew the women saved the water that collected in hollow stumps. It was supposed to make their hair luxuriant and shiny and resistant to gray. A few more women lay in the grass, napping in the shade of fragrant magnolia trees. Others plucked the hairs on their faces or rubbed their thick manes with the red covering of sumac berries to make them even blacker.

Six or eight chased each other through the meadow. Some were dressed. Some wore only short skirts. Some had dispensed with clothes. They were throwing strawberries and trying to rub the red juice on each other. Baskets of fruit dotted the meadow. Raven lay feasting on it all. Jackson considered this hardship duty. If he only knew. There was only one thing hard about it, and Raven was lying on it at this moment. He shifted to give himself more room in his tight trousers.

"Hu-uh-uh-uh!" he gasped, and his growing enthusiasm shriveled and tried to retreat up into his body. Chills shook him as a torrent of icy spring water splashed over his back and head. He rolled over in time to see a laughing figure retreat from the ledge. He chased her through the grass, scattering screaming, giggling women and girls. His quarry raced away like a panther, her short doeskin skirt showing long, magnificent legs. *A thoroughbred's legs*, Raven thought. Her hair streamed out behind her, and her bare soles flashed mockingly at Raven.

She leaped a large log, and as he followed Raven heard a rip and felt a sudden draft between his legs. *Damned army pantaloons!* Never mind he'd had them tailored so the baggy seat was much tighter than regular issue. His dignity was the victim of his vanity.

His attacker led him a wild chase as her laughing friends pelted him with strawberries. He tackled her at the edge of the meadow and grabbed her as she tried to squirm away. He threw his body across her, pinning her to the ground. With one hand he brushed the long, tangled hair from her face. For the first time in his life, Raven was speechless.

"*A'siyu*, brother," she said. "You run well for a ghost."

"Grandmother!" He panted with exhaustion. *Good Lord! She's a stunner!*

Tiana lay serenely under him, breathing only a little heavier than usual. He wondered if she had been playing with him, leading him along like a mother bird will do a snake. It was possible. The old mockery was in her eyes. And what eyes. Under dark, arched brows they were the color of sky darkened by storm, where wisps of gray thunderclouds begin and sunlight still pours through them.

Her golden-brown cheeks were flushed and her full mouth was stained with strawberry juice. There was a sensual, yet strong line to her delicately curved lips. Her teeth were white and even. Her narrow nose had a slight hook to it, that added to her determined look. She wore the old-style dress of the Real People. In Raven's opinion, the worst the missionaries had done was replace it with European clothing.

Tiana's skirt was short, and now it was hiked almost to the tops of her thighs. In the warm weather she had dispensed with leggings and moccasins. Raven knew from past experience that she probably wore nothing under the skirt and that the region between her thighs would be plucked smooth of hair. Her calico bodice was short and pinned in front with a brooch. It was cut low enough to show Tiana's rounded breasts and short enough to expose a few inches of glorious golden belly.

As Davy Crockett would say, she was glorification enough, even without spectacles. She was the woman a man might dream about all his life and never meet. Raven could feel her body rising and falling, her breathing in rhythm with his own now.

Her body! Raven rolled hastily off her. Surely she must have felt him growing hard against her. His confusion grew in direct proportion to her insouciance. Hands on hips, he stood glaring down at her as she sat up. She laughed and pointed to the rip that went from one end of his crotch to the other, showing his linen drawers.

"Is that why they call them breeches?" she asked innocently.

Swearing under his breath, he took off his soaked shirt and tied it around his waist. He blushed as she stared at his broad, hairy chest with open admiration. He had forgotten how it was to deal with women directly, without prudery, especially this woman. It was disconcerting.

"Hell-fire, Grandmother! You never ease up on a man, do you."

"I only stop to draw breath. If I let up, you'd all think you were lords of creation. Most of you do anyway," she muttered under her breath. She stood and tugged at her skirt. Now it was Raven's turn to watch, fascinated. In Nashville a man was lucky to catch a glimpse of an ankle, much less legs like Tiana's.

As they walked to retrieve Raven's knapsack, Tiana brushed the leaves and dried grass from her hair. She brought the heavy mass of it around in front of her and ran her fingers through it to smooth the tangles. Raven wanted to plunge his hands into the depths of it, twine it around his fingers and never let go. The suddenness and intensity of his feelings shook him.

Tiana quickly plaited her hair into one long braid and wreathed it on top of her head. She fastened it with pins from the leather sack she wore at her waist, then she picked a spray of wild purple orchids and tucked it behind her ear. She moved with unconscious ease and grace, and her laugh reminded Raven of mountain creeks. *Tiana. Diana. The huntress, goddess of the moon.* It was the first time he had thought about her English name. He wondered what else there was about her he'd never noticed before. He limped a little as his thigh wound throbbed.

"What's the matter?" asked Tiana.

"A wound from the Horseshoe. It still hasn't healed."

"I'll look at it later."

"The hell you will!"

"Ah, I forgot. You must be civilized now. It is permissible for civilized people to peek at nudity in stealth, but not regard the human body openly."

"Your English has improved." He changed the subject.

"I have a good teacher." And she too hastened to talk of something else. "When they carried you away three years ago, Drum said you were wasted, and trapped in evil dreams, raving at your demons. We thought never to see you again, although Drum knew you'd come back someday. As usual, he was right."

There was no accusation in her voice, but Raven hung his head.

"I've been traveling. The army sent me here and there." He waved his arm vaguely. "They were trying to heal my wounds. If I had a dollar for every doctor who said I wouldn't live, I'd be a rich man now. Some damned Scotsman in Knoxville refused to treat me. Said I would die anyway and it would be a waste of money."

"I can heal you." She said it simply, not as a boast but as a statement of fact.

"I've been some wonderful places in the last three years, Grandmother." He ignored her offer. He couldn't imagine baring himself for treatment. Or rather, he could imagine it only too well, which was disturbing. In many ways she was the same hoyden he had always known. In other ways she was a stranger. He decided to treat her as a younger sister until he could get his bearings.

"Some day you must see New Orleans," he said. "You must sip coffee and cognac at the Cafe des Réfugiés and watch Napoleon's exiled generals plot. There's a masked ball twice weekly, with palm trees and promenades." *You would take New Orleans without a seige or a shot, my Indian princess. You would be the most beautiful dusky face and form in a city full of them.*

"And I saw the ruins of Washington City, still smoking after the British plundered and defiled it," he went on. "It fair made my blood boil. I chalked 'The Capital and the Union Lost by Cowardice' on the Senate wall. And New York City! What a metropolis!"

Tiana put a hand on his arm and a finger to her lips. She pointed upward. Raven peered into the trees ahead of them.

"I don't see anything," he whispered.

"There." Finally he spied the big black bear lying along the branch of a fir tree. The limb seemed far too small to support his weight, which added to the absurdity of his being there in the first place. An animal that large and ungainly had no business in a tree. He looked like he had been left by a mischievous wind.

Unaware of them, the bear stretched and yawned, then climbed down the tree, tail first. He landed with a thump on his hindquarters, rolled, and ambled toward them. Raven's gun was empty and he was for retreating. But Tiana held her ground and stayed him with her hand. The bear stopped to overturn a log and root for insects. He licked the crushed ones off his paw with a blissful expression. He looked like an overgrown, good-natured dog, until he realized he wasn't alone.

Sniffing the air, he laid his ears back and stared at them. The three of them stood motionless for what seemed to Raven a long time. Then the bear charged. Raven would have fled if Tiana hadn't held him by the arm. The bear stopped fifteen feet away. Raven could see the gnats buzzing around his eyes and the gray hairs sprinkling his muzzle.

The Real People believed the bear clan had been men once. The intelligence in this one's eyes made it easy to see why. It was as though a man were trapped in that great, hairy body and peering from the eye sockets. The bear huffed, blowing air in gasps. Then he slapped the ground and snarled.

"Let's go." Raven tried to tug his arm away.

"He's bluffing," she said, still holding him firmly.

"*Maybe* he's bluffing." Raven continued to struggle, but tried not to seem panicked. With one hand he brandished his rifle like a club. "I don't fancy ending my young life as bear bait."

The bear snapped his powerful jaws, making a succession of loud clicks. He slapped a tree trunk, ripping away bark in a shower of pieces. Then he charged again. Still, Tiana stood serene. Raven closed his eyes and clenched his teeth and tensed for the fight he knew he couldn't win. He could hear the bear's heavy steps. He could smell the bugs and blueberries on his breath when the bear finally veered sharply and lumbered off through the trees. Raven opened his eyes and tried to regain control of his quaking knees. He loaded his musket with trembling fingers.

"You see, they're all braggadoccio," Tiana said.

"Woman, you're as crazy as Spearfinger."

"How do you know Spearfinger is crazy?"

They were a mile from Hiwassee Town when Drum met them. He must have run the whole way. His round face was bright red and he gasped for breath as he hugged Raven. Raven dreaded the moment when he would have to deliver his message from President Monroe. He was grateful for the Cherokee custom of approaching business slowly and obliquely. He knew he would receive a courteous, dignified hearing, no matter how repugnant his words.

"I would have met you at the ferry, my son," said Drum. "But I was arranging a feast." Drum turned to Tiana. "Daughter, your provider is looking for you. I think someone told him the news. It's impossible to keep a secret in Hiwassee Town. I'm sorry. I know you wanted to tell him yourself."

"Her provider?" asked Raven.

"This one's husband," said Drum. He beamed and put an arm around Tiana's shoulder.

"Her husband?" Raven thought he had misunderstood. It had been three years since he'd spoken Cherokee.

"You didn't tell him, daughter? She's carrying someone." Raven knew that meant she was with child.

"Congratulations, Grandmother," he said. But he felt as though someone had kicked him in the chest. He wanted to shout, "No!" She was meant for him. He had known her for years. She couldn't marry someone else. He felt like a starving man who's been given a feast, only to have it snatched away before he could taste it.

Chapter 24

"So, my son, you have come back to ask us to go to the Nightland."
Drum shook his head sadly, as he accepted the pipe from Jack
Rogers. Overhead, shadows from the fire danced on the latticed
ceiling of the council house. "You ask a hard thing."

"This one doesn't ask it, Beloved Father. General Jackson asks it.
And Father Monroe in Washington City. And Governor McMinn.
They have the welfare of the Real People in their hearts."

"You lie, my son." Raven didn't take offense at being called a liar.
He knew Drum was only saying he didn't know the facts. But Drum
was closer to the edge of anger than Raven had ever seen him. It
was lucky old Standing Together was away. He would have made
Raven's job even more difficult.

"Do you know what Governor McMinn called the headmen of
the National Council?"

"This one has been away. He—"

"He called us 'unprincipled.' He called us 'A set of the most
finished tyrants that ever lived in a land of liberty.' What does he
know of liberty? He wants the liberty to take our country from us.
We're unprincipled because last year we refused to cede land signed
away by a few bribed headmen."

Drum might be isolated. He might appear bland and indifferent
to life off his island, but Raven was often astonished by the breadth

of his knowledge. Whites seemed to think they were dealing with ignorant savages, a favorite phrase of theirs. They didn't know how wrong they were. Raven tried to calm the waters.

"McMinn spoke without thinking. It's a habit of the white man, as you well know. He doesn't understand the ways of the Real People."

"No, he doesn't." Drum regained his composure and smoked a few moments in silence. "He understands nothing but avarice."

"White people consider paper talk sacred," said Raven. "What is written down and signed cannot be changed. Those who sign are honor-bound to comply."

"You lie again. The Seven Clans have never broken an honest treaty. The whites have never honored one. And what of Jackson? We made a treaty defining our territory a year ago. It included land he had bought on speculation and it was not to his liking. He said it was a 'wanton, hasty, useless thing' and the height of his diplomatic ambition was to undo it. He bribed Pathkiller, Sour Mush, even The Just to abolish that boundary treaty. How sacred was it to him?"

"And what of the annuities and gifts that were promised in last year's treaty?" asked Jack Rogers. "And the treaties before that? Where are they? The Real People gave away one million, three hundred thousand acres of land. For what?"

"List the items and the amounts due you, and The Raven will see that you receive them. You have his word." Raven had expected more help from Jack. He was, after all, a very practical man.

"Skatsi," Raven used "Scotsman," the Real People's name for Jack. "You've seen how desperate whites are to settle, to farm, to own land. The hope of it brings thousands to our shores every year. The flood is irreversible, like the river's flow." Raven saw Jack nod slightly. "Every year there will be more."

"Aye. You can damn them, but you cannot dam them," said Jack. "In what currency will the Real People be paid? Not those worthless Indian Trade Office notes. They're always under par and take forever to redeem."

"Each family will be paid for the improvements on the Cherokee land—houses, barns, stables, smoke houses, orchards, and the like. Payment will be in United States Treasury notes or bank drafts."

"On a Philadelphia bank, not those fly-by-night places in Washington City," grumbled Jack.

"On a Philadelphia bank."

"I'd prefer cold coin I can jingle in my pocket," he said.

"You know the treasury's in a state of penury after the war. They don't have that kind of cash available."

"Aye. I know what state the treasury's in. That's why I want cash."

At least they were discussing the method of payment. That was a good sign.

"The emigrants will receive an acre of comparable land on the Arkansaw for each acre they give up here. And each will get a rifle, ammunition, a blanket, and a trap, or a kettle for the women. There's good hunting on the Arkansaw."

"The white fathers tell their red children hunting is uncivilized and that they should farm," said Drum. "Now Father Monroe tells them they should give up their farms and hunt."

"Beloved Father, don't play with me like a cat with her catch," said Raven gently. "This one is not a foolish treaty commissioner whose sole notion of Indians is what he sees carved in the tobacconist's shop. You understand the situation well. The simple fact is that the White Father in Washington City cannot control his children in the wilds. They are too many and too determined. They settle where they will and do as they wish. Is it not the same with the Real People? Didn't a British officer once say Cherokee warriors were like the devil's pig, they would neither lead nor drive?"

Drum had to chuckle. He was familiar with the saying.

"General Jackson is a wise man to have sent you on this errand, my son. Is there then no choice for the Seven Clans?"

"None that this one can see, Beloved Father. It grieves The Raven to bring this talk to you. You could stay here a few years longer. But eventually the flood will crest. The mountains will hold it no longer. Every day more boats arrive, full of white people from across the Great Water. If you leave now, the government will pay you well. You will have first choice of the rich country on the Arkansaw. The White Father promises you those lands forever."

"Forever is a long time," said Drum mildly. "Last year, the government promised us *these* lands forever."

"This one will need your help to persuade the National Council." Raven saw the flicker of annoyance pass over Drum's face only because he had made a study of that face. "Raven knows you dislike traveling to the Council meetings at Ustanali, Beloved Father. He knows the way is long and your wives complain that they'd rather stay home. He knows the ground where you dream at night is damp and makes your joints ache. He'll find a wagon for you to travel in. He'll bring provisions for everyone. He'll see to all the details."

"It is not the journey, although that is tiresome enough. They're making changes at Ustanali. Tsan-usdi, John Ross, and his people have invented something called a committee. Drum doesn't understand committees. 'Standing Committee,' 'Executive Committee.' We don't have words for these in our language. How can we understand them?"

"They'll make the National Council more efficient, brother," said Jack. "The committees will reason out our proposals, then present them to the entire council. We won't have to listen to many days of disorganized discussion. The consent of the entire Nation will still be necessary for changes to become law. And any individual or group or town that disagrees won't be bound by the law. It's the same as it was."

"Drum doesn't like the changes. He doesn't like efficiency. Why is everyone in such a hurry? For hundreds of years our way worked well for us. It was slow, but at least we were sure everyone was heard." Drum thought a few minutes while Raven waited patiently. Finally he spoke.

"Last year there was no summer. The season came and went and it never grew warm. The crops were stunted. It was an omen. Drum might as well give you an answer. He will go to Ustanali and argue in favor of moving. He will do this for his son."

"Thank you, father." Raven sighed in relief. Drum was leader of one of the most influential clans. His opinion was important. Each clan would discuss the question and come to a decision to present to the National Council. The argument there could go on for days, even weeks. But at least the plan was in motion.

Now Raven had to bargain with Jack Rogers alone. Charles Rogers' second wife was the granddaughter of *Ghigau*, Nancy Ward. If Rogers threw in with Raven, perhaps *Ghigau* would too. She rarely traveled to council meetings now. She was almost eighty. But she sent her walking stick to represent her and her vote.

Andrew Jackson had given Raven authority to offer Rogers what the government called a "silent consideration" to support the move. It wasn't exactly a bribe. There was talk of making death the official penalty for anyone ceding the Real People's land without consent of the entire tribe. Passions ran high on the subject. Headmen who signed treaties like this were risking their lives as well as their reputations. They deserved some sort of recompense. Raven intended to funnel extra money Drum's way under one pretext or another.

Oh hell, thought Raven. *It's a bribe.* In Jack's case the money would be a salary. Jack would be paid for services rendered as an agent of the United States government, if he would agree to help with the removal. Removal. The whites persisted in calling this sort of travesty a removal. It had an ugly sound. As though the Indians were merely obstacles in the white man's path, or stubborn stumps in his fields.

Raven thought he could enlist Jack's help. He was a practical man. He knew the inevitability of white settlement. He would do everything he could to protect his interests and assure his family the most comfortable relocation possible.

The government had authorized special considerations for others too. Maybe that was why the Cherokee had managed to be so honest before the white men came: they had no money. Well, they had it now. And if Raven was successful, his government's money would have many of the headmen running with the hare and holding with the hounds.

Two years before, as Raven had drifted in a small skiff down the Mississippi toward his assignment in New Orleans, he had read the days away. He'd gone through Shakespeare, the Bible, *Robinson Crusoe, The Vicar of Wakefield, Pilgrims's Progress*, and the poetry of Akenside. A line from Akenside came to him as he planned his next maneuver. "Each man has his price." The folks in Maryville put it another way. "Money will make the pot boil, though the devil piss in the fire."

Tiana's hands trembled as she unfolded the stiff sheet of paper James had just given her.

"Why me, brother?" She scanned the tiny, jumbled handwriting.

"*Ghigau* couldn't come to this council, but she sent a paper talk in English. Such as it is," he added ruefully. "Drum knows you hear the voice of the talking leaves and you understand *Gilisi*, English. You only have to read what's on the paper. You don't have to make a speech."

"But there are two hundred headmen in there. And another hundred people besides. And General Jackson." Actually, General Jackson was the only one Tiana worried about. "Why don't you do it, brother?"

"Drum wants you. He thinks a woman should read *Ghigau's* words. Don't be afraid. I've seen Jackson with his drawers down. He's only a man like the rest of us."

"He despises us."

"He doesn't. Our warriors saved his hairy arse at the Horseshoe. Jackson would never have breached those walls if we hadn't attacked from the rear and divided the Creeks. And if he had lost the battle there, it's doubtful he would have led the forces at New Orleans."

"I've been watching his face, brother. He does despise us."

"I haven't time to argue. Drum needs me to translate. And since I'm deputized to sign this treaty, I should know what's being said."

"When must I do this?"

"Now."

"But I haven't even had a chance to study it yet. The writing is difficult. There is no punctuation." Tiana was desperate. She would rather face the dreaded General Jackson with a blowgun than this piece of paper. She had seen his patience deteriorate as the days went by and the council continued deliberating. He wouldn't be happy with Nanehi Ward's letter.

"I'll signal you. Then just stride up to the benches in that majestic way of yours and read the words."

"Brother, please."

James held her forearms and stared her in the eye, a trick he had learned from his father. It was useful for intimidating someone.

"You and the other women complain that your voices are no longer heard in council," James said. "Drum wants to change that. He knows you can do it. I know you can. And in your heart, you know you can too. Whether they heed you or not, you must be heard." He shook her gently. "Will you read the letter?" She nodded. "I'll signal you," he said.

Tiana pushed through the crowd gathered around the pavilion. The open, seven-sided shelter had been built for these treaty talks. Two or three hundred people were packed on the benches inside. Twice that number overflowed into the surrounding meadow. Tiana wished the council had been held somewhere besides Hiwassee garrison. If it had, she probably wouldn't have gone. And Drum couldn't have asked her to do this.

It was early July. Tiana felt faint from the heat. Nausea swept over her, and she laid her hand tenderly on her swelling belly. She steadied herself against a post until she saw James raise a finger and beckon. She took a deep breath, closed her eyes briefly, and repeated a charm to dispel enmity. Then she walked calmly between the rows of benches until she stood before the one where Agent Meigs, Jackson and McMinn, Merriwether and Pathkiller, the principal headman, sat.

Pathkiller looked shrunken and almost asleep. He seemed weighed down by his heavy bracelets, earrings, gorget, and medals. He wore a huge sword strapped to his waist. *He's old,* Tiana thought. *No wonder John Ross is leading the council these days.* And John Ross was not here.

Jackson looked old too, but his haggard face was angry and imperious. His glare was cold. *The brother to Blue Man, Winter,* she told herself. The others didn't matter much. Tiana knew Jackson was the one who would force the Seven Clans to accept this theft of their homeland.

"You have something to say, my dear child?" Jackson's high-pitched voice seemed loud and grating and out of place here. Tiana heard the irritation in it.

"This one speaks only the words of another, Beloved Father," she said. She kept her eyes politely on the ground as she spoke. "Our Beloved Woman, Nancy Ward, has sent a talk. She has always held the red people and the white people by the hand."

"Read us her talk then. Time is fleeting."

Tiana cleared her throat and began.

" 'The Cherokee ladys now being present have thought it their duty as mothers to address their beloved Chiefs and warriors.' " Raven stared at Tiana as she spoke, devouring her with his eyes. Could this be the child he had known? She read slowly, but without faltering. Her voice could be heard clearly to the last benches and beyond.

Our beloved children and head men of the Cherokee nation we address you in council we have raised all of you on the land which we now have, which God gave us to inhabit and raise provisions we know that our country has been extensive but by repeated sales has become circumscribed to a small tract and never have thought it our duty to interfere in the disposition of it till now. . . .

She stopped to catch her breath and control her emotions. When she went on, she took care to insert punctuation, but she didn't change *Ghigau*'s words. If the grammar seemed strange to the white men, the Real People understood it. And they knew something Nanehi Ward didn't mention. Only a portion of the Seven Clans' homeland was to be ceded. But that portion included *Ghigau*'s village of Chota, an ancient Beloved Town and a sanctuary. The territory also included Hiwassee Island and Rogers Branch and farm. When Tiana paused, she heard weeping from the women standing at the outer rim of the pavilion.

> We do not wish to go to an unknown country. This act of our children would be like destroying your mothers. Your mothers, your sisters ask and beg of you not to part with any more of our lands, but keep it for our growing children. Keep your hands off of paper talks for it is our own country. If it was not they would not ask you to put your hands to paper.

There were more pleas to keep the land, as though *Ghigau* hoped to make her talk more effective by the sacred repetition. Finally it ended.

> Nancy Ward to her children Warriors to take pity and listen to the talks of your sisters, although I am very old, yet cannot but pity the situation. I have great many grandchildren which I wish them to do well on our land.

"It is signed, sirs, by Nancy Ward, Jenny McIntosh, Caty Harlan, Elizabeth Walker, Susanna Fox, Widow Gunrod, Widow Woman Holder, Widow—"

"We haven't time for a list of names," said Jackson abruptly. Tiana was so startled by his insolence she almost stared at him. No one ever interrupted someone speaking in council.

"We have patiently listened to memorials and objections from your headmen, but letters from your women try our indulgence. You may leave, miss."

Tiana walked slowly back between the benches, toward the brilliant sunlight. It took all her effort to keep from crying. She knew she and Nanehi Ward had failed. Jackson would have his way. She already felt like she'd been exiled to the Nightland. She didn't hear a woman call softly to her as she passed. She only turned to look when the woman tugged at her skirt.

"Beloved Woman," she said. "Will they sell our homes? Our country?"

Tiana shook her head slightly.

"I don't know," she said, finally. "But I fear so." She walked past those standing outside, and went to the forge. It would be hot there, but at least she would be with her love.

Sam anxiously watched Jackson's temper rising. By now he knew the signs well. Old Hickory wasn't used to being thwarted. He defied the Secretary of War, other generals, the President, anyone who had the temerity to stand in his path. Raven could imagine what he would say when he left here. He would rail about petticoat government. He would accuse the Indians of being a shifty bunch, unwilling to look a man honestly in the face.

Raven had tried to explain the Real People's customs before coming to this council, but Jackson hadn't paid much attention. "Your kind, gentle friends scalped Captain Demere alive and made him dance till he died," he had said. The fact that Demere had died fifty-seven years before didn't matter. Now Raven winced whenever the general rudely called a headman by name. This distasteful affair had dragged on for days. Raven prayed it would end soon.

It didn't end soon enough. By afternoon Jackson was purple in the face and shouting at the headmen. Raven could stand it no longer. He left the council house and walked through the silent watchers until he reached the edge of the meadow. He hunkered with his back against a tree, crossed his arms on his knees, and laid his forehead on them. Even then, he could hear Jackson berating the venerable leaders of a proud nation as though they were recalcitrant children.

James found Raven sitting there hours later, when the dark meadow was lit with cooking fires. He sat beside him.

"Is it over?" Raven asked.

"No. It's just beginning."

"The headmen didn't sign?"

"Oh yes, we signed." Raven heard the slight emphasis on "we." "We signed on the understanding that the treaty will have to be ratified by the National Council."

"They'll never do that."

"I know. But we had to say it. Our lives are in danger now, for signing away the Nation's land without the Council's consent. The ink is barely dry on the paper and Jackson is talking with Meigs about transportation to the Nightland."

"But Congress probably won't get around to ratifying it for months." Raven had had experience with the slow wheels of Congress.

"No matter. He's determined to get those of us who signed killed, your General Jackson."

"Surely not. Things aren't that serious."

"Yes, they are, brother."

Chapter 25

David stood with an arm around Tiana's shoulders as she leaned against a tree and vomited. She hadn't eaten breakfast, so there was nothing to purge but bile. Still she heaved convulsively until she gagged. And she shivered in the chill wind of late October. David feared for the unborn child who would jump down in a couple months. That he could only watch helplessly made David feel wretched and inadequate.

Jennie stood nearby with the rest of the decoction of maddog, skull cap, and leaf cup roots that brought on Tiana's nausea. Elizabeth was laying red and white beads on the white cloth that was Drum's payment for this ceremony. Drum would use the beads to ask the spirits about the baby's future, then he would keep them too as payment.

As David held a gourd of cool water for Tiana to rinse her mouth, he tried to control his anger. He came here with her to the river to bathe every morning. It was expected of an unborn baby's father. And David didn't mind. He enjoyed it, actually.

He patiently observed the taboos. He didn't wear a kerchief around his neck or a belt, so the baby wouldn't suffocate on its umbilical cord. He hurried through doorways, so the birth would be a quick one. He trapped animals so Tiana wouldn't have to eat meat gotten by bloodshed and risk bleeding to death when the baby arrived. But he had come to dread these early morning sessions at each new moon.

As Drum went through the divination ritual to ask for success in the birth and in the baby's life, David stood by with a neutral expression on his face. But he was scowling inside. Tiana said this falderol of the purgative was necessary to clean out her body, to get rid of spoiled saliva, as she put it. But it seemed cruel to David.

When it was over, Jennie rolled up the cloth for Drum to take back to Hiwassee with him and they all walked toward the house. At least this would be the last such ceremony here. They would be leaving for the garrison today, and then for the west. The Nightland.

As they approached the front gate of the Rogers' wigwam, Tiana saw a sullen group of three women, a man, and a few children standing in front of it. David drew closer to Tiana, and put a protective arm around her shoulders. He was tense. There had been so many threats against the Rogers that any strangers made David nervous.

"We should have taken the back trail," he murmured.

"Don't worry," Tiana answered. "They're neighbors, from across the branch and down five or six miles. They're probably on their way home from the garrison."

"*A'siyu*, friends," Drum called out. The people only stared at them. One spit into the dust.

"Do not think evil, friends." Tiana advanced toward them. "Our hearts cry for the loss of our beloved homes. We did not wish to sell them." David watched her anxiously.

"Wife," he called softly. "Come. They will not change."

A small boy stepped suddenly in front of his mother and hurled a rock. With an ugly, crunching sound it struck Tiana on the cheek just below her eye. Tiana put a hand to her face, and David, without thinking, chased the child. The women only glared at him, but the man lowered his musket from his shoulder. The boy tried to hide behind his mother's broad skirts, but David scooped him up. He marched him, kicking and struggling, close to Tiana.

"Tell her you are sorry," he said in Cherokee. In his anger he shook him. "You have wounded a lovely, gentle person who would never do you harm." The boy only glared at them both from under straight, black bangs. The man rattled his gun and grunted menacingly.

"Never mind, my protector," said Tiana. "The worm of anger is in his heart." She regarded the boy sadly. "It will eat at your vitals, my son," she said. David let him go and the boy ran to stand defiantly next to his father.

One of the women shouted at them, her voice shrill with hatred. "Your path will be black. You will be covered with dog dung. You will die soon and while you live, your souls will be heavy stones in your breasts."

David hurried Drum and the women toward the house. He felt something hit him in the back and smelled the odor of fresh dung.

"Betrayers! Thieves! Filth!" screamed one of the women after them. "Filth! May dogs shit on you!"

Jack and Elizur and John appeared on the porch with their rifles leveled. James stayed discreetly out of sight. As a signer of the hated treaty he was a special target for people's rage.

"Begone, you ignorant blinkers." Jack waved his gun at them. "Damn you all to hell-fire for a set of confounded dogs." If they didn't understand his English they understood his weapon, and they moved off down the trail. Jack put an arm around each of his wives' waists and escorted them inside for a breakfast of cold corn bread and honey.

"Don't fret yourselves," he said. "We're almost loaded here and the sun's barely up. In a few days we'll be floating down the river with no one to say an unkind word."

After Drum had eaten, saddled his old horse, and left for Hiwassee Town, the others went back to loading the three extra wagons Jack had bought. Tiana climbed the narrow stairs to the upper floor. She braced a hand on each wall to push herself along. Even though her belly was large with the child, it was her mind and her heart that felt tired and heavy.

The upstairs rooms had been cleaned out, but they weren't empty. A worn moccasin, a threadbare rag, a shriveled apple, a stocking that was mostly holes, and a broken basket sat abandoned in the corners. Without the bed and washstand and trunks Tiana noticed the red dust that lay thick on the rafters, and along the tops of the logs in the walls. She noticed sunlight where the window frame had warped and pulled away from the wall.

She held Fancy's old cornshuck hat she had found in the small attic room. It was yellowed and brittle with age and heat. It smelled of dust. The brim's edges crumbled in Tiana's hands. But holding it, Tiana could see Fancy's dark face as she came in from tending the vegetables. "Child," she heard Fancy say. "You look as melancholy as last autumn's garden."

Nannie had married Looney Price and moved out. They had built a small cabin on part of Jack's farm. Susannah had been sleeping in the cockloft so David and Tiana could have the girls' old room. After James and Drum signed the treaty in July, David thought it wise to move back to the Rogers' wigwam. Many of the Real People who came to the fort were unpleasant to Tiana, or worse, threatening. Usually David woke at four, and after bathing in the river with Tiana rode to the garrison to work at his shop. But for the past week he had been helping the Rogers pack.

Now the old room held new memories as well as old ones. Tiana leaned on the wall to ease the ache in her back and the nausea that washed over her again from the morning's purification. She wished she could ease the ache in her heart as well. She felt a tiny foot kick against her swollen belly. She closed her eyes and listened to the room's silence, ignoring the distant sound of voices in the yard.

She could hear the laughter at the feasts they had once had, and the dances and stories. She even thought she heard the quiet talk as her family shared the fire's light on long winter's evenings. And she heard David whispering in her ear and the soft moan he made when pleasure overwhelmed him. She smiled then. At least she would hear that sound again, no matter where they were.

Suddenly, Spearfinger's face appeared, like a grinning demon, at the open window. Her gray hair had turned white. Wisps of it strayed like cottonwood fluff from under her bandana. To reach the cat slide she must have climbed the piles of boxes and barrels waiting to be loaded. She hissed and beckoned. Tiana squeezed through the window, and squatted on the sloping roof. The thick moss on the old shingles was furry under her bare feet.

Below them, Tiana's family bustled about the yard. Tiana felt invisible on the cat slide, in plain sight to anyone who looked up. She wasn't surprised that no one had noticed Spearfinger. The old sorceress knew a very potent hiding spell, One To Miss Them With. She had taught it to Tiana. In exchange for reading to her, Spearfinger had taught Tiana many things in the past year.

"Mother Raincrow, how did you come here?" Tiana asked.

"With the Sons of Thunder." As though in confirmation, thunder rumbled far away in the mountains. "Thunder tells Raincrow you are running toward the Nightland. He tells her there is anger against you and your family. Raincrow brings protection against the Holders Of Grudges."

"Thank you, Mother. There is indeed anger against us. And do you have a charm to protect the house? It will be empty and abandoned. Evil might come here to dwell."

As though she knew Tiana would ask that, Spearfinger handed her a gourd.

"Bury it in front of the door and say, 'The Velvettail Rattlesnake has just come to look into your soul. The Diamondback Rattlesnake has just come to look into your soul. The Ground Rattlesnake has just come to look into your soul. The Copperhead has just come to look into your soul.' " Spearfinger leaned over and bit Tiana affectionately on the ear, sending chills down her spine. "May you live in peace in the distant sunrays, granddaughter," the old woman said. "And may The Provider blow his warm, gentle breath on your abode. May you leave your footprints on the White Pathway."

"I shall miss you, Mother Raincrow. My heart will be blue with longing for you. Will you not come west with us?"

"In the Blue Mountains of the Sunland I originated. I will rest there with the Seven Clans," the old woman said.

She leaped over the edge of the roof, and Tiana hunkered at the eaves to watch her dodge among the piled goods. She hopped across the stones in the creek and onto the top rail of the zigzag fence on the other side. Balanced there, she waved before she jumped down and darted into the forest.

Tiana stared down at the gourd she had left. She knew it probably held the brain of *Huhu*, the Yellow Mockingbird, a powerful spirit. She would have need of a powerful spirit.

When she went downstairs, the large candlebeam still swung slightly. The squeak of its chain sounded hollow in the empty room. Jennie had been about to lower it to pack it, but Jack stopped her. She was crying softly as Jack and David tried to comfort her.

"There's no space for it, lass," Jack said. "The wagons are overloaded now."

"I shall make you another, mother, when we get to the Arkansaw," said David.

Now the candlebeam looked stark and ugly, not the festive giver of light it had been. It hung in the barren room like the bones of a stripped carcass.

"We're almost ready to leave, daughter," Jack said.

"I'll be there in a moment."

Tiana went outside with the gourd. As she buried it and chanted the charm, she cried. It seemed so little to protect the walls and roof that had sheltered her all her life. She said good-bye to the spirit of the house, and begged its forgiveness for forsaking it.

She had another spell with her too. She'd taken it from Seeth MacDuff's Preacher's Book, on the theory that it couldn't hurt to call on every possible source of magic. She murmured the charm four times over the freshly turned earth covering the gourd. " 'The curse of the Lord is in the house of the wicked: but He blesseth the habitation of the just.' "

"Wife, we're leaving. There's a storm brewing." David didn't ask why she was kneeling in the dirt, or why her hands were filthy from digging. He knelt beside her and held her close as she sobbed. "Have you said good-bye to the mountains?" he asked.

"Yes." He gave her a big handkerchief to blow her nose. "I found tobacco in the path this morning," she said. "I kicked it aside. I suppose someone has put a spell on us. A *diga'ghahuh'sdo'dhi'yi,* One To Remove Them. It's supposed to make us feel lonely and depressed."

"Then we mustn't let it," said David. "Come. They're saving a place for you in the wagon."

"I can ride a horse. I'd rather be with you."

"I'll ride alongside. I can reach out and touch you. Besides, they need you to drive Old Thunder." He smiled at her as he helped her to her feet. He wiped her eyes with his thumbs and smoothed her hair, then he kissed her lightly on the mouth. "Look!" He pointed toward the east, the Sunland.

The rising wind whipped Tiana's dress and hair about her long legs as she stared at the mountains. They were aflame with the colors of autumn, but that wasn't what David was pointing at. Slate-colored clouds had almost covered the early morning sky. Only a shimmering ribbon of golden-pink light outlined the silhouette of the smoky, blue-gray peaks. As Tiana and David watched, the clouds moved in, narrowing the golden line until it disappeared and gray met gray. A gentle rain began to fall over the peaks.

"Good-bye, my friends," Tiana said softly to the mountains. "Please don't weep for us."

Many of the people of Hiwassee Town had come to the garrison's landing to say good-bye. They would be leaving too in a couple of months. The Raven and Drum had been organizing the move. It wasn't easy to arrange transportation for three hundred and fifty people. Fortunately for Raven, The Real People were short on worldly possessions.

Those who weren't going to the Nightland lined the margins of the river. There were no cries of good-bye from them, nor tears, although Tiana had known many of them for years. Tiana held her head high as she drove Old Thunder past them.

Jennie drove another wagon, Elizabeth the third, and Susannah the fourth. They had been joined by the wagons of Nannie and Looney Price, Charles and his family, and Aky and Annie and theirs. The Rogers men, their in-laws, and Elizur rode horseback, with their rifles ready. Cows and sheep trotted on lines behind the wagons, and the chickens and geese rode, protesting, in cages lashed to the wagons' sides.

When the wagons stopped in front of the dock, Drum's people rushed to meet them. Muttering and brandishing weapons and clubs, the others drew closer too. The soldiers who were scattered through the crowd to maintain order tensed as the rumbling and jostling increased.

Then Nanehi Ward walked from among the Hiwassee people. The mob hushed as she approached them. At seventy-nine, she still stood straight. Her white hair hung loose like long strands of the finest cotton. *Ghigau* sucked on a carved, red stone pipe and blew smoke toward the crowd. In a steady voice, she recited a charm to disperse emnity. People shuffled uneasily under it.

"We are all one," she said. "Red and white and black, we are created by The Provider. You are all my children. Would you lift a hand against a brother or a sister?"

"No, Beloved Woman," a few murmured, and the tension eased. Soldiers began helping the Rogers unload the wagons. Raven tried to take Tiana's heavy portmanteau from her as she walked toward the dock. She jerked it from him and glared contemptuously at him before she turned away.

There was a stir among the crowd as two boats rounded the bend. They yawed and swung on the end of long stern sweeps like dogs being wagged by their tails. Flatboats were designed to float down-river, using the current for propulsion. They were often at the mercy of the river's whims.

The pilots cursed as they tried to maneuver the cumbersome rafts toward the dock. The first boat swiveled slowly, maddeningly, and floated up to the pilings backwards. Raven was surprised to see there were passengers aboard.

"Who's that?" he asked. Drum stared with a small smile at the men who crowded around the stern opening.

"That's Ata'lunti'ski," said Drum. "My brother, He Throws His Enemy Over A Cliff."

"Hell-fire!" Raven blurted. Drum shook his head slightly. Without saying he was doing it, Drum had been coaching Raven in the sinuous craft of diplomacy. The weakness of Americans, Drum said, was that they were so eager to talk, to tell whatever was on their minds and to interrupt others.

"Father, you never mentioned your brother was returning from the Arkansaw."

"You never asked," said Drum.

Raven closed his eyes in exasperation. He still had so much to learn. Raven had been so intent on arguing the government's case, he had neglected to question Drum closely about the three thousand Cherokee already in Arkansaw County of the Missouri Territory. "Why is he here?" he asked.

"He'll tell us," Drum said.

Ata'lunti'ski led twenty warriors with grotesquely painted faces off the first boat. Above the feathers in his stiff scalplock, Ata'lunti'ski waved a black streamer. As he came closer, Raven could see it wasn't a banner, but a scalp. The skin was stretched onto a hoop and the hair fluttered in the breeze. Ata'lunti'ski gave a piercing, yodeling war whoop that was taken up by the hostile Cherokee on shore.

Damnation! This time Raven only thought it. He kept the expression on his face neutral. But there were gasps from those around him. Some shrank away from the grisly trophies the men carried. Some pressed closer for a better view. Raven doubted Ata'lunti'ski had dropped by to sing the praises of life on the Arkansaw. When a wheel started squeaking it wasn't because all was well with it.

Raven had spent months traveling, intriguing, bribing, threatening, promising, flattering, and cajoling. He had drafted countless letters for the Real People. He had even convinced fiery old Standing Together to sign. Now he understood why that had been possible. Standing Together was willing to move west so he could take to the raid trail again, and fight the fierce Osage.

Raven was tired. Getting the Real People to move at all was like trying to herd a flock of birds. For all his efforts only the Rogers and the people of Hiwassee Town were emigrating. Now even their departure was threatened.

As everyone rushed to talk to Ata'lunti'ski and his warriors, Raven saw the shaky agreement he'd built totter, like a chimney at the first quiver of an earthquake. He had to get the Rogers on their way. He could deal with Ata'lunti'ski later. Raven went in search of Jack. It was time for Rogers to earn the government's pay and hurry the loading of the boats.

Jack didn't disappoint him. He ignored the heated councils convening under the trees and the war drums that were starting. Ata'lunti'ski was causing a lot of agitation, something he was good at. He and his followers were complaining of conditions in the west, of unfulfilled annuity promises, cheating by the agents, boundary disputes, and warfare with the Osage.

But through it all, Jack doggedly supervised the loading. He knew it was only a matter of time before his adopted people no longer had a choice. He wanted to have first pick of the lands on the Arkansaw. He would be settled and able to supply the needs of those who came later. At a profit, of course.

For two days Raven helped stack and shift things. Then the men pulled heavy tarpaulins over the goods and lashed them so they wouldn't topple or slide in bad water. There was bound to be bad water. The Suck lay in wait to the south.

Raven couldn't blame the Rogers if they changed their minds after seeing the boats. Jack had been able to provide everything but space and comfort. Even divided between two boats, the thirty people would be crowded.

The flatboats were little more than rafts, forty feet long and twenty feet wide. The huge timbers of their decks had been squared to minimize leaks, but they were always wet. There would be little left in the oakum barrels by the time they reached the Arkansaw. Each boat had a low, flat-roofed cabin that covered three-quarters of its length. The bow area was fenced off for the livestock. The boats were beginning to look like arks. Guinea fowl and chickens, dogs and cats roamed in uneasy truce. There were horses, pigs, cows, and sheep in the fenced area.

Raven tried to curb his impatience as people wandered off for one last farewell, or to fetch forgotten things, or to eavesdrop on the councils with the western Cherokee. There was an added complication. The war party had brought captives with them. Adoniram, David's striker, had become smitten with one of them.

Ho'n Nika Shinkah, Night Child, looked about sixteen. She was small, with a plump, well-formed body and a round, innocent face. She wore a full skirt and a man's old shirt that fell past her knees. Her thick, wiry black hair was tangled. From the hunted look in her eyes, David was sure she had been raped, although he said nothing to Adoniram. Neither he nor Adoniram had been able to learn much about her, except her name and the fact that most of her family had been killed in Ata'lunti'ski's raid on her village.

Adoniram and David had spent the day bargaining with her owner for her, and Adoniram was beginning to look desperate. At first Night Child, Shinkah, had followed Adoniram with her eyes. But as it became evident he didn't have enough to buy her, she only looked at the ground.

David came to Tiana with the case. He wanted to give Adoniram their savings.

"David, we don't need the money," she said, "where will we spend it on the Arkansaw?" She kissed him lightly on the lips. "Besides, Adoniram will pay us back. And he'll help us when we get there. He's like family to you."

"That's what I was going to say." David grinned at her, his mouth falling into the uneven creases where one side habitually hitched up higher than the other.

When the girl's Cherokee owner saw his price was likely to be met, he raised it. Tiana backed him up against the side of a warehouse wall while his painted friends looked on, amused.

"My friend," she said in a steady, determined voice. "Who adopts captives into their clans?"

"The women."

"Who has final say in the disposition of captives?"

"I caught this one," he said, but he looked uncomfortable. "She is mine to keep or sell as I please."

"Sell her then, but do not be like *utsu'tsi*, the titmouse, saying one thing and then another." Tiana held out the bag of coins. The man took it, scowling fiercely.

Tiana took Shinkah by the hand and led her away.

"Adoniram has taken you into his soul," she said. "May you dwell there in peace." The girl looked at her mutely, understanding her manner, if not her words.

Raven had watched the bargaining because it was taking valuable time and because Tiana was involved. He had spent long, uncomfortable days in the army, many of them in pain. But this day had to number among the worst. When Jackson had proposed this removal, it had seemed a good idea. It would be better for the Real People to leave voluntarily than to have to fight for their land and lose, as they surely would.

But now he had doubts. It disturbed him to see soldiers protecting the Real People from each other. It pained him to see Tiana's cut and swollen cheek and know he'd been the cause of her hurt. Raven had neglected to count the cost to those who would leave and those who would stay. The tears and anguish, the bitterness and hatred and violence hadn't been part of his plans. They should have been. Would he ever be as wise as Drum?

James hugged Tiana. He wouldn't be traveling west yet. Ata'lunti'ski had asked him to interpret for his delegation to Washington. James was a good choice for the job. His English was excellent. He had interpreted for Raven throughout the months of negotiations on this treaty. At twenty-three he was so handsome, men as well as women took note of him.

He had finally let Jennie cut his hair in the short, disheveled Republican style. His red silk turban couldn't contain the tousled mass of thick, black curls. His smooth, brown skin and dark blue eyes looked elegant above his ruffled white shirt, open at the neck. He had the same patrician features as Tiana, the same full mouth and slightly hooked nose.

Finally Raven watched David and Tiana walk slowly up the dock. Stragglers boarded. Jennie and Elizabeth, John, Charles, Joseph, William, Aky, Annie, Nannie, and their mates and children, Susannah and dour Elizur and the Campbells stared toward shore.

Tiana waved sadly to those left behind. David stood with his arm around her shoulders. Raven felt an enormous loss, something else he hadn't counted on when he took this assignment. Tiana belonged to another. She had not given him a friendly word since she found out what his mission was. Even now she refused to meet his eyes. *She hasn't changed, really*, Raven thought. *She's still as fierce in enmity as she is in friendship*. If she hadn't been married, he would have raced up the plank to be with her, to share whatever an uncertain future might bring. His chest was tight with sorrow and longing.

David saw Raven staring at Tiana. He had seen him staring at her for weeks. The Raven. Was it only ironic coincidence that in the Real People's mythology the raven was a rival in love?

"Will you miss your old friend The Raven?" he asked Tiana as the boat swung away from the dock and people shouted good-byes.

"No!" There was venom in her voice. "He wrote a letter and signed it with Drum's name. It was shameful. Drum let himself be used by a man he calls his son. Raven sold his birthright like Esau."

"Perhaps Drum dictated the letter."

"No he didn't. It was claptrap. Fawning claptrap. It assured Father Monroe that we would stay civilized. They're sending us into a battlefield and they expect us to docilely plant and spin."

"Don't be too hard on him, beloved wife. He's only doing what seems right to him." The boat accelerated reluctantly as the current caught it.

"Father says the trip may take six months. Until April." There was a catch in Tiana's voice. "Husband, we'll never see springtime here again. Not the white blossoms of the service, or the red bud, or the mountains all covered in color, the new corn plants waving at us from the hillsides."

"There'll be springtime where we are too."

"It won't be the same."

Desolate, she leaned against him and watched the shoreline recede, the people there becoming smaller and smaller. In her mind she recited Spearfinger's hiding spell, One To Miss Them With. It seemed appropriate.

> *Now! Listen! This is the way it is.*
> *The wind will take me away,*
> *And no one but I alone will know it.*
> *Trees! Trees! Trees! Trees!*

Chapter 26

Jack Rogers stood on the cabin roof at the stern of the flatboat. David had built a windbreak of lashed-down sacks and boxes, but it didn't help much. Jack shivered under the blanket and the oiled cloth wrapped around him. The wind-driven sleet chilled him through and through. *Hell-fire, I'm too old for this.* He surveyed the water raging around a massive tangle of dead trees and sandbars and dirty ice floes ahead. Cramer's guidebook called this the Devil's Raceway.

Jack leaned against the thirty-foot sweep, fighting to keep it under control in the swirling millrace of the current. He stamped to get attention in the cabin below. He needed help. The boat bucked and plunged like a powerful animal. A submerged tree trunk scraped along the timbers with a tearing sound. The deck creaked with the strain. Jack could hear the children crying inside and the livestock lowing.

"Jack," shouted David, carefully picking his way across the pitching cabin roof, "we must tie up."

"There's no place," Jack shouted against the wind. He squinted and ventured one hand away from the sweep long enough to rub the icicles from his beard and brow. "Look!" He pointed to the red- and yellow- and black-striped Chickasaw Bluffs that rose high and forbidding. "Perhaps we can make the White River cutoff by nightfall." Jack knew he was being a fatuous optimist. They'd be lucky to make the next hundred yards.

"Tiana's time has come." David helped Jack with the sweep. "The women can't keep a fire going to warm her."

"Hell-fire and damnation!" Jack could see the worry in David's red-rimmed eyes. Already particles of ice were forming on his tousled hair, his long blond lashes and brows and heavy golden beard. He had neglected to put on his coat, and he shivered uncontrollably.

"Get you inside, man, before your jaws freeze tighter'n an oyster. Send Elizur up, put on your coat, and come back yourself. We'll tie up as soon as we can."

Jack turned and waved to Charles and John, who were trying to steer the boat behind him. He gestured toward shore, and Charles waved back. The canoes they used as lighters, to carry messages back and forth, bucketed along beside the boats. They were both battered and half full of water. They served mainly as drags, slowing the boats' careening course a bit. Jack knew he should cut them loose. As frightening as it would be to travel faster, they were in more danger now, at the mercy of the current.

The roar of the water, forcing its way through the obstacles ahead, grew louder. The channel through the barricade became smaller as trees, debris, and the wreckage of other boats washed against it. Rain mixed with sleet began to fall heavily, and lightning played around them. Now and then a forlorn raccoon or opossum drifted by in the branches of one of the huge, uprooted trees. Their eyes glowed yellow in the flashes of lightning. Logs surged through the water like battering rams.

Elizur and Adoniram pulled themselves across the roof and tethered themselves to rings on either side. With poles, they tried to fend off what debris they could. David stood at the bow between the animal pens and signaled which way to steer.

Jack cursed himself as the boat drifted toward the wall. The narrow opening bristled with ragged trees, broken boards, and masses of sharp roots. Maybe he should have waited until later in the season to make the trip. Had there been greed in his decision to leave early? He and his sons would have first choice of the land. Would greed be the cause of the death of his loved ones? No, he rationalized. They had to leave when they did to make the spring planting.

Jack could see the looming bulk of the barricade, black against the gray rain and sky and roiling river. Poking out of the curtain of rain was the arm of a sweep reaching upward, and a corner of the sunken boat to which it was attached. The limbs and roots ahead looked like fingers waiting to clutch Jack's frail craft and pull it under.

Branches scraped the sides of the boat and snatched at the men as the raft slid through the opening. Water sprayed over them, adding to the rain. Jack threw an arm up to protect his face from a jagged limb as they cleared the flume. The boat dropped, and the sweep whipped from his hand. He ducked instinctively as it passed over him and lashed back and forth on its fulcrum.

The boat lurched and began to revolve slowly, obdurately, in a wide eddy. As Jack threw his body across the sweep, it almost knocked the breath from him. He cursed again and slammed the heavy oak beam with his hand. Even through his sheepskin glove the cold made the blow sting, then ache. Tears burned his eyes.

Lord, help us, he prayed. *I don't ask it for myself, you understand. I'd not blame You for refusing me aid, hellbound sinner that I am. But consider the children, Lord, and the babe about to come into your world.* He wanted to cry with rage and frustration as the raft continued its stately turning, like an overweight matron at a cotillion. Jack had a sudden fear it would be sucked into the vortex. "Please, God, help me!" he shouted into the rain and the mocking roar of the river.

The boat broke free of the eddy. Pain stabbed through Jack's chest as he heaved against the sweep with all his might. Where was that damned Looney Price? As though in answer to his unspoken question, Nannie's husband appeared opposite Jack and tried to help him with the sweep.

"Tie yourself down, man," shouted Jack.

"Bad inside," Looney shouted. "Things all loose. Baby gonna jump down." Looney had a way of belaboring the obvious.

"Help David with the line. Tie it inland as far as you can. This current is consuming the bank at a prodigious rate." Looney looked at him blankly. Jack sighed. In his excitement he had forgotten Looney's English wasn't very good. "Long Man is eating the shore." Jack made scooping motions with his hand. Looney nodded.

The raft strayed closer to the edge of the Mississippi. They had cleared the bluffs and come into the flatlands. For mile after depressing mile stretched canebrakes, sawgrass, and snarls of stunted willows. The willows' raveled silhouette was black and shiny against the gray sky. With typical perversity, the raft gathered speed as it rushed toward shore. Jack braced his legs for the impact.

"Fend us off, Elizur," he shouted. "For God's sake, fend us off." They hit with a jar that started more wailing from the children. David disappeared inside, then rushed out wild-eyed.

"The baby's on the way!"

"It's all right, Davy, lad," said Jack. "We're safe." David's hands shook as he helped Jack storm lash the boat. Even here it was far from calm. As soon as the lines were secured, the men went inside. Jack tarried, checking the lines and knots and the lashed goods and tying the sweep into position in the center of the boat.

Finally, the rain and cold drove him inside too, but he opened the cabin door with dread. He hated being cooped up. He couldn't even stand upright under the low beams. It was bad enough under the best of conditions, which these weren't. Everyone bathed as often as they could. The women kept the cabin as clean as possible. But the stench from fifteen people and a dozen seasick cats and dogs hit Jack in the face and almost choked him. To make matters worse, the people were all sick to one degree or another. The smell of vomit was strong.

Jack squinted in the flickering light of rush torches and candle lanterns. The single room was shrouded with blankets that hung from hooks in the low ceiling. The blankets divided the twenty-by-thirty-foot cabin into cubicles to give the families the illusion of privacy. They also conserved heat from the coals that burned in kettles of sand or in foot stoves. Jack worried constantly about fire.

He stepped over little Moses Price, Nannie's firstborn. The child gurgled happily and pounded a cracked wooden bowl on the floor. Jack winced. His head throbbed with a dull pain that seemed to beat time with the pounding. Jack slipped his boot under the belly of a cat that was managing to nap through the chaos. He lifted her onto his instep and flung her. He got some satisfaction from the astonishment on her face. Tecumseh had been right about getting rid of cats, he thought. They were insolent creatures.

The cold from Jack's wet clothes had seeped through to his bones. His entire body ached, except where he suffered sharp pains. The light of the lanterns and rush torches danced wildly, exaggerating the rocking of the boat. George Hicks, Aky's husband, lay seasick and bundled in furs in a corner. Looney was toweling his lean body on one of Nannie's skirts.

Elizur and Adoniram finished relashing the boxes that had come loose and smashed three baskets of Jennie's pottery. Adoniram's Osage woman knelt on the floor and picked up the shards. She was a mum chit, Jack thought, but apparently not dangerous. She didn't seem inclined to scalp them all in their sleep.

Nannie, Jennie, Elizabeth, Aky, and David were all crowded between the blankets that curtained off Tiana's and David's space.

Aky's children, Aaron and Nannie, peered between two of the blankets. Jack felt embarrassed and irritated. Even though he had fathered eleven children, he had always managed to be elsewhere when they were born. The whole idea made him uncomfortable. "Poor planning," he would mutter as he helped some long-suffering cow with a breeched birth. *Ought to drop seeds and grow children in dirt. Water them, spread a little manure.*

Jack was also irritated about being ignored. He had just saved them all from drowning and no one had even a kind word for him, much less a mug of hot tea with whiskey and sugar in it. *I'm shaking like a wet spaniel and no one cares.* He knew the sulk was irrational, but he indulged it anyway. No one would notice, that was certain.

He stepped behind the woven mats that screened off a small area near the door. He felt slightly less trapped here, because in better weather he could leave the door open. Being on a boat was like being in prison, Jack always said. Except in prison he wouldn't have to worry about drowning. The mats were as good as a redoubt at keeping all of the children but Moses out. The rest of them sooner would have crawled into a den after a mother badger than invade Jack's sanctuary.

A long flannel nightshirt and two pair of thick wool stockings were hanging over the curved handles of a plow. A jug of hot toddies stood next to his blankets. Jennie and Elizabeth hadn't forgotten him. He put on the nightshirt and socks and the cap that warmed the spot on the back of his head where his hair used to be. Then he crawled into the nest of furs he had hollowed out among the lumpy sacks of seed corn. A small forest of bare fruit tree seedlings grew in burlap bags behind him. Jack's mouth watered for a plum. The thought of salt pork and dry government biscuit made his stomach churn.

Jack's pipe, tobacco, tinder box, and books were in a covered waterproof basket by his head. He took his spectacles from their wooden case and propped himself against a sack. He pulled the blankets and furs around him. He perched his spectacles on the end of his nose and tied them behind his head with the ribbons attached to their straight stems. He opened Zadoc Cramer's book, *The Navigator*, and turned to the section describing the next thirty miles of the river.

Tiana gulped air in great gasps and panted as the cramp knotted her bowels. She felt the pressure of the baby pushing against the delicate tissues of her vagina. David sat on a chair he had nailed to the floor. He held Tiana on his lap with his arms around her waist. She was fully dressed with her skirt tucked up and her legs spread. Aky gave her a warm drink made from the bark of the wild cherry. Maybe it was the bark, maybe it was the warmth, but it seemed to ease the pain.

Jennie was bathing Tiana's genitals with a decoction of spotted touch-me-not to scare the child down the birth tunnel. Elizabeth had tried luring it out with promises of a toy bow and arrow or a sieve and loom. Now she was scaring it out.

"Yonder comes Old Flint," she said, talking to the opening between Tiana's legs. "He's rising in the Nightland and coming to eat your liver. Come fast, O child, and we will run away together. We will run to the Sunland."

David rocked Tiana gently and kissed the top of her head. He laid his cheek against her hair and crooned softly to her.

"I see the head." Jennie worked her fingers into the opening, stretching the taut skin a little more, and pulled gently. Elizabeth held a cloth in which to wrap the child. The women crowded around and made little cooing noises as the wet, furry head pushed into the open.

Tiana saw the baby drop into Elizabeth's hands. "Is it a bow or a meal sifter?" Tiana asked.

"It is a sifter, a girl." Jennie drove the blood from the placenta to the child by running her thumb and index finger along the umbilical. Then she tied the cord close to the baby's body and cut it with her knife. She held the child up so Tiana and David could see she was a girl. Then she washed her in warm water, packed puffball fungus over the knot and the navel, and wrapped a cloth around the baby's stomach to keep the fungus in place.

She bundled her in a piece of blanket worn soft with age and gave her to Aky to hold. Elizabeth warmed her right hand over the coals in the squat kettle nearby. She rubbed Tiana's abdomen and recited a formula to bring down the afterbirth. When it finally came, in a gush of watery blood, Elizabeth wrapped it in a cloth, then looked perplexed.

"Grandson," she said to David. "I was going to teach you the formula to recite when you bury this in the mountains. If you carry it across two ridges and sing the song before burying *udi yadon*, That Which Has Remained, your next child will come in two years. But we are far from the mountains. And perhaps you think our customs strange. I don't know what to do."

"When I go ashore," said David, "I'll carry it over two hills."

Elizabeth smiled shyly.

"My granddaughter was wise to marry you," she said. "There is no evil in your heart."

David helped Tiana to their bed of woven mats covered with blankets and furs. Aky handed her the baby.

"Stay with me, husband," Tiana murmured.

"Nothing could make me leave, beloved." He arranged sacks and pillows so he could recline against them. He put an arm around Tiana so she was leaning against his shoulder and chest. With their heads together they stared at the child. Outside the blanket walls, they could hear the talk of the women as they fixed the meal, and the men as they smoked.

With his free hand David ran his fingers so lightly over the child's face and arm he barely touched it at all. He cradled the tiny fist in his own huge palm.

"Beloved," he said.

"Yes."

"I know your *ulisi* will name her in a few days. But might I give her a name too?"

"Of course. What do you want to call her?" Tiana looked fondly up at him. She had never felt so at peace. It was as though the ugliness of their departure, the sorrow, the cold, the storms, the uncertainty no longer existed. She was warm and safe and loved, and she and David had just created this magical being.

"I would like to call her Gabriel."

"Like the angel Gabriel in the Preacher Book?"

"Yes. It was my mother's name."

"It's a good name. I like it." She turned to him. "David, where is your mother, your family?"

"Dead. Gone to the Nightland."

"All of them?"

"Except for my daughters."

"My heart is sad for you."

"There is no need. I have you and Gabriel."

"Someday you'll see your other daughters again."

"I hope so."

"Maybe you can send a paper talk to them when we're settled. Life will be good on the Arkansaw," said Tiana.

"Of course it will," said David.

"I opened Seeth's Preacher Book today. Can you guess the first words I read?"

"No. I didn't know the Bible mentioned the Arkansaw."

"*Gha*! Listen! 'The wilderness and the solitary place shall be glad for them; the desert shall rejoice, even with joy and singing.' Isn't that lovely? 'The solitary place.' "

"Yes, it's lovely."

Tiana and Gabriel soon fell asleep. David lay awake long afterwards, staring at them. There was a smile on his face.

When Elizabeth went to tell Jack a girl child, a meal sifter, had jumped down, she found him asleep, his chin on his chest. His spectacles had fallen onto the open book in front of him. Little Moses had crawled in next to him under the blankets. He too was asleep. Jack's mouth was open and his face haggard. Elizabeth laid a finger lightly on his bristly cheek.

It didn't matter to her that time had battered them both. He was still her champion. Her bold, charming, young British officer. She would willingly follow him to the Nightland.

"Houston, have you disgraced your commission!" The Secretary of War's face was livid. The silky gentility with which Calhoun had treated Ata'lunti'ski had vanished. The Cherokee delegation had just left for the President's Palace and their talk with Monroe. The door was no sooner closed on them then Calhoun went for Sam's throat.

"How dare you appear dressed as a savage before your commanding officer?"

Sam stared at Calhoun in astonishment. It was clear to him that if the Cherokee considered the government's emissary as one of their own, the negotiations would go more smoothly. Sam's friendship with Drum and his brother had been invaluable. But apparently military punctilio was more important to Calhoun.

"I thought it in the best interests of my country, sir."

"You're a disgrace." Calhoun waved a handkerchief at him. "Feathers and animal skins, bells, a filthy blanket. Have you taken leave of your senses?"

"The blanket is clean, sir."

"Don't be impudent."

Sam kept his mouth closed, but with difficulty.

"There's something else of an even more serious nature," Calhoun said. Sam wondered what could be more serious than his clothes.

"Members of Congress have told me you're involved in the dastardly business of slave smuggling."

"What!" Sam was stunned.

"This is a serious charge, Houston. You may well be court-martialed and sentenced if it's true."

"It's not true. I caught some smugglers while in Tennessee. I turned them and their pitiful plunder over to the commander of Hiwassee garrison. You can verify the story with him. Or with James Rogers, Ata'lunti'ski's interpreter. He was with me when I arrested the scoundrels."

"He's also your friend. And so may be the commander of the garrison. However—" He held up a hand to fend off Sam's reply. "The matter will receive a fair investigation."

Sam was cleared of the charges when it was discovered they originated with members of Congress who were themselves involved with the smugglers. They were the slavers, "friends in high places." But there was no prosecution of them, nor was there an inquiry into why they would want to ruin a lowly lieutenant. There was no apology from John Calhoun for the callous treatment of a dedicated officer wounded in the service of his country.

Sam was too angry to worry about punctuation when he wrote his letter of resignation from the army. Then, dressed in his buckskins, Sam rode west with Ata'lunti'ski and his people. As the tree-shaded furrow of the trail rolled under their horses' hoofs Sam complained of the callous treatment he had received.

"Don't speak to me of ingratitude," said James. "If you lie down with dogs, you rise up with fleas. Remember when your esteemed Jackson reviled the men who'd saved his arse-end at the Horseshoe."

"You know how Old Hickory is. He puts on those shows to get his way."

"Yes, I know how he is. You, I fear, do not," said James. "What will you do now?"

"I intend to study a course of law in Nashville."

"A good choice. You'll make a persuasive lawyer. We'll call you *ditiyohihi*," said James.

"Quarreler?"

"That's our word for lawyer."

Raven laughed, and James didn't mention the obvious. Nashville was where Jackson lived.

Sam looked gloomily around him as they rode along the path toward Hiwassee Town. The usually neat fields were disheveled and bare. There had been no spring planting.

He must have been very preoccupied not to look up as he passed under Spearfinger's tree. She dropped on him, of course. She landed on him like a hungry owl on a hapless mouse. Though she looked more like the mouse attacking the owl. Sam's horse jumped and sidestepped and snorted as Sam wrestled gently with her.

"Mother," he said. "The feet of those of my clan are treading the Night Path. Black loneliness covers me. Do not torture me more." But Spearfinger only babbled on and continued chewing his ear. Her skeletal arms were wound around his neck in a stranglehold.

"James, help me," Sam called. James laughed and pried Spearfinger loose. He and Sam lowered the tiny old woman to the ground.

"Has everyone fled toward the Nightland, Mother Raincrow?" Sam asked politely, rubbing his sore ear. Spearfinger cocked her head and stared at him with bright black eyes.

"The Nightland has eaten the Seven Clans," she screeched before she darted off into the bushes. Sam left some of his dried venison and parched corn for her.

"I suppose that means they're gone," he said sadly.

"I suppose so," said James.

"There are twenty people in this group," he said. "Why did she jump on me?"

"She likes you," said James. Sam spurred his horse forward at a fast trot.

"What's your hurry?" James called after him.

"Drum might still be at the garrison."

"Brother, they left here a month ago, judging by the signs."

But Sam hurried anyway. He didn't stop until he reached the fort. He dismounted at the dock and walked to the end of it. For a long time, he stared down the empty river.

"Good-bye, father," he said in a low voice. "I shall miss you. Good-bye, Grandmother. Fare you well."

WEST

The Nightland

1818

The United States is unfortunate in having the worst of people on her frontiers where there is the least energy to be expected in civil government.

—JAMES SEAGROVE,
Indian Agent to the Creeks
1789

You have bought a fair land, but you will find its settlement dark and bloody.

DRAGGING CANOE,
Cherokee Leader
1775

Chapter 27

Tiana tucked a stray lock of hair behind her ears. She had gathered her unruly mane at the nape of her neck, doubled it, and tied it in a club with a dried eel skin. The eel skin was supposed to make her hair longer and thicker and blacker. David always said it was a case of gilding the lily. When he said it he wound a hank of it around his hand, pulled her, laughing, to him, and kissed her on the mouth.

She could hear him now, singing as he smoothed the top logs of the half-finished cabin walls with short, sure strokes of his adze.

> *Her hair it was as black as jet,*
> *in ringlets hanging down.*
> *Search the universe all over, and*
> *her equal can't be found.*

Tiana had pulled the hem of her skirt up and tucked it under her belt. A white woman might also have her skirts pinned up in the heat of a late May day, but she would have left her petticoats hanging modestly down. Tiana didn't wear petticoats. Her bare feet and slender brown legs were scratched with briars and marked with insect bites. She wore a pistol tucked into her belt, a knife in its sheath, and a bag slung at her left hip.

She squatted in front of a glowing heap of embers and sniffed, testing the smell of the bread baking under them. Nearby, Gabriel slept in her basket cradle hanging from a low limb of a big willow. Tiana had draped cotton gauze over the basket to protect the child from deer flies and the ugly black ticks that thrived here.

With a wooden spatula, Tiana brushed the coals off a large, upside-down pottery bowl, and slid the edge of the spatula under the lip of the bowl. She lifted it away from the fire and released a fragrant cloud of steam from the round loaf of corn meal and rye underneath. When she tapped the golden crust with the spatula, it made the delicate hollow rapping sound that meant it was done. She put it into a shallow basket and dripped honey over it. The heat sent the honey flowing in sweet rivulets across the crust and down the sides.

"The bread is ready," she called. As she crossed the cluttered ground around the cabin, she whistled along with David's song.

The stump-filled clearing on top of the hill was littered with stacks of firewood, unfinished logs, and squared timbers. There were mounds of clay and sacks of buffalo hair and dried grass to mix with it to make mortar. Stones for the chimney and springhouse lay piled next to the wooden sledge David had made to haul them from the fields. Oak logs had been rolled onto rails to season for a year. Next spring they would become the cabin's floor. The clearing was paved with the wood chips that flew from David's and Adoniram's axes.

The big grindstone, in its heavy frame, sat complacently in the middle of it all. When people came to visit, they brought their tools to be sharpened. And there were many visits. The Old Settlers, those who had followed Ata'lunti'ski and The Bowl to the Arkansaw years before, came by to offer help and to loan or give them things. Already David was doing a brisk business at his new stone forge under its temporary shelter.

Tiana climbed onto one of the squared timbers to look out over the countryside below. At the foot of their hill, Frog Bayou flowed through a narrow valley. The trees were a deeper green along it. Thickly forested hills extended as far as Tiana could see. Spring did indeed come here. There were redbud trees and serviceberries.

Thousands of birds greeted each sunrise. At noon the shrill crepitation of the "stocking weavers" and cicadas almost hurt her ears. In the mornings, if the light was right and a blue haze hung over the steep hills, and if Tiana squinted a little, the countryside looked very much like the foothills she had left.

It seemed quiet with just the four of them and Gabriel. Tiana's five brothers had left a few days ago to work on the cabins of their other sisters. They helped each other too, but brothers felt especially obliged to build their sisters' homes for them. The cabins would belong to the women when they finished.

They had helped David and Adoniram cut the logs and snake them to the cabin site behind David's patient horse. They had cleared the brush around the huge trees still standing. This year, Tiana and Shinkah would plant corn in the hacking, the area around the stumps.

Tiana and Shinkah had helped David and Adoniram push and haul the logs up poles leaning against the walls to a height of four and a half feet. Then David had left word at Fort Smith, twenty miles away, that they would need help to finish. Friends and family would be arriving within the next few days. So they had all been working hard to prepare the huge logs for the raising, and still clear fields and plant crops.

With his usual thoroughness, David had squared the timbers. It took him two hours to finish each one. When notched and fit together with lock mortices at the corners, the logs would need only a little chinking. David planned to use the timbers later as sumpter pieces and joists for a frame house. In the meantime, they were building a dogtrot cabin, two eighteen-foot rooms connected by a covered breezeway. When they finished this room, Tiana and David would help Adoniram and Shinkah build their house on land they had chosen, twenty miles away.

Now the two men were planing the upper logs of the wall, readying them for the next row. As David chopped toward himself with quick, hard swings of his adze, he saw the worried look on Tiana's face. He folded one foot up behind him at the knee and stood, storklike, leaning on the handle of his adze.

"If I err and amputate a limb," he shouted down to her, "carve me a hollow leg and put pebbles in it. I can keep time for the dances." She laughed. Both he and Adoniram had stripped to moccasins and breechclouts. Their muscular bodies glistened with sweat.

Adoniram's coarse black hair was pulled back and tied with an eel skin like Tiana's. The sun had bleached David's straight hair in streaks of honey and gold and white. The white of his eyebrows and lashes were reflected in the flecks of light in his brown eyes. His face was darkly tanned. He and Adoniram stopped work and sat with their legs swinging over the edge of the wall. Tiana handed the bread basket to David and climbed the wall, putting her toes in the spaces between the logs.

"Little sister." Tiana waved to Shinkah as she worked in the hastily cleared field down the hill. Shinkah shouldered her digging stick and unhooked the crook-shaped gourd from the branch where it hung. Air circulating around the gourd kept the spring water inside cool. Tiana had already planted a gourd patch. As the gourds grew, she would bend the necks into shapes for ladles and cups, spoons and canteens and bird houses.

For the corn planting, Shinkah had painted her face with red and blue lines on her forehead and cheeks. As Tiana handed her a piece of bread, she noticed again the small spider design tattooed on the backs of Shinkah's hands. Someday she would ask her what they meant. There was much she wanted to ask Shinkah, but even questions that seemed innocent often brought tears to her eyes.

Shinkah broke off some of the dried venison from the pouch at her waist and shared it. The meat was braided and tough as leather. It had a rancid taste, but Tiana was developing a liking for it.

"There's only a scantling of corn meal and hominy left in the barrels," Tiana said.

"When it's gone we'll just have to dry turkey breasts and grind them for bread," said David. "We'll get by. The game's thick enough to stir with a stick here."

"Lots to eat," said Shinkah. "Food all around." It was true for Shinkah. Tiana recognized many of the edible plants in the Nightland, but Shinkah seemed to know them all.

David ate the last of his bread. Then he took Tiana's hand. Grinning at her over it, he licked a bit of honey from her fingertips. She leaned toward him and kissed him on the cheek. Adoniram and Shinkah, discomfited, studied the landscape in front of them.

David held Tiana's hand a moment in both his. It was rough and calloused. Those long, tapering fingers should be playing a piano, or embroidering a delicate piece of linen. Not chopping and digging and hauling.

"The big house will have a stone cellar," David said. "And clapboard walls. It'll have a staircase and a second-story piazza and glass windows. I can see you coming down the stairs in a long, white dress."

She put fingers to his lips.

"I will love this house, dear one, because we all built it."

Tiana knew David didn't want the staircase for himself. He'd be content to sleep on a bearskin at his forge. As long as he could shape metal into things well made for a specific purpose, he was happy. What he built would be for her and Gabriel.

"Father Monroe should give us the tools and food he promised," said Adoniram.

"We can survive without the government," said David.

"That's not the issue," said Tiana. "They promised us corn and tools. They haven't kept those promises. We have a right to them. They took our homes, our land."

"I know," said David. "The issue is your beloved justice."

"Look!" Shinkah, pointed and crows began to caw raucously.

"Company." David jumped down inside the walls. He and Adoniram checked their rifles.

"Little sister," said Tiana. "Bring Gabriel." She began loading her pistol with trembling fingers. There was something alien about the outlines of the distant riders. She and Adoniram and David waited behind the chest-high wall. Shinkah darted in and put the cradle in the far corner. Tiana could hear Gabriel gurgling to herself.

"*Pi'sche!*" Shinkah said. "Bad." She ran out again and hauled in the two cows and the horse that grazed nearby.

"Who is it?" asked Tiana. Shinkah stood on a keg so she could see over the wall. Her eyes were the best in the group, perhaps because her people spent so much time on the open plains.

"Ni-U-Ko'n-Ska. Children of the Middle Waters. The Little Ones." She grabbed Adoniram's broad-brimmed hat, twisted her hair onto the top of her head, and jammed the hat over it. It came down over her ears, but it hid her face. With the heels of her hands she scrubbed as much paint off as possible. She laid her digging stick across the log wall and motioned the others to do the same with their guns. Her stick was black with dirt and sweat. From a distance it might look like a gun barrel. It might fool the keen eyes of the Little Ones, the Osage.

"They are your people," said Adoniram. "You can return to them if you want." He tried to keep the pain out of his voice.

"Stay," she said, her eyes following the riders.

The five Osage halted just outside the rifles' range. One of them held up his hand.

"Tse-To-Gah Wah-Sh'n-Pische, Bad-Tempered Buffalo," whispered Shinkah. "Bad," she said again.

"*Nuwhtohiyada*, peace," said Bad-Tempered Buffalo in Cherokee. The Osage warriors were the first Tiana had seen.

The men were tall, most of them six feet or more, and they were handsome. They wore only loincloths and moccasins. Their lean chests were tattooed in intricate geometrical patterns. Their eyebrows and ears were painted red. Their heads were shaved except for a high, bristling crest of hair that ran in a ridge from their foreheads to the napes of their necks where their scalplocks were. The crest was heightened by hair from deer tails and the beards of turkeys. They were armed with shields and bows and arrows. Knives and hatchets hung from their belts. Bad-Tempered Buffalo carried his war standard, a crook wrapped in a trumpeter swan skin.

"Peace, I'n-Shta-Heh, Heavy Eyebrows," he said again.

"Peace, Children of the Middle Waters," said David. "*Gado usdi isgidu'li'ha?* What do you want?"

"*Tsalu hi'a a'gwa'du'li'ha,* Fire In The Mouth, I want this," said Bad-Tempered Buffalo haltingly. David took three black twists of tobacco from his pouch.

"That's the last of it," said Adoniram.

David pitched the twists over the wall.

"Take it in peace," he said. "And carry our friendship to your father, Clermont. When you smoke it, our breath will mingle with yours and float to heaven together."

Bad-Tempered Buffalo rode well into the range of their guns. Tiana looked straight into his fierce, piercing black eyes separated by a long, aquiline nose with flaring nostrils. Leaning down from his horse's back, he picked the tobacco up and rapped it against his leg to shake off the dirt and sawdust.

"*Gali'eliga,* I am thankful." He turned his back on them and rejoined his companions. They all wheeled and cantered away. Eagle feathers spun above the tall roaches in the men's hair. Across Bad-Tempered Buffalo's back hung a bag with a scalp and an eagle's tarsus with outspread claws dangling from it.

The four young people watched until the Osage rode across the valley floor below them. Then they hunkered in the shade of the wall and passed the water gourd among them. Tiana's tongue felt as though it would stick to the roof of her mouth. The crows finally stopped their clamor, but their alarm still echoed in her memory. The green hills no longer looked friendly.

"Were they sniffing the air?" asked Tiana.

"Yes," said David. "They scented too many of us."

"*Wah-hopeh,* War medicine." Shinkah pointed to her back, pantomiming Bad-Tempered Buffalo's bag with the eagle talon and scalp.

"Will they be back?" Adoniram asked.

"Maybe yes. Maybe no. Little Ones hunt little brothers, the buffalo, soon. Far away."

"I'll get some geese," said Tiana. "They'll warn us." She picked Gabriel up and loosened the neck of her blouse so the child could suck. The feel of the tiny mouth pulling at her and Gabriel's small, contented grunts calmed Tiana.

"Damn the government." David threw his adze up on the wall and prepared to go back to work. "They sent women and children here to occupy land another tribe claims, and will kill to defend. And they haven't made a pretense of surveying the boundaries yet." The fact that his wife and daughter were in danger and the government would do nothing to protect them infuriated him. He ran his hand through his tousled hair. Then he rolled his bandana and tied it around his head.

"They don't care what happens to us," said Adoniram bitterly, taking up his own adze. "They drove us to the Nightland. We're ghosts. We no longer exist for them."

"We exist for each other," said Tiana. "And the Real People are to blame for this warfare too. John Chisholm dashed a child's brains out at Claremore Mound. They castrated the boys and raped—" She stopped. Shinkah might understand more than they knew.

"Cheat Little Ones," said Shinkah as she replaced the paint on her forehead and cheeks. Her round face had large, sad eyes and a full, wide mouth. She rarely smiled.

"What do you mean?" asked David.

"Agent Lovely want land. Say land for white man, to live between two tribes." She explained with drawings in the dirt. "So tribes won't fight. Clermont make X on talking paper. Lovely give land to Cherokee, Those With That Thing On Head." She pantomimed a turban. "They all lie to Clermont. Their words fall to earth." She led the horse and cows out.

Tiana put Gabriel back into her cradle and smiled down at her. The child stared up solemnly with wide blue eyes. Tiana emptied the priming from her pistol and tucked the gun into her belt.

"I will help you plant," she called to Shinkah. Shinkah helped Tiana tie Gabriel to her back with the carrying cloth and walked beside her toward the field. Tiana wished she could talk more to Shinkah. She missed the company of women. At corn-planting time, she felt especially bereft.

She had tried to maintain the ritual of the planting of the corn. But her farm was too far for a priest to come to bless the fields and ask Mother Selu's help. The Real People were so scattered it was impossible to plant together, as they had in the Sunland. Tiana had gone to the feast and dance in the nearest village, but it was a meager affair. The only people still living in villages were the poorest, those who hadn't the ambition to clear and plant farms on their own. Besides, Tiana didn't know them. She had left before the festival was over and had ridden sadly home.

As she worked, Shinkah sang, beating the rhythm with her feet and digging stick. Her small flat feet almost danced along the rows as she patted time. Tiana didn't understand the words, but she was entranced by their hypnotic repetition.

> *I have made a footprint, a sacred one.*
> *I have made a footprint, through it the blades must push upward.*
> *I have made a footprint, over it the blades float in the wind.*
> *I have made a footprint, over it I pluck the ears.*
> *I have made a footprint, over it the tassels lie, silver and gold.*
> *I have made a footprint, smoke rises from my lodge.*
> *I have made a footprint, there is cheer in my lodge.*
> *I have made a footprint, I live in the light of day.*

When the field was planted and the sun was too hot for heavy work, they all went to the river. Their favorite spot on Frog Bayou was dappled with late afternoon sunlight. The stream ran deep there, and was a clear aquamarine color. Wind whispered far up in the towering sycamores. The sound of it made Tiana feel cooler even before she dove into the water.

The men smoked and talked quietly while Tiana sat with her feet and legs dangling in the stream and nursed Gabriel. Shinkah waded in the shallows, poking with a stick in search of lotus roots and collecting the tangy, emerald-green watercress. Beech ferns lined the shore. Flowers pushed up through the fallen leaves. Mayapples sprouted from the forest mold like green umbrellas.

A crane stood one-legged, studying the water for prey. White pelicans flew over. A frog gave a call like a hungry calf. High up on the face of a limestone cliff, martins flew in and out of nests around the opening of a cave. Water moccasins lay like ropy, black grape vines in the water.

As the afternoon shadows lengthened mosquitoes began to sing and bull frogs started booming. Passenger pigeons darkened the sky as they headed for their roosts. Tiana and her new family walked up the hill toward home.

That night she lay next to David on their bed of fragrant pine boughs. She had laid fresh wood chips on the floor of their dug-out and they too smelled wonderful. She listened to the sad, haunting call of Adoniram's cedar flute outside the lodge Shinkah had made for the two of them.

Shinkah's lodge had seemed to grow under her hands. She had cut hickory saplings and stuck the butt ends into the ground in an oval. She bent them over and tied them with hickory bark, then used more hickory sticks for cross pieces. She covered the sides with elm bark and the top with mats of cattail stems sewn together with bark fibers. Tiana was constantly surprised by Shinkah's resourcefulness.

She also envied Shinkah her ability to fall asleep peacefully at night. Tiana lay awake, thinking and listening and missing her family. She reached from under the covers and put another stick on Little Father, as Shinkah called the fire. The brighter flame comforted her a bit.

What was it that kept her staring wide-eyed at the dirt ceiling each night? Partly, it was the worry about what they must do and what they must do without to survive. Even now, in May, she worried about the coming winter. She realized she had always taken for granted the comforts her father and mothers had provided.

Noises, amplified and intensified by the darkness, kept her awake too. The cracking of limbs was a familiar one. The weight of passenger pigeons was breaking them, just as they had back east. She knew the rustling that sounded like a dozen men crashing through the bushes was probably only a skunk. The frogs creating cacophony in the bog were like old friends. There were more wolves howling, but she knew about wolves. The coyotes' eldritch song had frightened her at first. She had thought them demons peculiar to the Nightland until Shinkah told her about Brother Coyote.

It wasn't the noise that kept her awake as much as the silence. She feared what she couldn't hear, what she wouldn't be likely to hear, even as it killed her. She feared the Osage and what they might do. She longed to be a hawk, circling high overhead. She wanted to be able to see for miles in every direction, able to warn her loved ones of danger.

She nursed Gabriel, who was fretting, and finally fell asleep. She awoke with chills running down her spine as she did every morning before light. Shinkah was chanting her song of death to the morning star. She sat outside her lodge with her blanket over her head and gave an unearthly cry that subsided to a moaning. She was singing for her mother and sisters who had been killed by the Cherokee and who had ridden west, toward Mo'n'ha, the Cliffs, the Little Ones' spirit land.

"O-hooooo. They have left me to travel in sorrow," Shinkah cried. "Ah! The pain, the pain! A-e, they, hey, Ah-hey, they, hey. It is I who take from them their last days. Ah, hooooo."

After a few minutes of it, Shinkah's mourning stopped abruptly, as it always did. There was silence in the forest around them, as though the birds and insects had hushed to listen.

David sighed and leaned over to kiss Tiana lightly. He put on his billowing white shirt and moccasins and she her long dress. Tiana picked up Gabriel, and David carried the willow cradle. Together they walked through the swirling ground fog toward the river.

Six deer drifted silently across the path. Wild turkeys prattled in the distance. Tiana caught a glimpse of an elk's antlers, and watched a trumpeter swan soar, white against the gray sky.

Each time she recited the morning incantation, she dipped Gabriel in the water.

> Gha! *Listen! She will make footprints on White Pathways.*
> *Lightning will go in front of her.*
> *She will stand beautiful in the sunrays.*
> *As much as is the Sun, she is covered with the Word.*

When the sun rose over the hills, Tiana held Gabriel up toward it. It felt as warm and comforting as it ever did in the east. It helped her forget her night fears for a time.

"Grandmother Sun," she said. "We greet you, my daughter and I. Shine on us, this day. Carry my words to The Provider, Grandmother. Ask him to bring us peace."

David came here with Tiana every morning, and he knew when she had finished. While Gabriel slept in her cradle, he and Tiana laughed and splashed each other. As they walked back to the cabin and their day's work, the birds serenaded them. The Nightland wasn't home, but Tiana had to admit it had its own special beauty.

Chapter 28

David fiddled with his hat. He had the feeling that what seemed reasonable to him, wouldn't strike others that way.

"Major, I'd like to recommend Adoniram Wolf as blacksmith here at Fort Smith." Mild astonishment displaced the usual stern look on Bradford's narrow face.

"He's an Indian," he said.

"He's a good blacksmith. He's worked for me for eight years."

"He wouldn't do." Bradford saw the anger in David's eyes. "Look, Gentry, some of my best friends are Indians. Many of them are fine people. Finer than the average white man out here, I can tell you. That's the problem. Things are rough here."

"Adoniram can take care of himself."

"He'd have to do business with white people. The fullbloods aren't cut out for that. They're too decent, if you want to know the truth. The whites won't like dealing with him. And I can assure you he won't like dealing with them. They'd insult him. They'd cheat him. They'd debauch him." Bradford raised his hand wearily when David started to protest.

"I know what you're going to say. Your boy isn't like the others. He won't take to drink. Believe me, in time, they'd get to him. And they'd get to his wife. The French pox is rampant. And the Indian women usually succumb to licentiousness, if not by bribes and presents then by force. Hell, I don't like it. I'm doing my damnedest to stop it." Bradford was a busy man, but David's guileless eyes seemed to draw him out. Bradford shook his head wearily.

"I assumed that once the army made its presence felt, the situation would improve. But more soldiers only seem to mean more buyers for the rotten whiskey these scoundrels sell. It's the whiskey more than anything. And Indians are easy prey. Well, I shan't bore you with a jeremiad. Your boy would be unhappy, believe me."

A sergeant burst into the room and saluted hastily.

"Beggin' your pardon, sore," he said. "Lieutenant Billings is after killing a trader, that Litten feller. Said he had his way with his wife. And the Indians are for getting out of hand. A regular gallimaufry it is."

"Excuse me, Mr. Gentry."

David followed Bradford outside. He blinked in the bright sunlight and walked across the crowded parade ground. Within a week after their arrival six months before Bradford's men had completed a hospital, a storehouse, a provision house, and the tiny cabin that served Bradford as headquarters. Other buildings had gone up since, but trouble between the Osage and Cherokee had stopped progress. The two stockade walls facing the land had been completed, but the sides fronting the fork of the Arkansaw and Poteau rivers gaped like missing teeth.

David stood on the tawny bluff in front of the fort and looked out over the rivers below. He could see the camps of the Real People, the Old Settlers, lining them on both sides. It was a gallimaufry, all right. Even from this distance it was evident that many of the people down there, white and Indian, were drunk.

The waterways were aswarm with boats. Each trader had a skiff or a fleet of them to ferry potential customers across the river. Canoes and bullboats darted among the flatboats and keelboats. But the Arkansaw was too treacherous for steamboats.

The Cherokee had gathered to ask for their long overdue annuities and to visit the post exchange, the only store for fifty miles. But they were there mainly to greet Drum and the people of Hiwassee Town. Makeshift stores had already appeared on wagon tailgates and under awnings and tents or just laid out on the ground. The main item for sale was whiskey, although one had to go into the woods to find it.

Like sharks circling a helpless victim, the licensed traders and moonshiners, the land speculators, drifters, and freebooters smelled the plunder that went with warfare. They were sucked into the vortex that had Fort Smith as its center. Major Bradford had his work cut out for him.

From across the busy drill field, David watched a group of soldiers watch an Indian woman toil up the slope from the river. There was hunger in the men's eyes. Their gray tunics gave them the look of fresh West Point cadets, but their faces were hard and definitely not young. *Stop the pox*, David thought wryly. *It's a wonder Bradford even manages to make them shave.*

As the woman came closer, David saw it was Susannah. One of the men caught her eye and she flashed him a coy smile before she ducked her head. The soldier sauntered up to her and playfully tugged one of her braids. She giggled into her hand. He caught her arm and dangled a bit of tinsel lace in front of her. David started across the drill field on the run, just as Tiana, carrying Gabriel on her hip, rounded the corner of a building near the men. She saw the soldier reach out and caress one of Susannah's large, firm breasts under her cotton blouse.

"Sister!" Tiana shouted. Susannah and the men turned to stare at her.

"Oh, Lord!" David breathed and he ran faster, dodging around the mounted patrol passing between him and Tiana.

With her free hand, Tiana grabbed her sister's arm.

"Go back to the camp *Tsu'tsan*," she said in Cherokee. Susannah started to object.

"*Hena*! Go!," Tiana said again. "*Nu'la*! Hurry!" Susannah pulled away from the man's grasp and started down the hill.

"Now, girls, there's no need to fight," the soldier stared appreciatively at Tiana. "There's plenty to go around." Tiana backed away, her hand on her knife sheath.

The soldier didn't see David hit him. The others watched amused as he picked himself off the ground. He swung at David, but missed. David grabbed him and held him easily by his tunic front at the length of one powerful arm. Tiana had never heard her husband raise his voice, and he didn't raise it now. She knew he was angry only by the way the creases around his mouth grew deeper and whiter than his tanned face. He shoved the soldier and sent him sprawling back in the dust.

"I'll get you," the man shouted. David gave him a brief, humorless grin, like a wolf showing his teeth. He included all the soldiers in his steady gaze.

"If I see any of you touch a Cherokee woman, you're dead men." He put an arm protectively across Tiana's shoulders. "I asked you to stay with your father or brothers. It's dangerous here."

"I came looking for you. You needn't worry. I can take care of myself. It's Susannah I fear for. She has no judgment where men are concerned. I must talk to her."

David's reply was interrupted by a shout from the wharf.

"They're here! Husband, they're really here!" Tears streamed down Tiana's face. The people of Hiwassee had brought the sacred fire.

With Gabriel bouncing on her hip, Tiana ran down the slope toward the river. The crowd at the dock began to shout. Men fired their guns or pounded with sticks on drums or barrels or trees.

Drum stepped from the boat onto the dock and into the noise. He carried a brightly polished copper warming pan. The wooden handle of the pan was decorated with beads and feathers. The noise grew when people saw it. Tiana just stood quietly crying in the midst of it. Drum had kept the sacred fire burning throughout the long voyage.

Drum also brought three hundred and fifty people with him. Soon there would be so many members of the Seven Clans the Osage wouldn't dare attack them. Tiana would be able to live without a pistol in her belt. There would be dances and ball games and nights of story-telling. There would be gossip to catch up on while the women gathered cane by the river or picked berries or worked together in the shade of the trees. She would hear the rhythmic thud of corn mortars in the twilight, and Drum's call to work in the community fields.

The Old Settlers were expecting a formal ceremony to receive the sacred fire. But in the years that separated them from their kin in the east they must have forgotten what Drum was like. As he walked down the plank, he held the warming pan in one hand. In his other arm he carried a small child, about three years old and black as three o'clock in the morning. She was Drum's favorite among the slave children.

While the men made their solemn speeches of welcome, the child, Martha, pulled at Drum's side whiskers. She blew in his ear, and set his mouth to twitching. He bounced her to distract her and only succeeded in distracting the headmen. They gave up, took the warming pan, and passed it to someone who would guard it until Drum could prepare a place for it.

Ceremonies were impossible anyway. Tiana spent the rest of the day helping to unload, and laughing and talking with her friends from Hiwassee. Gabriel was passed from hand to hand among the women. And Tiana inspected the new children who had been born since she left the Sunland eight months before. That night there was a huge feast and dance that went on until dawn. A game of ball play between the Old Settlers and the Hiwassee team was scheduled for the afternoon.

By the second day the celebration turned ugly. More and more of the men became intoxicated. Fights broke out, something that almost never happened among the Real People. Tiana saw white men offering women trinkets or a surreptitious drink and then leading them off into the forest. When she could stand no more of it, she wandered up a narrow trail along the river until she couldn't hear the drums and shouting and guns anymore.

After a frantic search, David found her there under the overhang of the bank. She was nursing Gabriel and rocking in the big loop of a sycamore root exposed by the water's erosion.

"This section of the river reminds me of the Hiwassee," she said. David heard the sorrow in her voice before he saw the tears on her cheeks. "The trees and bushes are just as thick and green, and there are small islands here."

"Beloved cooker." From the bank he bent to kiss the top of her head. "Please cease your hidling ways. Solitude here is dangerous. These aren't your peaceful hills and forests of home, no matter how much they remind you of them."

"I can't let them steal my liberty. They have no right."

"I ask it for my sake. My God woman, you're making me old before my time." He sat on a flat boulder and chucked pebbles into the swirling, reddish water.

"You saw them, the traders."

"Yes, I saw them."

"They're like magpies picking at the raw flesh on a horse's back, feeding off the living. They're getting people drunk, then selling them things they can never use—old wigs, clocks that won't run, wool clothing. Wool clothing, in this heat."

"Come here, my love." David smiled at her and she moved to sit between his outstretched legs. She leaned against his chest and stared into the churning waters. The cloth of his yellow calico shirt was soft with wear. He encircled her and the child in his arms, and she stroked the material in one of his full sleeves. He sighed in contentment, his breath stirring her thick hair.

"Sally Ground Squirrel says the women want me to represent the Long Hairs in the women's council."

"I'm not surprised." David wanted, suddenly, to keep Tiana and Gabriel here, safely encircled by his arms. He wanted to protect them, to separate them from the disappointments he knew waited for them. There was no going back, either to the Sunland or to the past. The Real People were becoming civilized. Their women were becoming, like it or not, just as circumscribed as white women. Where would a ferociously free spirit like Tiana's fit in?

David hugged her closer. She felt his lips brush her neck, sending chills through her. As he sang Gabriel to sleep, his soft voice lulled her too.

Hush, little baby, don't say a word.
Papa's going to buy you a mockingbird.

Sam glowered as he studied the cast list for the next play. He didn't like the look of his assignment. "The porter." The porter! It was an insult. He regretted joining the Nashville Dramatics Club. That cunning fox, Ludlow, had made them all swear to accept his casting of parts before he would agree to be stage manager. Sam was trapped. But perhaps he could bluff his way out of it.

"Ludlow, my boy." Sam assumed his best military stance and voice. After all, it had intimidated recruits in his army days. "What is this you've got me up for in the afterpiece?"

"Sam, I'm about to test the versatility of your genius." Ludlow was no slouch at manipulating people either. "That character is a very fine bit of low comedy. Short, but all fat." From the full height of his six feet two inches, Sam stared down at the bewhiskered Ludlow.

"What!" he said loudly. "Low comedy? Sam Houston in low comedy? By the Eternal, man. What are you thinking of? Surely you're not serious?"

"I am." Ludlow was unperturbed. Noah Ludlow was only twenty-three years old, two years younger than Sam. But he had performed in towns and hamlets on the frontier for three years. He had had a lot of experience with amateurs. That was why he made this group swear, on their honor, to accept their parts. He knew this role would rankle the young law student. Sam prided himself on his looks, and with good reason.

"By the Eternal, sir, people will hiss me."

"No, they shan't." *If they didn't hiss you in the last play*, thought Ludlow, *they won't hiss you now*. Noah had remarked to his wife that Sam Houston was the *largest* member of the company, if not the most gifted in dramatic ability. "If anyone should be so rude, I will go before the audience and take responsibility."

"I shall hold you to that." Sam was hardly mollified. "I'll attempt the character only because I pledged not to refuse."

Sam kept his pledge. The porter's role was small, only two scenes. And the character was a drunkard. Sam submitted to the costume Ludlow laid out for him—a checked shirt, buckskin breeches, red vest, long red wig, bulky stockings, clumping brogans, a red kerchief, and a hat with the brim torn from the crown and hanging down his back. He even submitted to Ludlow's painting his nose red. He probably would have gone on stage without a fuss if there had been no mirror in the green room.

As the audience milled and murmured outside, during the break between the evening's play and the farce that was the afterpiece, Sam caught sight of himself, full-length.

"By the Eternal!" he roared. The other actors jumped. "By the Eternal. Can this be Sam Houston? Somebody tell me who I am." He rolled his eyes and looked wildly around, lunacy in his stare. Everyone doubled over with laughter, but Sam wasn't amused. He paced the floor like a caged ape, waving his arms and raving. "I swear by all the gods, I won't go on stage like this. What will Mrs. Grundy say?"

People laughed until they were holding their stomachs. The previous summer Noah Ludlow's troupe had performed a play in which a Mrs. Grundy was mentioned often, but never seen. The actors didn't know that Judge and Mrs. Grundy were prominent Nashville citizens. Nor did they know that her religion forbade her attending the performance. Every time an actor said, "What will Mrs. Grundy say?" the audience tittered. The line had become a byword in town.

"Let someone else do it," Sam said. "I'll be damned if I will."

"Oh no, Lieutenant," said Ludlow mildly, using the former military rank Sam affected now and then. Perhaps it would remind him of honor and responsibility. "You'll be damned if you don't. You gave your word. The audience expect it of you. They'll not accept anyone else. Eaton, talk sense to him."

John Eaton took Sam aside. He was educated and urbane, one of the few men Sam looked up to. There were several moments of loud whispering and frantic gestures. In the end, Sam gave in. He had no choice. He had given his word, and that was iron.

"Look here, Ludlow," he growled. "If the people hiss me tonight, I shall shoot you tomorrow."

"Agreed." Noah Ludlow smiled to himself. If he was right, there was a comedian in Sam that few people knew about.

Sam's brogans made the floor quiver as he stamped off to sulk until time for his entrance. Ludlow pulled Eaton, the house manager, aside.

"John," he said. "Make sure Houston's well applauded."

"I'll attend to it." Eaton nodded and winked.

Sam stood in the wings, peeking through the painted folds of the portable proscenium curtain. The theatre had been made by converting an old salt house. The stage was temporary and Sam's tread was a test of the workmanship in it. The crude benches of the pit and the hastily constructed seats were all filled, and people lined the walls. There must have been four hundred in the audience.

They were dim in the flickering candlelight from the hundreds of wall sconces. But Sam knew most of them. Almost four thousand people lived in Nashville now. In his nightly ramblings from tavern to tavern, Sam had met most of those who counted. And most of those who counted were here tonight.

It was humiliating. Sam's mentor and idol, Andrew Jackson, was in the crowd. Not to mention Sam's drinking cronies and the ladies. *Good Lord*, he thought. *The ladies*. The ladies who blushed and dropped their eyes and fluttered their lashes when he bent over their limp fingertips. This role would follow him around Nashville like a can tied to a dog's tail. Who would hire a buffoon for a lawyer? He was ruined.

He fumbled with his itchy wig. Damnation. He was to be dishonored because of his honor, his pledged word. Well, there was no way out but across the stage.

Over the actors' lines and the raucous laughter from the pit, he almost heard the beat of drums and the song of the Booger dance.

He remembered waiting for his entrance signal outside the council door. Maybe the laughter triggered the thought. Laughter was the same everywhere.

Squinting, he dimmed the houselights even more and in his mind's eyes transformed the feathers in women's hats into the egret plumes in the turbans of the men in the council house. He smiled. He'd give Nashville a show for its money. He shouldered the trunk that was his prop and lurched out onto the stage.

"Your nights here are as black as pitch," he roared. "Why don't you subscribe among you for a moon? Bless you! I've got the hiccups." Mugging outrageously, Sam staggered about the stage. Many of his lines were almost drowned out by laughter.

"Good night!" he slurred when his scene was ended. "Damn it, how weak my knees are. Anybody to see me might almost suppose I was in liquor. Steady!" He pretended to trip and teetered on the edge of the stage. Women in the front row shrieked and tried to hide behind their escorts. "Good night! Steady!" And he left the stage. The audience stamped and whistled so, Ludlow feared for the seats. But Sam refused to go out for a bow.

"Damn their souls!" he raved. "They're mocking me."

"Nonsense," said Ludlow. "They're applauding your fine acting."

"Fine damnation, sir! They mean to ridicule me." Sam was trying to hide his mortification in anger. He ripped off the hat and wig and threw them. He ran his hand through his thick, disheveled auburn hair. Then he rubbed the red paint off his nose.

Fortunately, there would be only one performance of "We Fly By Night." Ludlow could see he would never convince Lieutenant Houston to repeat his role. Still, he had done a wonderful job.

"Ridicule you? Not at all," he said. "They mean you have acted the scene to perfection. And may I say that you have, Sam. I have never seen that part done so well."

Sam shrugged. And to Ludlow's surprise, he winked at him. Then he turned and left the room.

Chapter 29

It was Mulberry Month, late May of 1819. Shinkah called May Little Flower Killer Month. The small flowers may have died off, but the big ones were still blooming in profusion. A flock of irridescent indigo buntings had flown over. Tiana could hear the *kuk-kuk-kuk-kow* of the yellow-billed cuckoo. On the hills below Tiana's cabin, smoke trees bloomed. Their masses of fuzzy, gray-blue flowers looked like smoke rising above the green canopy of the forest.

As she was doing now, Tiana often sat in the shade of her cabin's central passage, the dog trot, and stared toward the Sunland. Even though she knew it was impossible to see her homeland from here, she couldn't stop trying.

As Tiana pounded corn for the next day's bread, David played with Gabriel. Only Gabriel could persuade him to take a break from his work. Most of the day she followed her mother around, trying to help. But now and then she would totter off to stand in the doorway of the forge and beg her father to play with her.

She usually had her way. As soon as he could put down what he was doing, he would ride her on his back to the river or hunt berries or make flower wreaths or practice ball play with the tiny pair of ball sticks Tiana had made her. Now, with the child on his shoulders, he was whinnying and galloping madly through the grass and flowers. Gabriel clutched fistfuls of his hair to hold on and shrieked with laughter as she bounced along.

"Aunt is coming," Gabriel called.

As Shinkah rode from the woods, she looked around at the work David and Tiana had done. The clearing spread farther down the hill in the year since Shinkah and Adoniram had helped cut the first trees. David had built a springhouse and smokehouse, cleared another field and started a barn. He had traded smith work for a wagon bed and had added the wheels and tongue. It stood now next to his shop. The shop itself looked like it had been there for years. There was already a mound of horseshoes out back. Stacks of tools and hardware and wagon parts waited to be fixed.

"*A'siyu*, sister." Shinkah dismounted and untied a leather satchel from her saddle.

"*A'siyu.*" Tiana smiled and put down her pestle. "How big you're getting! You must be carrying someone large."

"Not big like you." Shinkah gestured broadly in front of her. Tiana's child would jump down in three months. Shinkah had five months to wait.

"Is Adoniram well?"

"He very fine. But I lonely. My heart aches to see my sister again."

"My heart has missed you too." Tiana knew Shinkah was lonely. There was little love for the Children of the Middle Waters among the Real People. The war faction, led by old De'gata'ga', Standing Together, and Ata'lunti'ski, kept the hatred simmering. They did it partly in retaliation for the Little Ones' raids and horse stealing. But it was also an excuse for forays into Osage country after horses and scalps and war honors. So Shinkah had few friends outside the Rogers family.

"Sit." Tiana pointed to the bench in the shade of the dogtrot's overhang. "I'll bring you something to eat and wash the dust of the trail from your feet."

"I bring food." She opened her bag, and Gabriel appeared at her knee as if by magic.

"*Sali*?" she asked.

"Yes, pretty girl, I bring persimmon cakes." She broke off a piece and gave it to Gabriel. Then she shared some with Tiana and David. Tiana poured them each a mug of parched corn dissolved in water and sweetened with pulp from honey locust pods.

Shinkah always brought the cakes when she visited because she knew Tiana loved them. Shinkah had spread a hickory board with buffalo tallow, then a layer of the seeded fruit. She spread on more tallow and more fruit until she had four layers of each. She cooked the cake on the board, over coals.

"I have something for you too, sister." Tiana went inside and came out with a beaded belt of woven buffalo hair. "It will make the child jump down easily, so you will feel no pain."

"Will you show this one what to do for baby?"

"Yes, we can go to the river tomorrow and I'll try to work for you." Tiana was always careful not to claim too many magical powers. A young curer who boasted was likely to have her work spoiled by an older conjurer.

They all heard Flint Lock before they saw him. Or rather, they heard his wagon creaking and squealing in the woods.

"Flint Lock is coming," David said.

"Good. You were almost out of charcoal."

"Who is Flint Lock?" asked Shinkah.

"He's a charcoal burner. He and his partner have a pit about ten miles from here," said Tiana.

"Some say he's Old Horny, the devil himself." David lowered his voice conspiratorially. "And his pit is a burning chute to hell. Some believe his feet are cloven, and he can light fires with the tips of his fingers."

"I say he's a lonely, bitter man," said Tiana.

The wagon crawled into view. It was pulled by a mangy, patient pair of oxen named Soot and Cinder. Lock halted next to the forge shed, and by the time David got there he had already begun shoveling the charcoal into the large bin David had built.

When they finished unloading, Flint Lock followed David inside the cabin. He reminded Tiana of a dog who knows he's where he shouldn't be and expects to be chased with a broom. He perched gingerly on the edge of the bench by the table.

It was obvious Flint Lock was unacquainted with bathing. He was dark anyway, though whether it was from birth or from the sun or from ground-in coal dust or a combination of all three, Tiana couldn't say. He had a dusty cast to his dark skin. He always wore the same filthy felt hat, or at least, the crown of one. His hair might have been black. Or brown. Or blond. It was long and thin and greasy. His angular features led many to guess he was at least part Indian, but he never said so. And people on the Arkansaw didn't ask into a man's past.

The Real People allowed him to stay because they needed what he sold, and few were willing to produce it. But his eyes bothered folks. He had a shifty, hunted look, the evil eye, some said. But Tiana didn't fear him. She and her family and her house were protected by Spearfinger's charms. Besides, Flint Lock traveled all over the country delivering charcoal. He was a bottomless well of news, if one ventured into his murky depths after it.

As Tiana cut slices of smoke-cured bear meat and warmed up pone and poke greens, she chatted with him as though he were holding up his end of the conversation. Sometimes she could surprise him into giving her information. Amused, David watched her at work. The misanthrope was yet to be born who could resist Tiana.

Lock hunched over his trencher and ate with both hands. The two-tined pewter fork lay idle next to it.

"How's your partner, Mr. Lock?" Tiana asked.

"Dead," he mumbled around a mouthful of bear meat.

"I'm sorry to hear it. The fever?"

"Naw. Found a mull. Charred him from the feet up. Slow like. I heerd him screaming a mile away. I tole him to wait till I uz there to look fer them mulls." Mulls were soft spots in the hill of burning wood. They were formed by burned-out cavities in the stacked billets. The collier risked his life each day by jumping up and down on the mound to locate the mulls. The small ones could be tamped down, but the big ones had to be dug out and refilled with wood. If a mull didn't get him, a careless collier could die in the explosion caused by gases that built up in a poorly vented dome. It was hard, lonely, dangerous work.

"Life is precarious," said Tiana.

"Only death's a sure bet, missy," said Lock. "Anyways, hell's got no surprises for *him*. The devil'd best look to his buttons when my pardner knocks at the gate. He'll be telling Old Scratch how to build a hotter fire." Flint Lock gave a spectral chuckle.

When Lock left, they followed him to his wagon.

"Ef I was a religious man, I'd say she resembled an angel." He nodded at Gabriel. He looked as though he'd like to pat her golden curls, but thought better of it. Gabriel waved with one hand and clutched the grimy piece of sugar candy he had given her. Tiana recognized it as the kind her brother John sold at his store near Fort Smith.

As Tiana was clearing the table, she found a folded piece of paper under Lock's trencher. It was the first issue of *The Arkansas Gazette*.

The editor insisted on writing Arkansas without a *W*, and already that spelling was catching on. Lock must have hooked this issue from Fort Smith. But Tiana didn't care. The paper had seen hard use, and it was covered with coal dust besides. Tiana unfolded it carefully so the fragile sheet would tear as little as possible along the creases.

She took it outside to read to David and to Shinkah, who was sweeping the yard with a sedge broom. In the pale light of late afternoon, David played horseshoes with Gabriel. He had made her a tiny set of them and had driven stakes a few feet apart. The two of them played often.

Tiana read everything on both sides of the paper twice. She even sounded out the articles written in French for the Creoles.

"I'm going to visit Fort Smith with Gabriel," she announced when she had finished.

"You heard what Flint Lock said. The sickly season has started early. A third of the garison has bilious fever."

"I'll not stay long at the garrison. We'll visit my father and mothers and Nannie and Susannah and James and John."

"I can't go with you. There's too much to do here."

"Adoniram coming," Shinkah said. "We all go."

"Good." David was relieved. He didn't like to argue with Tiana, but he didn't want her traveling to Fort Smith alone. It was far too dangerous. He sat on the bench next to her and bounced Gabriel on his knee. "We can load the wagon with gopher peas and beans and dried pumpkin. We haven't much else to spare, but Lock said supplies are low at the fort. Adoniram can bring back some pig iron."

The last slanting rays of the falling sun played across the hills. Shadows stretched outward from the dark ravines and narrow valleys below them. They stayed outside and watched the sky fill with stars.

"That's called *Gi'li'utsun'stanun'yi*, Where The Dog Ran." Tiana pointed to the Milky Way.

"Why?" asked Gabriel.

"This is what the old women told me when I was a girl," Tiana answered. "Once a dog stole some corn meal. The women were angry with the dog. They chased him and whipped him until he ran off, howling, into the sky. He left behind him a white trail of corn meal."

"We call it Heaven's Path," said Shinkah. The child stared up at the magnificence of the stars.

"Each of us has an ancestor in the sky," Tiana went on. "Each star represents one of those ancestors. The ancestor decides what kind of person her great, great grandchild will be. And she watches over that child. Someday maybe you'll learn which star is your ancestor's."

As the evening chill settled, they moved inside by the fire. Shinkah sat on a buffalo robe on the floor. She sat as she always did, with her legs straight out in front of her. Gabriel settled into her soft lap. Tiana's was too big these days for comfortable sitting. The dried tobacco and apples and strings of pumpkin made the room aromatic. Several ax handles were charring and seasoning next to the fire.

Shinkah began an endless story. At least Tiana had never heard the end of it. Shinkah translated it roughly from the tales of her own people. Gabriel had heard it before, but she loved it, and she knew the ritual. Shinkah would stop now and then and say, "Ha'n." Gabriel would reply, "Ha'n." When Gabriel stopped answering, Shinkah knew her trick had worked. It was the Little Ones' way of putting their children to sleep.

David picked the child up. But instead of putting her in her own small bed, he stretched out on his, with her in his arms. He was soon as fast asleep as she was. He worked hard and usually fell asleep early.

Shinkah stared fixedly into the fire and spoke more than Tiana had ever heard her do. Tiana was lulled by her low voice and the crackling of the fire, the wolves singing far away and the mice squeaking in the rafters. The cheerful comfort of the cabin made Shinkah's story seem more horrifying. For the first time, Shinkah talked about the Cherokee raid on her family's village while the men were gone.

"They chased the boys to a hill near the village. Raped the girls. Cut off the boys' . . ." She searched for a word. "Their manhood. I could only revenge my mother."

"You took revenge?" asked Tiana.

"Yes. But only one. I could kill no more. My sister is unavenged. Adoniram knows nothing of it. He is a good, kind man. I could not tell him. They were his people, the ones who did this thing."

"You killed someone?"

"Yes. The last one who took me." She said it simply, as a matter of fact. "I tried to kill him as I was taught. I am *Wa-ca-be*, of the Bear Clan. Bear women can kill like this." She wet her right index finger and pointed it well away from Tiana and David and Gabriel.

"One says to one's enemy, 'You will die.' But he did not die. I am unworthy to be a Bear Woman." Shinkah drew a deep breath. A tear made a gleaming path in the fire's light. "I bit him here." She pointed to her neck, her jugular vein. "Sometimes I wake in the night. There is the taste of blood in my mouth. I had no knife to take his scalp. But my mother is avenged, I think."

David waved as the wagon left the farm. Already Gabriel was asking when they would get there. To distract her, Tiana began a story of Tsi-stu, the Rabbit.

"The rabbit was the leader of them all in mischief," she said. She and Gabriel and Shinkah turned to wave gaily until they were out of sight. Then they settled down to a day of story-telling as they traveled.

They entered Fort Smith to the sound of muffled drums and "Roslin Castle" being played on the fifes. Fifty soldiers marched behind a rough pine casket.

"What happened?" Tiana asked the sentry.

"Ague," the man said.

As Adoniram flicked the whip at the horses, two men dragged a third from Bradford's office. The man in the middle twisted and tugged. He jerked free, ran a few paces, and fell. On his hands and knees he vomited into the thick dust of the parade ground. Then he fainted, sprawling in his own bile. One of his companions turned him over with his foot and took his arms. The other grabbed his feet and they carried him toward the low building that served as a hospital.

"Don't go in there." The sentry nodded toward the hospital. "No one goes in there and comes out alive. It's bewitched, that place." There was fear in his eyes.

"Adoniram," Tiana said. "We'll leave this food with Major Bradford, collect the pig iron, and go immediately to my mother's house. We'll be safe there."

When they returned to the farm a week later, David knew something was wrong. He dropped his hammer and ran to the wagon. Tiana sat next to Adoniram on the seat. She held Gabriel. Shinkah rode alone in the rear of the wagon. In the heat of the June day, she had a blanket draped over her head. She sat as close to the tailgate as she could. She rocked back and forth and moaned in a low voice.

"What is it?" David asked. Tiana stared past him, her eyes unable to focus. She shook herself to attention.

"She's ill."

"Shinkah?" David peered over the side of the wagon at Shinkah.

"No. Our daughter. Shinkah says women of the Bear clan cannot get near the sick. They cause death to them."

David reached up and took Gabriel from Tiana's arms. Her eyes seemed a bit larger than usual and sunken in their sockets. And her blond, curly hair was plastered to her head with sweat. But she smiled at him.

"*A'siyu, sgidoda*," she said. "Hello, father." David gave a small laugh of relief.

"She's all right now. Was she very sick?" He swayed back and forth, smiling down at his daughter. Tiana climbed wearily from the wagon seat and Adoniram drove toward the half-finished barn. In the past five days Tiana hadn't slept more than a few fitful hours. She was weary to her marrow. She walked toward the house.

"Look at her. She'll be fine. What did she have?" David called after her.

"*Uhyugi*, an Intruder. They call it ague at Fort Smith. *Ulisi* is dead."

"Oh, my God. I'm sorry, my love." David put his arm around her waist. Behind him, he could hear Shinkah's voice rising in song to appease *we-lu-schkas*, the Little Mystery People who cause sickness among the Little Ones. The song chilled him.

"Drum tried to save her," Tiana said.

"Grandmother Elizabeth?" David asked.

"*Ulisi* and Gabriel." Now that Elizabeth was dead, Tiana would never again say her grandmother's name. One didn't call spirits by name and risk drawing their attention. "Bradford gave us laudanum. It was generous of him. They hardly have enough for themselves."

"My beloved." With his free hand, David hugged her closer to him. "My heart can't tell you how sad I am about your grandmother. But Gabriel will get well. She's not going to die."

"I looked in the water. A dry leaf moved. She will die."

"She won't!" David shouted. He lowered his voice. "That's superstitious nonsense, that divining business. Nonsense."

"I hope so." She put her arms around them both and cried quietly against his chest. Her cheek lay next to Gabriel's. She could feel the fever starting again. The first time Gabriel had seemed to return to normal, Tiana had rejoiced, just as David was doing. But after a day, the chills had started again. The child began vomiting until she was throwing up blood. The pattern continued: a day of remission, then the disease worsened, then another day of false recovery.

Yellow fever was a particularly cruel disease in the hope it tauntingly held out. White men had no clue as to what caused it. The Real People knew it was caused by vengeful insects. But they didn't know it was the mosquito. Neither Drum's medicine nor Tiana's nor The Just's had worked for Elizabeth Rogers. Tiana was afraid it wouldn't work for Gabriel either. There were too many evil spirits here, toward the Nightland.

Adoniram put a hand on David's shoulder.

"I can do your work at the forge," he said.

"No," said David. "You have work of your own to do. We'll get along here."

If Adoniram seemed relieved, it was only because he knew Shinkah wanted to be away from the ill child so she wouldn't cause her to become worse.

"Beloved Wife, you're exhausted," said David. "I'll watch her. Sleep."

Tiana woke ten hours later to Gabriel's screaming. David paced the floor with her.

"Hush, my angel, my sunlight," he murmured. "Mama's sleeping." When Tiana raised up on one elbow, David sat next to her on the bed and looked at her desperately. The child stopped crying only when a paroxysm of chills wracked her. Excruciating pain caused her to draw her knees toward her stomach.

"I've tried cool baths and warm baths," David said. "I've given her honey with a little spirits. She has the flux and she's vomiting blood. What can we do?"

Tiana laid a hand on the child's cheek and felt the heat from it. Then she ran outside and down the hill, away from the trampled yard. Behind the cabin the clearing had turned into a meadow. Tiana stared out over the plants, and prayed for the right one to nod to her. But there was no wind, no movement. Only the intense June heat and the still grass.

"Sisters," she said. "I come to you as a friend. Help me. Tell me what to do. My daughter is dying." She waited patiently for what seemed an eternity. Still, nothing spoke to her. She heard Gabriel scream again. With tears streaming down her cheeks, Tiana ran back inside.

Gabriel's face twisted in agony. Then she went rigid.

"Dear God!" David began to sob. "She's not even two years old." He said it over and over, his voice breaking. Gabriel stopped screaming. Her face became peaceful, and she seemed to be sleeping. David laid her gently in her cradle. He sat on the bed next to the cradle and rocked it.

Tiana knelt by the big basket trunk and took out the small set of horseshoes and ball play sticks. She would bury them with Gabriel so the child would have something to play with in the Nightland. She tore a hole in the big basket she had just finished. She was killing it so it would make a proper coffin. While she moved quietly about the cabin, picking up the bloody rags and burning them in the fire, David sang and rocked the cradle gently.

> *Hush, little baby, don't say a word.*
> *Papa's going to buy you a mockingbird.*

Chapter 30

David, Adoniram, and James stood in front of Major Bradford's desk. Jack Rogers sat in the only chair other than Bradford's. It was August, and the heat was almost more than Jack could stand. *Hot as hell's hinges*, he thought. He wiped his forehead with his bandana and breathed heavily as he listened to the argument.

"The captives must be returned, gentlemen," Bradford said. "There will never be peace with Clermont's people until their women and children are returned. My God, that's not so difficult to understand, is it?"

Adoniram followed the conversation anxiously. His dark eyes shifted from one person to another as each spoke. His English was not very good, and it was terribly important that he understand everything.

They could hear the keening of a Cherokee woman outside. Someone in her family must have died of the fever. She had come to the fort for help, but there was still no doctor. One third of Bradford's force had died or was in the hospital. There had been no supplies for months. Desertion was a constant problem. There had been no annuities or promised provisions for the Real People either, and they were angry.

Bradford was gaunt. His eyes in their sunken sockets seemed to skewer David as he spoke. He maintained control over the chaotic situation by strict discipline and by making no exceptions. David could understand the man's position, but he had to plead Adoniram's case.

"This woman is happy where she is," said David. "She and Adoniram Wolf are married. They're expecting a child. She doesn't want to leave him. Most of her family is dead anyway."

"Her father and brother aren't," said Bradford. "They want her back. Anyway, most of the captives have been adopted by you people. Yet they must be returned."

Drum said something in his mild, reasonable way and James translated.

"One woman won't make that much difference. Perhaps her father could be paid something extra for her. And what about the furs the Osage stole last fall?"

Bradford slammed his fist down on the rickety desk top. His stone ink well jumped into the air.

"Now listen here, Mr. Jolly. You have asked me to help end this war. Yet the Cherokee persist in prolonging it. And you play me off against the governor of the territory." James spoke quickly to translate for Drum, even though he knew Drum understood most of what Bradford was saying. "Whenever you don't like something," Bradford continued, "you hie yourselves to Saint Louis to complain. You know the Father in Washington will do anything to keep you people mollified and start the others moving west. And you take advantage of it. And the *last* time you and the Osage met in Saint Louis for treaty talks"—Bradford's voice rose a little in his fury—"your young men stole Osage horses *on the god-damned way back* from the talks. You can gull Governor Miller, but you can't gull me!" He glared over the desk at all of them.

Drum remained unruffled. Jack watched him and Bradford with amusement. Drum made a lengthy speech which James translated, using the third person, as Drum did.

"Major Bradford, John Jolly understands that being the headman of a war town such as Fort Smith is a very difficult, thankless task. Only a strong, wise person like the Major could do it." Bradford refrained from telling Drum to stop shoveling manure and hoe corn. Instead he sighed, rotated his ink well abstractedly, and waited for Drum to finish circling the point.

"De'gata'ga, Standing Together, leads the young warriors. He says the Osage are singing birds, liars. It is true they have stolen our horses until we are forced to plow with our bare hands. Standing Together is a stubborn old man. He is solid in his ways, like the oak that wrinkles and twists with the years. Like the oak, Standing Together cannot now assume another shape."

At least you can chop down an oak and stack it for firewood, thought Bradford, uncharitably. But in a way Bradford preferred dealing with De'gata'ga, or Taka-toka, as he called him. As belligerent as he was, at least a man knew where he stood with the old warhorse.

Drum continued. "Major Bradford is wise to see it is the hot-blooded young men who sing Standing Together's war song and follow him on the war trail."

"Then you must convince Taka-toka to listen to reason."

Drum had to smile at the impossibility of that.

"John Jolly will try, Major. He will try."

"And what about the captives?" David asked.

"They must be surrendered. Clermont and his people are coming to a council here in a week. They'll bring the furs they took. They expect the captives and their horses to be returned. They've waited two years while your headmen have stalled. They will have their relatives back if I have to send a detachment of soldiers to the villages to get them. Do you understand?"

"Yes," said Drum. When the men filed from the room, Bradford motioned for Jack to stay. Bradford's face softened until he only looked tired.

"Yes, Billy?" Jack said.

"Jack, we're desperate for beef. I'll pay you four cents a pound for all you can supply. And seventy cents a bushel for meal. We're existing on roasting ears and rabbit food, greens from the garden."

"I'll try, sir."

Bradford laughed as Jack gave a mock salute. Five months before, in March of 1819, Arkansas became a territory. Its first governor, James Miller, docked at Fort Smith with great ceremony. On the mast of his keelboat flew a pennant with his motto, "I'll Try, Sir." It had become a joke around the garrison.

"Thanks."

"And have those squatters we reported to you left?"

"My men and I ordered two hundred families off Indian land. Some of them with crops in have been given permission to stay until October to harvest them." Bradford shook his head. "We'll keep trying. But I reckon they'll be back. They, or more of their ilk.

Former soldiers are flocking out here to collect land as bounty from Madison's war. Speculation is frenzied. Men claim settlement rights, preemption rights, Spanish grants, even something they call New Madrid claims, for Christ's sake. It's like dealing with a particularly virulent form of lunacy."

"Thank you for trying." Jack picked up his hat and started to leave.

"Jack," Bradford said. "I haven't had a chance to tell you how sorry I am about your wife and granddaughter. It's been a terrible summer."

"Aye, Billy," said Jack. "It has." As he left, there was a stoop to his shoulders that Bradford hadn't noticed before.

Ata'lunti'ski, He Throws His Enemy Over A Cliff, was dying. At least a hundred people had gathered in the meadow and woods around his small cabin. Relatives who lived two or three days' travel away were still arriving. They had been filing through the small cabin to pay their last respects. The men squatted or sat on logs and smoked and talked. The women stood quietly in groups twenty or thirty feet away.

The fever was still taking its toll. But Ata'lunti'ski didn't have the fever. No one knew what he had. The new doctor had come from Fort Smith to see him. But he had left, mystified.

Standing Together, Drum, Jack Rogers, and some of the headmen sat in the shade of a big elm. It was the end of August of 1819, and terribly hot. The men mixed cool spring water in their whiskey and poured the rest of the water over their heads. While they waited for death to fetch their friend, they reminisced about their days as soldiers with him.

"Those were good times," Drum observed with a certain wry nostalgia. He was talking to avoid thinking about his older brother's dying. "We could shoot at Americans then." Drum sounded a bit wistful.

"The Osage are good enough enemies." Standing Together shook the cool water from his soft mane of silvery hair, still decorated with a scalplock and feathers. At sixty-five, he was slender and erect and agile.

"I was a boy, maybe ten summers," he said. "And Ata'lunti'ski not much older, when The Little Carpenter saved Bushyhead at Fort Loudon. We went with him on that hunting trip, when he stole

Bushyhead from those who would kill him." Everyone had heard the story a hundred times and more, but they listened attentively. Those who had recorded the story with their blood were dying. Soon there would be only the stories, told by men who had never been there.

"His hair stood out like this." Standing Together held his hands out from his own head. "Bright red it was, like flames. The women thought his head was burning, but they loved him anyway."

The women loved him. The men loved him. I loved him, thought Jack. How long had he been dead? Thirty-five years? It hardly seemed possible.

"My father told me about Fort Loudon," said Drum. "The warriors cut off the treacherous captain's hands and feet and stuffed dirt into his mouth. 'You want our land so much,' they said. 'Here it is.' Almost sixty seasons ago. And nothing has changed. All that bloodshed changed nothing. They still want our land."

There was a murmur among the crowd as Tiana rode into the yard. Ata'lunti'ski's twelve-year-old grandson, the messenger who had been sent for her, rode beside her. Jack Rogers rose and helped his daughter dismount. Her clothes were soaked with sweat and she looked tired. Her second daughter had jumped down only a week before.

"You shouldna' come, lass," Jack said as he walked with her to a bench in the shade. "It's too far and too hot."

People crowded around to look at her, and Jack waved them back impatiently. They knew Ata'lunti'ski had sent for her, but they didn't know why. They assumed she must be a very important person. There were few Hiwassee people there. Most of those who had come to wait for death with their headman were Old Settlers. One of Ata'lunti'ski's daughters brought Tiana a dish of berries and cream, a bowl of stew, and a drink of sour hominy gruel, cooled in the spring.

"Daughter," said Jack, settling himself next to her. "You can't go riding off, helter skelter, to help everyone who asks it of you." He knew a lot of people asked it of her. "You've had tragedy enough of your own, and a husband and child who need you at home."

"Ata'lunti'ski is a Beloved Father," she said. "He is dying. How could I refuse his request?"

"What would he be wanting with you?" Sometimes Jack himself couldn't understand why people came to Tiana for advice and curing.

She was lovely, yes, but only a woman, after all. And in Jack's eyes she would always be as much his harum-scarum little hoyden, with scraped knees and tangled hair, as a grown woman. He passed her his whiskey mug and she took a sip.

They looked up as Dik'keh, The Just, stood in the open doorway of the cabin. He looked exhausted. He had been praying and chanting over Ata'lunti'ski for five days. Ata'lunti'ski's wife followed him. She pushed through the crowd of women waiting to comfort her and hurried to Tiana.

"What is it, mother?" Tiana asked.

"*Kalanu Ahyeli'ski*, Raven Mockers," she whispered, afraid to say the words out loud.

"Are you sure?"

"Ata'lunti'ski says they're coming for him. He says you can recognize them."

"I've never seen one. How can I recognize them? Surely The Just would be better able to frighten them away."

"My husband wants you to do it."

Tiana fought back panic. Raven Mockers. They were the most dreaded of all the evil spirits. They were witches who robbed a dying person of life. They could be of either sex. Tiana had heard of sick people who had their hearts stolen and eaten by Raven Mockers.

"Why me?" she asked. "Why does he want me?"

"Back in the Sunland, Mother Raincrow told him you have magic. She said you'd recognize them. Very few people can. The Just says he is too tired. In his weakened condition, they might get by him."

Tiana followed the woman into the house. Word that Raven Mockers might be in the neighborhood passed through the crowd like the wind blowing by and many people left. No one wanted to be near when they came. Sometimes the witches traveled in groups, flying through the sky in a ball of fire with arms stretched out and sparks streaming behind. They cried like ravens when they arrived. They liked to torment their victim by throwing him out of bed before eating his heart.

Tiana stood in the doorway and peered into the spartan, windowless room. Aside from a few baskets and clothes on pegs, the only adornment was a gaudy uniform jacket and the shiny Removal rifle over the mantle. She crossed to the bench along the wall where Ata'lunti'ski lay in a heap of skins and blankets.

"Beloved Man," she said. "How can I be of service?"

"Daughter of Jennie Rogers of the Long Hair clan?"

"Yes, Beloved Father."

"Are you having your monthly bleeding?"

"No." Tiana didn't take offense. She knew Ata'lunti'ski was making sure she was free of taboos.

"Have you eaten food cooked by a bleeding woman, or have you touched anything that one touched?"

"No."

"Are you carrying someone?"

"My child jumped down a week ago."

There was silence while Ata'lunti'ski pondered that.

"I think it is safe," he said finally. "You must guard the door for me." His voice was weak. "If they see you there, they will know you can recognize them, and they'll flee. They know they'll die within seven days if recognized. You have nothing to fear, niece."

Ata'lunti'ski reached a trembling hand from under the covers. Tiana held it firmly.

"You were always a brave girl," he said. "Now you are a brave woman. I have heard stories of your deeds. And Rain Crow told me you know the songs of the old ones, and they hold you in their hands. You need not be afraid of Raven Mockers. They will be afraid of you." His voice faded and he dropped back onto the bed. "Please, niece, do this for me. I have never feared an enemy as I fear these."

"Of course, Beloved Uncle. I will guard the door." Tiana hesitated, then asked something that had been bothering her. "You talked with Mother Rain Crow before you left Hiwassee?"

"We sang together. Not many know the old songs anymore."

"Was she well?"

"She was very well. She was preparing for her journey to the Nightland. She may have left already. Soon I'll join her there. She is my mother's sister, you know."

"No, I didn't know. Then she is Drum's aunt too."

"Yes. There are those who say her parents performed the rituals when she was a child, to make her a witch. But it is not so. Some evil sorcerer spoiled her saliva and drove her mad."

"She was a grandmother to me. May she dwell in sunlight with the spirits in the Seventh Heaven." Tiana tucked Ata'lunti'ski's hand under the covers. "I will guard the door for you, Beloved Uncle."

"And you know what to look for?"

"Yes. They make a rushing noise, like the wind just before a storm. They cry like the raven. They look old and shriveled because they've added so many lives to their own. Most people can't see them."

"When I reach the Nightland, I will smile down on you." He breathed with difficulty. "I am like the sun going down. My night is coming. If I still breathe when next Grandmother Sun rises, will you work for me?"

"My head is not gray, father, I cure only simple cases, where the Intruder is not very powerful."

"But you will work for me?"

"I will try."

But she knew he would probably not see Grandmother Sun again. The Just left not only because he was tired, but also because he didn't want to be there when his patient died. As Jack would say, it was bad for business.

Tiana went outside and found a chair waiting for her by the door, under the overhang of the roof. Ata'lunti'ski's children and second wife stood anxiously under the trees. Only his first wife stayed inside with him. As Tiana sat down, she noticed the crowd had thinned considerably. She wondered if those who stayed did so to see a mortal confront the Raven Mockers. It made her feel like a piece of bait.

Nannie approached cautiously with a cane-bottomed chair. Susannah followed, carrying a stool.

"We've come to keep you company," Nannie said. Tears stung Tiana's eyes. She herself hadn't realized how alone she felt, facing an unknown enemy that was pure evil.

"My heart is touched, sisters. You're brave to do this."

"No braver than you are," said Nannie.

"Not as brave," said Susannah. She placed her stool as far from the door as she could and still be with the other two. She was seventeen now, and Tiana suspected she was carrying the child of an invisible father. If it was true, Tiana wondered who the father might be. There were a lot of possibilities. The women of the Real People were not prudish, but they were modest. Susannah lacked discretion and judgment where men were concerned. Tiana knew her younger sister was often the subject of gossip. But Tiana felt a wave of affection for Susannah as she sat on the edge of her stool.

She was ready to flee at the first rush of wind that signaled the coming of Raven Mockers.

"We brought light and some provisions." Nannie held up a basket and a handful of lighter-wood splinters. "And bear grease to protect us from the flies and mosquitoes. The sweet potatoes are still warm."

"I'm not hungry."

"You're too skinny, sister. You haven't enough lap for more than one child to sit on." Nannie saw the grief pass over Tiana's face like a swallow skimming dark water at dusk. "I'm sorry, sister." She took Tiana's hand and held it. Nannie now had a lap big enough for two children. Three, if they were small.

"Where's Shinkah?" asked Susannah.

"She's staying away from the village and the fort," said Tiana. "She doesn't want to go back to her people. Beloved Father, Drum, has been stalling all summer. Shinkah hopes if she stays out of sight, they'll forget about her."

Their voices dropped lower as it became darker. Finally, the last of the pine splinters burned out, and Nannie and Susannah fell asleep. Tiana heard them snoring lightly. She sat in the dark, listening to the night sounds, the crickets and the lonely cry of an owl, the whicker of a horse from the blackness.

She missed David. She wished he were here next to her. She wouldn't fear anything if he were. But he had been angry when she left, and he hadn't even offered to come with her. No, now that she thought about it, she knew he wasn't really angry. He was hurt. He acted angry to hide it.

Every week people came to Tiana's cabin asking for cures. Sometimes she could help them there. Sometimes she went with them to their isolated farms to work for a patient too sick to travel. At first David had been understanding, but after Gabriel died, he began to resent her leaving.

Her mother had tried to warn her, on the day of her marriage. *There will be times when you'll be terribly alone.* But Jennie hadn't told her the unhappiness she would cause the one who loved her most.

Nanehi Ward had once said, *When your life is in balance, your soul will be light.* Tiana's soul didn't feel light. It was heavy in her breast. She sometimes felt as though people were tugging at her, holding her down. Would she ever be able to balance her love for David with her duties to her clan and her people? *Why me?* She asked herself that whenever another weeping woman stood timidly in the yard. The women usually had sick children strapped to their backs in carrying cloths. They were usually poor, but they always offered her some small gift in exchange for a cure.

Why me?

Because not every clay vessel can hold embers from the sacred fire. We choose only the best. The voice was so loud in her head, Tiana looked around for her grandmother.

"*Ulisi?*" she whispered. She was tired and her mind was open to the voices of the spirits. She could hear her grandmother talking.

You are never alone, granddaughter. You contain the life force of every one of our people who've run to the Nightland before you. All the way back to your ancestor in the stars.

"I wish you could have seen my child jump down, *Ulisi.*"

Gabriel is here with me. We are not far from you. There are some advantages to living near the Nightland. Even in the country of the dead, Grandmother Elizabeth hadn't lost her sense of humor.

Tiana sat in silence, but the voice didn't speak again. It didn't matter. She sensed her presence close by. She felt as though her soul were floating in a vast river. Each drop was another soul, and they were all traveling together toward some unknown destination. She felt connected to her grandmother and her daughter, to Raincrow, and to everyone who had gone before or who would come after. She sat in silent communion with them for an hour or more.

About midnight, she was startled by a voice from the darkness.

"Daughter."

"Father?"

"James and I have come to relieve your sisters."

James drew the stool closer to Tiana and Jack. He tilted it against the cabin wall and propped his boots on an upturned log. He folded his arms across his chest and grinned at her. His teeth flashed in the light of the flickering torch Jack had brought.

"Midnight's my favorite time of day," he said. "The prairie flies have finally gone to bed and pulled the covers up under their vicious little jaws."

"Arkansas is the only place I know where flies have teeth," growled Jack.

"Father, you must be tired. You don't have to stay with me. You don't even believe in Raven Mockers." Tiana had noticed lately that Jack's eyes were sinking into a mass of fine wrinkles and there were dark half circles under them. His hair was wispy, like winter grass. She wondered when he had become so old.

"If Ata'lunti'ski fears them, they're as real to him as the worst of his enemies and twice as formidable. And as for being tired, I can stay awake longer than both of you put together."

"He took a long nap this evening," said James. "He fell asleep in council. Everyone politely ignored his snoring."

"A man has no secrets." Jack began to hum "The Minstrel Boy" softly under his breath. Tiana knew why he and James had come. Midnight was the worst time. It was when evil was most powerful. Jack may not have believed in spirits, but he knew Tiana did.

James talked in a low voice of his recent trip to the Red River country with Bradford and a squad of soldiers. The trip was to evict white settlers from Indian land, and James went along as interpreter.

"The more things change, the more they stay the same," Jack interrupted his low humming to observe.

"John and I are going to the Old Country," said James. "To arrange shipment of goods for our store. And John's to bring back the two captive Osage children. Have you any messages to deliver?"

"No, unless you'll be seeing Mary and David's children."

"We won't get to Georgia. But we may see The Raven in Tennessee."

"I have nothing to say to him. He is like the Raven Mockers, stealing the lives of others to enrich his own." Tiana considered the possibility of returning to the east. Then she rejected it. Strangers would be living in her mother's beloved house on Rogers Branch. Hiwassee Town would be abandoned, probably cannibalized by squatters looking for building materials. No, she couldn't go back.

Just before dawn, a wail rose from the cabin. Ata'lunti'ski had died, and his wife was mourning. The other women took up the cry. "*Al' skudi-ga'*, he has ended!"

Tiana rose, stretched, and smiled sadly at Jack and James. Without saying anything, she walked toward the river to greet the sun.

Chapter 31

James and John walked their tired horses down the tree-lined path from the Nashville Road to the Hermitage. They had passed acres of Andrew Jackson's cotton fields. The fields looked as though a heavy snow had fallen. Jackson's slaves, their heads bound in bright blue and red bandanas, bobbed and stooped among the drifts of cotton. They pulled the bolls with both hands, clipping the stems with long thumbnails and tossing them into burlap sacks on their backs.

It was Saturday. The slaves glanced heavenward from time to time. When the sun hung at the midday position, an eerie call went up. It echoed from field to field, signaling the end of the work week. Men and women moved toward the driver, whose whip hung over his shoulder. The women walked first in a file along the narrow path between the fields. They laughed and sang as they walked, carrying their huge bags of cotton easily on their heads.

They all knew the afternoon and the next day were theirs, or rather, almost theirs. They were expected to feed the stock, do plantation chores, and tend their own gardens. Later in the fall, they would have to gin cotton every night until almost midnight. But not on Saturday night or Sunday. Not at the Hermitage.

James and John dismounted at the brick shell of a two-story house that stood half finished in a low field surrounded by cedar trees.

There were piles of lumber and sand, bricks and shakes. A white-haired slave in a neat red jacket, baggy white pantaloons, and bare feet appeared from behind the building. He bowed perfunctorily and eyed James and John suspiciously as he took their horses.

"You'all come to see the General?" He pronounced general with a great *G.*

"Yes," said James.

"He's over at the blockhouse." As he led the horses toward the long stables, the slave nodded over the new house, indicating that the old one was behind it.

"So much for apparel proclaiming the man," said James.

"He seems to think we'd scalp him," said John. He inserted a finger into the front of his tight, high collar and pulled it out for relief from its stranglehold.

"Maybe he thinks we're Seminole," said James. "There are more than a few of them who'd like to scalp the General."

As they rounded the corner of the new house, they heard music floating across the meadow that separated the two buildings. Andrew and Rachel Jackson and a crowd of their friends and relatives were lounging on the porch in front of their large, two-story cabin. Two smaller cabins, for sleeping and storage, were connected to it by covered passages twenty-five feet long. A kitchen stood off by itself. A half dozen small black children flocked with the chickens at the kitchen door. Officially, they were part of the "trash gang" responsible for keeping the plantation free of litter. But nowhere was cleaner than the kitchen dooryard. They knew where their bread was baked as well as buttered.

The slaves' quarters were separated by a line of trees. At the edge of the field, near the stables, was a fenced paddock. A black trainer was exercising a pair of Jackson's prize horses. Discreetly out of sight in a dip in the terrain was the cock pit, where the general and his friends spent many hours. He had cleared a race track too, for his own amusement and to test his horses for the bigger races at the Clover Bottom course outside of Nashville. Beyond the paddock were orchards of a thousand apple and peach trees.

Jackson was pale and drawn after a hard campaign against the Seminole in Florida. At fifty-three, he looked ten years older. His stiff crest of hair was almost white. His lanky legs spanned the porch, his manure-caked boots resting on the top railing.

He was playing a banjo while one of Rachel Jackson's many relatives accompanied him on the fiddle. Sam Houston was experimenting with a limberjack. He bounced the jointed wooden figure on his thigh, making a rhythmic clacking in time to the music. Ten-year-old Andy Jackson was teaching him the technique. Seven-year-old Lincoyer Jackson and a slave child about the same age were buck dancing, setting up a complex counterpoint on the floor boards. The women sat at the far end of the gallery, away from the blue clouds of cigar smoke.

The gallery was crowded with men, women, and children, all tapping the toes of their boots or the tips of their fingers. Rachel Jackson, bundled up in a shawl and lap robe, sat in a rocker. Her head was wreathed in smoke from her small clay pipe. A tiny slave child and one of her grandnephews, three-year-old John Coffee Hays, nestled in her soft lap.

Slaves in starched dresses hovered as noiselessly as the hummingbirds sipping sugared water from gourds hung in the trees. The slaves refilled the men's glasses with bourbon, relit their pipes and offered cigars, and fanned flies away from the ladies.

"Mr. Jackson," said Rachel. "We have company." The music stopped. Jackson set his banjo aside and rose from his chair. He seemed to unfold at the joints, looking like the limberjack Sam tossed to Lincoyer.

"James! John! You old sons." Sam cleared the stairs in one lunge and waded through the pack of hunting hounds lounging in front of the porch. He grabbed both friends at once in a bear hug. When he pulled back to look at them, he felt a wrench at his heart. James looked so much like his sister, and Tiana had haunted Sam's thoughts for two years now.

"We'd best surrender," said James. "He has us surrounded." James cocked one eyebrow, stroked his beardless chin, and walked slowly around Sam, as though inspecting a horse at auction.

"Hell-fire. Look at him." John held out a warning hand. "Don't come too close, Raven. You'll get mud all over that velvet suit of clothes."

"The road was boggy enough at the river to mire the saddleblankets." James was embarrassed by his travel-worn appearance. He lowered his voice so the people on the porch couldn't hear. "And our stink would kill a snake."

Sam laughed. He knew the old Cherokee story about a hunter who was caught in the coils of a giant snake. The hunter freed one hand and wiped it under his armpit. Then he held the hand in front of the snake, and drove it away with the smell.

"So, you've turned into a dandy and a princock," said James. It was Sam's turn to be embarrassed.

"It's for appearance's sake. For my law practice in Lebanon. It's one of the ironies of the profession that to become prosperous, one must first look prosperous. Besides, a friend provided me with the duds." Sam took each one by the arm and led them to where his friends waited.

"Greeting, James, and John. Captain John now, isn't it?" Jackson extended a bony hand and James took it with misgivings. But in spite of himself, he was flattered Jackson remembered him. The last time the two of them had met, they had glared at each other across the council fire at the treaty talks. Jackson still wore his long hair pulled back in a queue and tied with an eel skin. He wore it that way in defiance of the army, which had been trying for years to make its soldiers cut their hair short.

"Allow me to introduce you," said Jackson. "My beloved wife, Rachel. Mrs. Grundy." Jackson introduced the ladies first. Each of them managed to give the impression of curtseying, even while seated. Several stared demurely, and a few not so demurely, over their fans at James. Sam felt a twinge of jealousy. He was used to being the cock of the flock. "William Carroll, John Eaton, William Fulton, Felix Grundy, John Allen of Gallatin." Each man nodded as his name was spoken.

"Excuse our disheveled appearance, Mrs. Jackson." James gave a courtly bow and a sweep of his arm and hat. His black curls tumbled into his eyes as he kissed the air over her plump and workworn fingers. The two children in her lap stared wide-eyed at him. "We meant no disrespect to you. Our way has been long and dusty."

"Pish tosh." Rachel smiled like a girlish grandmother. "Don't fret yourselves. We're plain folk here. Dinner will be served before long. You can make your toilet before then." Jackson found two extra seats and sat back down himself.

James preferred to stand, leaning against a post with one leg up. He and John had spent many days in the saddle. As James flexed his tired muscles, he was aware of his audience on the distaff side of the porch.

"What do you think of your old friend Raven, the barrister?" asked Jackson.

"He looks fat as a candle and twice as slick," said James. His gallery laughed. John was content to watch James perform. He had done it often enough before. James took care of the amenities with grace and wit. John made sure he himself was in charge of more serious affairs. With a smile, James accepted a glass of bourbon. He made a show of inspecting Sam again.

"General, I'd say he's stepping high as a rooster in deep mud. It's clear the Maker wasn't your tailor, Sam. Your skin doesn't fit you as well as those trousers." Sam blushed and the women laughed, delighted at the chance to be scandalized.

"You ought to be ashamed of yourself, James. I taught you educated English and you turn it against me." Sam smiled to show he was jesting. "Wait here." He ducked inside. At the Hermitage he didn't have to watch his head when he went through a doorway. The lintels were taller than usual, to accommodate Old Hickory. But Sam ducked anyway, out of habit. He returned, buffing a bell-crowned beaver hat on the sleeve of his plum-colored waistcoat. James had to admit The Raven looked very fine indeed.

"You may be a foppish dog, Sam," he said. "But you're a handsome one."

"A pretty severe colt," said Jackson. "He finished an eighteen-month law course in six. And he's been busier than a bee in a tar bucket ever since. He's Adjutant General of the state militia now. Colonel Houston." Jackson gave a mock salute.

"Congratulations," said James and John.

"Oh, Mr. Rogers."

John didn't bother to turn around. He knew the young woman was calling James. She was the prettiest of the lot. And she knew it. There was gilt scroll work around the invitation in her eyes.

"Mr. Rogers, do you have an Indian name?"

"Yes, Mademoiselle, I do."

"And what might it be?"

"It might be Sixkiller or Grizzly Bear or Coon Hound, but it isn't."

"It might be Woman Killer," Sam muttered to John. John only grunted.

"Don't toy with me, Mr. Rogers." She stamped a foot under her full skirt and pouted. "I will know. It must be something romantic."

"I'm not at liberty to say. It must remain locked inside me. Though if beauty were bullets, my fortifications would have fallen already."

Sam raised his eyebrows. He was used to hearing James's patter in Cherokee, but not in English.

"Careful, brother," John muttered in Cherokee. But he was secretly amused. The belle thought to make a conquest of a simple savage, but she had met her match. James had laid waste to more than a few fortifications in his time. His favorite of Poor Richard's sayings was "Neither a fortress nor a maidenhead will hold out long after they begin to parley."

But John didn't worry unduly. It wouldn't be politic to play fast and loose with Jackson's hospitality. He was too influential, and James knew that. And for all his flirting, James was faithful to his beautiful new wife, Suzie. A fidelity John doubted was reciprocated. Suzie was a source of contention between John and his brother. Not only was John sure she indulged in some green gowning on the sly, but she was of their mother's clan, and strictly taboo. James quoted his father on the subject, and claimed the clan restrictions were no longer valid. He pointed out that John Ross's wife was of his own clan. But James's marriage boded ill as far as his brother was concerned.

"Why cannot you tell me something so simple as your name?" The young woman tapped her nose with her fan, a sign she thought James was teasing her.

"One of the Real People never tells his secret name, Miss Donelson. That would allow another to steal his soul."

"I should think a girl would rather steal your affections." She held her fan dangerously close to her mouth. To kiss it and look at James would be a declaration of love.

"Lincoyer," said Jackson, clearing his throat loudly. "You and Jefferson run to the kitchen and tell Dolly we shall dine in an hour." Jackson knew about his niece's flirtatious nature. He preferred to spare James any embarrassment from it. "Do you remember Lincoyer?" Jackson asked, after the Indian child and the black one had gone.

"Is he the orphaned Creek baby you saved at The Horseshoe?" John asked.

"He is indeed," said Rachel. "He's part of our family now. He's such a dear boy. He seems quite fascinated with you two. He sees so few of his kind here."

"You don't suppose he's related to that nasty Weatherford fellow," said Miss Donelson.

"I would hope so," said Jackson. "Weatherford was a noble foe. I shall never forget the day he rode up to my marquee." Jackson relit his pipe so he wouldn't have to interrupt his story. "He was tall and light-skinned, bare to the waist, excuse me, ladies. He was unarmed, in the midst of his enemies. I must have been distracted or I would have recognized his horse at once. The Weatherfords were noted for their horses.

" 'General Jackson?' he inquired in a refined voice and perfect English. 'I am Bill Weatherford.' I was outraged. I had searched for that devil for months and he had found me." Jackson stood and paced the porch. " 'How dare you, sir, ride up to my tent after having murdered the women and children of Fort Mims?' 'I tried in vain to stop the slaughter there,' he said. 'I have nothing to ask for myself. Kill me if you wish. I come to beg you to send for the women and children who are starving in the woods. I did you all the injury I could. Now my warriors are killed and I am done fighting. Send for the women and children. They never did you any harm.'

"The soldiers had heard of his arrival. They crowded around the tent crying, 'Kill him! Kill him!' I rushed out to face them. 'Any man,' I said, 'who would kill so brave a one as this, would rob the dead.' "

"How thrilling!" trilled the niece.

With the side of his face turned away from the ladies, James winked at Sam.

A slave woman came and stood at the edge of the piazza. "Aunt Rachel, ma'm," she said. "One of my chi'runs is varsal sick."

"Oh, dear." Rachel set the two little ones on the floor. They followed her, hanging onto her skirts as she left with the woman. "Is it Terrance or Samantha?" James heard her say before she was out of hearing.

During the Creek war and at the treaty table, James had had ample opportunity to study Andrew Jackson's face. Even at rest, Old Hickory looked like a hawk scanning for prey. Now, as Jackson watched his dowdy little wife walk across the meadow toward the slave quarters, his face was full of love. The naked vulnerability astonished James.

"Here come the fry," said Sam as a horde of children, black and white, charged across the yard. Nine-year-old Eliza Allen, her blond curls bouncing, raced up onto the piazza. Her pinafore was full of sweet chinkapins, which she dropped into Sam's lap.

"Payment," she giggled. "For rescuing my cat yesterday." Then she fled with the others.

The adults talked languidly, mostly of horses and politics. From the kitchen the sounds of Dolly's pots and her scolding rose to a crescendo that ended with the clanging of the dinner bell.

After dinner there was the usual concert. The niece played Rachel's harpsichord and her sister sang, skills they had learned at the Nashville Female Academy. The other ladies arranged themselves around the room, rather like the cut flowers in the vases. Rachel's settee and parlor chairs, her harpsichord, and the queensware on the table seemed out of place in a log cabin. The room's heavy beams were blackened by years of smoke from the huge fireplace.

The men stood politely, their thoughts on the cigars and brandy that waited for them when the concert was over. Some of them were beginning to stir restlessly when the niece winked at her father, the fiddler. She began pounding out "Possum up de Gum Tree" on the delicate instrument, and her father joined her.

"Give us a dance, Aunt Rachel," everyone cried, clapping to the music. Andrew bowed and held out his hand. Together, they bobbed and whirled around the room. They were quite a sight. He was so tall and lanky he had to bend almost double to put his arm around her middle. She had been a beauty when she was young. Now she was too stout to have a waistline.

Afterward, James and John walked with Sam along the paths of Rachel's extensive garden. From the porch the voices of the men floated like the fireflies that rode the currents of the night. Now and then one of Andrew Jackson's "By the Eternal's" rang out. Far away a hound sang on the trail of a raccoon. A whippoorwill called loudly and incessantly, so close Sam scanned the bushes, even though he knew it was almost impossible to find the bird. Perhaps its elusiveness was why the Real People considered it a bad omen.

"Well, brother," said Sam. "You seem to have made a conquest of Miss Donelson."

"Are you sparking her?" For a moment James feared he had committed a terrible breach of etiquette.

"No, not at all. But she started acting like a spaniel on the scent when you appeared."

"The difference being, that with Miss Donelson the fun is only in the chase."

"Don't be so sure, brother," said Sam. "There was a glint in her eye."

"White women are too hard to find under all those skirts. Besides, if I sullied the fair white flower, Jackson would set his dogs on me."

"*Gha*! Listen, brother," said John, when he thought the amenities had been observed. "We have a reason other than friendship for searching you out."

"I'll do what I can. I haven't much influence except the patronage of General Jackson."

"No small consideration," said James. "I think your general will be president one day."

"I wouldn't hitch my sulky to a losing horse." Sam grinned into the darkness. "What's the favor?"

"Drum wants you to come to the Arkansas as Cherokee agent."

"Me? Why me?"

"You understand the Real People. They trust you. The last agent was a son of a bitch."

"Was?"

"Drum convinced him to resign."

"That's difficult to believe, even of Drum," said Sam. John pulled a piece of foolscap from his pocket.

"A copy of his resignation," he said. "But Lewis was only one of the problems. He was undoubtedly pocketing our annuities and selling us short on goods. And settlers are already overrunning our land. But at least they're not killing us. The Osage are. No one seems able to stop the warfare."

"Drum's people are hungry," said James. "Once the government removed us from our eastern lands, they forgot us. The promised tools and seed corn and food haven't arrived. Letters to the War Department are ignored. It's been root, hog, or die."

"I'm not surprised," said Sam. "That damned Calhoun is only interested in his own aggrandizement." Sam had never forgotten Secretary John Calhoun's treatment of him over the slave-smuggling issue.

"Even father hasn't been reimbursed for the expense of transporting his family west," said James.

"There was a drought this year. And sickness. People are saying the Arkansas is truly the Nightland," said John.

"The future looks promising for me here," said Sam. "My law practice is growing. The Adjutant General position is a nuisance, really. It requires a lot of time spent poring over scrambled records in Murfreesboro, but it's a boot up. I have friends here. Important friends."

"Drum needs you desperately, brother."

"Surely he and Ata'lunti'ski and Standing Together—"

"Ata'lunti'ski is dead. And Standing Together is part of the problem. He's keeping the war with the Osage well stoked. But he likes you, Raven. He might listen to you. People are dying," said James.

Sam walked a while in silence.

"I'll go," he said. "It'll be good to see Beloved Father again. But I'll need time to take care of things here first."

"Thank you, brother," said James.

"And how is your family?" Sam asked casually.

"Our mother died of the fever this past summer."

"I'm sorry. Give Jack and Jennie my condolences. And Grandmother, how does she fare?"

"Tiana?" said John. "Her second child jumped down just before we left. Her first died of the fever also. But David works hard. He's built them a comfortable home."

Sam was glad it was dark. James and John couldn't see him wince at mention of David's name. He wanted to ask if Tiana was happy and if she was as beautiful as ever, but he couldn't bring himself to do it. Soon enough, he would find out for himself.

Chapter 32

It was September, 1819. Tiana sat with her sisters on mats on the porch of her mother's new house. Jennie and Jack were sharing it with John and his wife Elizabeth and their children and Susannah. It would take a while for the house to be as grand as the one they had left, but Jack had ambitious plans for it. Tiana and Susannah were stringing leather breeches, green beans. Then they would dry them in the sun for several days, and hang them from the rafters.

It was obvious Susannah was carrying someone. David had been helping her brothers build a cabin for her, not far from her mother's. Susannah was making wedding plans, but everyone in the family would rather she remain single than marry the ne'er-do-well white man she'd been consorting with.

Jack raged at Susannah, telling her the man was only wedding her for her property—the house she would soon own and the farm Jack and his sons were clearing for her. But she was determined to have him. Her sisters had tried to talk her out of it, and now they just avoided the subject.

Annie and Nannie and Elizabeth were combing cotton, a tedious process they all disliked. Heaps of it lay around them. Sally Ground Squirrel occupied one end of the porch with her pottery. She was surrounded by carved paddles, hammerstones, her waterworn pebble for smoothing and polishing the clay, her gourd saucers, buckets of water, and baskets of crushed corncobs to smoke the pots.

Sally Ground Squirrel always seemed to require more room than the average person. She attacked her pottery like she attacked everything else in life, with vigor. She was pummeling a loaf of clay, kneading it and pounding it and slapping it onto a large, wooden tray. She separated a lump of it, rolled it into a ball, and gouged her spatulate thumbs into it.

She pressed and turned the clay so fast one would have to watch carefully to see what she was doing. When she had formed a small bowl, she wedged it into a cloth-lined hole in a basket of sand. Using it as a base, she began building up the sides. The reddish coils seemed to writhe with their own life under her thick hands.

In the yard, some of her pots were firing in a hearth of flat stones. She was baking them today because there was no wind. A breeze might have cracked them. Almost an hour ago she had set them, mouths down, on the embers and covered them with dry bark. Soon the bark would burn away and the rounded bottoms of the pots would stick up from the ashes like big red eggs.

Jennie was trying to get Tiana's new daughter to suck a rag soaked in a tea made from the roots of the Devil's Shoestring. The child was struggling and crying lustily. James had brought the roots from the Old Country. They would make her granddaughter strong.

Finally Jennie gave up. She handed her back to Tiana by way of every other woman on the porch. Each of them hugged the child or held her up and admired her. No matter how many children might be born to them, each new one was a source of wonder. Tiana loosened her blouse so her daughter could nurse. Tiana cradled her tenderly in her arms and looked down at the black fuzz on her head.

"Jo'ine'i," she murmured, testing the sound of the name. Jennie had given it to the child the day before, when they took her to bathe in the river and held her up for Grandmother Sun to bless. It meant third. "Why do you want to call her that?" Tiana had asked. "Because she looks like you," Jennie had said. "And you look like me. This one is the third." David called her Joanna, which was fine with Tiana. If everyone called her Joanna, her real name would be obscured. She would be better protected from any who might wish her evil.

Meanwhile, the gossip had resumed around Tiana and her daughter.

"Will you not bed your husband for a year, sister?" Susannah asked her.

"If I had a husband that good-looking, I'd not wait two days before bedding him again." said Aky.

"If she loves him before a year is up, her milk will spoil," said Sally Ground Squirrel, as though that settled the matter.

"My father says that's supersitition," said Nannie. Tiana didn't know if it was a superstition or not, but she had already felt David's caress on her skin and his body inside hers. So far, Joanna seemed to consider her milk sweet and good.

"Your father would deny anything that got between him and his pleasure." Sally Ground Squirrel winked at Jennie. "Is that not so, sister?" Jennie laughed. She and Jennie and Jennie's children were of the same clan and could tease each other. Tiana kept quiet, hoping Sally Ground Squirrel wouldn't notice her. When she got started in this vein, no one's dignity was safe.

"I think white men have bigger penises," she went on conversationally, as though she had made a study of it. "How big is your husband's stalk, daughter? When he bathes at the river I try to see his equipment, but he's shy, that one."

"He's big enough to fill the pot, mother," Tiana said.

"And bring it to a boil too, I'll wager." The women all laughed as Sally Ground Squirrel heaved herself to her feet. Tiana thought how good it was to hear laughter in this house again. There had been little since Grandmother Elizabeth had died.

"The biggest one I've seen, though, was The Raven's." Sally Ground Squirrel made an obscene humping motion with her vast hips that sent undulating ripples up through her pendulous breasts and ended with a quiver of her chins. She cupped her hands between her thighs, as though supporting a huge cock and scrotum. She pretended to stagger to the edge of the porch under the weight of it.

"And hairy, too." She said. "Looks like a bear's pizzle, or a pair of pumpkins in the tall grass. A tall, sturdy cedar of a penis. One could lie in its shade on a hot day. I think maybe one of us has already slipped that warm knife into her sheath."

Now it was Annie's turn to blush. Sally Ground Squirrel walked across the yard, talking about the possibility of The Raven returning to his father. Tiana knew Drum was expecting The Raven to come. But she didn't want to see him ever again.

She had considered singing a *diga'ghahuh'sdo'dhi'yi* spell, To Remove Them With One. The spell she knew was simple, although it required remade tobacco. She had only to form an image of the unwanted person in her head and while she sang, blow the smoke toward where he lived. *Now the Black Crows have just come to frighten you away. They have just come to surround you. You will go lonely through the country of the Seven Clans. Gha! Gha! Gha! Gha!*

But she wasn't sure if it would work to keep someone away rather than force them to leave. And even though the loneliness it induced dissipated when the person left, it was still negative magic. *U'dano ti*, a person of soul and kindness, wouldn't use it. She had decided to be patient and wait like the spider. Only she wanted the insect to avoid her web, rather than fall into it.

At least she knew the charms would work for her again. When first she had moved toward the Nightland, she'd felt lost. But as time passed and she listened to the voices and the silences of her new land, power began seeping back into her. *Ulaniguhguh*, the energy from the lightning and the running water, the spirit in plants and animals, was just as strong here. She had only to open her heart to them.

She was shaken from her thoughts by the women laughing again. She had missed Sally Ground Squirrel's last story. But there was another one. Sally Ground Squirrel always had another one.

"My mother told me the biggest pizzle in the world belonged to A'sik Ta'mas." Sally Ground Squirrel pulled her pots from the fire with a hooked stick. She tapped them and discarded one that didn't give a clear, ringing sound. It was cracked.

"Isaac Thomas? The prisoner Nanehi Ward helped escape?" Tiana blurted it out. She had heard about Ghigau rescuing the white trader and sending him to warn American settlers of a Cherokee attack. Ghigau always said she did it to stop the warfare and killing. Tiana had never heard this version before.

"The same one." As though deliberately keeping her audience in suspense, Sally Ground Squirrel dropped a handful of crushed corn-cobs into each pot while it was red hot and tossed burning brands into them. She tipped the pots to distribute the flaming material, then poured it out and inverted each pot over it. While the inside became smoked so it would be impervious to water, Sally Ground Squirrel went on with her story.

"His stalk of sugar cane was that long." She held her hands twelve or fifteen inches apart. "He and Nanehi Ward were lovers of course.

The white settlers probably didn't know they owed their lives to the penis of A'sik Ta'mas."

Sally Ground Squirrel seemed ready to share more secrets, but she was interrupted when a wagon pulled into the yard. The driver was a tall, gaunt white woman with short, steel-gray hair combed back from her face. Sally Ground Squirrel and the women on the porch stared at her. They were used to seeing white men in the Real People's country, but not their women. Tiana walked down the steps to meet her.

"*A'siyu*," the woman called in a deep, gruff voice.

"Hello," Tiana said. "May I help you?"

"I hope so. My name is Lovely, Percis Lovely."

"The agent's wife."

"Yes, God rest him. Is Mrs. Gentry here?"

"I am."

"Good." Percis jumped down from the wagon seat in a flurry of brown skirts and went around to open the tailgate. "Your brother, John, brought this little one with him from the east. She's one of the Osage captives. Her name is Lydia Carter."

That may be what you call her, Tiana thought. *But I doubt it's her name.*

"Bradford ordered your brothers to drag her back here," Percis Lovely continued. "Over that godforsaken rough country at the height of the sickly season. She's terribly ill. I'm going to take her to my place until better arrangements can be made, but I doubt she can survive the trip in this condition. I wondered if we might rest here a bit."

After Mrs. Lovely's husband died, she had been allowed to stay in her house, built on land contained in Lovely's Purchase. When he was Indian agent, William Lovely had bought the territory as a buffer between the warring tribes. There may have been squatters there, but she was the only white person, or any person at all for that matter, legally living in the hill country between the Osage and Cherokee lands. Shinkah said the Osage liked her and wouldn't harm her. Still, Tiana had to admire her courage.

"Of course. You may stay here as long as you like." Tiana turned to translate, but Jennie had already gone inside to get the visitors something to eat and prepare a place for them to sleep.

Tiana picked the child up to carry her inside. She looked about nine years old, but she was emaciated, and there were dark circles around her eyes.

"They tell me you speak some Osage, and also that you know a great many simples, that you're a curer." Percis kept pace with Tiana's long legs.

"I know some simple simples," Tiana said. Percis laughed, a rusty, hawking sound, but pleasant anyway.

"I have the gift to stop bleeding, myself. But this malady mystifies me. Perhaps you can help her while she's here."

"I'll try. She seems very ill."

"Much too ill to be exchanged, the poor little waif. And such a dear child too. Always talking about Ji'sa, Jesus. Spent the past two years with the missionaries. Your brothers say they were loath to part with her."

"Are the Osage captives to be exchanged finally?"

"Oh, yes. Clermont insists on it. They'll be going back to their families soon."

Tiana's heart sank. She would lose Shinkah soon.

All summer and into the fall of 1819, Standing Together and Drum avoided returning the captives. Drum used sickness as an excuse, then the necessity of harvesting crops. Standing Together didn't bother with excuses, other than the "personal reasons" that kept him from the treaty talks. Finally Major Bradford had had enough. He threatened to march a squad of soldiers through the villages and take the captives by force. Standing Together capitulated. He was stubborn, but he wasn't stupid. He wasn't willing to take on the United States Army.

The talks were scheduled to be held at Three Forks, the Place of the Oaks, where the Verdigris, the Neosho, and the Arkansas converged. It was a fitting spot, where east met west. To the east, towering forests of scarlet oak, hackberry, and ash thinned as they approached the Verdigris. Acres of nettles on the river's bottomlands provided cordage for Osage weavers. Miles of dense canebrakes grew along the Verdigris and Neosho rivers.

On the western side of the Verdigris, the great prairie began abruptly. The grass there was three feet high and tangled with saw briars that formed an impenetrable barrier. The grass-covered hills, dotted with small copses of trees, stretched to the horizon.

It was October, a time of gold and amber. Shinkah stood between

Adoniram and nineteen-year-old Tiana, whom she had begun to call mother. Tiana held her hand tightly and balanced two-month-old Joanna on her hip. Shinkah was eight months pregnant. A satchel with her few possessions hung from the burden strap she wore around her forehead. Adoniram held the beautifully woven cradle Tiana had made for her.

Even now, the three of them couldn't keep from hoping something would change Clermont's mind. That somehow Drum or Standing Together would be able to persuade him to allow Shinkah to stay with her husband. But Clermont, Arrow Going Home, was adamant. Major Bradford feared he and old Standing Together would come to blows before the talks were over. They faced each other like roosters in a cock pit.

Standing Together was decked out in his usual finery. Clermont wore a regimental jacket and a military tar bucket hat trimmed with tarnished silver braid. He was imperious, and his temper was short. He had been waiting a long time for this day. He and his warriors had rubbed themselves in clay, then bear oil scented with sassafras. Their shaven scalps gleamed in the autumn sunlight. Their deer hair roaches stood high off the crowns of their heads.

Clermont gave a short speech welcoming the captives home and expressing sorrow for two years of suffering at the hands of their murderous tormentors. Drum and Bradford had to hold Standing Together to keep him from attacking Clermont. Some of the captives ran to meet their weeping relatives. Some, like Shinkah, held back. Clermont advanced on them until Tiana could smell the sassafras and grease and sweat that stained the armpits of the wool army jacket.

Shinkah stood her ground, and Tiana didn't let go of her hand. Shinkah spoke rapidly in Osage. She always seemed to sing her language rather than speak it. Clermont replied.

"He says I must return with him." There were tears in her eyes. "He says my father waits for me. Every morning and every evening my father and brother rub mud on their faces and weep for my return."

Adoniram stepped forward. Tiana was surprised at how loudly and firmly he spoke. As large as Adoniram was, he was a quiet man.

"This is my beloved wife," he said. "She carries our child. I ask you to allow her to stay with me. I will care for her and love her until we travel the road to the Nightland together."

Clermont spoke to Shinkah again.

"He says it is my duty as a woman of the Bear clan to go to my father and comfort him. He says if you truly love me you will not forget me. In a year you can come for me."

"I will."

"Do not weep, mother," Shinkah said to Tiana. "A year is no more than a beat in the pulse of Wa-kon-da, the Giver of Life. We'll greet Grandmother Sun together in the next Deer Breeding Moon." She gave Tiana a package wrapped in a cloth of mulberry bark. The bark had been dried in the sun, then beaten until the woody part separated from the fibers. The fibers were bleached, then spun into coarse twine. Shikah had stretched the cord between stakes, fastened doubled cords to it, and woven a weft into them to make the cloth. Inside it was a blanket of soft turkey feathers, their quills twisted tightly into strong double threads of hemp. It was warm and soft and light as smoke.

"For your daughter," Shinkah said.

"My heart is heavy," said Tiana. "But when you return, it will be as light as this gift."

Clermont growled at them, but Shinkah ignored him. She had learned something of independence as a woman of the Real People. She laid a hand on Adoniram's arm, her good-bye to him.

Shinkah's unborn child added more weight to her small, well-fleshed frame. But Tiana knew that behind her low voice and soft body, like a partridge, was a warrior's courage. Shinkah wore a bright yellow shirt over a red skirt and blue leggings. She wore beaded bracelets on her wrists and above her elbows. Her hair hung loose down her back as a sign to everyone that she was married. As a woman of the Bear clan, she had tattooed herself, drawing the designs on her breast with a red-hot nail and charcoal. There were white burn scars around the blue lines of the tatoo.

She didn't look back. Tiana heard a choked sob from Adoniram. She moved to stand closer to him as tears ran unheeded down his cheeks.

"She will return," Tiana said.

"Until she is with the Real People again, the child will be an orphan," he said.

"The child will have Shinkah."

"Osage children belong to their father's clan, not their mother's, as ours do. The child will have no father among them. No one will protect or teach it." Adoniram stayed where Shinkah had left him until Clermont and his people had ridden out of sight.

James rode into Tiana's yard one sunny day in early March of 1820. David was working in his shop and the chime of his hammer rang in the clear air. Tiana was enjoying a rare few moments of leisure. With charcoal she had drawn circles and diamonds in a hide, tied it to a broad tree trunk, and was throwing her knife at it. She waved at James as she collected her knife and walked back to throw it again. James noticed the slits in the hide target were all clustered at the small black circle in the center.

He also noticed that David had replaced the window shutters with much heavier ones. He had built a long covered shed from the double cabin to the spring house, so they could get water without being exposed. He had added small slots, big enough to shoot through, near the eaves, and cleared the brush around the cabin far down the hill.

"*A'siyu*, brother," Tiana said. While James fed and watered his horse, she brought hominy mush and honey and stewed apples to the bench in the dogtrot. She held Joanna and rained questions on James as he ate. She hadn't visited her mother's house in over a month and she was curious about the gossip.

David joined them on the bench and leaned against the wall with his eyes closed. With one hand he reached out and groped until he found Joanna's foot. He gave it a squeeze and, still holding it in his big hand, turned to smile at her and Tiana.

David called Joanna his pixie. And she did indeed have an impish look about her. Her golden-brown cheeks were tinged with pink. She had a curved, red bud of a mouth and an upturned nose. If her big, dark blue eyes seemed mischieveous, it was because her curiosity often led her places where she shouldn't be.

"When I look at Joanna," David said to James, "I feel as though I'm seeing my wife as a baby. It's a rare privilege to enjoy your loved one through two lifetimes."

David knew what James wanted to talk about and he was avoiding the subject. Bad Tempered Buffalo and an Osage war party had killed three Cherokee hunters recently. There was talk of revenge and the Rogers were worried about their daughter and her family. After a few pleasantries, James came to the point of his visit.

"Father, mother, all of us, want you to choose another piece of land, one closer to the fort."

From the opening of the dogtrot, Tiana looked out over the farm. She thought of the labor she and David had put into it. She remembered the nights when her hands bled from broken blisters and her back seemed not flesh at all, but only pain made solid. As hard as she had worked, David had worked twice that much.

"We can't give this up, brother."

"Your farm is directly east of the Place of the Oaks, the heart of the Little Ones' territory," James said. "David, speak sense to her."

"We love it here," David answered. "We will not admit defeat and run from Bad Tempered Buffalo and his ruffians."

"What of your daughter? Will you endanger her?"

"We'll be careful," Tiana said. "We'll come to the garrison if there's any trouble. Perhaps I'll go soon anyway, to talk to Drum about stopping this endless raiding and killing. The Women's Council asked me to speak to the council of headmen."

"Talk to Bad Tempered Buffalo," James said.

"If I have a chance to, I will," she answered.

Chapter 33

Drum watched Tiana pace nervously outside the open pavilion that served as a temporary council house. He seemed amused by her anxiety. Inside the pavilion, three or four hundred people were finding seats on the benches. Tiana turned to Drum and tried once more to decline the honor of mixing the sacred Black Drink.

"Surely there's another who can do this better than I, Beloved Father. Sally Ground Squirrel should do it."

"She and the headmen want you to do it."

"But I have lived barely twenty-one seasons. I have no gray hairs. I haven't the experience for such a responsibility."

"Nanehi Ward was nineteen when she was selected *ghigau*." Drum answered Tiana patiently, although he had heard all these arguments from her before. "You shot a man who threatened your grandmother. People have been asking me when you would visit next. Many of them want you to work for them, cure their Important Things. You rode into the Osage camp to bring Shinkah back. And James tells me you lectured Kula'wo, Clermont, to follow the peace trail." Drum laughed and shook his head. "Do not tell me, daughter, that you have no experience nor right to mix the Sacred Drink. The headmen elected you *ghigau* for good reasons."

"What if I make a mistake?"

"You won't." Drum turned his attention to the crowd in the

pavilion. The Great Medicine dance would begin soon. People had gathered from miles away to bathe together in Long Man. Their farms, with neat cabins and orchards, pastures and well-tended fields, lined the Poteau and Arkansas rivers. There were still very poor families, clustered in tiny hamlets, remnants of the villages they had known. But in spite of the hardships, the Real People were prospering here. They had a lot to celebrate, this third fall in the Nightland. If they could only end the war with the Osage, they could make a good life.

While Tiana waited, she adjusted her white doeskin skirt and jacket. She smoothed the feathers of her white swan's wing wand.

"Niece."

She turned to find Sik'waya at her shoulder.

"Have you any messages for people in the Old Country? I'm returning there soon and I want to carry talking leaves with me. I have finally devised a system of drawing words."

"That makes my heart happy, uncle. But I have no messages." Tiana knew better than to ask about Sik'waya's writing. He had claimed to have solved the mystery of the talking leaves many times in the past eleven years. If given the slightest encouragement, he would discourse on the subject for hours, and she had enough to think about right then.

"Can you carry my words to my son, The Raven?" asked Drum. "You can find him as you pass through Na'si whil." That was as close as Drum could come to pronouncing Nashville. He wandered off to solicit more messages.

"I will gladly carry your words," said Sik'waya.

Tiana looked over at James, who shrugged. Drum had never lost faith in his prodigal son. He had been overjoyed a year ago, when James and John delivered Raven's promise to come west. But the months dragged on. Spring came, then summer and fall. Finally Drum received a letter, which Tiana had just translated for him. With the usual flourishes, Raven expressed regret that he couldn't join his beloved father on the Arkansas. Unavoidable responsibilities kept him in Tennessee, even though his heart was with his Cherokee family.

As Drum walked into the open council house to begin the ceremony, Tiana turned to James.

"What are the 'unavoidable responsibilities'? Is he marrying someone? Or is he only a singing bird?" She was angry that Raven would hurt an old man's feelings so cruelly. James was reluctant to answer.

One might tease a brother and give his children ridiculous names. One might play jokes on him, but one didn't criticize him to others.

"He's been appointed Prosecuting Attorney of the Nashville district. And he's been promoted to Major General of the Tennessee militia. A year older than I am, and he's already a general. He's becoming known as a good quarreler, a lawyer. Many people come to him and pay him well. Raven's joined the pack of hounds licking Jackson's boots. I doubt we shall see him again."

"I hope you are right, brother." Then Tiana saw Drum wave to her. She walked among the benches and into the open space at the center of the council house. She was nervous not only because she would be making the Black Drink, although that was an awesome enough duty. She had asked Drum's permission to do something else before the ceremony started.

She looked for Shinkah who was sitting with the Rogers family. She and David, Adoniram and James had ridden to Clermont's village to take Shinkah's father the bride price and to bring her back. It had been a dangerous undertaking, but well worth the risk. Tiana smiled at Shinkah.

"*Gha*! Listen, People of the Seven Clans," Tiana said loudly, and everyone in the council house quieted. "I tell you that the Osage captive, the mate of Adoniram, is now a member of my clan. She is my sister. She is a Long Hair and her children will be Long Hairs. Her footsteps will be on the White Path and the Seven Clans will not climb over her." Tiana beckoned to Shinkah who handed her young son to Nannie. She walked slowly and reluctantly into the center of the dance ground and stood looking at her feet.

"You will not be lonely," Tiana said, laying her white swan's wing on Shinkah's shoulder. "Your very soul will not be lonely. You will live happily in the country of the Seven Clans."

Shinkah's answer was almost inaudible. Only Tiana or Adoniram would have understood it anyway. Shinkah was reciting one of her people's sacred poems.

Truly, at that time and place, it has been said in this house,
They said to one another: what shall the people place on her wrists?
It is a bond spoken of as a captive's bond, that they shall place upon
   her wrists.
Truly, it is not a captive's bond that is spoken of.
But it is a soul that they shall place upon her wrists.

Chapter 34

Colonel Matthew Arbuckle was exhausted. He was forty-six years old, not a young man anymore. The strain was beginning to show in the lines of his thin face. It emphasized his hawk's nose, sharp chin, and receding hairline. He had been struggling to get the men of the Seventh Infantry Regiment to Fort Smith. They had traveled by flatboat, sloop, and steamer. They were making the last leg of the journey up the Arkansas under their own power. From his chair under a makeshift awning, Arbuckle watched them pole the clumsy keelboats. The men grunted in unison as they leaned into the long poles and started their weary journey to the stern of the boats.

The countryside along the Arkansas looked peaceful enough. The river was lined with the Cherokee's snug cabins, fenced pastures, and orchards, all nestled in a quilt of snow. But Arbuckle knew they weren't as prosperous as they looked. He had sent his quartermaster to barter for food and there had been little to spare.

A shout went up as men spotted the flag fluttering over the low log buildings perched high atop a bluff. Arbuckle was relieved. Just let him get himself and his men off these floating pestholes and he could handle anything. He rose, pulled the high collar of his great-coat up around his ears, and stood at attention.

As they edged toward the fort's docks, they passed silent Indians lining the river on both sides. The Osage were dressed in their best clothes and fully armed. Feathers fluttered from their shields and lances. Arbuckle realized he was passing in review.

Bradford was as relieved to see Arbuckle as Arbuckle was to see Fort Smith. The two men walked through a gently falling snow toward the headquarters building. Bradford waved his arms around, detailing the work that had been done and the work that needed doing. When he got no response, he glanced over to see Arbuckle staring at a young woman whose long blue cape swirled around her as she disappeared into the post store.

"Diana Gentry," Bradford said.

"I'd like to warm myself by her fire," said Arbuckle.

"She's married. Her father's an old trader. Throw some business his way whenever you can. Jack Rogers is his name. Hell-Fire Jack. He's a bit crusty. Has some odd crotchets. But he's good company when he warms up. He's been a good friend.

"You'll need friends," Bradford went on. "The Indians'll hate you for not stopping the war they keep fighting. The whites'll hate you for throwing them off Indian land. Government officials will hate you for not giving them special privileges. The junior officers will hate you for the discipline that keeps this madhouse running." Bradford didn't seem to mind being hated.

"An unenviable position," said Arbuckle. "Is she happily married? Rogers' daughter, I mean. I hear a lot of these Indian women kick over the traces and run a little wild. Split the blankets. Especially the breeds."

"Her man's a blacksmith."

"Ah. I make it policy never to tangle with blacksmiths."

"This winter's been unseasonably cold. Raids disrupted the Osage hunts last fall. The Cherokee burned or stole much of their food supply. The enrollment's up at the mission schools."

"What does that mean?"

"The Indians take their children to the schools so they'll be safe when the killing starts. I hope the snow continues to fall. It might keep them home."

A batman had stoked the fire in Bradford's office. He had thoughtfully left a jug of warmed brandy and two glasses on the desk.

"To the fair ones." Arbuckle downed his brandy and closed his eyes to savor it. He kept them closed a beat longer than usual, even for brandy. He loosened his coat, but didn't take it off. It was only slightly less cold inside than out. Their breaths left clouds of steam.

"I take it your trip was not pleasurable," said Bradford.

"You take it correctly. But you know how it is. Everyone has travel stories and horse stories and Indian stories."

"Have you Indian stories, Colonel Arbuckle?"

"A few. I fought Seminoles with Jackson."

"I served with him in the Creek War." Bradford felt his leg aching in the cold from his old war wound. Bradford gestured grandly at the bare, splintery walls of his small office. "This is your reward for service."

"The army has never been noted for gratitude," said Arbuckle without malice. "Who should I expect the most trouble from, among the Indians?"

"No contest. Standing Together by daylight."

"A young brave?"

"An old fart. A god-damned, gander-shanked old firebreather. You'll meet him. His cohort, John Jolly, that's the one to put the screws to. He can collect a lot of support if he wants. But he prefers to sit at home with his wives."

"On a night like this," said Arbuckle, "who can blame him?"

Bradford smiled ruefully. An easy commanding officer, this one. Good-natured, inclined to indulge his senses. He might not last the season. This post required discipline, not a womanizer.

On the other hand, he might make it. There was a look to the mouth and eyes, some subtle etchings in the lines of his face that showed inner strength. In any case, he would be a change from the command the post had operated under the first four years.

Tiana carried Joanna in the cloth sling strapped across her back and led her crippled mare. A gale howled across the high, steep hills. But here, along the river bottoms, the wind was milder. She pulled her blanket tighter around them both to keep the cold from seeping in to Joanna. The child slept peacefully. She was used to being carried as her mother worked.

David had objected to Tiana's going to Fort Smith to see her father, who was sick. But in spite of the bitter cold and her lame mare, Tiana was glad she had gone. Jack had been delighted to see her. She had read to him by the hour from his latest book, a series of droll stories by someone named Geoffrey Crayon. She had joked with him and teased him as she had never dared do when she was a child. It seemed to cheer him.

But she was alarmed at how he had shrunken. He huddled in blankets near the fire most of the time, while the wind howled around the house and through the chinks in the walls. She couldn't remember her father ever being sick. He wasn't used to it. He had seemed defeated by this Intruder. Tiana worked for him, and her remedies helped. He'd looked much better when she left. He'd walked with her to her mare and told her to go to John's or James's and ask one of them to accompany her home. But as she rode away, she heard his ragged, wracking cough.

She had ignored his order. She had rubbed her feet and Joanna's with ashes and had sung a song asking the wolf, the deer, the fox, and the opossum to protect them from frostbite. Then she had started out on the twenty-mile trip alone. It wasn't as dangerous as it once had been. There were cabins now between the Gentry farm and the fort. Tiana had passed the last one an hour and a half ago, about an hour before her horse had started limping. David's thirteen-year-old striker, Mitchell Goingsnake, lived there with his family. He usually stayed with Tiana and David during the week.

She had decided against turning around. It was about as far back to their cabin as it was to her own. And she was eager to be with David in front of her own warm fire. So she'd strapped eighteen-month-old Joanna to her back and had set out to walk the last six or seven miles along the frozen river.

She and the wolves saw each other about the same time. Tiana stopped and stared at them ahead of her and up the slope of the hill. She willed her heart to beat slowly. Many believed wolves could smell fear. The wolves stared back. There were six of them, and they were gaunt, their fur long and shaggy. They looked huge to her. They were digging in the snow, uncovering a frozen elk, but they stopped work to watch her. She considered her alternatives.

She had her pistol and her knife. She could dispatch one, perhaps two of them before they pulled her down. A shot might scare them away. She studied their sunken sides. They were starving. Once they charged, it wasn't likely they would stop. She couldn't outrun them. Even if she were as fleet as a deer, they would chase her in relays.

She could break the thin ice and swim the river. But Joanna would probably die before she could warm her again. She thought of rigging a harness and hauling Joanna into the safety of a tree. But if Tiana were killed, the child would be left to die of exposure. The thought was so horrible it made Tiana's eyes sting with tears. Or, she could continue walking as though they weren't there.

If only David would come striding over the ridge, whistling cheerfully. But he was home, serene in the belief she'd have better sense than to set out in this weather. *You should have better sense than to think I have better sense, beloved.*

The mare rolled her eyes and laid her ears back in fear. Joanna stirred.

"Are we home?" she asked.

"No, daughter. There are wolves, but they won't hurt us." She turned to the mare. "I have magic. I will protect us." Then she faced the wolves. *"Gha!* Listen!" she said in a voice as clear as the ice patterns at the river's edge.

Now! In front of me the sea dragon walks, breathing flames.
Now! In front of me the Red Mountain Lion walks, his head thrown
   back.
My name is Hawk.
I am of the Long Hair clan.

The mare quieted enough for Tiana to lead her forward. The wolves might sense the horse's fear, but Tiana had to take the chance.

In single file the wolves trotted not toward Tiana, but toward the path she must follow. About fifty feet from the trail, the leader wheeled and sat facing her as she approached. The one behind him did the same, then the next and the next, until all six sat in a straight line, parallel to the trail, and with their heads cocked and eyes bright. The black circles around their eyes made them seem even larger than they were, and alive with a human intelligence. Tiana felt the hair at the back of her neck stir. They behaved like trained soldiers, drilling. Tiana lifted her moccasins high so she wouldn't seem to be struggling in the snow.

When she was close enough to see the greenish tint of their eyes and the shades of gray in their pelts, the leader raised his sharp, black nose skyward and howled. The rest did the same. Then they looked at Tiana again, as though to see what effect it had. She threw back her own head and howled at the overcast sky. She felt like a sister to the wolves. Joanna laughed and tugged her mother's hair and barked like a puppy, as they sometimes did in play.

" 'Yea, though I walk a path through the valley of the shadow of death, I will fear no evil. For Thou art with me, Provider.' "

As she recited the charm, the wolves watched her pass. When she was out of sight, they ambled back up the hill to continue pawing the elk carcass.

Tiana arrived home at twilight and led the mare to the small barn. Joanna ran along the beaten path David had dug from the barn to the house, while Tiana rubbed the mare and fed her. It was warm in the barn, and the air was heavy with the smells of the animals. She patted each of them and spoke to them. She turned to find David standing in the doorway.

"It's good to be home," she said.

"Joanna tells me you saw wolves."

"Yes," she said, as though it were of little consequence.

"They could have killed you. You shouldn't have come back alone. You should've waited until someone could come with you."

"Aren't you glad to see me?"

David didn't answer. Instead, he picked her up easily and threw her over his shoulder. He carried her up the ladder carved into a huge log.

"David, what are you doing? What about Joanna?"

"She's asleep already. And yes, my love. I'm glad to see you. Are you glad to see me?"

"Why do you think I came home in the snow?"

He laid her gently in the sweet hay of the small loft. She took off her blue-and-white trade blanket and her long blue cape and covered herself and David with them. He opened her jacket and blouse and covered her bare breasts with gentle kisses. She twined her fingers in his unruly hair, darker now that he didn't spend his days in the hot sun.

"When you go away, there's no joy until you return." He murmured. "I live in fear that something will befall you, where I can't help you. If that happened, I couldn't go on. I love you more than life."

She closed her eyes to experience the sensuousness of his touch more intensely. She unbuttoned his heavy wool shirt and stroked his broad chest with her cool hands. She ran them down below the waist of his trousers. He moaned and held her close, burying his face between her breasts. It grew dark as night fell, and they delighted in the warmth and softness of each other's bodies without the distraction of sight.

When they finished, they walked with their arms around each other to the cabin.

While Tiana talked about her visit and news from the fort, David brushed her hair. He held it and stroked it, braiding and unbraiding it and running his strong fingers through the length of it. This was something David liked to do, but even he would never allow anyone else to see him at it.

"How is your father?"

"He seems better, but he's growing feeble. It saddens my heart to see it."

"And your mother?"

"She doesn't change much from season to season. A few more threads of gray in her hair. A few more lines in her face. She sends you her love. I brought something special for you," said Tiana.

"You already gave me the tobacco and coffee. What could be more special than that? I haven't seen coffee in two years."

"The coffee was from John, really. He saved it for you. As soon as he put the rest out for sale, it was gone."

She pulled a folded sheet of paper from the side pocket of her saddlebag. She opened it and held it up. "Look."

"It looks like writing," said David. "But none I recognize."

"It's a letter from Mary, written by Elizabeth."

"My daughter, Elizabeth?"

"Yes. Sik'waya's new system works, it really works! Do you realize what he's done?"

David studied the paper. "Good God, he's done what no human being has ever done, to my knowledge. Invented an alphabet."

"It's called a syllabary. He's made a character for each sound in our language. There are eighty-six of them."

"No wonder it took him so long. Good God," David was awed. "Your uncle is a genius!"

"I think so. Do you want me to read the letter?"

"You mean you memorized it?"

"No. Sik'waya taught me the syllabary."

"But you were only gone a week."

"I learned it in four days."

"That's preposterous."

"I did. Any child can. Everyone's learning it. He brought a whole bundle of letters from the Old Country. He taught them to read and write there too. Do you realize what this means?" Tiana's eyes were bright with excitement. "We can speak to each other directly, over hundreds, thousands of miles." She shook the piece of paper. "It's as though we've been mute, because so many of us haven't learned the white man's speech and writing. Now we can write our own language. These are my sister's words. Your wife's words." She faltered a bit on that.

"She's my wife no longer."

"She says she misses you. Her man left her, but she has another husband."

"Mary was never long without a man," said David ruefully.

"And, my protector." This was the part Tiana dreaded. "She says Patience and Isabel are gone."

"Gone?"

"To the Nightland. Measles." She turned and knelt with her arms around him. He hugged her and stared into the fire.

"I don't know them anymore. It's been five years with no word. Elizabeth must be fourteen now. A woman."

"Father sends you the best present of all." She found what she was looking for in her saddlebag.

"A book!"

"It's a collection of pieces by someone named Geoffrey Crayon. He's wondrous droll. We can read it a chapter a night and savor it through the winter. You start." She handed it to him. David pulled the chair closer to the fire and opened it to the title page. Tiana sat on her blanket, her cheek on his thigh and one arm wrapped around his leg.

"This is really by a writer named Washington Irving."

"How do you know that?"

"I spend time in the taverns at Fort Smith now and again. His work is mentioned often."

"Why doesn't he use his real name?"

"Why don't you write your real name?"

"Because—" Tiana stopped in confusion.

"Maybe, like you, Mr. Irving thinks someone will steal his soul if they see his name. Beloved, it's late. You must be tired. Are you sure you want to read this now?"

"Yes."

Outside, the wind howled and the wolves had long since started their nightly chorale. David turned the thin book over in his large hands. He opened it again gingerly, careful not to strain the binding. He read aloud every word on the title page. Then he turned to the first story.

" 'The Legend of Sleepy Hollow,' " he read. " 'Found among the Papers of the Late Died, Rich Knickerbocker.' " He began the outrageous adventures of Ichabod Crane.

It was a long story, but neither of them could stop reading it. They laid more wood on the fire when it burned low, and kept on with the tale.

" 'It was the very witching time of night,' " David read. Tiana clutched his leg a little tighter, as he described the silent horseman who rode behind Ichabod Crane.

On mounting a rising ground, which brought the figure of his fellow-traveler in relief against the sky, gigantic in height and muffled in a cloak, Ichabod was horror-struck on perceiving that he was headless! But his horror was still more increased on observing that the head, which should have rested on his shoulders, was carried before him on the pommel of the saddle.

"Oh, no!" Tiana shuddered. David patted her head.

"Your imagination will be your undoing," he said. "Should I stop?"

"No, no. Keep reading. Just don't leave me alone."

It was late when Tiana set the closed book on a small shelf with Seeth's Preacher Book. She felt rich indeed. She could take the book down and enjoy the story whenever she wanted to.

She took the warming pan from its hook on the wall and filled it with coals, while David banked the fire. Holding the pan by its long handle, she rubbed it over the sheets to take the chill from them. Then she put a hot soapstone wrapped in toweling at the foot of the bed with their clothes folded neatly next to it. She and David and Joanna would giggle and fumble to dress in a tent made of their blankets the next morning. David put on his nightshirt and she her gown. The child would sleep between them all night.

Tiana fell asleep immediately. She was worn out from the long day and the hard journey. David lay awake, thinking of his children, three of them dead. He threw his arm across his youngest daughter and his beloved wife. He stroked Tiana's hair, which he'd braided into one long plait for the night. She was affectionate and intelligent. She was a wife and mother beyond reproach. He had no doubt that she loved him. But David knew she didn't feel for him the passion that he had for her. *I can bend iron to my will,* he thought. *I can shape it as I desire. But I can't change something as soft and fragile as a heart.*

Chapter 35

The winter of 1822 and 1823 was worse than the year before. To escape the gales that scoured the plains, buffalo came east to within fifteen miles of Fort Smith. Wolves were seen on the parade ground at night. The fact that Sam Houston ran unopposed as Congressional representative for Tennessee was of little importance on the Arkansas.

The fact that Andrew Jackson had announced his candidacy for president mattered much more. The discussion in the council houses was of the possible consequences of Old Hickory in the presidential palace. The prevailing opinion among the Real People was that it would be a good thing. After all, they'd fought with him. They'd saved the day at The Horseshoe. If he had been ill-tempered with them at the treaty talks of 1817, that was just his way.

How time distorts memory, thought Jack when he heard the talk. Jack spent a good deal of time with Drum and Arbuckle. They smoked away the winter nights, either in one of their cabins or in the tavern, and toasted their feet in front of the fire. They listened to the wind whistling around the building and Jack coughing in long, wracking spasms.

Spring finally came, just when everyone had begun to speculate it never would. The hillsides were covered with white dogwood blossoms. The huge oak trees dangled long, golden tassels. The hawthorn trees were covered with white petals. The glade on the next slope was carpeted with flowers. Migrating birds squabbled deliriously in the trees. The sun flashed from the white breast of an osprey wheeling high overhead.

The forests seemed to vibrate with life. A month earlier Tiana and Joanna had heard the "peent" of the courting woodcock as he strutted and danced. They watched him rise in ever widening spirals into the twilight sky. At first the eerie twittering rustle of his wings in the evening gloom startled Tiana. But in the past two years she had come to listen for it.

Adoniram came to Tiana's cabin on Frog Bayou to pick up his share of the pig iron David had brought from the garrison. He and Shinkah stayed for a few days' visit. He was at the forge, starting on orders that had been awaiting the iron, while David and Tiana took the afternoon off. They'd taken the old wagon horse and ridden toward their favorite swimming hole, two miles away.

Little Chief and Joanna galloped on cane ponies through the tall grass in the yard. Like an Osage child, Little Chief's head was shaved except for three strips of hair across the crown and one lock dangling down his back. Shinkah kept one eye on the children as she hoed weeds in the garden.

Her stubby, bare feet poked out from under the dusty hem of her homespun dress. To hold her hair out of her eyes she wore a bandana, Cherokee style. A heavy wind had blown the night before, so while she worked, she silently recited one of Tiana's simple charms to help the plants stand up again. *Here, I have just come to find you lying down. I think you will soon stand upright.*

She picked a praying mantis off one of the plants and called the children. She knelt in the warm dirt so they could see it.

"The stick bug is one of the wise little old men. He can tell you where the little brothers, the buffalo, are."

"How?" asked Joanna.

"Squeeze his middle very gently. Like this." As she applied pressure to the insect's abdomen, he turned his head. "The buffalo are there." Shinkah pointed in the direction he was looking.

"But that's the Sunland," said Little Chief. "Buffalo aren't there."

"Do you think Mr. Stick is a singing bird?"

"Aunt," said Joanna. "Look."

When Shinkah turned, she recognized Bad-Tempered Buffalo.

She held up her hand, palm outward, and smiled. Another warrior ghosted from behind the seven-foot-high woodpile. Before Shinkah could speak, his arrow drove into her chest.

Four more painted men, with feathers bobbing at the crests of their shaved heads, slipped into the forge barn. They split Adoniram's skull and Mitchell Goingsnake's too before either could reach his weapon. They mutilated the men's bodies and scalped them. The one who had shot Shinkah kicked her and decided she was dead. He scalped her and hung the dripping trophy from the surcingle strap on his horse.

The Osage ran from building to building, taking what they could use and destroying what they couldn't. Bad-Tempered Buffalo recognized Little Chief's haircut and scooped him up. The child struggled and fought, but Bad-Tempered Buffalo tied him onto the back of his horse.

Another warrior caught Joanna. He lifted her by the ankles, and considered her a moment. She screamed as he swung her with all his strength against the logs of the cabin wall. He battered her again and again until her skull was smashed. Then he flung her body away and mounted his horse.

The other four men threw bundles of burning hay into the cabin, the barn, and the other outbuildings, and onto the roofs. They scattered the coals in the forge barn until it too began to burn. Then they lit the hay ricks. In a matter of minutes the men were gone. Thick black smoke billowed and rolled over the surrounding hills.

David and Tiana had bathed and made love. They were dressing slowly when Tiana sniffed the air.

"I smell smoke," she said.

"A whiff of it," David answered.

They finished dressing in a hurry and mounted. They kicked the horse's sides and he broke into a clumsy trot. When they came in sight of the farm, Tiana fought back panic. The smoke was so thick it was hard to see what was burning, but the entire crest of the hill seemed to be ablaze. They raced up the slope toward the forge barn, the closest of the buildings.

"Dear God in heaven," whispered David.

Tiana looked into the burning shed and saw the remains of Adoniram and Mitchell. She gagged and tasted bile in her mouth. She began to whimper, far back in her throat. David dismounted and ran toward the cabin.

"Joanna," he called. "Shinkah! Joanna!" The only response was the crackling of the fires as the flames devoured the dry, seasoned wood of the buildings. The hay ricks sent sprays of blazing straw into the air. Tiana felt the heat pulsing against her face as she led the horse toward the cabin. David waved her away, but she came on. He grabbed her upper arm in a grip that sent a spasm of pain to her shoulder.

"Go to the Goingsnakes for help."

"But Joanna, Shinkah." She tried to tug away from him, to give her arm some relief. David only gripped her tighter and shook her.

"Go!" He screamed it at her. His brown eyes were suddenly those of a stranger. Tiana stood dazed, until he shoved her down the hill. She stumbled and fell sprawling. When she got up, she saw him drop his shirt over something, mount the horse, and gallop down the path that led west. He was going alone after the raiding party.

Tiana picked herself up and stood, bewildered, until the smoke cleared briefly near the garden and she saw Shinkah's body. The heat from the burning hay was like a wall that kept her from reaching her. It had singed Shinkah's clothes and what was left of her hair. Tiana grabbed her ankles and pulled her away from the fire. Then she knelt over her.

"Sister!" she called. "Can you hear me?" The top of Shinkah's head glistened with thick, red blood. Her face and chest were covered with it. Because her scalp had been cut, her cheeks sagged grotesquely. The arrow still protruded from her chest. Too distraught to think clearly, Tiana tugged futilely at the shaft. She tried frantically to remember the proper chants to help Shinkah. But they'd been erased from her memory.

"Grandmother Sun," she called. She looked up, as though help might come from the sky. "You Great Wizards! Help me. Don't let her die!"

Shinkah raised a hand slightly and let it drop. Her lips moved. Tiana bent close to hear her over the fire's noise.

"Bad-Tempered Buffalo," she murmured. "Took Little Chief."

"I'll cure you," said Tiana through her sobs.

"I am on the trail to Mo'n'ha, the Cliffs, mother. Wah-kon-dah has me by the hand," she whispered. "Adoniram? Dead?"

"Yes, sister." Tiana looked around wildly. "Joanna? Where's Joanna?" But Shinkah's spirit had left her. She was dead.

Tiana tried to clear her mind and decide what to do. If she went for help, the buzzards and crows and ants would tear at her sister's body when the fire died. She couldn't bear the thought of it.

With Shinkah's hoe, she pushed her as close to the hay rick as she could. She took logs and kindling from the wood pile and threw them over the body. She threw her skirt over her head and, with the hoe, pulled burning hay from the rick onto the wood. It caught, blazing up until she could see only one of Shinkah's hands. With the tip of the hoe, she pushed the hand into the fire.

With the sound of her heart in her ears, she walked slowly to where David's shirt lay. A tiny foot protruded from the hem of it. Whimpering again, she lifted the shirt with the hoe. She recognized Joanna only by her bloody smock. In a daze, Tiana walked back to the garden and picked up a shovel. Ignoring the flying embers and the heat from the burning cabin, she stepped over the low wrought-iron fence around Gabriel's grave. She began digging methodically next to it.

Mitchell Goingsnake's father and older brother, James Rogers, and several other men from around Fort Smith found her as she was finishing the hole. She had wrapped Joanna's body in David's shirt and stood holding it in her arms. The air was permeated with the smell of roasting flesh from the forge and hay rick. She looked blankly at James as he put an arm around her. Her large, dark eyes were red-rimmed. Tears had left tracks through the soot and dust on her face. Her hair was tangled.

"Sister, my heart weeps for you." James was at a loss for anything better to comfort her. "We came to warn you that Bad Tempered Buffalo was in the area." He touched the bundle she held. "Your daughter?" Tiana nodded. He moved to take the bundle from her, but she hugged it tighter and half turned away. "Bury her, sister," James said. "We'll wait." Tiana fell on her knees rather than knelt. She gently lowered the body into the small, deep hole and began pushing dirt into the grave with her hands. James took the shovel and helped her. Then he knelt next to her.

"Where's David?" he asked. She nodded toward the west. She rose and walked calmly toward the east, past the men. James let her go. He knew she wanted to be alone to mourn her child.

From the woods into which she disappeared came a wail that sent chills through the men. It has followed by a second cry, then another and another. Meanwhile, the timbers of the cabin and barn crashed inward, sending showers of sparks heavenward.

Chapter 36

Major Woolley was livid as he stomped into Arbuckle's office.
"Did you see how they have that old man decked out?" he
shouted.

"I know what he's wearing, yes," answered Arbuckle with a patient sigh. He'd been expecting this. At least Woolley was consistent.

"We can't give him a military funeral in that uniform. It's British,
for God's sake. It's against regulations."

"That's the way Mrs. Rogers wants him buried. And that's the
way he will be buried, with full military honors. Here. This afternoon." Arbuckle pulled out his bulbous pocket watch. "In about ten
minutes."

"You can't—"

"Woolley." Arbuckle rose and took his tar bucket from the peg
and jammed it onto his head. He buttoned his dress coat, the one
that had no patches and was only a bit frayed at collar and cuffs.
He tied his purple sash at his waist. "Woolley, stuff your regulations
in the seat of your pantaloons, next to your brains. There should
be plenty of room." As he strode past his second-in-command he
paused to polish the toe of each boot on the opposite pantaloon leg.
Then he pointed a thin finger at Woolley.

"I've borne your insufferable stuffiness and your sapping of the
officers' morale. I've borne it because even an incompetent officer is

difficult to replace here. But if you do anything to obstruct or mar this funeral, I will see you transferred to the new cantonment on the Kiamichi River. And I will see that you stay there until hell freezes over and the devil sells indulgences."

Woolley's mouth snapped shut. Arbuckle might be able to do it. Under that easy, carousing exterior was byzantine cunning. He had just foiled the officers who had come west with him and had filed charges of negligence on the trip. He'd conveniently assigned all the witnesses to various duties in the field. He and Jack Rogers, the deceased waiting to be buried outside, had only recently been drinking in celebration of the acquittal.

Colonel Arbuckle strode into the gray afternoon. He joined the Rogers family, clustered around two coffins of raw pine boards. David Gentry's coffin was already sealed. His widow stood next to it. The group that had gone after the Osage war party had brought David's body in the day before. But though David would accompany his father-in-law to the cemetery for services, he wouldn't take his final rest there.

His coffin was loaded onto a wagon. Tiana insisted on taking him back to the hill where he'd lived and worked and dreamed. She would bury him facing the Sunland; he would sleep with his children. She didn't want him in a military grave. Arbuckle remembered the look on her face when she told him her husband was a warrior, but not a soldier. *The same might be said of her*, he thought. *Old Hell-Fire was always especially proud of that one.*

Arbuckle took a last look at his friend before the lid was nailed down. Jennie had dressed Jack in his ancient tartans, the uniform of the 71st Highland Regiment. She had included his canteen and dirk, his cartridge box and powder horn. His rusty bayonet and hatchet were strung through loops on his bayonet belt. She'd rubbed the belt with soot to make it black again.

The only incongruous feature of his shroud was the pair of moccasins over his trews. His uniform boots had long since worn out. Jennie had clubbed his wispy gray hair in a neat queue at the nape of his neck and set his black tam-o'-shanter with the plaid band at a jaunty angle on his head.

His children filed past the coffin and left more pieces of his old British uniform. Tiana put in his deer amulet and rotting knapsack. The other children added his gun worm, tobacco, a pint of his best whiskey—the last batch he'd made—and presents of jewelry and clothing. He would need them on his journey to the Nightland. Jennie carried his 1770-model Brown Bess cradled in her arms. The gun was almost five feet long. She laid it gently next to the body.

Tiana had nothing of David's to put in his coffin. Everything they owned had been destroyed. And there had been no time to make a new suit of clothes for burial. Summer came early on the Arkansas. The heat didn't allow for niceties. She had laid her small bag of precious medicine items in his hand.

"It's all I have to protect you on your journey," she had whispered to him. "That and my tears and my love." Then she had plaited her long hair into a single braid down her back. She had taken her knife and sawed through it, at the nape of her neck. She tied a red ribbon around each end and laid it beside him. It stretched from his shoulder to his knees. David's casket was closed now. None but Tiana, Arbuckle, and the men who'd brought him in had seen David's mutilated body.

The garrison's carpenter closed and nailed the lid on Jack's coffin. Jack's sons and sons-in-law lifted it onto their shoulders. The drums began a steady roll, hollow sounding on the loosened drumheads. The men of the fort lined up by companies, their guidons snapping in the rising wind.

Arbuckle had chosen members of Company C to escort the caskets. Company C was made up mostly of the remnants of the hand-picked Rifle Regiment that had built the fort. They were now the old-timers, the garrison's aristocracy. Even without the gold C on their coats, they could be identified by their world-weary air as they sauntered about the grounds. Now they stood smartly at attention.

The three young drummers had freshly painted their scarred old instruments for the funeral. Large white stars gleamed on the bright, navy-blue shells. As the drummers and fifers waited behind the escort, their white plumes fluttered in the wind. Tiana was touched by the trouble to which Arbuckle had gone. He couldn't realize how much more difficult his kindness was making this for Jack's family.

In the privacy of their own farmstead, Jack's widow and children could have sobbed out their grief, as the Real People did. But this six-mile-by-two-mile rectangle was United States territory. White ways prevailed here. Displays of emotion were out of place.

Finally, James strode to the front of the escort. His kilt blew about his knees. He wore his great-grandfather's tartans, the red-and-blue war plaid of the clan Grant. And he carried the pipes. Their voice rang out over the noise of the flags snapping and the wind moaning around the corners of the long barracks. James and the escort stepped out to the slow dirge of "Roslin Castle," played on the pipes. They marched to the hollow thud of the drums.

Tiana tried to concentrate on the music, on the faces, on the leaves dancing on the wind. She looked up at the gray clouds scudding across the sky. She tried to concentrate on everything but David as she had seen him last.

Her brothers and Arbuckle had tried to talk her out of looking into the coffin.

"My dear," said Arbuckle. "It was several days before the scouts found him. His body had been exposed to the elements and the beasts. And the Osage . . . they did what they usually do to enemies." He didn't mention that David probably hadn't died quickly.

"I appreciate your concern, Colonel," Tiana had said. "But I must see him. Else I'll always wonder if he's truly dead."

Oh, he's truly dead, miss, Arbuckle thought. But he stood aside and let Tiana lift the lid. He prepared to catch her should she faint. As she stared into the coffin, the color drained from her face. She swayed, but she didn't fall. After she had placed something in the box with David and had cut off her hair, she closed the lid with exaggerated care.

"Thank you, Colonel," she said. "You've been kind." She walked regally from the office.

But now David's face haunted her. To imagine him as she had just seen him was terrible. But to imagine him as she remembered him, laughing and singing and holding her close, was worse. She heard Drum's few simple words and Arbuckle's eulogy as noise, with no more meaning than the wind. While James played "The Minstrel Boy" friends and relatives walked by the hole and dropped more presents in on top of the casket. They hoped Jack would carry the gifts to their loved ones already in the Nightland.

Drum came to stand beside Tiana.

"Beloved Father, why do kind people die so horribly and evil people live to kill them?"

"If I knew, daugher, I'd be as wise as the immortals." The first clods of earth thudded onto the coffin lid. The six-pounder began firing. "You are welcome in my wife's house," Drum said, between the shots.

"Thank you. Mother and I will stay on at her house, with John and Elizabeth." Tiana paused, then said, "Why did this happen, uncle? You and Ulisi and the One Who Talked To Ghosts always told me I had magic, power for good."

"Sometimes the magic doesn't work," Drum answered sadly.

When the soldiers had been faced about and quick-stepped back to the barracks, Jennie and the other women began keening. Drum squatted at the edge of the mound of earth. He drew his blanket over his head and moaned. Tiana knelt next to him. She crossed her arms over her breast, and bent over until her head touched the earth. She was trying to collect her misery into the smallest possible package, trying to wrap herself around it as though to contain it. She sobbed for hours.

Tiana stood in the doorway of the small upstairs bedroom. Jennie had had John and James and Charles carry the girls' old bedstead there for Tiana. She looked at it now through a mist of tears. It seemed smaller than she remembered. She crossed the room and sat on it, smoothing the worn sheet with her hand.

She recognized the sheet from her childhood too. When bedclothes wore so thin in the center they could no longer be patched, Jennie pieced together the outer, less fragile parts of two of them. Tiana knew each stain and tear, each irregularity of Grandmother Elizabeth's weaving.

For an instant, she thought the past five years hadn't happened. Perhaps if she concentrated on the bed, on her childhood, she could wipe the sorrow from her memory. Then a scent of smoke brought it all back with such intensity she shuddered and began to sob. She buried her head in the feather pillow so she wouldn't upset the rest of the family. It took little to start Jennie crying again.

John and James were burning everything that had belonged to their father. Jennie insisted on it. If they allowed his possessions to stay, his soul would be reluctant to leave them. He would be unable to travel toward the land of the dead. Tiana had smelled the smoke from the fire in the yard. She cried until James knocked softly on the door lintel.

He sat beside Tiana and stroked her cropped hair. She sat up and he gave her a handkerchief to wipe her eyes and nose. She went on crying, but more quietly. Her hair stood out in dark clouds around her beautiful face. She leaned against James and he put his arm around her.

"You must come to the dance tonight," he said.

"I cannot."

"You must. The people have planned it to cheer us." They both knew recently departed souls tried to lure their loved ones to the Nightland with them. Sorrow and memories of the dead could cause the living to waste away. It was vital that Jack and David's families be distracted.

"I have nothing to wear."

"Yes, you have." James went out and returned with a huge bundle of clothes. "People have been leaving gifts on the porch for you all day—baskets, utensils, cloth, food. They know you lost everything. Surely there's a dress here that will fit you."

"Brother," Tiana said suddenly. "What is it like in the Old Country now?" She caught her breath and willed her tears to stop so she could talk.

"I've told you the land is being settled by white people. And that you do not want to see our old house. It would add to your sorrows. The people of the Seven Clans there are under constant attack from the government, trying to make them leave their homes."

"At least the government isn't killing them."

"Not yet." There was bitterness in James's voice.

"I know I can't go back to the farm on Rogers' Branch. But there must be villages where people still live in the old ways. There must be better places than this. There's only death here."

She walked to the tiny window that looked out over the front of the house. The people from Hiwassee were gathering from every direction. They would camp under the trees, and spend the next seven days feasting and dancing, to help the Rogers through their sorrow. Gently, James led Tiana downstairs to join the festivities.

By the end of the first night of dancing, the grief in Tiana's heart had been softened by the love around her. She was surrounded by the faces of her friends, laughing and teasing and singing to the constant beat of the drums. The sinuous lines of dancers moved in graceful rhythm with each other and with the world.

Tiana could feel the power of the group magnify as more and more dancers joined the lines and stepped in time to quickening drums. As they circled from the east toward the west, they seemed to be reaffirming and accepting the pattern of life, celebrating the cycle from birth to death. Tiana felt as though her heart were beating in time with everyone there. And each person was as strong as all of them together.

Between dances, people reached out to touch Tiana and talk to her, to give her gifts or tell her how much they would miss her husband and father and child. But Tiana began to hear other talk too. The young men were muttering about revenge, promising to cover the bones of the dead. The belief that an unavenged soul could not reach the Nightland was still strong.

Maybe the talk was good for Tiana. Anger made her forget her sorrow. She took the ceremonial white swan's wing from one of the covered baskets brought from the council house and strode to the center of the dance area. She held the wing over her head, and turned to face in each direction, until everyone quieted.

"Children," she said in a loud voice. Grief had released its stranglehold on her throat. And she chanted her talk, giving it power by repeating lines. "You have called this one Beloved Woman. You have asked her to mix the sacred Black Drink that purifies you. She asks now that you listen to her talk.

"Your sisters weary of carrying their babies on one hip and their pistols on the other. Your mothers weep to see their sons carried back to them, their bodies cold, their spirits gone where they cannot follow. Your mothers and sisters do not want more killing, and ever more killing. They do not want revenge. This one, from whom war has taken her beloved husband and child, does not want revenge. She wants peace. She wants peace now. She wants it forever. She has just come to ask of you only peace. Surely that cannot be so difficult, my children." She was trembling when she sat down and Drum took her place.

"The old ones here, the ones with gray on their heads and memories in their hearts, remember my brother, Skatsi, the Scotsman. "Drumsard." They know his skin was white but his soul was red. They have listened often to his wise counsel. They remember his bravery in the war between the Red Jackets and the Americans. He was never afraid to fight.

"But as his sons grew to manhood, he began to see with a father's eyes. He said he did not want his sons to die. He did not want their young bodies to decay. He did not want them to become the flowers of the forest that he sang about, the young men who die in battle.

"We old ones remember Skatsi singing. We did not always understand his songs, but we knew they were good, because there was goodness in his heart. He was my brother for a lifetime. My heart will weep until I join him in the Nightland." Drum's voice broke and he sat with his head bowed.

The evening's caller circled the cleared area, announcing the singers for the next performance and the one who would lead the dance. Tiana felt sadness wash over her again and walked away from the dance ground. She wanted to be alone for a while. Grandmother Sun would be rising soon.

A woman clutched a thin, patched blanket around her shoulders and stared fixedly at Tiana's chest. Tiana sighed. She could detect the anxiety under the stolid gaze. She had seen it before, on other women who stood thus in the yard of her cabin.

The woman gestured with her head. Tiana followed her into the deep gray morning.

Without a word, the woman set off at a brisk walk. Tiana had to hurry to keep up with her, even though the woman was many inches shorter and many pounds heavier. They walked for six hours. The sun was well up when they finally arrived at the tiny cabin hidden in a steep, narrow valley. The smell of skunk hung heavily about the place, and Tiana noticed a fresh grave away from the house. The skunk carcass was rotting over the lintel to keep plague away. But it obviously hadn't been effective.

The woman pushed open the warped door, and Tiana followed her inside. She blinked to adjust her eyes to the dimness. When the low door was closed, the only light was from a small fire in the center of the room. Smoke that didn't leave through the hole in the roof was layered against the ceiling. There was no furniture other than a few frayed mats on the dirt floor.

Pottery jars and baskets of corn and beans, dried vension, and pumpkin lined the uneven log walls. Clothes hung from elk antlers. A teenage girl tended some deer brains drying on a splintery board propped in front of the fire. Few of Tiana's close relatives tanned their own hides with brains anymore. These were fullbloods, clinging to the old ways, the ways she had said she wanted to go back to. These were people who thought whites bleached themselves with soap.

Tiana knew at night the door would be shut against the wolves and the hordes of malevolent ghosts and witches that swirled about. The air in the cabin was thick with the smell of skunk, old food, green hides, smoke, and the effluvia of people living in close quarters. Chickens roosted on the single puncheon shelf that served as a bed. The tattered blankets were stained with their droppings. The chickens shared the shelf with four children of varying ages. They must have been told not to leave the cabin until their mother returned. There was no man about. Tiana assumed his was the grave in the woods nearby.

"My daughter is broken." The woman spoke for the first time. "Will you work for her, Beloved Woman?"

"I will try." Tiana had already spotted the child with the broken arm. She probed it gently. The girl whimpered, but did not cry out, although the pain must have been excruciating. The arm hung at a strange angle. It was swollen, and the taut skin was blue and purple. "What caused this?" Tiana asked. "And when did it happen?"

"A swan attacked her yesterday morning," the mother said. Tiana nodded. It happened often. While playing near the river a small child would stumble into a swan's nest. The bird's powerful, flapping wings could easily snap a tiny arm.

Tiana was glad for the excuse to leave the cabin and go in search of plants for medicine. She built a fire outside and began boiling down the roots and leaves of the mullein into a tea for the child to drink. By the fourth day it would be the right consistency for the poultice.

Tiana bathed the arm with an astringent of water and powdered alum root from her medicine bag. She explained to the child what she was doing and warned her it would hurt. Then she sang to her as she set the arm the way she'd seen the doctor at Fort Smith do. The chant not only appealed to the spirits for help, it also distracted the girl. Tiana ripped off a strip of cloth from the bottom of her skirt to tie the thin wooden splints in place.

She worked for the child the prescribed four days. At night, she slept in a brush shelter by the fire. She said it was so she could watch the medicine simmer, which was true. But she also couldn't bear the thought of sleeping in the crowded cabin. She had already felt the fleas and chinches that infested the blankets and the dirt floor. She would rather take her chances with the wolves.

On the fourth day, she unwrapped the girl's arm and inspected it. She recited a charm, sipped some of the infusion of mullein, cardinal flower, and alder, and spit it onto the sore area. She applied a poultice for a few minutes and rewrapped the splint. When she left, the mother gave her a pair of moccasins she had made while Tiana worked.

"Mother," Tiana said, "I will tell the people of your trouble. They'll come help you here."

"My heart sings with gratitude, Beloved Woman."

"You must leave the cloth in place for at least a moon."

"I will."

But Tiana doubted she would follow the instructions. The Real People didn't bind broken bones. This child's arm would probably be crooked, as many were.

As Tiana walked down the trail, she thought about the past four days. There were families like this hidden away throughout the Real People's Nation. Maybe her purpose was to spend her life helping them. It seemed as though there was nothing great enough to balance the weight of her grief. But perhaps what little good she did would begin to lighten her soul.

Chapter 37

The Girth's wife, Tojuhwa, Redbird, lumbered by Tiana and the four girls with her. Mumbling to herself she set an erratic course for the river. She was a big woman anyway, and these days she was always chastely enveloped in yards and yards of calico.

Redbird spent a great deal of time half submerged in the river or throwing water over herself. James said she looked like a buffalo in a wallow. But Tiana couldn't laugh at her. Redbird stayed near the water because she was terrified of fire. More exactly, she feared being burned alive. She feared it so much she kept a bucket of water by her bed. From time to time she woke up screaming and poured water over herself.

Redbird had attended classes at the mission school. When she was ill and faced with the afterlife, she must have panicked, because she asked to be baptized. But her holier status gave her no peace. She began to worry about hell and about lakes of burning sulphur and brimstone.

Before she lost her sanity, she had confided to Tiana that she'd been much better off as a heathen. Then she had been innocent of the black robes' Word and things would have been better for her in the afterlife. Now that she knew the Truth, she was bound to that straight, narrow track the missionaries called the Good Life. It was too much responsibility for her simple mind.

One of the children with Tiana was the black slave child, Martha. Martha scratched Ꮁ Ꮅ Ꮞ Ꮣ Ꮎ, *nudanhtuhna*, insane, in the dirt with a stick. Tiana rubbed it out with the toe of her moccasin before the other three girls, Redbird's daughters, could see it. She knelt and whispered in the child's ear. "A person of kindness and soul doesn't make fun of the unfortunate."

"I'm sorry, Ghigau." Martha hung her head.

"Beloved Woman," called Duwe'ga, Spring Lizard. "The ashes are sifted." She held a basket of them over her head.

"*Atsu*! Very good! Pour them into the kettle. Now, A-wi'akta, Deer Eyes, add the shelled corn." The black child emptied her basket of brightly colored kernels into the kettle with the simmering water and ashes.

"What can I do, Beloved Woman?" Five-year-old Rebecca tugged at Tiana's skirt.

"Stir the kettle with this long stick. Be careful not to burn yourself or turn it over. When the skin loosens on the kernels, tell me. Spring Lizard can stir the beans."

Redbird's children looked like urchins. Their mother wasn't caring for them. And their father, The Girth, had gone to search for someone, which was the Real People's way of saying he was looking for a second wife. Tiana doubted he'd have much luck. The Girth's second wife would have to live with a simple husband, eight children, and another wife who might wake up screaming in the middle of the night and pour water over her head.

"Beloved Woman," said the slave child shyly.

"Yes, Deer Eyes."

"My name is really Martha."

"I know." Tiana took her small face in her hands and with her thumb rubbed a smudge of ash off the smooth, coffee-colored skin. "But you have eyes as large and as beautiful as a deer's. A person can have as many names as she wants. Do you mind if I call you Deer Eyes?"

"No. I don't mind." The child grinned, her white teeth brilliant in her dark brown face. She was neatly dressed in a smock made from sacking. Her hair was plaited in tiny rows all over her head. Her mother and father were planting The Girth's fields. They belonged to Drum, but he had loaned them to The Girth to help until another wife could be found. In the meantime, Drum and Tiana were trying to find out the cure for Redbird's insanity.

Now Tiana sat cross-legged on the ground in Redbird's cluttered yard. The dust felt warm under her cotton skirt. Grandmother Sun warmed her back with a pleasant heat. Tiana could smell the parched plants, the smoke from the fire, the boiling beans, and the baking dung from the pasture. Chickens tiptoed archly around the yard, pecking at places where insects might be. The hens maintained a soothing, staccato clucking as though gossiping *sotto voce*. The bees set the air to vibrating with their constant hum. The new colt was frisking in the pasture, and learning to whinny.

A quarter of a mile away, down the river, someone was grinding corn. Tiana could hear the steady thump of *akanona*, the mortar and pestle. The women who lived close enough talked in code with their mortars. The talk went on all day, because there was always someone grinding corn.

Tiana took out two of the combs that held her hair in a pile on her head. She gave one to Martha, and the two of them began unsnarling the younger girls' tangles.

"Beloved Woman, will you tell us a story tonight?"

"Yes."

"Will you tell us how the buzzard got his bald head?"

"Yes."

"Beloved Woman, the skin is falling off the kernels," called Rebecca.

The children had started calling her Beloved Woman after the headmen voted her the title of *Ghigau*. "For most people, age brings wisdom," Drum had said. "But once in a while, someone is born knowing. Don't ask me how this can be. But a few children know the ways of the world just as birds know how to find their way back to their nests. Our daughter Tiana is such a one."

Somehow, word spread to even the remotest of cabins. She walked or rode from one farm to another, helping those who were sick and in need, and everyone knew her. Children flocked around her wherever she went. She often had trinkets for them from John's store, but that wasn't why they followed her. If she no longer had a farm or children of her own, she was adopting the entire band.

"Beloved Woman." Rebecca was tugging at Tiana's skirt again. "The corn is ready."

"Good." She put a large basket sieve on a flat rock and poured the kettle's contents into it. The ashes and water seeped through and into the dusty earth. "Now we wash the corn at the spring to rid it of skins. Fill the kettle with water and put it on the fire again."

The four girls gathered around the rim of the great wooden log mortar while she pounded the damp kernels into meal. She stopped now and then so they could run their fingers throught the meal to see if it was fine enough.

"We have to work fast so it doesn't get cold." Tiana emptied the meal into a shallow pottery basin. She poured the beans and their water into the meal. She worked the mixture with her hands, then formed it into balls. She flattened the balls and laid them on a flat rock by the fire.

She wrapped the flattened bean cake into one of the broad corn leaves that had been dipped in hot water to make it supple. She tied the package with a flexible river reed and laid it aside. "Now you try it." Each of the children dipped her fingers into the mass of dough and made her own flat cake. Then they dropped their cakes into the simmering water.

"They'll boil an hour or so," Tiana said. "Why don't you all bathe in the river while I clean up here."

They ran off squealing and laughing. Tiana walked back to the spring and pulled up a small plant she had noticed growing there amidst the damp moss and rocks. Its small clusters of white flowers and its narrow, toothed leaves looked like the water parsnip. But it wasn't. It was water hemlock and very poisonous. A bit of its root would kill a child if she mistook it for the edible parsnip.

Tiana turned it over in her hand. When she had stood on that bare hill three years ago and laid flowers on the graves there, she had considered eating some of it. As she'd walked among the desolate ruins, her own future seemed charred and broken.

It had been a mistake to go back to where David and the two girls were buried. The Real People believed one shouldn't visit gravesites. Witches gathered there to eat the livers of the dead. Spirits of the dead might try to lure their loved ones to join them. She hadn't gone there again. She had brewed a tea of the thimbleberry shrub, brought from the Old Country. It was supposed to pull memories of loved ones from the mind. There was a great demand for it here.

Even now, after three years, Tiana's eyes filled with tears at the thought of David and her daughters, and of Adoniram and Shinkah. But mostly she missed David. He had been so good. She had known he would always love her, always be there for her, and she regretted not telling him more often that she loved him. If she ate a bit of the plant, she could join him and escape this devouring loneliness. She brushed the black dirt off the pale root, dug a piece out with her fingernail, and sniffed it.

She was startled when The Girth's dogs began barking frantically. A man was leaning down from his horse to peer into Redbird's open door.

"Call off your hounds or I'll shoot a few," said a second man.

The dogs stood behind her and snarled from around her legs. Tiana was sorry her pistol and the rifle were inside the cabin. These men smelled of evil. It was more than just body odor. Most white people smelled bad. These had a sour aroma of menace in their sweat. Tiana felt her own lip curl like the dogs'. "What do you want?" she asked.

"The squaw speaks proper English, Bill." The man's face was dark with the stubble of several days' beard. Both his front teeth were missing and he had a tic over his left eye. His clothes were all the same shade of gray-brown.

"We thought you'uns might offer some hospitality. You Injuns is supposed to be hospitable people." The second man leered at her. His belly hung well over the waist of his baggy pantaloons. "Looky for heap strong man, squaw?" He pulled up his sleeve and flexed his pale flab. "Me give you good fucky-fucky." He patted his groin with a self-satisfied air.

"Go away!"

"Now, miss, ain't no need to alarm yourself," said the first man, apparently the diplomat of the two. "We just passin' through. Lookin' things over. Shoppin', like."

"There's no store here. Nothing for sale."

"Looks to be plenty of real improvements here, Bill," the first man continued. "Smokehouse, corn cratch. Peach trees. Lacks a barn. How many acres you'uns got under the plow, missy?" he asked Tiana.

The fat man leaned over the pommel of his saddle and went on undressing Tiana with his eyes. She could feel rage expanding inside her. If only she had her gun.

"You're trespassing." She tried to keep her voice steady.

"Naw." The thinner man spit a stream of tobacco through the gap in his teeth. "Naw. Way we look at it, you'uns is the ones trespassing. This country's for white people. We aim to have it.

territorial legislature's gonna vote to throw you out. We can't have a pack of dirty savages squatting in our country."

Tiana began edging toward the house. If she could get around them and inside, she knew the guns were loaded.

"I think she's about to invite us inside," said the one with the belly. The front of his pants was bulging and he shifted in his saddle to ease it. "Hot damn!" He dismounted. Tiana pulled her knife from its sheath at her waist.

"If you touch me I'll carve my name on your testicles."

"Testicles? Hear that, Cyrus? Testicles. We got us a educated squaw." Then his face contorted with anger. "You ain't gonna do no such. You gonna lie still and I'm gonna do you a favor. Iff'n you're real lucky you might have a remembrance of me—a snot-nosed, half-breed brat."

"You shall not touch me with one slimy, fat finger."

"We'll just see . . ."

With a hard, deft flick of her wrist, Tiana threw the knife. It sank to the hilt into the fat of his upper thigh, just missing the shrinking bulge in his pantaloons. He howled and doubled over.

"You filthy bitch." His partner pulled his rifle from the boot on his saddle and aimed it at Tiana. Tiana's fear left her. She stared at him calmly.

"You can only kill me," she said. "And of course, my clan will not rest until you are dead. It's our law." Tiana knew that technically, she was lying. The National Council had long since outlawed clan revenge. But there were laws and there were laws. The old law of blood was more compelling than the new paper law. "My clan is very large and very powerful. They will find you, no matter where you go. Shall I tell you some of the ways my people kill a man?"

"You bitch," he said again. But he was wavering. She wasn't the hysterical, helpless victim he had expected.

"Help me, Cyrus," called the fat man.

"I will, soon's I figure out what to do with her."

"Throw your piece down." James stepped into the open, his rifle leveled. A tattered figure followed him.

"This is none of your affair."

"She is my sister. She is of my clan."

"Oh, shit," murmured Gap Tooth. He spit another stream of tobacco to collect his thoughts. He had heard of Cherokee clan revenge. He realized his natural superiority as a white man might not save him from being skinned alive or burned at the stake. He dropped his gun into the dust. Tiana slipped inside and returned with her pistol.

"We was just passing through and the little lady here took fright. You know how women are." Gap Tooth tried to take refuge in mutual male arrogance. James half cocked the hammer on his gun. Gap Tooth hurried on. "My partner's hurt. We need to get to Cantonment Gibson. See a surgeon."

"Hold them, brother, while I get my knife." Tiana walked to the fallen man and pointed her pistol at his right eye.

"Don't shoot me, miss. You wouldn't kill a man."

"I'd sooner kill you than scratch lice," said Tiana. "Don't move."

"I shan't."

With the gun still pointed about six inches from his eye, she planted a foot on his belly and yanked the knife out with her free hand. Blood followed in a gush. She wiped her blade on his trouser leg and stuck it back into its sheath. The man groaned. Tiana tossed a clump of dried moss onto his stomach.

"Stuff that into the hole," she said.

"Then be gone or be dead," said James.

Tiana fired Gap Tooth's gun into the air to empty it. She poured dirt down the muzzle and pounded the firing mechanism against the log ends at the corner of the cabin wall until the hammer and frizzen snapped off. She pulled the fat man's rifle from under the straps that held his rolled blanket, and did the same to it.

"You'll hear about this," said Gap Tooth. "I'll have the law on you."

"Colonel Arbuckle is the law between Fort Smith and Cantonment Gibson," said James. "And if you're lucky, he will only laugh at you."

The men left, mumbling and threatening. Tiana felt her strength draining out of her. James put his arm around her.

"Your husband would be proud, and so would father."

Drum's slaves arrived out of breath, their hoes ready for attack. The girls tumbled into the yard. They had all heard the shots. How could Tiana tell the children they mustn't run carelessly into the open like that? She didn't want them to live in fear. But how could she explain the difference between fear and caution?

"There were intruders," she said. "White men who strayed. We'll report them to Colonel Arbuckle."

The man who had come with James walked slowly toward them. His horse had a wide, filthy collar of woven basswood bark with a mangy tuft of red-painted hair dangling from it. He was an Indian, but he looked like a vagabond on the tramp. His white men's clothes were ill-fitting, torn, and dirty. He was emaciated and hollow-eyed. His stiff black hair was all of one length and stood out around his head. He was a tall man, but his shoulders were bowed, as though weighted by a burden. There was something unsettling about him. Something familiar.

"Sister," said James. "This is Bad-Tempered Buffalo. But now he calls himself Moses." James's eyes pleaded with her to bury the hatchet of her hatred.

"I remember him," she said evenly.

"He gave himself up to the soldiers rather than bring retribution down on his people. He did it knowing he might be hanged."

Tiana remembered that too. She also knew of the Little Ones' horror of strangulation. Hanging would trap his soul so it could never reach paradise.

"In jail he tried to cut his throat with the edge of his pewter spoon," James said. "He had sharpened it on the stone wall of his cell. But they caught him in time. The governor pardoned him several months ago." James seemed determined there would be no hatred, no ugliness here. Bad-Tempered Buffalo held out a thin, shaking hand. He looked as though he were suffering from some sort of fever. Tiana looked at the hand, then at the gaunt face above it, and finally at James.

"Don't ask me to do this, brother," she whispered. "He killed my man, my child, my sister, my friends."

"The hatred and the killing have to stop sometime," said James. "You have said it yourself. The Osage have been forced to move again, to make room for *us*." James nodded at the spectre between them. Bad-Tempered Buffalo, now Moses, patiently continued to hold his hand out. "The missionaries at Hopefield told him about God. He went on a vigil, fasted for seven days. He said he couldn't find God. He asked Reverend Montgomery if *he* had seen God lately. Now he seems to be searching for Him. I found him almost starved."

Slowly, reluctantly, Tiana held out her hand. She took Bad-Tempered Buffalo's fingertips in her own. A wisp of a smile appeared on his face. Tiana stared into his eyes, searching for a trace of the arrogant, handsome warrior who had taken tobacco from David so long ago. Bad-Tempered Buffalo rubbed his fingers on the back of his other hand. It was the sign that meant "I am poor."

"Amanda," Tiana said.

"Yes, Beloved Woman," said Drum's slave.

"The girls and I made some bean dumplings. They're boiling over there. Please bring them. We'll eat them with venison. Come, Moses." She took Bad-Tempered Buffalo by the arm and guided him toward the cabin. "You look hungry and ill. Perhaps I have some herbs that will help you. Deer Eyes, take the horses to the pasture and rub them with grass. Rebecca, run to the river and tell your mother to come eat. And call the boys. They should be there trapping fish." She turned to her brother. "What brings you, James?"

"I wanted to see how The Girth's family was doing. Help out. And I have a letter for you from Mary."

After supper, and after Tiana had read Mary's letter aloud and told the story of how the buzzard got his bald head, she had to go outside. The tiny cabin was crowded with nine children and five adults. Even Drum, whose cabin was always overflowing, would have said he had no place to spread his blanket. James followed her.

"I want to hear what those men wanted," he said.

"Then let's go to the river. Long Man is handsome here."

The night had a warmth to it, like black down. The half moon had a haze around it that made it seem fairylike. As they walked, Tiana told him what had happened. "What did they mean, about the territorial legislature voting to throw us off?" she asked.

"There's talk of whites settling Lovely's Purchase. But it won't happen. It was promised us as an outlet to the hunting grounds to the west. We have a right to be there."

Tiana looked out at the quiet water, black and silky, with a strip of moonlight across it like a shirred silver ribbon.

"Right is nothing when white people want land. You heard Mary's letter. The Georgians blame the government for civilizing us and making us want property." She didn't try to keep the bitterness from her voice. "We're damned if we do and damned if we don't, as father used to say. But damned in any case."

"Sh, sister. Don't think of it." He put his arm around her and they stood, silent, watching the reflection of the moon.

"People expect too much of me, James. They expect me to be always calm and wise and fearless. Sometimes I'm so frightened and confused and lonely."

"I am too." James's wife, Suzie, had run away with the hired man and taken their new baby with her. James had no idea where she or the child were. "Sometimes I wake in the night to drums," he said. "And it's only the sound of my own heart pounding with fear . . . for you, for mother and Susannah and her daughter who must live with that wretch, Miller. I fear for our people."

"You're a man."

"Men fear. Even Drum and Standing Together have fears."

Now that the afternoon's crisis was well over, Tiana's calm began to scatter. Loneliness and anxiety swept over her. She began to cry in deep, gulping sobs. James held her close, and felt the sobs shaking her. He stroked her soft hair. It had grown until it reached the center of her back.

"Hush, sweet sister. Many men love you and desire you."

"None of them touches my heart. None of them walks in my soul. There's no one to hold me, protect me. And I can't fight evil alone. There's too much of it."

James refrained from telling her she wasn't alone, that her family and hundreds of friends loved her. He knew she was saying there was no one set apart for her. There was no one to walk the White Path with her.

"I want to stay here longer. I cannot face them all now," she said when her grief subsided.

James took her hands and squeezed them. "Be careful."

"I will."

As he walked slowly up the path, the moon painted his shoulders and dark, curly hair with pale light. Perhaps someone had put a spell on his sister. Some unknown man was trying to make her lonely so he could force her to love him.

> *I just took your heart away from you.*
> *Throughout the night, your soul will be lonely.*
> *Now! The Black Raven has just come to cling to you!*
> *He has just come to draw away your soul.*

Had the stealthy Black Raven brought remade smoke on his wings and let it drift over her while she slept? Had he taken her soul with him, leaving her empty and bereft?

Chapter 38

O'Neale's tavern, near the Capitol, was crowded. Andrew Jackson's cronies were singing and waving their tankards in time to the music. Beer sloshed onto the floor and soaked into the sawdust there. Outside, a cold, December wind howled along the broad avenues of Washington City. It drove ice and rain against the wide front window of O'Neale's. Flames roared in the twelve-foot fireplace. Men sat around it with their feet propped on chairs and elevated over their heads. It was a custom foreigners often remarked on.

The firelight and the candles gave the wooden furniture, ceiling, floor, and walls a sepia patina, softened even more by a haze of smoke. Heaps of steaming coats and scarves hung on brass hooks near the entryway.

The men's song was accented by the occasional ring of tobacco juice hitting a brass cuspidor.

> *I 'spose you've read it in the prints,*
> *How Packenham attempted*
> *To make Old Hickory Jackson wince,*
> *But soon his schemes repented.*
> *For we with rifles ready cocked*
> *Thought such occasion lucky;*

And soon around the hero flocked,
The hunters of Kentucky.

Sam gathered himself for an assault on the chorus.

Oh, Kentucky! The hunters of Kentucky.

He had to bellow to drown out his friend, Junius Brutus Booth. Booth was British and insisted on singing the original words, a bawdy ballad about Unfortunate Miss Bailey. When the last note had finally been permitted to die, Andrew Jackson leaned his banjo against the wall and rose from his chair near the fire. His small blue eyes seemed to focus light as he looked out over the room. He raised his brandy glass and waited for what passed for silence at O'Neale's.

Peg O'Neale Timberlake went on serving customers and keeping Jackson's circle well supplied with Monongahela toddies. Her cheeks were pink naturally, but the cold and exertion had deepened their color. She and her full skirts and low-cut bodice maneuvered gracefully around the crowded tables. Jackson cleared his throat for attention.

"To the patriots of Seventy-six," he said in his high, thin voice. "May we ever cherish their principles and carry on their struggle for liberty."

"Hear! Hear!" the men cried. John Eaton stood next.

"To Independence. May we hold on to its substance and scorn its shadow."

"Hear! Hear!"

Peg Timberlake stopped and held up a small hand that clutched six full tankards by their handles.

"To the next Congress." Everyone hushed to hear her soft voice. "May they encourage domestic manufactures and be contented with forty-two dollars a week." Congressmen hissed and everyone else cheered.

Sam Houston stood, his tall form visible from everywhere in the large room. He held up his glass.

Let her be clumsy or let her be slim,
Ancient or young, I care not a feather;
So fill up a bumper, nay, fill to the brim,
Let us toast all of the ladies together.

Junius Booth stood next. He was a slender, dark man with a narrow moustache and an aristocratic air. When he spoke it was with a British accent and a flair for the dramatic that had been thrilling audiences in American theaters.

"To the boulevards of your fair capital. May they not always be as deep as they are wide."

"I'll second that, Junius." A bull of a man had entered and was searching for a place to hang his dripping coat. His deep, powerful voice carried easily over the hubbub. "O'Neale's Dearborn is practically up to its running boards in mud. It's as cold as Henry Clay's poker stare out there." As usual, Daniel Webster was dressed in blue coat and pantaloons and a buff-colored vest, the colors of the Revolution.

"Welcome, Daniel," said Jackson. "Join us." The chair creaked when Webster sat in it. He wasn't tall, but he was solid. Sam had once remarked, though, that if he shaved the bushy thatch of hair from his head he'd probably be skinny underneath.

"The mud's bad," said Sam conversationally. "I picked up a hat in the middle of a mud hole near the Capitol this morning. And, by the Eternal, there was a man's head under it. 'Howdy, ol man.' I said. 'You're in the way of a bad fix.' 'Hell,' he said. 'That ain't nuthin' to the fix this mule under me is in.' "

"Peg." Across the room, a customer waved his empty tankard. "Fill this until it overflows as prettily as your bodice."

He must have been a stranger. Talk ceased. To a man, the members of Jackson's crowd rose. Their chairs made an ominous scraping noise across the floor. Jackson put out an arm to keep John Eaton from storming over to assault the scoundrel.

"Sir," said Jackson in his thick Tennessee drawl. "You will apologize to Mrs. Timberlake for your base remark, or your life is forfeit."

"I meant no offense. I was saluting the lovely Mrs. Timberlake's charms." The man bowed deeply in Peg's direction. "I apologize, Madam, for any offense my careless, but admiring tongue may have incurred."

"I accept your apology, sir." Peg passed close to Jackson's corner on her way to the bar. She glanced up at Jackson and Eaton, both of whom remained standing. "There will be none of your childish dueling over me, do you hear? Washington will never stop chattering about it," she said in a low tone.

"Yes, Mrs. Timberlake." Jackson saluted her and jackknifed back into his seat. Peggy tossed her thick black curls and swept off to refill the tankards. With his eyes, John Eaton followed her swaying skirts. It was obvious, even to strangers, he was in love with her.

He wasn't the only one. The nephew of the Secretary of the Navy had killed himself over her. Two officers had challenged each other. An old general was captivated by her. The latest gossip was that while Peg's husband's duties as Navy purser kept him on long voyages she found solace in the company of the elegant, erudite, and wealthy Mr. Eaton.

"As a stranger to our shores, Junius, you should be warned about the gossip in this city," said Sam.

"For instance," said Webster, "if you bathe in any of the clear streams hereabout, keep it a secret."

"Explain," said Booth.

"Well," said Sam. "Our Chief Executive—"

"Former Chief Executive," said Eaton.

"Our soon-to-be-former Chief Executive, the frosty Mr. Adams, is in the hasbit of bathing alone every morning in the waters of the Potomac. Last summer Anne Royalle, one of Washington's reporters of the fair sex, followed him there. She writes books full of news her subjects would prefer no one read. Miss Royalle found the President's clothes and sat on them."

"Sat on them?"

"Yes. She parked her crinolines on them and refused to move until he granted her an interview. Mr. Adams seemed to think it beneath his dignity to be interviewed by a female. And so they parlayed, he submerged in the moat of the Potomac and she from the citadel of his clothes. After two hours he became cold and capitulated." Sam turned to Jackson. "Speaking of brazen females, I heard you met Kate, the witch at the Bell plantation."

"Yes. A most sobering experience. She quotes scriptures, tells jokes, tweaks noses, plays havoc with the bedclothes. I didn't believe the stories until she stopped my wagon." Jackson sat with his chair tilted back until it was perilously close to toppling.

"Did she speak to you?" asked Booth suspiciously. He had been the victim of Tennessee blanket pulling before.

"Indeed she did. She said, 'You may go now, General. I'll see you later.' By the Eternal, it was worse than fighting the British. No offense, Junius."

The door opened again and Sam jumped to his feet.

"John!" He rushed toward John Rogers and Sik'waya. "Captain

John, you old son! And Mr. Gist. *A'siyu, igali'i*. Greetings, friends. What an honor." Sam guided John and Sik'waya to his table. John was dressed like the men around him except that his coat's cut was a few years out of fashion. "What brings you east?" Sam asked.

"Treaty talks, as usual." John looked glum.

"As interpreter?"

"No, as a headman."

"You must be doing well."

"You know what my father always said."

Sam laughed and imitated Hell-Fire Jack's brogue.

" 'Much may be made of a Scotchman if he is caught young.' Gentlemen," Sam said to the men at the table. "Allow me to present friends I haven't seen in almost ten years. We are honored to have among us Mr. George Gist, a genius and the Cadmus of his people." Sam bowed to Sik'waya. He didn't worry about offending him by naming him. He knew Gist was the name Sik'waya reserved for white people. "And Captain John Rogers, veteran of the Creek War. Actually, both these gallants fought at the Horseshoe." Jackson stood and extended his bony hand. Sik'waya took it gravely.

"We are honored indeed, sir." Jackson bowed to Sik'waya. "I have heard of your remarkable accomplishment."

"Mr. Gist invented the alphabet that led his people out of the darkness of illiteracy," said Sam. "His invention is worth more than a handful of gold to each of his nation."

Sik'waya smiled in his serene, cryptic way. Through the years he had learned to accept insults and compliments with the same grace. His gray hair was hidden by a turban of calico, printed with roses. He had on a dark blue-and-white-striped hunting coat over his white linen shirt. His beaded belt held a large knife. He wore leather leggings and high moccasins, coated with mud. He carried a long white bag on a strap across his chest. He stood out in the room full of tousled haircuts, high collars, and waistcoats.

A silver medal hung from a thong around his neck. It was his one concession to vanity. The National Council had had it struck for him two years before. On one side was his likeness. On the other was the inscription, "Presented to George Gist by the General Council of the Cherokee Nation, for his Ingenuity in the Invention of the Cherokee Alphabet, 1825."

As he listened to the garble of English around him, he took his pipe and tobacco out of his deerskin bag.

"Junius," said Sam eagerly. "Show Captain Rogers and Mr. Gist your instantaneous lights." Booth produced a box of the new British friction matches from among the wine bottles, tobacco, snuff boxes, pens, paper, sand-pounce boxes, and ink pots on the table.

"What are those?" John leaned forward to see better.

"They're called Prometheans or Congreves." Booth held one up for inspection. "Each splinter of wood is coated with sulphur and tipped with mucilage, chlorate of potash, and sulphide of antimony. Each box comes with a piece of glass paper." Booth was a tragedian of the first mark. He knew how to squeeze every bit of drama from a scene.

"Here, Junius." Easton handed him one of the infamous coffin handbills. The opposition claimed the dead men pictured on it were Jackson's victims, killed in duels or as a result of his military discipline.

Booth twisted the paper and held it and the match aloft. With a flourish, he pulled the match across the glass paper. Sik'waya gave a cry of delight as the flame appeared magically at the end of the splinter. Booth lit the paper, then John and Sik'waya's pipes.

When the talk turned to the Creek War and the battle of the Horseshoe, Sam leaned over and whispered to John.

"Is your family well, brother?"

"Father was lost five years ago."

"My hearts weeps. I didn't know."

"He lived a long life. It was his time." *John never was sentimental*, Sam thought.

"My son," said Sik'waya. "We must speak with you alone."

"Of course." Sam was grateful to change the subject. "Peg," he called. "May we use the small room?"

"Of course, Sam. The fire's laid. Use one of Mr. Booth's Congreves to start it. The place may be a bit chill."

"Excuse us, gentlemen," Sam said. "We have years of talk to catch up on."

When they were settled and the fire blazing cheerfully, John spoke.

"Congratulations on your election as governor."

"Thank you," said Sam. There was another awkward silence. Sam had been so busy campaigning and running Tennessee, he hadn't written his friends on the Arkansas in years.

"They want us to move again," John said. Sik'waya remained silent. He couldn't get used to the white way of leaping into business instead of easing into it with pleasant talk. But John understood the system. It was better to let him proceed.

"Where?"

"To Oklahoma Territory, across the border from Arkansas."

"At least it's not far."

"Not far!" John fought to keep his temper in check. It was his biggest handicap in negotiations. "It might as well be the ends of the earth. We've settled on the Arkansas. We've cleared fields, built houses, planted orchards. It's our home. How often must we leave all we've worked for because of white greed?"

"'We've become too successful," said Sik'waya sadly. "The white men crowding the edge of the Nation are envious. They want what we have, but they do not want to work for it. They prefer to take the harvest of our labor."

"It won't happen," said Sam. "The land was promised to you. I helped write the treaty."

"James likes to quote your Mr. Benjamin Franklin," John said. " 'Mad kings and mad bulls are not to be held by treaties or pack thread.' You are as naive as the Real People, friend. Georgia passed a resolution giving itself the power to take Cherokee lands any way she chooses. The eastern division of the tribe is taking the state to court to win legal title to its own lands."

"I heard about the case. It sounds like a wise move."

"It's foolishness. We had a short meeting with Father Adams today."

"What did he say?"

"He said the 1818 Lovely Purchase promising us an unbounded western outlet for hunting grounds were unreasonable. He said, 'It is very embarrassing and scarely imaginable that the President and Secretary of War should have assumed so unwarranted an authority and given so inconsiderate a pledge.' Drum has written Adams time and again, but to no avail. We and a few others came east to try to reason with him."

"Three-fifths of the land they propose to give us is broken, barren country." As he spoke, Sik'waya stared into the fire. His eyes were bright with tears. "It's fit for nothing. Why cannot they leave us in peace with what is ours?"

"Already the Arkansas government is settling whites in our country. They assume they'll have their way."

"If you sign the treaty and move, perhaps you'll finally be left alone," said Sam.

"Maybe. If the land is barren enough," said John bitterly. "But if we sign, we may pay with our lives. Ridge and John Ross wrote a law making death the penalty for signing away tribal land. We in the west make many of our own laws. But we also obey the laws made by the National Council in the east."

"You shan't be murdered. They must still answer to the laws of the United States."

"We have our own laws and our own enforcement of them," said John. "All your paper talk will not change that. Anyway, it's against the United States law for whites to settle on Indian land. Yet Governor Izard is doing it, and no one is stopping him. White men's laws are like spider webs. They catch the small flies and let the big ones go."

"My son," said Sik'waya. "You are headman of Tanassee. You have spoken often in the white man's council here in Wasuhda'no'i, Washington. We need your advice."

"I'm no friend of Father Adams, or Calhoun or Clay. When Father Jackson is elected principal chief, then we can help you."

"And will he win?" asked John.

"Of course. Our campaign theme is 'Vindication of a Hero Wronged.' Adams is a cold fish, unliked here. This will be the first election that truly reflects the will of the people.

"Now tell me about Drum and Sally Ground Squirrel and James. Are they well?" Sam didn't ask about Tiana. He assumed she was still married and prospering. It didn't occur to John that he might be interested in her.

Tiana stared at the tall pole set in the rocky ground in front of Sik'waya's ramshackle cabin. She was furious at whomever had planted it there. The top of the sapling had been sharpened. When she had asked Sik'waya what it was for, he said "I think it's to set my head on."

He had continued to load his few possessions into his old wagon. His youngest daughter, Guhnage'i, Black, chased the chickens about the yard in a great commotion and clouds of dust. Sik'waya's patient wife, Sally, drove the family's three cows into the yard. Their son came from another direction with the pigs. The horses grazed nearby, mowing neat circles whose radii were the lengths of the tethers. The yoke of oxen stood placidly at the front of the wagon. Tiana had often thought Sik'waya must be brother to the oxen. He had their fatalism.

"What do you mean, to set your head on?"

"When they cut it off."

"Who?"

"Whoever put the pole there. We found it when we came back from the saline."

Tiana tried to rock the pole with her hands, but it was solidly set. She looked around for a hatchet.

"Leave it, daughter," said Sik'waya. He went on packing his pipe collection and small pottery pieces and silver work into a barrel of corn meal so they wouldn't be damaged on the trip. It wouldn't be a long journey to their new land farther west, but the roads were bad.

"But what if they come?"

"If they come, it won't matter whether the pole is there or not," said Sik'waya mildly. "Have you seen the talking leaves from the Old Country, daughter?" he asked her. "Buck wrote a wonderful talk on conscience. It's here somewhere." He began rooting in the clutter of baskets and sacks and bandanas tied at the corners to hold things.

"I can read it later, Beloved Father." Tiana looked around nervously. Her pistol was in her saddlebag and her horse grazed under the drooping trees. The air was heavy with dust. It was hot for May and Tiana's temper was short. She was glad to see Sik'waya's sons-in-law were helping the family move. She noticed they kept their weapons close at hand.

"Buck says a good conscience is a sweet perfume that spreads its fragrance over everything near it without exhausting the supply of it. Isn't that a lovely talk?"

"Yes, it is," said Tiana. "Beloved Man, I shall go to the Light Horse. They'll protect you along the road."

"The Light Horse's duty is to carry out the Nation's laws. The law is that those who sell or sign away the Nation's land must die." He carefully unfolded the tattered sheet of paper he had finally found. He beamed at it with pleasure. He never tired of seeing his characters on the talking leaves.

This first issue of *The Cherokee Phoenix* had been printed February 28, 1828, three months earlier. It was mostly devoted to the Cherokee nation's Constitution framed by delegates at the new eastern capital, New Echota. Tiana had noted that according to the constitution, only Cherokee men would be allowed to vote or sit in council.

Tiana helped one of the boys heave a bushel basket of coarse,

sparkling salt onto the bed of the wagon. The boy jumped aboard
and pulled the basket back until it nestled among the lumpy sacks
of seed corn. Richard Gist, an older son, threw three woven fish
weirs after the salt. Then he laid the heavy wooden mattocks along
the side of the bed. Sally's spinning wheel followed.

Polly Gist held the chickens while E'yagu, Pumpkin Setting There,
tied their feet together. They hung the poultry, protesting loudly,
along the outside of the wagon. Polly's husband, Flying, went from
wheel to wheel, tarring the axles with pine pitch. E'yagu's husband,
George Starr, carried out the new rifles the government had given
the men for enrolling to emigrate. The guns were wrapped in bright
blankets, also part of the enrollment pay. The government probably
hadn't intended the weapons to be used to protect the signers from
their own people.

If Sik'waya wasn't disturbed about his death sentence, his family
was. They shouted instructions at each other louder than usual. Pigs
squealed as the boys caught them. The dogs tied to the back of the
wagon barked continuously.

Polly Gist Flying's daugher, Annie, struggled from the cabin with
a large covered basket. The basswood bark rope holding it shut
broke, scattering the contents. The child began to cry as she knelt
to pick up the clothes. Tiana helped her gather the patched, threadbare dresses and shirts. She shook the dust from them and put them
back in the basket. The girl sat on the lid while Tiana retied it with
another piece of rope. As Tiana worked, she hoped Sik'waya would
buy his long-suffering family some new things with the five hundred
dollars the treaty promised him.

Sally rolled and tied the mats that usually covered the floors and
walls, and stowed them in the wagon. Her oldest son carried out
the only feather ticking. Sally scolded him for dragging the end of
it in the dust. She scolded everyone, but they all knew it was to
keep from crying.

Finally they were packed. Sik'waya left the cabin door open, as
it had always been when he had lived there. He sat on the passenger's
side of the wagon seat. With his spectacles perched low on his
aquiline nose, he read the latest issue of *The Cherokee Phoenix* Tiana
had brought him from Fort Smith. Next to him, Polly suckled her
baby. Sally sat in the driver's seat. Tiana rode up beside her.

"Mother, avoid Fort Smith if you can."

"Is it bad there, Beloved Woman?"

"Very bad. The white men are selling whiskey and useless trinkets. They wait like carrion crows outside the house where payments for people's improvements are being made."

"We'd planned to stop there. We need the money."

"It would be wise if you went in with Sik'waya only. If you need help, ask my brothers."

"Thank you, Beloved Woman," said Sally. "We'll be careful."

Tiana didn't mention that her brother John was selling whiskey too. He was becoming more and more interested in his own profit. In an unguarded moment, when Drum had had one brandy too many, he had confessed to her that John had inherited his father's love for money, without Hell-Fire Jack's wit or charm. "I miss your father, Tiana," he had said. "His advice was good and his company warmed the cold nights. There are few like him now."

One of Sik'waya's grandsons returned from a quick trip to the woods to relieve himself. Sally cracked the whip over the oxen's broad backs. The wagon started with a groan and a creaking, like old bones. It looked misshapen under the huge salt kettles, chickens, buckets, skillets, and gourds that hung along its sides. They rattled and clattered as the wagon moved over the rocky yard.

Two boys rode on top of the feather ticking. Their job was to catch anything that seemed about to fall. The other children rode two or three to a horse. They were surrounded by bags and sacks strapped behind them or hanging from the surcingles. Black made a run and leaped onto the ox's back. She settled herself there, holding onto the wooden yoke. The adults walked, each carrying a bundle.

Tiana rode with the little caravan as far as the rough trail that strung together the Real People's scattered farms and settlements along the Arkansas. The track was narrow. There wasn't a wagon in the Indian Nation that didn't have streaks along its sides from scraping between trees. When Sik'waya and his family turned north-west, toward Fort Smith, Tiana headed in the other direction, toward Sally Ground Squirrel's house. The trail was crowded with wagons and horses, mules, oxen, herds and flocks and foot traffic.

Drum's farm seemed more crowded than usual too. There was a strange wagon in the yard, and Drum and his family were gathered around it. Tiana's hand dropped automatically to her pistol.

"Beloved Woman," Drum called to her. "Translate for us." A white family sat in the wagon. They had fewer possessions than Sik'waya. But there were fewer of them, and they weren't exactly starting with nothing here.

The man was of medium build. His rusty black suit and wilted white collar were out of place in the heat. The woman next to him wore a dress made when she was thirty pounds lighter. It pulled across her ample bosom. There were three children in the back and an old woman, apparently blind. She had been napping, propped against the sacks, and had just waked up.

"What's all this gibbering about?" she asked in a quavery voice. "Are we home yet?"

"Yes, mother," said the man patiently. "We're home. These good people are the former owners of the farm."

"Savages?" she snapped. "Are we among the unsaved? We'll be killed."

"Hush, mother Thompkins," said the younger woman nervously.

"You are safe, Mother," said Tiana. She was still mounted and she leaned over to touch the old woman lightly on her thin, wrinkled arm.

"Who is that?"

"My name is Tiana," she said in her musical accent.

"Beautiful name." The old woman reached out her spidery hands and Tiana leaned farther forward so she could run her fingers over her face. "Beautiful. Are you a wild Indian, child?"

"I suppose I am."

Her son turned to Tiana.

"Please tell this gentleman that we apologize for any trouble we may have caused him." Tiana smiled at him. He had no idea the trouble he and his kind had caused. He hurried on. "We were told you would be given good land farther west. And that the money we paid for this farm would provide education for your children." Tiana nodded. The man seemed eager to convince them of his good will.

"Tell him not to worry himself," Drum smiled gently. "We give him the land and the house with the wish that The Provider will bless them and the fields for him and his family."

"Thank you, kind sir, thank you," said Mr. Thompkins. He extended his hand and Drum shook it. Drum pulled a small piece of paper from inside his shirt. It had been folded many times until it was almost lost in Drum's big, square hand.

"This is a charm," he said, through Tiana. "It will make your corn stand upright after being beaten down by wind or hail. I have heard the wind is strong in the new country, and I was going to take it with me. But I want you to have it. The instructions for using it are written in Sik'waya's characters. You will not need a Curer Of Them to read the charm for you. Someone at Fort Smith can probably translate it."

"Won't you need this?" asked the man.

"I can remember it." Drum held his hand up, palm outward in friendship. Then he climbed heavily into the lead wagon. This was a bigger caravan than Sik'waya's had been. Many members of Drum's family had built their cabins as close as possible to the quarter-mile land boundary required by the Real People's new law. They wanted to be near Drum's help and advice. Now they would move with him.

Tiana watched the horses and wagons pass. She counted heads to make sure everyone was there. She also watched the white family, curious to see what they would do. She expected to see the man tear up Drum's magic paper as soon as Drum's back was turned. To her surprise, he unfolded it, stared at it, then carefully refolded it and put it inside his baggy coat. She saw his wife nod toward the cabin and heard her say, "Do you suppose it smells in there? There are probably enough bugs to carry us away while we sleep."

From here, the caravan would pass Jennie's house and add her family. Jennie's sons had been helping her pack. Tiana called to one of the younger girls who trudged ahead of her. She held out her hand and pulled the girl up in front of her. The child maintained a respectful silence. Tiana remembered how awed she herself had been of *Ghigau*, Nanehi Ward. It was strange to think this child might regard her the same way. To put her at ease, Tiana began telling her the story of Stonecoat and the seven maidens. She often talked with the girls, asking them questions, gauging their answers. She was looking for a special one to whom she could pass her knowledge.

Talking helped ease the leavetaking. Tiana didn't look back at the farm where she had spent almost as much time as at her mother's. In a way, she wouldn't be sorry to start over on a place with no memories.

Chapter 39

Susannah Rogers's husband, Nicholas Miller, left her and their eight-year-old daughter, Melzie. Miller had been nothing but trouble since he'd married Susannah. The family was glad to see him gone, even if he did take the only two good horses and whatever else he could steal. The Rogers had moved into Oklahoma Territory a few months before, in the spring of 1828. Nicholas and Susannah and Melzie had been living in the hastily-built dogtrot cabin with Tiana, Jennie, James and his new wife, Nannie Coody, and whomever needed a roof over their heads.

It had been difficult enough clearing fields for a summer crop and building shelter without Susannah's troubles. She and her husband fought constantly. Between their bickering and the enervating heat, the cabin seemed far smaller than it was. Tiana often heard James mutter that a good hanging would save a bad marriage.

But Susannah had been distraught when Nicholas failed to return from one of his frequent trips to the taverns around Cantonment Gibson. A few mornings later, when the family woke up, Susannah and Melzie were gone. Now Tiana, James, and John were searching for them. Charles, William, and Joseph had set out to look in another direction.

Tiana suggested trying the settlement near the cantonment where Miller went to drink and gamble, and probably to wench. Even though it was obvious he didn't intend to return to his wife, she might have gone after him.

The trail led through Gibson, but Tiana and her brothers didn't dally there. When they found out Susannah had not been seen, they moved on. They didn't even stop to drink from the clear spring that supplied the camp with water.

Four years earlier, Arbuckle and his men had begun the cantonment on the Grand River at the end of the Fort Smith road. It was in the middle of the country contested by the Little Ones and the Real People. Arbuckle had done the best building job he could under the circumstances. His men had cleared the matted nettles, head-high weeds, and dense stands of oak, ash, and hackberry from the site. And they had hacked away the solid barrier of canebrakes, two miles wide along the river. Arbuckle had assumed that once his men left Fort Smith behind, they would enjoy better health. He was wrong. Soldiers died, in increasing numbers, of malarial fevers and the flux. Already Cantonment Gibson was being called the Charnel House of the Army. And this was August, the worst of the sickly season.

Tiana and her brothers rode southwest to the juncture of the Verdigris, the Grand, and the Arkansas rivers where Clermont's villages had been. The Little Ones too had been displaced by the constant jostling of tribes, as the government moved them farther and farther west. The area was also called Three Forks, and traders had built stoves there. Clustered around them were the taverns and shanties, the tents and lean-tos of those who made their living off the Indians and trappers and the soldiers. The settlement sprawled haphazardly among the stumps of the forest that had been cut to build it.

As Tiana rode past the first makeshift shelters, she kept her face impassive, only difficulty. She was used to seeing poverty, but this was poverty of a different sort. Her people were poor in material goods. These people were poor of spirit.

This was where gamblers and whiskey peddlers, white drifters and rogues and the off-castings of the Indian nations collected. White men were supposed to have permits to even pass through the Real People's country, but it was almost impossible for Arbuckle's men to check the hundreds who sneaked in illegally.

Trappers, reluctant to take off their fur hats and leather shirts even in August, lounged in whatever shade they could find. The hawk bells on their leggings jingled and the bear claws and silver coins of their necklaces clanked when they moved. Men shouted at each other in French, Spanish, English, and a patois of various Indian languages.

No one was legally allowed to sell liquor to the Indians, but many lay unconscious by the sides of the trail and others reeled among the buildings. Dogs, hogs, and chickens competed for the garbage rotting everywhere in steamy, redolent heaps.

What disturbed Tiana were the women. A few of them were respectable, the wives of enlisted men or laundresses for the fort. The bushes around the laundresses's shacks were covered with clothes spread out to dry. But most of the women weren't respectable. Even some of the laundresses did a more fundamental business on the side.

Most of the women were Indian. Their shrill, unhappy voices hurt Tiana's ears. Their dirty, naked children played in the mud. Tiana breathed a charm to protect Susannah. She prayed she and her brothers would go home and find their sister safe there.

She stopped near a white man sitting on a stool in front of a particularly ruinous hovel. James waited patiently for her. John merely waited. They were used to trips with her becoming more like royal progresses than anything else. If she wasn't stopping to talk to people, they were stopping to talk to her.

"What are you doing?" she asked.

"Blinding this here stool pigeon." He held the blue-gray passenger pigeon in one large, dirty hand. With thick fingers he stuck a needle through the edge of one of the bird's lower eyelids. He knotted the thread and brought it over the bird's head and through the lower lid on the other side. He pulled the thread tight to draw both lids closed and hold them there. Then he tied the thread on top of the head.

"That's cruel."

"Naw, 'tain't. Birds don't feel nuthin'." He patted the pigeon roughly and put her in a crude willow cage. He took out another one.

"How do they eat?"

"I feeds 'em. Ain't gonna let 'em starve. Cost me a heap of work, catching 'em, training 'em. This one here," he jabbed a stubby finger through the cage at a bird whose eyelids had permanent holes in them. "He's worth five dollars, hard money."

"You train them?"

"Surely. Not every bird can be a stool pigeon. Have to be able to keep their balance on the stool, this perch here. Have to flap just so when the stool drops. Makes 'em look like they's landing to feed. Decoys the rest of the flock to 'em so I can drop the net over 'em. It's hard work, missy. Look at that callous." He held up a hand with black blood caked in the creases and under the nails. Tiana stared at it, like a rabbit at a snake.

"I got those callouses from the peenchers." He pointed to a pair of blacksmith's tongs. They'd never looked malevolent to Tiana before, but they did now. "I squeeze their leetle necks till the blood pops out their eyes, and trickles down their beaks. Has to wade knee-deep in mud and blood and birds. Has to kill thousands of them, quick like, before they spoil. It ain't easy. Sometimes, I jest peench their heads with my fingers. I got strong fingers, but it's exhausting." It hadn't taken him long to notice Tiana was probably the most beautiful woman he'd be likely to see in his lifetime. So he was laying on the charm.

"I can give you some of the catch, if you like, in exchange for a bit of your . . . time." He jerked his head toward two wagons, full to the brim with carcasses of pigeons. "Most of 'em will spoil anyways, 'fore I can sell 'em. Only gonna feed 'em to the hogs. I stand to lose on this batch."

"Sister," John said it loudly, and in English. He rattled his rifle for good measure.

Without another word to the pigeon hunter, Tiana joined her brothers.

"Did you hear that?" she asked them.

"I've run into his kind before," said James.

"I pray I never do again," Tiana answered. She felt the need to go to the river and purify herself, just from being near him.

"Where do you think we should start looking?" she asked.

"The taverns," said James. "Like everyone else, news stops there first."

"You two ask on that side of the road and I'll ask on this." John nodded to both sides of the trail dividing the settlement roughly in half.

"I'll ask the women," Tiana said. She knew the women wouldn't want to talk to her brothers. It was customary for Indian women to avoid speaking even to the men they knew.

"One of us should be with you."

"I can take care of myself. And I'll stay within hailing distance."

James and John knew she could take care of herself under ordinary circumstances. But these weren't ordinary circumstances. And as her brothers it was their responsibility to protect her. They also knew how much attention she attracted. At twenty-eight most women had long passed their prime. But Tiana seemed ageless. The years only added an intangible quality to her beauty. She had a combination of confidence, intelligence, and serenity that drew people to her, even ones her brothers would rather stayed away. Frequently, some smitten brave or a soldier from the cantonment would come to the house and plead for her hand. She firmly, quietly, turned them down.

Now she led her horse among the cooking fires and wash tubs, the corn mortars, piles of furs, and discarded wagon parts and other lumber that littered the settlement. The women were evasive. Some claimed not to have seen Susannah and her daughter at all. Some said they had seen them, but didn't know where they were. Finally she asked a large black woman who was scrubbing clothes at a stream. The woman spoke Osage and French, and she answered Tiana honestly.

"I saw your sister," she said. "Three, four hours ago. Five white men pass by here with her and the girl. I think maybe they tell her they know where her husband is. She goes with them."

"Where?"

"That way." The woman pointed to a narrow track leading off through the woods. "I think maybe there's a buffalo camp five, six miles, toward the prairie."

"Thank you, mother," Tiana said.

"I think maybe they bad men," the woman observed as she went back to her washing.

James and John and Tiana galloped into the camp, to find it almost deserted. A lone figure sat by the charred logs of the cooking fire.

"Tsu'tsan!" Tiana cried. She leaped from her horse and ran to her sister. Susannah looked at her blankly. Her dress was half torn off and her face and arms were bruised. She was very drunk.

"Sister," James said, shaking her gently, "have they hurt you badly? Where is your daughter?"

"They took her," Susannah said, as though from a great distance.

"They took us both. Many times." She pulled her shredded skirt down tight over her knees, drew her knees up toward her chin, and wrapped her arms around them. She sobbed in great hiccupping gulps as she rocked back forth. Tiana put her arms around her and held her close. They rocked together.

"Dear Jesus, God in heaven," swore James. "The hell-fired bastards."

"I'm going after them," said John. "The trail is fresh. They may have the child with them still."

James started to protest. He wanted to kill them himself, but someone had to escort the women home. Tiana knew how he felt. She usually counseled against revenge but in this case it would be very sweet indeed. She was sorry she never learned some of Raincrow's darker magic, a spell to Return Evil To Them By Fire.

She and Susannah rode double and James followed them back through the settlement. The usual noise stilled somewhat. The Indians there knew instinctively what had happened. They noticed John was gone. They knew revenge would be taken.

When he passed the pigeon hunter's cabin, Tiana saw he was gone, and she dismounted. She opened the cage and took each pigeon out, one at a time. With the tip of her skinning knife, she cut the threads that held their eyelids closed and gently pulled them through the holes. She whispered an apology to each and stroked its velvety, blue-gray feathers. Then she opened her hands and gave the bird a slight toss to help it fly away. She watched them all go before she remounted and headed for home.

John came back a day later. He carried Melzie's body wrapped in his blanket. He unfolded a piece of buffalo hide and shook it. Five bloody scalps fell into the dust of the dooryard.

"I killed them with my knife, while they slept. I am sorry I was only one and could not cut their genitals off while they lived and burn them to death slowly." He said it simply, and went inside to eat.

James picked up the five matted clumps of hair and wrapped them again. He would dispose of them quietly. There would be no dance to celebrate John's bravery. There would be no boasting about this, no mention of it at all. James knew John would have hidden the bodies well. And it was likely no one would miss the buffalo hunters or grieve them. But they *were* white. The authorities had a way of summarily punishing any Indian who killed any white man, no matter what the circumstance.

Tiana carried Melzie's body inside, and she and Jennie began preparing it for burial. She found herself wishing the missionaries were right, that there was a hell. That evil would be returned to those men by fire, even after they were dead.

It was a cold, gloomy morning at the end of 1828. The clouds looked heavy enough to fall from the sky by their own weight. But they weren't heavy enough to depress Sam's spirits. He whistled to himself as his big dapple-gray racked along the narrow shortcut to Gallatin and the Allen estate. The horse knew the route well and hardly needed guiding. Sam held the reins lightly with one hand and warmed the other in the pocket of his voluminous wool surtout. The coat's broad, stiff collar was turned up to protect Sam's neck and ears from the wind. His tall beaver hat was pulled down tightly on his head.

He had reason to be happy. In spite of a vile campaign by his opponents, Andrew Jackson had been elected President of the United States. He would take office in a month. Perhaps as president he could extract payment from those who had dragged in Rachel Jackson's good name, calling her a bigamist and a woman of easy virtue. The unjust accusation had caused her untold grief.

But all that was over now. No one would be hurling accusations at the president's wife. Sam himself had just decided to run for a second term as governor of Tennessee.

With that out of his mind, Sam had time to consider an even more important decision. He intended to discuss it with his friend Colonel Allen when he got to the plantation. The Allen place was another reason for his light heart. There would be a warm fire and hot toddies, a big breakfast, and a certain smile. Sam anticipated the Christmas festivities at the Allens'. Next to Mrs. Polk, they gave the best parties in the area.

Sam's revery was interrupted by galloping hoofs. A rider pulled up sharply in front of him, handed him a sheet of paper from his pouch, and speeded on.

"Wait!" Sam yelled after him. "What happened?"

But the man was already around a bend. The message on the handbill was simple. "Mrs. Jackson has just expired." Sam read it several times, trying to understand it.

He yanked the gray around and kicked the animal with his heels. He sped along the forest track, then burst onto the main road. As he came closer to the Hermitage, the track grew more and more crowded. Everyone was headed in the same direction. They walked or rode horses or farm mules. They drove whatever buggy or shay or wagon they had. Black and white, young, old, rich and poor, they streamed toward the Jacksons' plantation.

When Sam couldn't move fast enough in the press, he jumped a fence and galloped across the stubble of the fields. He left his gray with a weeping house servant and leaped up the steps to the entry- way. The parlor was crowded with sobbing relatives and servants.

"Hannah, what happened?" Sam grabbed Aunt Rachel's maid by the arm.

"She's gone, Mister Sam, she's gone."

"When? How?"

"I think . . ." Hannah looked around her, then drew Sam into a corner. "I think she died of a broken heart. You know she didn't want no truck with that big empty house off there in Washington Town. I was with her when she passed on. She said, 'I'd rather be a doorkeeper in the House of God than to live in that place.' " Hannah began to cry again.

"Where is she? Where's the General?"

Hannah nodded toward Rachel's bedroom. "He's grieving in there. The poor man's heart is like to be torn from his breast."

With his hat in his hand, Sam looked in the bedroom door. Jackson seemed about to expire himself. His long knobby fingers were buried in his bristly hair, which stood out in spikes around his head. With his other hand, he stroked Rachel's cold forehead.

"Thirty-seven years, Sam. She's been my life for thirty-seven years." Jackson's face hadn't looked this haggard since the ter- rible days of the Creek War. And he was fifteen years older now. "I ran a race and I won it. And what has it gained me if I've lost my life? My joy? She lived only to help others. And she suffered the vile slander of those who would hurt me through her."

Outside, Sam could hear the steady moaning and chanting of the hundred slaves Rachel called family. Of the thousands who filled the grounds, some came to pay respects to the deceased wife of the new president. Most came because they knew Aunt Rachel or had been helped by her. Many brought food for the family and the mourners. Fires burned around the grounds as people cooked. Ten thousand people came to see Rachel Jackson buried the day before Christmas. That was twice the number living in Nashville.

Sam led the rest of the pallbearers down the curved path to the garden. It had been Rachel's favorite spot in life, and it would be her resting place. She would lie near the grave of her adopted Creek son, Lincoyer, who had died of consumption two years before. Jackson followed the coffin. He leaned on his cane and was supported by his old friend, John Coffee. As Sam listened to the long eulogies, he wondered if Jackson would ever recover enough from this blow and take the presidency he had just won.

For once, the eulogies were accurate. Aunt Rachel had been as close to a saint as Sam had ever met. As a cold mist began to ghost through the branches overhead, Sam thought about Rachel's sad life. She had been hounded because of her first husband's carelessness in finalizing their divorce. She had married Jackson thinking she was a free woman. The name of bigamist had followed her for almost four decades. And she had never been able to have her beloved husband for herself. She had had to share him with a nation that devoured its heroes. It maligned them, adored them, but almost never granted them privacy.

Jackson began to speak. His first words were an apology for the tears that ran down his face. His voice trembled.

"I know 'tis unmanly, but these tears are due her. She has shed many for me." He went on in a louder voice. "Friends and neighbors, I thank you for the honor you have done to the saint whose remains repose in yonder grave. She is now in the bliss of heaven and can suffer no more here on earth. But I am left without her, to encounter the trials of life alone.

"In the presence of this dear saint, I can and do forgive all my enemies. But those vile wretches who have slandered her must look to God for mercy!"

As Sam stood in the rain, he searched the crowd for a special figure. Her lower face was hidden by the white lace handkerchief she held to her eyes. She had taken the ruffles and flowers off her wide-brimmed hat and had added a black net veil. It shrouded her blond hair and upper face but Sam would have recognized her anyway. He had studied that slender body and tiny waist from across the room at many of Mrs. James Polk's cotillions.

Even in black and heavily veiled, Eliza Allen was beautiful. Aunt Rachel's death had changed Sam's mood, but not his mind. He was still determined to ask Eliza to marry him. Sam was more careful about his speech these days. He was trying to refine his image. But back in Russell's tavern, with his boots up among those of his friends, Sam would have said he was arse over teakettle in love.

Chapter 40

After the funeral, the Christmas holidays at the Allen plantation were muted. Aunt Rachel had visited there often. She brought small gifts and news or just sat by Mrs. Allen's bedside and chatted. Mrs. Allen had been an invalid for as long as Eliza could remember. "Female troubles" was the only reason Eliza had ever heard. And it never occurred to her to ask for details.

When Eliza needed a mother, she turned to Dilcey, her mammy since Eliza was a baby. Dilcey had held her hand when she was frightened at night. Dilcey had crooned her to sleep and waked her in the morning. Dilcey had brushed her hair each day until her scalp tingled, and had pulled back the thick hanks of it to make sure Eliza had washed behind her ears.

Eliza was the only daughter and the youngest child in the Allen family. She was the apple of not only her father's eye, but her brothers' and her uncles' and all the house servants' and most of the field hands. She had been pampered but not spoiled. She had managed to emerge from her silk-wrapped cocoon of childhood as a graceful, demure young woman of eighteen.

She knew she was beautiful. People had told her so from the time she was a baby. Suitors swarmed around her. But she wasn't particularly vain. She knew all the right answers to the polite questions asked in genteel society. If she knew the answers to few other questions, it wasn't important.

She sewed a neat stitch. She knew how to direct servants. But at eighteen, she was still a child in many ways. The women talked of marriage in her future, but the future had never been further away than the next party or dance. When the ladies gathered, their marriage talk was just a soothing hum over her head as she sewed.

When Governor Houston visited, after Rachel's funeral, Eliza chatted un-self-consciously with him as he led her into the small sitting room. Her hand rested lightly on the velvet sleeve of his deep green redingote. He may have been governor of the state, but he had been her father's and her uncle's dear friend long before that.

"How magnificent you look tonight, Governor Houston." And that was true, Sam wore a snowy white ruffled shirt under a black satin vest. His loose black trousers were in the new style, baggy at the waist and legs and gathered at the ankles. His beige doeskin gloves were stuck into his waistband. His silk stockings were heavily embroidered and his black leather evening pumps had silver buckles. He wore his hair in the short, careless style that showed off his thick auburn curls. The current fashions were flamboyant, and Sam excelled at flamboyance.

"Where did you find such cloth, Governor?"

"In Washington City." Sam tried not to stare at her. Her delicate beauty made him feel overgrown and clumsy. Her waist was so tiny he thought he could encircle it with his hands. The thought made his neck and face feel hot.

"I would love to see Washington City. I hear the ladies have the most gorgeous dresses there. And they have balls and banquets every night."

"That they do. You'll see Washington City, I promise you."

"Law, I think not. I'll die in this quiet pond of a place while somewhere there are fast rivers running into the ocean. Have you seen the ocean, Governor?"

"Yes. And please call me Sam, Eliza." Sam watched helplessly as the object of his adoration picked up a small stick from a pile by the hearth and fed it into the fire. The fire's light glowed on the intricate sculpture of her blond hair. It had been carefully molded over a wire frame and a few ringlets had been allowed to escape down the back of her neck.

"I reckon I can call you Sam, if it pleases you, Governor. Will you be at the races Saturday?" Eliza was beginning to sense Sam's unease and she looked longingly toward the door.

"Will you accompany me to the races?" Sam asked her.

"Of course. We are all going."

"I mean, will you honor me by going as my betrothed?"

"Betrothed?" Eliza looked at him in bewilderment.

"Will you marry me, Eliza?"

"I . . ." Words deserted her. She stared at him.

"I love you. I'll do everything in my power to make you happy."

"I can't say, Governor Houston. I must ask my father." She toyed with the heavy curtain to hide her confusion. "I'm so young."

"And I'm so old?" said Sam.

"Oh no, you're not, sir."

"Age makes no difference. Not in love."

"I will think on it, sir," said Eliza. Dazed, she left Sam standing in the middle of the room.

Sam's heart was pounding wildly. For the past ten years he had gotten whatever he wanted. He was toasted and hailed all over the state. He couldn't go anywhere without being recognized. People flocked around him when he graced dinners and parties and drawing rooms. They laughed at his stories and hung on his words. He knew Eliza would marry him and that she would make him happy.

Eliza was used to others arranging her life for her. She consented to marry Governor Houston because her parents wanted her to.

Sam fretted through the festivities on the afternoon of the ceremony. There were races and contests of all kinds. Tables were loaded with food for the hundreds of people who came. As evening approached the cream of Nashville society gathered in front of the curved staircase in the huge central hall. Hundreds of candles glowed there and in the main drawing room, where the ceremony would take place. White bunting draped the walls. Branches of fragrant cedar and shiny magnolia decorated the mantle tops and cornices. Sam's breath caught in his throat as Colonel Allen appeared at the head of the stairway with his daughter.

Eliza seemed to float down the stairs in a cloud of white tulle and silk. Sam didn't know she had spent the day locked in her room upstairs, where she cried in Dilcey's arms. As the hour of the ceremony drew near, Dilcey had sent out for food, dried Eliza's face and her own, and laced her into her corset. She tried to repair the damage done by the tears. She fussed and scolded. She bathed Eliza's face with milk and powdered it. Finally, she just hoped the veil would hide the bride's red nose and eyes.

The ceremony seemed to go on for hours. The reception lasted the better part of eternity. Finally Sam found himself alone with Eliza in her room. It was disconcerting. Too lacy and pink for his tastes.

"I'll be back," Eliza said in a low voice.

"Where are you going?"

"Up to Dilcey's room to put on my nightgear."

"Hurry back." Sam held her shoulders and kissed her lightly on the forehead. He ran a hand into her elaborately coiled hair to loosen the pins that held it.

"Mr. Houston." Eliza was truly horrified. "I can't. Not here. It wouldn't be right. I shan't be long." She fled.

Sam began to pace. Most of his friends knew two kinds of women, the ones they paid to enjoy and the ones they married. Sam divided women into three categories: the brown-skinned girls he had known as a boy along the languid Hiwassee River, the ones he paid for, and the ones he had courted in a desultory manner, with vague thoughts of marriage. He had had no experience with the present situation. He had assumed their mutual passion would carry them off to bliss.

While he waited for Eliza to return, he took off his boots and jacket and vest. He stood with them in his hand and looked for a place to put them. He finally draped the jacket and vest over a delicate chair and lined the shoes up neatly under it. He unbuttoned his braces and put them on top of the vest. He tried to sit in the Hepplewhite by the fire, but it seemed too fragile for his big frame.

He fumbled with the buttons on his trousers, thought better of it, and sat on the edge of the four-poster, with its gauzy canopy of hand-woven netting. He felt foolish in his embroidered socks. He really hadn't thought much about what he would wear to bed on his wedding night. He had supposed he would sleep in the long, loose shirt he wore for the ceremony.

Eliza finally returned. She was ethereal in her flowing white gown with her golden hair cascading around her.

Sam put his arms around her and held her close. She was so slender he feared he would crush her. He could feel her trembling.

"Are you cold?" he asked.

"No," she whispered.

"I shall try not to hurt you."

Eliza started to cry.

"What is it?"

"I cannot lie with you here. My mother sleeps just beyond that wall."

"You're my wife."

"Please." Eliza began to cry harder. Sam was afraid someone would hear her. He wiped her eyes with the tail of his shirt.

"The room next to Dilcey's in the garret is empty. You can sleep there. Please. Tomorrow we will be together."

"As you wish, my love."

Sam kissed her on the cheek and lit a candle from the fireplace. He gathered his clothes and boots and padded out the door, closing it softly behind him. Below, he could hear the sound of music as the reception went on. He passed Dilcey, wrapped in a comforter and apparently asleep on the floor by the door. He didn't see her follow him with her eyes as he walked silently down the hall and up the narrow stairs to the attic. Then she stood, wrapped the comforter around her, and let herself into Eliza's room. She spent the night lying next to her young charge, holding Eliza until she had cried herself to sleep.

After a leisurely breakfast, the Allen family waited in the cold of the January morning while Eliza's bags were loaded on the backs of the two horses that would carry them to Nashville. Her considerable wardrobe would follow in a wagon a few days later.

Eliza hugged her father and uncles and brothers. She threw a kiss to her mother, who pressed her face against the thick windowpane above. She clung to Dilcey while Sam and the men made small talk to avoid watching the leavetaking. Sam helped her onto her horse. She arranged her skirts and took the reins in her gloved hands.

The two of them were an hour from Nashville when the wind became too bitterly cold to go on. They stopped at Locust Grove. The owners of the plantation were old friends of Sam's and of the Allens. Sam knew he and his bride would be welcome there.

That night, Sam's heart was thumping so loudly he was sure Eliza heard it as he pulled the bulky covers back and slid in beside her. She lay, silent and shaking, as he tried to calm her with his big hands. He stroked her small body as he would a nervous filly, but his touchs only seemed to increase her distress.

"I will not hurt you for long, my dear." He nuzzled her neck. He ran his hand down her leg and lifted the hem of her gown, tugging at it to get it up to her thigh. She didn't raise her body to help him. Instead, she became rigid and stared wide-eyed at the ceiling. As Sam tried to gauge her reactions to each of his movements, he wondered why there was such a premium on virgins. On the one hand, the thought of another man doing this to Eliza was intolerable. On the other, it was intolerable to Sam that he should frighten her like this.

He decided there was no alternative but to get the ordeal over with and hope it would be better the next time. He pulled his own nightshirt up and rolled on top of Eliza. He began pushing against her as gently as he could. His member had always been a source of admiration to the women of the Real People, but now it seemed far too big for the task at hand.

Eliza whimpered in pain, but he did not stop. He couldn't stop. All the frustration and longing he had kept in check broke loose. With his fingers dug into her shoulders for leverage, he thrust and battered until he broke through the shield that kept him out. She was dry and tight, but he plunged deeply into her. She cried out in agony and he in groaned as his passion was finally released. Then remorse took over. He withdrew slowly and tried to caress her. She pulled away and turned her back on him.

"No more, please," she sobbed. "No more."

Eliza heard Sam stirring the next morning as she pretended to sleep. She looked so peaceful and chaste, Sam's spirits lifted a bit. Surely she would soon get used to the carnal side of matrimony. As he put on his trousers, he didn't notice her open her eyes briefly.

When she saw the raw sore on his upper thigh, near his groin, she closed her eyes and tried not to grimace. His large, hairy body was bad enough, but the open sore was more than she could bear. The subject of Sam's old wound had never come up except as an occasional remark on his limp when it pained him. Sam had hoped his bride would love him too much to care about it. He kissed Eliza on the top of her head before he tiptoed from the room.

She followed him down an hour later. She heard Sam's laughter outside.

"Did you sleep well?" asked Mrs. Martin as she showed the kitchen slave how to knead the dough for the day's bread.

"I am well," said Eliza, smiling at her.

"We're so happy you and the governor stayed with us. He's such a fine man, Sam is. You must both be very happy."

"Yes, we are," said Eliza.

Eliza opened the back door. She stood in the cold on the back stoop and watched Sam and the Martins' two youngest daughters pelting each other with snowballs.

"That Sam Houston certainly is a handsome man," called Mrs. Martin. "Perhaps you'd better go help him before the girls get the best of him."

"I wish they would kill him," Eliza murmured, unaware that Mrs. Martin could hear her. "I wish from the bottom of my heart they would kill him."

Three months later, on the night of April 23, 1829, Sam stood with a single companion on the deck of the *Red Rover*. As he looked up at the lights of Nashville on the bluff above the steamboat wharf, he could see the the torches burning in the square there. The mob was ugly. He closed his eyes, trying to shut out what he had seen the past few nights.

His life was in rubble around his feet. The mob was crying for his blood. *Let them have it*, he thought. *It's worth nothing to me*. He hadn't seen his effigy burning in Gallatin. The few friends he had left tried to keep him from finding out about it. But someone in the crowd that gathered nightly in the Nashville square to jeer him had shouted the news. He pictured the lifeless form, in flames, revolving slowly in the wind.

He had been posted as a coward. The rumor was that the Allen men were threatening to kill him. He had boarded the boat tonight under cover of darkness. He had left incognito not because he feared bodily harm, but because he couldn't face so much hatred. Most of Nashville seemed to be his enemy now. Even the ministers he'd gone to for counsel had turned him out.

What would Andrew Jackson say when he received word of this? Sam's reputation, his career, his friends, his wife were gone. The woman he loved more than life itself was weeping at her father's house. And he was the cause of her tears. He gripped the railing until his knuckles were white and stared at the water sliding by as the boat moved away from the dock.

The scene kept playing in his mind. His rage, his shouts at Eliza, accusing her of infidelity. That was the worst. One did not war on women. How could he have frightened her so? His own hurt had made him insane for those moments. He saw, again and again, her tears. He heard her small voice trying to defend herself. *Houston, you ass! You monumental ass!* he thought. He shook the rail in his frustration and despair.

He had tried to repair the devastation his jealousy had created. Eliza would receive no correspondence from him, but he had written her father, pouring out his heart in remorse. "I do love Eliza," he wrote. "That she is the only earthly object dear to me God alone will bear witness."

But the situation became worse. Rumors flew—that he beat her, that she was adulterous. Sam realized now, with painful clarity, that she simply didn't love him. She never had. And because of his pride, he had ruined not only his life, but hers as well.

Chapter 41

Jim Bowie stood with one arm resting on the polished bar top. As he sipped his whiskey, he looked around the boat's saloon. The room was decorated with white-and-gilt scrollwork. The round polished tables squatted on thick, rococo legs. Heavy red curtains hung at the windows. A huge picture of a scantily clad Liberty, eyes blind-folded and hand holding a set of scales, hung behind the bar. But it was poker that held Bowie's attention. He was watching for an opening at a table. There were twenty cards in a deck, so only four men could play at a time. Bowie was assessing which game was being played at a level where he would be likely to win.

One quartet caught his eye, perhaps because the men around the table were so disparate. One was obviously a professional. He wore a ruffled white shirt with the collar open in the new style. He wore a red satin vest with big gaudy flowers on it and green spectacles, probably to shield his eyes from scrutiny.

Bowie judged the man across from the gambler to be a planter. He was more conservatively dressed, in trousers of black domestic and a plain vest. The collar of his linen shirt was held high on his neck by a green silk cravat tied in a flowing bow. The third man was Irish, not long off the boat by the sound of him. He was of medium height and slender build, a good-looking fellow with a jaunty air and no end of droll stories. The night before, Bowie had listened to him while his companion drank until he fell unconscious across the bar.

The Irishman's companion was the fourth man at the table now. He was fashionably dressed, but his clothes were rumpled and stained. His thick auburn hair was tangled and he had a week's growth of beard. He was handsome enough, well put together, and almost as tall as Bowie. But he was a drunkard. Since Bowie had boarded the day before, this was the first time he had seen the man away from the bar. Sometimes he drank silently and sometimes he raved about empires in the west.

Tonight he seemed more in control of himself. He drank steadily as he played, and he lost just as steadily. But he was drinking and losing stoically, as though that were what he was put on earth to do. No one noticed him touch his fingertips to his lips and transfer a bit of saliva and chewed tobacco to them. Nor did they notice his lips move. They wouldn't have understood the charm if they'd heard it. It was in Cherokee. It was a charm to bring wealth.

> Now! Listen! You rest above, Red Man!
> You have an abundance of wealth. You have just
>   put it in my lap.
> As high as the treetops, He will be walking.
> I stand as bright as the sunburst.

Suddenly the planter pulled a huge knife from the waist of his pants. Before anyone could react, he slashed it downward in a blurred arc that ended in the dealer's hand. The knife pinned the hand to the table, palm down. It also pinned the cards the dealer had been about to give himself. The gambler stared at the knife while the other two men stood so fast their chairs fell backwards with a crash. Talk hushed.

"My friend." The planter's voice was as silky as Kentucky bourbon. "If there is not an ace under your hand, I owe you an apology."

The gambler clenched his teeth and pulled the knife loose with his free hand.

"You dog," he said. But his hand trembled as he dropped the bloody knife on the table. The planter turned the torn cards over. Among them was one with a single spade on it.

"I marked this one." He held the ace up so they could see the slight crease in the corner. "I have been following its progress in this game. Our colleague has been keeping more in the ruffles of his sleeves than his wrists."

The planter picked up his knife, wiped it carefully on his handkerchief, and put it back in his waistband, under his coat. He put on his flat-crowned hat and gave a mock salute, touching the brim of it as he left the room. The Irishman and his friend righted their chairs, then wove an unsteady course to the bar.

"Faith, and I need a sip of the amber," said the Irishman.

"I'm buying." Bowie had a shock of sandy hair and an engaging smile. But his large hands were scarred with knife cuts. "A dram might settle the nerves."

"My nerves are settled." The Irishman's tall companion spoke slowly, and with great concentration. "But I accept your generous offer of a taste of the golden waters of Lethe. I have much to forget."

The Irishman held his glass in front of a candle and studied the light passing through the liquor.

"To *usqebaugh*, the water of life," he said.

"May the skin of your bum never cover a drum," said Bowie. The third man swayed as he held up his glass.

"Here's a health to poverty. It sticks by us when our friends forsake us." He held his hand out to Bowie. "Samuelson's my name. My friend here is Harry Haralson. He still has the mud of Ireland on his boots. He has not only kissed the Blarney stone, but, I suspect, has had his way with it, and left it making wedding plans in the morning."

"I'm pleased to meet you. My name is Bowie, Jim Bowie."

"Some relation to the knife, I shouldn't wonder," said Haralson.

"Not by blood." Bowie grinned. "However, my brother, Reason, originated the design."

"We'll each be getting one when we get to Arkansas," said Haralson. "We hear they make the best ones there."

"Look up James Black. He learned the secret of Damascus steel from a blacksmith with the Cherokee." Bowie leaned his elbows on the bar. "Arkansas Territory is passable, but the country of milk and honey, the Land of Goshen, is Texas. Either of you gentlemen ever been to Texas?"

"I joined the Texas Association a few years back," said Samuelson.

"I've heard of them. A group backing colonization there. All under Spanish authority, of course." There was a touch of irony in Bowie's voice.

"That's them." Samuelson leaned closer and lowered his voice.

"Tell me, Jim, what do you think the possibilities are for annexing Texas?"

"Sir, Texas belongs to Mexico. It's a rich province. The Spanish will not part with it under any circumstances. I myself have taken an oath of allegiance to them. My wife is Spanish."

"It was merely an idle question. There's talk of an empire waiting in the Rockies for the man strong enough to win it."

"I know nothing of empires." Bowie smiled. "My wife's family is highly placed in the government. We are prospering. I have no cause for complaint. Nor any reason to search for the chimera of an empire in the sunset. The only dynasty I care about is the children who will someday play around my knees." He had to pull himself back to the present. "And will you gentlemen stay long on the Arkansas?"

Haralson looked up at the ornate ceiling and Samuelson stared into his glass as though there were a fly in it.

"We don't know." Samuelson scratched his patchy new growth of beard. "We're pilgrims, adrift in the world, with no port in life's storms."

"Awash in the world, you might say." Haralson drained his glass.

"We're like Diogenes with his lantern, searching for an honest man. Or at least one we can trust. I hope you have many friends, Jim, friends you can count on when you need them most. There's nothing more valuable." Bowie wondered what could possibly have filled this man's voice with so much bitterness.

"Tell us about Texas," said Samuelson. Bowie obliged him. They passed the evening discussing this and that. Haralson's brogue thickened as he became more inebriated. He made even Samuelson laugh when he described Andrew Jackson's inauguration.

"Those who spent time on the American desert," he said, "likened it to a stampede of buffalo. The unwashed were after climbing on the official furniture in their muddy clodhoppers and craning their chicken necks to see the Hero of New Orleans." Haralson climbed onto a chair and peered over the crowd in the saloon.

"I meself saw two gentlemen pushing a lady of astonishing corpulence through a very small window. The press was that thick. People were fainting. And punching peelers. I nivver saw the like. Not even at the best of wakes."

"The old aristocrats, Adams, Clay, and that ilk, were appalled," said Samuelson. "Or so I heard," he amended hastily. "For myself, I've put politics behind me."

When a group sitting nearby began to sing, Samuelson's eyes misted and his mouth twitched. Bowie watched him fight to control the emotions that raged under his ravaged face.

"Well, and we've been drinking a smart drop," said Haralson. "It's time to step off nimble for bed." He laid a hand on his friend's arm.

As they left, Samuelson's head was bowed. He looked, even from behind, a broken man. Bowie listened to the song, paying attention to the words for the first time.

> *'Mid pleasures and palaces,*
> *Though we may roam,*
> *Be it ever so humble,*
> *There's no place like home.*

The next morning, Bowie stood in line behind Haralson as they waited for the toothbrush hanging on a chain near the pitchers of river water. While Bowie held his place, Haralson peered into the pitchers, deciding in which the silt had settled the most. When they finished their toilet, they strolled toward the saloon that was now the dining hall.

Haralson whistled to himself as he leaned on the railing and looked out over the water. He seemed to be drinking in the scenery, the people, the boat, the river, the whole of the country in huge gulps.

"Your friend seems unhappy," Bowie ventured cautiously.

"Aye. He is that. A most unhappy man indeed. Do you know who he is?"

"No."

Haralson paused to consider the confidence he was about to make.

"You seem a likely sort," he said. "Not one to betray a friend. And we're getting off the boat this afternoon anyway. He's Sam Houston, the former governor of Tennessee." Haralson laughed at the expression on Bowie's face. "I'd not be lying to you," he said.

"I'd heard something about it. There was some tiff between Houston and his wife, wasn't there? Some hint of scandal?"

"Tiff? Hint? Aye, and more. You know the way of folk. Neither Sam nor the lass would speak of it. 'If my reputation cannot stand the shock, then let me lose it,' Sam says. He's an honorable man, that one. But, in the absence of truth people will invent lies. Sam fell victim to those respectable thieves and murderers who steal one's name and assassinate one's character."

"I heard he resigned in a cloud of mystery. Surely a domestic matter can't be that serious."

"A lady's honor is serious in Tennessee. They hung him in effigy in Gallatin. Threatened his life in Nashville. And for what? No one knows. Some say he accused his new bride of infidelity. But he says if anyone utters a word against Mrs. Houston's purity, he'll write the libel in the blackguard's heart's blood. He refuses to speak of it, and so does her family and the lass herself.

"All anyone knows for sure is that he was away campaigning. When he returned, he found his bride had fled in tears to her father's house, less than three months after their wedding. Sure and it was a sad day for him. His rivals have made the most of it. And the clergy who claimed, in better times, to be Sam's friends, refused him baptism when he s at his lowest ebb."

"It's as the Good B k says, 'Wheresoever the carcass is, there will the eagles be gathered together,' " said Bowie. "Do you think he mistreated her?"

"Sam? Surely not. He has a temper, mind. But there's no doubt he loves her as life itself. A good deal more than life, right now. In fact, I'd best go find him. He might throw himself overboard."

"If you or . . . Samuelson get to Texas, ask in San Antonio de Bexar for me. Everyone knows me thereabouts."

"I shall that!" Harry climbed down the ladder to the deck below. Bowie leaned over the rail so he could watch the man clamber over and around the boxes and bales. Haralson's full tenor floated up.

> *The turban'd Turk, who scorns the world,*
> *May strut about with his whiskers curled,*
> *Keep a hundred wives under lock and key,*
> *For nobody else but himself to see;*
> *Yet long may he pray with his Alcoran*
> *Before he can love like an Irishman.*

Haralson reached the bow of the boat. He braced one boot on the coaming, grabbed the tall spar of the loading derrick, and leaned out over the water. He pretended to sight out to sea as he roared the last line again. "Be-fo-o-ore he can love like an Irishman."

If a man were in need of cheer, thought Bowie, he could do no better than to have Haralson as a companion. Haralson might never amount to much in the world's eyes, but he would never want for anything friends could provide.

As for Sam Houston, Bowie contemplated him as he watched the yellow water slide by. Sam perked up soon enough when the talk turned to Texas and empires. It was an ungenerous thought, but Bowie wondered if the man was enjoying his despair. He did seem to have an overdeveloped sense of drama. He had talked the night before about hearing an eagle scream and seeing it soar off into the sunset as he'd boarded the boat to exile. Houston claimed it meant his destiny lay to the west. Well, eagles were carrion eaters. The omen could be interpreted in more than one way.

Chapter 42

Sam and Harry debarked at Cairo, Illinois, where the Ohio met the Mississippi. Gambling and whiskey had taken a good deal of what little money they had. Even the general cabin fare on the steamboat was too much for their thin purses. So they stalked along the clamorous waterfront, looking for a keelboat to hire.

They stepped carefully, avoiding the piles of manure left by the huge dray horses that pulled the wagons jamming the waterfront. They dodged bales and crates flying through the air at the ends of loading cranes. Nearby, a mule brayed loudly. The cacophony made Sam's ears ring pleasantly. He felt lighter in the head and heart than he had in months. The wild medley of odors was too complex to sort out. But the strongest smell was the hemp and tar of boat lines. It triggered longings for distant country and reckless adventure.

"Bedlam," shouted Harry over the din. "This is bedlam."

"You said you wanted to see the backside of the country. You wanted to see how people live beyond the sway of hot shaves and cold juleps."

"So I did." Harry grinned.

"*Petit Puce*." Sam read the name off the last of the keelboats in line. It had been pulled up on shore, and its prow was buried in the thick mud. "This is it." Sam walked gingerly out onto the planks laid end to end across the red morass. The wood sank under his weight until the mud oozed over his boot toes. Harry followed, peering around Sam to see the boat. It looked as though it had been recently salvaged from the river bottom. The algae on the exposed hull was as thick as a lawn.

Two huge dogs of indeterminate breed raced to the prow of the boat and snarled and raged at them. Their sides were scarred and their back hair bristled. Harry would have estimated the length of their teeth at six inches.

"Sam, where did you hear of this, this . . ." For once Harry was at a loss for words.

"In the tavern, while you were flirting with the barmaid. They say the owner doesn't charge much for passage down the Mississippi. When he reaches New Orleans, he loads up with firewood and lashes the boat alongside a steamer. When the wood runs out, the steamer cuts him loose. He cuts more wood, finds another customer, and so on."

"Inventive."

"Eh, you!" Sam and Harry whirled around. "What you boys want wit' my boat?" Jacques's huge, faded plaid shirt made him seem even bigger than he was. His baggy canvas pants were gathered under a hand-woven belt that had once been colorful but was now frayed and dirt-colored. His black eyepatch made him seem ominous, as though he had more to hide than an empty socket. His long hair and beard were grizzled. He couldn't have been less than fifty-five years old, but Sam wouldn't want to tangle with him.

"We want to hire your boat, as far as the mouth of the White River cut-off to the Arkansas."

" 'Ow much money you got?" Jacques slogged through the mud, which didn't quite wash over the tops of his high boots.

"Not much."

"Come aboard. We talk."

Sam and Harry eyed the dogs warily as Jacques walked up the plank that led to the pitted deck. The plank bowed under his weight. The dogs continued to snarl from around his short, thick legs.

" 'S'okay," Jacques called down to them.

" 'S'okay," Sam repeated softly with a French accent.

" 'S'okay," Harry mumbled to himself, wishing he had a stout shelaighleigh.

For a week the three men drifted down the brass-colored river. When Sam wasn't taking his turn at the sweep or tarring leaks or bailing the bilge, he read to himself or aloud to the others. Harry preferred to spend his time fishing. Jacques played his fiddle. When the dogs weren't scratching, they were comatose around the men's legs.

Sam was sorry when the trip ended and Jacques left them and their baggage at the wharf of the ragged hamlet of Little Rock, the seat of government for Arkansas Territory. Jacques had insisted on taking them that far up the river, although they earned their passage by cutting wood. They used Jacques's ploy of selling the wood to steamboats in exchange for a ride alongside.

"We're almost there," Sam said as he and Harry watched *Petit Puce* diminish down the river.

"And it's glad I am to hear it. How many more miles?"

"Only a couple hundred."

"A couple hundred!" Haralson was incredulous. "A couple hundred. Why, if I were in Ireland and took a trip like this, I'd end up in darkest Mongolia, eating goat cheese with the Khan."

"You may eat goat cheese yet before we're through," said Sam. "We can float and starve, or we can ride and eat. Riding, we can hunt for our meals."

"Riding it is, then." Harry didn't seem at all unhappy about the prospect of hunting. He went off in search of a gunsmith to rifle his old musket barrel while Sam looked for horses to buy or hire.

Sam studied the rental stock at the livery stable and argued with the owner.

"Take the three by the door, or leave them. It's all the same to me." The liveryman went outside.

"Third one's got a bad pastern," someone said. A large black man was shoveling manure nearby. Sam sauntered over and leaned on an open stall gate.

"Which one's good?" he asked the man softly.

"Fifth." He rattled the water bucket to cover his voice.

"Coffee!" Sam shouted. "Coffee, remember me? Sam. The Raven."

"Houston, Sam Houston? Lordy, how could I forget you? You saved my life."

"What's going on?" yelled the liveryman from the doorway. "I'm paying that man to work, not chitchat."

"Ain't paying me," said Coffee. "Slops from the table and a pile of dirty straw to sleep on ain't pay for a man." As though throwing a spear, Coffee hurled the shovel across the stable. It hit the wall and fell with a clatter.

"You uppish nigger." The man stalked toward them, his pitchfork raised. "Stand back, stranger. I'm putting this high-talking darkie in his place, six feet under a white man's feet."

"Now, sir," said Sam. "Don't agitate yourself."

"No cause to get involved," Coffee said. He held a mule hame in front of him. Pitchfork and all, the stable owner hesitated.

"Now, gentlemen." Sam moved between them.

"Don't put me in no class with a nigger," said the man.

You aren't in a class with him, Sam thought. *I was flattering you.*

"This rogue belongs to a friend of mine," Sam said. "I've been looking for him."

"He owes me the rest of the day's work for his meals and last night's lodging."

"I don't owe you a brass-plated fart."

"Now, now," said Sam placatingly. "I'm sure we can reach some sort of agreement. I can see you've been sorely tried by this saucy fellow."

"Sorely tried, sir."

"Well, I'm prepared to make restitution."

"I don't give a shit about that. I just want my money's worth."

"My friend is anxious to have his nigger back. I'll give you an extra ten dollars, and take this scoundrel with me, as well as the first two horses in line and that fifth one."

The man hesitated. He was torn between the desire to do bodily harm to Coffee and the knowledge that he'd die trying it.

"Let me at him," he said unconvincingly.

"I'll beat you to horse shit," said Coffee cordially.

"The townspeople will tear you to shreds for it."

"I'm sure that will be a great consolation to your widow." Ignoring the pitchfork the man still held, Coffee advanced a few steps.

"Coffee, get your no-good black arse outside and wait. If you run again, I shall cut you down."

"You and the army." Coffee's voice was heavy with menace. He turned in the doorway just long enough to wink at Sam.

"What's happening?" Haralson arrived and Sam motioned him to be quiet.

"What do you say?" Sam asked the stable owner.

"I say he should be flogged inside out."

"Oh, I assure you, he'll get what's coming to him."

"If he's a runaway, I oughta get more reward than ten dollars."

"I'm offering forty dollars for the hire of three horses and the chance to rid yourself of a dangerous man. You know how these primitive people can carry a grudge."

"You only get two saddles. The third animal was for pack, you said. And I want coin, not shin plasters or gilded moonshine."

Actually, Sam only carried coins. He didn't trust the bank notes either. There were too many enterprising counterfeiters producing gilded moonshine, as the bills were called.

"Pay the man forty dollars, please, Harry."

"But, Sam, we haven't—"

"Please, Harry."

The three men didn't tarry long in town. They distributed their luggage as best they could among the horses and sold what wouldn't fit. Coffee had only a small satchel with an extra shirt and a new glassed carpenter's level, a present from Seeth. As they rode along the narrow, winding Indian trail through the wild Arkansas valley, Sam and Coffee talked.

"What lured you to the Arkansas?" Sam asked. "Surely you must know it's dangerous for you here."

"Surely I do know it. I was for going to Africa. Some folks in Connecticut were raising money for me and Fancy to go. They're setting up a colony there, for former slaves and free persons of color."

"Last I heard, you were living in Canada."

"We were. But it was too cold up north. That was why I wanted to go back to Africa. But it wouldn't really be the land I came from, not my tribe. And Fancy wanted to come here. She never got over missing the Rogers. She figures she can help Miss Tiana."

"Why does Tiana need help?"

"I thought you must know, being an old friend of the family. We received a letter from her a year ago. Her husband and child were killed. And her father died."

"I didn't know," said Sam. "Where's Fancy?"

"I sent her ahead. On a steamboat. We had only money for one passage. We figured she'd be safer on the boat. The captain seemed a good man. He promised to look after her. I stayed behind to earn passage or work my way to Fort Smith."

They had to travel the last hour to Louisburg in the dark. Lightning played across the horizon and thunder rumbled. They pounded on a cabin door outside the small town, just as the rain was beginning to fall. The door swung open suddenly and Sam stared down the double barrels of a shotgun.

"Howdy, stranger," he said meekly. "Could you spare shel—"

"*Procul hinc, procul este, severae!*" roared the small man at the other end of the barrel.

"What did he say?" whispered Harry.

"Stay hence, stay far hence, forbidding ones," murmured Sam from the corner of his mouth. "Ovid, I think." He never took his eyes off the gun barrel, which wavered a bit as its wielder swayed in the lighted doorway. The man squinted to see out into the dark. With the light behind him, his face was a black mask.

"*Ave, Imperator, morituri te salutant.*" Sam brought his hand very slowly to his forehead in a salute. "Those about to die, salute you."

"Eureka!" shouted the man. He lowered the gun and peered out at them. "You're not part of the ignorant banditti that infest this place. I can forgive them being banditti, but ignorant, ah, that I cannot forgive." He seemed to have trouble focusing. "Enter, gentlemen, enter. *Hic vivimus ambitiosa, paupertate omnes.* Here we all live in a state of ambitious poverty."

"That's correct." The large woman behind him lowered her rifle. "Except for the part about ambitious." She spat into the fireplace, causing a sputtering and steaming among the coals.

"Linton is my name." Their host pushed things off two extra chairs and onto the cluttered floor. He had a cultured, Virginia Tidewater accent, albeit a bit slurred. "John Linton. And this is my spare rib, Bertha."

After introductions and a sparse dinner, Sam and John Linton gorged on the classics. In the morning, Linton insisted on riding with them to Fort Smith.

"'Tis only common courtesy," he said, saddling his old horse, Bucephalus.

"But it's a hundred and twenty miles," said Harry.

"One hundred and twenty-seven," said Linton. "I wouldn't think of letting you ride all that way unescorted. You'd think us a rude lot indeed. And we can talk. My God, man." He turned to Sam. "Do you know how I've thirsted in this desert for the cool, refreshing words of the ancients? The local officialdom here doesn't know Catullus from corn shucks."

For a man head over heels in misery, Sam had a rather rollicking time of it. When their small casks of whiskey ran dry, there was always someone along the way to refill them. Every settler in Arkansas seemed to be in the distillery business. They were happy to trade their merchandise for freshly killed game or labor. Sam didn't even sober up long enough to succumb to the Blue Pukes, as he called them.

When they ran low on ammunition, Sam's proficiency with a cane blowgun and darts impressed everyone.

"Where did you learn that, Samuelson?" Linton asked.

"With the Cherokee, as a boy." Sam stared into the thick greenery around them, and up into the massive trees towering overhead. "When Houston looks back over the wastes, there's nothing half so sweet to remember as that sojourn among the untutored children of the forest."

"Houston?"

"I'm not who you think I am, John."

"Well now, to tell you the truth," hiccupped Linton, "I didn't think you were who I thought you were."

"*In vino veritas*," said Haralson. "There's truth in wine."

Sam confessed the real reason for his exile, although he didn't say why his wife left him.

"I'm like Nebuchadnezzar," he finished. "A homeless exile."

"*Stat magni nominis umbra*," said Linton. " 'There stands the shadow of a great name.' But don't despair. As Publius Syrus once said, 'Not even a god could love and be wise.' "

To cheer them, Harry recited an old dialogue between an Irish innkeeper and an English traveler. He punctuated each two lines with a chorus of nonsense.

" 'Halloa, house,' shouted the Englishman. 'I don't know anyone of that name.' 'Are you the master of the inn?' 'Aye, sore, when my wife's from home.' 'Have you any porter?' 'Aye, sore. Pat is an excellent porter.' 'No, I mean porter to drink.' 'Oh, sore, he'll drink the ocean, nivver fear.' "

Then he taught them part of his endless repertoire of bawdy songs. They bellowed "The Boys of Bedlam" for miles as their horses ambled along.

It was twilight and raining when they reached the outskirts of Fort Smith. They were enjoying each other's company too much to ride straight into the settlement. It was a dreary place in any case. Since the garrison had pulled out, it had fallen to rack.

Sam claimed an abandoned cabin in the name of Bacchus and sprinkled a few drops of whiskey in each corner, while John and Harry protested the extravagance. Coffee, who'd stayed sober, brought in dry wood from the crumbling porch. After sweeping the mouse turds from the hearth, he laid a fire.

While the fire caught, he skinned the three rabbits Sam had shot with his blowgun.

The others rolled in the two wooden casks and uncorked one. They camped in front of the fire, lounging on their blankets and leaning against their saddles.

"I feel sorry for the lasses," said Linton. "They don't drink. What kind of life must it be, not to drink?"

"So, I'll sing, bonnie boys, bonnie mad boys," Harry began to sing softly. The others joined him.

"Bedlam boys are bonnie. And they all go bare and they live by the air, and they want no drink nor money."

"To Bacchus!" John raised his mug. "The god of wine and good times."

"To bonnie, bare-arsed Bacchus," said Harry. "And to the bonnie boys of Bedlam."

"I propose a sacrifice to Bacchus," said Sam.

"What sort of sacrifice?" asked Harry.

"The shirts off our backs. A man who is willing to part with the shirt from his back is a worthy son of Bacchus."

"Hear! Hear!" said Linton and Haralson. Coffee shook his head in amusement and continued whittling a stick. He fed the curly shavings into the fire.

"Here are the terms of the sacrifice. Each in turn must quote a line from the classics and feed an article of clothing into the fire. Then he's permitted a drink."

"Agreed," said Linton.

"I am a midding scholar at best, gentlemen," said Harry. "I am the product of a hedge school. The British think education gives an Irishman delusions of self-government."

"You own a vast store of verse and wit," said Sam. "Recite what you know. I shall commence." Sam stood, favoring his aching thigh. Hours on horseback always set it off. " '*Nihil tam absurde dici potest quod non dicatur ab aliquo philosophorum.*' 'Nothing so absurd can be said, that some philosopher has not said it.' Cicero." And he shied his hat into the blaze. The flannel curled, then shriveled and flared. Sam tossed his head back and emptied his mug.

"Bravo! I'll go next." Harry stood. " '*Amo, amas*, I love a lass, as a cedar tall and slender. Sweet cowslips's grace is her nominative case, and she's of the feminine gender.' O'Keefe." Harry threw his hat after Sam's and took a long pull on his drink.

" '*Varium et mutabile semper femina.*' 'Woman is always fickle and changing.' Virgil."

"Coffee, will you join us?" asked Sam.

"Naw, Sam. Most of my learning's been Bible verses. Besides, you boys been three times around the track with your drinking and I'm still at the gate. I'll keep the fire stoked."

"I'll continue then," said Sam. And he did. An hour before dawn, he and Harry had sacrificed all the clothes they wore. They sprawled naked in front of the roaring blaze. Harry was asleep. John Linton wore only his long white shirt. He stood shakily to recite.

" 'Let schoolmasters puzzle their brains, with grammar and nonsense and learning.' " He hiccupped and swayed dangerously. " 'Good liquor, I stoutly maintain, gives genius a better discerning.' Goldsmith."

"Now the sacrifice," said Sam. But Linton balked.

"This is my only shirt, Houston."

"The gods must be appeased, sir," roared Sam. He attacked Linton and tore the shirt from his back. He watched as it blazed up, then turned to stiff ashes. "What do you say to that?" he asked Linton. But John, knocked against the wall by Sam's rush, merely slid down it. His bare rear end bumped along the logs, picking up splinters, as he went. He was asleep before he hit the dirt floor. Sam sighed and passed out too.

He woke up the next morning, dressed and laid across the packhorse. His head was throbbing. Ahead of them, Coffee slouched in his saddle and whistled a gospel tune with a spritely beat.

"By the Eternal, Coffee, untie me."

"Surely, Sam. I was afraid you might fall off." Coffee stopped the horses and came back to untie Sam and Harry. Harry groaned.

"Where are we?"

"Almost to Fort Smith. Time to spruce up and be presentable. The packet to Fort Gibson will leave in an hour or two, I hear."

"What happened to John?" Harry was holding his head. His eyelids looked like the only thing in the world they wanted was to close and stay that way. Coffee laughed with delight. Sam winced at the sound.

"I reckon he should be waking up any time now. And naked as Adam in the garden."

"That's right," said Sam. "We . . . uh . . . we did burn some clothes last night."

"You surely did. I had the devil's very own time getting you two dressed this morning. But you had plenty of clothes in your bags." Coffee nodded toward the luggage that surrounded them.

"Did you leave any for poor Linton? He had nothing with him but the clothes on his back."

"Naw. I reckon he's wearing sackcloth and ashes now, without the sackcloth. I forgot about him. I was in such a hurry to get you gentlemen to the dock before *Facility* leaves."

"*Facility?*"

"Captain Pennywit's boat. Man we passed back a ways says Pennywit's always needing roustabouts."

"Why?"

"Oh, I don't know." Coffee was evasive. "Something about the chances he takes. He's a good pilot though."

Harry started to laugh hysterically.

"What is it?" asked Sam.

"Linton," Harry managed to choke. "Naked."

The picture of John waking up one hundred and twenty-seven miles from home with no clothes hit them all. They laughed and sang as they cantered toward the rundown shacks and decayed and cannibalized barracks that had once been Fort Smith.

So I'll sing bonnie boys, bonnie mad boys,
Bedlam boys are bonnie.

Chapter 43

Steamboats were still a novelty on the Arkansas, especially north of Fort Smith. Not many could get across Satan's Skillet, a stretch of rapids where spray hitting the rocks looked like water dancing in hot oil. Heavy cargo often had to be unloaded, then packed around the shoals so the lightened boat could pass over them. An enterprising farmer used his oxen to tow boats off the bars and charged five dollars for the service. But he rarely had the privilege of towing Philip Pennywit.

Tiana smiled as she stood among the excited crowd at Webber's Landing and listened for Pennywit's distinctive whistle. She had ridden *Facility* once. Pennywit had caught her leaving bits of food in the corners of the cabin.

"What are you doing?" he had asked.

"Feeding the rats."

"Feeding the rats?"

"To encourage them to stay."

Pennywit had laughed until his eyes watered.

"Have you so little faith in my vessel? You think the rats might leave and we'll sink? Come, come with me."

He took her to the glass-enclosed pilot house. She stared down at the rocks and water almost thirty feet below.

"Does it frighten you?" Pennywit had asked as they neared the Skillet.

"No. I once rode a flatboat through The Suck."

"Tennessee? Near the Lookout Mountain?"

"Yes."

"Then you're an old hand indeed."

The stewards knew what to expect. They stationed themselves near the lanterns hanging in the saloon. The boat's deck was so loaded with goods they blocked the windows and the lanterns were lit even during the day. As *Facility* gained speed, passengers on the promenade of the boiler deck watched in dismay. Women screamed as the spoon-shaped bow hit the shoal with a shudder that passed through the vessel. The stewards and the seasoned passengers stoically held the lanterns so they would swing less wildly. Women and men were thrown in heaps against the walls.

Tiana had waited for the boat's old hull to split like an overripe melon. Pennywit turned to see her clutching the back of the faded settee with the black horsehair stuffing oozing out the split seams. She was grinning from ear to ear.

"You like this, do you?" he'd shouted over the din from the boiler deck and the wooden hull scraping on rocks. She grinned wider. "If you ever want to sign on, I'll teach you to navigate this pathway to perdition." He nodded at the half-submerged trees whose roots seemed to be combing the water for victims. "When the water gets too low, we tap a few kegs of beer and ride on the foam."

Tiana had never taken him up on his offer, although she had been tempted. But she and the captain were still good friends. The few times they were at Cantonment Gibson together, they played whist. Now she was waiting for *Facility* at Webber's Landing, twenty miles south of the fort.

The landing was a maze of cargo, some of it rank. Many of the trappers were careless in the tanning of their hides. The hot June sun stewed the odor out of them. The huge bundles of deer and buffalo skins, otter and beaver pelts were set downwind, but the smell was still strong.

Watt Webber's men stood guard over the powder keg and ax boxes that held Mexican silver dollars, the preferred currency of western traders. Watt was half-Cherokee and half-white and all business. His trading post, ferries, and plantation were worth a great deal of money.

Some hogsheads held pecans and saltpeter and coarse, glittering salt from nearby salines. Others were full of smoked sides of bacon and the beans that formed the bulk of the garrison's menu. There were whole deerskins, bloated with honey or beeswax, and baskets of dried apples and peaches, bags of snake root and sarsparilla. There were sacks of corn and upland rice and gopher peas, and boxes of the trinkets soldiers liked to send home as presents. The bowls and pipes and beautifully polished arrow heads were carved from the gleaming black argilite that made up the shelf of rock called Webber's Falls. And there were acres of cordwood to fuel the voracious steamboats.

There was more confusion than usual at Webber's Landing. Runners had brought word that Drum's famous son, Kalanu, The Raven, was aboard *Facility*. Drum, three hundred of his people, and a huge crowd of the Old Settlers had come to meet him. Tiana hadn't seen Drum this excited since Arbuckle's soldiers had challenged his young men to a game of ball play. Drum had won a king's ransom in goods from the soldiers and he had been expansive in victory. He offered to let the soldiers play the women the next time.

The Real People were dressed in their best and brightest clothes— reds and blues, greens and yellows, a wild melee of checks and stripes and flowers. Feathers and plumes bobbed from turbans. Drum wore his full ceremonial regalia, with a huge crescent gorget on his chest and heavy silver earrings dangling from his distended lobes. Children played hide-and-seek among the boxes and barrels.

When twilight darkened into night, slaves lit torches. Dancing began under the trees, along with a quantity of surreptitious drinking. For a while Tiana held Fancy's hand to keep her from chewing her nails down any further. Fancy tried to meet every boat that stopped, on the chance Coffee was aboard it. Her nerves were wearing thin, and Tiana had come along this time to comfort her in case he wasn't on *Facility*.

The two of them had been living at Sally Ground Squirrel's farm. Jennie and Susannah were staying with James and his wife, Nannie. Susannah had become deeply melancholy. Tiana visited her often, trying to cheer her up, but she didn't want to live in the same house with her.

Besides, she felt more useful with Drum and Sally Ground Squirrel. The town house was near the farm, and the women's council often asked her to speak to the headmen. Many of the women were unhappy about the new laws that were being passed to exclude them from speaking in council.

Sometimes Tiana became discouraged, when the men listened politely and did the opposite of what the women counseled. But she couldn't give up the struggle. Besides, there were always crowds of children at Sally Ground Squirrel's. And Tiana never stopped looking for the one with whom she could share her knowledge.

"What's keeping that boat?" asked Fancy.

"Sawyers, snags, and shoals," said Tiana.

"Lordy." Fancy was beginning to pace like an animal when they heard Pennywit's whistle. Pennywit always blew a low tone first, booming and pulsing until it vibrated Tiana's marrow. Then he added a piercing blast and three descending notes, ending in a wild, barbarous chord that made Tiana's scalp tingle.

A shout went up as the crowd surged down to the wharf. Slaves with torches lined the shore for hundreds of feet downstream. The drumming intensified as the boat glided toward the dock. Twin gouts of red and gold cinders blew from *Facility*'s two stacks and glowed against the sky. Fancy searched for Coffee among the roustabouts who lined the lower deck's railing and waved their hats. Their usual call and response song was drowned out by the noise on shore.

"Ka-la-nu! Ka-la-nu! Ka-la-nu!" Everyone but Fancy and Tiana seemed to be chanting Raven's name. He had been a headman among the whites and a friend of the White Father, Jackson, in Washington City. If he wasn't a messiah, come to save them in time of trouble, he was close enough for government work, as Arbuckle was fond of saying. People rushed the boat before the broad plank was well seated. It took all of Tiana's strength to keep Fancy from running after them.

"Let me go. I think I saw him." Fancy tugged to break free.

"Wait, sister. Pennywit must have his prank first." Just as Tiana knew he would, Pennywit cleared his mud valve with a deafening roar and a cloud of steam. People screamed and ran in all directions. It wasn't a foolish panic. Steamboat explosions were common. Tiana pushed Fancy into the press.

"Go find him," she shouted. Fancy sprinted up the plank and was soon lost in the billowing clouds of steam.

Tiana put her forearms on top of a stack of crates and rested her head on the backs of her hands. A man's hat shaded her face and dark blue eyes, but she could see the ceremony about to take place. She watched for The Raven. As long as she was here, she might as well see what changes time had made.

She would have missed him altogether if Drum hadn't rushed forward and grabbed him in a tight hug. They walked toward Tiana until they were almost close enough to touch. Tiana was surprised to see tears glistening in the torchlight that shown on Raven's haggard, bearded face. *He's old!* she thought in astonishment. He must be near forty now. Thirty-seven, anyway. It didn't seem possible this was the confident young man who had seen them off at the wharf over ten years before.

"My son." Drum's voice carried to the edge of the crowd. "My soul greets you. The winters have been many and cold since last I looked on you. We have heard you were a great headman. We heard a dark cloud covered the white path you walked. We are glad of it, my son. The Seven Clans are deeply troubled. The Provider has sent you to advise us. My wife's house is your house. My food is yours. My people are yours. You are home."

Tiana was almost touched by the despair she saw in Raven's eyes. Then she remembered his betrayal, his forsaking them when they needed him. He hadn't even written in years. If he was suffering now, it was part of life's balance. He had achieved his success partly at the expense of them. Now he was paying the price.

"Rest with us, my son," Drum continued. "I will bathe your feet after your long and sorrowful journey." Raven and his traveling companion were soon hidden by the hundreds of people who pressed forward to see and touch the former general, Congressman, and governor.

"Sister, he's here!" Tiana jumped at Fancy's voice. In spite of herself, she had been craning to catch one more glimpse of Raven.

"My old friend!" Tiana began to cry as she hugged Coffee to her. "Sister," she said to Fancy. "I left a satchel of clothes at your cabin in the quarters. I want to stay with you tonight. In the morning I'll ride to the mission."

"Why are you going there?"

"Father Washburn promised to teach me French. It's time for me to go. They've offered me hospitality for as long as I want to stay."

"They still think they'll lead you to their path, don't they," said Fancy.

"They do. Imagine thinking there's only one path through life."

"When will we see you again?" asked Coffee.

"A month or two. There are many people to visit. In the meantime, you can work for Drum. He'll protect you. There are unprincipled people outside the Nation who would steal your liberty."

Tiana lay awake on a pile of sacking that served as her bed in the loft of the slave cabin that night. She ignored the faint rustlings and sighs and voices that drifted up through the cracks in the loft floor. She was used to sharing a house with many other people. And she felt so removed from physical love it was difficult to imagine it anymore.

A hundred feet away, Raven stared at the smoke-blackened ceiling. Sally Ground Squirrel's double cabin stood in a grove of tall sycamores and cottonwoods. It was furnished just like the old one in the east, although there were a few more things here, like a set of china and pewter silverware. There was even the traditional dugout for sleeping in the winter months. But Drum planned to make this house much larger, adding a second story and separate kitchen.

Raven wanted to do what he could for his adopted people. It was his only purpose in life now. He had already written Jackson that he would accept no situation in the government. That he wished nothing from him but friendship. He offered to try to keep peace among the Indians and to let the president know of injustices done them.

As he lay there, he heard the rasp of a dry corncob. Someone was scratching insect bites. It was such a small, long-forgotten, yet totally familiar sound.

The misery of his long, tragic journey faded a little. He felt like a weary wanderer returned at last to his father's house.

Colonel Arbuckle stared into the square, black hole. He probed the bottom of it with the fifteen-foot pole his lieutenant sheepishly handed him.

"I'll be god-damned." In spite of his exasperation, Arbuckle chuckled. Sweat beaded at the line where his kinky slicked-back gray hair met his high forehead. A drop of sweat dangled from the tip of his large, hooked nose. He squinted, trying to see the bottom of the hole.

"I'll be god-damned," he said again. "Captain, how many feet did you say were entered in the log book?"

"Four hundred and sixty-five, sir. A few feet a day for the last eighteen months. I don't know how it could have happened, sir," the lieutenant stammered.

"Well, you aren't to blame. After all, they've gulled every Officer of the Day for a year and a half. You're the one who finally caught them. I'll be damned." He laughed out loud. "Those scoundrels are clever enough to be officers. Lower me down." He waved to the privates standing at parade rest.

Two guardhouse prisoners had been given the duty of digging a well on the hill where the garrison moved each year for a summer encampment. The cantonment itself was on low ground. It was a dangerous place in the hot summer months. There were more men buried outside the walls than stationed inside them.

The surrounding hills were healthier, but water had to be hauled from the river far below. The two original prisoners had worked steadily, winter and summer. When their sentences were up, two more replaced them, then two more. Each pair had reported their progress. But they'd stopped digging at about fifteen feet. Then they'd hollowed out a cavern, cool in summer and warm in winter. They'd carried down a lantern and whiled away their time playing cards.

Arbuckle was reluctant to come back to the surface.

"I just might set up my summer office down there," he said as his men heaved him out of the hole.

"Colonel Arbuckle, sir, allow me to introduce myself."

Arbuckle squinted into the sunlight. He took in Raven's fringed and tasseled Indian hunting coat, his turban and painted leather leggings.

"You don't have to." He wiped his dusty hand and shook Raven's. "General Houston, your reputation as a . . . as an imaginative dresser has reached me." He didn't mention that word was also out from the president himself to keep a close watch on Houston. Apparently, some of Raven's drunken talk of empires had blown east.

"Did you lose something?" Raven peered over Arbuckle's shoulder toward the innocent hole.

"About eighteen months, times two," said Arbuckle. "I've been expecting you, . . . General. Or should I call you Governor?"

"Call me Sam."

"Fine. I'm Matt. Pleased to make your acquaintance at last. I hear old John Jolly put on quite a show for your arrival a month ago. Tell him to visit more often. I miss our talks."

"He sends his regards. He thinks highly of you."

They walked toward Arbuckle's quarters at the head of the rows of neat, if dingy, tents. The encampment covered hundreds of acres.

Tents and fenced pastures rode the crests of the cleared hills. It was as though the camp, once released from the confinement of the palisades, was reveling in the freedom. The bivouac was a model of precision, though. Everything was laid out in those satisfying lines and squares that the military felt gave order to the universe.

It was hard to miss Arbuckle's red-and-white-striped marquee with scalloping along the edges where the peaked roof met the walls. Three flags, one for the United States, one for the Territory, and one for the regiment, hung limply out front. Brass-tipped poles held up the tent flap at a rakish angle and provided shade for a pair of camp chairs. Cigars, two glasses, a decanter, and the latest issue of *The Arkansas Gazette* were set on a brass-bound wooden chest between them. Arbuckle settled himself into one and waved Sam into the other. He offered him a cigar, then drew the other under the generous overhang of his own nose and sniffed deeply.

"In the matter of a helpmeet as compared to an aide, I find it difficult to choose. The one has her, uh, feminine charms, the other his silence. But then, I've never had a helpmeet, and I've had any number of aides, so I may not be the best judge."

Arbuckle waved his cigar at the tent behind him. The sun shining through the striped roof and walls made bar patterns of shade on the dirt floor inside. "I think the army requisitioned this from lawn party surplus. There should be white-gowned virgins nudging wooden balls through those little wire arches, and blackamoors circulating with pitchers of switchel."

"This is the bug's bum, all right." Sam swatted a lazy mosquito. He looked out over the magnificent view of rolling hills and forests and the deep green stripe of trees hiding the river. Sam was grateful to be sitting down. He had eaten too little and drunk too much on the trip to the Arkansas. Since his arrival he'd hardly stopped traveling and talking to headmen of various tribes. He was beginning to feel the strain of the past few months.

"You're lucky you debarked at Webber's when you arrived last month," Arbuckle said. "*Facility* caught fire farther up stream."

"Indeed?"

"Yes. They were lighting the cannon to signal their approach here and it exploded. Killed several rousters and burned up some cargo. Pennywit escaped injury though. Thank God. He keeps us alive. He's one of the few who can make it here, no matter how low the water gets.

"Couple months ago a floating peep show arrived." Arbuckle blew smoke rings and studied them as he talked. "Barrels of whiskey aboard, and a few accommodating women. As if the hog ranches around here didn't cause trouble enough, they have to float sin in on the tide. Can't get supplies, just doxies." Arbuckle grinned at Sam. "Ah, well, you're only too aware of the burdens of command, I'm sure." He refrained from mentioning the scandal that had brought Sam to the Arkansas. "I expected to meet you earlier."

"I've been traveling a lot among the tribes. And there was a summer hunt on the outlet."

"The former outlet. The government doesn't think the Indians should have all that good land just to hunt on. Did you bag a buffalo?"

"Could hardly help doing it. We saw a herd pass for hours. If it wasn't such a thrill to bring down something that large, it could hardly be called a sport. Just point your gun and fire."

"No doubt my old friend Jolly has been filling your head with talk of his confederation of tribes, a wall to the east to keep out whites, et cetera."

"He has."

"You must realize the government would never stand for it. Standing Together raved about it for years, until he died. Funny, but I miss that old son of a bitch."

"I know how the government feels. But the Cherokee also have complaints about DuVal."

"Ah yes. Agent DuVal. I just had a set-to with him myself. I seized his unauthorized whiskey last month, as the law says I should. But neither the territorial district attorney, nor the marshall would press charges. And your Secretary of War, Mr. Eaton, has just ordered me to return it."

"He's not my Secretary of War, Matthew," said Sam mildly. But Arbuckle was tightly wound now.

"Enforcing that damned law has always been difficult. This affair with DuVal has made it impossible. Almost every boat that comes up the Arkansas is selling whiskey to the Indians and the enlisted personnel. The Arkansas border being so close to the Indian Nation is very convenient for them. Catch a man with a *hogshead* of it and he says it's for his personal consumption, or that he's intermarried into the tribe and therefore exempt. And among the worst offenders are your friends, the Rogers. Charles has a distillery and John continues selling it at his store.

"Try to stop the sale and a cry of injured outrage goes up. Traders are threatening to sue me for damages for 'interfering with the rights and privileges of the free democratic citizens of the Territory of Arkansas.' And your Cherokee aren't any help either. The most exercised word in their vocabulary is *duyukduh*, justice."

"*Duyukduh*." Sam laughed. "I've heard it often."

"They say it's their right to drink if they choose. Why should white people be allowed whiskey and Indians not? I can see their point, actually."

"But it does loose ravening havoc among them," said Sam.

"And I suppose Jolly has told you about the annuity frauds and the broken treaty promises, the land grabbing and the war with the Osage." Arbuckle slouched resignedly farther down in his chair. When it came to the Indians' problems he felt like Sisyphus rolling the boulder up the hill, only to have it fall back down on him.

Arbuckle was prepared to be wary of Houston. He didn't relish the idea of an outsider arriving and proclaiming himself an instant expert on the Indians' intricate problems. He could interfere badly. But Houston seemed witty and likable enough. Intelligent and well read too, from what he'd heard about him. If the man had been a convicted ax murderer, being a good conversationalist would still earn him respect in this misbegotten society. Arbuckle had a feeling he was going to enjoy the peculiar ex-governor's company. *Perhaps this place has made me a bit peculiar myself*, he thought.

Chapter 44

Tiana covered her mouth, but not quickly enough to catch an elusive giggle. Reverend Cephus Washburn continued his sermon while his interpreter translated it for the congregation of eight bored Cherokee. Mrs. Washburn pumped out "Abide with Me" on her foot organ while the congregation approximated the tune and words, using the small hymnals printed in Sik'waya's syllabary.

Then they filed out of the church. They headed for a table to collect cider and raisin cakes, their reward for sitting through the service.

"Mrs. Gentry," said Washburn. "What was so humorous about my sermon?"

"I don't like to snitch, Beloved Father."

"I know my interpreter takes liberties with my words. What did he say?"

"He said, 'Father Washburn tells me to say to you that in the sight of God there are but two people—the good people and the bad people. But I do not believe him. I believe there are three kinds; the good people, the bad people, and the middle kind, like myself.' " Washburn shook his head, as much as his high, stiff collar would allow.

"I suppose you agree with him."

"No, I don't agree with him."

"You don't!" Washburn turned to her with hope in his eyes.

She pitied him. He was so certain he was right. And he was so unsuccessful at convincing her people of it. At best they merely added hell and the devil to their own assortment of demons and fairies.

"No," she said. "I think there are as many kinds as there are individuals. Each has his or her own measure of good and evil. I can't imagine the measures ever being exactly alike, because each of us has different experiences to add to the one or the other. Some people live longer, and so their measure of each is greater."

"Ah, my child, you've been here two months now, and I wonder when you will see the light and join our church."

"The world is my church, Beloved Father. How can one collect holiness and put it in an ugly wooden building?"

Reverend Washburn started to object, and Tiana held up her hand.

"You have tried to explain it many times," she said. "But it still makes no sense to me. It makes no sense to my people. We cannot understand why you Christians guard your religion so jealously. You treat it as a jewel to be put in a box and looked at only on Sunday morning. This jewel is for the Loud Talkers. No one else may look at it. This one is for The Ones Who Go To Water, the Baptists. And this one is for the Presbyterians. To capture sacred spirits and keep them in a house is impossible. That would be like trying to capture the air we breathe, the clouds, the trees, the running water. All of these things are holy."

"You're an intelligent young woman, Mrs. Gentry, surely—"

"Beloved Woman." One of Drum's many grandnephews rode up, out of breath.

"We don't shout on the Sabbath, son," said Washburn. Dirtthrower Tiger looked at him blankly. Tiana translated.

"Tell the Black Robe I apologize for interrupting his sorcery." The child looked frightened. "Am I in the path of his smoke?"

"No, you aren't," said Tiana. "Why have you just come looking for me?"

"Beloved Father says to come home quickly. An Intruder has attacked The Raven. Beloved Father needs you."

"What is he saying?" asked Washburn.

"He says General Houston is sick and John Jolly wants me to help care for him."

"Why doesn't he go to the cantonment? There's a surgeon there now."

"I think the surgeon died of the fever."

"Well, no offense to your people's traditions, Mrs. Gentry. But General Houston should receive civilized medical care. The Cherokee think fevers are caused by vengeful insects. It's a preposterous superstition."

"If Beloved Father asks me, I must go." As far as Tiana was concerned, the missionaries' most annoying trait was condemning any beliefs that weren't their own.

"You've come along so well with your French," Washburn said. "And we'll have students soon. You can help translate for us."

Tiana wavered. It was beautiful here, high on a bluff near the mouth of the Illinois River. She could see for miles in all directions. And Reverend Washburn had been kind to her. In spite of their limited understanding, he and Reverend Palmer were true friends to the Real People.

But she missed the music and the talk and the company at Drum's. She missed her mother and her family. Besides, the missionaries' approach to life was depressing. Tiana's French teacher, Jerusha Johnson, was constantly reprimanding her for this and that. And Jerusha was ten years Tiana's junior.

"A whistling woman and a crowing hen always come to the same bad end," she would say. Tiana whistled anyway, but the pleasure had been taken from it.

"I'll gather my things and come with you," Tiana told Dirt-thrower. "We can ride double."

On the trail from the mission they met Sik'waya. He was coming to pick up his monthly copy of *The Cherokee Phoenix* that arrived there with the mail packet from Cantonment Gibson. Sik'waya usually spent the night at the mission, then rode home. Or rather, his old horse plodded home, while Sik'waya sat in the saddle and read and reread his paper.

As Tiana rode past the corn and the cotton and tobacco in Sally Ground Squirrel's half-cleared fields, she wanted to turn around and go back to the mission. Why should she help Raven? What right did he have to show up here, after abandoning them, and expect to be treated like royalty? Her conscience rebuked her for being so spiteful. Surely Nanehi Ward never felt this way. A real *Ghigau*, a

Beloved Woman, wouldn't be petty. But Tiana didn't call herself a *Ghigau*. Others did.

And why had Drum called for her? He could cure someone as well as she could. Drum was sly. He was probably trying to drag her into a reconciliation. *It won't work, Beloved Father.*

Sally Ground Squirrel had cleared out the penthouse, the large, airy room tacked onto the back of the second cabin. Tiana found Drum sitting there by Raven's bed. He was dressed in his best clothes, to assure the spirits of his respect for them.

"My heart rejoices that you have just come, daughter," Drum said. Tiana had never seen him so distraught.

"Dirt-thrower told me there was an Intruder, an Important Thing."

"Yes. I thought you might have learned something at the god-school. I hear they have powerful medicine there."

Tiana pulled a small flask from the leather bag at her waist. She uncorked it and held it out for Drum to sniff. His nose wrinkled, recoiling of its own accord.

"What is it?"

"Venice Treacle."

"What's in it?" Drum was always interested in new medicine.

"Vipers, wine, opium, herbs and spices, licorice, roses, St. John's wort, germander, the juice of rough sloes, and honey."

"Does it work?"

"Beloved Father Wasuh'huna, Washburn, said it might. It tastes vile, so it must have some effect." She pulled a chair close and stared down into the sleeping Raven's face. "The Important Thing seems strong. Why isn't he at the soldier place?"

"He made me promise not to take him there. He said he wanted to die here, with those he loved." Drum's voice caught, and his hand trembled as he lit his pipe with a rush light.

"Go to sleep, Beloved Father. I'll watch over him. At dawn we can take him to water. Maybe the two of us can convince the Important Thing to leave." Drum nodded.

"My heart rejoices that you've returned to us, daughter. The house is lonely without you. The people come here daily, to ask you to work for them. We miss your voice in counsel. The Raven asked for you."

Drum plodded from the room, but he didn't go to sleep. He circled the cabin in the dark, chanting and ringing it with the sacred smoke of remade tobacco, and enclosing his beloved son in its care.

Tiana turned her attention to the patient. The room smelled. Raven had suffered diarrhea and vomiting for three days. He had been carefully cleaned up, but the odor lingered. Tiana took some peeled cedar twigs from a pile of them on a shelf. She brushed off a dusty, shallow pottery bowl, lit the twigs, and put them in it. They would sweeten the air, and they would rid the room of *anisgina*, malevolent ghosts.

Raven began to breathe more quickly. He moaned and twisted in his sleep and shook violently. Tiana pressed her long fingers gently into one side of his neck. His pulse was speeding up. Another attack was coming. With her other hand she felt under his long white shirt. His spleen was enlarged. He began to mumble and toss.

"Hush," she murmured, although she knew he couldn't hear her. "Hush, old friend."

"Eliza," he muttered. "I believe you, Eliza. Please." He sobbed as though his heart would break. "So cold. I'm sorry, Mother." His words tumbled out in a jumble. He raved for an hour while she sat, holding his hand and trying to soothe him. Finally he fell asleep again. She felt the heat radiating from him. Fevers usually intensified at night. That was when witches, night-goers, roamed and tormented the sick.

Tiana got up and went outside. She sharpened four sticks and drove them into the ground at the corners of the house, with the pointed ends projecting outward. She was protecting The Raven from witches. In his weakened condition, he would be easy prey. She chanted one of Raincrow's charms, luring the witches to impale themselves on the stakes. Then she went back inside.

She bathed Raven's head and chest with the cold water Sally Ground Squirrel had left. She poured a little on his parched, raw lips. She knew his head and muscles must be aching. His fever was terribly high. Surely he couldn't survive this.

She propped her elbows on her knees and stared down into his face. She felt so helpless. If she only knew which insect or animal caused this, she could appeal to that creature's enemy to help. He seemed to have what the white doctors called the Intermittent. With luck, the fever would abate in eight hours, near dawn. He would either recover, or fall ill with another attack in a day or so.

When she pulled his shirt up to bathe his chest, she noticed the open sore on his thigh. He had refused to let her cure it many years before, but he couldn't refuse now. She took linn bark from her bag and went outside to pound it on a stone. She boiled it over a small fire, and bathed the wound with the ooze. The rest she let simmer. By morning it would be the consistency of jelly and she could make a poultice of it.

Tiana kept vigil all night, singing softly to herself to stay awake. She sang the Real People's songs, and she sang the ones her father and David had taught her. From time to time, Drum would peer in.

"You must sleep," she scolded him lightly.

"I can't."

When the first faint glow of dawn tinted the blue-black sky, Drum appeared again.

"It's time," he whispered. "How is he?"

"He'll probably wake in an hour or so." She straightened the blanket under him and grasped the corners at his feet. Drum took the corners by his head.

"I can ask for help," Drum said.

"We don't need it. He's much thinner now. We can carry him." They took him to the river, upstream from where the family members would soon be taking their morning bath. They laid him gently in a tiny meadow of soft grass and positioned him so he faced the water and the rising sun.

Drum dropped pulverized tobacco into water heated by the seven coals he carried in his kettle. He filled his mouth with some of the water. He stood facing east and calling silently on the gods of the winds. He blew the water over Raven, then he closed his eyes and chanted again. He repeated the rite four times.

> Gha! *Listen, O Great Whirlwind.*
> *You have just come to sweep the Intruder into the swamp.*
> *You shall scatter it in play!*
> *It shall utterly disappear. All is done.*

Raven stirred and muttered in his sleep. Drum sprinkled water around his blanket.

"He's just waking," said Tiana softly. "I pray he doesn't sicken again. The Intruder plays with us like cats play with mice in the corn cratch." When they'd carried Raven back to his bed, Tiana yawned and stretched wearily.

"Beloved Father, I'm going to sleep," she whispered. "Then I'll be cutting cane along the mouth of the creek. Send the black child, Martha, for me if he worsens."

"He won't worsen. Look, his fever's abating and he's waking. He doesn't look as yellow as before."

"Yes, Beloved Uncle." Drum had seen at least as many victims of ague as she had. He knew it went, only to come again. But he chose to ignore his experience.

Tiana walked out into the cool of the morning. Already she could feel currents of warmer air, like the breath of some large spirit animal. High above her the leaves of the tall sycamores and cottonwoods fluttered slightly. They would trap the cool night air and hold it against the heat of the day, when the women sat out here to do their work.

"Sister, how is he?" James held his horse's bridle. He had just arrived.

"He's just walking into the light now. But the Intruder still lurks in the shadows."

"I rode as fast as I could." He hurried inside.

Other family members and friends were gathering outside the door as Tiana walked away. She didn't plan to leave the prognosis to chance. When the sun rose the next morning she would float her divining needles in a still pool to see if Raven would live or not.

Being able to read the future was a frightening talent. She almost never resorted to it. More than once Tiana wished Spearfinger had never told her she had it, nor taught her how to use it. She couldn't read details, only general tendencies. She only knew if a thing would turn out well or badly. And even that was often ambiguous.

> *You, Provider,*
> *I ask You.*
> *You know.*
> *Tell me the way it is.*

As she drifted off to sleep, she planned to hang some of the family's mats on Raven's walls. The bright birds and flowers and geometric designs painted on them might cheer him. She was lulled by the soothing whir of a cousin's spinning wheel in the corner and the board that creaked rhythmically under the woman's bare feet. Out-side the open window, chickens and geese clucked. The latest litter of pups growled as they tussled in the dust. From far off came the tic-toc of axes and the whoomp of mortars and pestles.

There was also the faint sound of voices from Raven's room behind the wall where Tiana slept. Raven had trouble focusing as he rose out of the black pool of sleep.

"Father?"

"Yes, my son. I'm here. So is your brother."

"Greetings," said James. "I bet John you'd be racing Drum's new mare by the end of the week."

"Why not this afternoon?" asked Raven. But his voice was thick with fatigue and his eyes were sunken in their sockets. Pain pulsed in his temples, and his body felt as though someone had been beating him with clubs.

"Maybe tomorrow. You look tired now."

"Is there no one else here?" Raven squinted. The sunlight through the open doorway was blinding. It made his head throb even more. He closed his eyes to give them some relief.

"No. Do you want me to bring someone?" asked Drum.

"I must have been dreaming. I thought I heard a woman's voice. She sang to me."

"Tiana was with you through the night."

"Grandmother? She's here? She came back from the mission?"

"Yes, son. You'll see her." It pained Drum to know his favorite niece refused to see Raven. And it pained him more to know Raven sensed it. Raven had said nothing of his woman who lived toward the Sunland, and Drum didn't ask. He knew his son would tell him everything eventually.

Tiana avoided the house when Raven was awake. She and Fancy spent one day at the river, chopping at the dense, green stand of cane that grew for miles. They brought home a huge bundle of it, wrapped in old hides and dragged behind the horse. Another day they took the children in search of summer grapes and sunflowers, raspberries and plums. Tiana and Fancy also gathered baskets of nettles. Later they would strip the fibers from the stalks and make rope of them.

There was always work to do, but Tiana and her sisters and cousins found time to have fun. They picked flowers and wove them into diadems, and lazed in the shade of the massive scarlet oaks and ash. One especially hot day Tiana and Fancy and a small horde of girls, Drum's and Sally Ground Squirrel's granddaughters and nieces, carried the laundry to the river. They did their duty, beating the clothes with walnut paddles and getting thoroughly soaked in the process. Then they laid the clothes out to dry on the drift grass around the willow trees.

Tiana lay naked in the shade chewing on a juicy grass stem and watching the girls play. As she listened to their laughter and watched them splash in the river or pick berries, she suddenly remembered Spearfinger. She smiled to herself when she pictured Spearfinger's wizened face appearing like a demon and frightening her as a child. Now she understood that Spearfinger had been looking for the special one, testing her.

As she grew older, Tiana too looked for the one to whom she could pass her arcane knowledge. She loved all of the children, but none of them seemed to be the right one. At times she despaired of ever finding her. Then she considered how old Ulisi and Spearfinger and Ghigau had been when they taught her. At twenty-nine, Tiana felt old sometimes, but there was still no gray in her hair. *One must learn patience from the spider*, Ulisi always said.

For a few moments Tiana allowed herself to drift back into the past, to be with that long-legged, skinny child of the snarled hair and the scraped knees. As though she were accompanying another person, she went in memory with her to the lovely hills and secret places where she had played. She remembered the fairy world that child had lived in, close to the Little Ones under the bushes and closer even to the spirits than she sometimes felt now.

Was it possible for the memory of her younger self to call to her like the ghost of one dead? Tiana was overcome by a longing for a time and a place that were gone, that she could never see again. Even if she went back it wouldn't be the same. *You can't go back*, she told herself, fiercely. *You must find happiness here. Now.*

Two of the children threw themselves down beside her and set a wreath of flowers onto the thick black hair that reached her waist now. The hair made a perfect frame for the blue-eyed grass and bluebells.

"We picked blue flowers because they match your eyes," said Tsgoya, the child they called Bug. She had probably been named by a mischievous uncle. James had asked Tiana to name his girls, because John liked to tease him with the names he would give them.

"You have the most beautiful eyes I've ever seen," said Bug's sister, La'lu, Jar Fly. Definitely named by an uncle, Tiana decided.

"You make my heart glad, daughters." She smiled at them. She pulled a bluebell from nearby and held it out to them. "My father called these Witches' Thimble or Harebells, because in his country witches could change themselves into rabbits. But I think they're too beautiful to belong to witches."

The three of them leaned back in the grass and looked for shapes in the fluffy clouds flowing overhead. The undergrowth wasn't nearly as lush here as it had been in the mountains of the Blue Smoke. The wind blew incessantly, and summers were a trial. The Real People had settled in the eastern part of their new land, clinging to the hills and trees of the low mountains. But the open glades and flowers and the bluestem grass under the huge trees made the countryside seem like a park.

Cabins were being built and improved. Orchards were spreading. The fields were beginning to look like more than just ragged openings in the forest. As Tiana lay in the grass, with the children beside her and laughter riding the breeze, she dared hope her people would finally find peace here.

Tiana had been up most of the night, helping one of Sally Ground Squirrel's slave women with a difficult delivery. She hurried along the path to the river. Grandmother Sun would be up soon and Tiana wanted to be there to greet her.

She stopped at the edge of the trees near the small waterfall where she met Grandmother Sun each morning. Someone had arrived before her.

Raven stood alone in the shallows of Long Man. His clothes lay in a heap near Tiana. He faced away from her, toward the sun, which was just beginning to show above the trees. She saw him raise his arms and heard him chant Drum's morning song.

Tiana silently repeated her own song to the sun. She was annoyed to see him there. She couldn't greet Grandmother properly now, and he disturbed the tranquility and solitude. She had so few chances to listen to silence, so little opportunity to be by herself. She treasured these moments with the birds and the dawn, the sun and Long Man. She also caught herself studying his tall, muscular body, which annoyed her even more. It had been a long time since she had looked at a man like that.

She was about to shorten her usual ritual and go home when she saw Raven sway. He fell to his knees at the edge of the water and pitched forward until his elbows and head rested in the gravel of the shoreline. When he didn't move, Tiana became alarmed. She went to him, squatted beside him and touched his shoulder. He flinched.

"I'm sorry I startled you," she said. "You should be in bed."

"Grandmother?"

"Yes. I come here every morning."

"Forgive me. I didn't know. I didn't mean to interfere."

"Don't worry yourself. The sun will rise tomorrow. Can you stand?"

"My clothes."

"Here." With eyes averted, she waited while he dressed. He laid a hand on her shoulder to steady himself while he put on his pants.

"You're still weak, brother," she said. It wasn't as hard to call him that as it had been. He was gaunt and hollow-eyed. His handsome face had a yellowish tinge. His strong body was much leaner than it had been when he arrived. And he had been thin then. Now his clothes hung on him. She couldn't hold a grudge against someone who had suffered so much. Perhaps he had paid for the evil he had done and his life was back in balance.

"I had the fever a few years ago," he said. "It comes back now and then."

"We thought perhaps you would journey to the Nightland," she said. "Although the divining stones indicated you would live." She walked with her arm around his waist and his around her shoulder. He leaned heavily on her.

"I wished I could go there. I've wished it many times in the past six months."

"Hush. Don't talk of dying."

"I've been lost for such a long time, Grandmother. I forgot what's important. I forgot about the silence."

"You were living with white people. They don't like silence."

"Drum always said that. He said their talk made his ears ring. He said we can best know our own hearts in solitude, where there is no reflection from others."

"Perhaps you were trying to see yourself in the reflection of others."

Raven stared for an instant into her eyes. She was right. That was precisely what he had been doing, patterning his life after Andrew Jackson's. Then he realized he was being rude, and looked ahead again. A man could become lost in those blue-gray-violet eyes and never find his way out.

"Perhaps I was." He gathered his courage. Apologies didn't come easy to Raven. "Perhaps I was trying to lose the reflection of myself in your eyes, that last time I saw you in the east. I was ashamed of the man you saw in me."

"We won't talk of those days. We of the Seven Clans renew ourselves each year at the Green Corn ceremony, so we don't have to live with the regrets of a lifetime." She smiled in his direction. "When you think of it, it's one of our better ideas."

"White people could learn a lot from the Seven Clans."

"White people are *tsundige'wi*, closed anuses."

Raven laughed, for the first time in weeks. It hurt, but it felt good too. At last he began to think he would really live. *Tsundige'wi*. He had heard the term long ago. It meant They Have Them Closed, Stopped Up, Blind. But the inference was plainly what white people might refer to as having a tight arsehole.

When they reached the cabin, Tiana helped Raven onto a bench under the trees and ran inside to get him something to eat. Drum and the rest of the family had returned from their morning bath at the river. They stopped eating and stared at her. Tiana thought she detected a grin under Drum's solemn look.

"How is the patient?" he asked.

"He tried to go to water this morning. He's still very weak." She ladled some thin hominy gruel into a bowl and poured a bit of milk and honey on top of it. She was going back outside when Drum called to her.

"Daughter." He handed her a folding canvas camp chair. "Kalanah Ah'wuka sent it." Colonel Arbuckle had given Raven various small items to help his recuperation. But Drum was saving the brandy and strong cigars until Raven felt better.

Sally Ground Squirrel carried the chair outside, while Tiana took the bowl and horn spoon. When Raven was comfortably seated, Sally Ground Squirrel squeezed his arm and shook her head.

"*Ulesoda*," she said. "Thin."

Raven reached up and pinched her round cheek.

"*Galijohida*, fat," he said.

Sally Ground Squirrel laughed and left. The women set up their work under the trees, but away from Tiana and Raven. They were all hoping Tiana would make her peace with him and they didn't want to interfere.

Tiana settled down beside him and asked him questions about life in the white man's cities. Now that she had reconciled herself to forgiving him, she was rather enjoying getting to know him again. He was still the charming story-teller she had once known. In a way, it was as though the past twelve years had never happened.

"James says there are enough white men in Philadelphia alone to eat all the Indians if made into a pie," Tiana said.

"James is about right."

"Why are there so many?"

"They're just following the instructions in the Preacher Book. 'Be fruitful and multiply and replenish the earth.' "

"The earth is full enough. It doesn't need replenishing."

"Well, you know how prudish white people are about loving each other. The Preacher Book gives them an excuse to do it without feeling guilty. Reminds me of a story."

Without thinking about it, Raven had slipped into his old habit of talking to her as a friend. He had forgotten the taboos and circumlocutions he'd had to use in conversing with white women. But he also had to force himself to keep his voice casual. He felt like he was approaching a beautiful but unpredictable wild animal. He was terrified of offending her and sending her away from him again. Perhaps this time forever.

"Tell the story." Tiana was always ready for a story.

"Seems a newcomer was in a tavern and struck up a conversation with an older man. After discussing this and that, the newcomer said,'You're awfully pert for a fifty-year-old man.' 'Did I say I was fifty? Friend, I'm seventy years old,' said the geezer, hitting a fly with a spray of tobacco juice. 'And proud of it.'

" 'Well, I'll be' said the stranger. 'If he were alive today, I'll bet your pappy would be proud to have a son so young-looking.' 'Did I say my pappy was dead?' asked the old man. 'Why, he's ninety-five years old and busy as a barn fire.'

" 'Ninety-five!' exclaimed the young man. 'That's amazing! I'll bet if *his* pappy were alive, he'd be proud to have a son like that.' 'Did I say my grandpappy was dead? No, sir. Stranger, he's a hundred and twenty years old and getting married next week.' 'Getting married! Now why would a hundred and twenty-year-old man want to get married?' The old timer looks at him kinda sly and says, 'Did I say my grandpappy *wanted* to get married?' "

Tiana threw back her head and laughed. It was music to Raven. It had been a long time since he had heard such a laugh of pure, un-self-conscious delight.

"Now you must tell me a story," he said.

"What do you want to hear?"

"Why the buzzard is bald." He folded his hands across his lap and leaned back with his eyes closed to enjoy it.

"I should have known you'd want that one."

As the days went by, Tiana spent as much time as she could with Raven. At first she told herself she was only helping a patient recover. Then she admitted she enjoyed his company. He was wittier than anyone she had ever known. But there was a darker side to him too. Perhaps it was connected with his woman in the Old Country, the one he never mentioned. But she suspected it went deeper than that. What he didn't talk about tantalized her as much as what he did.

And he had a lot to talk about. He had traveled in the highest circles in the country. She listened to story after story of his escapades, and he never repeated one.

Then, as Raven's strength began to return, more and more headmen came to see him. They came not just from the Seven Clans but from the Creeks and the Choctaw. Word had spread that a friend of Father Jackson was living with Drum. Tiana was able to spend very little time with him. And she was sorry about it.

She began finding excuses to be near him. She began watching him from the corner of her eye. Asleep and awake, she began dreaming about him, his eyes and his smile and the curly, red-gold hair on his chest. At times her longing for him was so intense she suspected sorcery. Surely this preoccupation for a man couldn't be natural. She kept alert for signs that he had employed someone to bewitch her, but she could find none. Whenever her eyes met his she looked quickly away, and felt warmth spreading over her face and neck. He must have someone working for him. No man had ever made her feel this helpless confusion.

Raven was feeling the same way. At times, while sitting in council, the voices around him would become a senseless garble. He would be with Tiana again, laughing under the trees or strolling along the river.

He had asked no one to work for him to ensnare her. But he was working for himself. Several times a day, even while in council, he would softly repeat a charm he had learned as a boy. The Real People had many like it.

You will be unable to glance away.
Your thought is not to wander.
At my back upon the Eternal White Road will be the sound of your
  footsteps.
I have just come to draw away your soul.

Chapter 45

A score of drums throbbed with a steady pulse. The hawk bells and tortoise shell rattles strapped below the women dancers' knees, rang in the clear night air. The caller in the center of the dance ground chanted a line, and the hundred and fifty singers and dancers sang the response. Their voices blended in the hypnotic, sensuous chant that had been going on for an hour.

Raven's face was solemn as he watched the pheasant dance, but he was happy. He finally felt like he was really home. The missionaries had tried to stop the Green Corn ceremony. Drum had listened politely to their arguments and had gone on with the arrangements. This was the biggest festival the Old Settlers had ever had.

The dance ground and open, seven-sided council pavilion were in a depression, a bowl surrounded by gently sloping hills. The hillsides were covered with people all dressed in their best clothes. Torches and campfires flickered like fireflies in the blackness. Hundreds had been camping for a week in the forest around the new council house. As usual, they were a cheerful sight. Fortunately, the missionaries hadn't been able to persuade them to stop wearing the brightest colors available, and mixing them wildly.

Raven shared the front bench of Drum's clan section with the beloved men, the clan advisers. He was the only full-blood white man there, although there were whites at the fringes of the crowd. Some of them were officially intermarried into the tribe, but most were whiskey traders or drifters. Sitting behind the Beloved Men were the ball players, each with his own clan. As always, Raven felt himself being swept along by the rhythm, the swaying dance, and by the overwhelming feeling of unity and well-being that prevailed.

It was early September, 1829, the time of annual renewal. It was when all crimes but murder were pardoned, all debts forgiven. If an adulterous couple had managed to stay hidden throughout the year, the two could now live openly together.

For a week, people had been arriving at the small village nearest Drum's farm. It had a communal granary, the open council house, a *gatayusti* field and ball play area, as well as the dance ground. But the village wasn't what it had been in the east.

For years the missionaries and the government had preached that prosperity could only come to people who farmed their own land. Community fields were a fraction of what they had once been. The headmen of the National Council had passed a law prohibiting people from farming closer than a quarter mile from each other, to encourage individual initiative. Those who still lived in the villages tended to be poor and conservative, unwilling to change the old ways.

But the council house and the sacred fire were here. For days people had burned mats and stools and gourds and replaced them with new things. The night before the ceremony, all fires had been extinguished. Today, hundreds of people had filed through the airy council house. They had murmured their thanks to Drum and to the spirits as they received embers to ignite the dried moss or shredded bark in their containers.

The communal storehouse was full. Still people left more food there, the first fruits of their harvest. Baskets and sacks and mounds of food lay piled around the entrance. For a week, the village, with its humble cabins, had reverberated with laughter and singing.

Raven had been escorted from one feast to another, and he had gained back the weight he'd lost. There had been shooting matches and gambling, foot races and gambling, horse races and gambling, and ball play and gambling every day until it became too dark to see the ball. And there had been a great deal of drinking.

Drum had huffed his way up a ladder to the top of the council house each dawn. He had sucked in a deep breath and roused all of them from their beds with an eerie yodel. He said it was to frighten away evil spirits. But Raven figured he enjoyed scaring everybody.

Raven had been ill for so long that feeling well made him think he could do anything. Drum and James had a difficult time persuading him not to join in the ball play. He became indignant when James pointed out it was a young man's game, and Raven was no longer a young man.

Each night the moon grew fatter as though it too were enjoying the harvest. Tiana said it looked like a sleek, silver cat basking by the firelight of the stars. She and Jennie, Susannah and Raven and Drum's family had been sitting out under the trees and watching shooting stars blaze across the night sky.

Tiana. Raven thought of her now, as he often had in the past few weeks. He was so preoccupied with her he hardly noticed when the music and dancing stopped. Then Tiana herself moved gracefully to the middle of the dance area. Raven drew in his breath and leaned forward on the bench. Around him people murmured, "*Ghigau*, Beloved Woman." As Tiana strode into the fire's light, she strode into his heart and filled it.

She wore a tight jacket of thin white doeskin that stopped a few inches above her narrow waist. Her knee-length skirt was woven of black feathers and edged at the hem with white swan's down. The feathers seemed to breathe with life of their own, stirring as the skirt swirled around her long, slender legs. Her dense black hair hung loose to her waist. It swayed heavily from side to side as she moved. Long red and yellow ribbons had been plaited into it at the crown of her head, and they fluttered when she walked. She wore plain white deerskin moccasins and fringed leggings that hugged the contours of her legs. The flames of the large fire brushed her honey-colored skin with gold.

The hundreds of people on the hillsides and in the council house hushed. Raven saw Tiana's full lips move as she chanted something heard only by herself. Raven couldn't have taken his eyes off her if his life had depended on it. His love for her had been growing daily. Now it took hold of him completely. As the Real People put it, she had drawn away his soul. He was unable to think of anyone else.

Surely she was a sorceress. She was clothed in magic. How else could he explain the force that held him her prisoner. It wasn't just John's whiskey that made his head spin and his blood pound in his temples.

His heart ached with longing for her. He didn't see how he could bear the pain of it. The Real People called it *uhi'sodi*. "Loneliness" was the only English equivalent, but *uhi'sodi* was much more than that. It was a supernatural melancholy, a desperate yearning that seemed to afflict the Real People more intensely than others. The feeling tugged at his insides and shook his heart like a pupa rag.

Raven felt at the wristband of his shirt until he found the piece of paper hidden in the folds of his sleeve. Drum had given him a charm written in Sik'waya's syllabary. It was written in the margins of a stern letter from the new Secretary of War, John Eaton. Raven had to chuckle about what Eaton would say if he found out how the paper of his letters was used. But then, perhaps Eaton would understand better than most. He was certainly a prisoner of his love for Peg O'Neale Timberlake.

Drum knew what was troubling his son. He had always known. He didn't mention names when he gave Raven the charm, but he had a mischievous look in his bulging eyes.

"It's to attract someone," he had said. "It's to inform the Great Raven. He's a powerful love spirit. Almost as powerful as the Spider. But I can't give you Spider charm."

"Why not?" Raven had asked.

"Because Spider charms are too powerful. They ensnare. They create *uhi'sodi*. Incantations that call up *uhi'sodi* are unpredictable. They can cause unpleasant things to happen. I'll give you an example of a spider charm, but you must never use it. At least you'll be able to recognize one if you hear it."

"But what if someone doesn't want to be attracted?" Raven asked glumly.

"Drum thinks someone is lonely. That she walks the Blue Pathway of loneliness. Throughout the night her soul is empty and cries like the lonely hawk."

"She doesn't seem lonely."

"She is." And Drum went back to rolling strips of moist, aromatic tobacco into a long rope.

Now Tiana seemed far above loneliness or any other worldly concerns. She threw a handful of coarse salt at Drum's feet, and more into the fire. The flames flared a cold blue color. She waved a large white swan's wing over the water simmering in the big kettle. She picked up a basket and emptied its contents, leaves from Drum's holly bushes, into the water. The smell of the Black Drink filled the air. Raven remembered the rush of ecstatic feelings and visions the drink caused. Then Tiana began to speak.

"The people of the Seven Clans must remain united," she said, her voice carrying into the hills beyond the dance ground. She turned slowly to face each of the seven clan sections. "There are those who would divide us and turn us away from the path we have always followed. They have separated us from our land. They have separated some of us from our brothers, the animals, whose forgiveness is no longer asked when hunting them.

"Their whiskey separates us from our dignity and reason. They have divided the old from the young who no longer listen to their elders. They try to separate us from our religion and from our friend, Thunder. They encourage us to make new laws, separating the men from the women, laws that deny women their rightful voice in councils. They tell us to accumulate wealth so the rich can scorn the poor. They would have us guard our wealth rather than share it, so we learn to mistrust each other.

"We must not heed those who would divide us. They do it to weaken us and steal our land. We must think of each other as family. We must not abandon the ways that made us strong and happy. Else we will be lost in a fog and wander a path that leads to destruction."

When Tiana had finished and sat down, the drumming started and the ball players began their dance. They leaped and dodged, imitating the game, until their naked bodies gleamed with sweat, from exertion and the heat of the fire and the effects of the Black Drink. Now and then they would leave to vomit into a small ravine set aside for the purpose.

When they left the dance floor, two hundred eagle dancers swooped and rose and whirled, like eagles soaring and diving. They held their arms outstretched and eagle feathers in their hands. It was a long, exhausting dance. When it was finally over, The Girth and James Rogers appeared.

They wore bearskins, and they shuffled and whoofed around in the circle of firelight. They roared and threatened each other by stamping and slapping the ground. Then The Girth pretended to turn over logs in search of grubs, and James sat placidly eating invisible berries. When other dancers pretended to stalk them, the children shouted warnings to them. There was a loud struggle when the bears rushed the hunters. Someone fired two shots into the air, and James and The Girth fell. They rolled and quivered and pretended to die.

Their dance meant the serious part of the ceremony was over. The chatter and laughter rose as people settled down for a long, good time. The drummers slowed their beat. Raven heard the distant jingle of bells and rattles. The first singer seated in the center of the dance ground began the chant of the friendship dance. The clear voices of the women dancers answered from the darkness, and everyone turned to look for them. Their high, sweet song gave Raven chills. He took another sip of the flask James had given him.

He saw Tiana lead the line of women into the torchlight. Their long white dresses looked like light from the moon overhead. Tiana had changed her feathered skirt for a pale doeskin dress, decorated with fringe and beads and colored ribbons. Her legs were bare but for the strings of hawk bells tied below her knees.

The women moved in a graceful, shuffling trot around the edge of the dance ground. As they went, each woman selected a partner from among the men. When Tiana stopped in front of him, Raven could only stare at her. She smiled, her white teeth flashing in her dark face. She beckoned with a toss of her head, but Raven's legs refused to move. His legs knew as well as he did what happened in the friendship dance.

The old half-smile flitted across her face as she surveyed his new beaded shirt, his yellow leggings, the silk turban with the plumes nodding over it. She took his hands in hers, pulled him bodily to his feet, and put his hands on her shoulders. When she rose on her toes, she could almost stare him in the eye.

Facing their partners and moving sideways, the men and women followed Tiana and Raven counterclockwise. Tiana pulled the circle of dancers into a spiral that wove toward the central fire like a moth's flight into a candle. But the heat Raven felt wasn't from the fire. There was a stirring in his groin. He wasn't aroused as much by her hands gently gripping his shoulders as he was by the knowledge of what was coming.

The first singer finished his song, and the dancers and audience whooped. The second singer began. Raven's heart beat faster. The pantomime was about to begin. Raven had a moment of panic. *Oh, Provider*, he prayed, *don't let me do anything foolish tonight*.

At a signal from the singer, each pair of dancers held hands. Then they crossed their hands, bringing Raven closer to Tiana. He felt as though he were falling into her dark blue eyes, tumbling helplessly head over heels. Her hands were warm as she moved them so her palms lightly touched his. He felt her finger lightly brush against the inside of his hand. It was the most intensely erotic sensation he had ever felt.

The old teasing look was in her eyes, but there was something else too. The two of them moved together, following the singer's directions almost unconsciously. They were aware of nothing but each other, lost in the sensual beat and the swaying of bodies.

Tiana put her forearms on his shoulders, and he did the same. Yet still their bodies didn't touch. Raven's heart beat in time with the drum, with the pulse of the earth under his feet and the star-strewn sky above him. Tiana stroked him under the chin, and he did the same to her. Her skin was so soft, so smooth. He was eager for the next part of the dance, and frightened of it too.

As though to prolong the tension, Tiana broke the sequence of steps. She raised her hands, palms in, to shoulder height and made a quick half-turn to the left, then to the right. Raven and the others followed her lead.

Then the two files of dancers crowded together, so their movements would be hidden. Tiana reached out and ran her hands over Raven's chest. He stroked her firm, round breasts. Their full curves were so perfect, so delicate, he had trouble breathing. Under the thin, velvety doeskin he could feel the nipples harden. A cold sweat formed on his forehead and at the base of his spine.

Raven felt Tiana's hands stroking his cock, which throbbed at her touch. He caressed her upper thighs and ran a hand down the triangle of her lower belly and into her groin. Her full lips parted, and her eyes filled with desire. To be so alone and intimate with her, yet surrounded by hundreds of people, was tantalizing to the point of insanity. Raven had done the friendship dance before, when he was much younger. It had been a light-hearted, teasing thing then. It had been nothing like this.

The third singer began, and there was another whoop from the dancers. The files backed away from each other and the couples held hands again. They zigzagged after Tiana and Raven, who circled the area one last time. Raven was frantic at the thought that this would end soon. Concentrating on Tiana's lovely, untamed face, he silently repeated the charm Drum had given him.

Like the Red Lightning . . .
Like the Fog . . .
Like the Panther . . .
Like the Red Wolf . . .
Like You, Red Raven, you Great Wizard.
I will be walking in the very middle of her soul.
Now! The smoke of the White Tobacco just surrounds her.

The dancers separated, and Tiana went to sit with her clan under the pavilion. Raven heard her bells jingle as she untied them and put them under her bench, on the other side of Drum. Drum decided to sit back in his chair, leaving a clear view between his adopted son and his favorite niece. And Tiana stared at Raven. He felt her eyes on him, and he concentrated on the flask of whiskey as the booger dancers burst through the crowd.

They didn't distract Tiana, however. *Damn her*, Raven thought. *She was a single-minded child, and now she's a single-minded woman.*

Raven forced himself to sit still under Tiana's scrutiny. He did not know she had been studying him for weeks. She had studied his face and his body as he slept or raved with fever. She had studied him while laughing with him under the trees or scooping hominy mush from the same bowl. Inside the man he was, she found the boy and the friend he had been.

But this was unexpected. Her body still tingled from his touch. There was a pulsing heat, an ache in her groin. She glanced over at him again. His wild, russet hair was caught in a long braid down his back. But locks of it escaped and curled around the edges of his silk scarf and tumbled into his eyes. His nose was straight and strong. Tiana wanted very much to run her fingers over his lips, then down his neck and chest and abdomen. At thirty-seven, and without ever really working at it, Raven had a magnificent body.

He turned and looked at her. Tiana flushed and stared him in the eye. Drum pretended to see only the booger dancers. They were running through the crowd, scattering people in all directions. They sprayed water and scattered humus, shouting it was dung.

Tiana stood and began to work her way out of the mob. Raven drained the flask in one long drag and hurried after her. He was afraid of losing her in the confusion, afraid his intentions would be obvious to others, and afraid he had mistaken her look.

He saw her dress, pale in the moonlight, flitting ahead of him through the trees. It was a relief to leave the noise and the smells of bile and dust, sweat and tobacco smoke and the sassafras odor of the Black Drink. The cool night air cleared his head a bit, but he was still giddy. His ears rang and his groin throbbed.

Tiana headed for a moonlit meadow near the river. She turned and waited for Raven, who walked into her arms.

"Beloved," he breathed into her hair. She unwound the scarf from his head and loosened the hair from its braid. She buried her fingers in his thick curls. Then she ran her fingertips lightly across his mouth. He caught them and kissed them, then he kissed her palms.

She held his face in her hands and brought his head down until her lips could brush his. She searched his eyes once more, to reassure herself this was the right thing to do. Then she kissed him harder. He held her tightly against him, lost in the feel of her, and ran his hands down the smooth slope of her back.

Reluctantly, he let her go. He untied his belt and took off his buckskin coat and laid it on the grass. Before he could do anything else, she had run her hands into the opening where his leggings were tied to his loincloth. She caressed the back of his bare thighs and ran her warm hands up under the curve of his strong haunches. He shuddered at her touch.

She untied his loincloth thong, and it and his leggings dropped. While he tugged the leggings over his feet, she pulled her dress off in one, quick motion. She stood naked, glowing in the moon's light. Her shoulders and the tops of her breasts were dusted with silver. Raven was afraid to touch her, afraid she would disappear like some teasing sprite. A woman this beautiful was a possibility, one this free was not.

Tiana touched him first, stroking the scar on his thigh where the wound had finally healed. He picked her up easily and laid her gently on his coat. They made love slowly as if this were the only important thing in the world and they had a lifetime to do it.

Finally, they lay side by side on their backs. Tiana threw Raven's shirt over them to keep the dew off. She rested her head on Raven's shoulder, and he laid his head on his other arm, which was crooked behind him. Tiana ran her fingers gently along his thigh and leg.

"I think I love you," Raven said. He shuddered. "But is this love, or is it malaria?" She laughed lightly.

"You are walking in the center of my soul," she answered.

Overhead, the moon seemed to be caught, like a ball of fire burning in the branches of the cottonwood under which they lay.

"Grandfather Moon looks like *Atsil'dihye'gi*, Fire Carrier, trapped in a web," murmured Tiana.

"You've caught me in your web, Spider Eyes," said Raven.

"Spider Eyes?"

"You've bewitched me," said Raven. "You've asked the White Spider to help you."

"Do I need help?"

"No." He laughed. "You need no help." He kissed her smoky-smelling hair. He inhaled the fragrance of the columbine seeds she chewed and used as perfume and the sassafras of the Black Drink she had had. "A poet once said, 'Our souls sit close and silently within, and their own webs from their own entrails spin; and when eyes meet far off, our sense is such that spider-like, we feel the tenderest touch.' "

"Who was the poet?"

"Dryden. An Englishman. He lived long ago and far away."

"No matter. He could have been one of the Seven Clans."

"Yes. He was wise enough and word-weaver enough."

They lay listening to a mockingbird imitating an entire flock.

"So much music in such a tiny creature," Tiana said softly.

"No wonder he's believed to be magic."

The mockingbird cycled through a seemingly endless series of calls and whistles and warbles, some shrill, some melodic. When Raven and Tiana had been quiet a while, a cricket began singing close by. Tiana could picture him in his dark, solitary hole, his serrated legs vibrating urgently. She tried to imagine what it must feel like to be a lovesick cricket, and she giggled.

"What is it?" Raven had been almost asleep, and stirred.

"I'm just happy."

"I didn't know there was any happiness left," he said. "I thought I must surely have it all."

They watched the moon fall through the cottonwood's branches. Torchbearer, the morning star, rose. Raven felt absolutely at peace. There was no need to fill the silence with chatter. He and Tiana finally fell asleep with their arms around each other.

When dawn came, Raven rolled over and murmured to her. He opened his eyes and realized she wasn't there, although her dress was over him. Naked, he padded to the river. She stood with her back to him and faced the east. He waited silently while she greeted Grandmother Sun.

As she came back up the path, she spotted him sitting cross-legged on a flat boulder. She laughed and beckoned with her head. With their clothes in their hands, they walked to a spring-fed pool trapped in a limestone basin. It was tucked into a deep crease in the hills and surrounded by dense brush and tall trees. They chewed dogwood twigs and brushed their teeth. Raven smiled as Tiana casually stirred the pool with a long stick.

"*Laecedaemon*, my love?" he asked.

"What?"

"A mythical lake monster. You're educated, Spider Eyes. Surely you don't fear the Great Leech." He came to stand beside her on the rock ledge rimming the pool. The two of them were mirrored in the shimmering, blue water.

"If I do fear him, it's your fault."

"My fault?"

"Yes. You threw me into that dreadful, watery pit, long ago. I never forgot it. You should be ashamed, terrorizing an innocent child."

"You were never innocent."

"Liar!" She shoved him with her shoulder so he fell sideways into the pool. Arms and legs flailing, he landed with a huge splash. He shuddered as the cold water hit him, and he surfaced snorting and blowing. He grabbed her ankle and pulled her in with him. They roughhoused like children, each struggling to duck the other.

They waded from the water, the drops beading and gleaming on their bodies as the morning rays broke in golden stripes through the trees.

"I feel like Adam and Eve in the garden, before Uktena, the Great Snake, spoiled the party," said Raven. They were drying each other with Raven's stroud loincloth when the bushes parted.

"*A'siyu*, sister," said Tiana cheerfully. Annie looked startled and guilty. "Starting early?" Tiana asked as Annie backed out of the small glen. They heard a man's voice somewhere behind her. Tiana shook her head and laughed. "That one's fooling her husband again," she said. "And she has a whole year before she can be forgiven."

Raven stood behind Tiana and put his arms around her waist, pulling her to him.

"And have you forgiven me?" he whispered in her ear. "Do you still hate me for sending your people here?"

She turned and held him close, giving him the answer with her body.

Chapter 46

Drum stared off toward the east, the Sunland, as Tiana read her sister Mary's letter to him. She often translated letters for him. Drum had never learned Sik'waya's syllabary. His attitude toward writing was ambiguous. He recognized its power. He treasured charms written in it. He often had Tiana transcribe his own incantations.

He hid the scraps of paper along with his other medicine, his sacred tobacco, and his powerful but terrifying red-and-green tourmaline crystal that was the eye of the Great Snake, Uktena. They were all carefully wrapped and buried in jars in the yard or hidden in the rafters. Drum changed the hiding places every so often. In the case of Uktena's eye, it wasn't so much to keep others from finding it as to keep the eye from escaping and coming after him to do him harm.

Drum said he was too old to learn such strange skills as marking, the Real People's word for writing. But Tiana thought that was an excuse. In a sense Drum considered writing both sacred and profane. Capturing spirits and imprisoning them on leaves was a precarious practice, likely to irritate them. It was something he was content to let others do. The care and feeding of his crystal, the eye, was as much responsibility as he wanted.

For Tiana, the chore of translating was double-edged. She knew

all the news, official and unofficial. That was good. But the news
was usually bad. An outsider wouldn't have detected much anxiety
in Mary's letter. It was terse, yet filled with the circumlocutions the
Real People used.

It spoke of the birth of a granddaughter named Annie, the illness
of a neighbor, two dollars and sixty-five cents that Mary owed Drum
and promised to repay, with interest. Her letter had the false stops
that many of the Real People included in their correspondence. And,
as with many letters, the meat of the matter was in the postscript.

"Now! That is what I, Mary, have just stopped writing," she said.
But the letter continued.

> Now I greet you this morning from far away. *Ata'la dala'nigei*,
> the yellow metal, has just been found nearby. It is not easy
> here. That is all I have just written you, Beloved Uncle, for
> my sister to read.

It is not easy here. In the dappled shade of the trees and the laughter
of those around her, the words chilled Tiana. Drum too knew what
they meant. He sat in silence a long time while Tiana waited with
the paper folded in her lap. *Ata'la dala'nigei*. Gold had been discovered in the place called Lick Log. Lick Log was part of the Cherokee
Nation, but it was in the territory the Georgians claimed as theirs.
There had been a lot of speculation in council about the consequences
to the people who lived there. The only thing white people coveted
more than land was the soft yellow metal.

Soon Drum would take the letter, committed to memory after
two readings, and join the group of men sitting under the trees. But
Drum had thoughts he wanted to mull over before he presented the
letter. At times like this he often discussed his ideas with Tiana, as
a sort of rehearsal. He spoke now in English, his accent heavy with
the lilting *l* sounds and the confusion of *D* and *T*. He seemed to be
reciting something.

> Congress wants none of your lands, or anything else which
> belongs to you; and as an earnest of their regard for you, we
> propose to enter into the articles of a treaty.

"What is that, Beloved Father?" asked Tiana.
"The Treaty of Hopewell, made toward the Sunland, long, long

ago. I was there. I was a young man." His voice took on a sad, faraway tone. "War was exciting then. We were so confident. But the old men wanted peace. The Beloved Woman, Nanehi Ward, spoke. The old men took the hands of the white men in friendship. The Tassel spoke. He said, 'I have shown you the bounds of my country on my map and on the map of the United States. If the commissioners cannot do me justice in removing people from the fork of the French Broad and the Holston Rivers, I am unable to get it myself. Are Congress, who conquered the king of Great Britain, unable to remove these people?'

"The Tassel is fortunate perhaps. He is living in the settlements of the Nightland. I hope the hunt is good there and that he has no time to look down at us. It would make his heart heavy to see how we have fared. I fear for our people in the Old Country, toward the Sunland." Drum rose heavily to his feet.

"But they are going to plead their case in the white man's high council," said Tiana. "They have good quarrelers, lawyers. They'll prove the land is theirs by right."

Drum shook his head as he shuffled toward the men who rose to greet him. Tiana realized he looked old. His usual smile and the glint in his eyes were gone. He paused and turned to stare at her.

"My ambition was to wander a white path. I wanted only to smell the flowers along the way, without disturbing the flow, the pulse of the seasons, whose breath is the wind. That was the only ambition I had. I wanted to harvest enough to share with all who came to my door.

"I once thought war was the greatest test a man could face. I was wrong. This peace is much more difficult. This," he fumbled for words, "this destruction of our pride, this seduction of our men with whiskey and of our women with favors. Beloved Daughter, if you and The Raven have children, guard them well. To watch them grow up in a world such as this, it is a sad thing." He turned and went to join the other headmen in their informal council under the trees.

It was so tranquil here in the shade of the huge sycamores and cottonwoods, Tiana tried to forget Drum's words. Here, now, there was laughter around her. It was the time of the Great Medicine ceremony. Everyone from the neighboring farms had gathered, as in the old days, to stand in the cauldron of Long Man and be purified for the coming year.

They had walked in groups along the green tunnels over the paths that converged on Sally Ground Squirrel's snug cabins. They came with the family dogs trailing behind them and children in tow or on their backs.

Some of the women carried on their shoulders enormous bundles of carded wool wrapped in sheeting and pinned shut with thorns. The huge bundles looked burdensome, but weighed little.

While they were here, the men sat in council or entertained themselves with ball play and races. The women visited with each other and made their work lighter by sharing it. They gossiped and sang and took a break now and then to gamble at Black Eye, White Eye.

Tiana sat between the roots of a sycamore, away from the bustle, yet relishing it. She leaned against the rough trunk, crossed her long legs in front of her, and closed her eyes to listen to the sounds.

There was the hollow patta-patta-pat of Nannie's carved wooden paddle against an unfired pottery jar. She heard the thunk of wooden ladles against the sides of an iron kettle as two women stirred the cloth they were dying. Others sat in a patch of waving cane splints, the woof of their baskets. To sit with basket makers was like being in a field of dry grass with a gentle wind blowing, but the sound was too subtle to carry over the noise in the yard.

Other women showed the children how to string slices of dried pumpkin and the twisted green beans. Some pounded corn or sewed. Tiana heard Fancy humming to herself as she scraped kernels of hard corn off the cob. Fancy's humming and singing were among the pleasantest sounds Tiana knew.

Harry Haralson was having the most fun. He wore a blindfold and groped around, trying to catch the young women who taunted him. They darted in to touch him or tug at his clothes. The tail of his shirt had pulled out in back and flapped after his slender body.

"Ha'li, Ha'li," the young women called. "*Na, na.* Here, here." Harry always said there was no such thing as an ugly woman, only some a bit less favored than others. And the women of the Real People, he said, were surely among the most favored of all the fair beauties he had seen in his travels. He loved them and they loved him. If they called him Ahyelsdi Kayuhsoli, Knife Nose, behind his back, it was with affection.

Tiana tried to separate Raven's voice from among the jumble. But he was hard to hear. To his credit, Raven listened more than he talked in most of these councils. She looked over at him and found him staring hungrily at her. He winked slowly in her direction. He could let his mind wander. Despite the clouds of tobacco smoke over the group of men, no serious issues would be debated until after the meal.

Tiana could smell the food simmering now. *Salo-lu-gama* was a special stew of young squirrels roasted in hot ashes, then boiled with hominy. The picnic would go on all day. People would sleep in the cabins or in wagons or under shelters in the yard and begin again in the morning. Tonight, as they had for the past two weeks, Tiana and Raven would sleep together in the room where she had nursed him through his illness. But she and Raven had been planning a cabin of their own. James and John and Coffee promised to help with it.

Raven had observed the correct etiquette in asking for Tiana's hand. He had enlisted Sally Ground Squirrel to speak with Jennie about it. He waited for Jennie to give her permission before he began living openly with her daughter. There had been no wedding ceremony. But that was usual for two people who had been married before. *Let it continue this way forever, Provider*, Tiana breathed.

There were stifled screams as the young women around Harry scattered. Harry took off his blindfold and looked up at a half-naked Osage sitting on a horse.

"*Oeh*," said the warrior.

"Oh, shit," said Harry. "Sam," he called over his shoulder.

"*Oeh*," the man said again.

"God save you, God save you kindly." Harry bowed and smiled. He backed toward the safety of the men, and the grim Osage followed. His tall roach bobbed as he dismounted. He was obviously dressed in his best clothes, but they were tattered, like gentility gone to seed. His loincloth was frayed at the edges and his moccasins patched. There were beads missing from the design on them. His musket was ancient, but polished lovingly. His horse looked jaded. Drum approached him with Raven behind him.

"*Oeh*," the Osage said once more.

"*Oeh*, welcome, friend," said Drum. Harry sat with a thud at the base of a tree.

"Lordy," he said, to no one in particular. "And it was my life I thought he'd be having, sure."

The Osage drew a string of wampum, polished purple and white shell beads, from his saddlebag. "For Kalanu," he said.

"Daughter," called Drum. "We need you to interpret." Everyone gathered to listen while the Osage messenger read the pattern of the beads, and Tiana translated. The designs symbolized hands of peace and friendship to the Cherokee. When the brief council was over, Raven and Haralson went to saddle their horses, while Drum hurried around collecting what they would need for the trip.

"Raven, don't go," Tiana pleaded with him. She was suddenly and painfully aware of how David must have felt when she went riding off on some mission or other. But she feared more than just loneliness now.

"I must go, Spider Eyes. The Osage want to talk to me."

"They may kill you."

"What's that?" asked Haralson. "And is it a dangerous thing we're doing then?"

"No," said Raven.

"Yes," said Tiana.

"Oh, good," said Harry. "That's settled." He tightened the saddle cinch. "We're after destroying ourselves."

"They don't want to kill us. Be reasonable, Spider Eyes. I won't be gone long." He saw her eyes glisten with tears. "I'll be safe."

"They're so unpredictable. They killed my friend and sister, one of their own. They hate us, Raven."

"I have to go." He hugged her and kissed away the single tear that ran down her cheek.

"I've just found you," she murmured against his chest. "I can't lose you. I've lost so much. Losing you would be more than I could bear."

"I'll be back, in a few days. A week maybe."

"My son," called Drum. "The Little One waits."

"Then I'll go with you." Tiana turned and strode toward the shed where the saddles were kept.

"No." Raven ran after her and took her gently by the arm. "I understand," he said. "I know about your dreams. I hear you cry out in the night, calling the names of your loved ones. You will not lose me. I feel there's no danger here. But if there is, they can only kill me. They can do worse to you. I cannot take that risk." He kissed her forehead. Then he mounted and cantered to catch up with Harry and the messenger, who seemed to be in a hurry.

Through a blur of tears, Tiana watched them go. Then she headed for the pasture.

"Daughter," said Drum. "*Gha*! Listen! When you go after him, will you take something for me?" Tiana laughed. She linked her slender arm through Drum's thick one.

"Of course, Beloved Father. What is it?"

"The ceremonial wampum and my peace pipe. I'll tell you how to interpret the wampum and you can teach Raven."

"It's not too late. You can send someone else to catch him."

"You might as well do it, since you're going after him anyway. You have always had a way of appearing where you were not wanted. Like a fly in the hominy. My son has been too long with the white people. He thinks he can give a woman an order and expect it to be followed."

"Please hurry with the wampum, Beloved Father." Tiana knew how Drum could putter when he began searching through his medicine and valuables. He had a way of forgetting the hiding place of the particular item he was seeking. He spent a lot of time sorting through everything else, reminding himself of the charms that went with them, the uses and the taboos.

She packed food for the trip and her ceremonial clothes, in case she attended a council. She rolled her blankets into a flexible cane mat that would shed water, and tied it behind her saddle. When Drum brought the wampum, she handled it carefully. It was old and very beautiful. Sally Ground Squirrel had repaired some of the weakened sinews on which the beads were strung.

This particular wampum was a wide beaded belt with five narrower beaded strips hanging from it. The geometric patterns of the bead work represented friendship, accomplishments, buried hatchets, and welcomes for the rising generations. When she had learned what the symbols stood for, she rewrapped it reverently. It had been at Hopewell, so many years before. And it had been at many councils since then. Its opalescent purple and white beads had been polished to a soft sheen by the years of handling.

Tiana caught up with the men in the middle of one of Harry's long monologues that had Raven laughing helplessly. Even the Osage looked faintly amused, although he couldn't understand a word. The average Osage spoke a little Cherokee by necessity, and French by preference, but disdained English. Harry had given this one a precious cigarette. The Osage had regarded it intently, trying to comprehend its function. Finally he had carefully unrolled it, put the tobacco in his pipe, twisted the paper, and used it to light the pipe.

Raven was glad to see Tiana. As the trail between them had lengthened, he had regretted not letting her come. Even Harry's ridiculous stories weren't enough to keep him from thinking of her.

"Where are we going?" Tiana asked when they were headed north again.

"As best I can understand, we're going to Colonel A.P. Chouteau's domain."

"I've heard of him," she said.

"Everyone's heard of him. He seems to be a bit reclusive though," said Raven. "I don't know what to expect. Lisa, Astor, most of the men in the fur business can be a ruthless lot. Stay close when we get there, Spider Eyes."

"What has everyone heard about Chouteau?" Harry asked.

"That his father settled Saint Louis," said Raven. "That the family made a fortune in the fur trade. That the Osage revere Auguste Pierre, the brother we're going to visit. I think Auguste Pierre graduated from West Point, though it's hard to say. There are a dozen or more brothers and half-brothers, all named Auguste or Pierre or Auguste Pierre or Pierre Auguste. There is one named Auguste Aristide and one named Rene Auguste. Their mother must have been feeling fanciful when those two were born. At any rate, it's difficult to keep them straight."

The hills around the small party were steep, but the country was more open, the trees shorter than farther to the south and east. Their Osage guide hustled them through the twisting valley of the Neosho River. He wouldn't even let them stop to chase the herds of deer that crossed their path. That was almost enough to throw Harry into a sulk.

They approached Chouteau's trading post late in the afternoon of the second day. The post was a good-sized village of fifty or more cabins scattered through the forest. From the rolling houses at the wharf where the hogsheads were stored to the cabins and huts, the area was teeming with activity.

Tiana lifted her feet higher in the stirrups to keep them out of the reach of the Osage dogs. The dogs looked like a pack of starved wolves. They had pointed ears and fierce, slate-colored eyes. Each one's mangy skin was stretched over the frame of his rib cage.

The long hair on their tails fluttered like tattered banners in the wind. The fur along the sharp ridges of their backbones was raised and stiff, like the tall, bristling crests of their masters. They snarled and snapped around the horses' legs. At the same time, they seemed to be quarreling among themselves as to who would have the first bite.

Some of the trappers' Osage wives were skinning and tanning hides or stretching them on willow withe frames. Hickory coals burned in shallow pits under the drying frames. The fragrant smell of the hickory smoke almost overpowered the odor of dung and rotting meat, sweat and stale bear grease. Babies hung in bark cradles from low branches. Children ran in troops and got in everyone's way.

As the women watched the party pass, some still held their bone awls, or brooms of turkey wings or cooking ladles or bloody skinning knives. Others carried huge piles of dry brush in the burden straps that passed across their foreheads. It was warm for October. Many of the younger women wore only moccasins, leggings, and breech-clouts. Tiana could see the black, geometric tatoos on their breasts. The older ones wore tunics that passed under one arm and attached at the opposite shoulder. Others were dressed in a wild assortment of Indian and white clothes, mixed with little regard for color or function.

Their husbands were preparing for their trips into the high coun-try after the thick winter pelts. Their traps hung in grim clusters, iron jaws gaping, from the cabin walls. The men were even more colorful than the women. They were a mix of many tribes and nations, but they all looked Indian. They wore their greasy hair long and loose or braided and wrapped with ribbons and fur. Their leather clothes were covered with tassels and beads, fringe and the occasional scalp. The hawk bells on the garters below their knees jingled continually. Even the horses were painted and decorated with plumes woven into their manes and tails.

Tiana slowed her horse to look around her at the new sights. The Creole trappers lounging in the shade kissed the air in her direction. The Osage called Frenchmen who had become like the natives Walk-ers Over The Earth. There were many of them here.

"*Ma petite lapine*, my little rabbit, let me stroke your fur," one of them crooned to her.

"*Bons garcons*," the Osage said laconically.

"Indeed, they do seem jovial lads," said Harry. "Wonderful view Monsieur Chouteau is after having." The colonel's house stood at the crest of a sweeping slope of lawn, planted with ornamental shrubs and flowers. Below, along the river, Indian women bathed in the warm afternoon sun. Most wore no tops, and their skirts clung wetly to their bodies. They laughed and splashed with the children.

An old slave opened the gate. He grinned at the four of them and bowed as they entered, leaving their entourage of dogs behind. More blacks ran to shake hands and greet them in pidgin French.

"*Gha!*" Tiana breathed, looking up at Chouteau's mansion. She had not seen anything so elegant since the Vann house back east. It was a two-story double log house, like Sally Ground Squirrel's. But it was much bigger. And it was covered completely with whitewash. The stairway in the open central hall led to the upper floor. Great stone chimneys hugged each end of the house. There was a wide veranda and a second-story gallery across the entire front.

"*Danser.*" The Osage pointed to the second floor and pantomimed a waltz. He seemed as proud of the house as if it were his own.

"He says, 'Dance'," Tiana said. "But I don't know what he means by it." As they came closer, Tiana saw the logs in the house were beautifully squared. Her throat tightened briefly. David would have done work that fine. A buffalo skin hung over the veranda railing.

A small, dark man in dirty canvas coveralls directed two slaves in planting a scrawny young tree while he himself bound wooden stakes in place around another one.

"*Bienvenu,*" he said as they approached. "You will pardon me if I don't shake hands. I have dirt on them." He gave a courtly bow to Tiana. The Osage spoke to the man, then disappeared into the circle of Indians squatting around a roasting deer carcass.

"General Houston, I am so pleased to make your acquaintance." From somewhere not too far away a pig's shrill squeal decended into a gurgle as its throat was cut.

"This is Tiana Gentry, niece of John Jolly," said Raven. "And this is my friend, Harry Haralson." Chouteau clicked his heels and nodded to Harry. He wiped his left hand on his coveralls, took Tiana's fingertips in his own and kissed the air over them.

"Ah, my dear, your loveliness is a fragrant, cool cascade on a hot day. You honor us with your beauty. Even here, in this humble, remote outpost, we have heard stories of the beautiful Beloved Woman of the Cherokee. May I say, the stories fell far short of the truth."

"*Merci, monsieur.*" She spoke in a throatier voice than Raven was used to.

"*Parlez vous français, Madame?*" asked Chouteau. As they headed for his house he guided Tiana gently with a hand on her elbow.

"*Non, monsieur. Petit peu.*"

Raven cleared his throat and danced a little to arrive on Tiana's left side. At forty-one, Cadet Chouteau was almost effeminately handsome. His short, black hair was carelessly combed forward onto his high forehead. His dark eyes were luminous under thick lashes. His nose was aquiline. His cropped, curly black beard framed a thin, sensual mouth. His small body was wiry and looked twenty years younger than it was.

Harry trailed behind, staring around in delight. Here was more dash and panache, as he would say, than even he had expected.

Chouteau turned for one last look at his precious new paradise trees. He was just in time to see an Indian throw a bridle rein over the branch of one. Chouteau let out a string of oaths in French. The Indian shrugged, picked up the reins and led his horse away.

"I am so glad you could come," Chouteau said to the Raven. "There are so many urgent matters to discuss. But business later. You and your friend and your lady must be tired, General—"

"My friends call me Sam."

"And my friends call me Cadet. West Point, class of Oh Six. Sixth in a class of fifteen. Sam, you and your beautiful wife will share that cabin. We entertain in this one. Harry, you can sleep upstairs. There are extra pallets we can put in the ballroom."

"The ballroom?" As they walked onto the front gallery, Tiana glanced up at the second floor, which was at least sixty feet across.

"*Certainement*," said Chouteau. "We have our little *fandangos*, as they say around here. Have you perchance read Rabelais or Voltaire, my dear?"

"No. The Black Robes who taught me didn't approve of them."

"Pity. They miss the fun of life. I weep for them. '*Si Dieu n'existait pas, il faudrait l'inventer.*' 'If God did not exist, it would be necessary to invent him.' But forgive me. You have ridden long and hard to get here. There is water drawn for you, and towels and brandy on the table in your room. 'I drink for the thirst to come,' as Rabelais would say. Ah, *mon dieu*, if he were only here. If you need anything, ring the bell next to the brandy. A servant or one of my wives will come.

"The large bell outside will signal dinner. The dining room is behind the house, next to the kitchen. Now." He clicked his heels again. "I will tear myself from your charming company so you can rest. I anticipate dinner with delight." Bowing, Cadet took Harry off with him to show him around. Tiana could hear them laughing as they walked across the lawn.

"I think there is no danger," she said into the vortex created by Chouteau's departure. She kicked off her moccasins and bounced on the high bed, testing the thick, down mattress. "*Gha!* Do we have this whole room to ourselves? Look at this."

"I see it." The large room was filled with heavy, dark furniture. The whitewashed walls were covered with animal heads and antlers, Indian pipes and amulets, bead work and painted shields, European paintings and tapestries. Raven poured himself a glass of brandy, downed it in a gulp, then poured another. He pushed Tiana gently back into the billowing mattress. The purple satin comforter felt cool under them.

"I smell like a horse," she said weakly.

"We both do." Raven jerked upright as the door slammed open. A black man stood there with their bags. He grinned and set them on the floor. Raven latched the door behind him and pulled in the string. On his way back from the door, he closed the shutter in the painted face of a Little One who peered in at them. "Where was I?" Raven asked.

"Here." Tiana patted the bed beside her.

Raven kissed her eyes, then brushed his lips against hers. He lay on his stomach, propped himself up on his elbows, and stared down into her face. With one finger he smoothed her heavy, black eyebrows.

"Did you know your eyes are the color of the sky at late twilight, when there are lavender flecks? And your mouth . . ." He stroked her soft, full lips. "Just the thought of your mouth makes my stomach feel like there's a salamander in it."

"Do you love me then?" She nibbled his fingers.

"Like a razorback loves rattlesnakes."

Chapter 47

An hour before dinner, two of A.P.'s slaves arrived at the door of Tiana's room with shoes and a dress. Cadet had sent them with his compliments. They chased Raven out while the two of them fitted and altered the gown on Tiana. They only had to look at her to know the corset they had brought wouldn't be necessary. Tiana was relieved. She had already decided she wouldn't wear it, even at risk of offending her host.

Once the women had gotten her into the gown, fastened all the hooks down the back, and dressed her hair, they went to the door and called Raven. He reappeared immediately. He had been pacing up and down the veranda, trying to make casual conversation with Cadet and Harry, while imagining what Tiana would look like. She stood self-consciously in front of him.

"Do I look acceptable?" She had never worn such a dress. She was afraid she looked slightly ridiculous. There was no large mirror in the room to tell her otherwise.

"No, you don't look acceptable," Raven said. "You look ravishing. Turn around." She obliged him. "Lord," he breathed. "You are the enchantress. You are surely clothed in magic." Raven was at a loss to tell her just how beautiful she was. The pale purple silk gown shimmered in the candlelight, and caught the flecks of lavender in her eyes. It was cut in the French fashion, and its neckline was far lower than any Raven had seen in the east.

The short puffed sleeves framed the soft swell of her breasts above the tight bodice. The bodice itself came to a point just below her waist, making it look even narrower and her hips fuller. The skirt reached her ankles in front and trailed into a short train at the back. A small bustle added a voluptuous accent to the curve of her haunches. Her hair had been caught up with mother-of-pearl combs, then allowed to fall in wavy cascades across her shoulders and down her back. It seemed to shine with an irridescence.

As though approaching a rare object of art, Raven put his hands carefully on her shoulders, under her hair, and kissed her lightly on the lips.

"I am indeed the most fortunate of men, my princess. Honor me by allowing me to escort you to dinner."

"You look more than handsome yourself," she said. And Raven did. His white linen shirt was open at the neck in the new style. The ruffled, deep V of the collar set off the mass of curly russet hair there. He wore the shirt over his leggings and loincloth with one of Tiana's bright woven belts, and a red silk sash across his chest. He wore red-and-blue beaded bands on his upper arms, and a silver gorget made by Sik'waya. His high moccasins were elaborately beaded and fringed.

He showed her how to put her arm under his and lay her hand on his forearm, but he didn't have to teach her how to move in her new finery. She walked slowly and regally, partly because of her natural poise and partly because she feared stumbling in the strange, pointed silk shoes.

The table was sumptuously set with fine china, crystal, and silver. Auguste Pierre and Harry rose as Tiana and Raven walked arm in arm into the dining room. Harry gave an involuntary whistle.

"Thank you for the loan of the gown." said Tiana. "I had not brought anything suitable."

"It is not a loan, but a gift. For another to wear it after you would profane it."

Raven cleared his throat again. As his friends would have said, A.P. knew how to shovel the soft fodder. Raven felt a twinge of jealousy. He remembered, just in time, to hold Tiana's chair for her. She slid into it with a whisper of silk, as though she had been schooled in the best of salons. Raven shouldn't have been surprised by that. She had counseled the most influential headmen of her nation. She had addressed Andrew Jackson, for that matter. And she did everything, from pounding corn to leading a dance, with the same poise and grace.

With a slight flourish, Chouteau produce a pale blue scarf, the weight of a spider's web, and gave it to Tiana.

"*Merci*, Monsieur Chouteau." She smiled at him.

"Call me A.P. or Auguste or Cadet and make me a happy man." Cadet Chouteau wore black sateen pantaloons, a gleaming, starched white shirt and high collar, a brocade vest and blue silk cravat.

Chouteau's two Osage wives, Rosalie and Masina, sat silently at the table. It was easy to see from their almost identical, round faces that they were sisters. They seemed accustomed to being mere decoration, and content to be relieved of the burden of entertaining guests. They reminded Tiana of Shinkah, and she decided to make their acquaintance later, when there were no men around. If they were at all like Shinkah, they would have a great deal to say.

Rosalie and Masina were dressed in the latest fashion. Perhaps Cadet's legal wife and cousin, Sophie, had picked out their gowns. She lived in St. Louis, but she must have known about this arrangement.

The dinner was as mismatched as Chouteau's life. It was a mix of roast venison and Indian corn, fricaseed turkey, French cakes, and Spanish coffee. Tiana's favorite delicacy was beaver tail, skinned and threaded onto a green stick and roasted over the fire. When the meal was over, servants cleared the dishes and Masina and Rosalie disappeared.

Raven and Cadet, Harry and Tiana sat in front of the fire in the main room of the double cabin. Tiana was given the seat of honor, and she reclined on an elegant sofa with red satin upholstery and lyre-shaped arms. She and Cadet sipped claret. Raven and Harry attacked the difficult task of lowering the level in the largest of Cadet's whiskey barrels, which sat like a taciturn guest in the corner.

"I feel like a princess in one of those fairy tales my father used to tell," Tiana said. "My heart is as light as my head from this claret, monsieur."

"We try to have a few ameneties, even in the wilderness."

"I hear you have productive salt springs near here," said Raven.

"Ah, *mais oui*. They are very salty, those springs. But I am looking for a buyer for them."

"Why?" Raven was interested.

"I am not so young anymore, *non*. And I have opened that post at the Falls of the Verdigris at Three Forks. There's a ferry there and a boatyard, as well as a store. My brothers help, but it is difficult. Times are hard. The game is not as plentiful as it was in the old days. My men travel farther and return lighter each year. Would either of you gentlemen be interested in buying a saline?"

"It's grateful I am for the opportunity, but it'll not be me." Harry held up a large boot, showing the holes in the sole. "My feet twitch and grow exceeding restive if I'm for staying too long in one place, Eden though it may be."

"I shall consider your proposal," said Raven. "I am in a dangerous state of penury."

"You will never want," said Tiana. "The Seven Clans do not let their own starve." It bothered Tiana to hear talk of money, as though it were a thing to possess in and of itself. It was one of the major points of disagreement between herself and her brother John.

"A man cannot accept charity."

"It's not charity. You write letters for the council and give advice and serve as interpreter."

"Still, I need an income, so I won't have to depend on others."

"To the tale that is life." Cadet raised his glass and interrupted what sounded like the start of an argument. "May it have a happy ending."

"Hear! Hear!" said Harry.

Without knocking, seven half-naked Osage filed through the door. They were led by an old man, six foot five inches tall and ramrod straight. His skin was the color and texture of papyrus long buried in desert sand. Each man spoke a low greeting to Chouteau, then sat or squatted on his heels in a semicircle in front of the fire. Each had painted his shaved head, ears, and eyelids red.

Raven wrapped his trade blanket around his waist as they did, and sat with them, his long legs crossed in front of him. The old leader, Pawhuska, White Hair, began assembling his pipe and tobacco. On occasions like this he still wore the sparse powdered wig that gave him his name. It nestled in his deer hair roach like a molting quail in tall grass. Forty years before, he had grabbed a white soldier by the queue, expecting to scalp him. When the hair came off in his hand, he considered it powerful medicine. He also wore a buffalo robe painted with his hunting boundaries. Unfortunately, they were boundaries the whites now considered theirs. Tiana saw Harry wrinkle his nose.

"Sweat and sassafras," she whispered to him. "They rub their bodies with buffalo marrow mixed with sassafras."

"Aye, and it's the sassafras that puzzled me then," said Harry. "I recognized the sweat."

"We were speaking of poverty, Sam," said Chouteau in English. "*Ni-U-Kon-Ska*, The Children of the Middle Waters, are experts at it. They have had long practice at being poor. Hamtramk, their agent, would teach them to be even more proficient. He throws them into the depths of poverty as you would throw a child into a deep pool to teach it to swim. He steals their annuities and allows white men to slaughter their little brothers, the buffalo. The white hunters throw away a thousand weight of meat for twenty pounds of tallow."

"Where did the name Osage come from?" asked Tiana.

"*Wah-sha-she* is but one division of the tribe," said A.P. "But they were the first Marquette encountered when he entered their lands. When he asked them their name, they of course said *Wah-sha-she*. Since then it's become Osage. It is one of life's tantalizing little ironies that *Wah-sha-she* means Name-Givers. And who can say God has no sense of humor?"

The Osage glanced at Tiana from time to time as they engaged in their own form of fidgeting—tamping their pipes, pulverizing their powdered tobacco even finer, checking the seating of their hair roaches, and elaborately studying the construction of the ceiling.

Tiana finally realized she was the only female in the room. Among her own people that wasn't strange. The women rarely mixed with the men, true, but as Beloved Woman she could enter any council. But the Osage, like the whites, looked at it differently. There would be no serious talk until she left. She rose and smoothed her skirt, as much to feel the cool, glossy texture of the silk as to rid it of wrinkles.

"I'm tired from the trip, Cadet. 'Destroyed riding,' as our friend Harry would say." She graced Harry with one of her dazzling smiles. Not for the first time, Harry felt a surge of envy for Raven. "Please tell your wives that the meal was *superbe*." She gave the last word a French pronunciation. As she took a candle and left the room, Cadet rolled his eyes.

"May I presume to say, Sam, that you are among the luckiest of men."

"I know."

The Indians each gravely accepted a tin mug of whiskey from

Chouteau. Cadet had long ago learned not to serve his Osage friends whiskey in glasses. They broke glasses, and they didn't care what container the whiskey came in.

"White Hair is the *Ki-He-Kah Tonkah*, the big chief. He wants you to write a letter to Jackson."

"About Hamtramk?" Sam asked.

"No. That will come later. This concerns a missionary. He cannot meet a man in the road but what he must grab him by the nape of the neck and attempt to force-feed him religion as though fattening a goose for market. He's been a trial for the Little Ones. I could do it, but they know you are a friend of Jackson. Do you mind? I'll translate."

"Of course I don't mind." Raven stood at the tall desk and wrote in his looping hand as Chouteau dictated. While he spoke, White Hair sat with his chin up and his eyes closed. His warriors did likewise.

Father, we moved our people toward the setting sun and left the missionaries two days' march toward the rising sun.

Father, one of them followed us and has been living on our land, though we gave them land enough.

Father, he has quarreled with our men and women.

Father, we have enough of white people among us without him, even if he were good. He disturbs our peace.

Father, we hope you live long and be happy.

Solemn as a prelate, White Hair took the last pen and, with a flourish, scratched a large, shaky X at the bottom of the page.

In her room, Tiana listened to the low voices of the Little Ones who weren't privileged to join the council with A.P., The Raven, and White Hair. Instead, they sat back on their heels in the open hallway outside her door. Their pipes made tiny points of light in the darkness. She heard Raven's laughter from the other room. Somewhere, a concertina wheezed out a tune and a dog howled in sympathy.

Tiana stared at the beams overhead, ghostly in their whitewash. She considered her love for Raven. That he loved her she didn't doubt. But she knew, in her heart, there was still a darker part of him she couldn't see. And he would have many vying for his time. This love of theirs might prove a wild horse to ride.

She set her mouth in a determined line. Be that as it may, she would ride it, until it threw her off or gentled to her hand.

When Tiana woke, just before dawn, Raven was sleeping deeply beside her. He had been drinking and talking most of the night. A.P. Chouteau was an engaging and literate man. And he had a fine stock of ardent spirits. Tiana blew softly across Raven's ear, and he swatted at it.

"Will you greet Grandmother Sun with me?" she asked.

"Mmmmph."

"What language is that?"

"You have but one fault, my dear," Raven mumbled. "You are cheerful of a morning. Give Grandmother my fond regards and tell her I'll speak with her at a more reasonable hour. I'm sure she'll be hanging about heaven for at least the rest of the day."

"You are fortunate we do not believe in hell. You would surely go there."

She kissed him lightly behind his earlobe then nibbled it and gave a cackle. He was rubbing the spot when she pulled on her simple dress of homespun and belted it. She looked wistfully at the silken gown draped over a chair. Chouteau had said it was hers. But where would she wear it? As much as she liked the dress, she was glad to be back in clothes that allowed her to breathe. By the time she had put on her moccasins and padded outside, Raven was asleep again.

She found Masina or Rosalie, she wasn't sure which, and another woman waiting for her on the veranda. Masina/Rosalie spoke to her in broken French.

"*Oeh*, greetings." When Tiana answered her in Osage, her black eyes lit up, transforming her plain, solemn face.

"You have knowledge." The woman stated it as a fact, speaking quickly in her own tongue. "My friend's child is ill."

"I have a little knowledge of *We-lu-schkas*, the Little Mystery People who cause illness."

Cadet's wife beamed at her.

"You understand our medicine?"

"A dear friend taught me something of it."

As Tiana followed the two through the village, the usual pack of dogs collected around her. She heard the Little Ones beginning their morning song to Wa-kon-da. No matter how many times she heard it in her life, it would always bring gooseflesh. And no matter how often she confronted Osage dogs, she would always wonder if this batch would call her bluff.

The child looked to be five or six seasons. She was suffering from flux, which was caused by two teams of Little People playing ball in the child's stomach. Perhaps the Little People were not so different from the Osage's Little Mystery People. While Tiana examined the girl, her mother brought black medicine, coffee, which Tiana sipped politely although she didn't like it.

This would work best at sunrise, which was about to happen. She hurried to cut a piece of root from an agave plant. A.P. had planted them as a fence around his garden and now they were cropping up here and there. Tiana was glad to see them. They were powerful medicine for flux. And she had only to chew the roots, not simmer them for days. A circle of women had gathered to watch her work, but they stood well back when she faced the child toward the rising sun and began to chant in her own language. No one wanted to be in the path of foreign magic.

> *Listen! On high You dwell.*
> *On high You dwell, You dwell, You dwell.*
> *Forever, You dwell.*
> *Relief has come, has come.*

She mixed the chewed root with a mouthful of water and sprayed it over the child's belly.

"Sister," she said to the mother. "I will work for your daughter tomorrow at sunrise and the two days after that. Give her some of this root to chew."

"Thank you, Medicine Woman." The girl's mother shyly handed Tiana a beaded belt woven of wool painstakingly unraveled from an old blanket. Tiana smiled and thanked her.

Tiana had been right about Chouteau's wives. By the end of that first day, she knew a lot about them. One or both spent the day with her introducing her to the women in the village. And they talked constantly. Tiana knew better than to ask their names directly. But she soon learned one was called Walks In The Firelight and the other Gthe'-Do'n Wi'n, Hawk Woman, and that they belonged to the Upland Forest People, Clermont's band.

She heard in great detail about the perfidy of the Thorny Valley People, led by White Hair. The two headmen had been feuding for years. While she shared a meal of corn batter fried in oil, she was caught up on the past year of village gossip. Like Shinkah, Walks In The Firelight and Hawk Woman were shrewd, with a sly sense of the ridiculous. Tiana laughed until her sides ached at their imitations of the missionaries.

On the second day there were three women waiting for Tiana when she walked out into the dawn, and more the day after that. She spent most of the next week helping those who came to her. It was good she kept busy. She and Raven, A.P. and Harry spent one rainy afternoon playing billards. But she usually saw Raven only at meals and occasionally before she fell asleep at night. He spent hours in council with the Little Ones. He listened to their grievances and promised to write Father Jackson about them.

The night before Tiana and Raven were to leave, Cadet arranged one of his famous *fandangos*. He had sent runners to the French settlements, and people began arriving a day earlier. They carried dance clothes in their saddlebags and led their best horses to race on Chouteau's track.

They were a merry lot. Tiana could understand why the Osage preferred the French to the British and Scots. They had an enthusiasm for life that was hard to resist. But they didn't have quite the stamina for the kind of good time the Real People enjoyed.

By four in the morning, most of the revelers had wandered or staggered downstairs to sleep. The rest had passed out around the edges of the ballroom. Harry had left in the company of a charming French/Osage lass. For all intents and purposes, Raven and Tiana were alone in the huge ballroom, except for one sleepy, inebriated fiddler. He yawned and somehow managed to take quick swallows from a jug while he sawed on his cracked instrument.

No music had ever sounded sweeter to Tiana. With Raven's arm around her waist and his hand in hers, he taught her to waltz. Tiana had never waltzed before, and she was thoroughly intoxicated with it. It was headier than whiskey or the Black Drink or the hemp her brothers had once given her to smoke.

They grew more confident and their bodies began to move as one to the slow, eldritch song of the fiddle. As they gathered momentum, Raven held her away from him to create an outward pull until it seemed to Tiana they were standing still and the walls were spinning in a magical blur around them.

She wanted to dance like this forever, in an empty ballroom, with

Raven's arms around her, and the music filling her. But the fiddler finished his performance by falling face forward and lying motionless on the floor. He left Tiana and Raven clinging to each other and laughing as they waited for the world to stop spinning.

"I felt like a hawk soaring," she said.

"I feel like a man mighty in love."

He kissed her long and hard, then led her off to their room. There were others sharing it tonight. But they would all be sound alseep. And the French were very understanding anyway. Tiana and Raven finished making quiet love just before Grandmother Sun rose. Then they went to the river to greet her.

Chapter 48

Tiana stood in the doorway of the blacksmith shop, one of the dozen ramshackle buildings at Chouteau's trading post near Three Forks. It was November, 1829. The Osage were gathering at the nearby agency for the distribution of their annuities. They were joined by the rag-tag and bobtail of the frontier. Tiana had seen far more wholesome creatures under rocks.

She had come to the blacksmith shop to escape the noise and confusion outside. Usually the smithy was the center of activity. There was more cursing and swearing at the boatyards, but building a flatboat was a slow process. It wasn't like watching a man shape glowing iron and spray sparks with his hammer. Now, even the blacksmith couldn't compete with the horse races and dog fights, the knife-throwing contests and brawls of annuity time.

Tiana usually avoided the blacksmith shop. There were memories there. And she avoided memories. It wasn't good to think about loved ones who had made the last, lonely journey to the Nightland. Homesick ghosts entered the thoughts and dreams of those left behind. They caused them to pine, to waste away and die of sorrow and join them. And Tiana could never enter a blacksmith shop without thinking about David.

But there was nowhere else to go. Chouteau's office was full of headmen sitting in council. Even his loft was littered with Indians that Cadet's employees had dragged there to sleep off their binges safely. Over the ringing of the hammer on metal Tiana could hear shots and drunken laughter and the chanting of an Osage wise one, one of the Little Old Men, as they were called. His poem could have fourteen hundred lines and take all day to recite.

Tiana had just left Raven and her brothers, John and Charles. They were shouting at each other about whiskey. Charles distilled it and John sold it and Raven disapproved of the Indians having it. Like their father, John and Charles equated liquor with liberty. They would allow no one to tell them they couldn't make it and dispense it as they wished. At least their whiskey was safe to drink. An Osage had already been blinded by someone's bad batch.

Hamtramk wasn't stopping the illegal whiskey sales. Nor did he seem interested in preventing traders from giving the Indians worthless baubles in exchange for their certificates of indebtedness. The government gave the certificates in lieu of money for the annuity payments. They could be cashed later, but as far as the Indians were concerned, they were useless. The headmen were sure Hamtramk and the other agents were gathering quantities of the certificates for almost nothing and planning to redeem them later.

Raven had been voted an official member of the Cherokee Nation. Drum had entrusted him with thousands of dollars worth of the certificates to keep them safe. That made Tiana uneasy. Raven was causing the agents a lot of trouble. They were looking for excuses to discredit him. His having so much of the tribe's money made him suspect. And it was a terrible temptation for any man.

Tiana sat on a bench against the wall of the shop. She leaned her chin despondently on one palm and drew designs in the sawdust with the toe of her moccasin. With her free hand she absentmindedly scratched behind a hound's ears.

To cheer herself, she thought about waltzing with Raven in Chouteau's vast, echoing ballroom. She closed her eyes and tried to will herself back there, instead of here. Raven himself slipped in the door and sat down heavily next to her. The dog at Tiana's feet growled.

"I have just been looking for you." Raven spoke haltingly in Cherokee. He practiced it with Tiana and insisted on speaking it in council with government officials. It wasn't mere affectation on his part. It was his way of forcing the whites to recognize the sovereignty of the Real People's Nation. "Then it occurred to me that I might find you here." Raven never asked her about David. She didn't know whether he wasn't curious or he didn't want her asking him questions in return.

"The noise, the fights, made me unhappy."

"I shouldn't have brought you. I should have known this would be worse than the Real People's distribution. The Little Ones aren't as civilized. And they aren't your people."

"I wanted to come. I see so little of you."

"I know." Raven put his arm around her and the hound bristled.

"Easy," Tiana said. "This is Unli'ta, Long Winded, my beloved husband." Tiana had started calling Raven that because of the time he spent in council. Even Cherokee women usually showed their husbands a little more respect, but Tiana still considered Raven the friend she had known in her childhood. And she had inherited much of her father's irreverence. She and Raven leaned their heads against the wall and stretched their legs out in front of them. The hound put his muzzle in Tiana's lap so she wouldn't have to go out of her way to scratch his ears.

"There's so much to do," Raven said wearily. "They think I'm a savior or magician. Roly McIntosh and his Creeks dictated a nine-page letter to me, listing the wrongs done them by their agent. The Real People, the Osage, the Chickasaw, the Choctaw all have complaints.

"The indemnities haven't been paid. The boundaries haven't been run on the Real People's land. No preparations have been made for the emigrants from the east. Their seed corn and tools aren't here. Winter's coming on. The Comanche and Pawnee and Kiowa are raiding. And who can blame them? Their hunting grounds are being overrun by the eastern nations.

"Then there are the white settlers. Getting rid of them is like trying to pick ants out of molasses. You never get them all, and more come anyway."

"You can't solve everything yourself," Tiana reminded him.

"Jackson could."

"He's far away."

"Yes, he is." Raven brooded about that a moment. "*Gha*! Listen! Will you talk to John? He only gets his hackles up when I try to. I hate to involve you in this, but he's in trouble with Agent DuVal. Something about a gambling debt John incurred while in his cups. The man expects DuVal to pay it because John's his interpreter. And DuVal won't and John won't. You know how he is about money and principles. And he's been drinking and he's making threats."

"I'll talk to him."

"Good. You can talk sense into his thick Scottish skull while I saddle horses. A Scotsman and a Cherokee. What a combination." Raven shook his head at the enormity of it.

"Where are we going?"

"Surprise. *Nu'la*. Hurry. I can't stand much more of this myself. If you can't calm John down by the time the horses are ready, I'll demote you from Beloved Woman to Beliked Woman."

Half an hour later the two of them had left the noise and confusion behind. They crossed the quiet Neosho River on Chouteau's ferry and walked their horses down the trail that disappeared toward the southwest and the Texas settlements along the Red River. Arbuckle's troops had laboriously hacked the path through the mile of dense canebrakes near the river.

In effect, the Neosho divided the woodlands from the plains. Beyond the brake was a prairie of bluestem grass. The gentle hills were slashed by a valley filled with the oaks and ashes and hackberries along Bayou Menard. There the trail was bordered in places by hundreds of acres of nettles. Tiana didn't envy the men who had cut through them.

"Gambling," Raven said. He must have been thinking of John. "Did I ever tell you about a gambling feller I once't knew?"

"No." She grinned at him. When he broke into backwoods English, she knew there was a story coming.

"Well, this particular gambler was on his deathbed. He was taking serious leave of his physician. 'Son,' said the doctor, 'you'll not live past eight o'clock tomorrow morning.' The gambler took the news bravely. He exerted what small strength he had to beckon the doctor closer. He had to bend down to catch the dying man's last words. 'Doc,' he said." Raven lowered his voice to a hoarse whisper, and Tiana leaned toward him to hear.

" 'Doc, I'll bet you a buck I last till nine.' " He stretched forward and kissed her. She laughed. It wasn't possible to stay unhappy around Raven.

"Did you calm John?" he asked.

"No. I might as well whistle jigs to a milestone as talk to him in that condition. Sally Ground Squirrel always told me to avoid doing the impossible. It takes too long."

"Then where is he? He was headed for trouble."

"I had Drum send him on a fool's errand back to the courthouse at Tahlontuskee. It's a thirty-mile ride."

"I wish he didn't hate me so. We used to be more than friends. We were brothers."

"He doesn't hate you. He's envious of the influence you have with the headmen. Spend more time with him. Ask his counsel. Where are we going?" Tiana slipped that in casually, to trick him into answering her.

"To Comanche country. I figure if anyone can charm them into talking peace, you can."

"Seriously, Unli'ta. Where are you taking me?"

"You can't stand to be in the dark, can you?"

"Bats and cutpurses prefer the dark. I'm neither."

"Only another mile." They passed the two-mile marker, cut from the local pinkish-orange stone. A mile later, Raven turned his horse from the road and cantered up a gentle slope to a meadow. Below them the Neosho curved among the hills. Closer by was the stream called Skin Bayou.

"This is it. How do you like it?"

"What is it?"

"This is where our house will be. We can put an orchard over there."

Tiana rode up beside him. She sat with her leg brushing his as she looked out over the wide, brown hills. Here there were trees, but farther west she could see only small copses of them. It was barer than any place she had lived. She stared toward the horizon, the Nightland, wondering what it would be like to ride out across those hills until she came to the high mountains or the big water she'd heard about from old Nathanial Pryor. Pryor had been on the Lewis and Clark expedition and he never tired of talking about it.

Her long silence made Raven uncomfortable. He dashed headlong into it.

"I know it's a hard day's ride to Sally Ground Squirrel's and your mother and sisters. But I'll be going to the courthouse at Tahlontuskee often and you can go with me. You can visit while I'm in council."

"It's fine." What use was it to remind him he hadn't asked her opinion? That he gave no thought to her wishes. That this place was closer to Cantonment Gibson than she would choose to be. She knew he wanted to please her. And he was so excited about his surprise, she couldn't spoil it for him.

"I searched a long time to find just the right place." His enthusiasm was boiling over. He dismounted and paced off the dimensions of a cabin. "We can build here," he went on. "The wigwam will face east, of course, toward the Sunland. Coffee will help us build it. And James and John offered to help, and your other brothers too, of course. We'll start on it as soon as I get back."

"Where are you going?"

"I have to go to Washington City."

"When?"

"In the next few days. Drum and the headmen asked me to go with a delegation." Drum had sneaked this one by Tiana.

"Wonderful," she said. "I can pack in no time."

"Spider Eyes, you can't go."

"Of course I can. I can visit my sister Mary in Georgia. And I've never seen Washington City. She laughed in delight at the prospect of a trip.

This was going to be difficult. Tiana wasn't used to being thwarted. It was one of the very few things she wasn't good at.

"Spider Eyes," Raven said, "only men will be going."

"We'll say I'm coming along to do your cooking, like on an old-fashioned hunting trip."

"It's impossible. You see . . ." *Damnation, how to explain?* "By white law, I'm still married to Eliza."

"You've split the blanket. You're no longer man and wife."

"It's not that simple. And there are appearances." That was the wrong choice of words. Negotiating with the Comanche would be easier than this.

"Appearances! Oh, yes, I suppose appearances would be bad. Sam Houston, a friend of the president, with his brown squaw. 'Nigger.' That's the word to describe my 'appearance,' isn't it?"

"You know that's not it."

"Then what is it?"

"There are those who would discredit me, and through me, Jackson. They hounded Rachel Jackson to her death with charges of bigamy. Now they've set up a clamor over Secretary Eaton's wife, Peggy. They're like hounds to the scent, the good folk of Washington."

"True. Bigamy would be the issue. There's not much to a white man living with a squaw."

"I wish you wouldn't use that word."

"It's not like a white woman consorting with a red man. Look at Galagina, The Buck's poor wife. Burned in effigy by the good Christians of Connecticut. Called a criminal, a *criminal*, for debasing herself with someone of an inferior race."

"Spider Eyes," Raven put his arms around her and hugged her while she cried softly. "Spite ill-becomes you. And where did you hear about Buck Boudinot and the citizens of Connecticut?"

"I read the newspapers. And in her letters Mary spoke of meeting Harriet Boudinot. Mary says she's wonderful. Not like a white person at all." Tiana wiped her eyes. "When will you be back?"

"In the spring. In time for planting. Where shall we put the corn? You'll notice I picked land that has the fields already cleared."

"Yes," she said. "The fields look cleared all the way to the Nightland. I'll put in some apple seedlings now. And we'll have indigo and squash and melons. I want sheep, for the wool, and we'll plant some cotton."

"We'll have it all. And a horse for racing."

"I'll ride him for you." She was beginning to catch his enthusiasm. Raven took her face in his hands and stared into the deep blue springs of her eyes.

"Spider Eyes, your voice and your face and the memory of you will warm me when Blue Man's winds blow through Washington this winter. I'll come back to you as soon as I can. While I'm in the east, I'll begin arrangements for a divorce so we can be married as soon as possible. We will let the business of our lives be love."

James Rogers was going east too. Drum was sending him as an emissary to the people of the Seven Clans who were stubbornly resisting all the attempts of the Georgia legislature to dislodge them. James enjoyed the steamboat trip with Raven and Harry. Free from the problems in the west and not yet embroiled in those of the east, they fell into the pattern of their youth. Travel always had that magical quality of suspended reality. When traveling, only each day's adventures were important.

The three of them talked through the clear, cold nights. They told endless stories, and drank, sang, and gambled the days away. And they played practical jokes. Pennywit and the other passengers soon learned to look to their flanks when the three were around. It started as they watched the rock ledge of Cantonment Gibson's landing diminish. Harry was scratching frantically at his armpits, his rear end and groin and the backs of his knees.

"Chiggers, Harry?" asked James.

"What are chiggers?"

"Passion bugs," said Raven. "I've had 'em many a time."

"You've been green-gowning in the tall grass, I take it." James winked.

Harry looked like the cat caught in the cream jug.

"The wages of sin, Harry."

"The sin was worth the price," said Harry. "But what are they?"

"Tiny bugs. They burrow under your skin and set up house-keeping." James was going to enjoy this trip. Weeks of bedeviling Harry.

"This late in the year?"

"It's been a mild autumn," said James.

"What shall I do about them, then, darlings?" asked Harry. "For they're sure to be driving me to distraction soon."

"There are lots of remedies," said Raven. "One of the most effective is whiskey."

"Taken internally?" Harry asked hopefully.

"No," said James. "You rub the whiskey over the bites. Then you sprinkle sand over them."

"The chiggers get drunk and throw rocks at each other," said Raven. It took Harry a full five seconds to realize he'd been taken. "There's another remedy. A real one. Very effective," Raven went on.

"I can't say I believe you fellows," said Harry.

"Trust us." From his coat pocket Raven pulled out a cigar and a block of congreve matches Arbuckle had given him as a going-away present. "The object is to smother them. You can do that by holding a lighted cigar close over them." Raven lit the cigar and puffed on it.

"Oh, no you won't!" said Harry.

"I assure you, it's quite scientific. The fire saturates the air with phlogiston so it can no longer support life. Or maybe it robs the air of phlogiston. I can't remember. But it works anyway."

"This will do it, Harry, lad, you have my word." Harry stared hard at James. The Cherokee didn't lie, as far as he knew.

"All right. But most of the bites are on me bum."

"It's too dark for surgery in the cabin. The ladies never come out here among the cargo. We'll just clear a spot in the bales and boxes. Take your trousers off, Harry." Raven was all sincerity and business. "James can keep watch and I'll perform the operation. I swear, on my mother's honor, I won't hurt you."

Harry lay, belly down, across a sack of corn. Raven handed his trousers to James, who immediately walked away waving them like a captured enemy standard. Raven put the lit cigar in Harry's mouth.

"Harry, old sod," Raven said, affecting an Irish accent. "And it's an urgent matter I'm just after remembering I must do, darlin'. I'll be back, till Tuesday is a week." He too disappeared over the boxes. Harry stood in outrage.

"You bloody bastards!" He waved his fist after them. Giggles and squeals overhead made him look up. He had forgotten that the ladies promenaded on the upper deck each afternoon. They crowded the railing and stared down at him.

"I'll get you, you blackguards," Harry shouted after the retreating heels of James and Raven. Then he tugged his shirt as far down as he could to hide his skinny, white knees. As he pulled it down, he felt it creeping up in back, and a draft hit him there. Ah well, nothing to do but brazen it out. Harry flicked the ash from the tip of the cigar and doffed his hat to the balcony. Someone threw a silk flower from her bonnet and it landed at Harry's feet. He picked it up and kissed it. The ladies cheered. Then he went cat-footing it in search of a pair of trousers and his erstwhile friends.

"Where did the good times go?" Raven asked James, a few days later. He and James and Harry were leaning against the boiler deck railing. As they smoked, they looked out at the black silk and diamond night.

"We signed the good times away with the treaties," said James. "Along with the bribes and the other gifts that aren't spelled out. The laughter went with the land, with our innocence. We have no time for it, John nor I nor you either. We're too busy trying to keep more from being stolen from us.

"Now Jackson says it is impossible to have a country made up of sovereign tribal nations." In his anger, James clenched the railing. "We should have killed him at the Battle of Horseshoe Bend."

"And how history would have changed," said Raven.

"Indeed," said James.

"But you would have lost the land in the east anyway. You must realize that."

"Yes. I know it." James paused. "I'm working as an agent for Eaton. Did you know?"

"Are you?" Drum had told Raven, but he had finally learned not to show how much he knew.

"He has promised a liberal reward. It will place myself and my family in easy circumstances for the balance of my life. And it's only to do what Drum and the other western leaders want. To persuade the Ross faction to give up and join the western nation. To unite here and make a stand. They can't win in the east. The situation is becoming increasingly ugly in Georgia."

"Brother, you don't have to defend yourself to me. In these times a man does the best he can and looks out for his own." In his pocket, Raven fingered the letter he had written at Drum's dictation. It was to be delivered to Father Jackson. It said in part, "My son, The Raven, General Houston, has walked straight. His path is not crooked. He is beloved of all my people." It wasn't easy to walk a straight path these days.

James kept Raven and Harry company as far as Nashville, then he went on alone. As he rode into the new Cherokee capital of New Echota, he was impressed with it. Untouched by the frantic gold fever further east, the town looked peaceful and prosperous. There was a print shop for *The Cherokee Phoenix*, a courthouse, stores, a school, homes, a church, a tavern, even a shoe store. They were all scattered along the fifty-foot-wide streets that had been neatly surveyed into blocks.

The tranquility of the place didn't fool James. He had no illusions. He would earn the money Secretary Eaton offered him. Feelings about ceding land ran high. The message James carried would undoubtedly bring him verbal abuse, and maybe physical harm as well. Major Ridge and John Ross had written a law that made selling land without consent of the National Council a dangerous business. "They shall be viewed and treated as intruders," the law went. James was an intruder among his own people.

Tiana stood with legs spread and one foot propped on the log she was trimming. She swung the planing ax with considerable skill, but she couldn't keep up with James. Chips flew from his ax.

After Raven had left for the east five months before, the men in Tiana's family gathered to fell trees and drag them to the cabin site to season. Tiana had been there every day, working along with the men. She wanted the cabin finished when Raven came home. It was early May. He should be arriving any day. There were nights when she woke in a cold sweat, her heart drumming in her ears. What if he didn't come back?

"Sister, let's rest," said James. They walked to the tree where Fancy, huge with child, sat shelling corn. She had her legs spread and scraped the kernels into the trough made by her skirt. Tiana and James took long drinks from the hanging canvas bag. James dribbled some of the water on his bare shoulders, chest, and back. Then he squirted some at Tiana. She laughed.

"Look out, now!" Fancy wiped off stray drops. "This child of mine will be born a fish, what with all the water you two are throwing around."

"How's Mary? Is she still in Georgia?" Tiana asked James as they lounged in the shade and listened to Fancy sing to herself. Tiana hadn't had a chance to hear all of James's news from his trip east. She missed being able to listen to the men's discussions at the new council house near Sally Ground Squirrel's cabin. She missed translating letters for Drum. There were many things she missed. She missed The Raven most of all.

"Sister Mary is well. She has a good man with her. She seems to have calmed considerably." He didn't mention that she had aged considerably too. "Her granddaughter is bright as a copper penny. Reminds me of you at that age."

"And how are things toward the Sunland?"

"Not well." James leaned back and wiped his face with his bandana. "Worse than that, really. Whites are invading the Nation's land. They know no law. Their miserable shanties are sprouting everywhere, like mushrooms in manure. Drinking, brawling, stealing, killing."

"Sounds like annuity time."

"Worse. These men are so base, so consumed with greed, they make the sharks out here seem tame. The Georgia legislature has made it legal to kill us."

"Surely that's an exaggeration."

"They've extended their laws over the Nation and nullified all of ours. Our people can't mine gold. They can't speak out against removal or meet in council. Worst of all, they cannot testify in court against a white man. Think of it, sister. All any white has to do is make sure there are no white witnesses and he can do as he wishes. And they have divided the country of the Seven Clans into one-hundred-and-sixty-acre lots. There's talk of a lottery for them."

James didn't mention the scandal that had involved Raven. That he was investigated by Congress for trying to use his friendship with Jackson to receive ration contracts at highly inflated prices. He had been acquitted, and maybe he had been falsely accused. His friendship with Jackson brought him enemies who would do it.

"And what of Tsan-usdi, Ross?" Tiana asked. "How did he and the National Committee receive Drum's proposal about moving west?"

"As expected. They called Drum a traitor."

"James, Tiana," called Coffee. "The cats are ready." Coffee had dug clay and mixed it in a pit with crushed cattail stalks. He had added water to make a gooey mortar. It was time to plaster the wooden frame of the chimney. Later, when there was time, Coffee promised to build them a proper house with stone chimneys.

Coffee stood on the scaffolding as they built up the wall of mud around the sticks. Finally James and Tiana had to make large mud balls, wrapped in straw, to fling up to Coffee. The balls were called mud cats. Now and then a stray cat would fall on them. They all laughed as they became covered with mud and straw.

"Lovely," said a woman's deep voice behind them. Tiana looked around to see a tall, gaunt white woman with short, steel-gray hair combed back from her face.

"Of course," Tiana said. "I remember you. We met at my mother's house, over ten years ago."

"I didn't think you'd remember. We're neighbors now. I still live on Lovely's Purchase, only ten miles that way."

Percis Lovely hadn't changed much in ten years. She had reached that stage in life where time seemed to stop. Her face and hands were darkly tanned and deeply creased. Her gingham dress was faded, but she had that indefinable quality Raven called "class."

"I was on my way to Cantonment Gibson and thought I'd stop to visit, welcome you to the neighborhood. Here." She handed Tiana a bundle wrapped in a yard of cloth with the four corners tied together to make a bag. Inside were four white china cups with blue rims, each wrapped in cotton.

"Mrs. Lovely—"

"Percis."

"Percis, they are beautiful. Thank you."

"Pish, my pleasure. And what shall I call you? I know your people don't like being referred to by their real names."

"You may call me Tiana. That's not my real name."

Tiana and Percis, James and Fancy and Coffee sat under the tree, drinking cold spring water from the cups. Fancy and Tiana shared one. Suddenly, Tiana stiffened, listening. She put a finger to her lips.

"I hear the cannon."

"Are you sure?" asked James.

"I'm sure. Pennywit is arriving. Percis, I must go to Gibson, quickly. Forgive me. I'm expecting someone on that boat."

"General Houston, I suppose."

"Yes."

"Well, run along, child. I'll follow."

Without saddling, Tiana leaped on the horse and beat his sides with her heels. She was glad she had cleaned up for Percis's visit.

From the pilot's house on *Facility*, Pennywit saw her racing along the cantonment's high bluff. He blew his whistle in greeting.

"*Unli'ta!*" Tiana called, and waved. "My beloved talker!"

Raven stood on some of the boxes at the bow of the boat. He was alone. Harry had drifted off on some new adventure. Raven jumped from the deck before the boat landed, his long legs spanning the water. He hit hard and sprinted up the dock. Tiana dismounted and ran to meet him. He grabbed her, lifted her off the ground, and spun her around.

"Diana, my huntress, my goddess, I've missed you more than I can say."

"And I've missed you."

Raven kissed her long and hard. There was whiskey on his breath.

Chapter 49

It had been raining for a week. Tiana felt the weight of the clouds and the August heat and the moisture in the air. She was beginning to feel like a prisoner in the new cabin she had so proudly shown Raven three months before. She and Raven had gone to Cadet Chouteau's uproarious Fourth of July celebration the month before. The Fourth may not have been a French holiday, but they were delighted to celebrate it anyway. The feasting and dancing, the interminable toasts and the horse races had lasted for the better part of a week. Tiana and Raven had been among the last to leave. And they had sung and laughed all the way home.

Now they were being overly polite, striving not to get on each other's nerves. Tiana always had enough to keep her occupied. But Raven was different. He had spent some of the week in Nicks' tavern at Cantonment Gibson. But it was the sickly season and Cantonment Gibson was not a pleasant place to be. So he stayed home, drank steadily from the huge stock of liquor he'd had shipped from the east, and wrote letters to his friends in Washington and Tennessee. Or he paced the floor, composing his latest article for *The Arkansas Gazette* and reading the response to his last one.

His articles, written under the name Standing Bear, had incensed so many officials that their outraged responses had to be printed in a special dueling supplement. Raven's accusations of fraud and incompetence were making him many enemies in Arkansas Territory.

When he finished writing, he checked the account books of the store he stocked with the goods that had accompanied the liquor. Tiana caught him poring over *Paddick's Bank Note Detector* and she knew he was bored. He usually despised trying to remember the current discounts on individual bank notes. They didn't see that many of them in Raven's trading post anyway.

As much as she loved Raven, he vibrated with tension these days, ever since he had returned from the east. Tiana sometimes felt like she was trapped with a caged animal. He seemed to pace even when he was standing still. Tiana considered various plans of escape—to her mother's, to Sally Ground Squirrel's, to Chouteau's or Percis Lovely's. But they all required traveling. And the roads were a quagmire.

Finally the sun came out. It dried the mud around the cabin and cracked it.

"Let's go."

"Where?" Raven looked up from his desk.

"Out." She dropped his boots, with a loud thud, next to his feet. She carried baskets for berries and he brought his blowgun.

The rain had washed the dusty landscape and turned the fields and meadows and forested hills brilliant shades of green. The insects were deafening. The bluestem grass was tall enough under the trees to be cut for hay. The meadows were choked with berries. Tiana found a damp spot of ground around a seep. She hunkered down and pushed the bushes aside.

"What are you looking for?" asked Raven.

"Golden doves, columbine. See?" She held a branch of the delicate flowers in her fingers. Their long, swooping petals did look like a cluster of doves in flight. "I chew the seeds and blow them onto clothes. Makes them smell good. Or if they're pounded in a mortar, a young man might try to steal them to rub on the palms of his hands."

"Why would he do that?" Raven hunkered down next to her and blew into her hair.

"Then he tries to shake hands with a young woman so she'll fall in love with him."

"Silly superstition," Raven said. But he made a show of rubbing the seeds in his hands, then caressing her.

"Don't you believe in magic?" she asked.

"Of course I do." He picked a fragrant white flower that swayed, though there was no wind. The bee that was moving it flew away. Raven touched the center of the flower and held up a pollen-dusted finger. "A tiny creature makes honey of this, without a mill or a factory. That is magic. If the bee can do that, anything is possible."

It wasn't hard to fill Tiana's baskets. There were wild strawberries and raspberries, sour choke cherries, gooseberries, and summer grapes, whose vines grew up into the trees. Tiana and Raven climbed a low chinkapin and filled a sack with nuts to make into soup.

"Why don't you get scratched picking berries?" Raven held Tiana's hands out and inspected her arms. "I always look like I've been wrestling a bear in a briar patch."

"You go at it wrong. You should hold your hand under a cluster of them and tease them into your palm with your fingers, like this." She cradled the bulge of Raven's balls inside his pantaloons. He smiled at the wicked look on her face. "If the berries are ripe, they tumble into your hand," she said.

"Spider Eyes, you're so swasivious." He tried to pull her down into the tall grass.

"We'll be covered with honey dew."

"Then we must take our clothes off so they won't get sticky." They draped their clothes over the baskets. Their moccasins and the hem of Raven's pantaloons were already soaked with the sweet liquid secreted by aphids. They made love tenderly, not minding the grass or the insects or the musty smell of the damp earth under them. They were part of it all.

"You'll be the death of me, woman," he said when they had finished. "I'm not a young man any longer."

"Part of you doesn't know that."

"What part would that be?"

"*Wautoli*." She touched his penis, slumped and shriveled now. "And *tse-le-ne-eh*." She stroked his testicles. "And *tsu tla'mohi*." She ran her fingers through the curly hair of his loins.

"This is the way to learn a language." Raven rolled over on his side, propped himself on one elbow and began touching her body as he named parts of it. "*Kanasa'duhii*, toe. *Kanigeni*, knee. *Ganuhdi'i*, breast." When he reached *aholi*, her mouth, he popped a strawberry into it.

Tiana lay on her back and lowered her eyelids until she was looking through narrow slits. She liked to see the silhouettes of the grass that way, each one outlined against the bright sky. She watched two ravens tumbling and chasing each other overhead. Above them, turkey buzzards wheeled in lazy circles. Raven tickled her by dragging a grass blade across her neck.

" 'Fair Venus' neck, her eyes that sparkled fire,' " he recited. " 'And breast revealed the queen of soft desire. When first entranced in Cranae's isle I lay, mixed with thy soul, and all dissolved away.' "

"Pope." She blew the grass blade away. "*The Iliad.* 'Mixed with thy soul and all dissolved away.' That's very nice. Your Mr. Pope isn't all bombast."

"You're an excellent pupil."

"You're an excellent teacher."

With their baskets in their hands, they walked to the river. They lay in the cool water a long time, letting it flow over them. They washed off the sticky honey dew and tried to drown any chiggers they might have picked up. They were dressing when a raccoon ambled down to the water in search of crayfish or frogs. Before Raven could reach for his blowgun, Tiana had thrown her knife and sunk it into the animal's skull. She skinned and gutted him with the same knife.

"Baked raccoon and sweet potatoes tonight." She grinned up at Raven. Reluctantly, they headed home.

"Coffee," Tiana shouted from the stile. "We're loaded with swag. Help. How many for dinner?" She handed a basket over the fence to Coffee.

"Only the Colonel, so far." Most of Raven's white friends and some of his Indian ones affected the title of colonel. But "The Colonel" could only be Matthew Arbuckle.

"Only the colonel?"

"That's right."

It was impossible. There were always people passing by or coming to visit. Perhaps the soupy roads were keeping them away. The passersby were more often than not settlers bound for Texas. Raven and Tiana put them up, but it made Tiana uneasy to see Raven's eyes as he stared after them when they left in the morning. Once or twice a week delegations from one tribe or another would appear at the door. Tiana fed them and Raven talked to them. Then they retired with dignity to the pavilion Raven and Coffee had built for them. Many a night Tiana went to sleep with the sound of their talking and singing and drumming in her ears.

"Is he here on pleasure or business?" Raven asked in a low voice.

"He's wearing his formal stock, the one that's too tight around his neck. And his new boots."

"It's business," said Tiana.

"Greetings, Matt." Raven waved at Arbuckle, who stood in the doorway of the cabin. "You're just in time. Berries and cream now and baked raccoon later."

"Greetings, Sam. Good afternoon, Mrs. Gentry." Arbuckle gave Tiana his usual courtly bow.

"We'd be pleased if you would stay for supper," Tiana said.

"Thank you, dear lady. But I can't stay long."

While Arbuckle and Raven settled themselves under the trees, Tiana put the raccoon carcass to soak in salted water. Fancy brought cream from the spring house and they served the men mugs of persimmon beer and strawberries in blue porcelain bowls.

Arbuckle talked of this and that, troubles at the fort, the weather, the raid the Texas Cherokee made on a Pawnee village. Finally, he came to the purpose of his visit.

"I dislike presuming on our friendship, Sam," Arbuckle said around a mouthful of fruit. The cream clung to his moustache. "But the law is the law. You'll have to turn in your ardent spirits. I understand you have nine barrels here."

"Those spirits are for myself and my guests."

"Nine barrels?"

"Yes. Not one drop shall be sold to the Indians. I entertain too much respect for the wishes of the government, too much friendship for the Indians, and too much respect for myself to make traffic in the baleful curse."

"And the license for your trading operation there?" Arbuckle nodded toward the shed that held the stock Raven had ordered on his last trip east.

"I intend only to give goods at honest prices. I am a citizen of the Cherokee Nation, with all rights. I need no license. Besides, I'm intermarried into the tribe."

"Then you have your marriage certificate?"

Raven hesitated. They hadn't had the ceremony yet. The spectre of bigamy haunted Raven, and getting a divorce from Eliza was proving not to be a simple matter. Divorce had to be granted by the Tennessee legislature and petitioning for it would mean reviving the entire unhappy situation. Also, the rumor was that Eliza didn't want a divorce. There was even talk, in Tennessee, of a reconciliation. Raven knew that was impossible, but he dared not say so and offend her family all over again.

"We have no certificate, Colonel," said Tiana. "We don't need one. That ritual is only some magistrate's words. It has nothing to do with the understanding between two people."

"By your own law, Tiana, you need a certificate. It's a wise law, made for your protection."

"I need no protection from Raven."

"Perhaps you don't. But other women do. There are white men who cohabit, then claim their women's property as their own, under white law."

"I know it."

"Well . . ." Arbuckle trailed off into an embarrassed silence. *Good God,* he thought. *I'm suggesting this man commit bigamy as well as live in sin.* "You ought to obey the laws of your own National Council," he finished lamely. "Sam, the Secretary of War has written about your case." Arbuckle squinted at the letter he produced from his coat. " 'An Indian tribe does not have the right to confer on such citizens any privileges incompatible with the laws of the United States.' You can obtain a license at my headquarters. Until you do, I must ask you to stop selling to anyone."

Raven's jaw set in the stubborn line Tiana had learned to recognize.

"I'd advise you to be comfortably seated while you wait for my visit. It will be a long time coming." There was more than Raven's personal gain at stake. He knew he could easily get a permit and trade. But in doing so, he would be denying the Real People's authority over their own territory.

"I'm not a young man, Sam. My job is not an easy one. I ask your cooperation." Arbuckle rose, his knees creaking. "Diana," he bowed to her again. She was always amused by his easygoing manner behind his martinet's face. "My sincerest apologies for introducing such unpleasantness into the pleasantest of surroundings." He pretended to speak in confidence to her, but they all knew he meant Raven to hear him.

"I know I may speak frankly with you. Your man is a brilliant statesman, a convivial drinking partner, an entertaining wit, a passable if ponderous poker player, and a more than mediocre scholar in a sea of ignorance. He is also an enormous boil on the behind of my authority. Speak sweet reason with him, will you?" Arbuckle smiled, the creases deepening around his beaked nose.

"Houston," he said. "You are half again a fool to be traipsing around the countryside with this beauty sitting home alone. Good day to you both."

Raven walked alongside Arbuckle's horse as far as the gate. Arbuckle spoke in a low voice so Tiana wouldn't hear.

"If you don't turn in your liquor and get a trading permit, I shall have to confiscate your stock."

"You and the United States Army."

"Precisely."

After Arbuckle left, Raven drank steadily from the whiskey barrel. He seemed determined to prove that the entire amount was indeed for his personal consumption. Tiana parboiled the raccoon in milk and water. Then, while Raven read aloud to her from one of Irving's *Sketchbooks*, she stuffed the carcass with crumbled corn bread, herbs, and diced pepper grass. She laid bacon strips over the outside and baked the animal under a pottery bowl, with coals heaped on top and around it. While they waited for it to cook, they ate sweet potatoes, steaming in their stiff skins.

"I can't believe we have the whole evening for ourselves," said Tiana. "Teach me to play poker."

"What have you to bet?"

Tiana shrugged.

"What I have is yours anyway. And what you have is mine."

"We have to bet something." His face brightened. "Clothes."

"What?"

"We can bet our clothes. Every time you lose a hand, you take off something."

"You have to do the same."

"Absolutely."

They began. They laughed and drank wine and accused each other of cheating. Frowning intently at her cards, Tiana sat cross-legged on the thick buffalo rug. The fire's light glowing on her skin was more than Raven could stand. She wore only a loincloth and her thick, black hair, sparkling with irridescence.

"I surrender," Raven threw down his cards. "I forfeit." He grabbed for her.

"Oh no you don't." Tiana's head spun pleasantly. As she stared at Raven's handsome face, she thought her heart would burst with love for this madman. "You still have your moccasins on. You should have gotten rid of them first. You have no shame."

"You torment me, woman." Raven dealt another hand, but it was impossible to concentrate.

"Maybe this form of poker will become popular at the cantonment," Tiana teased.

"I doubt the stakes would have the same appeal if the other players were old Nate Pryor or Two-Drinks-Scant Nicks or Matt Arbuckle."

Drum and all his friends and relatives were celebrating a visit from Tiana and Raven. Everyone was dressed in party clothes and getting ready for a night of dancing when they heard the faint whistle of a steamboat approaching Webber's Landing. The party was adjourned and everyone set out in laughing, chattering groups to meet the boat. They knew emigrants would be on it.

Any steamboat's arrival was cause for celebration. They brought news from the outside, letters from the east, new trade goods, and sometimes old friends and relatives. This one was supposed to have five hundred old friends and relatives.

"What is it, Beloved Father?" Tiana noticed the worried look on Drum's face.

"Where shall we put them?"

"There's room here." Raven gestured to the hills around them.

"For these, yes. But what of those who come after them? There are fifteen thousand of the Seven Clans left in the old country. We need more land. Much of what we've been assigned is stony and barren."

"We'll take care of them," said Tiana. "We always take care of our own. You've been begging them to come for years. Now they're here and you look unhappy about it."

"You're right, daughter." Drum smiled at her. "We must make them welcome."

Drum and Raven, John and James and the other headmen stood at the end of the dock as the boat edged closer and the rousters jostled to put down the plank. Tiana craned to see those aboard. The deck was full of people, yet strangely still. And the roustabouts weren't singing as they usually did. They huddled at the bow, as far from the emigrants as they could get. Those on shore fell silent and watched anxiously. The wind was off the river and it carried a stench.

"What is that?" asked Tiana. Raven stared, heartsick.

"Just people," he said. "I've seen it before, on the Mississippi. Boat captains give deck passengers space, but that's all. No food, no shelter, no medicine but what they can provide themselves. The government paid these people's passage. They should have been better cared for than this. Damn them!" Raven was angry, but he felt guilty too. The furor over the ration scandal he'd been embroiled in the year before had caused all ration contracts to be cancelled. These people suffered because of it.

"There's more than just the smell of people forced to live too close together," said Drum.

"You know something we don't," said Tiana.

"A bird told me something I've told no one else." He was interrupted by the roustabouts pushing to leave the boat. There were no cabin passengers on the upper deck. From somewhere in the crowd on the lower deck, a woman begain to wail.

"Cholera." The word passed through the people on shore like a night wind through tree tops. A lone white man stood among the desolate people on the lower deck. He handed a baby to its mother and walked wearily down the plank. Two Cherokee men pulled the plank back, leaving the passengers still aboard.

"Is John Jolly here?" the white man called. His eyes were sunken. His filthy clothes smelled of vomit and excrement.

"I am John Jolly," said Drum.

"Doctor Manning. I was told to find you. That you could help."

"Doctor Manning," said Tiana. "It's criminal to force them to travel like this."

"This is better than the first part of the journey. At least they have air on deck. They had to travel from the Tennessee to the Ohio and down the Mississippi on flatboats. With bastards selling them whiskey at every stop." Manning's eyes took on a haunted look at the memory. "Women, children, drunken men all crammed into tiny, close rooms. The heat was unbearable. The sick were stepped on by the well. At one time there were eight of the afflicted creatures stretched out dead near me. It was terrible. I can't tell you how terrible it was." It was plain he would never forget how terrible it had been.

"The cholera?" asked Tiana.

"No. Not then. Fevers. Flux. Various illnesses. I treated them with what camphor and quinine I had. The cholera broke out before Fort Smith. The few paying passengers debarked there."

"We must see to them," said Drum. "What do you suggest?"

"I'll go with you," said Doctor Manning. "They should all be quarantined. I'll do what I can for them. I don't expect anyone to want to help."

"I'll help," said Tiana.

"Spider Eyes . . ." Raven fell silent. He knew Tiana did as she wished.

"They have nothing," said the doctor as they walked toward the boat. "Even before they left, whites made unjust claims and took their property and goods. My God, it was like foxes in the hen house. The traders took what little was left."

In the days and weeks that followed Raven began drinking more and more. The pavilion and the yard around Wigwam Neosho, as he called the cabin, were filled with destitute people. They were waiting for the provisions the government had promised them. It was too late to plant and winter was coming on. In desperation, many of them sold their promissory notes in exchange for anything they could get to live on. There was no lack of speculators willing to take advantage of them.

Raven extended as much credit as he could at his store. Drum gave away food until he worried that he wouldn't be able to feed his family. And still people came to his door for help. He and Raven and the other headmen railed at Arbuckle and their agent. But they were helpless too.

Raven lay awake one night, brooding. Outside, a late summer rainstorm pounded on the shingles of the roof. They knew it must be driving in under the eaves of the pavilion and soaking the people camped there. But the cabin was already wall-to-wall children, asleep in heaps, under blankets and clothing, buffalo robes and rags.

"I should have stayed longer in Washington," Raven said in a low voice, so as not to awaken them.

"You did what you could."

"It wasn't enough. Davy Crockett stood up to Jackson on the Removal Bill. On the floor of the House he said he thought the people kind enough to give him their suffrage supposed him to be an honest man. And if he should be the only member of the House to vote against the bill, and the only man in the United States who disapproved of it, he would still vote against it. He said it would be a matter of rejoicing to him till the day he died, that he had given the vote. It was a good speech.

"Think how this must affect his constituency. They hate Indians.

The hatred's bred into them, like blue eyes and wheat straw hair."

"Yes, I know."

"He said he knew many Indians and nothing could force him to vote to drive them out. 'Be sure you're right,' Crockett used to say, 'Then go ahead.' And by God, he did. Maybe if I'd lent my support to Crockett . . ."

"And lost the patronage of Jackson."

"Jackson's friendship is all I have back east. Crockett can speak from the floor of Congress. I'm nothing. So the Removal Bill passed. And the Seven Clans will be forced to emigrate. This mob was only five hundred, and look at the strain they've put on the Old Settlers. There are thousands in the east. What will happen?"

"It will be difficult. It's always difficult beginning over. Many of them will be lost and confused, uprooted and carried away like an oak in a flood. It may take years, Raven, but we'll overcome it all. We'll prosper again. The people of the Seven Clans are strong. And at least we'll all be together."

"If only I had some position from which to speak, to tell the country what's being done to the Indians."

"There are your articles in the *Gazette*. The eastern papers reprint them. Thousands of people are reading them."

But it was as though he didn't hear her.

"Crockett, that backwoods jokester with not six months of education, represents twenty-two thousand people. Twenty-two thousand people. And I'm nothing. I'm a voiceless exile."

Chapter 50

The men with Raven had arrived at that ineffable stage of intox-ication where everything said was sensible, sage, or witty. Or all three at once. They were in Colonel Nicks' tavern at Cantonment Gibson. On the table in front of them stood a forest of empty bottles.

Over the noise in the small tavern, they could hear the new cap-tain's wife practicing the pianoforte in the officers' quarters upstairs. It was an incongruous sound that made Raven feel good. Cantonment Gibson was the last post on the Arkansas frontier. The 1830 sickly season was just ending. It had justified calling Cantonment Gibson the graveyard of the Army, the hellhole of the southwest. But there was culture here. Where there were women, there was refinement, and a cool, soothing hand to aid the ailing in body and spirit.

"To music," said John Nicks. He liked to sample his own wares. He said he had to be sure the quality was high. And besides, God had made him two drinks scant. "From the first squalling song of a newborn babe to the dirge that sings us to the grave."

"To music." The men drained their tankards of rum and Mrs. Nick refilled them. Then she went back to polishing the bar already rubbed to a sheen by elbows and forearms.

"Did I ever tell you boys about the first pianoforte in Arkansas?" asked Sam. His hand wove a bit as he lit his cigar.

"Careful, General," said Matthew Arbuckle. "You don't want to set fire to your goatee."

"I shall never forget the excitement that seized the good folk when it was learned a pianoforte had arrived," said Sam. "It was owned by a new family that had failed in the east but was of gentle stock."

"I didn't know Houston lived in Arkansas," old Nathanial Pryor whispered to Captain Bonneville. Bonneville shrugged, not taking his eyes off Sam. In his high, stiff collar, Bonneville's round face and bulging eyes made him look like a frog being swallowed by a snake.

"Now, boys," Sam continued. "Everyone was familiar with the word piano. But none could say just what it might be. Someone had read of a *soirée*, at which Mr. Nuisance would preside at the piano.

"They presumed this to mean Mr. Nuisance would stir the piano with a pole, as the showmen did the lions and elephants. I remember one old fellow remarking that if they would tell him what a *soirée* was, he'd tell them what a piano was and no mistake."

Through the long story, Chief Bowl, just arrived from the Cherokee's Texas settlements, sat across from Sam. He nodded sagely as though he understood every word. His cocked Spanish officer's hat was beginning to slide down over his forehead as he slumped lower in his chair.

He looked like a harmless, drunken old man. It was difficult to imagine that his war party of Cherokee and Creek braves had just dumped sixty Pawnee scalps on Arbuckle's desk. With Bowl's gray eyes and sandy hair, it was difficult to even distinguish him from a Creole or white trapper, tanned dark under a thousand suns.

"The village had a resident oracle, one Moses Mercer, who had been all the way to Little Rock," Sam continued. " 'Yes,' he said. 'He reckoned he knew all about pianos. He'd seen more pianos in Little Rock than woodchucks.' It's a musical instrument, played by ladies,' he said. 'The way the dear creeturs can coax music out of a piano is a caution to hoot owls.' Now, you have to understand that Moses didn't know everything. And he had a way of filling in details with his imagination.

"He had a disciple, a certain Latch, who considered Moses the font of all knowledge. Latch confided in Moses that he was consumed with a passion to see the thing itself. So Moses marched him up to the family's door. No one was home. But a fantasmagorical contraption sat at the end of the gallery. It was a maze of bars and rollers and paddles and wooden gears.

"Moses turned to it as cool as an icicle in the north wind. 'There it be,' he said. Latch's eyes threatened to pop from his head. With resolution that would enable a man to be scalped without flinching, Latch reached out and turned a crank. Well, a delicious clamor and grinding arose from the machine.

" 'Beauteous!' breathed Latch. And he raced into town to tell everyone about it."

The story was interrupted again by a snore from The Bowl. He slid down until his chin rested on the table. His large hat covered his wrinkled face. Raven grinned at him and continued.

"Soon after, the entire village was invited to a party at the home of the failed newcomers. The invitations announced that Miss Patience Doolittle would perform at the piano. You can imagine the stir. Everyone was in attendance. They looked around the living room curiously, but couldn't see anything resembling a piano.

"Finally, the grand moment came. Moses allowed as how his friend, Latch, would be glad to give the machine a turn for Miss Patience. She graced the blushing Latch with a smile and said she admired people with musical taste. Poor Latch fell into a chair, all chawed up. Moses was as complacent as a newly painted sign.

"Miss Patience whipped the covering from an awkward, thick-legged table sitting in the corner. She opened the the lid and presented the astonished multitude with a dandy arrangement of black and white keys, brighter than a salesman's smile. 'Miss,' said Latch. 'What is the instrument Moses showed me on your gallery? The one with the crank and rollers.' 'Why, Mr. Latch—' " Raven paused for effect. " 'That's a Yankee washing machine.' I do believe Moses found employment in a distant city after that."

"Is that a true story, Sam?" Nathanial Pryor was having trouble focusing on Sam's face, much less the story.

"As true as preaching," said Sam.

"That leaves a lot of play on the line," said Arbuckle.

"Who's for cards?" Nathanial Pryor produced his grimy deck. As the hour grew later, the tavern gradually emptied. A party of surveyors bedded down on the floor with their boots pointed toward the fireplace. Mrs. Nicks made ready to go to bed herself. She straightened the sign behind the bar. It read, GENTLEMEN LEARNING TO SPELL ARE REQUESTED TO USE LAST WEEK'S NEWSPAPER. No one wondered how gentlemen who couldn't spell could read the sign.

There were hints of Mrs. Nicks all over the rough room. Her own woven rag rugs covered part of the sanded floor. Calico curtains hung at the window. A shelf held her collection of nutmeg graters, decanters, and punchbowls. A few books and newspapers were stacked neatly on the tall desk in the corner. There was good walnut and cherry furniture. And the communal towel was changed daily. Or at least, every other day. Some people said Sarah Nicks was responsible for the fortune her husband was amassing. Few could believe old General Nicks was sober often enough to tend to business.

Sarah snuffed out most of the tallow candles. The men hunched over the cards, illuminated by a soft pool of light in the darkened room. Sarah stood at Sam's shoulder.

"General Houston," she whispered. "Your woman is waiting for you outside."

"Tell her to come in, Mrs. Nicks. I shall only be a few minutes more."

Sarah Nicks walked slowly into the cool night. A gentle wind had blown away the insects.

"Good evening, Mrs. Gentry," said Sarah. She had seen Tiana there often, waiting at the stone well, her horse cropping the grass that grew thick and green around it. Sometimes Tiana was singing softly to herself in a full, alto voice. Sometimes she was just staring up at the sky or toward the wedge of dim light spilling from the tavern door.

"Good evening, Mrs. Nicks," said Tiana. Her dark face and hair blended with the night. Her voice, with its strange accent, seemed disembodied.

"General Houston says to go inside and make yourself comfortable."

"Thank you. But I'm comfortable here."

"Child, the night humors will make you ill. At least stay with me. I can understand your not wanting to consort with those ruffians. They become boisterous in their cups."

"Thank you again. But I like the night. The stars are our ancestors. They watch over me. And I might miss his leaving. He fell once and hurt himself."

"They are a trial, aren't they, dear?"

"Yes, they are," said Tiana.

"You know where my house is. I worry about you, out here alone. There are those around who can't be trusted."

"No harm shall come to me. Thank you, Mrs. Nicks. Sleep well."

No harm shall come to me, Tiana thought. *I am magic. But not magic enough*.

"Good night, dear."

"Good night."

As Sarah walked wearily to her cabin, Tiana began her endless song again. It faded, and Sarah heard only the night birds and insects and the swish of her own voluminous skirts around her broad hips.

About one in the morning, Tiana heard the scraping of chairs and saw the light from the doorway darken when the men snuffed the candles. As they crowded arm-in-arm through the low, narrow door they were singing.

> *My head, oh my head! But no matter, 'tis life.*
> *Far better than moping at home with one's wife.*
> *The pleasure of drinking I'm sure must be grand,*
> *When I'm neither able to think, speak, nor stand.*

"Husband, I have your horse here." Tiana knew calling Raven husband made him uncomfortable. She did it now deliberately. She was angry with him.

"My beloved Spider Eyes," Raven called in Cherokee. "You find the Raven like a lodestone finds north." Raven wove across the parade ground toward her.

"Like north, you are usually in the same place," she said.

"Good night, General," called Raven's friends. Arbuckle and Pryor carried The Bowl between them.

"You damned fine," Bowl mumbled over and over. "Damned fine."

"The Flowing Bowl." Raven waved one arm toward the old headman. The gesture made him lose his balance. Tiana caught him, and he hugged her clumsily to him.

"You boys keep it quiet," slurred Arbuckle. "I can't have rowdiness on the post. It sets a bad 'sample for the men."

"John," Pryor called to Nicks. "Have a care when you go home. Enter through the door." The men laughed. The week before, John Nicks had tried to crawl in the window, so as not to disturb his sleeping wife. He found Sarah sitting up in bed with his rifle leveled at him. It had almost sobered him up.

"Can you ride?" asked Tiana, standing by while Raven hoisted himself into the saddle.

"Of coursh." They rode slowly toward home, Tiana carrying a pine knot torch. They stopped at the river.

"Ho, Charon," Raven shouted. "Here is a dead soul to ferry over Cocytus." He turned to Tiana. "Did you know Cocytus is the river of lamentation?" The ferryman's dog began barking hysterically. "Hush, Cerebus, shhhh. Do you know who Cerebus is, Spider Eyes?"

"No." Tiana was no longer angry with him, just disappointed. She was used to men drinking a lot. Almost everyone she knew did. But with his usual extravagance, Raven carried it too far. And he seemed destined for a better life than that of a drunkard.

"Cerebus is the hound at hell's gate. He lets souls in, but he doesn't let them out again. The dead souls can never return to the land of the living, the Sunland. Exiled forever from life. In the Nightland.

"Cerebus has three heads." Raven clenched his fists, held them up at right angles to his forehead and waved them around, as though they were looking in different directions. "Ho, Charon, my good immortal, he bellowed again. "I have your passage money here, on my cold lips." Raven tilted his head back and tried to balance a silver coin on his mouth.

A light appeared as old Punk Plugged In, the ferryman, carried a frying pan with burning pine splinters in it. He was used to these late calls, but he didn't like them. Tiana paid him twice the fare to mollify him. The creak of the hempen rope through its pulley lulled her almost to sleep.

"Spider Eyes, my beloved," mumbled Raven as they ambled along the trail toward home. "I love you. Have I told you that today?"

"No."

"I do. You are Grandmother Sun and Grandfather Moon and all the furry stars. You are the crown jewel in the diadem of heaven. And I love you. Truly. You are a superlative woman. When I get you home I'll take all your clothes off and show you how superlative you are." Raven had trouble with the word, *superlative*, but Tiana caught his meaning. The sad truth was, Raven was a much happier man when he was drunk. Drunk or sober, he was far wittier, more loving, and more charming than other men.

And unlike some men, alcohol in no way diminished his enthusiasm for loving or his facility for it. He made good his promise. When dawn came, he reached up and slid the shutter back on its

runners to let in the morning light. He pretended to wave the sunshine inside, as though splashing water over Tiana with his hands
and bathing her in it.

"The golden sunlight suits your golden skin, my Spider Eyes.
'You are a woman clothed with the sun, and the moon under your
feet.' That's in the Preacher Book, you know." He leaned down and
tenderly kissed each firm, upturned breast on the velvet nipple. He
was sobering up. "My Beloved Woman," he sank down on top of
her. "What's to become of me?" He fell asleep before she could have
answered, if she had tried to.

Tiana got up and went to the river to bathe and greet the sun.
She milked the cows and fed the chickens. Then she wandered over
to Fancy and Coffee's cabin. Smoke drifted comfortingly from the
chimney and she knew breakfast would be ready. Coffee was already
gone, searching for stray cattle in the canebrake.

"You look whupped," Fancy said as Tiana came in. "There's corn
dodgers and bacon warming. And mush with honey." Fancy was
heating several irons on a rack over the coals. She would use one to
iron her cotton dress. When it cooled, she replaced it on the rack
and took up another.

Tiana relaxed on the pile of quilts on the pallet near Fancy. Coffee's
cabin was plain. Most people asumed he and Fancy were Raven's
slaves. It was the safest way for them to live, even in the Real People's
Nation.

The National Council at New Echota was enacting harsher and
harsher laws concerning black people. Now neither Coffee nor Fancy
could legally earn money or own property. Fancy and Coffee had
their cabin and their cattle, and Coffee kept the money he earned
as a carpenter. But it was a secret. Tiana often came here for company
when Raven went to Cantonment Gibson. And she and Fancy worked
in the fields together.

"Your child will be jumping down any time now," said Tiana.

"Can't jump down too soon to suit me." Fancy patted her bulging
stomach and arched her back. She and Coffee had given up hopes
of having a child. Now Fancy was euphoric at the prospect. "You
and Raven must have arrived late last night."

"Yes. He asked what's to become of him."

"He'll be all right." Fancy nodded toward the dress she was ironing. "He always has extra irons in the fire, that one. He has more
schemes and more friends in high places than a hen has mites. It's

you I worry about, trying to do your work and his too. You just lie down there and rest a spell."

"There's corn to pound," Tiana said. But her eyes closed of their own volition. Before she went to sleep, she thought of Raven's schemes. He did have a few. The farm, the store, the saline he was planning to buy. Then there was that letter to Jackson. "When I left the world," he wrote, "I had persuaded myself that I would lose all care, but it is not so. For as often as I visit Cantonment Gibson, where I can obtain newspapers, I find that my interest is increased rather than diminished. It is hard for an old Trooper to forget the note of the bugle." Every week, on mail day Raven rode to the cantonment to wait for it to arrive. He would lounge about Nicks' store and stare at the slots in the big mail desk.

Tiana finally went to sleep to the lullabye of Fancy, crooning Seeth MacDuff's spirituals over her ironing. It seemed like she had only been asleep an instant when Fancy shook her awake.

"It's happening. It hurts."

"When did the pains start?"

"About an hour ago."

"Be calm, sister. Lie down." Tiana went outside and dipped a rag in the water gourd hanging by the front door. She paused to look up at the sun. Almost noon. Raven's horse was gone from the pasture. It was mail day at Gibson.

Tiana knelt by the pallet and bathed Fancy's face with the cool water. When Coffee arrived, she sent him to get Percis Lovely. He didn't want to leave Fancy.

"I'll need her. She's the closest."

"What about the doctor at Gibson?"

"Fancy said she doesn't want a white man attending her. Please hurry. Percis has the gift, I know it. I've talked to her many times. We may need her magic."

All afternoon Tiana sat by Fancy. She bathed her with cool water after each surge of pain. She changed the bedclothes when they became soaked with sweat. She washed between Fancy's legs with a decoction of spotted touch-me-not to scare the child down the birth tunnel and into the world.

She mixed a drink made from steeping slippery elm bark, touch-me-not stems, and pine cones. The elm was to make Fancy slippery so the child would slide out easily. The touch-me-not was to frighten it into jumping down, and the pine was an evergreen and would bring long life. Still Fancy writhed and moaned, and there was no sign of the baby. Tiana almost cried with relief when Percis entered the cabin with Coffee close behind her.

"She's a thin thing, poor dear," said Percis. "I feared this."

When the birth fluid finally gushed, it was after midnight. Coffee was outside, chopping firewood by torchlight. It was dangerous, but at least it gave him something to do. Tiana stood behind Fancy and lifted her to a slanted position, with Fancy's long, thin legs spread straight out. Percis squatted in front, waiting for the baby, but it didn't come.

"Percis," said Tiana. "I want to pray for the child to jump down. Will you hold Fancy." While Percis supported Fancy in a sitting position, Tiana stood in the east corner of the room.

Gha! *Now!*"

She called.

> *Come out at once, thou boy!*
> *Yonder in the Nightland, old Flint has risen.*
> *He is terrifying as he runs this way.*
> *We will run fast, away from old Flint.*

Then she stood in the other three corners of the cabin and repeated the chant. She substituted "thou girl" for "thou boy," and went through the process again.

"Tiana," called Percis. "The baby is coming." Fancy's face was contorted with pain as the child's head emerged.

"Just a little more, sister," whispered Tiana. She began to croon one of Fancy's spirituals. Percis lowered the tiny body onto a cloth and murmured a short prayer over it.

"Is it a boy or a girl?" asked Fancy, trying to see. "A bow or a meal sifter?"

"Dear child, it is stillborn."

"Oh Lord, no!" Fancy began to sob. And she began to bleed. The blood flowed out in a rush, bright and glistening red, like liquid rubies. Tiana had helped with many births, but she had never seen so much blood.

"Coffee!" shouted Percis. Coffee rushed into the room and held

Fancy his arms. He rocked back and forth with her, ignoring the blood that soon covered them both.

"Percis, can't you do something?" Tiana begged. "She'll die."

Percis knew she had the gift to stop bleeding under ordinary circumstances. She stood, eyes closed, and spoke Fancy's name and the location of the bleeding. Then she silently recited verse six, chapter sixteen of Ezekiel. She recited it again and again, but to no avail. "The Provider wants her," Percis said. "He must have need of her."

"I need her," sobbed Coffee. He continued holding her as she bled. She bled for a long time.

"Beloved Woman," said Fancy. Her voice was weak.

"I am your sister and your friend." Tiana leaned closer to hear her.

"Is it bad in the Nightland?"

"No, sister. It will be good there. You'll see my father and *Ulisi* and your new baby. Will you give my love to my husband and my children and friends?"

Fancy nodded and tried to smile.

"I'll miss you, dear Coffee," she said. "It will be lonely there without you. I'm running toward the Nightland." Fancy closed her eyes. A shudder went through her.

Tiana felt the pulse in her neck flutter, then stop. She wondered what the journey would be like. Fancy looked no different than when she slept.

" 'Behold a pale horse,' " The words from Seeth's Preacher Book came unbidden to Tiana's mind. " 'And his name that sat on him was death.' "

They washed Fancy and her child and dressed them, Fancy in her best clothes and the baby in the tiny white gown Fancy had made for her. Then they laid boards across the backs of two chairs and draped a white sheet over it. They stretched Fancy on her back on the platform, with the child in her arms. Percis tied a cloth around Fancy's chin to the top of her head to keep her mouth closed when *rigor mortis* set in. Tiana placed coins on her eyelids to hold them down until they set. Percis covered the single small mirror in the cabin. To look in one with a corpse nearby meant death. Coffee folded a blanket to serve as a pillow and put it under Fancy's head. Then he went to find flowers. He moved as if asleep.

Percis sat in the only other chair. Her head fell on her chest as she napped. Tiana went to the river to bathe and to say good morning to Grandmother Sun. She squatted on the bank and cried for a long time. Then she washed, letting the cool water ease the throbbing in her head. She fed the animals quickly.

"Percis," she called in at the door. "I'm going to Cantonment Gibson to fetch Raven. Coffee will be here if you need to go home."

"My hand can feed the stock. I'll wait."

"Thank you. You are a friend indeed."

"We all do what we can. And Coffee needs company."

On her way out, Tiana passed Coffee, sitting on a stump, staring at nothing. She leaned down from her horse and gripped his shoulder. He covered her hand with his own huge, calloused one. They didn't speak. Wrapped in a mantel of grief, she rode slowly into Cantonment Gibson. In the Nicks' tavern there were only two men, drummers peddling their wares, by the look of them.

"He's around back, Mrs. Gentry," said Sarah Nicks. "Passed out, they tell me." She leaned over the bar and spoke in a low voice so the peddlers couldn't hear. "I refused to sell him any more liquor last night. Made him angry. Started quoting the Greeks and Romans, so I wouldn't understand what he was saying. He'd never insult a woman, though. He is a gentleman, whatever people might say. Anyway, he must've gotten some bad whiskey after he left here. Captain Bonneville's off duty. He can help you."

"Thank you, Mrs. Nicks."

"Child, he's exhausting you. He's a wonderful man, in spite of it all. I understand how you must feel about him. But he isn't worth worrying yourself to death. Look at you. There are dark circles under your eyes."

"I didn't sleep last night. A friend died."

"I'm sorry to hear it. Would you like some hot tea? I have a few cakes left over here. Eat something."

"Thank you. But I'd best find General Houston."

Tiana walked around to the back of the tavern. There was a gully there. Colonel Nicks had thoughtfully lined the top of it with a wooden railing for men to hold onto when they puked into the garbage-littered ravine. Flies buzzed there in the early autumn sunshine. Raven lay stretched on his back next to the rail. As Tiana approached, a buzzard sidestepped away from him. The bird ducked his head at her and hissed. He had been delicately picking morsels out of the vomit that covered Raven's hunting shirt. Tiana backed away and went in search of Benjamin Bonneville.

She found him in his quarters, relaxing and investigating the new sextant he had just received in the mail. He was planning an exploring expedition and was collecting things for it. He wore socks, his uniform trousers, and his white undershirt, the collar off and the neck open. He hastened to put on his jacket when Tiana knocked and stood in the doorway.

Captain Benjamin Louis Eulalie de Bonneville's bachelor cell was a small room in the row of officers' quarters along the north wall. He had a narrow bed with a straw mattress and a solitary chair, worn to fit the contours of his ample backside. A letter of gratitude from Marquis de Lafayette to his young secretary, Benjamin Bonneville, hung in a frame next to the stone hearth. On the other side was Bonneville's diploma from West Point.

His rifle and pistols and hunting knife all dangled from pegs over the mantle. Uniforms, gardening coveralls, and a few civilian clothes hung on other pegs along the wall. His boots swung from the rafters in a vain attempt to keep mice from gnawing them. The floor was made of planks rather than the dirt of the enlisted men's barracks. A small window provided cross-ventilation with the door. His two shelves of books were his one extravagance. He had found a comfortable, if not luxurious, niche in life.

"Mrs. Gentry." He was flustered at the presence of a woman in his sanctuary. She was, in all likelihood, the first female to have ever entered it in the six years he had been there. "What can I do for you? Do sit down." He quickly dusted the seat with an old cloth, realized it was a pair of torn drawers and became more flustered. "You look tired and distressed. Did the general not arrive safely last night? Mrs. Nicks suggested he go home around midnight."

"He found someone to sell him liquor. He's drunk and sick and snoring behind the tavern. Providing lunch for the buzzards. I need help putting him on his horse."

She certainly doesn't mince words, Bonneville thought. "I'll happily be of assistance. Let's get that general of yours back in the fray." As he followed Tiana out, he couldn't help staring at her slender, graceful body. Her hair swung almost to her knees.

The rumor was that she was over thirty years old. No chicken, as Jonathan Swift would say. But Bonneville found it hard to believe. Women aged quickly out here. He had known this one for over five years, and she didn't seem to age at all. Without thinking about it, he brushed his thin, light brown hair forward to hide the fact that it was retreating from his bulging forehead.

Tiana stopped at the well and drew a bucket of water. Bonneville helped her carry it behind the tavern. A small crowd of children stood in a ring and watched her pour the water over the fallen hero. Raven sat up with a start, held his head, and groaned. Together, Tiana and Benjamin stripped his shirt off and loaded him onto his horse. He lay, face down, along the animal's neck.

"*What a piece of work is man,*" thought Bonneville. *And this particular piece of work has slid about as far as he can slide.*

"Thank you, Captain Bonneville."

"Think nothing of it, Mrs. Gentry. I hope you won't be needing such assistance again."

As they rode out of the cantonment, Tiana followed Raven's horse, who was headed for home and the pasture. The cantonment was busy, as usual. Tiana knew their progress was being watched. She held her head high and looked neither to the left nor the right. Her pride was not a flimsy thing, to be propped up by the approval of others, nor torn down by their censure. The stares and whispers and laughter didn't touch her. But her heart ached for the man who rode with her. Perhaps someone had spoiled his saliva. She resolved to begin working for him, to return the evil.

Chapter 51

The winter of 1830–1831 was harsh. Snow came early and fell far deeper than usual. The lead-colored days and starless nights dragged by. And it seemed to Tiana that her life had narrowed until it encompassed the area fifteen paces by fifteen paces, from one cabin wall to the other, and the frozen dooryard. It was a treat to wrap in a blanket, bend into the constant wind, and trudge to the barn.

Tiana wandered in the aromatic gloom and the steam of the animals' breath. She brushed them and fed them and talked to them. She soothed them when the wolves lamented their hunger. Or she listened to the mice scurrying in the hay overhead. That such tiny, fragile creatures could exist and multiply in the teeth of winter was a comfort.

Much of the time, Tiana stayed where she was now, wrapped in a blanket, working or reading near the fire. She sat on a thick buffalo robe and leaned against one of the whiskey barrels Raven had rolled inside. Outside, the wind mourned in concert with the wolves. A bare branch rattled against the eaves. Coffee had covered the chinks between the logs of the walls with crude, hand-sewn boards. But enough wind blew between the cracks to set the flames of the rush lights dancing.

Coffee was asleep in the loft. A destitute emigrant family was staying in his tiny cabin. Eight men sat around the table. *Like flies on a pasture pie*, Tiana thought. Four of the men had overstayed their welcome. They had been on their way to Texas and had stopped for the night a week ago. It seemed they were determined to stay until either the whiskey or the winter was gone, whichever happened first.

The Bowl was with them. He was returning to the Cherokee's Texas settlements along the Red River. Bonneville was studying his cards too. The light polished his round cheeks like the apple he was eating. The seventh card player was a white boy, a pimply drifter who had showed up at the door like a stray puppy. Raven had made him a clerk in the store. But Tiana was sure he was stealing stock. It was more trouble to watch him than to tend the store herself.

The talk was of Texas and politics. The game had been going on for days. There were fifty-two cards in this deck, allowing more than four people to play. A New Orleans gambler had brought the idea in on the last steamboat before winter arrived. The game had caught like hay in hell, as Raven said.

Raven and the new clerk had cut rectangles from stiff leather and burned pictures of spades, hearts, diamonds, and treys on them with a hot nail. It had taken them hours, but they stuck to the task with a dedication wanting in more worthwhile endeavors. Raven's representations of royalty were imaginative, if not artistic. There were cards for each suit, from one to ten now. The irregularities on the cards' surface made it easier to cheat, but no one complained.

Tiana concentrated on the latest issue of *The Cherokee Phoenix*, from December, 1830. She felt like old man Campbell. She remembered how he had refused a hearing horn because, he said, the news was all bad anyway. There was little of cheer in the paper, except for the religious homilies of the editor, Elias Boudinot, as Buck called himself. The most depressing was Father Jackson's second annual message to Congress.

> It gives me great pleasure to announce that the benevolent policy of the government, steadily pursued for nearly thirty years, in relation to the removal of the Indians beyond the white settlements is approaching a happy consummation.

"A happy consummation." Old Major Ridge had been right, when he wrote Drum. "That chicken snake Jackson can crawl and hide in the luxuriant grass of his infamous hypocrisy." Jackson had obviously never seen the hungry, stricken faces of the emigrants as they filed off the boats.

That wasn't all. Georgia had divided the Cherokee lands within her alleged jurisdiction into forty-acre gold lots and one-hundred-and-sixty-acre farm lots. There was to be a lottery to distribute them to the whites. Many whites were not waiting for the lottery. They were driving the Indians out now. The Real People were being arrested for mining gold. Their equipment was destroyed and their lands confiscated, while whites were allowed to mine unmolested.

The eastern Nation, under John Ross, was taking the state of Georgia to court again. Justice Marshall was expected to give a ruling soon. In the meantime, the state was ordering all whites living on Indian land to register. The only ones who seemed to be the target of the law were the missionaries, who were supporting the Indians in the fight for their land.

By the time Tiana read the last page, her hands were shaking with rage. The men's voices began to grate on her nerves. They were loud. They were drunk. They encouraged Raven to shut her out, to lose himself in the unreal world alcohol created. Suddenly she hated them all, even Bonneville, who had always been kind to her. She folded the paper with deliberate precision and laid it on the shelf that served as Raven's desk.

"I'm going to the hen house." She shook the cats from her blanket and draped it over her shoulders.

"This time of night?" Raven's fine, blue eyes were bloodshot.

"Yes."

"Hurry back. We'll want something to eat soon."

Tiana picked her way through the jumble of the men's blanket rolls, guns, and gear. The cabin would have been crowded even without them. The rafters were strung with dried pumpkins and green beans, squash and peppers. There were baskets of apples and beans, corn and nuts, salted fish and acorns. As Tiana went out, she checked the vinegar that was souring in a keg. The hound, with her liver-spotted puppies, was asleep in a boxed-off corner. Tiana opened the door, sheltered the battered tin lantern with her blanket, and stepped out into the cold.

At least the stars were out. They sparkled like splinters of ice. She heard a cackling and commotion from the chicken house and hesitated. It was probably just a fox. No sense calling Raven. He was too drunk to be of much help anyway. And she couldn't stand the thought of all those men coming outside and breaking the spell of the wind and the night. She snuffed the lantern and, with one hand on her knife, let her eyes adjust to the dark. Then she walked quietly toward the shed that sheltered the chickens.

A small figure raced around the corner and collided with her. The chickens in his hand flew away, squawking. The lantern fell with a clatter and the force of the collision knocked the intruder sprawling. Without thinking, Tiana pounced on his chest, pinned his arms with her knees, and held her knife to his throat. He struggled desperately until she pricked his neck with her knife.

"Quiet," she said in Osage. "I will not hurt you." She had felt the fuzzy top of his head where his hair had been shaved and was growing out. "You must be cold on the ground. You're wearing so little and you're so young. I will not hurt you," she repeated, trying to remember what Shinkah and Chouteau's wives had taught her.

"Are you hungry?" There was no answer. "I will feed you. I will give you food for your family. Do you understand me?" Still no answer. "I am not an enemy. I am a friend." The child was shivering convulsively from the cold. "You do not believe me. Stand then, and run away."

She helped him to his feet. He had trouble standing. His legs were bare and his feet must have been numb. "Here," she said. "Here is my knife. Kill me with it, or take it. Or come with me to eat and be warm." She pointed toward the cabin. She made eating motions and pretended to wrap a blanket around her and sleep. He stared at her, then at the knife she held out to him, handle forward.

"Friend?" he asked, in a low, shaking voice.

"Friend."

He didn't take the knife and he didn't run.

"Follow me. I will feed you. But I must do something first." She took a sack of down she had been saving in the hen house. It was to be for a mattress. The boy followed her.

She entered the cabin almost unnoticed, except for some muttering about the cold air she brought in with her. The boy shrank back in fear at the sight of so many white men. Tiana pointed to the loft, and he climbed the ladder.

"Who's that?" asked Raven.

"A lost, cold traveler."

"Looks young."

"Yes." Tiana put a cloth over her face and began feeding handfuls of the feathers into the flames. As the stench filled the room, the men looked up from their game.

"What are you doing?" Raven pushed back his chair.

"Think I'll step outside for some air." Bonneville sensed a storm brewing. He had never seen Mrs. Gentry lose her temper, but he figured it would be quite an experience. He led the retreat outdoors. Raven followed to explain there was some mistake. Choking and coughing, Tiana slammed and barred the door after him. The hound looked accusingly over the edge of her box. Raven pounded on the door and shouted.

It didn't take long for the fire to sweeten the air again and Tiana called the boy down. Coffee slept with his blankets over his head. When many people shared a cabin, they learned not to see or hear what didn't concern them.

"Sit." Tiana gestured to a place in front of the fire. She threw a few more logs on and rubbed his filthy feet to warm them. "You poor child," she murmured, offering him some dried beef and hominy mush. He wolfed it down, and she gave him a bit more.

"There's more later. Eat too much, sick." She imitated vomiting. He seemed to understand. He looked apprehensively toward the door. Raven's shouts were getting louder. Tiana piled blankets around the boy's bony shoulders. His ribs showed under his grayish skin and the tattered shirt he wore. His loincloth was thin with wear.

"Woman, open this door immediately."

"I will let you in, if you promise that your friends will sleep in the barn."

"That's outrageous!"

"Their blankets are in here. Promise or I shall chip the ice off you in the morning."

"You can't drive a man out of his own house."

"This is *my* house. Do you promise?" There was a low mutter of voices as the men conferred. Tiana had to smile. Raven would be beside himself.

"I promise," he called, finally.

"On your honor."

"On my honor."

"And you won't allow any of those men to come in here and disturb our rest tonight?"

"I promise." Raven's teeth were chattering.

"What is your name, child?" Tiana asked the boy.

"Mon-sho-dse-mon-in, Traveler In The Mist."

"Traveler, open the door slowly, and stand behind it." She pantomimed. "Do you understand?"

"*Han-hai*, yes, mother," he said. He couldn't be more than ten years old. What was he doing alone, so far from home?

Three things happened at once. The door swung open. Raven charged through it. Tiana's knife flew past his ear and buried itself with a loud, vibrating *whump* in the lintel. Even drunk, Raven knew the knife missed his ear only because Tiana intended it to. Now she stood at bay, with the big iron skillet held in both hands like the bat in a game of Old Cat. She began kicking bundles of blankets and saddlebags toward the door.

"I must be going, Mrs. Gentry," Benjamin Bonneville called through the latch hole. "Thank you for your hospitality." There was no irony in his voice. Women were so alien to him that nothing they did surprised him. "My bags are the Osage ones, with the beading and fringe on them." Raven pitched the bags and blankets through the door. The Osage boy helped him.

"Good night, boys." Raven shut the door, latched it, and whirled on Tiana. It was one thing for him to humiliate himself in front of his friends. It was quite another to be humiliated by a woman.

"How dare you insult me!"

"How dare you treat me like a serving wench!"

"I am a person of some consequence. I will not be humiliated."

"And I am *Ghigau*. I hold the highest office a woman can have in my nation, though I've been of little use to my people lately. I must spend all my time seeing that you don't hurt yourself in a drunken stupor, or allow your enterprises to founder while you gamble at Nicks' tavern. "I will have peace in *my* house, one night," she said. "If I have to fight for it."

Even the spider loses patience. Tiana braced herself for Raven's wrath. She welcomed it. She leaned into it as into a cool breeze on a scorching day. Coffee lay on his stomach and hung his head over the edge of the loft hole. He had never heard Tiana raise her voice. The alien sound of it had wakened him. He was fascinated. The Osage child snatched two apples from a basket and retreated back to the warmth of the hearth. He squatted on his heels, out of the line of fire, and stared from one to the other as he munched.

"*Nulla fere causa est, in qua non femina litem moverit*," Raven shouted. Roughly, it meant "Women are always causing trouble."

" 'One that hath wine as a chain about his wits, such an one lives no life at all,' " she answered.

Damn her! thought Raven. Educate them and they become insufferable. And she had the advantage of being sober.

"How dare you insult my friends!" He took a more direct approach. His tanned face was flushed with rage.

"Friends," she shouted back. "Friends! Drain that whiskey barrel," she pointed with the skillet, "and see how friendly they are. Except for Benjamin Bonneville, Coffee, The Bowl, and myself, you had no friends here tonight. How could anyone be your friend? Look at you. You're disgusting. You smell like a stable. Your face looks like last year's cornfield." Raven ran a hand across the stubble on his chin. "And your eyes, your beautiful eyes, they're empty and red."

"I have been a United States Congressman and a general and a governor. Now I am but a lowly shopkeeper at the arse-end of the world. I drink to forget that I'm an exile, far from home and friends."

Tiana swung the skillet, and with all her considerable strength, she heaved it at Raven's head. He ducked as it crashed against the door with a satisfying clamor. It made her feel so good, she grabbed a pot of apple relish and threw that at him. The relish ran down the door in lumpy rivulets. Raven looked stunned.

"Don't *ever* use that word again in my hearing," Tiana was trembling with anger. "What do you know of exile? You left of your own free will. You've never been hounded from home, the land your people have lived in and loved for centuries. You don't know what it's like to be told you're not good enough to associate with *civilized* people. That you taint the country just because of your skin color. We're all exiles here, twice over. While you, you revel in it. You posture at misery. You solicit pity like a shameless beggar."

"I do not."

"You do." Tiana slumped, her anger burned out. "Raven, I fear for you. You cannot continue like this."

"I know it." He sank onto a bench, and put his head in his hands. "My dear Spider Eyes, you have a tiger's heart wrapped in a woman's hide."

"Come here, warm yourself by the fire," Tiana said in a quiet voice.

She put a kettle of water on to heat. Then she whetted his long razor on the wide leather strop that hung near the mirror and stand with the basin and pitcher on it. Raven sat disconsolately, with a blanket draped over his shoulders. He looked tired as he stared fixedly into the flames. Tiana lathered her hands with the lye soap and warm water. Sitting on a stool in front of him, she wet his face with part of a towel, dipped into the water. She held his chin with one hand and began shaving his cheeks and trimming his curly side whiskers.

"Who's the boy?" Raven asked.

"An Osage. I caught him stealing chickens."

"Pryor and Cadet say the Osage are starving." With sorrow in his blue eyes Raven studied the child.

"From the looks of this one, I'd say they were right." She spoke to the boy, who answered shyly. "As well as I can understand, he says his father is sick and his family is hungry. He thought he could bring them some food." Tiana spoke again and the boy climbed up the loft ladder, trailing a train of blankets.

"We'll give him as much as he can carry," said Raven. When the child had disappeared into the loft, Raven caught Tiana's hand and held it. "What's your name?" He stared intensely at her. He was still drunk.

"Tiana. Diana. Spider Eyes."

"And *Ghigau*, Beloved Woman," said Raven. "An appropriate name, that one. But what's your other name?"

"Stop talking. I can't work."

"What is it?"

"It's not important."

"It is important."

"What someone scribbles on a tierce of tobacco, for shipment, doesn't necessarily describe what's really inside. It doesn't tell if the goods are fresh or spoiled."

"You're avoiding the question."

"One doesn't tell one's other name."

"Just as one doesn't sign one's name to letters or documents?" Tiana's insistence on signing everything with an X bothered Raven. He couldn't make her admit it was irrational to believe a signature gave others power over her.

"A secret name, a spirit name, is an old custom."

"But you're not an old woman."

"I'm as old as the memory of my people. And as young as their children yet unborn."

"I'm your husband, your lover, your friend, your soul's mate. You can tell me."

"I cannot."

"You won't."

"I won't then. I did it once, as a child. But I was young and didn't know better. Why do you care so?"

"Because it's a part of you that you won't share. You've shut me out." She finished shaving him and began running a comb through his thick, tangled curls. She plaited it into a queue that hung to his shoulders.

"I love you," she said.

"But you don't need me."

"I need you very much."

"You'd do just as well without me. Better perhaps."

"That's not so. You are the sun rising in the morning for me. There may be days when the sun rises and the day is cold and dreary, rainy, maybe. But it's still a new day and good things can happen. And I give thanks for it. You're not easy to live with. The sunlight in you sometimes hides under clouds. But I wouldn't want to live with anyone else. Besides," she tugged his braid. "You always say you like an independent woman."

"A lot of men like independent women. Until they have one."

"There's warm water left. We can bathe and read a bit until the fire burns down, then sleep."

"That sounds like anyone's idea of heaven."

They lay in each other's arms, watching the coals glimmer and wink in the darkness.

"There are cities in the east that look like that," said Raven. "I have stood on a high hill in Philadelphia and looked down on thousands of lights, all in a lily-low. The streets are lined with torches, so people can find their way home. And candles wink in windows. We need a window of real glass. Remind me to order one," he said sleepily. Tiana lay a few minutes in the dark, listening to him breathe.

"Hawk," she whispered, finally.

"Mmmmm?" He mumbled.

"My name is Hawk."

Raven hugged her to him, then relaxed and was soon breathing deeply. She didn't know if he had heard her or not. Her own breath stirred the wispy curls on his cheek.

.   .   .

Loaded with food, the boy left the next morning. As was the Osage custom, he gave no word of thanks. And as Tiana had heard Shinkah do so often, she thanked him instead, for allowing her to share with him, and for honoring her house with his presence.

Raven was more considerate at the Wigwam Neosho after that night. In case he forgot, there was a pale stripe of splintered wood where the skillet had hit the door. Raven and Tiana still entertained often, but there were fewer all-night poker games. Arbuckle and Bonneville were frequent visitors. They seemed to bask in Tiana's hospitality.

Raven and Tiana visited Cadet Chouteau and old Nate Pryor. They stayed with Drum and James and John Rogers whenever Raven had to go to the council house at Tahlontuskee, which was often. When Raven wanted to gamble or drink seriously, he rode to Cantonment Gibson. With their feet up and goblets of brandy balanced on their stomachs, he and Bonneville spent hours in the captain's room. They discussed the classics or the fortunes that lurked in the mountains farther west. Bonneville had what Harry Haralson called "The Itch." He had requested leave for his exploring expedition, and was having difficulty waiting for approval of it.

Sometimes Raven drank at the officers' mess or at Nicks' tavern. Or if no one congenial could be found, he drank by himself. Many mornings Tiana would find him sprawled by the trail asleep. Often he had been dumped there, out of the way, by the first detail to leave in the morning.

Still, Raven wore his ignominy with grace and a certain brooding aura of mystery and loss. When he strode through the cantonment in his turban and plumes, his fringed buckskins and bright calico hunting shirt with tiny bells tinkling, he drew the officers' wives to their curtains. Washerwomen looked up at him from their steaming kettles and tubs. There were few men more alluring than a handsome one with a look of tragedy, especially tragedy that involved love.

Everyone knew a scandal had shaken him from high office and driven him here. Eveyone knew it involved a beautiful woman. His political enemies, here and in Tennessee, kept the issue alive in the papers. They were not convinced the lion was declawed and helpless.

But there were never any details, although the women in particular scanned each article carefully for them. Nor would The Raven, even at his drunkest, say a word about it. So, there was a great deal of speculation.

Finally, in exasperation, Raven sent a proclamation to a Nashville paper. It was copied in others.

I, Sam Houston, do hereby declare to all *scoundrels whomsoever* that they are authorized to accuse, defame, calumniate, slander, vilify, and libel me to any extent. Be it known for the especial encouragement of all scoundrels, that I do solemnly propose to give the author of the most *elegant, refined and ingenious lie or calumny* a handsome gilt copy (bound in dog) of the *Kentucky Reporter* since its commencement.

The *Kentucky Reporter* had been one of the shrillest in its attacks on Raven.

Drum and Tiana and Raven's friends and followers watched anxiously as he drank his way stolidly toward oblivion. Drum had even assigned some young men to trail him and keep him from hurting himself. Raven had nominated himself for representative of the National Council and had been voted down. He had not taken the disappointment lightly. Drum watched Raven now, as he sat in council.

Raven had been drinking, as usual. He swayed on the bench. There was a stir at the door of the council house. It was no longer the dark, dome-shaped building of the old days, but an airy log cabin, set up higher than the surrounding ones. It had two doors for cross-ventilation, and shuttered windows. It was only three miles from Drum's farm. Not far away, work was in progress on a courthouse. When it was finished, it would be a building of which to be proud.

Drum heard laughter and shouting outside as a crowd of the younger men led in a large, black slave. He was built like The Raven, broad of shoulder and narrow of waist. He was dressed in a wild costume of ribbons and jewelry, medals and fringes that dragged the ground. He wore a ruffled shirt and coat, moccasins that were too large for him, and a huge, gaudy turban with plumes. His face had been painted white.

He had been well coached. He struck a pose everyone recognized as Raven's and made an eloquent speech, totally in gibberish that managed to sound like Latin. The council house was in an uproar. People rocked with laughter and looked at Raven to see how he was taking it.

If Raven had been sober, he probably would have admired the man's acting. He knew the Real People's sense of humor. If he had felt better about himself, he might not have taken offense. But he was neither sober nor feeling good about himself. Drum moved closer to head off trouble. Raven was usually too much of a gentleman to brawl, but the whiskey and his temper might get the better of him. Drum tried to lead him away, tugging gently at his sleeve.

With a sweep of one big hand, Raven knocked Drum over. The old man hit his head on a bench and lay unconscious. Howling, the other men leaped on Raven. Benches overturned in the melee. They dragged him outside and beat him until he lost consciousness. Drum woke up and staggered down the steps. Squinting in the bright sunlight, he clawed and elbowed his way through the mob around his son. He grabbed one man who had his foot cocked to kick Raven in the ribs.

"No, my sons," shouted Drum. Everyone drew back. They had never heard Drum's voice raised. "His feet are on the Dark Path." Drum knelt beside Raven's body and checked gently for broken bones. The rest began drifting away, many with heads hanging. For as long as any of them could remember, there had never been violence in council. Only James and John and a few of the older men stayed to help Drum.

Raven woke up in Drum's bed. The old man was sitting beside him and chanting in a low, guttural voice. He stopped when he saw Raven stir.

"How do you feel, my son?"

"Worms are eating me, father. And not because of these bruises." Raven looked down at the purple marks on his body. "Do not trouble yourself to cure these lumps. They should stay to remind me how bad I am."

"I was not chanting to cure the lumps, Raven, but the dreams. You have been having bad dreams. Dreams cause sickness."

"Father." Raven took one of Drum's hands in his own, "Please berate me. Be angry with me. I don't deserve your compassion."

"Perhaps your Preacher Book is right about that, as in so many things. Pity can be a worse scourge than a whip."

"Husband," called Tiana from the doorway. "I brought a letter from the cantonment. It's from your brother, John." She sat on the edge of the bed and touched his bruises lightly.

"I'll put a poultice of mullein leaves on these."

"Was my copy of the *Gazette* there?"

"Yes."

"There must be something bad in it of me or you would have given it to me right away."

"Yes."

"What is it this time?" Raven was almost smiling. "Go ahead. Tell me. They've made up so many lies it's becoming a joke. Don't they know I can't hurt them any longer?"

"No, Raven," said Drum. "They don't know that."

"They said you're a 'green-eye monster, a slanderer of men and a deceiver of women.' " She didn't mention their words about his Indian wife, "his unholy alliance."

"Puny stuff. But how they hound me. They've driven me to strike the man who loves me most in the world." With tears in his eyes, he looked at them both. "I have drunk the cup and only the dregs remain for me."

"A great deal more than that remains for you, my son," said Drum. "If this act was necessary to make you realize the error of your path, then my few bruises were worth it."

As he read his letter from John Houston, Raven's face paled under its dark tan.

"My mother is very ill. She's asking for me. John says they don't expect her to live much longer. I'm to hurry."

"Then you must go at once," said Drum.

"As soon as I apologize to the council for what I did."

Chapter 52

A cold March rain beat against Tiana's back. She rode hunched over her horse's neck to keep as much of it out of her eyes as possible. The trail was a morass of gluey red mud. She passed a stranded wagon of Texas emigrants. The wheels of their overloaded vehicle were mired to the axles. A sad-faced woman and her litter of children watched Tiana as she rode by.

Tiana saw the misery in their faces, but she couldn't feel much pity. These people were heading into Texas where they would displace and anger the plains tribes more. And the Indian nations here would suffer for it. Even now, the Osage women and children were camped within three miles of Fort Gibson. They feared the Pawnee, who were threatening to attack. The Osage men and their former enemies, the Creeks, were allying to fight them. It seemed that only war with some new tribe would end the one between the Osage and their neighbors from the east.

At any rate, Tiana knew she would more than likely find this mob waiting in her yard when she returned from the fort. Perhaps she would ride on to Sally Ground Squirrel's farm or stay with her mother or brothers. Raven was with one of Drum's delegations in Washington City again. And Tiana's cabin was cold and lonely. She had left Coffee at the farm to watch the stock and keep an eye on the store's clerk. Coffee had a new woman, named Malinda. She was small and quiet and kind. She would never replace Fancy, but she was easing Coffee's grief.

The blanket draped over Tiana's head and shoulders was sodden. Her long hair was heavy and stuck to her cheeks and forehead and back. She was chilled to the marrow of her bones. Coffee had tried to dissuade her from coming. The cold rain had been falling for days and the roads were nearly impassable. Old Jack plodded dolefully along, his hoofs weighted with the balls of mud that formed on them.

It was mail day at Fort Gibson. There might be a letter from Raven. Tiana led Jack onto the ferry and stood in his lee to keep off the pelting drops. The ferryman, Punk Plugged In, rarely spoke to her. He was dour by nature and he was a full blood. Usually the men of the Seven Clans didn't speak to women unless necessary.

"One wonders when Kalanu will return from the Sunland," he said, as though his question had nothing whatever to do with her. He stared intently at the frayed hempen rope he hauled on to pull his ponderous raft across the river. He always stared at it. He seemed to think his will alone kept the rope together for one more trip.

"This one doesn't know." Tiana also looked off in another direction. "Perhaps there will be a letter with news of him today."

"Someone misses him," said the ferryman. "He always makes one laugh, even when one is sleepy and angry with him for the lateness of the hour." That was news to Tiana. She had known Punk Plugged In for twenty-five years, and she had never seen him smile, much less laugh. "And he always asks about one's family, and he pays well. May he return soon."

Tiana saluted the guard at the palisade gate and smiled at him. He knew her well. Her smile was the brightest thing he was likely to see that day. Tiana noted how rotted the logs in the wall were. Each year Arbuckle asked Congress for funds to rebuild. Each year his request was turned down. Instead, Congress officially elevated Gibson's status from cantonment to fort. Arbuckle would have preferred the money.

It didn't escape Tiana's notice that the government forgot not only the Indians once they were shipped out here, but everyone connected with them. Tiana led Jack along the corridor formed by the roof of the second floor porch of the officers' quarters. Jack's hoofs rang on the planking and his head dropped so low his large bottom lip threatened to brush the boards. She tied him to the hitching rail and flung her blanket over his back. Even in the cold, he was steaming.

In the center of the parade ground, a wretched soldier rode an ungainly wooden horse with a backbone constructed at a sharp angle. Sitting on the horse was painful at best, mutilating at worst. The soldier held two bottles of whiskey in his outstretched hands, and he wore a board around his neck. "Whiskey seller" had been etched into the board with a hot nail.

"Gracious, child." The Widow Nicks looked up as the wind blew Tiana through the door. "You'll catch your death."

"My death will have to catch me first, Mrs. Nicks," said Tiana. "Good day, Colonel." She smiled at Arbuckle. She wasn't surprised to see him here. Since John Nicks' death of pneumonia three months earlier, Matthew had been courting the plump and pleasing Sarah. "An extraordinary make of a woman," he would say to Raven. "And active in business." Not only was she active in business, a good cook, and soft as a feather mattress, she was rich. The fact that Two-Drinks-Scant Nicks had left her twenty-five thousand dollars didn't discourage Arbuckle's ardor.

Tiana scanned the tall postal desk that took up half of one wall. Its shelves were divided into numbered slots. Tiana never got over the thrill of seeing the heavy brown and white sheets of paper, folded, sealed, and slid at precise angles into their compartments. They were wrapped around the talks of people Tiana didn't know. She tried to imagine who some of them might be as she waited for Sarah Nicks to hand her the letter.

"You have a package from the general too," said Sarah. "When you finish reading your letter, go on over to my house and set a while, dry out. Sadie just baked bread and there's applesauce. Here's a cup and some tea shavings. Hot water's on the stove."

"Thank you." Tiana took the letter and the small, battered wooden box to the corner where two chairs stood near the stove. She poured hot water into her teacup and warmed her hands around it. She basked in the heat from the stove as she broke the seal on the paper. Raven had returned to her in October after his trip east to bury his mother. Tiana knew he had changed when he stepped off the boat. He didn't smell of liquor.

Drum had persuaded him to go east again in December, this time to ask the government to make the promised restitution for livestock stolen by whites when the Real People moved from Arkansas. The council also wanted increased annuities and more land to accommodate the increasing number of emigrants.

"My dearest Spider Eyes," the letter began.

You should soon receive a pair of contrivances manufactured to tame a woman's hair. Here, women twist their hair and sculpt it into fantasmagorical shapes, *à la chinoise*. However none of them can can compare with your tresses, left in their natural state.

As usual Raven spoke of his longing for her and for the tranquility of the Wigwam Neosho. He told her about life in Washigton City. Of the drunk who wandered into the president's big white mansion and fell asleep on a couch. He told her about the fashions the women were strapping themselves into. "I must surmise," he observed,

That they have some machine, such as we use to press furs into a tight bundle and bind them. For I see no other way they can possibly condense their waists into the gowns they wear. I fear that someday, when a bevy of them is crowded into the balcony of the Senate or House, one of them will burst, to the great consternation of all.

He told of the curious new custom, lately imported from Europe, of tipping waiters, to insure promptness. He called it a bribe to avoid starvation.

"You ask of Washington City," he wrote.

How shall I describe it? It is like no other city. It is made up of thoroughfares which begin in fields and end in fields and are bare for most of their lengths. Public buildings are miles apart, and set in those selfsame fields. It looks rather as though the populace had decamped and taken its houses with it.

Raven told Tiana about the scandal, the Eaton Malaria some called it, that had sent former Secretary of War Eaton to Florida as governor. Jackson had tried for two years to force the wives of his cabinet members to accept Eaton's new wife, Peg O'Neale Timberlake, the tavernkeeper's daughter. But without success. He could conquer the Creeks, the British, the nullifiers, and the assassin who made a foolish attempt on his life and was soundly caned by Old Hickory. But he couldn't conquer the ladies. All their banquets and balls and teas conspicuously lacked the Secretary of War and his lovely wife of the tarnished reputation.

Like malaria, the Eaton scandal kept returning tő plague Jackson. There were even some who speculated that Eaton had had Peg's husband, Timberlake, murdered so he could marry her.

Raven was not just indulging in gossip. He wanted Tiana to know that the people of Washington City were catholic in their prejudice. They could despise anyone, regardless of race, color, creed, or station in life.

Raven didn't mention that he too was an object of gossip. He could hardly be otherwise when he appeared at social functions in full Indian dress. Someone in Drum's delegation had given Raven a magnificent buckskin coat with a beaver collar. But it became wet and stained and it shrank during the trip east. Raven wore it anyway, because he had no other. If the plumes nodding in Raven's hair didn't attract attention, the bells tinkling on his leather coat did.

He also wore his moccasins and blanket and, occasionally, his leggings. The leggings particularly fascinated the ladies. Word had gotten around that leggings weren't made like trousers and that Raven's long hunting shirt covered a set of bare buttocks and thighs. In a society that covered its piano legs, speculation about what was under General Houston's shirt was heady stuff.

When Raven wrote Tiana, at the beginning of March, 1832, he himself didn't know how drastically Eaton's exile to Florida would affect him. On the last day of March, while Tiana sat by the Widow Nicks' stove and read Raven's letter, William Stanberry delivered in the House of Representatives scatter-shot criticism of Jackson. He included a question: "Was not the late Secretary of War removed and sent to Florida because of his attempt fraudulently to give Governor Houston the contract for Indian rations three years ago?"

The local hangers-on raced to O'Neale's tavern to tell Raven. They did it with the same relish gamblers will coax dogs to fight. Raven didn't disappoint them. He left a wake of overturned chairs behind him in the tavern. O'Neale's post coach was waiting patiently for its driver to finish his Tom and Jerry, a drink of brandy, rum, egg, sugar, nutmeg, and hot milk.

Raven climbed into the driver's seat, took the reins and whip, and clattered off toward the Capitol. The messengers posted along behind. They didn't want to miss any of the fun. Raven drove the coach wildly through the fields, taking shortcuts between the aimless boulevards. He arrived at the Capitol, which looked itself like something of an exile. Under the dreary sky, it brooded majestically among the flocks of sheep and the copses of trees surrounding it. Raven vaulted the broad marble steps two at a time and burst into the foyer of the House chamber. James Polk was waiting for him.

"Sam." Polk grabbed his arm.

"I'm going to settle this account now," shouted Raven. Startled ladies and aides, gawkers, petitioners and snuff-sniffing representatives turned to stare.

"Listen to me, Sam." With great difficulty, Polk steered him back outside where a raw wind was blowing. "You'll only bring more charges down on Jackson. Everyone knows you're his man. If you create a scandal here, they'll only go for him. You can't indulge your ire."

"Indulge my ire! Sir, I've been falsely accused of dishonesty on the floor of Congress. I've been publicly humiliated by poltroons for the last time!"

"Then send a second around. Call him out. Do it properly."

"I shall, by the Eternal. I shall. Will you be my second?"

Polk faltered. He envisioned Raven demanding he deliver the note on the floor of the House. Besides, dueling was illegal.

"Never mind." Raven brushed him aside. "What can one expect of a man who drinks water?"

But Stanberry seemed to prefer verbal battles only. He refused the note Raven's second delivered. He did, however, arm himself with two large pistols. Raven began carrying the large hickory cane he had carved. There was an air of disappointment around Washington when nothing more happened for two weeks.

One dark night, about the middle of April, Raven and two friends left Felix Grundy's rooms. They had been drinking, in honor of spring, but they weren't very intoxicated. They strolled down the broad avenue toward their lodgings in Brown's Indian Queen Hotel.

The stumps had finally been cleared from the avenues, and the farmers had been convinced not to plant their gardens in the middle of them. The police force had been doubled, raising it to two men. Washington was becoming civilized. In the dim light of the flickering gas street lamps, Raven thought he saw Stanberry leave a tavern.

"Are you Mr. Stanberry?" he asked.

"Yes, sir," Stanberry answered.

"Then you're a damned rascal!" Raven's right shoulder still pained him, deep down where the bone had been damaged. So he swung his cane with his left hand. The wood resounded against Stanberry's head with a loud crack.

"Don't!" Stanberry staggered and threw up a hand to protect himself.

But Raven was beyond reason or entreaty. The years of pent-up anger and frustration boiled over. He was striking out against all those who had slandered him, humiliated him, driven him from his home, ruined his career, shamed his wife in Tennessee, hurt his woman in Oklahoma, and caused the sorrow in his mother's eyes when she died.

Stanberry was a big man, almost as large as Raven. But he turned and ran. Raven leaped on his back and dragged him to the sidewalk. Stanberry screamed for help. He pulled a pistol from the waist of his trousers and pressed the muzzle to Raven's chest. When he pulled the trigger, the lock snapped and sparks flew, but nothing happened. Raven wrenched the pistol away and threw it into the nearest pile of manure in the avenue.

Raven stood and thumped the groveling Stanberry a few more times with his cane. Then he lifted the man's feet, exposing the dirty seat of his trousers. He kicked the representative's rear end hard, then dropped his feet. He straightened his clothes and strode off into the night without looking back.

Come what may, Raven no longer felt helpless. He had done what he needed to do, and the devil take the hindmost. As a man who had lost everything, he was at least free of the fear of loss. He had to restrain himself from breaking into an undignified whistle.

The affair wasn't allowed to slink off as a common street brawl.

"Most Daring Outrage and Assault," the headlines read. The House voted one hundred and forty-five to twenty-five to arrest Raven, although Polk protested that it wasn't legal for them to do it. Raven was given forty-eight hours to prepare a defense. He engaged Francis Scott Key as his attorney.

Washington City's social center was not the theater, or the race tracks, the opera or salons. For pure entertainment, nothing could beat the proceedings in the elegant halls of the Senate and House. A government and a society were being invented there on a daily basis. People flocked to watch the drama.

Since Andrew Jackson had taken office, the solemn chambers had become a great deal livelier, if also more uncouth. There was a small sign at the head of the stairs leading to the upper gallery: GENTLEMEN WILL BE PLEASED NOT TO PLACE THEIR FEET ON THE BOARD IN FRONT OF THE GALLERY, AS THE DIRT FROM THEM FALLS UPON CONGRESSMEN'S HEADS. Dirt was a tactful way of saying mud and horse manure tracked in on boots or bare feet. Ladies had to master the skill of holding their skirts high enough to keep their hems from dragging in the tobacco juice on the floor, yet still not show any ankle.

On the last day of the trial, a bright morning in May, Raven stood straight and quiet before the Speaker's dais. His back was to the concentric rows of desks. Above the dais was a vaulting arch draped in folds of red linen. It framed a sculpted figure of Liberty and an eagle in flight. Flags hung over pictures of Washington and Lafayette. Raven could feel the excitement in the large hall behind him. The gallery had filled two hours before the day's trial was to start. Everyone who was anyone was present.

Many Congressmen had gallantly given their seats to lady friends. Raven could hear the rustle of their crinolines and their whispers and low laughter. He imagined them inspecting the snuff boxes and writing implements supplied each representative and wrinkling their noses at the brass cuspidor under each desk. The displaced Congressmen sat in extra chairs, or on piles of documents. Some stood with the rest of the crowd between the pillars along the wall. Others stood on the sofas to see better.

It had rained earlier that morning. Raven smelled wet wool and leather, tobacco and dirt and the lavender and rose scent of the ladies. He heard the nervous coughing, and stifled the urge to cough himself. For the past two weeks the business of running the country had slowed to a crawl. Newspapers had to carry long articles about the trial to satisfy their readers. Raven had what he'd wanted, the entire country with its ear cocked. He was about to give the most important performance of his life so far. And he was relishing it.

If looks could win this case, Raven's victory would be assured. Jackson had called Raven into his office two days earlier.

"Have you no clothes but those?" he roared at Raven.

"No, sir."

"By the Eternal, man. You can't go before Congress in those savage rags." He had tossed a silk purse with long tassels onto the desk between them.

"I can't accept this, sir."

"Yes, you can. It's not you they wish to injure, Sam. They wish to injure your old commander. Dress like a gentleman and buck up your defense. I won't have you convicted because of that bungling attorney, Key. He's a better songwriter than a lawyer."

"I'm sorry for whatever trouble I may have caused you, sir."

Jackson sat back in his chair. His wide mouth split suddenly in a grin.

"Trouble? Sam, after a few more examples of the same kind, members of Congress will learn to keep civil tongues in their heads. It must never go beyond this room, but I'm proud of you, boy."

"To tell the truth, sir, I felt meaner than an Osage cur after I struck that man. I thought I'd gotten hold of a great dog, but found instead a contemptible, whining puppy."

"No matter. Just get you a good suit of clothes. I know how you look when you're dressed up." Jackson skewered Raven with his stare. "I won't have you losing this case. Do you understand?"

"Yes, sir."

Raven had gone to the best tailor in Washington City. Now, over tight, buff-colored trousers, he wore a burgundy-red coat reaching his knees. He wore a white satin vest with a gold watch chain. He carried the infamous cane and a wide-brimmed, low-crowned white beaver hat. He had curried it until it gleamed in the sunlight that poured through the glass dome sixty feet overhead.

Raven looked far better than he felt. His head ached and his stomach churned menacingly. He had been drinking into the morning hours with friends, and his system wasn't as used to it as it once had been. He had awakened with a bad case of what Hell-Fire Jack called the Blue Devils. He had ordered the barber to show up early with coffee and shaving traps. He had shown the man a pistol and a purse.

"If the coffee doesn't stick when I drink it," he had said, "shoot me with this pistol and the gold is yours." Raven would rather die than be sick and fail in his summing-up speech. It had taken three tries that morning, but the coffee had finally stayed down.

Now, he wondered if Stevenson, the Speaker of the House and presiding officer at the trial, felt as queasy as he did. Stevenson had been one of the celebrants in Raven's room at the Indian Queen Hotel the night before. He had passed out on the couch sometime after midnight. Felix Grundy had ceased to be interesting shortly after that. James Polk, sober as usual, had left early. Raven had put a pillow under the snoring Grundy's head and left him where he was, sprawled between the bed and the washstand.

"What will Mrs. Grundy say?" Raven had muttered before he fell asleep.

Raven was startled from his reverie by silence. It was his turn to speak in his own defense. He bowed to Speaker Stevenson.

"Mr. Speaker." Raven's normal speaking voice carried to every corner of the room. "Arraigned for the first time of my life on a charge of violating the laws of my country, I feel all the embarrassment which my peculiar situation is calculated to inspire. I disclaim, utterly, every motive unworthy of an honorable man. If, when deeply wronged, I violated on impulse the law, I am willing to be held to my responsibility. All I ask is that my actions be pursued to the motives which gave them birth." He turned to face the hushed audience. The hall was patterned after a Greek theater. It was a fitting place for Raven to make his defense.

"I stand before this House branded as a man of broken fortune and blasted reputation. I can never forget that reputation is the high boon of heaven. Though the plowshare of ruin has driven over me and laid waste my brightest hopes, I have only to say

> *I seek no sympathies, nor need;*
> *The thorns which I have reaped are of the tree*
> *I planted; they have torn me and I bleed.*

Even for The Raven it was high rhetoric. The crowd burst into applause. Lord Byron had served Raven's purpose well. Raven waited for the noise to die. "That man, Stanberry, has slandered me and refused to answer a polite note. I have chastised him as I would a dog. And I will do the same to anyone who insults me."

He went on to argue that by meddling in the affair, Congress was invading his private rights as a citizen. He spoke for half an hour about the dangers of a legislature that took too much onto itself. He cited Greece and Rome, Cromwell and Bonaparte. Finally, he glanced up at the flag draping the portrait of George Washington.

"So long as that proud emblem shall wave in the Hall of American Legislators, so long shall it cast its sacred protection over the personal rights of every American citizen. Sir, when you have destroyed the pride of the American character, you will have destroyed the brightest jewel that heaven ever made. But, sir, so long as that flag shall bear aloft its glittering stars, so long, I trust, shall the rights of American citizens be preserved safe and unimpaired—till discord shall wreck the spheres—the grand march of time shall cease—and not one fragment of all creation be left to chafe the bosom of eternity's waves."

He gave a small bow to Speaker Stevenson, then to the people in the hall. A woman's voice rang out in the silence that followed.

"I had rather be Sam Houston in a dungeon than Stanberry on a throne." She leaned over the gallery railing and tossed a bouquet of roses at Raven's feet. He retrieved them and bowed over them with eyes lowered. Then he sat down and stared straight ahead throughout the storm of applause that went on for several minutes.

Junius Brutus Booth made his way through the mob and threw his arms around Raven.

"Houston, take my laurels." He shouted to be heard over the noise. "What a performance," he said in a lower voice.

Raven stood at the railing of the steamboat's boiler deck and looked out into the night. He had made this trip so many times, the Mississippi was like an old friend. Raven had entered Washington City in disgrace and left in triumph. There were only two situations that caused him pain. Both of them involved women.

Raven had seen Eliza. It hadn't been easy. He had bribed Dilcey, her slave. It had taken all of his charm and some of his silver to convince her to help him. She had lured Eliza into her cabin on some pretext or another, and Raven had watched through a wide crack in the floor of the loft.

Raven had heard the rumors that Eliza wanted him back. But did he want her? She was as beautiful as ever, but she seemed much younger than he remembered, and spiritless. Raven decided the word spiritless described her well. There was no flash of life in her eyes, no magic in her. She had been replaced so completely in his heart by someone else, she seemed a stranger. And he wondered what madness had driven him to behave as he had.

When she left, he had come down from the loft, thanked Dilcey, and disappeared into the night. Once again, he was leaving Tennessee behind, but it was no longer home. His mother was dead, and so was his passion.

That brought him to the second problem. He felt a warmth in his groin just at the thought of Tiana. Could he bring himself to leave her?

A young man walked up to stand beside him. He too stared out at the black waters, glittering with luminescence.

"You have a magnificent country, General Houston." The man spoke with a heavy French accent.

"Indeed it is, Monsieur de Tocqueville."

"It makes one almost sympathize with Americans' suffocating patriotism."

"Are we so much more patriotic than Europeans?"

"*Mon Dieu*! The entire populace of Europe can't, how do you say, it, muster the patriotism exhibited by the lowliest American rag and bone peddler. Let a stranger criticize this country and he risks bodily harm. One cannot speak of anything except perhaps the soil and the climate. Even then, Americans defend both as if they had cooperated in producing them."

Raven laughed. He rested his back on the railing and faced the lanky Frenchman. De Tocqueville's beak of a nose was outlined by the saloon lights.

"Well, Monsieur de Tocqueville, you may speak to me of anything you like."

"Even the president's Indian policy?"

Raven laughed, ruefully. "A delicate subject, indeed. It has divided the country. I shall not offer you bodily harm for criticizing Old Hickory's policy. But I must warn you that my attachment to him is firm and undeviating."

" 'My country, right or wrong,' as your Admiral Decatur would say."

"Perhaps he would have said it," said Raven mildly, not wanting to give offense. "But he didn't. What he actually said was 'Our country! In her intercourse with foreign nations, may she always be in the right; but our country, right or wrong.' Don't feel badly about it." Raven offered a cigar and match. "Americans never quote it right either."

"But what of imprisoning missionaries? Surely you can't defend that."

"Jackson didn't imprison them. The state of Georgia did. And they weren't entirely blameless, Worcester and the others. The government told them they must get permits to stay in Indian country. They chose to ignore the law. Samuel Worcester is a stubborn man with a desire for martyrdom."

"But in a good cause, it seems to me. Did not Justice Marshall of your own Supreme Court say Georgia was wrong in imprisoning the missionaries and harassing the Indians?"

Raven turned to look out over the water again. For a foreigner not long in this country, de Tocqueville had a rather thorough understanding of the situation. His English was excellent too, if stilted and bookish.

"And did not your president say, 'John Marshall has made his law, now let him enforce it'? Surely, sir, you, as a friend of the Indians, must realize the gross injustice of the case."

"I'm not claiming it's just or that Jackson was right in saying what he did. He's a man of quick tempers. He says what occurs to him at the moment. But he's also a realist. Monsieur de Tocqueville, you cannot know the hatred the Georgians harbor for the Indian. That the Cherokee are often more civilized and prosperous than they only adds fuel to that hatred."

"The less a man's station here, the greater his arrogance."

"The Indians cannot coexist with the people of Georgia. If the Cherokee do not remove, there will be war. The country is already torn by the question of states' rights."

"*Oui*," said de Tocqueville dryly. "Your illustrious president threatens to hang the South Carolina nullifiers."

"When Jackson talks of hanging, you can look for a rope."

"Yet, he strangely ignores the fact that Georgia nullifies the Supreme Court decision and keeps Worcester in jail."

Raven turned again, to look de Tocqueville in the eye.

"No one is more in sympathy with the Indians than I. They are a race of people I'm proud to say have called me brother. All the injustices and pains I have suffered in this life have been at the hands of whites, not Indians. The man I love as a father is a savage king, living in the ways of his ancestors. It is he who wants the eastern members of the tribe to go west and join him, to halt the advance of the whites."

"Impossible, it seems to me. The Georgians say they must have the territory of the Cherokee. Yet Georgia has seven persons to each square mile of her state. In France we have one hundred and sixty-two inhabitants per square mile."

"That's why the Georgians live in Georgia and not in France. They don't like being crowded."

"*Touché*. And are the missionaries helping the Indians?"

"Are you collecting material for your book, Monsieur? I thought you were studying America's prison system."

"Forgive me if I am being impertinent. I do find your country fascinating. I only want to learn as much as I can."

"Do I think the missionaries help the Indians? Sir, I do not. To send missionaries among them is a very poor way to go about civilizing them. My friend Colonel Chouteau says one can always tell when one Indian has been twice as long at the mission as another. He's twice as good for nothing.

"The missionaries take people who already have a refined sense of right and wrong, and an enviable style of government and moral suasion and pervert them." Raven realized his voice was becoming bitter. "Some wag carved a bit of doggerel on one of the pews at Dwight mission. My . . ." Raven hesitated, then went on. "My Indian wife saw it there. It's about one of the Black Robes, a pompous, stingy, self-righteous man." He recited.

> *The eloquence of William Vail*
> *Would make the stoutest sinner quail.*
> *The hissing goose has far more sense*
> *Than Vail and all his eloquence.*

"Tiana says her brother once saw the man refuse to sell food to a starving Indian because it was the Sabbath. He wouldn't *give* the woman any food either."

"Is she fair, your wife?"

"Fair doesn't begin to describe her. She is my solace amidst the lights and shadows of forest life. She's like molasses, rather than honey. Dark, sweet, but with a bite to her. Monsieur, I recommend Cherokee women above all others."

"And what are your plans when you return to Indian country?" It was an innocent question, but Raven's guard went up.

"I have no definite plans. My fortunes have been at the ebb, as you may know."

De Tocqueville nodded. Everyone in the country knew about Sam Houston's fortunes.

"A group of corrupt politicians and Indian agents tried to ruin me," Raven went on, "I was dying out. Had they taken me before a justice of the peace and fined me ten dollars it would have killed me. But they gave me a national tribunal for a theater and that set me up again. I shall find something to do, I promise you that."

De Tocqueville drew a thin notebook from inside his coat.

"General Houston, would you be so good as to tell me about the Cherokee?"

"My pleasure. What would you like to know?"

Chapter 53

When Raven got off Pennywit's boat at Webber's Landing, Drum was there to greet him. He hugged his son and stepped back to admire his finery.

"Someone is visiting my woman and me," he said. Raven was happy to see the old mischievous twinkle back in his father's eyes. "But I did not tell her you were coming on this boat." Raven knew Drum had heard the boat was coming. The women's cabins stretched for twenty-five miles downriver. They relayed the information as they pounded corn. And there were always children Drum could send to fetch Tiana wherever she was. Raven knew if he was patient he would find out why Drum wanted him to go find her.

"Where is she, Beloved Father?"

"At the river, where we dig mussels. Do you remember?"

"Yes."

"Then go. Don't stand here talking to an old man."

Raven started off at a run.

"Take my horse," Drum called after him. "Those clothes weren't made for running." *Nor riding either*, Drum thought. He shook his head. It would take a week or more to re-educate his son. It always did. It took that long just to get the odors of the white man's cities off his skin and the babble of their incessant talk from his mind.

As Raven cantered along the tree-shaded path toward the river, he met a crowd of Tiana's cousins and nieces, young and old. The small girls' mouths were stained with berry juice. Everyone's hair was wet. Some of the women carried fish weirs or baskets of berries or fish. Two swung a huge basket of clean, wet clothes between them as they walked. Some balanced their babies on their hips or carried them in cloth slings on their backs. The usual pack of dogs ranged along the trail, sniffing everything. Everyone crowded around Raven's horse, laughing and teasing and asking what he had brought them.

"Wife, where is your sister?" Raven asked. He used the teasing expression for his sister-in-law, Nannie. He knew that as far as Tiana's family was concerned, he and Tiana were married.

"Gigging mussels."

"Is she alone?" He had a horror of something dreadful happening to her. She was in the habit of roaming the countryside alone.

"Elizabeth and Nannie are with her. James's and John's wives."

"I know, sister. I've not been gone that long."

Before he saw the river, Raven smelled the water on the wind blowing through the willows and cottonwoods and the bluestem grass. He heard the garble of turkeys, hidden in the tall buffalo grass of a nearby prairie. A jackrabbit burst from under his feet when he dismounted. Overhead, a golden eagle wheeled lazily in a shimmering blue sky. Crows and magpies squabbled in the trees.

Raven crept through the thick bushes and trees to the pool where the mussels were. He called softly to Nannie and Elizabeth Rogers as they dug clay. Stifling their laughter, the two women moved off silently down the trail toward home.

Tiana's clothes were draped neatly over a bush near the shore. She lay on her stomach on a small raft in the middle of the pool. She was staring so fixedly into the water she didn't notice Raven hiding in the bushes. He waved at the mosquitoes swarming around his face. Whenever he was away, he forgot about the heat and the insects here. Already he could feel itchy welts.

Tiana wore only a cotton loincloth looped under her woven belt. Her long legs flowed into her slender brown hips, her sides, shoulders, and outstretched arms in one sinuous curve. Her bare buttocks were carelessly draped by the end of the loincloth, covering only enough to tantalize Raven. Her knife sheath was on her belt. The insects must have been bedeviling her, but she didn't move.

Tiana wasn't so much aware of the wind and the birds and insects around her as she was part of them. She felt weightless and suspended in the spirit world. The hardness of the raft against her body made the mystical quality around her more intense, yet kept it in balance. The rough wood was a contact with reality that helped her appreciate her euphoria all the more. Moments like this, when she could forget everything but immediate sensations, were few and fleeting. She remained motionless, because she didn't want to disturb this one and because she seemed to have lost contact with her muscles.

As she gazed into the clear water, she thought she could see each buff-colored grain of sand and pebble on the bottom. She watched a mussel raise the edge of its gray-brown shell out of the sand and open it slightly. She knew she should insert the pointed end of her gigging stick into the crack. When the shell clamped shut on the stick, she should lift it into the basket of mussels that sat next to her on the raft. She should do that. And she would, after she had enjoyed doing nothing for a few more seconds.

"Spider Eyes," Raven shouted.

In a flash, she was over the side like a startled otter and her heart was dancing in her chest. She clung to the far edge of the raft with her knife drawn. When she realized who it was, she was happy to see him, but irritated with him too. And to her own surprise, she had a fleeting feeling of resentment, as though a bit of freedom had been taken from her.

"Someday you will startle me and I will kill you before I know what I'm about."

"If someone doesn't kill you first. How many times have I told you not to go around half-naked? Three-quarters naked?"

"You've been among civilized people too long. You're preoccupied with nakedness again."

"Someday you'll provoke someone when I'm not around to save you."

"That's certainly true." She pushed the raft in front of her as she swam toward him. "I mean it's true about your not being around."

She waded ashore, the water beading on the bear grease that coated her body. She had perfumed the grease with columbine seeds. The result wasn't unpleasing. Dripping wet, she threw her arms around Raven. He kissed her and smelled the faint odor of resin. She must have been chewing *No-tsi Usdi*, Little Pine, to spit on the raft and gig to lure the mussels.

He had only a brief moment of chagrin at holding a naked woman in the bright sunlight. And an even briefer moment of regret about his good clothes getting wet and greasy. He had hoped to impress her with them, forgetting that clothes never impressed her much anyway. He ran his hands down her bare back and pressed her hips against him. She began unbuttoning his trousers.

"You're pale," she said. "You've been shut away from Grandmother Sun." She noticed something else about him too. There was a look of determination, a sense of purpose, that hadn't been in his face before. It made him even more attractive, but her heart grew heavier. Even as he talked, she sensed some part of him was far away.

They bathed, then made slow love in the sunshine. When they had finished, Tiana lay on her back with her eyes closed and her hand on Raven's thigh. She felt Grandmother Sun's warm fingers on her eyelids and Raven's warmth under her own hand.

"When you are gone," she said in a low voice, "it seems I shall never see you again. Never feel you. It seems like this is but a dream. Then, when you're here with me again, it seems you were never away. And I want to hold you forever."

"I have missed you more than I can tell you. I longed for the time I could lie with you again and hear the voice of silence. Sometimes, while talking with the most important men in the country, my mind would fill with you. I knew you were sending your spirit to me."

"I did send it, every day."

"And I received it. Your love is a White House that shelters me wherever I go. You've led my feet to a White Path. I live in the center of your soul." He kissed her lingeringly. Then they bathed again, dressed, and carried the basket of mussels to where Tiana had tied Jack.

"What happened to Jack's tail?" asked Raven.

"Wolves," said Tiana laconically as she tightened the rope that secured the basket to Jack's broad back. "They were bold this winter. I'm sorry I wasn't at the landing to meet you. Many more vessels reach here now that the snag boats clear the channel. I met every one for months. But many of them carried emigrants from the Sunland. I think the world has reversed itself." They rode side-by-side along the trail.

"What do you mean?"

"It seems the Sunland has become the Nightland. The people

from there tell terrible stories. The white men drive them from their homes and burn them or steal their crops and stock."

"I've heard the rumors," said Raven.

"They're not rumors. Those people don't lie."

"No. It's a skill the Real People haven't learned yet." Raven rode in silence a few minutes. "Spider Eyes, I'm sorry I was gone so long. I became involved, all against my will, in an affair of honor."

"We read about it. The trial before the big council, the debate about the ration contracts. Drum was pleased with your speeches. He said you've learned well."

"I had a good teacher. I pretended I was trying to persuade a stubborn group of headmen. I brought you presents. You'll be the most beautiful woman east or west of the Mississippi."

"Drum and Sally Ground Squirrel will have a feast tonight."

"Of course. I only go away so Drum can celebrate my homecoming. He enjoys it so. Is there any news I should know? Beloved Father wouldn't even talk to me. He sent me here straight from the boat."

"You just missed Benjamin Bonneville."

"He actually set out on that wild-eyed exploration to the western mountains?"

"A month ago. And Colonel Arbuckle is still suffering from the flux. I gave him medicine, which he took politely, and threw away, I'm sure. At any rate, he's still in a crankus mood. He and John Drew have been battling over the barrels of liquor that belong to the two of you. John is threatening to shoot the colonel if he tries to confiscate them." John Drew was Tiana's nephew-in-law and Raven's new business partner.

People were already gathering for the feast when the two of them reached the house. A slaughtered steer, venison, and pigs roasted on spits. Large, round-bottomed clay pots of stew were propped in the cooking fires. The yard was filled with smoke, but it discouraged mosquitoes. Children, black and red, raced around.

After dinner, Raven told stories about life in the white man's cities. James and John swore the tales were true.

"Raven does not lie," James said. "There is an iron horse that runs on a metal trail. John and I rode it in Baltimore. It can race as fast as a horse. But it makes clouds of black smoke and has a loud call. If you think me a singing bird, I shall show you the soot in my ears from the iron horse's nostrils."

"And we saw a rolling show," said John. "With elephants and black-and-white-striped horses and birds so large a man can ride them."

No one believed them, but everyone loved the stories anyway. The women wanted to know what styles white ladies wore now and how they fixed their hair. Several of them had leghorn bonnets and followed eastern fashions with a singleminded fervor the local missionaries found distressing. But then, the missionaries had always disapproved of the Cherokee's love of frivolity and fun.

Raven waved his hands in the air above him as he tried to describe the complicated hairdos of the women in Washington City. Finally he took an old calico shirt and some vegetables and managed, with James's help, to construct an outlandish artifact on his head. Before they finished, everyone was helpless with laughter.

The women discussed bouffant sleeves and bustles. They laughed and twisted each other's hair in imitation of the styles Raven described. The men smoked and talked politics. Raven sat comfortably in the center of it all. In a corner, Tiana sang a lullabye to James's youngest child curled in her lap. "*Ha'wiye' hyuwe'*," she sang. "*Ye'we yuwehe' Ha'wiyehyu' uwe'*. The bear is bad, so they say. Long time ago he was very bad, so they say." She repeated it over and over until the child was asleep and Raven felt as peaceful inside as the little one looked. Tiana went to the other room to lay the child among the other babies who had surrendered to fatigue. When she came back, Drum was beginning a story.

"This is what the old men told me when I was a boy. The game we call *gatayusti* was invented by the great gambler, Untsiyi, Brass. One day a Son of Thunder played the game with Brass. With the help of Thunder's magic, the boy beat him. Brass had been so sure he would win he bet his life on it. So the boy and his brothers chased Brass all the way to the edge of the world.

"They tied his hands and feet with grapevines and drove a long stake through his chest. They planted the stake in deep water in a place called *Ka gun'yi*, Crow Place. To this very day, two crows sit on the end of the pole. Brass can't die until the world ends. He lies there still, face up, and he struggles to free himself. The beavers take pity on him and gnaw at the ropes holding him. But the crows feel the pole shaking. They caw and scare the beavers away." He paused to let everyone think about the horrible fate of Brass.

"I know a similar story," said Raven. "About a man called Prometheus, who lived long, long ago. He brought sacred fire to mankind and was punished by the gods. He was chained on a mountain where he suffered every night from the cold. And every day a vulture tore at his liver. It healed at night so Prometheus could suffer the same agony daily, throughout eternity."

When the stories were over, everyone rolled up the floor mats. There would be dancing all night. Tiana took Raven by the hand and sneaked out with him. They climbed the stairs to the new second story and found an empty room among the eaves. There were three or four pallets on the floor, all made up for guests. This room was used for storage too. The walls were lined with baskets of corn and beans and apples.

Raven knew that bushels of squash were stored in cool pits in the ground. The corn cratches would soon be full and pumpkin slices would festoon the ceilings. Drum and his big family would spend long winter evenings telling stories in front of the fire. Raven wondered where he would be while they did it.

He and Tiana made gentle love for a long time. If only life could be lived solely in her arms, he would have no need of ambition.

"This gets better each time we do it," he whispered into her smoky hair.

"Old fires burn hotter," she said.

When they finished and lay exhausted and happy, Raven gathered courage to tell her the news.

"Spider Eyes, I have to make another trip."

"But you just arrived." She propped herself on one elbow and stared into his face, a slightly paler oval in the darkness of the room. He stroked her long hair, losing himself in the smell and feel of her.

"Not right away. Months from now. This winter."

"Will you go back to Washington City?"

"No. Texas. Jackson asked me to find the Pawnee and Kiowa and Comanche and meet with them, to bring them to peace talks."

"I suppose he wants you to meet with the Texicans too, now that he knows the Spanish won't sell Texas. He can't get it honestly, so he intends to foment rebellion. Am I correct?"

"I've known you for almost a quarter of a century, Spider Eyes, and still I underestimate you."

"I read all the newspapers that come here. And men pass through on their way to the Red River. Gangs of them stop at Wigwam Neosho. They're scum, husband. The offscourings of the earth.

Arbuckle has given his patrols orders to stop them, but that's as impossible as stopping the whiskey traffic."

"I have to go. The president needs the information. I'll be back in the spring."

"You don't have to go. There are hundreds of men who could do what Jackson asks." She allowed anger to creep into her voice. "But you want to go. You are like A'sku'ya, Long Man, the River. You're always restless. You never stay in one place. You must always go somewhere bigger. Some place I'll never see."

She started to cry, silently, in the dark. "People come to me, because they think I have power. Perhaps I had power once. But it must be gone. I cannot live where I want. For when I do, the government comes and tells me to move. I cannot love whom I will. For when I do, he is killed or taken from me. I cannot protect my family. They die, in spite of my magic. My youngest sister made the journey to the Nightland while you were gone."

"I didn't know, beloved. My heart cries for you."

"I think she just wearied of life. Her saliva was spoiled and her dreams were bad after her child was killed and she was used by those buffalo hunters. Sometimes I wish I could join her.

"And you, Raven." She used his name deliberately, perhaps in a last effort to control him, to keep him with her. "My love for you has made me helpless. Sometimes I feel it's a trap that has caught me and holds me fast."

"You mustn't feel that way. It's you who have bewitched me. I want to go to Texas for you. I have seen friends from Texas. They say it's prosperous, a lovely region. Thousands would flock there if the government were settled. It's a land of promise. Sweet Spider Eyes, you've woven a web around my heart. I won't leave you long. There's an empire waiting there. I'll win it for you."

"I would rather share the Wigwam Neosho with you than an empire. Empires do not fall into one's hand, like ripe fruit."

"Texas will. It's ready for the plucking, I tell you."

"No, Raven. One must fight for empires. Many people die so a few men can rule territory so big they can never even see it all. That's what empires are."

"It'll be glorious. You'll see. For once I shall have the satisfaction of saying, 'I told you so.'" He put his arms around her and held her close. He felt the heat and wetness of her tears against his chest. "No matter what happens, you know I love you. You know you will always walk in my soul."

"Yes, I know it. No matter what happens. I'll cherish you while you're here and suffer *uhi'sodi*, loneliness, when you go."

"I won't be gone long. In the meantime, let's visit Chouteau. He can mix up a ball faster than a gnat can blink. And I brought you a dress that will blind them with its splendor. Jackson's niece helped me pick it out."

"And we'll waltz?"

"All night."

Raven burst into Wigwam Neosho one day in October of 1832. Tiana looked up from her vinegar making. She was surrounded by baskets of peeled apples. She was grinding them in a crude machine and putting the pulp in a sack. Already juice was dripping from the sack into a big bucket. Once the juice soured, she would strain it and let it stand six months. Tiana worked harder than usual these days, trying not to think of Raven's leaving again in two months.

"He's looking around the farm." Raven could hardly contain his excitement. His grin stretched almost into his curly side whiskers. "He'll be right in."

"Who?" Tiana tried to sort out the mess.

A short, balding man of about fifty entered the cabin. He looked like a middle-aged Puck, plump as a partridge and with round, pink cheeks.

"Tiana," Raven gave a snappy bow. "Allow me to present Mr. Washington Irving." It took a few seconds for the name to register. When it did, Tiana's face broke into an astonished smile.

"Mr. Irving. *The* Mr. Irving? Geoffrey Crayon?"

Irving nodded a little sheepishly. He should be used to this by now, but he had hardly expected to be recognized by an Indian woman in a cabin in the wilderness.

"This is an honor," Tiana said.

"The honor is mine, madam. You're even more beautiful than General Houston described. And please don't trouble yourself. It was rude of me to surprise you this way."

"I can't believe this good fortune. Warm yourself by the fire. The stew is ready, and there's hominy and honey. What brings you to such a faraway corner of the world?"

"My traveling companions and I are going with the Rangers and the Stokes commission. We're to explore the area to the south and west of here. Make contact with the wild Indians and hunt the noble bison, I trust. My companions are wild for it."

"He'll be riding with my old friend Jesse Bean, and the Arkansas Volunteers."

"My dear sir," said Tiana. "Do have a care. They're a barbarous lot, those Rangers."

"So I've noticed," said Irving. "They're a raw, unruly band. They have no tradition of military service to temper them. They appear to have no training, no uniforms, no commissary nor consciousness of rank, as far as I can tell."

"They're only volunteers, enlisted for a year," said Raven.

"The authorities expect trouble out here when Jackson has his way and empties the east of savages." Tiana smiled at Irving to show she said it without any malice toward him.

"I served with Jesse Bean in the Creek war," said Raven. "Grew up with him. He's as brave as they come. Just lacks polish."

"He and the Rangers lack anything *to* polish," laughed Tiana.

"Tiana took it amiss when I invited a few of them home for dinner and they didn't wait for her to clear the plates before they put their boots on the table and began to pick their teeth with their bowie knives."

"Mr. Irving," said Tiana. "I never would have thought the author of the *Sketchbooks* would one day sit in my cabin on the way to hunt bison. Are you a hunter as well as a scholar?"

"Perhaps a better hunter than a scholar, though indifferent in both pursuits. As a boy, I used to hunt in upper Manhattan. And my older brother was a fur trader with the Indians on the New York frontier."

"Your stories have given us more pleasure than you can know." Tiana set the table with her best blue porcelain as she talked. Irving watched her move gracefully and un-self-consciously about the room. She added elegance to the simple splintered table and rough walls, the furs on the chairs and beds, and the calico and beaded dresses hanging on pegs.

As she worked and chatted, Tiana felt at ease with the man whose words she had read so often. It would have been difficult not to be. Irving's hair was combed forward onto his forehead and cheeks. It was the style of the day, but with his turned-up nose and broad, full mouth, it gave him the look of a pixie. There was a droll sparkle to his eyes that made people instantly like and trust him. *A doux little man*, Tiana thought. It was difficult to imagine him chasing buffalo with Jesse Bean's unwashed ruffians. With a charming smile, he took the brandy Raven offered him. He was blissfully ignorant of the trouble it had caused. Arbuckle was still trying to confiscate it.

"I trust you'll spend some time with us," said Tiana.

"Would that I could, gentle lady. But the intrepid Captain Bean has already left. My companions and I must hustle to catch him."

"Then we shall have to make the most of what time we have with you." While the two men helped themselves to the stew and steaming corn bread, butter, honey, and preserves, Tiana propped her forearms against the edge of the table and leaned toward Irving. He was amused and charmed by the intensity in her look.

"Tell me, Mr. Irving," she said. "Where do you get the ideas for your stories?"

Irving smiled at her indulgently. He had heard that question before. He waved his fork vaguely.

"From life. I read men, not books. I fear I'm more of a doer than a contemplator." Already he was making mental notes to jot down later in his looseleaf. *Governor Houston—tall, large, well-formed, fascinating man. Low-crowned white beaver, boots with brass eagle spurs. Given to grandiloquence. A large and military mode of expressing himself.* As for his wife, she gave the lie to the old remark that persons of Indian mixture were half civilized, half savage, and half devil, a third half being provided for their particular convenience.

Chapter 54

Tiana' voice choked and her hands trembled with anger as she read the article in the *Phoenix* aloud to Drum. It was a copy of a letter written by Ridge. She and Drum both knew that although Pathkiller was Principal Chief of the Cherokee Nation, east and west, he wasn't really in charge. John Ross, the President of the National Council, and Ridge, the Council's Speaker, were directing affairs in New Echota. Even though it was distressing, Drum asked Tiana to read the article again.

It told of what was happening in Georgia. Tiana remembered how elated they had all been when they'd read Justice John Marshall's decision in favor of the Cherokee. "The Cherokee Nation is a distinct community occupying its own territory, in which the citizens of Georgia have no right to enter but with the assent of the Cherokee themselves." Since Andrew Jackson refused to enforce Marshall's ruling, the Georgians were making the Real People's lives a nightmare. Ridge's letter said, in part,

> The usual scenes which our afflicted people experience are dreadfully increased. They are robbed and whipped by whites every day.

There was more. Ridge detailed raids on the Real People's live-stock, the terror of night riders, the overwhelming feeling of frustration and helplessness. No Cherokee could testify against a white man in the Georgia courts, and Georgia refused to allow them to hold their own courts. And they couldn't fight back. That would give the Georgians the excuse they needed to declare the Indians dangerous and to expel them. So they were powerless to stop the attacks.

When Tiana finished reading, she and Drum sat silent for several minutes.

"Do you know what phoenix means, my daughter?" asked Drum.

"Raven told me," she answered. "It's a mythical bird that burns and rises from its own ashes."

"Buck Boudinot picked a good name for his newspaper. Like the phoenix, I pray we will rise from the ashes of this strife. We pray we will be purified by the sacred fire. It will be a purification paid for with our blood." Drum paused. "It is time for *E'lohi Ga'ghusduh'di,*" he finally said sadly.

"The Foundation of Life?" she asked.

"Yes. It is necessary."

"Think you we're in such danger then, father?" In all the troubled times they had suffered, Drum had never suggested that ritual. That he did so now made Tiana's stomach churn with fear.

"Our brothers and sisters toward the Sunland are in terrible danger," Drum said. "I weep for them. I will notify those with special magic in each of the clans. You must help me, daughter."

"I do not know the ritual."

"I will teach you." Drum rose heavily, pushing himself up from his low stool with his hands against his own knees. As he plodded into Sally Ground Squirrel's house, Tiana heard him repeating a line to himself. She assumed it was from the ritual. "From here I made my appearance in the Light of the Seventh Heaven: there the Seven Clans lie about . . ."

As principal headman of the western division of the Real People, Drum would be expected to organize the complex ceremony. Tiana knew only that it began at midnight, on the west bank of a stream, and ended at dawn. She also knew it was never resorted to except in the most extreme circumstances, when the entire tribe was threatened by war or some other calamity.

To dispel her foreboding, she waded into the mob of girls waiting for her. She had promised to teach them basket making while Raven,

James, John, Drum, and the other headmen met in council to discuss Ridge's letter.

As Tiana led the girls toward the river where they would cut cane, they crowded close. Several hung on each hand and several more wrapped arms around her waist. Her progress was slowed further by three-year-old Delilah Rogers, James's daughter, who clung to her leg. Because Tiana had named her, Delilah felt she had special claim to *Ghigau*. It made no difference to her that Tiana had named many of the girls there.

"Have you no respect for *Ghigau*?" Delilah's older cousin Cynthia tugged her away. John's daughter Cynthia was amiable enough, but ungovernable. Tiana suspected she and her cousin, Betsy, were sneaking off to meet white traders at night. They always seemed to have more ribbons and knickknacks than the others.

Where are the special ones? Tiana asked herself, as she studied the girls laughing and talking around her. Were they *all* being changed by the whites and their gaudy goods? Had their steps strayed so far from the old Path they would wander lost in the world? Would they be neither white nor Indian?

When parents asked Tiana to name their babies, she took the task very seriously. She used many names from Seeth's Preacher Book. Not only was the poetry in it beautiful, it was very holy and the white people's main source of magic. White people's magic was obviously strong.

Besides, she felt she was protecting the children by giving them Christian names. They would have to deal with whites more and more in years to come. Tiana believed non-Indian names would throw white people off the track. They would hide the child's real identity and blunt the evil power of calling her by her name, as white people so rudely did. As soon as the children were old enough to understand, Tiana sat each down and explained the importance of a spirit name.

Tiana worked hard to keep the flame of the old knowledge bright. But sometimes she felt she was trying to do it in a driving rainstorm.

Elias Rector waited patiently on a big black gelding while Tiana and Coffee said good-bye to Raven. Rector had met Raven at Fort Gibson and asked to ride with him toward the Red River until their trails forked.

Tiana adjusted the collar of Raven's shirt so it lay over his powder-horn strap.

"Have you the food I packed for you? You really should wear your heavier coat." She fussed to keep from crying. She had made him clothes for the trip, new hunting shirts and moccasins. His blankets were rolled in a mat and tied behind his saddle.

"No matter how much food or how many coats I take I shan't be warm or well fed until I see you again, my love." He took her slender hands in his large ones and kissed the fingertips.

Raven carried his bowie knife and pistol in his belt and his powder horn and cartridge pouch slung across his chest. His rifle rode in a boot by his right leg. Tiana's throat tightened as she looked at him. At times like this, she wished he were an ordinary man. She knew the rebellious faction in Texas had sent him letters begging him to lead them because he was so far above ordinary. But if he were ordinary, if he weren't such a rambunctious, complicated, impossible puzzle of a man she wouldn't love him as she did. It was a dilemma from which there was no escape. She could only hang on and ride the horns of it.

"Long-winded One," she tried once more to persuade him to ride their good horse. "Please take the bay. Leave Jack here."

"No, Spider Eyes. You need him. I will not leave you with a second-rate horse." So tailless Jack wore the fine horsehair bridle Tiana had braided and decorated with red yarn tassels and tiny hawk bells.

"Have a care they don't scalp you," she said. Raven could tell from the look in Tiana's eyes she wasn't joking.

"I can't come to harm. I have a passport from Jackson."

"You have only to convince attacking Comanche to read it," she said. She hugged him one last time, trying to memorize the feel of him.

"Take care of her," said Raven as he shook Coffee's hand.

When Raven swung onto Jack's back, Rector had to smile. The old horse looked as though Raven should be carrying him.

"Hie, noble steed." Raven crouched as though for a charge. Tiana laughed, and it helped. Raven blew her a kiss as the two men rode toward the Texas trail. "I'll see you in the spring," he shouted over his shoulder. Tiana and Coffee waved.

In one of Raven's saddlebags was a pouch wrapped in waterproof, oiled paper. In it was a copy of Caesar's *Commentaries* and letters from Drum and others to friends and relatives living with The Bowl along the Red River. There was also a letter from one of Jackson's friends. It said, in part, "I do not believe Texas will long continue its allegiance to the Mexican government, and I would much rather see it detached through your agency than by purchase. It has been your fortune to engross more public attention than any other private individual in this nation. Daily, I am asked a hundred questions about this extraordinary man, General Houston."

Then there was the passport asking "all tribes of Indians to permit safely and freely to pass through their territories, General Samuel Houston. Thirty-eight years of age, six feet, two inches in stature, brown hair and light complexion."

Rector proved a good traveling companion. He claimed to get drunk once a week on whiskey and sober up on wine. For the two days they rode together he matched Raven, story for story. Before they parted, they sat for an hour under a tree and passed the last of Rector's flask. Raven and Elias watched Jack stamp and twitch to rid himself of flies.

"That damned bob-tailed pony is a disgrace," said Rector. "Take my black."

"I can't do that."

"Nonsense. It's the least I can do for Texas. I will be able to say, in the sunset of my life, that I traded horses with General Houston. You're quite notorious, you know."

"Am I?" Raven looked at him innocently. "Well, I thank you for the gift. I pray I shall prove worthy of it."

As Rector rode off on Jack and Raven was retying his saddlebags, he reached into the one with the letters. When he packed, he had noticed a small piece of folded paper in his passport. He opened it. He recognized Tiana's neat hand, but the charm for the protection of a traveler was written in Sik'waya's syllabary. Below the charm was a line in English, but Raven knew the sentiment was Cherokee. It said, "We shall make our souls into one forever." Raven's eyes stung as he read it. He refolded the paper and put it with his mother's gold ring in the small bag around his neck. He felt Tiana's love riding there, close to his heart.

Fewer and fewer women of the Real People practiced magic these days. But Tiana still did. She hardly fit the whte man's image of a witch. As he rode along, Raven pictured her by the river, facing the rising sun. She would be naked, even in the cold of a late November dawn. She would be clothed in light. She would glow with it. He imagined her that way now, her arms raised to Grandmother Sun. He knew that for the next two mornings she would chant the charm he carried with him. It was probably to protect him.

> Gha! *Listen. You have just come to hear, Provider.*
> *Ha! You have just come to place his feet on the White Path.*
> *Ha! Let his fine clothing be hidden from enemies.*
> *Listen! From the Sunland where you live, you hear me.*
> *Ha! Rise up now.*
> *Ha! Lift his soul to the treetops and ride on his right arm.*
> *Follow his steps. Listen!*

As Tiana followed the Osage woman through the small village at Chouteau's, the stench was so powerful she had to hold her hand over her mouth and nose. Chouteau's trappers were sometimes careless about the tanning of their hides. But she had never smelled such an odor of decay here before. Crows and buzzards circled noisily overhead.

She screamed in horror as a skeletal dog ran by. It was dragging a human head by the hair. Tiana's companion shouted and kicked at the dog. It dropped its prize and backed off, snarling, its tail between its legs. The woman picked the head up by the hair. It swung by her side as she hurried along.

"What happened?" Tiana asked her.

"Big victory. Come see. Come, hurry."

The bare earth in front of the village's main lodge was littered with rotting heads. Some were still in the brass buckets where they'd been thrown after the raid on the Kiowa village. Some had been dumped into piles as warriors argued over which belonged to whom. Men were methodically scalping them. The woman tossed the head she held into the center of the pile. The head had belonged to a child. The starveling dogs skulked around the perimeter, whining and growling.

Tiana forced herself to look closely. Most of the sixty or seventy heads were either women or children or old people. They stared up at her as though still alive. They were caked with dirt and blood and flies. The flies' loud buzzing made her ears ring and she tasted bile in her mouth.

"Big victory," the woman said again. She grinned and nudged one of the heads with her foot. Tiana choked and gasped for air.

When she felt a touch on her shoulder, she screamed and whirled, her hand on her knife.

"Mrs. Houston, I'm sorry you saw this. Come away from here. They will be decently buried as soon as all the scalps are taken." Cadet Chouteau looked tired and sad.

"What happened?"

"The Little Ones attacked a Kiowa village. The captives say the men were off raiding the Utes. And collecting their own scalps, no doubt." A boy and girl about ten and twelve years old were tethered to a post nearby. Chouteau pointed at them and gave a command in Osage. Reluctantly, the captives' owner untied them and led them toward Chouteu's house. "At least I can care for them.

"The warriors"—Chouteau said it with some sarcasm—"feared the return of the Kiowa men. So they hacked off the heads and brought them home in the Kiowa's own buckets."

"It's monstrous," said Tiana.

"It's natural," said Chouteau. "Do you condemn a cat when she proudly brings home a fledgling or a helpless mouse she's killed? *Non, ma chere.* It's her nature. Killing is these people's nature."

"You'll forgive me, Cadet, if I stay only long enough to eat and rest. I'm not sure I can even eat."

"I understand."

The image of those heads and their staring, sightless eyes, tormented Tiana after she left Chouteau's. She feared more than ever for Raven's safety. How could he convince the Kiowa to talk peace when they returned home to find the decapitated bodies of their wives and children? The horror of it invaded her sleep. She began dreaming of Joanna and David, Shinkah, Adoniram, and Mitchell Goingsnake as she had last seen them.

Now, as she hoed the field, she had to stop suddenly and lean on her mattock. She remembered Shinkah helping her plant, and she began crying. She cried for Shinkah and David and her children and father. But she cried for all the others too, for the starving Osage boy and all those who were hungry. She cried for the Kiowa mother searching for her child among the headless corpses. She cried for every victim and for the senselessness of the killing. For a terrible instant they were all her family, all her children. She was overwhelmed by it. She wanted to sink down on her knees in the dirt of the field and wail out her grief, as Shinkah used to do.

"Tiana," called Coffee. He nodded his head toward the Texas trail. "Looks like a fish swimming upstream."

A lone figure shrouded in a bright poncho and mounted on a big bay approached from the southwest where they had seen so many disappear. Tiana dropped her mattock and climbed to the second rail of the worm fence. She shaded her eyes to see into the afternoon sun.

"He's come back, Coffee, he's come back."

"Well, he said he would," said Coffee.

Tiana's skirt was hiked up and her feet were bare, as usual. She jumped the fence and ran down the dusty road to meet him. He stopped his weary horse and touched the brim of his wide Mexican sombrero, all glittering with silverwork on the band. His saddle and bridle were elaborately decorated with silver plates and buckles. Tiana took a running start and leaped up behind him. He half turned and wound his big hand into her hair. He pulled her to him and kissed her hard and hungrily.

She wrapped her arms tightly around his waist and pressed her cheek against the rough wool of the poncho. It smelled of sheep's oils and stables and dust. Mostly dust. Raven was lean and darkly tanned by the same sun that seemed to have bleached his eyes a paler blue. The squint lines around them had deepened. The muscles in his broad shoulders had hardened. He and the horse had traveled a long way.

That night, Raven and Tiana celebrated with the last of the brandy. She was so happy to see him, she drank more than usual. The room spun merrily as she lay with her head cradled on his shoulder on the buffalo hide in front of the fire.

"Tell me all about it," she said.

"There's a lot to tell."

"Good. Then you'll be around a while. Where did you stay when you weren't tracking the wild Comanche?"

"At the New England Retreat in La Villa de Nuestra Señora del Pilar de Nacogdoches. The hotel advertises baked beans, codfish, doughnuts, lottery tickets, and no fleas or rats. But it lies on all counts but the lottery tickets."

"Nacogdoches? The place where Matthew Arbuckle says the devil sends hell's rejects?"

"The same. They tell a story there of a man who went to see a lawyer about a terrible thing he'd done while in Nacogdoches. 'My friend,' said the lawyer, 'that is a very serious crime. You'd best leave town immediately.' 'But that's impossible,' cried the criminal.' 'Where would I go? I'm already in Texas.'"

Tiana laughed. Raven turned over so he could look down at her.

"I can't tell you how much I've missed that laugh," he said, and kissed her full mouth. Then he went on. "Parts of Texas are rough. All new states are infested by noisy, second-rate men who favor rash measures. Texas is overrun by them. What Texas needs is a leader brave enough for any trial, wise enough for any emergency, and cool enough for any crisis."

"And who might that be?" Tiana couldn't help smiling at him. He was as James had once described him. A magnificent specimen of a man and one commissioned by God for leadership. He was just the sort he said Texas needed.

"My dearest Spider Eyes. Texas is more than the border banditti. I had Christmas dinner with Jim Bowie and his wife in San Antonio de Bexar. You'll like Bexar. Life is gracious there. We'll spend afternoons on shaded patios drinking wine and listening to the guitars playing. The Spanish are like the Real People. They love color and music and dancing. They have fandangos and parties every other night.

"You can shop in the marketplace. Ursula Bowie said she'd show you how to prepare things. The sights and sounds and smells there will make you giddy. They have fruits that taste like perfume. And the houses, wait till you see them. They're made of huge clay bricks, plastered like the Real People's used to be. But they're warm in winter and cool in summer.

"Spanish is a musical language, like your own, only simpler. I'll teach you what I know of it. Mrs. Bowie can help you too."

It was a seductive life Raven described for her. A quiet life without warfare in a happy, languid country.

"What of The Bowl's request for title to his people's land in Texas?" Tiana asked. Raven hesitated.

"They were granted permission to live in Texas," he said.

"But were they given title to the land like the white settlers? Bowl went to Mexico City to ask for it."

"He didn't get it." Raven said. "But he will."

No, he won't, thought Tiana. *He'll have to be content with that ridiculous Spanish officer's hat they gave him. A trinket instead of anything of substance. Just like here.*

"The government in Mexico City is in transition now," said Raven. "When things sort themselves out, Bowl will get the title."

"And will things sort themselves out?"

"Santa Anna is in charge now. General Don Antonio Lopez de Santa Anna y Perez de Lebron. He's a liberal. He'll see things our way."

"*Our* way?"

"Well, I did draft the letter to him explaining our . . . the Texans' position. And I helped write the constitution they plan to present to him. You'd have laughed at those roughs trying to write a proper document. In exasperation, the man in charge finally grabbed one by the shirtfront and pointed his bowie knife at him. 'If you don't follow parliamentary procedure,' he said, 'I will start carving.' "

"There'll be war."

"I doubt it."

"And you talked with the Comanche and Kiowa?"

"Yes. They'll be here any day to meet with Montford Stokes and the peace commission."

"Mr. Stokes says you might as well try to collect the clouds as try to gather the Comanche now."

"They said they'd be here."

Tiana didn't argue with him anymore. Instead she asked him to tell her more about the Spanish and their customs, and about Texas. He was only too happy to oblige her.

But she couldn't forget the letter Raven had begun writing almost as soon as he got home. It lay on his desk now. It was to Jackson of course. It said, in part:

> The people of Texas are determined to form a state government. Texas can defend herself against the whole power of Mexico, for really, Mexico is powerless and penniless.

One line from the letter echoed in Tiana's head as she lay awake that night, long after Raven was breathing deeply beside her. "I may make Texas my abiding place. . . ." She knew he wanted her to return to Texas with him. But if she refused, he would go anyway. He never said so, but it was as certain as Grandmother Sun rising in the morning.

Montford Stokes, with his slow North Carolina smile and the wisdom that had come with his white hair, had been right. No Comanche or Kiowa appeared to meet with him and the peace commission. Raven wasn't the only one disappointed. Everyone at Fort

Gibson had been dreading and anticipating the arrival of the fierce horsemen. As May heated up for June, for summer and for the sickly season, the troops began to stand down.

When it was obvious the southern chiefs weren't coming at all, Raven became restless again. He began trying to convince Tiana to go with him to Texas. But it was to no avail.

"Damn it, woman!" he finally shouted. "You and I are too . . . " He searched for a word. "Too powerful for this place. We need more opportunity to show what we are, what we can do. Texas can give us that."

"I am powerful wherever I am. Where I am is not important. *Who* I am is important. If I am powerful, as you call it, that power comes from within, not without. I'm needed here. More and more people are coming from the Old Country. All of us who are settled and can help them must do so."

"I need you. Come with me. I beg you, Spider Eyes. I've bought land from Stephen Austin. You and Coffee and I can work it. They're talking of making me head of the army. What if I win Texas and lose you?"

"You said there wouldn't be war."

"I just received a letter from a friend in Texas. He says Santa Anna is swinging like a weathervane in a hurricane. No one knows what he'll do. But you'll be safe. Even if there is war, it'll be over before it starts. The Mexicans can't fight. They have no heart for it."

"No. The Texans are not my people."

"You could pass." Instantly he wished there were some way to recall the heedless words. Tiana's eyes went from the color of early morning haze in the mountains to gunmetal.

"Pass for what?"

"Mexican," Raven stammered, all too aware of his blunder.

"The Americans hate the Mexicans too. I won't be a stranger among people who hate me."

When Raven had packed, Tiana rode with him as far as Wilson's Rock on the Verdigris River. They didn't speak much. Tiana knew Raven would leave without her. But Raven still couldn't believe she would let him. He tried once more to change her mind.

"Spider Eyes, I'll file a petition for divorce as soon as I'm settled. Then will you join me?"

"No, beloved. I shall not be an exile again. Not even for you. You must return to your people. I must stay with mine."

Raven leaned over and put his hand up under her silky hair.

"The spider will wrap me in veils of loneliness until I see you again, my Beloved Woman," he said in Cherokee. "You are truly walking in my soul." He kissed her long and lightly. Through a curtain of tears she watched him ride slowly away, toward the badlands and Texas.

" 'We two are truly set apart.' " She murmured the ancient charm softly. " 'You will always think of me. You will think of me from your very soul. You will never forget that I walk the earth.' " Raven turned to wave. With her hand raised in salute, Tiana watched until he was out of sight around a bend in the trail.

She stood motionless a long time, thinking of her life, the joys and the losses. Ghigau Ward said a life lived well was in balance. The good offset the bad. Perhaps someday the pain of this would fade and prove her right once again. Tiana hoped so. But she also wondered if she would become like Spearfinger, surrounded by the ghosts of her memories.

Chapter 55

It was April 19, 1836. The countryside around Vince's Bayou was one vast bog. General Sam Houston pulled his battered slouch hat down over his forehead in a futile effort to keep the rain off. The water ran out of the three deep creases in the brim. Sam's threadbare black coat was spattered with mud. His snuff-colored trousers and high moccasins were covered with it. The Bowl's granddaughter, Mary, had made him the moccasins. He wore them to save his only pair of boots. Sam had recently written The Bowl a letter, telling him he hoped to see his old friend before the moccasins wore out. In return, The Bowl had politely told a Mexican envoy he and his people would remain neutral in this fray.

Sam pulled his big white stallion, Saracen, to the side of the trail to watch his dejected army plod by. The men trudged with their heads down and their rifles wrapped in blankets to keep them as dry as possible. "Army" was probably too dignified a label for them. There were less than seven hundred men. Many of them were ill with measles and dysentery. Few had had any kind of military training. Most of them called themselves Texans, but they represented eight or ten different nationalities. About all they had in common was their tattered clothing, their coating of mud, their long, matted hair and beards, and their lice.

Santa Anna, on the other hand, had three thousand well-equipped men and was expecting five hundred reinforcements. Sam knew that because Deaf Smith and the black freedman, Hendrick Arnold, had just captured a Mexican courier. Speaking slowly, so Deaf could read his lips, Sam complimented him on his new trousers. The Mexican's blue wool uniform pantaloons were much too tight for Deaf, but they were better than his old, mud-shellacked buckskins.

At least the rain was keeping the Kentucky contingent from trying to kill each other with their fists, as was their wont. And ten miles back, Sam's retreating army had finally parted company with the refugees who were fleeing toward the United States. It wasn't the responsibility of caring for so many civilians that Sam minded. He hated watching the women struggling along, mile after weary mile, with their crying children and their heavy burdens. He did what he could to help, but his own men had practically nothing and vehicles were scarcer than hen's teeth.

"General Houston." Sam recognized the woman's voice. He could hardly have traveled with the refugee column and not known it. Mrs. Pamela Mann was the sort to draw attention in any crowd, no matter how large. She was young and tough and beautiful. As she rode up to Sam, her two horse pistols hung in holsters from her pommel, within easy reach. Her bowie knife was in a sheath attached to her saddle.

"Good morning, Mrs. Mann."

"General, you told me a damned lie." So much for the amenities. "You said you was going on the Nacogdoches road. Sir, I want my oxen."

"Well, Mrs. Mann," said Sam. "We can't spare them. We can't move the Twin Sisters along without them."

"I don't care a damn for your cannons. I want my oxen." She jumped down from her horse and sawed through the rawhide that attached the chain to the oxen's harness. She cracked her whip over the animals. No one said anything as she drove them back the way she had come.

Sam's wagonmaster scratched his head.

"General," he said. "We can't get along without them oxen. The cannon is done bogged down."

"We'll have to get along as best we can, Captain Rohrer."

"Damn it, I'm going to get those oxen back." Rohrer spurred his own horse after her. Sam raised up in his stirrups and called after him.

"Captain, that woman will fight."

"Damn her fighting," the man shouted over his shoulder.

"Come on, boys," said Sam. "Let's get this cannon out of the mud." The goo almost washed over the tops of Sam's high moccasins as he put his broad shoulders to the wheel and heaved with all his considerable strength. He knew Rohrer would return without the oxen. He was right.

Mrs. Mann reminded him of Tiana, although she hadn't the Beloved Woman's serenity or intellect. Mrs. Mann was very much of this world. But Sam could imagine Tiana defying the army for *duyukduh*, her beloved justice. Sam had taken some pleasure in Mrs. Mann's company, although apparently Mrs. Mann hadn't taken enough pleasure to give him her oxen. He had been trying to blunt his loneliness and forget the stubborn woman who refused to join him in Texas. Sam looked down at his moccasins, misshapen with mud. He had to admit it was just as well Tiana wasn't here.

The rain finally stopped, but Sam was still coated with mud when he formed his army into a hollow square. He sat on Saracen in the center of the formation. His loud voice could be heard by the rearmost ranks. Across the prairie, covered with bright spring flowers, the men could see the smoke of New Washington as it burned. Santa Anna's forces were close.

"Victory is certain!" Sam shouted. "Trust in God and fear not! The victims of the Alamo and the names of those murdered at Goliad cry out for cool, deliberate vengeance. Remember the Alamo! Remember Goliad!" With a pang, Sam remembered Davy Crockett and Jim Bowie who had died in the Alamo.

"Remember the Alamo! *Recuerden el Alamo*!" his men shouted. If Sam had told them that they could only win Texas by jumping into the cataracts at Niagara, they would have leaped.

"There is no use looking for aid," Sam said. "None is at hand." Sam and his men had retreated as far as they were going to. The men who had died in the Alamo mission a month before had bought them as much time as they would get. Tomorrow, Sam's army would meet Santa Anna's soldiers at the pretty, rolling plain called San Jacinto, Saint Hyacinth.

Tiana stood in the open doorway of Wigwam Neosho. She pointed her pistol at the man who sat on his horse in the dooryard. Coffee and Tiana's slave, Peter, stood near the barn, ready to help if necessary.

"Get out of here, McGrady," she said.

"Diana, me darlin', it's sorry I am if I angered you last night. I had a bit of the juice in me."

"You have a bit of the devil in you. Clear off my land."

"Now, darlin', that's no way to be talking to your own husband. This is *our* land."

"You're not my husband, no matter what you tell your verminous friends. This is my land, and you'll be buried under it if you don't leave."

"Diana—"

"Now!" Her patience was gone.

Samuel McGrady flashed her his smile. He was a handsome one, and ever so charming when he wanted to be. And rotten at the core. It had taken Tiana a while to discover that. She had been blinded by his winning way and her own loneliness.

It was the spring of 1837. It had been almost four years since Raven had left. He had written her a few affectionate letters begging her to join him in Texas. She knew he had won the battle of San Jacinto and made Texas an independent republic. In return, the Texans had elected him president of it. But the situation there was still chaotic. There were rumors of another war with Mexico. There were Indian troubles and a huge debt. Raven spoke longingly of his reunion with her, but it was obvious that Texas occupied all of his time and most of his thoughts. She had not answered his letters, although she had read them so often she had memorized them.

McGrady had showed up at the door one day a few weeks earlier. What had his pretext been?

"Pardon me, ma'm," he had said, his hat in his hand. He had a trace of an Irish brogue that was appealing. His hair was a reddish gold. "I couldn't help noticing you when you were at the fort, Tuesday a week. My friends said you were working this big farm alone, with only a pair of negroes. I wondered if you'd be needing an extra hand."

It was planting time and there was more than enough for him to do. Tiana had hired him on a temporary basis. He slept in the barn. For three weeks he was a good worker. She would stop her own chores now and then to watch the muscles of his bare shoulders and back as he chopped wood. He had a boyish smile and an infectious laugh. When the weather turned cold and rainy, she hadn't the heart to send him out to the barn without warming himself by the fire first.

As she walked by him, he tugged at her skirt and pulled her down beside him. He wrapped the ends of her hair around his fingers and kissed them. She bent over his hand and brushed it with her lips. Suddenly, she needed to feel his touch. She needed to be held. She needed to feel him inside her.

They had coupled fiercely. In the morning, McGrady seemed to think they were married. Worse than that, he assumed that not only did he own Tiana's property but he owned her too. He did no work that day. He went off to Fort Gibson, spread the news that he had married the widow Gentry, and came home roaring drunk that night.

His reception was not what he expected.

"Where's my dinner, wife?" he had demanded as soon as he walked in. Tiana looked at him in astonishment.

"I want it now!" He wove to a chair at the table. Tiana quietly picked up his gun, his knife, and her own pistol and knife.

"I'm not your wife and you'll not stay here in that condition."

"I'll stay here if it pleases me. This is my house. We're cohabiting. You're my wife. What's yours is mine."

"If cohabiting makes a mate, then you'd best be kind to the cow, because you're sharing her barn."

"Woman, don't anger me."

Tiana pointed her pistol at him.

"Go to the barn, McGrady, then leave in the morning, first light. I don't want to see you here again."

He took a step forward and the gun didn't waver. He had come to know her well enough to believe she would use it.

"You'll reconsider, lass. You need a man. You're a hot one, you are. Well." He put his hat on. "You know where to find me."

He had shouted for her that morning, and she had thrown him his empty rifle. But McGrady didn't want to leave for a number of reasons. First, he had found a comfortable home here. He had been planning to use it as a base for his illicit whiskey business. Second, he had already been spending the money he expected to get from Tiana's farm. Third, he had told his friends he was married to the beautiful, elusive Mrs. Gentry. He didn't care to face their scorn when he came back a rejected suitor. Fourth, he couldn't believe she would turn him out after she had slept with him. And fifth, he had to have her. After one night he was addicted. He couldn't bear the thought of living without the touch of her lithe, golden body.

He started to dismount, and she shot his hat off. She reloaded while he retrieved it.

"Please, Diana."

"Go, McGrady."

"I'll be back when you're in a better mood, lass. Perhaps when you're ready for some more loving." He winked.

Even under normal circumstances, Samuel McGrady didn't think the word "no" applied to him. His attitude was strengthened by the fact that he had always had his way with women. Now, his persistence bordered on obsession. For the next six months Tiana held him at bay. She shot at him once, as he skulked in the woods near the house.

She stopped traveling alone. Coffee usually went with her, when he could be spared. Or she timed her visits to the fort to coincide with Percis Lovely's. Percis suggested she find herself another man. "A woman like you would have no trouble finding someone," she had said. "I can't," Tiana had answered, "Raven's memory warms me more than the arms of another man would." Percis had nodded. She had never remarried, for the same reason.

Arbuckle threatened to arrest McGrady, and he disappeared for a month or so. But he came back when Arbuckle took sick leave and went to Saint Louis. Tiana's brothers helped as much as they could, but they were busy with their own affairs. And her farm was thirty or more miles away. They tried to convince her to resettle near them or Drum. But she refused. "I won't have that *wetumpka*, that hog thief, drive me from my home."

When fall came and the crops were in, James appeared at her door. He talked her into at least going to his house for a long visit. Tiana left the farm in the care of Coffee and Peter.

When they stopped at Captain John's, they found a visitor from the east. John Ross, the president of the National Council, had come to see what the Nightland was like. The Real People in the east revered him as a savior. He and the Rogers and Drum talked most of the night. His news was even grimmer than the stories they had been hearing.

Ross was forty-six now. He had aged more than his years warranted since Tiana had last seen him in Hiwassee. But with his pale blue eyes and wavy brown hair and pug nose, she found it as hard to believe he was an Indian as she did twenty years ago. His Cherokee had improved, but it still wasn't the tongue he was most comfortable speaking.

"Schermerhorn duped Congress into believing his treaty was approved by the Real People," he said around his pipe. "A handful of headmen and their followers were there. Those traitors Ridge and Buck Boudinot signed. And their lands were taken out of the lottery and reserved for them. Now Van Buren says the treaty is law and we must leave our country within the year, will he, nil he."

"Will you come here?" asked Tiana.

"No. We'll go on fighting. We've collected thousands of signatures repudiating that treaty. When Congress knows the truth, they'll rescind it. Right now the Cherokee nation stands alone, moneyless, helpless, almost hopeless. But we have no intention of yielding."

There were people who accused Ross of fighting removal for personal reasons, to hold onto his extensive property and power. Some said he was a dictator who wouldn't tolerate any view but his own. Or perhaps he fought because of the inherited stubborness of his Cherokee and Scottish ancestors. Whatever his motives, he was obviously a man who had decided what course to take and wasn't going to deviate from it.

"What happened when you were arrested?" asked John. "Since the Georgians destroyed *The Phoenix*, we've little notion of what goes on in the east."

"I returned from Washington City to find my family had been turned out of our house. And my wife's an invalid. Georgians had taken over the plantation. They said they'd won it in the state lottery and we owed them back rent." Ross's voice broke and he stopped talking for a moment.

"We heard it was a beautiful, big house," said Tiana. "They had twenty glass windows," she told her sister-in-law. "And peacocks. Workshops, smokehouses, stables, slave quarters."

"A lifetime of work," said Ross. "Gone. Now a slovenly mob of trash lives there. In the dead of winter, my family and I had to take up residence across the line in Tennessee, in a drafty, one-room cabin with a dirt floor. The Georgia militia arrested myself and John Howard Payne there. They carried us back into Georgia and held us, tied to chairs, for twelve days."

"Across the state line?" asked James. "That's illegal." Ross only laughed.

"My friend, the Georgians know no law."

"Is John Howard Payne one of the Real People?" asked Tiana.

"No. He's a writer who's been moved by our plight. He's been helping me take our cause to the people of the United States. If they only knew the injustice we're suffering they'd rise up in outrage."

"Payne wrote that song, 'Home, Sweet Home,' " said James. He hummed a few lines and Tiana nodded. She had heard it often while waiting for Raven to leave Nicks' tavern. When the men reached the maudlin stage of inebriation, they would sing it.

"In Georgia, gangs of white ruffians roam the countryside at night. They steal our horses and cattle and terrorize our people. While Payne and I were prisoners, we heard the Georgia militiamen talking about it." Ross began pacing in front of the fire. He mimicked his captors' drawl, but there was anger in his voice. " 'Ah, there must have been some beautiful slicking done last night,' one of them said. 'Jeb and the boys tied an ox team to the eaves of the niggers' shack.' "

Tiana winced at the word. Ross went doggedly on with his story.

" 'First one timber fell,' the man said, 'and the family tumbled on their knees. One began to beg and the little ones squalled, and the old woman fell to praying.' Then the militiamen all pretended to cry like the frightened children. It was a great joke for them."

"James, John." Drum spoke into the silence that followed Ross's story. "One of you must go back to the Old Country with White Bird and see for yourselves how things are there. You must be our eyes." James and John looked at each other. It was a long, arduous trip, and they had both made it too many times.

"I'll go, Beloved Father," said James.

When Tiana finally went to bed her sleep was troubled. She woke late the next morning to hear Coffee calling from the yard.

"What is it, Coffee?" She leaned from the second-story window. Coffee's horse was lathered.

"That man McGrady, he took Peter."

"Damnation! Go to the kitchen and eat. I'm coming down."

Tiana threw on her clothes and ran across the empty sleeping pallets. Most of the family was already up. "What happened?" She arrived in the kitchen breathless and found Sally Ground Squirrel dishing up hominy mush and milk.

"McGrady came around, right after you left. He must have been watching. I was clearing that new field and Peter was chopping wood. McGrady walked right into the house and Peter went after him, to protect your things. They had a terrible row. McGrady put his gun to Peter's head and took him to the fort. I couldn't do anything."

"I know." The National Council had made stringent laws governing slaves and free blacks. The headmen said it was necessary. There were evil influences that affected the slaves. But another reason was to appear more like the whites, as far as Tiana was concerned.

"McGrady told the new man there, the one taking over while Arbuckle's gone, that Peter was his slave, that you'd given him to him and he had a paper to prove it."

"A paper?"

"Yes. He was waving one around. Said it was signed with your X."

"A forgery."

"Anyway, Peter's in the guardhouse."

"I'll go get him."

"Sister, wait." James stood in the doorway. "Is that the slave our brother sold you before he died?"

"Yes."

"Let John or William take care of it."

"They don't have to fight my battles."

"Dear sister, that's what your family is for. You've gotten into the habit of fighting all your battles alone. That's not our way. The men of the Seven Clans protect their sisters. Arbuckle's gone. And there's no telling what McGrady might try if he gets you in his grasp."

Tiana slumped onto a stool, buried her face in her hands, and fought back the need to cry. She remembered what Drum had once told her. "I wanted only to walk a peaceful path through life, without disturbing the flow." She felt bruised and buffeted by events that no longer flowed. They raged and raced out of control. At times like these she longed for Raven's presence. He always seemed to know what to do. What to say. Then she dismissed the thought. He was gone. He wasn't coming back. There was no more use thinking of him than if he had journeyed to the Nightland.

"James, I'm going with you to the Old Country," she said.

"You heard White Bird. It's dangerous there."

Tiana had to laugh.

"It's dangerous here. Remember the mob last summer." The Arkansas militia had gotten into a brawl at a house of ill fame near the fort. The Cherokee men there bested them, so they prowled the countryside for days beating any Indians they could find. Arbuckle had fined the Indian prostitutes who had started the ruckus. And he had punished the militiamen, but not before innocent people were hurt.

"And McGrady, who'll protect me from him? Besides, I want to see *Tsacona-ge*, the Place of the Blue Smoke, again. I want to see springtime in the mountains of the Sunland. And I'm worried about Mary. We've had no letter from her in almost a year."

Chapter 56

Grandmother Sun's smile was gentle and warm on Tiana's face. The river murmured along with her as she chanted her morning song. This was a special song asking for wealth for her sister Mary, and her family.

> Now! Listen! Gha! *On White Pathways they will be making their footprints.*
> *There will be no evil: for in front of them Lightning will be going and behind them coming.*
> *For their bodies are beautified by The Provider, and they will fade into this Red Tobacco which clothes them.*
> *Where the Seven Clans are, they have appeared: they are beautified.*
> *They stand in the middle of the sunrays, facing the Sunland.*
> *Now then, you who founded the Seven Clans, you have wealth near the water which they can keep.*
> *You do not need it: if it can be borrowed, they greatly wish to borrow it! Look! all of you!*

As Tiana sang it she glanced at Mary's eight-year-old granddaughter, Annie, who stood naked beside her. Annie's lovely face was serious.

This was David's granddaughter, the child of his daughter, Elizabeth. Annie was as dark as David had been fair. She had the elfin, sloe-eyed beauty of her great-grandmother Elizabeth and her great-Aunt Jennie. But now and then she gave a look or a gesture that reminded Tiana of David.

Whenever Annie stood with one hand on a hip and the opposite foot cocked to the side, and flashed a shy, crooked grin, Tiana felt a tug at her heart. The pose was so uncharacteristic of a woman of the Real People, yet so like David. Tiana didn't know how that could be. Annie had never seen her grandfather, nor heard much about him, as she never heard about her father who had passed on too. One didn't talk of those who had gone on to the Nightland. But David was inside her nonetheless.

Tiana had been excited to find Annie here, at Mary's tiny cabin in Georgia. Since she had arrived three weeks before, she had been watching Annie and talking to her. *This is a special one*, she thought now, as she and Annie, Elizabeth and Mary and Mary's third husband, Hunter, walked up the trail toward home. *The sacred fire burns brightly in her.* Tiana was excited, and relieved too. She was beginning to wonder if there were any left who hadn't been seduced by the white way. She had never put it into words, but as a woman she felt an added burden of responsibility.

The men were the ones making the changes in the Nation. They met in council to create laws imitating the white man's. The men strove to amass land and cattle and slaves like the white men. That left the women to carry on the knowledge as they had always done. Even though White Bird, John Ross, had far more white blood in him than Indian, he was fiercely proud of being one of the Real People. His mother had passed that pride to him, just as Ulisi and Jennie had passed their heritage on to their children. Now the duty was Tiana's. And she took it seriously.

It was May, 1838. It was planting time. Tiana worked in Mary's cornfield with the rest of the family. She smiled down at Annie as the child squatted next to the mound of red Georgia clay Tiana was building with her mattock. She had given Annie the task of planting the seven kernels in each mound, and Annie was doing it solemnly.

"Will your morning charm make us rich, Beloved Mother?" Annie asked.

"You already are rich."

Annie was silent. Tiana gave a short laugh. She knew Annie would never contradict her. It wasn't polite. But she knew the child didn't believe her either. She had only to look around her to understand why. Mary's cabin and farm were as impoverished as any Tiana had seen on the Arkansas.

Mary and Hunter seemed to think poverty was their only defense. If their farm was poor enough perhaps no Georgians would covet it and drive them away. Also, Hunter was as old as Mary. He suffered from rheumatism. During her visit Tiana had worked for him, frying the oil out of eels and rubbing it on his painful joints. But the labor required to eke a living from this tough clay was almost more than he could manage.

Tiana knelt in the warm earth and laid both palms on Annie's narrow chest.

"You are rich here," she said. "In your heart. In your soul. No one can steal that from you. If you are poor there," Tiana gestured to the shabby cabin, "you must be that much richer inside to balance it. For every bad thing that happens to you, find the good that keeps it in balance." Tiana took Annie's hand in hers and scooped up some of the earth with it. "This is yours. Wherever you go, there will always be earth to feed you and sun to warm you."

Annie held the dry, red soil reverently in her hands and pushed her thumb through it, crumbling it into powder. Tiana saw Elizabeth glance over at them. There was gratitude in the look.

Elizabeth was plain-looking, with a broad face whose features seemed to have been rolled out flat, and small, pale brown eyes. Her dust-colored hair escaped in thin wisps from under her bandana. She was a kind, gentle, loving soul who seemed weighed down by circumstances she couldn't change. She had confessed to Tiana that she worried about Annie's future. She had asked her to teach the child, to help her cope with this deadening poverty and the fear that haunted all of them.

"Shall I tell you a story?" Tiana asked.

"*Hayu*! Yes! Tell me how suli, the buzzard, got his bald head."

Tiana laughed. While she and Mary and Elizabeth told stories the rest of the day, the corn seemed to plant itself.

They bathed late in the afternoon and ate the usual supper of corn mush with beans and bits of rabbit meat in it. Mary spread frayed mats on the cabin's dirt floor. There were no chairs and only two stools. After the meal there was nothing to do but sit around the fire and wait for bedtime and listen to Mary cough helplessly.

This was the loneliest time for Tiana. She missed the talk and laughter at the cabins of her sisters-in-law and Sally Ground Squirrel. She felt isolated. The Seven Clans in the east didn't gather to celebrate anything. The Georgians considered any assembly a council to foment trouble. And councils were forbidden.

So Tiana stared into the fire burning in the center of the cabin floor. There was no chimney. What smoke didn't escape through the hole in the roof pooled among the eaves. She tried not to brood about the fact that her charms and medicines were having no effect on the disease that was eating away at Mary.

She tried not to think about what might be going on beyond the narrow, wooded valley that sheltered Mary's tiny farm. On their trip here, she and James had seen the blackened bones of burned cabins, and white people working farms built and cleared by those of the Seven Clans. She had seen the fear in people's eyes. She had heard stories of the night riders with black handkerchiefs over their faces.

James. What could be keeping James? He should be back from Washington City by now. As though she knew what Tiana was thinking, Elizabeth spoke.

"Why did uncle go to Washington City?"

"Beloved Father sent him with the other headmen to ask Father Tseksini, Jackson, about something being discussed in the white man's Big Council." How could she explain it? "They speak of making Arkansas a state 'when the Indian title there is extinguished.' "

"Extinguished." Hunter studied the bowl of his long, clay pipe. "That is a good word for what the white people are trying to do. They would extinguish our sacred flame."

"I wonder why he is taking so long to return." James's absence made Tiana uneasy.

"Knowing James, he's probably enjoying the feasting and dancing in Washington," said Mary. "He always did love a party. We hear from those who've been there that the white poeple give many parties."

It had been a shock to see Mary after twenty-two years and to remember how much she herself had loved parties. The vain, beautiful coquette had disappeared. In her place was this bent, haggard, sixty-year-old woman who coughed into the bloodied rag she hid in the bosom of her blouse. Her third husband seemed to love her very much, though. Hunter was a full blood, stolid and simple and good, and uneducated in the ways of the white men.

"He will arrive safely," said Hunter. "The people of the Seven Clans will protect him."

"Who will protect the Seven Clans?"

"White Bird will drive the white men from our land. He will lead us back to the paths of our ancestors. He will protect us. He will destroy that papertalk signed by those traitors, Ridge and Buck Boudinot."

Hunter and the others believed John Ross could save them, in spite of the fact that the soldiers massing at New Echota had already confiscated the Real People's weapons. They believed it in spite of General Winfield Scott's proclamation calling on all of them to report to the authorities and await transportation to the Nightland. They believed it because White Bird, John Ross, told them so.

As though to mock White Bird's promises, Tiana heard shouts and gunfire outside. The door vibrated as someone pounded on it with a rifle butt. Hunter opened it and faced a semicircle of bayonets. Beyond the Georiga militia with the bayonets, Tiana saw looters outlined by the torches they carried. They were rounding up the stock in the small pasture.

Other men scattered hay bales and set fire to them. Tiana could hear them complaining loudly that there wasn't anything here worth taking. Some rode back and forth through the fields, trampling the seeds and breaking down the fences. Others set fire to the corn cratch. Several crowded into the cabin and herded Mary and her family outside. Tiana heard the sound of crashing as someone ripped the sleeping benches from the walls.

"*Hena*, go." One of the men gestured with his bayonet. *Hena* was probably the only word he knew in Cherokee.

"Let us collect our things." Tiana could see it was useless to argue about going.

"No time for that." The man was surprised she spoke English. "You people should have been collecting your things long before now. You were warned."

"These are simple folk. They don't understand proclamations."

"Sister, I don't have time to chat. We have to clear this whole section. Now move." One of the militiamen prodded Hunter with his bayonet. Tears ran down Annie's cheeks, but she made no sound.

"That's not necessary." Tiana pushed the bayonet away and glared at the man who held it. "Lieutenant, tell them to let us get some blankets, and food. We haven't even any shoes on."

" 'With dispatch,' my orders say. And to tell the truth, missy, you'd best hustle along while the boys there are busy." He nodded over his shoulder at the rabble rampaging around them. "They're liquored up and in a hair-cutting mood. And they're talking about taking home souvenirs, if you catch my meaning." Tiana did.

She was glad Hunter and Annie and Elizabeth didn't understand English and that Mary had forgotten most of what she once knew. But they understood the man's manner well enough. They understood that there was very little to distinguish him from the lawless wretches in the mob. With their bayonets, soldiers began shoving Mary away from the house while others set fire to it. Annie charged into one of the men and began flailing at him.

"Stop it," she screamed. "Stop hurting *Ulisi*."

Tiana caught her around the waist. Holding the child's arms, she knelt in front of her and stared her in the eyes, a sign that the old rules no longer applied.

"We must bear adversity with dignity, my daughter," she said in the Real People's tongue. "That is what makes us better than they. That is what makes us worthy of the spirits' aid."

"Why aren't they aiding us now?"

"They shall, if we ask them correctly and behave with dignity and forbearance. Come with me." She took Annie's hand in hers and grasped Elizabeth's with her other one. She walked toward the path without looking back. Hunter and Mary followed.

"My chickens," said Mary, distractedly. "Who'll feed my chickens?"

"Look straight ahead, sisters," Tiana said. "Don't let them see you're afraid." She knew from the shouts behind her that the men had found Elizabeth's husband's grave. They were digging it up to take whatever jewelry might be buried with the body. They had come prepared with shovels for the task. Tiana talked to Elizabeth to keep her from realizing it. The thought of her husband's bones being left for wolves to gnaw might have made her try to fight the men.

Tiana and her family walked, barefoot, through the long night. When Mary slowed, a militiaman would swear and prod her with his bayonet. Tiana had to catch Hunter's sleeve to keep him from attacking them. Finally Hunter almost carried Mary. They were joined by others, militia and their prisoners, most of them silent.

Dawn's pale light washed over a long column of people, many of them weeping quietly. Some carried children or a few possessions in bundles or baskets, but most were empty-handed. Next to her a young woman's eye was purple and swollen shut. She walked gingerly, as though in pain. Tiana knew, from the look on her face, that she had been raped. Tiana tried to talk to her, but she refused to say anything, or even glance at her.

About midmorning, a wagon caught up with them as they rested and napped by the road. Militiamen fed them cold bacon and stale corn bread from it. The sick and infirm were loaded onto it. But Mary clung to Hunter and refused to get in. Tiana was glad. She hated to see Mary staggering along, but she feared their being separated. As the afternoon wore on, Annie began to stumble from exhaustion. Tiana carried her pickaback, while Elizabeth and Hunter helped Mary. That night, they slept on the ground, and huddled together for warmth.

The second day they neared the Hiwassee. The hills and trees were like old friends. As they passed the path that led to her father's farm, Tiana choked back tears. Most of the huge old trees had been chopped down. The place looked bare and ugly, like a beautiful woman with a shaved head. Junk littered the yard. One end of the porch had collapsed. She understood why James never encouraged her to come back here.

At Hiwassee garrison, the refugees were driven into twenty-eight pens with rough, open log walls and stout roofs. Each crib was about sixteen feet square. Tiana looked through a wide crack between the logs and beyond the ranks of soldiers. She could barely see David's old blacksmith shop, off to one side of her line of vision. She lowered her head onto the log and let the tears flow silently down her cheeks.

Mary squatted with her back against the wall and began to moan softly. Other women did the same. There was little talk. Everyone was still too stunned. Tiana wiped her eyes and sat next to her sister and niece and grandniece. Hunter stood over them, as though trying to protect them.

"Don't worry." Tiana took Mary's hand. "It's all a misunderstanding. James will find us and explain to the soldiers that we don't belong here." Tiana saw there was too much confusion to try to contact the commander now. When everything settled down, she would demand their release. At least the United States Army was in charge here rather than the militia.

A week passed. The weather grew hot. Each morning Tiana begged the guards to let them all go the the river to bathe, but they refused. So she greeted Grandmother Sun as best she could, looking out at her through the cracks in the log walls.

The log shelters became more and more crowded. Soldiers and the men of the Seven Clans built new ones, until the camp sprawled across ten square miles. But here were no facilities for the sick, and it was doubtful people would have let their relatives be taken to a hospital if there had been one.

Now Tiana squatted next to Mary and held out the rations the soldiers were trying, without success, to distribute. Mary only shut her mouth tightly and turned her head. She hadn't the strength to move more than that.

"Sister, you must eat." Flies buzzed around Tiana's eyes. The sick had to stay with the well. The odor of vomit and diarrhea in the pens was nauseating.

"She will not take their food," said Hunter.

"Talk to her, brother." Tiana pleaded with him again. But it was useless. They were all too stubborn and too frightened.

"White Bird says we must not cooperate with the soldiers," Elizabeth said. "They will banish us to the Nightland. We will become living ghosts, homeless and lost."

"An army of the Seven Clans is forming in the mountains to rescue us," Hunter added. His face was hollow with hunger. "And White Bird will convince the white man's big council to bury the paper talk and release us."

"Thunder will save us." Mary coughed.

"Those are only rumors, spread by singing birds. We must save ourselves. We must eat." Tiana was desperate and frustrated. They were all the same. No one would even talk to the soldiers. They refused to muster, to give their names. They refused not only the food but the clothing and shoes the soldiers tried to issue them. They believed if they accepted anything from the white men they would be accepting also the hated treaty that took their land.

People shared what little food they had brought, giving most of it to the children. When that was gone, they stared stolidly at nothing and starved. They ignored the men who brought the rations. Not until the children began to sicken and die did they take the food at least, although they still refused the blankets and clothing. The days were hot, but Tiana and the others shivered through the nights.

When James didn't appear after a few days, Tiana tried to see the commandant. But the guard only looked her up and down, undressing her in his mind. She knew the price for asking him a favor would be more than she was willing to pay. She almost cried with relief when she glimpsed a familiar face.

"Captain Armistead!" she shouted. The man turned around and Tiana realized from his insignia tht he'd been promoted in the twenty years since she had seen him. "General!" she called. "Over here." Armistead peered through the logs. Tiana laughed for the the first time in over a week. "I'm Tiana Rogers, Jack Rogers' daughter. General, I must talk to you."

"Miss Rogers, what are you doing here?"

"General, you must help us. There's been some mistake. James and I were visiting from the west and we were caught up in this. At least I assume James has been caught, else he would have found me by now. I have to get word to him. And my sister is sick. I have not been able to cure her. Please, she needs a doctor." In her joy the words tumbled out. Armistead took her by the arm and guided her to his office.

"How is your father? Lord, old Hell-Fire was one in a million."

"He journeyed to the Nightland, many years ago."

"I am sorry, Miss Rogers. Listen . . ." Armistead floundered, distracted by this personal complication in an already complex situation. "I can put you on a steamboat, pass you off as a relative or something. I could get court-martialed for it. But hell, you're my old friend Jack's daughter. And I'll try to find James. But to tell the truth, things are in a bit of a turmoil. Thousands of people are suddenly dispossessed under the most trying of circumstances. People have been snatched up off the trail, out of fields. James might already be headed west."

"But he speaks English. He's three-quarters white."

"Doesn't matter. If he's identified with the Cherokee tribe, he'll be deported. A large group has already been sent off. The army fears that if people have warning they'll break for the mountains. Then it'll be the devil's own time rounding them up."

"But this is barbarous."

"I know. God, I know. I never thought chasing Seminoles through the Florida swamps would look good, but it beat this."

"My sister is with me. And her husband and daughter and grand-daughter."

Armistead held up a hand.

"I can help you escape. Maybe. But I cannot let four of you go. The countryside is alive with militia hunting fugitives. And I use the word 'hunting' deliberately."

Tiana looked at him in disbelief.

"General, you know we're not dangerous. How can you be party to this?"

"I'm a soldier. My commander-in-chief, the president, has ordered it. I have no choice. If you have any things, you can go pack them. I'll send a sentry for you when it gets dark."

"And leave my family."

"They'll arrive safely. We're not barbarians. Our orders are to see that the emigrants get to the west."

"I won't leave them. When will a doctor see to the sick? People are dying." Over the years Tiana had developed respect for some forms of the white man's medicine. Besides, the Real People's spirits might be reluctant to come to this place.

"The doctor should be here tomorrow."

"And when can we expect to leave?"

"Soon. We're to move you out as soon as possible. Harris, see her safely back to her . . ." Armistead hesitated. He knew the conditions in the pens. He just didn't know what to do about them. " . . . quarters." Tiana turned to go. "Miss Rogers, I'm sorry."

She didn't answer. Captain Harris had to hurry to keep pace with her as she strode back toward her shelter. As she passed one of the pens, a hand reached through the opening between the logs and clutched at her.

"Beloved Woman," a woman cried, "My granddaughter is sick. I hear you are a Curer Of Them. Will you help her?"

"The white Curer Of Them will be here tomorrow, mother."

"I don't want a white sorcerer to bewitch her."

Harris started to say something as Tiana entered the shelter. Then he closed his mouth and waited patiently for her.

"Miss Rogers," he said when she came out. "If there is something I can do, please tell me. Ask for Harris, Jeb Harris." She looked him in the eye, to see if he told the truth, and to challenge him. What could he possibly do?

"I mean, if anyone molests you," he stammered, thrown off bal-

ance by the intensity and strength in her dark blue eyes. He knew
Cherokee women had a reputation for being beautiful, but he never
expected to find someone like her here.

"There is something you can do," she said. "They took my knife
when we arrived. It might be here somewhere. It's in a sheath with
red and blue and white beadwork. The blade's worn quite thin."

"I'll look for it. I promise."

Early one morning a few days later, Tiana was helping a mother
whose baby was about to jump down. Annie squatted at her side.
As she worked, Tiana explained what she was doing and Annie's
wide, black eyes took it all in. Tiana had put leaves under the woman
to protect her and the infant from the dirt. The heat was intense.
There was no shade other than the shelters. The trees had all been
cut to build them and to provide fuel. There had been no rain either.
The dust from so much activity hung in the motionless air. Flies
buzzed constantly.

When Tiana and Annie walked wearily out into the glare of the
day, Captain Harris was waiting.

"May I speak with you in private, Miss Rogers?" He guided her
away from the center of the compound. "Gather your family as
quickly as you can and meet me here."

"What is it?"

"There's no time to talk. Hurry. Believe me when I say, it's
urgent."

When Tiana returned with Hunter, Mary, Elizabeth, and Annie,
Harris shouldered his rifle and marched them toward the woods.
Tiana looked back at the camp, at the women cooking their morning
bacon and gooey flour cakes over small fires. They hadn't gotten the
knack of cooking with wheat flour. She saw a formation of soldiers
moving into the center of the compound, and she had a moment of
panic. Was everyone to be executed? Given what had already happened, it was possible.

"Where are you taking us? What's happening?"

"Boats are ready to leave for the west."

"Then we should be on them."

"No. There's cholera along the Mississippi. And smallpox." Harris
stopped them in a secluded grove by the river, three miles from
camp. "The soldiers' orders are to load the boats whether people
want to board or not."

"They don't want to go," said Tiana. "They still think they'll be
saved and they'll be able to go back to their homes."

"I know it. General Armistead knows it." There was pain in Harris's voice. He was thirty-five, a few years younger than Tiana. He had large, sad brown eyes, and a huge, bushy moustache. "Armistead's orders were to fill those boats, no matter what."

"But they'll resist."

"I know. It could be ugly. That's why I hid you. Here." He handed her her knife.

"You found it!"

"I couldn't believe it myself. But there it was, with the rest of the confiscated weapons." He watched Annie dabble her feet in the creek, which was much lower than usual.

"Why did you warn us, Captain Harris?"

"Four years ago, I was with the military escort for a party of five hundred emigrants. We went partly by water and partly overland. It was a terrible journey. I still have nightmares about it. Cholera, flux, fevers, drunkeness, bottomless despair.

"I couldn't bear to think of you as part of that. I've been watching you since you arrived, always helping others, always cheerful, when there's no cause under God's blue sky to be so. I just couldn't bear it." He took dried peaches and apples from his pouch. "Annie." He held them out to her. "*Suhkta*, apple; *kwana*, peach," he said in halting Cherokee. Annie smile a shy thanks and divided them with the others.

"I have a daughter about her age," Harris said wistfully. "Sometimes, in my nightmares, I see her caught in this."

While the women went upstream to bathe, Harris shared his precious tobacco with Hunter. Harris was right about the loading of the boats. When he marched them back that evening, the camp was in an uproar. Women wailed. Families huddled in fear like trapped animals. When the Real People had refused to board voluntarily, the soldiers had rushed them and herded six hundred people onto the boats. In the panic and confusion, children were separated from their parents and sent off to the Nightland alone. Husbands, wives, grandparents, siblings were lost.

The grief was terrible. In the days that followed, a new rumor spread through the camp. Someone had found out about the cholera. Armistead was faced with rebellion if he tried to force more emigrants to leave. He was relieved when General Scott sent word to hold his charges in camp. Scott had agreed with Ross and the National Council to delay removal until the end of the sickly season, or at least until rain fell.

For three months, Tiana and the others sweltered in the compound. Captain Harris helped as much as he could. He scoured the countryside for extra food and vegetables. But the drought had shriveled crops. There was enough to keep people alive, but barely that. So he brought Tiana food he had saved from the officers' mess, and watched her meticulously divide every morsel of it with those in her shelter.

Tiana got permission to take the women to the river to cut cane. They made mats to cover the dirt floors of their pens and hang on the walls to shield them from the sun. They laid the leafy cane tops down as beds. She spoke to the headmen in their weekly council in Armistead's office, and convinced them to allow their people to be vaccinated for the smallpox. Then she helped them convince the others.

But she couldn't cure her own half-sister. Consumption was an appropriate name for what Mary had. She seemed to be shrinking daily. Tiana chanted for her every morning, but it did no good. Her rain-seeking rituals were just as ineffective. She felt as though her magic had shriveled and died inside her.

Tiana worked day and night, attending the sick or showing women how to cook the strange white flour. Measles had broken out in camp, and there were a lot of sick. She grieved with those whose loved ones had died. Sometimes she just sat quietly with frightened families and told them about life in the west.

Everywhere she went, Annie followed, like a smaller, darker shadow. She had inherited her grandmother Mary's beauty, but not her frivolous disposition. And as Tiana worked for the ill, she explained her cures to Annie. Harris sent a soldier he could trust to guard them while they searched for the plants they would need in their cures. Annie constantly amazed Tiana with her memory for the plants and their uses, and her way with people. She was indeed a special one.

Everyone in the compound knew Tiana. Harris heard "A'siyu, Ghigau, greetings, Beloved Woman," a hundred times a day. Tiana kept the children amused with games and stories. She told all the Real People's stories she knew. Then she told her father's stories from Scotland and Shinkah's Osage tales and Seeth's Bible stories. Finally, the children couldn't even be coaxed to play. They lay listlessly in the shade, too weak and disheartened to wave away the swarms of flies.

Each day dawned hot and bright and dry. Water was rationed. There was barely enough for the fifteen hundred people in the camp to drink and cook with. Bathing or washing clothes was impossible. Tiana never complained aloud, but her skin felt stiff with dirt and dried sweat. Her hair was greasy. She had never been this dirty. She hated the filthy shell that was her body. She checked herself every day for lice and fleas. Sanitation facilities were terribly inadequate too, which was one reason so many suffered from the flux.

September came, and still there was no sign of rain. But the men's council in camp was busy. John Ross had finally admitted defeat, but he had won another concession. The Removal wouldn't take place under a military guard. The Real People would be allowed to go west by themselves. Arrangements for the journey were being made in the Hiwassee compound and the other camps. The compound's council elected two captains to be in charge of the column and a police force to maintain order.

Toward the end of September, wagons loaded with cooking equipment and blankets and clothing began to arrive. White Bird and the headmen were as good as their word. They were organizing and supplying their own exile. White contractors and freighters and steamboat owners who had been planning to get rich off the Indians' plight raised a howl of protest. But General Scott ignored them.

Tiana sang as she went from shelter to shelter, helping those who needed her. The spirits of the whole camp lifted and Tiana heard laughter again, when she thought she had forgotten what it sounded like. They weren't to be driven toward the Nightland like cattle. They would go with dignity.

Chapter 57

Tiana tilted her head back and opened her mouth to feel the drops of rain on her face and tongue. She danced with Annie and Elizabeth and splashed in the puddles with the children. Men and women ran out in it too, tasting the cold water, washing themselves, or just gazing heavenward.

In spite of the guards' protests, everyone thronged to the river to thank the spirits. Armistead let them go, although he lined the shore with soldiers. People from neighboring shelters asked Tiana to lead the Great Medicine ceremony and to ask the spirits' blessings.

As she waded into the swirling water, autumn leaves brushed by her or stuck wetly to her skin. Tiana felt magic surging through her. Joy welled up inside her, and spilled over in happy tears. Soon they would begin their journey. Soon she would be home. Soon she would see the family and friends she had left a year ago. The rain fell on October 10. When Removal began two days later, it was still falling.

The huge camp stirred before dawn as runners woke people and helped them organize in the steady, cold drizzle. Gradually, a long column formed with the wagons in the middle, and men on horseback ranged along the flanks. Captain Harris was bothered by the men on horses.

"The women should be riding," he said to Tiana.

"Pregnant women and the sick and the old are riding in the wagons. But someone has to patrol the line of march."

"The Cherokee themselves asked that no soldiers go with them." Harris had disapproved of General Scott's decision not to send a military escort with the emigrants. He feared for the Indians' safety.

"The people don't trust soldiers," Tiana said. "They would rather be guarded by their own." Tiana watched the column form as people slowly coalesced. Those who had lived near each other all summer tended to get into line together. Some carried their possessions in bundles or drove cows in front of them. But most were empty-handed.

"This many people will be strung out for miles." Harris pulled his hat lower over his eyes to shield them from the rain. He wondered how Tiana could ignore the cold and the drizzle. "And the whiskey vultures are already gathering. Can your Light Horse keep them in check?"

"They shall have to. Captain Harris, why aren't you in uniform?" In the bustle of preparations, Tiana had just noticed that Harris wore civilian clothes.

"I've asked for a leave of absence. I'm going with you."

"But you were looking forward to seeing your wife and daughter when your duty here ended."

"I've made this trip before, although by boat, not by land. I know I can be of service. I'll see my family when I return." Harris was too diffident to tell Tiana her people had come to mean a great deal to him. He didn't have the heart to remind her that winter would catch them far from their destination. He had to protect them as best he could, or he would never be able to sleep well again. He was also much too shy to tell Tiana he had fallen in love with her.

With eighty-year-old Going Snake at its head, the column began to move forward. Tiana grinned at Harris.

"I'm going home, Captain. I'll see my family at last." Tiana had made most of the trip east on steamboats, so she had only a vague notion of the territory through which they would pass. But she had confidence in the toughness of her people. They were a nation of walkers.

Her elation died quickly though. She was going home, but everyone else was journeying to the land of death. The grief around her threatened to engulf her. It was as if in losing their homeland, the exiles had lost the most beloved member of their family.

The people who had defended their land for centuries, with bows and arrows, with guns, with constitutions and laws, and finally with words in the white man's court, were at last being driven out at gun-point. Their departure was slowed even more by those who stopped for one last look at the hills of the Sunland. Annie turned to wave sadly. Mary clung, sobbing, to a gnarled old cedar while Hunter comforted her. No matter how bad the trip might be, it couldn't be as agonizing as this farewell.

"Beloved Woman."

Tiana turned to look at the woman who stood behind her.

"Will you make the road shorter for us?"

"I will try, sister."

Word spread that Ghigau would bless the trail, and a huge crowd of people gathered. As Captain Harris watched from a distance, he took a deep breath to ease the ache in his chest. There were a few silver threads in her hair now, but he couldn't see them from here. He stared at the curves of her body, where the wind and rain had molded her worn, linsey-woolsey dress to her.

The dress had come from the shipment of used clothing gathered by the headmen of the National Council. But she refused to wear any of the shoes mixed in with the wagonload of clothes. She said none of them fit and they were uncomfortable. She wore instead the moccasins of crudely tanned cowhide she had made during the summer. Harris knew the moccasins wouldn't last long on the rough trail ahead.

Tiana faced west instead of east. Harris couldn't know the importance of that, but everyone else did. They faced west with her. They knew she was telling them their destiny lay there now. Tiana stood straight and tall. She welcomed the cold rain in her face. Like a winter bath in Long Man, it made her aware of her skin and her body, and her union with the seasons and the elements. The wind wrapped her wet hair around her. Her clear, strong voice sent chills through Harris as she sang one of Drum's songs to make a journey shorter. She and the others would have need of it.

Finally, the stragglers caught up with the rear of the column and they all started on the thousand-mile journey. Many of the exiles still had no shoes or coats, and the weather had gone from sweltering to cold. But at least they were moving.

Two weeks later, the rain was falling again. It had been falling for days. Tiana helped Annie and Elizabeth up the slippery embankment and onto the main trail. Hunter followed them. Mary was riding in a wagon with the sick ones. The wagons that crossed the stream before them had left ruts two feet deep and filled with viscous, reddish water. The mud was treacherous, slick yet sticky, and they had to place each foot with care. It formed a crust that grew thicker and heavier on their moccasins with each step.

Tiana put her arms around Annie, who shivered in the wind. They were both wet from pushing wagons across the stream, but it little mattered. They had been wet almost the entire trip so far. At least now the mud had been washed off their moccasins and clothes. For a few minutes Tiana's feet felt light. She seemed to be walking on air. But she knew they would grow heavy with mud again as soon as she took a few steps along the trail.

Tiana rubbed her arms to warm them. But her skin was icy and clammy to the touch. She wondered how Annie, with her shorter legs, could keep going. She herself was stumbling with fatigue. None of them could sleep much when they camped. They huddled under soggy blankets that only kept the rain from falling on them as hard as it would have with no shelter at all. They napped at night when exhaustion numbed them to the cold and the rain and the hard, wet ground.

Tiana waited now on the bank of the stream and watched the last of the column struggle across. Men, women, and children pushed the wagons through the mud and the swirling water. It took two days for the fifteen hundred people, three hundred wagons, and five hundred horses and mules to ford this stream. Tiana wondered how many more rivers they would cross before they finished the last weary mile.

She heard the toc of axes coming from the forest crowding the sides of the trail. The men were cutting trees to lay across the swamp further ahead. Jeb Harris rode up beside Tiana. He despised being on horseback when most had to walk, but he spent his days searching the surrounding country for food and grain and medical supplies for his charges.

He also rode in search of the elusive disbursement officer who was supposed to deliver money for provisions, but hadn't appeared yet. And he ferreted out and threatened the whiskey peddlers lurking in the woods. When he rode with the column he was on the move ceaselessly, tending the sick and helping the Light Horse maintain order. Because of the whiskey, fights were breaking out constantly among the men.

"Miss Rogers, we might as well camp for the night," he said. "We can't go anywhere until the logs are laid. That quagmire would swallow a wagon without a trace." He started to ride away, then turned. "Mrs. Bear Meat's youngest looks bad. He has the measles. I administered pulverized ipecac and some of your miracle tea. And I said a short prayer four times, as you suggested. It seems to put the patient and family more at ease. But I think The Intruder will carry him to the Nightland tonight."

Harris worked so often with Tiana in ministering to the sick he was beginning to use her expressions. He didn't realize what an honor it was for the Real People to allow him to work for them at all. But because the Beloved Woman trusted him, they did.

"I shall sit with her, Captain."

She and Annie and Elizabeth made a shelter of their blankets with the Bear Meat family, while Hunter went to get Mary from the wagon. With a flint Tiana coaxed a spark, then a flame from the last of the dry moss she carried in a horn slung at her side. She leaned over it to protect it from the rain misting under the lip of the shelter and from the wind.

She fed it the driest twigs she could find, then bigger ones, until she had a very small, tenuous fire going. The wood hissed as the flames heated the water in it. Steam rose from the saturated blankets over Tiana and the others. Everyone crowded as close to the frail warmth as possible. Tiana held Cloud Bear Meat's two-year-old son to give Cloud a rest. The baby was covered with red spots and he cried piteously. While the salty bacon boiled, Elizabeth patted out small flour cakes to bake on flat stones.

"We should have asked the Little People to carry us under water too," said Cloud. "And hidden us there." She was younger than Tiana, but her face was haggard and drawn with care. "The people of one town did that, you know."

"What town?" asked Tiana.

"Oh, just a town near Shooting Creek, on the Hiwassee." Cloud was vague about details. "They prayed and fasted and the Little People took them under water where the white demons couldn't get them. They say you can see the round dome of their town house roof when the water is low. It looks like a rock, but it's really the town house. And people say you can hear them talking down there. Whenever anyone fords the creek near their village, they throw food into the water for them. And those who have fished there say their lines get caught and held by the ones underwater."

"I wish them happiness." Tiana had heard dozens of similar stories of people who managed to hide from the soldiers and escape exile. She allowed herself a fantasy of her own. As she watched Grandmother Fire dance and sing her hissing song, Tiana dreamed briefly about being warm and dry and safe. She indulged in the thought that this nightmare had never happened. She imagined waking up in her own bed in her cabin amid the cottonwoods on the lazy Neosho River.

"Beloved Mother, look!" Annie pointed up. The rain had stopped and the sky was bright with glittering stars. "You said when the stars came out again you would tell me the story of the seven boys who danced up to heaven."

"This is what the old women told me when I was a girl." And Tiana began the story of the Pleiades. When the tale was over and the meal was finished, everyone fell into a deep sleep, the first in a week. But even though they were both tired, Tiana and Annie sat up until the seven boys, the Pleiades, were well on their way from the eastern sky to the west. Tiana had a great deal to tell Annie, and she didn't want to wait until they reached the Arkansas.

Just as Tiana was preparing to crawl into her filthy, dank blanket, Captain Harris passed on his nightly rounds.

"Do you never sleep, Captain?"

"I might ask the same of you. How is the Bear Meat child?"

"I think you are right about him nearing the Nightland. He is very weak."

"Where's your other blanket?"

"My sister needs it."

"I'll get you another one. But I know you'll give it away."

"How was the day's foraging?" she asked.

"Not good." Tiana heard the despair and fatigue in his voice. "I've turned over every rock for twenty-five miles. I've knocked on every cabin door. I've pleaded and bargained. Folks are without provisions themselves. It wasn't a good summer for crops. We have enough for meager rations tomorrow, then the search starts again. Parties of emigrants have already passed this way and frightened off all the game."

"There was enough corn for whiskey," said Tiana bitterly.

"I know. We're doing what we can about that vermin."

Tiana had seen Hunter sneak off after his wife fell asleep. She knew he was probably spending his family's annuity money on liquor. He had come home very drunk the night before. One of the men who had been elected a captain of the Light Horse was drunk so often he had to be tied to his horse and driven along.

The next morning Tiana woke up to the keening of Cloud Bear Meat. The headmen delayed departure long enough to bury her child and two others who had died during the night. Although the rain had stopped, the wind in their faces made the next day's march difficult. Elizabeth walked, limping, next to the wagon in which her mother rode. Tiana carried Annie pickaback and taught her songs as they traveled. The child's bare feet were swollen and bleeding.

As the long file of weary marchers neared Nashville, Tiana saw white people lining the sides of the road. She set Annie down and put her hand on the knife at her belt. If they intended to taunt or throw rocks, she would fight them. She would rather die here than suffer any more injury at the hands of whites. Then one of the women waiting by the trail held out a basket of food to Tiana.

"For the child," she said. Tiana reached for the food and the woman grabbed her hand and held it a moment. "I wish I had more," she said, tears streaming down her cheeks. "Here." She took off her coat and draped it over Annie's shoulders.

"Thank you." Tiana said. "We won't forget your kindness."

"God bless you," the woman called after her. Others gave food and blankets, although not a fraction of what was needed. One woman handed Hunter a pair of worn, heavy boots. "My man's gone on," she said. "He won't be needing shoes where he is."

Old Going Snake died outside Nashville. His grieving people carved a monument for him and planted a white linen flag on a long pole so others passing would know of his death. As they walked by almost every person laid some tiny offering of food, or an item of clothing on the grave.

On November 17, it began to sleet. The sleet turned to wet snow. Tiana and a score of other people put their shoulders against the wagon Mary rode in and pushed it through the freezing, sucking mud. When the wheels finally pulled loose from the mire, Tiana leaned both hands against the wagon's sides to keep from falling with the dizziness that coursed through her head. For a moment it replaced the steady, throbbing ache there. She heard the groans of the sick in the wagon as it jolted over the craters and ruts in the road.

Then she caught up with Annie and Elizabeth, who held a blanket over them to keep off the worst of the wet snow. They shared the blanket, as they walked alongside the wagon again.

"You'll like the Arkansas, daughters," Tiana said. "There are buffalo in herds that stretch to the horizon. And elk and huge flocks of turkeys." She described the comfortable farms of the Old Settlers, and the feasts they had. "Things grow very big on the Arkansas. I planted beets once and didn't go back to harvest them in time. When I finally went to the field a week later, those beets were as big as cedar stumps." Annie laughed.

"You're a singing bird, Beloved Mother."

"How much farther must we go?" asked Elizabeth.

"Not too much farther. We're almost to the Mississippi."

"Miss Rogers." Tiana turned to see Captain Harris beckoning to her. He leaned down so no one else would hear and handed her a small vial. "Hunter has passed out back there. He's drunk. Wave this under his nose, will you? I have to check the rest of the line."

"What is this?" Tiana uncorked it, sniffed, and made a face.

"Tincture of Carbonate of Ammonia."

She finished rousing Hunter and trotted barefoot through the snow to catch Annie. She saw the hired wagoner lift his whip to strike Mary, who wasn't climbing back into his wagon fast enough. She saw Annie sprint toward them. Tiana yelled and began running. When the man raised his whip to strike Mary again, Annie grabbed it in both hands and swung on it.

The man swore and tried to yank it from her, but she had wrapped it around her arm and now sprawled on top of it in the muddy slush. She was shrieking at him not to hurt her *Ulisi*. He drew his foot back to kick her, so he was unbalanced when Tiana hit him with the full force of her body and threw him to the ground.

Oblivious to the screams of the women around her, Tiana knelt on his chest and jabbed her knife into his throat. Annie grabbed one of his hands and sank her teeth into his forearm. He struggled, but he wasn't a large man without his whip. And Tiana had the strength of rage. Blood was dripping from the puncture in his neck when men from the Light Horse dragged Tiana and Annie off him.

They helped him up and pointed back along the trail. It was clear he was being dismissed. Elizabeth helped Mary into the wagon. One of the men climbed into the driver's seat, and the column moved on. But Tiana was shaking. She had been about to slit the man's throat. Worse, she wished she had.

The convoy stopped for the night at the bank of the Mississippi. The headmen decided to camp there in a stand of cedars until the high winds abated enough to cross the river. Tiana calmed herself that evening by making her usual rounds. With Captain Harris following, she visited the entire length of the column, stopping to cheer those huddled around their fires or to help the sick. Each morning now the delay was longer as more bodies were buried.

Several of the children had come down with whooping cough. Many, young and old, were suffering the flux from drinking polluted water. Scorbutic infections from the poor diet had caused even the well to have raw, sore areas on their wrists and faces. The freezing weather had killed most of the plants, and Tiana found few from which to make poultices or teas. She had to rely on the incantations and the benevolence of her spirits to cure people.

She brought back the bits of food, pay for her services, and divided it among everyone in her camp. Annie was entertaining the younger children with stories and games of Black Eye, White Eye. Tiana smiled as she watched them nibble the fragments of dried pumpkin someone had hoarded and given her. The pleasure in their eyes was better than the pumpkin's sweetness would have been in her mouth.

Elizabeth had warmed her hands over their small fire and was massaging her mother's shoulders. Mary was wrapped in Tiana's blankets and still she shivered uncontrollably. "My saliva is spoiled," she said over and over. "I think I shall reach the Nightland before you."

"Then you can wait for us, sister," said Tiana. "You can carry our greetings to those who are there."

"Where is my husband?" Mary asked.

"He will return soon." Tiana knew she was being a singing bird, but she couldn't tell Mary the truth. The despair and guilt in Hunter's eyes had been growing as he watched his wife die. He had taken to disappearing for hours at a time and returning drunk.

Harris found Tiana there later, washing Annie's bleeding feet with warm water and rubbing them with a salve of pounded aster root. He squatted in front of the fire, drawing peace from Tiana's presence.

"Miss Rogers." Captain Harris held out a pair of moccasins. "I find you shoes and you give them away. Please wear these."

"Thank you, Captain."

He looked at her bloody, bruised feet, and the dark hollows under her eyes that seemed even larger than usual in her thin face. She ducked her head and coughed quietly. Harris wanted to put his arms around her and hold her to him, to warm her and to warm himself with her spirit. Suddenly a feeling of hopeless desolation overcame him. He put his head in his arms crossed on his knees and began to weep. Tiana reached out and touched him lightly on the hand.

"This is truly *Nunna-da-ult-sun-yi*, The Trail Where They Cried," she said. She had seen the fever in Harris's eyes. She put a cool hand to his forehead. His skin was hot to the touch.

"You're ill."

"I've been treating myself. I don't want people to know it. There's so much to do."

"Captain," she said softly. "You can't take the guilt of your whole race on yourself. No one blames you."

"It would be almost easier if they did."

Captain Harris's guilt and despair increased the next day when someone sold him tainted meat. Sixty or more people were in agony before it was discovered. They were taken to an abandoned cabin, where Harris and Tiana tried to ease the suffering. As Tiana moved among the sick, they reached out to touch her as though to receive strength from her.

"My heart is glad you are here, Beloved Woman," said one man. "This is an evil place. I fear Raven Mockers."

"They shall not enter, brother," Tiana said.

The small room was foul and reeking, but at least it provided shelter from the wind. The sick who couldn't fit lay out in the cold and sleet. Their relatives held blankets over them to protect them as best they could. People writhed and doubled over with the excruciating cramps. They vomited and suffered diarrhea. Tiana went outside to see to a woman who was giving birth in the freezing wind. She railed at the women around her.

"Why did you not take her inside?"

"There are ghosts in there, Beloved Woman."

"Help me carry her in. We can make room for her somewhere."

"Beloved Woman," called Elizabeth from the schoolhouse. "Come quickly."

Tiana ran back, to find Mary dead. She and Hunter and Elizabeth put her in a rough coffin with a dead child and another body. Like everything else, coffins were in short supply. Annie sobbed for her *Ulisi* while Tiana and the others hacked at the frozen earth. So many funerals had taken place along the way that few stopped to watch this one. Tiana kept digging with a tin cup long after the rest quit. She had seen the wolf-pawed graves of others along the trail, and she refused to let her sister's bones be dug up and dragged away.

When the winds calmed a bit, the column moved on, leaving the sick to come later in wagons. Besides graves, the ragged train of people left wagons, broken down, or helpless because the horses had been stolen. Now there wasn't enough room in the remaining vehicles for the sick and the old. Many hobbled along as best they could, supported by their relatives. Blood from bare, cut feet splotched the snow on the trail.

Hunter disappeared. With Mary gone, he could stand it no more. He ran away. Determined to return to their homes, others like him were fading into the forests and hills. Neither the headmen nor Harris tried to stop them. Harris was driving himself like one possessed. He seemed to be everywhere.

On December 5, they reached the Meramec River in Missouri. Snow began to fall more heavily. Elizabeth tore a blanket into strips to wrap around their feet. Tiana rubbed their raw, aching soles with ashes and sang the song of the wolf, the deer, the fox, and the opossum to protect them from frostbite. Even as she did it, she feared it was futile. Her magic seemed gone. She felt helpless and alone, deserted even by her spirits.

When Tiana finished treating Annie for frostbite, she wrapped the child's feet in strips of blanket and tied on the moccasins Harris had given her. In the shelter next to theirs, another woman moaned in childbirth. As Tiana helped her, she shook her head now and then to clear the ringing from her ears. Somewhere deep in her chest a pain nipped at her, and she felt a rubbing in her lungs when she drew breath. Far off in the white-shrouded hills, wolves howled.

In the bitterly cold days that followed, the men built small fires along the trail. People stopped to warm their hands and feet as they passed. Harris found Tiana huddled at one of them. Annie and Elizabeth crouched next to her with their arms around her. Tiana was coughing and her face was twisted in pain.

"Miss Rogers, are you ill?" Harris cursed the fact that he had no coat to give her.

"I'll be all right, Captain." She began coughing again. When she spit, brownish flecks of blood spattered the snow.

"*Dagwalela*, wagon," Harris shouted. He waved with his arm and supported Tiana with the other. "Bring a wagon here, quickly."

"There's no room in the wagons. I can walk."

"Shut up." Harris heard an ugly rasping sound when Tiana breathed and he became frantic. "Hurry up, damn you!" With his arm around her waist, he led her toward the wagon. "There are blankets in the wagon. You'll be warm there." Tiana began shaking with chills that sent spasms of pain through her body. Warm. She tried to imagine being warm.

"Will we ever be warm again, Captain?"

"Yes, you will. We're almost there."

"Almost home?"

"Yes. A few more days."

"What day is it?"

"December twenty-third."

"Captain, I want to go home."

"You'll be home soon, Tiana."

"I mean, I want to be buried there."

"Don't talk about burying."

"Promise you'll take me home."

"I promise."

Tiana leaned against the wheel of the wagon and vomited. Her cough was dry and hacking and her sputum was rusty with blood.

"It hurts." She shivered.

Please, God, Harris prayed. *I've never asked you for anything. But please, please, don't do this.*

As Harris helped her into the wagon, he noticed her fingers were white and peeling from frostbite. Her toes, exposed by the torn rags wrapped around her feet, were blotchy and swollen.

Word spread up and down the column that the Beloved Woman was dying. People filed by the wagon to speak to her and give her food or clothing or rags to help keep her warm. She lay shivering under a pile of ragged, dirt-crusted blankets. Harris and Annie walked by the wagon all day and sat with her all night.

The next afternoon, she called for Annie. Annie grasped her thin hand and rubbed it, trying to bring warmth into it.

"Daughter." The effort of speaking made Tiana close her eyes in pain. "Promise me you will learn the old knowledge. Promise me you will find a teacher. Speak to my mother or to Sally Ground Squirrel or Drum. Ask them who can teach you. Tell them I wanted you to learn the knowledge. You are a special one. You must carry the flame to the future. Do you promise me?"

"I promise, Beloved Mother."

"And if you see The Raven, tell him I love him. Tell him he walks in my soul wherever I am."

"I will."

A paroxysm of pain wracked her. Her breathing was fast and rasping.

"I'm going toward the Nightland. I'm going home."

Harris sobbed.

"Don't cry, Captain. My father is in the Nightland, and my grandmother and my children and loved ones. I'll be happy there." When she smiled at him, he caught a glimpse of her impish humor. "I'll make another home there. And not even the white men will be able to drive me from it."

She still had the smile on her lips when she died.

Epilogue

As Sam Houston paced, his brass eagle spurs jingled. The old wound above his right ankle throbbed inside his boot. After the battle of San Jacinto, the surgeon had dug twenty bone fragments from that ankle. Had it been only three years ago? It seemed like a lifetime had gone by. Sam sat to ease his ankle. A messenger had just arrived with a dispatch and a letter.

The dispatch said Texas's new president, Mirabeau Buonoparte Lamar, had ordered an attack on the peaceful Cherokee living along the Red River. When The Bowl's horse was shot from under him, the old headman was wearing the sword and red sash Sam had given him as a token of friendship. The Bowl was wounded in the hip, but he stood to face a company of soldiers. He died waving the sword.

Next, Sam opened the letter from James Rogers. James told of being caught in the Removal and forced to march west, along what was being called *Nunna-da-ult-sun-yi*, The Trail Where They Cried. As best as anyone could tally, four thousand of the Real People died on that journey. And more died after they arrived. There was a terrible struggle for power going on between the Old Settlers and the headmen of the eastern division. James said the word *duyukduh*, justice, was heard constantly.

After they arrived in the west, Major Ridge, his son John, and

Elias Boudinot had been brutally murdered for signing the hated treaty that sent the eastern nation into exile. No one knew who the assassins were. Sam remembered Tiana's speech at the Green Corn ceremony ten years before. The whites had indeed divided the people of the Seven Clans.

James reported the death of Drum in December of 1838, four months before. In the same month, A.P. Chouteau had died in abject poverty. Like his friends the Osage, he had been unable to adjust to the changes the Americans brought. Drum and Cadet were buried at Fort Gibson with full military honors.

Finally, James wrote of the young captain who delivered Tiana's body for burial soon after Christmas. He told of the story being spread by those who had traveled The Trail Where They Cried with her. They said her soul rose like a light, swooping and soaring until it disappeared into the clouds around the sun.

Sam read the letter through. Then he read it again.

He read the last part several times before he laid his head down on his battered desk and cried.